Casey Hollingshead

This one's got even
More sellswords. —

The Captain (Battle Brothers Book 2) by Casey Hollingshead

Very special thanks to,

The Battle Brothers community, Jan, Paul, Christof,

JC, Phil, Heron, Hannah, Mrs. G., and the family.

Chapters.

The man leapt. Beneath his feet, eyes watched. His friends captured him in dead stares. Such peaceful eyes. He desired their dark. Wanted it. Wanted the ease of it being over.

All the same, he hid behind a tree for even now he could hear the beast.

Eating. Ripping. Tearing. The unbearable crunching.

Worst of all – it was taking its time.

Holding his breath, the man crawled across the forest floor. Knees wet. Hands muddied. He found a lumberjacking axe. He carried it with him in clips and clops. Snot bubbled. Drool dangled. Tears plopped. It was quieter that way, to not wipe, to not swipe, to not run the water from his eyes. It was quieter to let the fear own him.

"Where is he?"

No. Friends can't talk. Not when they're missing all that.

A bush moved. Grass softly hissed. Moss curled. Footsteps followed him.

The man turned around. It was no beast.

"Where is he?"

The man's eyes went wide.

"Did he return to Marsburg?"

The man reeled backward until he fell against a tree.

"Or did he go north to the empty mountains of Sommerwein?"

The man threw down his axe. He knew not what he saw. He preferred the beast.

The beast he could understand. The little creature beside it, though?

"I already asked your friends. So now I'm asking you."

The man screamed. He covered his face.

Soft words rained upon him:

"Where is he?"

"Where is the hexenjäger?"

"Where is Richter von Dagentear?"

"Where is the one they call the Wight?"

"You don't know? That is quite alright. Never hurts to ask."

The beast growled and darkness followed and the forest quieted as it once was.

Chapter 1. A New Page.

"Richter!"

The boy leaned up off the cot. "Yeah?"

"Yeah? That's how you answer your commander?"

"Sorry sir."

"Get yer arse out of bed and meet me outside."

"Yessir."

"Whole army's on the march and yer in here farking snoozing."

"Yessir, sorry sir."

The lord shook his head and the tent flap closed.

Richter threw his legs off the cot and drove them into a pair of oversized boots and stood up. He double looped an oversized belt to cinch an oversized pair of pants and rolled the sleeves on his oversized shirt. As he hobbled about, he eyed the tent's shifting flap. With every curling glimpse of the outside, a new soldier could be seen passing by. The army moved on a steady march, an unending rhythm of boots and armor that despite its martial intents and violent ends could lull one to sleep. He sat down on the bed, listening in awe. The plodding boots, thumping in unison, the clinking and clanking of armor and weapons, the snorting of horses, the creak of wagons. All his life, everything he knew was simply what he could see and touch. Now he was in the middle of a great machine, himself a small element spinning with its centripetal forces pulled in from all over the world.

The tent flap flew wide and his commander peered in. "Yer arse has got five seconds."

"Yessir!"

Richter jumped to his feet and strode outside, his clothes billowing like a sail wrapping the mast of a listless ship, his legs folding the leather of his boots as they tilted ungainly beneath him. Quietly at war with his own clothes, he stood up straight and kept his chin high for here the army marched before the skin of his nose. Like himself, the men had an aura of hurry: one long line as far as the eye could see, but with men still adjusting their helmets or girding weapons to their hips. Some ate on the wing, using cocked elbows for plates as they chewed up half-cooked breakfasts while their spears clattered overhead. If they weren't eating, they were complaining, though these talks quieted as they neared the lords as if the noblemen were but holy tunnels into which sounds respectfully shrank. To the sides of the marching column stood the commanders on horseback. Nobles in steel plate and mail, their caparisoned mounts representing colors of powerful houses. Beside them hunkered a mob of scribbling scribes for it was surely a day meant to be heard, seen, and remembered in as much detail as could be captured. One even glanced at Richter and studied him as he wrote furiously.

The boy looked elsewhere and his eyes met those of his commander. He immediately looked away again, but the horse was already being turned. It moved with such firmness and authority it seemed as though a statue had come alive, beckoned by its maker, his bidding as rigid and focused as his masonry. Soon, the formidable horse stood over Richter. The boy remained steadfast, though he could feel the commander leaning in his saddle.

"Boy, you got any clothes that fit?"

Richter turned. "I lost them in the swamp, sir. Last scouting."

"You mean when them other boys didn't come back?"

Richter swallowed. "Yessir. I was the only survivor."

"Hmm. Tragic. Now tell us again what you saw out there."

"More greenskins—"

"*Louder* boy."

Richter cleared his throat. "More greenskins than could be counted, sir!"

"Can you count, boy?"

"Yessir. I've learning."

"But there was too many to count for you, eh?"

"Yessir."

"Louder."

"Yessir! The greenskins were like an ocean, sir!"

"Like an ocean you say." Grinning, the commander straightened up. He looked over to the line of other horsed commanders. "Hear that, men? More greenskins than can be counted! A green ocean swells before us! And what are we to do with this 'green ocean', men?"

The commanders and soldiers alike shouted back: "Turn it red!"

Richter cleared his throat. "Sir... if I may make a suggestion..."

Hiccupping with dying laughter, the commander slowly turned. "You say something, boy?"

"Yessir."

"And?"

"The territories west of here are swamps, sir. I noticed most of these men are heavily armored, and that you're riding horseback."

"Not just me, but a whole contingent of cavalry that will ride these greenskins flat. You know what contingent means, boy?"

"Do you know that a weighted horse will sink and get stuck in a swamp?"

Richter pursed his lips as soon as the words left them.

The commander sat upright and even his horse pinned its ears.

"Boy."

"Yessir."

"I'm going to go into them territories and lay flat these orcs and goblins."

"Yessir."

"When I come back, alive and well and full of honor, I surmise that my victorious men shall be in need some entertainment for the evening. Little in this world can match the glee that comes from killing greenskins, but I always try to do well by my men even in the quiet aftermaths."

"Yessir."

"And so I think I'm going to strap you to a tree and hide you raw with a whip until the squealing isn't fun no more. Hells, I think we may even put an apple on your head and have ourselves a shooting contest. Something for the guile bowmen to show off their skills with, understand?"

"Yessir."

"But!" The commander sat upright. "If you're right, well, then you got nothing to worry about at all. I guess we'll all just be somewhere out there stuck in a swamp, dying and wishing we'd done listened to the little grey boy from that shit town this world didn't want no more."

"Yessir."

Smirking, the commander nodded and then turned his horse. Its tail swished in the boy's face as it left, and the commander resumed his position with the rest of the nobles. They pointed and laughed while Richter stood staring straight ahead, but even in his blurred peripheral he knew they were fashioning him a proper punishment. A peasant should never backtalk to a noble. Highborn. Lowborn. These were the places. These were *always* the places. No matter how you turn a ladder, the first step starts at the bottom.

Richter watched thousands of men march by. As the tail end of the army started drifting out, the commanders lifted their reins and the horses turned in one smooth motion, the sun gilding their armored stride. His commander glared at him while a few of the other nobles mockingly tipped their helms like he was a princess standing there to see off the region's finest troop.

When they were all gone, a workmanlike quiet filled the camp as the camp followers moved about to roll up tents and stomp out campfires and empty crockpots. All the while, Richter stood fighting his own clothes, trying to stuff his ill-fitted pants into his equally ill-fitted giant boots.

As he struggled, a shadow fell over him.

He looked up.

A man stood there wearing a black coat and a black hat. He leaned forward with a smile. "Hello there. You are a pathfinder, are you not?"

"The last of them here," the boy said with a nod. "Name's Richter."

"Mhmm. The boy from Dagentear. The one they call the Wight."

"I don't really like being called that, but some do it anyway."

"Some."

"Yeah, like you." Richter stood in his boots like they were buckets. He looked up, shirt and pants billowing, appearing as a boy who fell naked through a fat man's washbin and came out clothed. "What do you want?"

"I heard what your commander said."

"Yeah, so? He made sure everyone heard."

The man in black smiled. He said, "I was in those territories near your scouting. The time you went out with a few and came back alone."

"You saw us?"

"Briefly. I kept quiet, obviously."

"What in the hells were you doing out there?"

"I was looking for a woman."

"You find her?"

"Aye."

"Well good on you getting your piece wet. You looking to celebrate?"

The man in black smiled again, this time looking up and about as though trying to share the smile with others. As he turned, his black coat opened briefly and a line of bandoliered glass vials caught the sun in blinding winks, the cascade of colors a rainbow's variety.

Richter took a step back. "I haven't seen you around here before."

"No, I wasn't wanting to be seen. Until now, of course."

"What do you want?"

The man held his hands out, palms forward. "I mean no harm, boy. I'm leaving this camp today. What you told your commander is true. You've no need to fear the whip because soon there will be no one left to hold it."

"Alright," Richter said. "And?"

"I think it best that you come with me."

"Come with you where?"

"To Marsburg."

"Never been to Marsburg."

"I surmise a few years ago you'd been nowhere else but Dagentear yet here you are. Do you know what surmise means?"

"Yeah I know what surmise means." Richter looked down at his boots. He looked at the camp followers slowly trudging about like spirits dragging anchors. He snorted and spat. "Alright. I'll come with if you got some pay."

"That I do."

"You try anything funny on the roads and I'll kill you dead."

"Aye." The man in black nodded. "Fair enough."

"Yeah," Richter said. "But if I'm wrong about the greenskins and my commander does indeed return… bounty hunters are liable to come looking for me. They'll draw me up. They'll likely even have a reward for me, too." The boy eyed the man closely. He added: "A big reward at that."

The man in black moved his hands and out of the crossing of sleeves he produced a small leather bag. He lofted it into the air and when Richter caught it a great jangling sounded that drew a couple prospecting eyes from the camp followers. The boy quickly secreted the crowns in the nook of his elbow.

"More where that came from," the man said. He looked skyward, judging the sun and where it was and where it would be. He seemed to catalog his findings with a grunt and then looked down. "I'm leaving now. You coming?"

Richter stared into the bag. A pile of golden Landon faces stared back. It was more money than he'd ever seen. He nodded. "Y-yeah… I'll go with ya."

"Good. Do you have a weapon?"

"There's probably a crossbow or two around here somewhere."

"Do you know how to shoot one?"

Richter shrugged. "I practice now and again."

The man smiled. "Well then. You go grab your weapon of choice and we shall depart."

"Wait," Richter said. "I don't even know your name."

"Ah." The man leaned as though to tell a secret: "Carsten Corrow."

Leaning back, Richter said, "Well alright, Carsten. What am I to do in Marsburg, help you look for more of your lady friends?"

Carsten smiled. "Aye, something like that."

~ ~ ~

Something like that.

Richter opened his eyes. Hobbs stood at the end of the bed.

Furrowing his brow, the man said, "I told you to let me rest."

"You stirred on your own. I'd just been sitting here doing nothing."

"Don't have better things to do?"

"Not right this minute, no. Nothing's all I got."

Sighing, Richter sat up and swung his legs off the side of his bed.

"You alright?" Hobbs said.

"Give me a moment."

Richter put his head into his hands. Outside the bunkhouse, the ferry town brimmed with woodworkers sawing trees and the creak of wagons coming and going. Morning birds chirped and fluttered. As the sounds ebbed and flowed, Richter touched his missing ear and, for the first time in a while, there was no pain. Merely scars touching scars.

"You alright?" the boy repeated. "You were talking in your sleep again."

Taking a great breath, Richter stood up.

Hobbs met him in a hurry, Carsten's old witch hunting hat in his hands.

"It's not good to talk in your sleep," the boy said, speaking as he tipped on his toes. "My father said a man could pass secrets doing that, and he said no matter how it came out, a secret told was a secret lost."

"This the father who beat you and named you after a dog?" Richter said. He flicked the lid of Carsten's cap and tussled the boy's hair. "How about you mind your own business, eh?"

"But can I ask… who were you talking to?"

"If it's worthwhile, you'll never have to ask someone what they were dreaming," Richter said. He nodded. "They'll just come out and tell you."

"It was Carsten, wasn't it?"

The tinge of joviality faded from Richter. "Aye. It was Carsten."

"What'd he have to say?"

"What do you think?"

The boy held out the guildmaster's hat. "So it's still about her, is it?"

Richter did not take the hat. Instead, he patted the boy on the cheek. "My dreams are nothing to concern yourself with, alright?" He walked to a wash basin in the corner and threw water into his face. He said through the splashes: "Nothing to concern yourself with, Hobbs, you hear me?"

"But she's out there still…" he paused. "You know… Claire."

As water dripped from his face, Richter glanced toward the bunkhouse's window. The silhouettes of peasants came and went, but every so often one would stop and point and its shadowed hand would press against its equally shadowed face and whisper, and despite all that dark and silent obscurity,

Richter knew what these folks whispered about: the Wight. A rumor running through the town like a rat scratching under the floorboards. And as the black shapes departed, Richter stared at the strange empty light their absence left behind. It seemed to him that even the briefest shadow could forever blemish the light which helped produce it. A chill hidden in all that warmth.

Richter looked down. His reflection stared back from the wash basin. Another Richter. Corrugated. Wobbling. A befogged visage rolling back and forth, beautified by the water's swirling mystery, and then the water stilled into a mirror and his face could be seen in full, blemished by the water's unflattering flatness, himself seen in gruesome clarity. Himself as perfect as himself could be mustered. Scarred. Sagging. Unkept.

"So, are you going to tell the company?" Hobbs said. "They should know who you're after, shouldn't they?"

Richter turned back. "Boy, did I not say—"

Hobbs stood at the edge of the bed with Carsten's hat on his head. He ran his little fingers along the brim as if he'd just bought it for himself.

In an instant, Richter crossed the room and swept it from Hobbs' head. When the boy reached out for it, Richter held it aloft, and when the boy leapt for it, Richter swung it further away and shoved Hobbs back onto the bed.

"What in the hells has gotten into you, Hobbs?"

"She's out there and, and… and you're not even talking about it!"

Grumbling, Richter reached into his jacket and pulled out a slip of paper. He unfurled it, showing a black and white drawing of a roguish man. He said, "You see this? It's the name, face, and price of a brigand by the name of Kantorek, the self-proclaimed 'King of Dragons.' He is in these woods and he is very real and I'm going to take his very real head and cut it off in exchange for very real money."

The boy sighed. He said, "I know how you think. I know what you're thinking about. And I know that Claire must—"

"Boy," Richter said, his voice elevating like a teacher's paddle.

Hobbs stopped. He held his hands up. "Fine. I'll leave it alone."

"Good." Richter rolled up the brigand's bounty. "Good. Great."

Sighing, Hobbs ducked past Richter like a wounded rabbit creeping across a naked plain. He went to the corner of the room and picked up his wooden toy sword. It never brought out of him the playfulness Richter had hoped it would. Instead, the boy held it upward and stared at it like he was waiting for it to point him the way to go. He then swung the sword, clapping its tip against the floor and bringing himself to lean on it like a cane.

Hobbs said, "Can I ask you something?"

"If you're smart about it."

"I will be."

"Alright then. Ask away."

"Just what sort of sellsword company do you think this will be?"

"A nameless one," Richter said, smirking. "At least for now."

Hobbs clucked his tongue and shook his head. "You know what I mean."

Richter walked to the opposite corner of the room. There tilted Adelbrecht's sword and he took it up and girded it to his hip. "It won't be like the Free Company," he said, cinching the leathers. "That I can assure you."

Annoyed, Hobbs clucked his tongue again. "That's a gimme answer."

Richter took his hand off Adelbrecht's sword and held Carsten's hat before him, slowly turning it around and around, memories turning with it, slowly and unseen but all too felt.

"You discuss matters that don't concern you," Richter said and he put on the hat and went for the door.

"Wait, Richter," Hobbs said. "I've one more question."

Sighing, Richter's hand fell from the handle. "What is it?"

The boy slowly crossed the room. "I understand you don't want to talk about her. I understand you think it's dangerous to announce to the world that you're hunting a princess. I very much understand that not everyone will even believe that she's a witch until they see it with their own eyes."

"What is your question, boy?"

Hobbs stood before Richter. "If you're *not* hunting Claire von Sommerwein, then what is this?"

The boy lifted his wooden sword and its point fell upon Richter's bandolier, clinking one of its many hexenjäger vials.

Richter looked down and slowly pushed the wooden sword away.

"The company comes first," he said. "You asked how good the company can be and I'll say this: it can be made to do what I need it to do. Even if they don't truly know, they can still be prepared to face whatever might come out of these woods. But, Hobbs, all of that depends on…" Richter paused. He thought of himself in the Battle of Many Names, a small voice lost to the machinery of war and the pride of men which drove it. But now he could change things. Now he could do what was right and proper.

He wasn't a small voice anymore. Now he was *the* voice.

"The company depends on what?" Hobbs said.

Richter smiled. "On just how good of a captain I can be."

THE DRUNK SLEPT in a wheelbarrow with his sword and shield limp across his lap and his legs draped over the ends of the wheeled and wooden bed. By that morning, three women had congregated about him, not for any improper reason other than they needed the use of that which had been gracelessly occupied. They held a whispering congress on how to evict the sellsword until a woodworker stepped out from his bunkhouse and marched over and said just kick him out, then this man looked at the drunk's armaments and he stood there a few moments in contemplation. Grunting nervously, he threw a dismissive hand and said let the sellsword sleep and went back inside and indeed the women also departed one by one.

As though disturbed by the sudden silence, the drunk snorted awake and fell out the wheelbarrow the only way that could be done: by forgetting he was in one and tipping it clean over and dumping himself in a clatter of shield and weapon and boots and curses. This roused a glimmer of humor in the eyes of onlookers, though none dared to outright laugh. All the same, the drunk stood up and patted himself down and gathered his things and ventured to the corner of Immerwahr's store and took a piss. When he came back to the road the wheelbarrow was gone. He looked left and right, realized where he was, figuratively and literally, and headed to the town's center and the two-story pub which stood there like a priory for the thirsty.

He entered and a few men playing cards at a table looked up at him and exchanged nervous glances but the drunk simply pointed toward the stairs, wordlessly announcing his intention to which the men nodded and offered peaceful gestures as though he were an esteemed guest. The drunk climbed the steps, sauntering from one side to the other, overcorrecting himself into the wall or against the handrail, cursing under his breath all the while, but in laboring time he came upon the penultimate step and righted himself, his back cracking in a long stretch.

"Morning, Dahlgren."

The drunk looked up. The homesteader looked down.

"Sophia," Dahlgren said. "Morning."

He smiled.

She smiled.

"Even for you, you're looking rough," the homesteader said.

"Oh you know me," the old man said. "I'm from around the way."

"Mhmm." Sophia crossed her arms. "Where'd you sleep this time?"

"Around." Dahlgren leaned, peering into her room. "Hobbs in there?"

"No, the boy's being more venturous lately."

"Oh?"

"Mhmm. Playing 'captain' with a couple local lads."

"I don't trust those kids. Thomas got an eye on him?"

Sophia nodded. "The servant's being watchful as always."

"Good. And where is our actual captain?"

"Doing inventory and I believe looking to hire fresh faces."

"Hm." Dahlgren took his good hand to his chin and rolled his mouth until the jaw cracked. Yawning, he said, "The roster could use new blood."

Sophia sighed. "Hopefully these ones will last more than a day." As the words left her lips, her eyes widened as if to try and net them back in. "Ah, I didn't mean to be so crude."

The old man dismissed her concerns with the wave of his hand. "Sellswording is the toughest business there is and it's quite a task to find a good fighting man to start with. You can't know until you know so you gotta keep hiring until you find the good ones. Speaking of knowing things, are Trash and Quinn in town?"

"Elletrache is on a hunt. Said he saw a deer and he wanted it and I suspect he'll get it." She pointed down the landing to another door which had a red sock adorned to its handle. "Quinn's asleep in there. Got two women with him. Or maybe it was three."

"Course he is and course he does." Dahlgren stared at Sophia, and her at him. He scratched the back of his head with the nub of his handless arm and nodded. "Ah, well. If Richter's pulling recruits, he'll be wanting me to bust 'em into shape. Run tryouts, all that shite."

Sophia looked out the door and then down the hall. She pulled the old man in. "I think you've time yet for other matters."

"Lady," Dahlgren said, taking the homesteader's rough hands into his leathered one. He leaned in. "Let's give it a moment, say when I come back from the day's work—"

"This is about as fresh I've seen you all week. Now's better than ever."

The old man smiled. He spoke drolly, "But the captain's waiting."

The lady pulled at his shirt. "Mean old Richter can keep waiting."

~~~

Captain Richter stared at the company's inventory strewn across a table.

"We got a couple aketon caps," Crockett said, the paymaster walking by with a quill pen and a sheet of paper. He picked one of the caps up by hooking a finger through a hole. "Looks like rats chewed on this one."

He dropped the cap and went further down the table, now and again pointing with his quill pen. "Couple full body gambesons to go with the caps… but the chest pieces also suffered some nibbling. Damn them rats really do go hard on the gambeson. Aside from those, we also got one metal helm belonging to Dahlgren. One chainmail also belonging to Dahlgren. He also has his sword, but he keeps it on his person. I paired the round shields and spears together as you requested, but the quality of their woodwork leaves a lot to be desired. I'm no strongman by any means, but I'm pretty certain I could break some of these just rolling over in bed, not that I fancy myself to sleep with spears and shields when I'm so up to my eyeballs in the ladies…"

Pausing, Crockett glanced at Richter to see if his attempt at humor had landed at all, but the captain only nodded as if to say, 'go on.'

The paymaster cleared his throat and did just that: "Here we got four small bows. One crossbow and Elletrache of course still that has that, uh, handheld ballista he menaces the local wildlife with. Quinn won't let me add his daggers to the inventory, but I suppose he's got four or five of them on his person. He's also been practicing with throwing axes lately much to the horror of many. The rest of it, well, we got handaxes, lumberjack axes, some pitchforks, wooden clubs, and whatever this thing is," the paymaster paused, picking up a slab of wood connected by a knotted string tied to another slab. "A cheap attempt at a flail, I take it?"

Richter nodded. It was a frequently used weapon by militias short on a blacksmith. Good for knocking a drunkard's skulls, not so great in an actual battle, much like a typical militia itself, in fact.

Throwing it back into the pile, Crockett said, "That about sums it up."

Richter walked up to the table and looked the weapons over, his hand bristling across their handles and dull edges. His other hand rested on the hilt of Adelbrecht's sword, its steel girded to his hip. He glanced down at it and the natural way its pommel rested into the curve of his palm. He slowly took his hand off it and crossed both arms.

"What we have here," Crockett said. "Is a mess in every sense of the word."

"Aye." The captain turned to his paymaster. "Now let's go get us some men to wield this mess."

Chapter 2. The Shapeup Line.

RICHTER DRAGGED over a slab of wood while Crockett rolled two stumps in tow, trotting from one to the other in a hasty yet stumbling ebb and flow. They combined their efforts to make a wobbly table and then they turned to a local and asked if they could borrow his porch chairs which he allowed. The captain offered a coin for the help, but the man declined and despite this charity he left the two with a few words of chastisement, of which "sellsword shites" were most common.

"Nice fella," Crockett said.

"There are worse ways for a town to treat sellswords," the captain said. He took a seat, running his hands on the chair's armrests.

Crockett settled into his own chair as he threw his ledger upon the table. He carefully arranged his quill pen and ink bottle beside it. Finished, he placed his hands in his lap and said, "I think we look official enough, don't you?"

A peasant walked by and said nothing but stared each man in the eye and spat at the ground, then pointed at his spit and then at the two men.

Richter nodded. "We look like proper mercenaries alright."

The two watched as the townspeople passed to and fro, most of the peasantry whispering the moment they saw the sellswords, others yet ducking their heads and quieting away. But much else was going on. Lumberjack axes snickered and snackered at the tree line surrounding the town. Elsewhere, hammers clogged the air with clapping echoes upon echoes as daytalers nailed up boards or slatted rooftops. Out everywhere, dogs laid sunbathing, their tails occasionally wagging to nothing and their eyes lifting now and again to watch the feral cats that sauntered about, and there was indeed always a cat sauntering, their own tails swishing with strange dismissiveness.

Amongst all this, a band of children sped forth in shrieking, reckless abandon. They brandished knightly toys from Immerwahr's shop, or carrots for swords which were easily eaten into maces and daggers. But the moment they saw the two mercenaries, they ceased all play and covered their mouths. This silence proved disturbing for suddenly quieted children was never a portend for good, and the dogs lifted their heads, and the cats froze, and the daytalers held their hammers high, and the axes quit. A woman swung into the road and gathered the little ones and ushered them away, and as she left things returned to what they were, noises and sights and all.

Crockett sighed. "And to imagine I thought they'd warm to us."

Richter had attempted to alleviate the townspeople's fear of mercenaries by doing as good of work as he could, and of course by keeping Quinn under control and trying to limit Dahlgren's drinking. But killing for coin was an inherently distrustful vocation. Yet, telling peasants that he was playing the part of a sellsword just to muster the forces needed to kill a powerful witch who also happened to be a young Sommerwein princess just didn't seem like it'd land well with the laity. If there were any lynching blood flowing in their veins, then that sort of conspiracy might surely energize it.

"I'd say it is a fine day, though," Crockett said, tilting back and forth in his chair, his burly weight testing its legs until he clapped forward. "Ah, wait. Maybe spoke too soon."

A throng of men approached the table, a disheveled lot so ragged that their complexion carried a sort of disdain for mortality: scars and blotches and moles all over the flesh, mouths that couldn't close, noses that wheezed, shapeless eyebrows burned or plucked away, receded hairlines on young men and wispy tails of it on the plain domes of the older lot, as though time itself served as an agent and amongst these men it aimed wildly and without regard for collateral. And these poor souls bumbled forward on busted knees and hobbled feet, altogether a collection of walking errors seeking answers of a world long exhausted of its kinder truths, such a strange assemblage of men it seemed their parts had been chosen at random, and oft for humorous effect at that, and in this regard Richter assumed some higher powers were indeed having a laugh at his expense as the mob soon closed in.

"By the old gods," Crockett said. "Surely this isn't the best of them…"

"Get that pen and ledger ready," Richter said.

"You can't be serious?"

Richter nodded. "We need every body we can afford."

Shambling and shuffling, they arrived at the table and one possible recruit held up a piece of paper that the paymaster had posted that morning.

"You the sellswords, right?" the man asked.

Richter counted the men at near to a dozen. He did not recognize a single one of them for Immerwahr's ferry town, caught between lands of war and lands of wilderness, carried an element of transience.

"My name is captain Richter," Richter said, then gestured down. "This is my paymaster, Crockett."

One of the men raised his hand.

"I'll be asking the questions," Richter said.

The man put his hand down.

Richter nodded. "Are there any soldiers or former soldiers here?"

None of the men raised their hand.

"Alright. How many of you have ever killed someone?"

The men glanced at each other.

"This is not an inquiry of law," Richter said.

One man scrunched his face. "A curiosity of what?"

Another piped in: "He said inquiry. Inquiry of law. That means he ain't gonna arrest us for nothing."

The scrunched face relaxed. "Oh in that case yessir, I done killed before."

"With what intent?" Richter said.

"You mean with what cause did I do it?"

"That's right."

"Well, wasn't much intent, really. See, I was a'roofin' a pub at the time. Twice as tall as this town's drinking hole! Each floor had its services, and the roof was a roof. I see you all know what a roof is, that's good. Well. They put this flagstaff out in front of the establishment and this drunk fella done thrown a bucket up on it. So it was at eyelevel with us roofers, that flagstaff and that bucket. It spent days just hanging there by its handle. Naturally, we turned to throwing rocks into it. You know, like a game and such."

"It's a fun game, rocks and buckets," a man said. The others agreed in murmurs. "Honestly the best fun I'd ever had."

The original man continued: "Yeah it's fun, but anyway someone bet me I couldn't land a brick in it without knocking it down. We wagered three points be fair if I made it. We were sporting bets at this stage of the roofing, you know? Roofing takes a while sometimes. Anyway. I attempted the throw. Wouldn't you know it! Yessir, that's right fellas: the shot landed plumb square in that'n bucket! Unfortunately, it broke the harness off the bucket and the damn thing fell straight down and killed this addled donkey that just been standing in the wrong place, standing there beneath the bucket that is. No ill omen, but in the descent of bucket and brick, you know, there was some evil speed involved. So that bucket struck that bastard donkey deader than dead, he didn't get out no hee nor haw. And yessir. That's what I killed."

"A donkey?" One of the men groaned before yelling out: "He asked if ye ever killed a *man*, fool!"

"Oh well shit you got me standing back behind everyone else how in the hells am I supposed to hear the question proper?" The donkey slayer rubbed his head. "Sorry sir, in that case… no, no I have not killed nobody."

One man scratched his ear. "Damn that tale had me confused from beginning to end."

Richter sighed. He raised his voice and said, "Is there a soul here who has killed something aside from a donkey? Or any other animal for that matter, er, no wait…"

Crockett leaned back, grinning. "They got you more twisted up than any witch's hut, Richter."

"Shut it, Crockett."

One man raised his hand. "Yer asking if any of us be un-law-abidin'?"

Another man swatted it down. "No he said this wasn't no such inquiry!"

One man in the back grabbed another man's arm and raised it for him, nearly yanking him off his feet. For extra measure, he pointed at the man's chest in case anyone didn't know who he was talking about. "This fella here is a poacher! On the run from the Landons I hear! Aren't you on the run? Tell 'em yer on the run."

The supposed poacher tried to shelter himself behind the others, but Richter's gaze seemed a lawman's sort and the men made a gap and there the summoned stranger stood almost nakedly alone.

"This is true?" Richter said. "You're a poacher?"

"Aye," the poacher said. "Just a couple of deer, that's all."

"Even one deer is a serious offense to the Landons."

"Aye sir."

"But they are not here. They are in Marsburg, hiding behind their walls."

"Aye sir."

"You have a bow, poacher?"

"Aye sir. And a quiver with some arrows. Good arrows, mind."

Richter looked at his paymaster.

"On it," Crockett said, scribbling into his ledger, estimating the cost of the man's equipment so as to properly compensate him were he to be hired.

"Poacher," Richter said. "I understand you have fled from Marsburg, but why are you not hunting Immerwahr's side of the woods?"

The man rubbed the back of his head. "Ahh, I don't like talking about it. Nobody believes me."

"Believes you about what?"

"L-like I said, I don't like talking about it."

Richter nodded. "You tell me, and you're hired."

The poacher's eyes lit up. He blurted, "There's a direwolf in the woods."

The rest of the group groaned, one of them thumbing toward the poacher. "This dumb fark's been peddling this'n lie for weeks."

"It ain't no lie," the poacher said. He nodded confidently to Richter. "I swear I've seen it, and there's just no way I'm wandering into the woods alone no more." He cleared his throat and stood up a little straighter. "You asked why I'm not hunting. Well, that's why."

The paymaster leaned over. "Elletrache did say monsters might flock to these woods in the absence of beast slayers and travelers. Wouldn't shock me if such a creature were afoot, though I certainly hope it is not true."

"Me too!" one man shouted. He gritted his teeth. "A direwolf can rip you apart with its teeth alone!"

"Quit this beast-talk," another said. "There ain't no direwolf."

"Hey I dunno. On my way in someone mentioned three lumberjacks had gone missing. Maybe the poacher is on'ta'somethin'?"

"They're amiss cause bandits own the Ancient Road you dullard!"

"Hey I'd heard some lass went up a tree and never climbed down."

"How in the fark does some girl's inability to fall out a damned tree prove there's a direwolf?"

"No I was just contributin', that's all."

"Yeah, there ain't no farkin' direwolf here."

"Y'all best shutup about the monster talk. I ain't sleeping enough as is."

"That's cause you sleepin' outside."

"Well we don't all got coin to buy a farkin' pile of hay you scamp!"

"Scamp? That's a big word for a man who wakes with the cats and dogs!"

"Listen, hey listen to me you shitter! One day I'mma earn enough coin and I'mma get one of them fancy rooms, and if I see you in there I'mma walk into *your* room and, well, you'll see, you'll see!"

"Why wait to see it? Show me what ye'll do now, just make sure'n'get them weevils out yer ears first."

The rest of the men took a step back and cooed excitedly like crows watching two cats about to fight.

"When I'mma done with you, you'll need to see a tooth doctor!"

"Oh is that right? Well you'll be needing a gravedigger!"

Richter slammed the table. "Excuse me!"

Two men with their fists raised slowly lowered them.

Crockett shook a purse of coins to fill the sudden silence, and also draw the men's collective attention span like babies to a rattle. Fists unclenched and mouths moved to form quick apologies.

Richter leaned forward, knuckling the table. "It was likely bandits that killed those lumberjacks, but a direwolf is something we will take into account. As for you, poacher, you're hired. Ten crowns daily with fifty upfront."

The poacher pumped his arms. "Oh by the old gods, I've myself a day!"

"Fifty!" another man yelled. He strode forward. "Hey! I-I'm a poacher! A really good one, too!"

The men started clamoring for attention:

"Don't listen to that man, he's got a clubfoot! Myself, well, my... uh, my uncle was a soldier in the Landon army! I learned a lot from his war stories!"

"Yer full'o'shit!" another man said and soon a shoving match started.

"I can swing a shovel real good!" another piped in. "There's some skill in shovel swinging! It ain't no sword, but when I get bored I sometimes pretend it is! And I get bored real easy so it's like I train all the time!"

"Just wanna remind everyone I had the skill to get that brick in the bucket, don't y'all forget."

"Hey I got a question. If one were to supposedly steal a chicken from a coop is that considered poaching or something else?"

"That's just theft, man."

"What's the penalty for that?"

"Depends how hungry the chicken's owner was, I suppose."

"It's all stupid shittalk anyhow, the whole reason the poacher got hired was cause he had a bow!"

"I've shot a chicken with a bow! It was easy! It just stared at me, then I shot it."

"Wow! I once knew this fella who stole chickens to fu—"

"Enough!" Richter slammed the table. A few passing peasants stuttered in their steps before hurrying away. The captain cleared his throat. "So you're not killers. I understand that now, quite thoroughly do I understand that. I've only one more question: how many here *wish* they could kill someone?"

The men glanced at each other and then back at Richter.

"You mean," one man said. "Like if I were given the opportunity… to kill someone I didn't like…"

"Would you do it," Richter said, "if you were paid to do so."

All hands shot up.

"Good," Richter said. He patted Crockett on the shoulder. "Very good."

"No offense, captain," Crockett said, lowering his voice, "but these are just daytalers and cripples and runaways. They're not fighters…"

"Observation noted," Richter said. "Now hire them all."

~~~

Richter opened the door to Immerwahr's store. Two boys holding foodstuffs stared at the captain and then glanced at each other. They put the items back on the shelves and made a quick escape as if they were caught stealing, which Richter knew very well that they were. A moment later a woman sauntered out from the aisles, picking up her dress and ducking away from the captain as though he might strike out at her like a cat's usual animus for innocent passersby. When she got out onto the store's porch she turned around and spat and said, "Mercenary bastard!" and spat again and added, "Killer!" She may have had more to say but the door finally closed.

The captain turned around. Rows of shelves had been added to the monk's store and some expensive windowpanes helped shower the room with a faint yellow glow, the light winking over metal trinkets and dimpling over wooden ones. For such a modest building, it had the allure of something grand, so long as one ignored the tilt in the foundation, the way the wood groaned at the slightest breeze, and the war of cats and rats that mewled and squeaked beneath the floorboards.

"Immerwahr," Richter said, taking off his hat.

"Just in the back my friend," the monk said. "In a state of… ergh, preoccupation!"

The voice was oddly elevated. Richter walked further in, passing shelves of vegetables and salted meats and leaf-wrapped fish heads. As he reached the back of the shop, he saw the monk up on a ladder stocking the top shelves with toy soldiers. Richter regarded him, hat in hand, as though the monk were up on his temple steps and the captain had with him an assortment of troubles which could not be tangibly held yet weighed ever so mightily. Before Richter could part with his woes, the monk spoke without so much as looking back:

"One of your sellswords got drunk and pissed on my building today."

Richter nodded. "I thought it smelled a bit fresh in here."

The monk paused and looked over his shoulder with a pensive stare.

"Alright," Richter said. "I'll talk my man."

"But I haven't even said which one it is."

"Drunkard. Pissing on your store. I got a good idea."

Immerwahr returned to stocking his goods. He continued with his complaints just as well: "And there's been considerable grousing about a man of your party imbibing young wives and then lowering their guard with humor and dance until they just so happen upon a bedroom. Now that I'm well aware you are, excuse me, *were* a determined witch hunter, do I need to explain that a wayward vagabond does not offer drink to settled ladies without some other notion in mind?"

"I'd argue that it is the woman's choice on how to behave."

The monk looked over his shoulder again. "I'd argue that their husbands don't see it that way."

Richter nodded. "Alright."

"While I appreciate the idea of letting the ladies frolic and do as they wish, we both know that watchful, familial eyes can carry considerable scorn. So it may be that a husband takes offense on a drunken wench's behalf and runs your man through with a sword. So it may be that I have seen this action with mine own eyes before and wish not to see it again, no matter how deserving the scoundrel."

"Understood."

"Good," Immerwahr said. "And may I hazard a guess that you again know the culprit?"

"You're talking about Quinn," Richter said. The thief had indeed gone through the womenfolk of the town like a rabid dog through a litter of kittens. "He has a taste for danger and… being something of an annoyance. He enjoys it when people look at him for all the wrong reasons."

Immerwahr turned around again, now holding a toy wolf and a toy knight in the balance of his hands. He bobbed them measuredly as he talked: "We all enjoy a little adventure in our own ways but, Richter, please. I am trying to maintain the peace here. Tell your sellsword to rub a few crowns together and go lay with the ladies of the night. That's what they are there for."

"I'll see to it," Richter said.

The monk started putting the final touches on the arrangement of toys, bringing them to sit at the edge of the shelf, faces out, glaring down like watchful, albeit tiny guardians. His fingers graced each one with a gentle, last touch. He said, "I would be wary of the town keeping better watch of your men than you are, Richter. I don't bring up these instances to humor you, after all. These reports come to me from the people themselves, and they were not given to me with, how do you say, narrative pleasantries."

"I understand."

Richter dawdled a few moments, hoping Immerwahr would not bring up a third issue. As he prayed for conversational clemency, he reached out to one of the lower shelves and tilted a wood sculpture carved in the shape of an animal he had never seen before. The creature looked like a horse with a puckered face, strange ears, and a spine cratered into humps. Richter ran his finger between the humps for of all the oddities present they were certainly the most unusual.

"Mmm yes, its peculiarity makes it rather entrancing to the uninitiated eye." Immerwahr stepped off his ladder and walked behind his counter. He nodded at the toy. "Although that one is not for sale."

"What is it?"

"They call it a camel."

"Is it a real animal?" Richter said, looking back at Immerwahr as he left a finger on the model.

The monk nodded with a smile. "Yes, it is a real animal and indeed a curious one, as you can tell by its shape. These beasts are acquainted to the southern deserts. My understanding is they can travel long and far on little more than a sip of water."

"Interesting," Richter said. He set the animal back onto its base. He touched it again, and then once more for no particular reason. If it carried any luck, he certainly sapped the lot of it. He turned away and also returned to business: "Just to let you know, I took the privilege of hiring some of the town's recent arrivals."

"You didn't happen to hire that minstrel who showed up, did you?"

"I'm not certain, but I very seriously doubt the group I hired had a minstrel amongst them. They were not of... poetic intelligence."

"Good." Immerwahr nodded to himself a few times. "Very good. Last thing I need is a pub without music. Not sure why these silly bards want to go off fighting so much, but every other one I meet always seems desperate to go join a band of mercenaries."

"I suppose for the ballads," Richter said.

"You mean battles?"

"No, I mean ballads."

Immerwahr thought for a moment. "Ah... ah! I see. You mean they seek real-world experiences so as to engross the artistic craft with tangible merit. That is admirable, I suppose. A genius song is oft laden with genuine life."

Richter shrugged. "It would seem better to put those experiences under your belt *and then* start in on one's artistry. What madman would deign themselves a minstrel without first seeing what all there is to sing about?"

The monk raised an eyebrow. "Richter, do you wish to debate the merits of minstrels?"

"Not really."

"Well," Immerwahr said, a hint of disappointment dripping off that lonely syllable. He cleared his throat. "Well anyway, absent of minstrel talk, are you any closer to finding our resident menace, this 'King of Dragons'?"

The company's second official contract: to kill a notorious bandit leader in the forests. Just as the monsters and creatures had returned to the woods absent of their hunters, so too did brigandage find territorial purchase in the absence of noble patrols. While the 'King of Dragons' certainly had no dragons to his name, nor a royal crown for that matter, Richter found the man to be impressively elusive. And while he may have been a figure more worm than wyrm, the brigand at the very least had a lot of snake in him.

"Richter?" the monk said, tapping his countertop. He tilted his head forward. "The King of Dragons, Richter, are you closing in on him or…?"

"The bandit's name is Kantorek," the captain said. "I would prefer you call him that instead of glorifying his existence with aerified nonsense."

"And why would I do that? Hells, Richter, why would *you* do that? When you find this rogue and put his head on a pike, wouldn't it prove far more impressive to claim, *here be staked the King of Dragons!* A simple, '*this is the head of Kantorek*' just doesn't have the same… energy to it. You'll find no more renown in it than in slaying a rat in a cellar."

The captain nodded. "Call him whatever you want, but to answer your question: yes, we are closing in on the brigand. He appears to have established many camps in the area and frequently moves from one to the other, but I think there is a pattern in these movements."

"A pattern articulated and rubricated by dead travelers on the roads?"

Richter took a step back. "I'm working as fast as I can."

Bowing hurriedly, Immerwahr said, "Apologies, Richter, I did not mean to come across in such a manner. That was disrespectful of me to say and I have full faith that you are expediting this… process."

"The bandit and his brigands will be taken care of, Immerwahr. I gave you my word on that," Richter said. "We'll be training the new hires today and then we'll go on patrol again."

"You think a day's worth of training is going to be enough?" the monk asked, his face a genuine expression of concern.

"To be honest, Immerwahr, the word 'training' is an exaggeration. These are tryouts if anything. Dahlgren could have a month with them and they still wouldn't be ready. Sellswords aren't soldiers. They learn the hard way, by getting into fights and coming out alive." Richter knuckled the countertop. "I do have a question for you."

"Go ahead."

"Have you heard anything about creatures in the woods?"

"Yes," Immerwahr said. "Yes, I have heard about that."

Richter straightened up. "And you have heard…?"

The monk smiled like a father dispelling his son's nighttime fears. "I have heard about a direwolf, a lindwurm, a dragon, a nachzehrer, a webknecht, a brigand, a wiederganger, a black clad cultist, I've even heard that the trees themselves have come alive and skewered men dead with their branches, and that mud creatures have risen from rainswept territories and swallowed travelers whole. Richter, please, the laity love to talk about all the ghouls and ghosts these woods hold. Until you see it with your own eyes…"

Richter nodded. "Alright. I got it."

"Mmhmm. Yes, well. As I had been hinting at earlier, the townsfolk are tiring of your presence." Immerwahr reached down behind the counter and when his hand returned it came with a sack. "So, to be terse, I don't want you training in the town anymore."

"Why's that?"

"It scares the townsfolk." The monk patted the sack. "You've yourself a hundred crowns in there. Good coin for a very simple job."

"That job being to train outside of town?"

"No," the monk said, then paused and bobbed his head side to side. "Well, in a manner. I actually want you to go to the ferryman. A couple of new people in town said that he was talking up a storm about something he saw on the opposite shoreline and I would like to know what has him so riled up. Now this is just hearsay, but supposedly he saw a man murder another man after getting off the ferry, but this was contradicted by another witness who said they saw both travelers stand and leave together. Who knows, but it's concerning enough an even that I'd like a little more info from the ferryman himself."

"I think I can ask him a couple questions," Richter said, nodding as he took the sack of money. "We'll train by the shoreline, then. Might be good to see to the ferryman anyway, ask him if he's seen any of Kantorek's bandits."

"Thank you, Richter. Oh! And one more thing."

"Aye?"

"The other day you inquired if any of the peasants have had a hard time finding herbs and shrooms in the forest."

"And?"

"They have been. More specifically though, it appears someone is picking all the mushrooms."

Richter raised an eyebrow. "Is this far from here?"

"Near the Ancient Road at the very least. Past that, I don't know. With Kantorek afoot, few dare to venture far."

"Do me a favor, monk, and tell your townsfolk to never cross that road." The captain put his hat back on. "And if these folk do truly dislike our presence then it's probably best to not tell them that order came from me."

Chapter 3. Training Day.

THE COMPANY TRAVERSED THE FOREST, passing through as a great sigh of men, a beleaguered composition on the march, heavy breaths choking and coughing, there before them and above them and beyond them the trees standing and trees fallen, and all the brush in between. They stuttered at the sight of a tree bit by lightning, black veins, static as they were, still yet seemed to violently spark across its denuded trunk. The sellswords nodded to the sight and as they passed every single man reached out and touched the charred remains and every single man had his own reason for doing so.

Further away from the ferry town, Richter spotted a patch of fresh mushroom with no caps. He looked for footprints but curiously found none.

"Something the matter?" Dahlgren said.

Richter nodded. "I think I'll scout ahead."

"I think not," Dahlgren said, rebuking in a snap.

"You think not?" Crockett said with a scoff. "Just who do you think is captain here?"

"Oh, that would be Richter, there's no question of that. But just because his is a pathfinder's heart doesn't mean it'll do the company any good if he wanders off and gets himself killed."

"Hey yeah, I agree," Thomas said, fumbling with his spear and shield, a somewhat humiliating allotment of gear for it were also the weapons given to the greenhorns. "I say we just let the fresh recruits stay on point."

Richter remembered captain Adelbrecht doing the same in the caravan from Walddorf to Marsburg. Let the fresh faces walk into the danger. He cringed at the reality that between his known men and those of the new recruits, it was indeed the right call to put the latter group on point.

"Alright," Richter said. He glanced at the newly hired men and gave a warbling, birdlike whistle to them, not too loud, but very inconspicuous. Too inconspicuous, in fact, for the men did not even turn to it. He tried again, but again the greenhorns marched on unawares.

"Hey dullards!" Quinn shouted.

One of the recruits stopped and looked back, and then tilted his head and gathered the attention of the rest. They started doubling back.

Dahlgren looked at Richter. "What bird sound was that?"

"Black woodpecker."

"Woodpecker?" Quinn said. "Maybe next time go and try knocking your head against one of these trees instead. They'll certainly hear that."

As the recruits neared, one raised his spear up like a guard approaching strangers. "What is it? Did we do something wrong?"

"No, we're just aligning assignments here. You're to go on ahead of us," Richter said. "Get on by about fifty paces. We'll move in two groups. Us in the back, you in the front. Keep your eyes and ears open, do you understand?"

"Is this an army thing?" another asked, turning back to Richter.

Richter shrugged. "Sure."

"Nice. And what if we run into something, what do we do?"

"Then you yell and run fifty paces back."

"So we don't fight?"

"You retreat." Richter pointed at the tree canopy, his finger tracing slants of light pillaring down. "Right now, the sun is on the back of our heads. If you need to run, make sure the light is hitting your eyes and you'll be fine."

"I think we can handle it," one of the greenhorns said, heaving up his shield and spear and clanking them together, and almost knocking both out of each hand in the process. He straightened up. "Y-yeah, we can handle it."

"Well," Dahlgren said. He clapped his hands. "Get to it!"

The greenhorns turned and went away, one of them counting his steps like a child traipsing a fallen tree trunk. After fifty-odd paces, they stopped and turned around and one gave Richter a thumbs up and the captain reluctantly returned the sign as if greeting a neighbor he didn't particularly like on a morning he didn't particularly want to wake to.

"Do they know what you intend?" Quinn said. "I thought to say something, but they seemed rather happy about the endeavor."

"What's he talking about?" Crockett inquired, pen in hand as if something revelatory would be said in response.

"Oh nothing much, only that the captain is sniffing an ambush and would rather it be them than us who walks into it."

"That's right." Richter turned to the thief and nodded. "I would rather it be them than us."

Quinn grinned. "Every man who says otherwise is a liar."

~~~

"So lemme get this straight," Quinn said, juggling an axe with one hand. "We go to the shore and we train these fellas for a day, and then tomorrow-ish we track down this Kantorek fella and send these scamps in face first?"

Richter climbed over a fallen tree and said, "Something like that, aye, and today we're also getting paid just to talk to the ferryman."

"Getting paid to chat?" Quinn said. "Shit I'm in the wrong business."

"Ferry masters see and hear a lot," Crockett said. "Ears and eyes like those are good to check in on. I'm sure Immerwahr would like an update."

"Crockett's intuition is correct," Richter said.

Wiping sweat from his face, Crockett said, "Thank you, captain."

Quinn eyed him. "Looking a little greasy there, Cricket."

"I know I could stand to lose a few pounds, Quinn," Crockett said. "Doesn't mean you have to bring it up all the damned time."

"Mhmm, way I see it, we should drop all this sellsword shit and sell Cricket here to a hogwallow barn'n'show! Strip this fat boy down to his altogether, grease 'em up a bit, and watch him run from some farm boys!" He tossed the axe up again. "Them rustic folk can scrounge up more coin than you'd imagine for such a display."

The paymaster turned. "One of these days I am going to beat the shit out of you, Quinn."

The axe's handle landed in Quinn's hand and this time he slowly lowered the arm as he turned toward the paymaster. "What'd you just say?"

Richter looked back. "Quinn, Crockett, that's enough."

"Hells," Dahlgren said. "I say just let 'em have it out."

Elletrache snorted and spat. He set his giant crossbow over a shoulder and said, "Yeah I'd be willin' to put money on the pig'un."

"See, even the beast slayer thinks him a hog," Quinn said. "Hear that, Cricket? You oink and Trash here might mistake you for a sow!"

Crockett took a step toward the thief, towering over him. "He's also willing to put money on me kicking yer arse."

"Now hold on a minner," Elletrache said, unyoking his crossbow. "Are we sayin' this here fight's gonna be by fisticuffs or with weapons and such?"

"There's not going to be a fight," Richter said.

Dahlgren laughed. "Shit, Trash, I figured they'd just brawl it out."

"If they're going in a proper pugilistic scrap then ol' Elletrache has it on the pig'un. But! You put steel into the fold and it goes to the boot thief."

"Aye," Dahlgren said. Grinning, he turned and pointed his nub of an arm at Richter. "Who you got, captain?"

Richter shook his head. "Nobody's fighting anybody."

"Hey yeah," Thomas said. "We, uh... lost, the, uh—"

"Are there idiots here seriously not going to put coin on me?" Quinn said. "C'mon, look at me. I'm a proper menace. No way I'm losing to this fat boy. I know Thomas has money on me, ain't that right Tommyboy?"

"Oh, uh, sure," Thomas said, shrugging. He pointed out into the woods. "But I just wanted to say we lost our recruits."

Richter leaned back. "What?"

"Yeah they just sorta kept on walking when we all stopped."

The captain jogged ahead, pushing the men out of the way as he ran up a half-fallen tree and looked forward. He stared through the foliage and saw absolutely no one. Just prints in the mud, tracks renting moss from trunks, and a couple of folded branches. The wake of men who had stolen out into the forest, bumbling like fools asking to be caught.

"I'll be damned," Trash said. "Those little snots dribbled right out from our noses."

"Dahlgren," Richter said, snapping his fingers. "We go quick now."

The old man nodded. He clapped his shield. "You two lovebirds say another word and I'll be hiding your arses. Let's move! Double time, fellas! Move move move!"

~~~

They heard the recruits screaming first.

Bracketing their yelps were the hoots and hollers of another party.

As Richter and the rest of the company barreled through the woods and out onto the Trading Swords' shoreline, they found four of the recruits huddled together with their shields and spears nervously stabbing outward. They were nearly surrounded by black clad brigands wielding swords and daggers and the wild grins of victory so imminent it could be savored, though the moment the captain and his men entered the picture all the brigands stopping having a laugh. They collectively retreated back a step.

"Sellsword shites!" One of the bandits used a bloodied dagger to point at a few bodies in the sand. "We already claimed two!"

Richter fell in behind the recruits and put his hands on their shoulders. They jumped and cried out, but as they looked back at the captain something in his stare calmed their nerves, and they glanced at each other as if to wordlessly ask if their fellows had seen it as well, and indeed they all had and they nodded at Richter who nodded back.

"Who did we lose?" Richter said.

"Th-the poacher and the donkey killer."

"Ahh," Quinn said. "I had such high hopes for those two."

"Hey," one of the recruits said. "Are we farked?"

"No," Richter said. "And if you try and run I'll kill you myself."

"That's pretty farked, captain," Quinn said, grinning wildly.

"Lotta chatter!" a brigand yelled. "Cheep cheep cheep, baby birds!"

Staring over the huddled group, Richter could see the poacher dead in the sands, face down, his vaguely protective armor of cloth cut to ribbons. Not far from him was the donkey killer, dead on his back, forearms cocked with the hands missing fingers. Just as Richter's eyes set upon him, a pale and bald brigand stepped forward, crouched down, and cut one of the donkey killer's ears off.

He lifted the ear and stared through its hole at Richter. Grinning, he said, "Like what you see, sellsword?"

"Ah c'mon," Quinn said. "That don't even make any sense!"

The brigand lowered the ear. He shouted: "Shields up!"

"*Hooh*!" The brigands disappeared behind a rise of round shields. "*Hooh!*"

Between his men good and new, Richter now had ten in total, and the brigands stood in equal number. The rogues had no spears, but instead wielded hatchets and daggers, now and again opening their wall of shields to let a cockeyed madman jump out and dance and hoot and holler, testing the mercenaries' resolve with his manic behavior.

"Dahlgren," Richter said, looking at the old man.

"Sir?"

The captain nodded. "Form the shield wall."

Dahlgren immediately drew up his sword and held it into the sky and stepped dead center of the formation.

"Alright you maggots! Around me! Shoulder to shoulder! Shoulder to shoulder! Here to there! Here to there!"

"Ow fark!" A recruit shrank from his neighbor like a boy from his brother's fist. When he looked over, Elletrache towered over him.

"Yar," the beast slayer said, nodding at his armor made of lindwurm scales. "Best not bump elbows with me, little greenhorn. Ol' Elletrache might not be sharp, but this here armor sure is heh heh heh."

"By the gods, what kind of outfit is this?"

"Quinn!" Richter shouted.

"Yeah?"

"Left flank. Kill anyone who tries to get around us."

"Gladly."

"Crockett and Thomas, right flank."

"O-of course," the paymaster said, and the servant looked as equally ready for the task.

"*Hoo-ahh!*" the brigands swung their shields open but this time it was no dancer, but a man planting his feet and hurling forth a javelin.

"Shields up!" Dahlgren and Richter both screamed.

A greenhorn shrieked and wheeled his shield just as the weapon blasted right through and slashed him across the cheek.

"I've been hit!" he cried out. "I'm dying!"

The brigands laughed.

"Yer fine," Dahlgren said as grabbed the man's shield and broke the javelin hanging out of it. He pushed the greenhorn back into the line. "Good as new, right?"

"H-how's my face?" the recruit said, turning his head, a slip of red pouring down his cheek.

"Improved," Dahlgren said. "Now get yer fuckin' shield back up and get back in line!"

"Hey!" One of the brigands called out, walking forward and pointing. "Hey you!"

Elletrache looked around.

"Yeah, you! One with the greenery! Those're lindwurm scales, are they not? How about we make ye a deal! You give us that armor, and we'll split! Everyone goes home in one piece! I think that's fair, is it not?"

"Elletrache," Richter said. "I'm not even going to consider—"

The beast slayer pushed Richter out of the way and unyoked his giant crossbow and leveled it at the mass of brigands. They clambered over the top of each other to get out of the way, revealing in the rear the pale brigand still fondling his prized ear trophy, and the man glanced at the change of decorum in his companions, and then his headless body toppled onto the shore as red mist and skull fragments swirled into the air behind him, Elletrache's harpoon making *whoop whoop whoop* whistles as it skipped and skidded clear across the river. The beast slayer lowered his weapon and knuckled his eyepatch.

"Haha!" Quinn shouted. "Brutal!"

"Sh-shoot 'em again!" a recruit yelled, hoping that this miracle weapon alone would remove any need for his being there. "Keep shooting!"

"Ah," Elletrache said. "It takes a minner to reload I'm afraid."

Covered in blood and brain, a brigand slowly turned back around. He pulled an indiscernible red string from his hair before looking at the mercenaries. "Ah-ahh… ch-charge! Charge them now! Kill them all!"

Richter did not think this man their leader – that man was in another world now, and even there presumably not in the sum of all his parts – but the terror of the beast slayer's weapon had done its job, and the whole mob of scapegraces came barreling forward in staggered confusion and fear, utterly disordered, albeit dangerous all the same.

The captain knew that he now had the upper hand if only his company could keep it together. Unfortunately, they were flagging already. These were ordinary men he had hired, not a killer amongst them, not a lick of military training, and not a minute of Dahlgren's instruction neither. But Richter knew these men from elsewhere: he saw them every single day, trundling to and fro, keeping themselves in this world out of some atavistic compulsion to eat and shit for as long as possible, murmuring and slurring and bumbling one day to the next, forever clinging to the smallest chance that things might get better. That they had ended up precisely where they were added nothing of value to this trajectory. No ordinary fool joins a sellsword company with a sound mind. They do it out of desperation and to see to it that, yes, maybe they could show this world what for, that they could give it a piece of their mind. The whole world chews on you long enough, you may want to stomp on a few throats before it swallows you hold. Richter knew this all too well.

One of the recruits gave his peace: "W-we can't take them!"

And another: "They're going to kill me!"

Indeed, Richter knew all of these men all too well. In a flagrant disregard for his own wellbeing, the captain strode to the front of his company and took Adelbrecht's sword and drummed it across the shields of his men. As the charge of the brigands stomped just behind him, the captain stared in the eyes of each man whether they be greenhorn or old brothers in battle and with unflinching ferocity he yelled: "This is your chance to prove yourselves worthy of the flesh and blood the old gods have given you! Men! Rise above the worms which haunt your feet! Raise your arms, men! *Be as one, and as one be a castle, and if you are but men of stone then let rage be your ramparts!*"

To a man, Richter's company roared with life and hardened their shields against their breasts and their spears steadied in sharpened points. Richter turned around and pointed his steel toward the flocking brigands, an out of formation mob swinging every weapon imaginable, gold and silver chains jangling from their necks, earrings glinting, gapped mouths swearing motherborne curses. The captain held his sword in both hands and braced.

In a moment, a collision. The black clad brigands slammed against the sellswords' line and the men all grunted as shields clattered together and spears strode up over and around, a porcupine of shafts going every which way and there came the sharp twang of steel gliding against steel and the shrill screams when they found purchase and the *thwips* of bows and crossbows being fired overhead and out of the corner of Richter's eye he saw a man with a pitchfork slamming it up and down like a shovel, and at the other side of the fight he saw a sellsword using his shield to batter a man's head in and of all things there, right in front of Richter, the captain realized he'd already crossed his sword with a toothless bandit and when their eyes met the brigand grinned and then suddenly Dahlgren's blade launched over the captain's shoulder and the man's eyes went crooked and his legs equally so as he crumpled like a marionette and in another moment came a rotation, the old man grabbing Richter and throwing him back behind the line and exchanging places with him all the same.

"Get yer arse behind the shields!" Dahlgren growled. "You think we can afford to lose you, captain?"

Before Richter could stammer so much as a word, the old man turned back around and rejoined the fray, his shieldarm bashing men to his left, his swordhand skewering those to his right.

The fighters fell on top of each other dead or dying, and the wounded were somewhere in the mud still yet having it out as if the battle itself had some economy of being and theirs was the land of cripples and beggars, their warfare eschewing steel for teeth and fists.

Richter saw a recruit flailing at the bottom of that hellish and he grabbed him by his boots and dragged him to safety. When the recruit turned over, Richter realized it was no sellsword at all but instead a brigand covered in blood. The man blinked and cocked his head as if to say 'you would truly save me?' and the captain answered by driving his sword through him. The man kicked back at the sheer pain of the puncture, but the steel found his heart and he calmed in an instant. One bad moment to buy an infinite peace.

As Richter drew the blade out, a voice hailed: "We won! We won!"

The captain looked up. In the span of moments, the battle concluded. Bodies heaped in stacks sometimes three high. Arms and legs protruding from the pile. Sometimes faces, their frozen eyes glaring. Above the twisted mound of corpses, bloodied survivors staggered about catching their breath.

"Hey!" Quinn yelled. "We got ourselves a runner!"

Beyond the battlefield, a brigand was fleeing up the shoreline, his pants halfway down his legs, his feet shuffling in a one-man sack race.

"I'll get 'im," Elletrache said, drawing up his crossbow.

Richter jumped to his feet. "We need him alive!"

The beast slayer gazed down his weapon, then sighed and lowered it.

Grabbing his own crossbow, Richter quickly aimed. The brigand looked back and yelped at what he saw and hurried ever faster. His silhouette moved in the sights of Richter's weapon, a black shape shifting unpredictably, arms flailing like a ragdoll held at a girl's side. Too many details... too many...

He fired.

A tuft of sand harmlessly kicked up at the heels of the brigand.

"Shit," Quinn said. "Guess I'll get the farker then."

The thief sprinted over the corpses with an axe in hand and his tongue sticking out of a grinning face. He planted his feet and hurled the weapon and it sailed end over end, rainbow arcing right onto its intended target. The brigand howled and fell to the sands, an axehead burrowed in his arse, blood, fat, and bone glistening in the floppy gash of a cheek.

"Holy shit!" Quinn pumped his fists. "I got him! I mean, I knew I'd get him. No doubt in my mind."

The brigand screamed and tried to get up but as his legs straightened his muscles tightened around the axehead and he shrieked and fell back down.

"Listen to 'im squeal," Quinn said, grinning. "Hit him right in the arse."

Richter snapped his fingers. "Go tie him up before he bleeds to death."

"Yeah yeah, alright."

As the thief scampered up the shore, Dahlgren sidled beside Richter. He drew up his shield – or what was left of it. Half an axe sat burrowed into its edge, the hand of the would-be killer still attached. The old man picked the hand off like a scullery maid unsticking an old dish rag from a washbin. He threw the hand and then threw the shield, too.

"Respectfully captain," he said. "Your aim's been off lately."

"Aye," Richter said. "Sight isn't what it used to be." He turned his hands, both scarred, one of them brutally so with lines crisscrossing every which way, wounds from when he had killed Adelbrecht with a wire mesh. "I think I got a bit of the shakes in my hands."

"That's alright. I get those, too."

"I think that's the drinking, Dahlgren."

"Wrong, the drinking is what makes it go away."

"Crockett!" the captain suddenly yelled, looking around. "You alive?"

A pile of corpses lifted and bodies drifted apart. The historian rose from between the rolling corpses, patted himself down, and then picked up his ledger. A dagger had been sheathed halfway into it.

"You alright?" Richter said.

"Ah, I think so."

"Very good." The captain pointed around the field. "Take account of who we still got and inform me of it as soon as you can."

Dahlgren leaned down and grabbed an arm and heaved the corpse up. "This is one of ours," he said before dropping it back onto the heap. He leaned back down and picked up another body and heaved it up. This time the body's knees curled up before awkwardly planting its feet. The old man grinned. He said, "This one's alive."

"Hey," Thomas said as he tottered. "Yeah. I'm alright, I think."

Richter looked around. "Did any of the recruits survive?"

The company glanced at each other and then at the bodies.

"Poor bastards all got it," Elletrache said. "To the last."

Crockett unsheathed the dagger from the book. He swung his girded ink bottle around and dotted it with a quill. He opened the ledger and started crossing out names.

Grunts and hollers came from up the shore. They turned to watch Quinn wrangle the brigand down like a ranch hand pulling a steer. The captain looked further up the shore to see the ferryman's house, its door oddly ajar.

"Alright," the captain said. "Let's at least see if our ferryman is still alive."

~~~

"Damn," Dahlgren said. "They even did in the birds."

The ferryman's front door creaked and tottered on old hinges. Beside the home, a dovecot lay in ruins. White and grey feathers swirled with the wind. Richter loaded his crossbow and moved ever closer to the hovel. Dead doves lay all along the way, gently scratching in the wind, nature herself cooing them to take flight, to join her in the skies, to depart the land, depart this cradle of gruesome creatures and their natures which had so brutally betrayed them.

"Anybody home?" Richter said. "You've got five seconds to come out or we're burning it down with you inside. Five. Four. Three. Two!—"

The captain kicked the cottage's front door off its hinges and it clapped flatly on the ground and a great cloak of dust swirled from its edges. White feathers danced in the dust as a terrified dove fluttered from corner to corner. The ferryman lay slumped against a wall with his head cocked to a shoulder and a crimson slit going across his neck. Sighing, Richter stepped back. The frightened dove joined him, flying out of the cottage and knocking his witch hunting hat right off.

"Ferryman in there?" Dahlgren said.

"Aye, he's dead."

Richter leaned down and picked up his hat. He knocked the sand off it and put it back on, the cloth coolly sliding over his missing ear. He looked toward the river. The last surviving dove sailed over it squalling and afraid.

"Alright then," Richter said. "Let's go ask our prisoner some questions."

~~~

Dahlgren and Richter stood at the length of a small dock which extended out over the Trading Swords river. The old man held the brigand in a chokehold, keeping him unconscious while Richter ran twine from a metal bucket to the brigand's teeth, lassoing each tooth with tight knots. Thomas meanwhile ran a thick sea rope around the man's arms and body, ensuring he'd not flail about whenever consciousness would return.

"Quinn," Dahlgren said. "Quit yer fancy footing and come over here and help."

The thief stood on the shore with his hands fisted to his hips, watching the rest of the company bind the prisoner. He shook his head. "I axed the man in the arse. I got him there. As far as I'm concerned, my job's done."

"What? Yer job's not done until the captain says it is!"

"He can't swim," Richter said.

The old man turned. "Huh?"

Nodding, Richter said, "A kid I knew growing up behaved like he is. Scared of the water, and the further everyone else went in, the further away he wanted to be from it."

Despite an unconscious man drooling onto his elbow, Dahlgren turned and calmy said, "That true, Quinn?"

"I ain't getting close," Quinn said. "One of you might throw me in."

Crockett laughed. "A thief afraid of water? But stealing from boats is a common tactic in that, uh, vocation. Quinn, don't you think you're cheating yourself out of a, dare I say, stream of revenue?"

Quinn pursed his lips.

"That really true?" Elletrache said, himself also standing on the shore, albeit because none of the company wanted to get too close to him and his sharp lindwurm armor. "Ye can't swim?"

The thief didn't answer but all the same admitted to the charge when he threw a dismissive hand and turned to stare at the very terrestrial tree line.

"Hells," Dahlgren said. The old man looked at the brigand. "He's purpled out, captain. He might not wake up if I don't soften this soon."

"Five more seconds," Richter said. The captain ran the final length of twine, getting it good around a molar. He tested the tension and nodded.

"Alright," he said. "Loosen up."

Dahlgren nodded. He slackened his arm and the brigand slumped.

"Hey, yeah," Thomas said. "He looks awful dead."

"Give it a second," Richter said.

And just like that, the brigand snorted and he jerked around as if still thrashing against a dream he was yet to leave. But he was in no dream, he was in a nightmare of his own making.

"You remember us?" Richter said, kicking the man's boot. "We're still here. And so are you."

The bindings kept him tight and so he wriggled in confusion before his eyes flashed wide and he looked from man to man to man and to captain. Slowly, the purple left his face and a stark red took its place.

He looked up at his kidnappers and grimaced. "Aw shit."

"Aw shit is right," Dahlgren said.

"Hey, I would like to—uh…" the brigand said, but as he talked his mouth chewed down on strings of rope that heretofore had gone unnoticed. He looked down to find fishing lines running from his mouth to a bucket sitting on the edge of the dock, the Trading Swords river rushing beneath its posts with murmuring ferocity like a thunderstorm in a jug. He opened his mouth and tongued his teeth, probing against the twine wrapped around their roots. He looked up with wide eyes. "What is this?"

"Call it incentive to talk," Dahlgren said. "Every single one of your teeth is tied to that bucket. We thought ourselves out of luck when we had so little string, but as it turns out you've little supply of teeth. I suppose some days just swing your way, you know?"

"By the old gods," the brigand said. His tongue went up again and probed the strings. "By the old gods!"

Richter nodded toward the bucket. "You understand what happens if I throw that in the water, aye?"

The brigand stared at the bucket. "It goes… downstream…"

Dahlgren said, "And it won't stop for nothing, but you'll stay right here."

"Y-you wouldn't!"

Richter put a boot on the bucket and tilted it toward the rushing waters.

"Oh by the old gods wait! H-hold on!" the brigand screamed, the strings bobbing frantically like a puppeteer losing his tempo. "L-let's not be hasty here, yeah? L-let's talk! I'd love to talk! See? I'm talking now! I love talking! Let me talk! Can't a man talk?"

"Aye," Richter said. He pointed toward the ferryman's hovel, the dead doves around it now being pecked on by crows, a few of the black birds wandering indoors for better pickings. He said, "Why did you kill him?"

"The ferryman?"

Richter drew down on the brigand. "Did you kill anyone else?"

"N-no, not yet. Well. Uh, no. The answer's truthfully no!"

Richter tilted the bucket. "Why the ferryman?"

"Oh!" A flash of remembrance came across the man's face. "We killed him cause he was trading information about who was comin' and goin'! The King of Dragons sent two men to go scout the western shorelines for value. When we asked the ferryman if he'd seen anyone, he brought them up. Now, those two told him to keep his mouth shut, yet there he was blabbering. We asked the ferryman why he didn't oblige their request, and he said it was because they weren't there anymore, the cheeky bastard. Naturally, we couldn't trust him to not speak of where we were coming and going so we… took care of the problem."

"Fucking savages," Dahlgren said.

When the brigand looked to the old man, Richter tugged on the strings. His head whirled back with a yelp and his attention remained on the captain.

"I want to talk about Kantorek," Richter said.

"Y-you mean the King of Dragons?"

Dahlgren spat. "He's no fucking king of anything."

Richter nodded. "Let's just call him Kantorek, aye?"

"Absolutely," the brigand said, nodding adamantly. "Let's do that. Kantorek Kantorek Kantorek."

"The last time we captured one of your sort he told us where Kantorek camps, except as it turns out, Kantorek doesn't stay in one place for long."

"Who does?" the brigand said, flashing a smile that died the second he saw his humor landed nowhere. "Uhh, right. Kantorek moves camps on a rotation of sorts, that's why info like that would be useless."

"I understand that now." Richter nodded back. "There is an issue, though."

"Hmm? What issue? There's no issue. Kantorek moves around. That's what he does, as you said."

"No, the issue is that these woods are far too dangerous to simply choose a place at random, so he must follow some sort of mapped schedule, aye? Places he trusts. Boltholes, hideouts, that sort of thing."

The brigand swallowed. "Uh... yeah. That's right."

"I know he doesn't stray too close to Immerwahr's town."

"Whose town?"

"The ferry town."

"Oh, no, of course not. Kantorek leaves that town alone."

"Doesn't leave its travelers alone," Dahlgren said.

The brigand cocked his head a bit as if doing some lively accounting. "Well, see, when a person leaves a town, they're no longer part of it—" he caught onto Dahlgren's glare and quickly rectified himself again. "Oh, you know what? You're right. They're still townsfolk even when on the road. We should stop, uh, complicating their lives. Wh-when I get back to the King— when I get back to Kantorek, I'll be sure to inform him of this."

Richter spat into the bucket. The brigand's eyes stared at it as if an assassin's arrow had landed just short of his feet.

"Kantorek avoids the destroyed priory," the captain said. "Aye?"

"Yessir," the brigand said. "I don't rightly know all the areas he stays, but that one he does indeed avoid. There's old lindwurm bones and totems of beastly creatures all over the place. Besides, holy grounds in that state of being... nothing good can come of it, I'll just say that much."

Again, Richter spat into the bucket. He wiped his mouth and stood up and looked out to the rushing Trading Swords river and nodded to nothing in particular. "You're telling us just what we want to hear, brigand."

"But that's all I know! I mean, all I know is what you're asking! I... uh..."

Richter crossed his arms and stared down at the brigand. "Marsburg's been under siege for a good clip now. Do you think they'll appreciate it if I send your teeth to its fisheries?"

The brigand's attention narrowed on the man with the black hat, his towering silhouette a stark nothingness, every inch of him hidden away behind sleeve or hat or coat, there leering a man as shadow, its authorship discarded, the darkness borne out on its own volition.

Slowly, the brigand slackened. "Wait, are you the one they call the—"

"My paymaster has a map," Richter interrupted as he looked up. He threw a hand at Crockett. "You tell him in detail every single place where Kantorek camps and we will blindfold you and set you down the shoreline with a walking stick."

Crockett briefly raised the ledger. "Ready when you are, brigand."

"Kantorek will kill me," the brigand said. "I know he will... you don't understand... and I'm new, alright? I'm new. They say they call him the King of Dragons because he flies the land burning its mice and rats. Now you want me to be a rat..."

Dahlgren spat again. "The fucker can't fly, you fool."

"He can!"

"You've seen it?"

"Well, no. But I've heard tales from those who have."

"Right. And is it Kantorek himself who has been telling these tall tales?"

"Yes! But he doesn't wish to show his true power! He says he weakens every time, and that he's awaiting a moment of true battle, a moment of direness, and he will then unfurl his wings and take to the skies and save us!" With every word the brigand's face lit up, like a drunk monk recounting a familiar sermon. "Yes! He will fly, he will fly! Yes he will!"

Richter crouched again. His fingers danced upon the tooth-twine and the slight tension brought the brigand to a quick silence. The captain curled one string and pinched it with his thumb and gave it a tug. The brigand snorted as he jerked forward.

Leaning, Richter said, "I understand your difficulty, brigand. I know that you think certain words will save your life. But I don't want you thinking at all. Do you know what I want? I want horror, brigand. I want violence. I want death." He looked around at his company. "And I want to get paid. Do you know how I get paid? By having the truth." He tapped the man's pate with a finger. "Whatever truth you have in here, you give to me, understand?"

Swallowing, the brigand looked toward the river then back to the captain. "Alright," he said. His voice changed. "I'll give you the truth. In fact, I'll tell you exactly where he is. No harm no foul, right? A-and maybe you'll succeed, yeah? Maybe you'll actually kill him and I won't have to live in fear. Maybe Kantorek really isn't the King of Dragons! Maybe he can't even fly!"

Richter smiled. He leaned over the dock and put his hands in the water. A brief redness mistily trailed away, then they were clean. Just like that.

"Alright," the brigand said. "I'll give you his sites as long as you can swear by my safety."

"You'll be safe." The captain nodded and held up his dripping hands. "I swear it upon my mother's grave."

Chapter 4. A Good Scrap.

LIKE MOST BOYS, Hobbs didn't know how to fight nor did whom he was fighting know how to fight, but in that vast gulf of ignorance, and as one blow came in after the other, the children created some fountain of knowledge almost preternaturally, and Hobbs knew something about it just felt right, and when the next bully's punch sought his face – a glancing blow that caught him in the nose and slashed across a cheek – well, what was that aside from another lesson learned? If he could have taken that strike and tattooed it or stuffed it and put it on a mantle somewhere, he would have.

Instead, the two boys fell to the ground in a heap of limbs and yelling and for some reason the dirt felt grittier and coarser than ever before, and the blades of grass crunched coldly against their backs. Even with autumn coming, the air seemed hot with their collective resolve, breathing in each other's faces, sharing angst and anger alike, huffing in patterns of victory and defeat as they rolled from advantage to disadvantage.

"I'll fark yer mother!"

"I'll fark yours!"

A girl piped in: "You two shouldn't use that word!"

Outside the two fighters stood a crowd of children, wholly unaccounted for with not a single adult in sight, making them perhaps the most devilish assortment of human beings possible, completely unstable individually and finding no purposeful organization in the whole. They cheered and roared and some emulated taking bets, the measurement of the trade mostly in imagination, things they had seen their fathers do in fighting pits or dog rings.

Others occasionally came forward to get their own licks in, usually a tentative kick to one of the combatants – against who mattered not – before a quick retreat lest the receiver saw who did it and remember their face.

As the children roared at the mayhem, the two boys went at it:

"Let go of my hair!"

"Don't grab down there!"

"You don't grab!"

"Alright I'm letting go!"

"Alright."

The boys rolled again in brief, oddly agreed silence. Then, the bully gained the upper hand and with it he returned to insults: "Fark yer mother!"

The girl stomped her feet. "Don't say that!"

"You… your mother…" Hobbs found himself in multiple quandaries. Raging, he screamed: "Fark all of you!"

They rolled again, a whirlwind of flying grass and dirt, the kids chirping with voyeuristic excitement, fun at its most skittish. Whenever the brawl rolled toward the crowd, the kids fanned out, chortling with oohs and ahhs.

Finally, Hobbs landed on top and put his knee into the boy's chest and started hitting him in the ribs. That's where his stepfather used to hit him. Never the arse. The arse was tender and a cushion, but the flanks? That's where things would sting and continue to sting. He did as he had learned, and a murmur of a dead man's violence curled into his fist and struck a blow again and again and the boy beneath him howled out and in his desperation he took Hobbs' ankle and sank his teeth into its flesh.

"No biting!" Hobbs screamed, tears filling his eyes. "No biting!"

He defensively swung himself around, but the kid wouldn't let go.

"I'll bite you, you arsehole!" Hobbs said, chewing into the bully's wrist.

"N-no biting!" the kid retorted. "Truce on the biting!"

Hobbs let the flesh free of his teeth and the bully tore away from the ankle. The boys fought on, albeit in more civilized ways with Hobbs delivering slaps here and there, and his opponent driving knees and elbows which clocked in like maces. But Hobbs still had the upperhand, his punches aided by gravity, the whole earth his battle brother.

Unable to get free and accumulating a series of hits that saw his lips and gums bleed, the bully grabbed a nearby mound of dogshit and slapped it into Hobbs' face. Naturally, Hobbs reeled away in horror. The throng of children *ooh'd* again and then burst into laughter as the boys started another roll, this time Hobbs ending up on the bottom of it.

"I'll smash yer teeth in!" the bully said.

"He won't miss 'em, those are just his baby teeth!" some kid yelled from the crowd, spurring the sort of laughter one would find hard to forget all the way to their death bed and Hobbs felt a tear or two emerging, no doubt pained on his future self's behalf.

Punches rained down. Hobbs' teeth went numb. But he took it with the resolve of a strongman. The bully's assault tired out before Hobbs gave up to it, and eventually the bully simply slid off his belly and sat astride him, sweating and laboring for breath. Silence fell over the throng of kids, quiet enough that the ongoings of the town itself seemed to refill the air, saws snoring, wagons creaking, animals barking, baying, howling, mewling.

"You two done?" one from the crowd asked.

"Keep going," another quickly added.

"Aye, don't stop! Why're ye stoppin'?"

The bully wiped his shit-stained knuckles on the grass. He pointed at Hobbs. "You had it coming. Hey, one of you hand me that toy."

Hobbs sat up. The bully was holding the toy sword Richter had bought.

"You and your sellsword farks should leave," the bully said, pointing the weapon. "Leave and never come back!"

"Yeah!" the rest of the kids screamed. "Go on and get out of here! Go!"

"We're helping you!" Hobbs said, tears in his eyes. "And I thought you were my friends!"

A girl piped in from the crowd: "My mother says you're dogshite on a sellsword's boot, no better, no worse!"

"Haha yeah, he's more like dogshite!" a boy added.

The girl stamped her feet. "That's what I said!"

"Dogshite!" another boy said, pushing the girl out of the way. "Yeah he's dogshite!"

Another strode forward, arms crossed with unearned authority. He said, "My father says sellswords aren't no different than common bandits!"

"My pap says they're killing brigands only so they can take their place!"

Hobbs wiped the tears from his eyes. "None of this is true... none of it!"

"Shut it, mercenary churl." The bully brought the sword up into both hands. "Now I'mma teach you a real lesson."

"Is that what you're doing?"

The words broke upon the children like a crack of lightning, each flinching and covering their heads.

Hobbs and the bully looked over.

The nameless sellsword company had returned, caked in blood, hair unkempt, armor nicked and sliced, and there behind them followed a murder of crows, black shapes huddled amidst the hanging woods like some clerical retinue biding its time. Before all this Richter stood front and center, his face speckled red, his hand upon the pommel of Adelbrecht's sword, his guildmaster's witch hunting hat sitting askew on a one-eared head.

"I asked," he said. "'Is that what you're doing?'"

A crow squawked and the kids cried out and took off in every direction. Richter watched their faces carefully before snatching the bully by his shirt and pulling him back. The kid screamed to his friends for help, but the little ones fled out into the town like a den of rats set aflame.

Richter looked down. The dried blood on his hand crackled as his grip tightened. He said, "You have something that doesn't belong to you."

The bully looked up at the captain, and suddenly swung the wooden sword. It thwapped against Richter's leg and they both looked at it as if an accident had transpired.

"Uhh," the bully said. "I-I'm sorry, I didn't mean to do that."

Richter looked at Hobbs. The boy got to his feet and wiped the dogshite from his face and then dusted off his clothes. The captain looked back at the bully and he took the sword from his hands and the boy yelped.

"Apology accepted," the captain said, and let the kid go.

The bully stood there a moment, glancing at the sellswords, his chest rising and falling in anger and fear. He snapped and screamed: "Yer destined for all the hells! All of ye is!" And as he turned to make leave on this statement, Quinn stuck a boot out and tripped the bully. When the bully turned over and howled about the crime Quinn simply kicked him again, sending the boy tumbling across the ground.

A few passing peasants paused and whispered to each other.

"That's a bit out of line," Crockett said. "Probably shouldn't be kicking kids, Quinn."

"I just wanted to say something," Quinn said, standing there with his hands on his hips. "You're the Fritz boy, yeah?"

The bully looked around. He nodded. "Yeah."

"Well if we're out here exchanging messages, I'd live to give you one." The thief grinned ear to ear. "Please tell your mother that Quinn said hi."

The bully stood and backed away, hands clenched, mouth tremoring in hate. He pointed and screamed: "Scapegraces!" And then he turned and fled.

"Goodness. That was dramatic," Quinn said. "What is there, a farkin' theater in this town? Where do kids even get that sorta gumption?"

Crockett sighed. "I find myself asking the same about you, Quinn."

"You should be asking yourself where all the foodstuffs strangely disappear to, you fat fark. Oh wait, mystery solved. It's your—"

"Enough," Richter said. He strode forward and handed Hobbs the wooden sword and patted the boy on the shoulder. He paused a moment, realizing he left a blood stain on the boy's cheek and so he licked his thumb and cleaned it off the kid.

Hobbs stared at the smudged blood and then looked up. He said, "Are you alright?"

"Aye." Richter nodded. "Are you?"

"I am now."

"Good."

"I'm glad everyone is doing great and all, but, uh…" Crockett counted tragedies on his fingers: "Our new recruits are already corpses, the ferryman is among their number, half the town thinks we're murderers, and Quinn is over here kicking children in full view of said townsfolk." The paymaster turned to Richter. "So… what do we do now?"

"We do what we have to," the captain said. "We hire some more men."

Chapter 5. Scapegraces.

"Next!" Crockett barked. "I said next!"

A man wearing a blue-and-white jester's cap pointed at himself. "Me?"

"Yes, you."

The man behind him leaned around. "If he's being dumb, can I go next?"

Crockett sighed. "Let's just keep it orderly."

"Agreed!" The jester finally strode forward. With bells jingling from three cotton cap horns, he bowed. "It is good to meet you, m'lord."

Sighing again, Crockett said, "I'm not royalty."

"Apologies. I pray my services have not been soured... captain, is it?"

"Paymaster." Crockett dabbed his quill pen in his inkwell. "Your name?"

"Minnesang, sir."

"Minnesang?"

"That's right. M-i-n-n—"

"I know the word." The paymaster leaned back, taking a good look at the jester's hat. "I take it this is a stage name?"

"Perhaps, perhaps not." The jester smiled smugly. "I'd rather not give away trade secrets."

"Your name is a trade secret?"

"Yes!" The jester barked, bolting upright with a wild grin. "Minnesang and always Minne-been... ang... hold on, I need to work on that..."

Shaking his head, Crockett put down his pen and said, "Alright then Minnesang, unfortunately for you I've been instructed to not hire the town minstrel. Immerwahr's instruction."

"Oh, but I am new here," Minnesang said. He defensively feathered his fingers against his chest. "And I am no mere minstrel, sir, I am… *a juggler!* And a jester. Although the former of the two is more, how do you say, appropriate for your company's needs."

The man's arms were out like a bird in a mating dance, all fingers flush and wiggling, the little bells in his cap tingling with the tiniest of shakes.

"You juggle, uh, what exactly?" Crockett said.

The jester crossed his arms with one hand planted under his chin as he thought. He said, "Axes, daggers, knives, stilettos, I can juggle whips and flails, too, though not on windy days, and I don't even mind juggling shields though the kite ones get a little hard on the hands, and also there must be absolutely no wind when it comes to those. I can juggle little kids, too. No fatties, of course. Not that you are, uh, rotund in shape. Hmm… I also juggle ordinary things such as plates, forks, non-human babies, so like puppies, kittens—"

"Great, I got it. You can put your arms down now."

"Ah, right. You get the gist, or shall I say you get the jest—"

"Thirty crowns upfront," Crockett said, picking up his quill pen and writing again. "We'll supply you a spear and—"

"Is that thirty crown-crowns, or crown-crowns as in for the head…"

"Coin."

"Ahh, wonderful. Landon mint?"

"Some."

"*Beautiful.* Any from the lowlands? I always liked that lowlander coin."

"Some." Crockett said again and with a beleaguered sigh he set his quill pen down. "Or if we keep going on like this it could be none."

Minnesang put both hands up in surrender, then used one to pinch his lips shut.

"Right," Crockett said. "As I was saying, thirty crowns upfront, and we'll supply you a spear and shield. You—uh, wait…"

Behind the juggler a trio of armored men walked past. They wore thick, uneaten gambeson armor and aketon caps, and they carried a mix of spears, hatchets, and a bow with a full quiver. Rucksacks packed with traveling gear. Most importantly, they appeared to give no care at all about the wouldbe sellswords or the paymaster or the town in general for that matter.

Crockett hurriedly got to his feet.

Minnesang stepped back. "Oh, do you need a demonstration? I can juggle for you!"

"What? No. You're hired, now move out of the way." Crockett pushed the juggler aside and rushed toward the trio while whistling for their attention.

The three men turned around in unison.

"Yeah?" one said.

Crockett held his hand out and introduced himself. They each shook it in turn, though as they did, they glanced at one another with knowing smirks.

One said, "So you work for the nameless mercenary company?"

"A name is being worked on, also a banner," Crockett said. "But that's not important. Would I be correct in saying you three are the fighting sort?"

"We were soldiers if that is what you're asking." He thumbed toward each man as he made declarations: "Landon army. Lowlander. Myself, well, I'm a bit of a mongrel."

"A man more mutt than mercenary," another said and the three laughed.

"So you are deserters?" Crockett said.

One of the soldiers straightened up. His fist tightened around the handle of his spear. He said, "Sure. If you wanna put it that way."

"Ah, uh, apologies. Let me get to business," Crockett said. "We can offer men such as yourselves a hundred crowns upfront."

The three men burst into laughter. "A hundred crowns?"

"Y-yes... that's more than three-times the amount we offer most. You would be the highest paid by far."

"Sir, respectfully," one soldier said. "We're going to have to decline."

"I once got paid thirty crowns just to run a tryout," one of the soldiers said. "If you want us, it'll be a thousand."

Crockett's mouth fell open.

Smirking again, one man slapped a hand onto the paymaster's shoulder and eyed the throng of miscreants lined up for hiring. "I wish you the best of luck finding the right men in this here hog wallow."

The deserter let his hand slide free and they turned and went away. As they got some distance, they looked back and smiled at Crockett, then shook their heads and burst into laughter.

Little bells jingled as Minnesang sidled up to the paymaster. He clucked his tongue and shook his head. "That was rough. Hey, do you mind if I go do juggling tricks on the side? You know, for extra coin."

Crockett turned. "Do you know a man named Quinn, by any chance?"

"Quinn? No, sorry."

"How about Quindiagan."

"That sounds like a long name for Quinn."

"It is." Crockett looked at the man's hat. "You two are an awful lot alike."

"I'll take that as a good thing."

"Eh, well…"

"Hey," Minnesang said. "Can I ask *you* something?"

Crockett looked back at the shape-up line to see the wouldbe new hires frog-jumping each other's backs until one twisted an ankle and fell to the ground howling. The paymaster nodded. "Sure, I suppose I have a minute."

The juggler crossed his arms and leaned in with conspiratorial whispering: "What's this I hear about your company having the man they call the Wight? Is that really true?"

"His name is Richter von Dagentear," Crockett said. "He's a sellsword captain. That is, *our* captain."

"So a myth in the flesh! And at such a prestigious rank!" Minnesang shook his head and grinned as his bells jingled and jangled. "Fascinating!"

~ ~ ~

"Now where do you get off carrying around somethin' like that?"

Sophia looked up from a log she was sitting on. A large woman stood over her, blocking the sun with her wide hips and rounded belly and a wide head full of unkept, waxy hair. Middle-aged or perhaps Sophia's age, though she assumed herself to be the younger, and even in caring about that thought she knew she most likely was.

The woman pointed at a black kite shield that Sophia was painting. She said, "So? Where'd ya get it?"

Sophia tilted it. "We got it in a fight."

"Ah, so ye are with the sellswords."

"I am." Sophia looked down at the half-painted shield. She said, "This fine article was pulled from the black cloaked brigands who killed the ferryman. Looks nice, right?"

"Yer men ain't no different than the brigands," the woman said. "How could we know it wasn't yer men that up and killed the ferryman?"

"I suppose you wouldn't ever know," Sophia said. "You can do with that what you will."

"Wouldn't ever know," the woman repeated. She spat a big gob and said, "You their whore?"

Sophia shook her head.

"I'd seen you slumming around with that older fella, the drunkard with the clipped wing."

[64]

"That doesn't make me a whore."

"No. I suppose it don't," the woman said. "But by the way he roses you and talks to you I know he ain't yer husband."

"My husband's dead," Sophia said.

"Mine too."

"Sorry to hear that."

The woman spat. She said, "Did you hear me say sorry about yers?"

"No."

"Then don't bother with saying sorry about mine."

"My sons are gone, too," Sophia said.

The woman nodded. She snorted and swallowed and looked off a ways then nodded. She said, "Well. Sorry to hear that."

Sophia set the shield in the grass. She rode a finger down its front and center. "I'm going to paint a white sword here. What do you think?"

"I think yer company killed the ferryman," the woman said. "I didn't come here to chat paint."

Sophia sighed.

The woman continued: "I want ye to stay clear of us womenfolk. I want ye to stay clear of the children especially."

"Sure, if it'll make you feel better, I can do that."

"Good. And I also see you got some boy in your stead."

"Hobbs."

"Don't give a damn what his name is. Now I know he ain't yer kin, so I'll say this as well: that dog-named runt best stay clear of our children, too."

"He's just a boy," Sophia said.

"No such thing as just a boy," the woman said. "He's being raised by jackals, he's gon' be a jackal. I don't want him near the children, you hear?"

Sophia stared at the black shield. She looked up and said, "I take it you've talked this out with the rest of the mothers?"

"Aye." Grinning a faint rind of yellowed teeth, the woman said, "Consider me to be speakin' on their behalf. The peaceful option, ye know?"

The woman picked up the bucket of white paint Sophia had prepped for the shield. Snorting, the villager whipped her head back to clear her hair out of the way, then leaned over the bucket and spat into it.

"Go on and paint your white sword," she said, dropping the bucket. "And while you do that, you sit there and think yourself wise to my words, woman, for I say them as a lady, and to ye yourself as a lady. The next one who comes this way with such words will likely be a man, and he'll say them as a man, and he'll treat you as one, too."

Sophia angrily leaned down and snatched the paint bucket and brush. In a matter of seconds, she dipped it and drew a shrewd sword with the hastily splashed crossguard dripping lines, as though a sword might wreath itself in a white cage. She threw the brush down and staked the shield between her legs and said, "You send that man any damn time you want."

~~~

Louis von Walddorf's finest spy looked south to Marsburg.

"Just get the hells out of here," Thomas said, kicking rocks at the edge of town. "You're no sellsword, you fool, and you're going to get found out the longer this goes on, that's if something doesn't up and kill your arse first."

"Whatcha talking about?"

Thomas nearly jumped out of his boots. He turned around to see Hobbs standing there, his face a bit scuffed from his battle with the bully.

"Ah, h-hey there, Hobbs."

"I scare ya?" Hobbs said, grinning.

"Little bit." Thomas nodded toward the boy's bruises. "I'm sorry I couldn't be there to stop you getting bullied like that."

"You had your own battle to fight," the boy said. "It's alright."

Thomas shook his head. "No, it isn't."

"It is," Hobbs said. "And if I say it is, it is."

They talked at the edge of town, standing in the shade of the bunkhouses like two daytalers stealing a break. Before them, trees swished and swayed with every breeze, the forest always peaceful if just taken at a glance.

A few townsmen circled around the bunkhouses carrying axes and knives and shortswords. They looked at Hobbs and they said a word between themselves and they looked at Thomas and shared another whisper.

"Hey," Thomas said, waving briefly.

The townsmen spat. One said: "I don't wanna hear word one, sellsword."

Sighing, Thomas put his hand down. The townsmen shook their heads and slowly clambered into the woods. Both Thomas and Hobbs knew they were going to see the 'issue' at the ferry for themselves. Few in the town seemed to believe that the ferryman had been slaughtered by the brigands, instead believing that it were the finders of his corpse that had made him cold. Sellswords were a universally despised lot, and Hobbs was slowly realizing that he may yet come to represent crimes he wouldn't ever dare to commit, simply by being what he was, and by being with who he was with.

Hobbs picked up a broken branch and then leaned against the bunkhouse, aimlessly drawing lines in the dirt at his feet.

"Thomas, can I ask you something?"

"Sure."

"How was it? The battle, I mean."

The servant cleared his throat. "Ah, hey…"

"You don't have to answer, it's alright. I shouldn't have asked."

"It was awful," Thomas said, almost blurting it out. "I'd been in a few brawls, couple fistfights, not unlike yourself. And men killing each other on the streets or in the comfort of a lord's hall, or even in a tournament... that's all fine. But this was something else. This was my first real taste of combat. I'd never even seen so much blood, and I didn't know some men took so much to die, but also at the same time... that some men took so little."

"I wanna know the details," Hobbs said. "I think I need to, anyway."

Thomas leaned against the bunkhouse. The forest facing them was alive with insects and birds and the rustle of the wind dipping into the leaves and branches. He said, "It was just chaos. No other way to explain it. I could see and hear and yell and scream, but really, I don't know if I was actually doing anything. My arms moved, my legs moved, but I don't think there was thought behind any of it. Almost as if I was just preserving myself by instinct alone. Like... like an animal, I suppose."

"Kill anyone?"

Thomas stared silently into the forest.

"You can be sad about it," Hobbs said. "I won't mind."

"No, it's not that," Thomas said. He blinked and shook his head. "Maybe I did, but it doesn't matter because they wouldn't be my first anyway."

Hobbs' eyebrows went up. He said, "Really? You? You've killed before?"

"Hey," Thomas said, grinning. "Just because I look like a skittish little rat doesn't mean I haven't snuffed the light a time or two."

"Well hells, if *you* could do it then certainly I could."

"There is so much wrong with that statement Hobbs that I don't even know where to begin."

Suddenly, a branch broke in the forest, and then another, and then the crunch of heavy boots and the hiss of bushes being pushed apart. Thomas leaned up off the bunkhouse and instinctively put his hand on Hobbs, holding him back.

"It's me," a voice gargled through the foliage. "Gatdamn jerky bastards."

A pair of deer legs swung into view, and then tilted away as the man that carried them appeared. Eyepatch, rounded shoulders, crooked gait, furs and pelts and lindwurm scales ever adorned, beastly teeth hanging from his neck by a string. He paired the deer's legs in each hand, the animal's neck lolling over a shoulder as though along for the ride. Elletrache turned and spat.

"My eye itches and this shit ain't farkin' light. Now one of you two gits can come over here and scratch m'eye or you can help with this here game, but ya sure as shite ain't just gon' stand there and do nothin'."

Thomas said, "I thought you had some help with you."

"S'posed to," Elletrache said. "But them townsfolk done run off wagging aspersions at yours truly. Seems they learned of my station as sellsword and took it in the crude sense. Well. I'll say this, that motley business done wiped clean all my time committed to helping feed these people ever again, ungrateful sonsabitches."

"Don't take it to heart, Trash," Hobbs said.

"I didn't intend to. Only matter now is this shit is still farkin' heavy and you two are still standin' there with yer thumbs up yer arses."

"Oh, right!" the boy rushed forward as Elletrache unlimbered the game. Hobbs crouched before the creature and ran his hand through its fur, his fingers stopping at the edge of a mortal wound beneath which the creature's heart had been pierced with a bolt. He looked up with a smile. "It's beautiful."

"It's dead is what it is," Elletrache said. He looked the boy over. "Where's your sword? I mean that wooden one you got yer arse kicked over for."

Hobbs stared at the deer's glassy eyes. He said, "Dahlgren borrowed it."

"Dahlgren? Huh? What would that dumb drunk want to do with a wooden sword?"

~~~

Richter looked toward the sun, and by the time he looked back down Dahlgren was sauntering around the bunkhouse corner.

"You're late," the captain said.

Dahlgren wiped foam from his mouth and grunted. "Apologies."

"Are you drunk?"

"What is this, a fucking trial?"

"Alright." Richter sighed. "Where's your sword?"

"My what—oh, uhh…" Dahlgren paused and looked down. His hands patted about his person. His steel sword was gone, and in its place, he had Hobbs' toy sword girded under a belt. He discovered it as though his hip were a shelf and the sword a forgotten mug. Smirking, he unsheathed it with drunken aplomb. "I guh-got this." A wry, almost stumbling smile awkwardly cut across the old man's face. "I thought it'd be funny to use."

Richter sighed again. "You're going to spar me with a toy?"

"Ohhh, I don't think it'll be a problem," Dahlgren said, turning the wooden sword left and right. "It's got a few nicks in it, but otherwise it's golden. The right man can do a whole lot with this lil' th-hic-thing."

"Ah, sure," Richter said. "But ignoring what might happen if my steel hits that wood, there's another problem."

"Oh?"

The two were hidden away at the outside edge of the ferry town, but peasants and travelers were coming and going, their shadows winking down the nearby alleys. The sounds of training would surely draw more cursory attention, luring those same shadows to come for a closer look.

Dahlgren danced the sword through his fingers. "What is it, captain?"

Richter cleared his throat. He said, "Dahlgren, if the peasants see me getting worked over with a damn toy, they'll think less of me."

"Oh. Well yar. I fully understand yer con-hic-concern, captain," Dahlgren said. He suddenly leveled the wooden sword firmly. "But don't you think it best to be a little embarrassed now than fully dead later?"

The captain sighed again. He drew up Adelbrecht's sword. "Alright, old man. Let's get to it."

"Now that's the sp-hic-spirit!"

~~~

Richter entered Immerwahr's shop and as the door clattered behind him a group of men inside turned their heads like owls to a barn mouse. One man had his hands on the 'camel' before he slowly set it back on the shelf. Another took a bite out of a carrot with strangely aggressive menace. Together they started coming forward. The captain counted five of them, as well as five hatchets, three daggers, some light purses, and a whole lot of heavy intentions.

"I'm here to see the monk," Richter said.

"That right?" one man said, chewing the carrot. He pointed with both prejudice and produce. "And what you got there with you, scapegrace?"

"A bag of money."

The carrot-man slowly grinned, orange bits smeared across his teeth.

"Lotta blood stains in that there bag o' money."

Richter nodded. "That's usually how it comes to be."

"Mhmm… you know, I heard you wasn't just no ordinary sellsword. I heard you was a witch slayer."

Setting the satchel down, Richter shouted, "Immerwahr!"

When the captain tried to step further inside the shop, the men came together, forming a blockade.

"Is it true?" the carrot chewer asked. "You kill old crones for pay?"

Another man leaned in. "I heard he's the one they call the Wight."

"He ain't no fark from Dagentear," another said. "Or maybe he is… he's got that face… but I don't remember the Wight having just one ear…"

"Excuse me," Richter said. "Unless you have a contract that needs fulfilling, you all need to step aside."

"'Step aside', he says." The carrot chewer smirked. "I bet he killed the ferryman himself."

Richter crouched beside his knapsack and undid its strings. He loosened its opening then grabbed its bottom and upturned it. A flood of brigand heads came rolling out and the men jumped back with frightened curses.

"I buried the ferryman by the shoreline," Richter said as the heads clopped and clattered, some coming to rest with their noses plugged between the floorboards, others tottering with bloodied faces glaring up at the living, tongues protruding in purpled clumps. The captain pointed at the collection. "These are the brigands who killed the ferryman. This is *their* burial."

The carrot chewer spat out his bite. "All these heads don't mean a farkin' thing. We know yer just as awful as the brigands, just waitin' on yer chance to get one over on us. I say we take this fool here and now while he's all alone!"

"Yeah," another said. "Then we get the rest, one at a time!"

Richter put his hand on Adelbrecht's steel and started unsheathing it.

"Alright that is plenty enough!" a voice called and there came a shrill, whirling cry behind it.

The captain slowly lowered the blade back into its sheath as Immerwahr strode forward through his store. He had a wooden stick in hand, and at the top of it was another stick which rode up and down a set of grooving notches, causing a curious birdcall to sound out. As he neared, the whistling wooshes picked up in pace, and the men started ushering themselves out.

"C'mon now, clear it out, clear it out!" the monk said. "I know you all aren't buying anything. Except you! You best pay for that carrot!"

The man threw a coin. "Of course, Immerwahr! I would never steal!"

"You swear by that?"

"I swear it! Or, at least, I'd never steal from you."

"Alright, I suppose that's well enough," Immerwahr said. He pushed the men as Richter stepped out of the way. "If any of you touch this man, I will see to it that the old gods hear of it!"

"Oh, by the old gods," one of the shrewder men said, his eyes wide.

Richter stood aside as the group walked past him.

"We've our eyes on you," one said as he stepped off the porch.

"Yeah, best—ack!" one interrupted himself as he accidentally punted a head with his foot, causing the bounty to spin across the floorboards and sail back outside where it rolled along the porch. A child screamed and a woman gasped. The punter straightened up as though none of this had transpired and he confidently pointed a finger at Richter. "Best… best watch yourself!"

Richter said nothing. He simply met their stares and nodded and waited until they were cleared out.

"Truly, Richter," Immerwahr said, staring at the heads. "You dumped this mess here?"

The monk sighed and walked out of the store and retrieved the head on the porch.

"Apologies, m'lady, apologies my little lady," he said to a woman and child outside. "This is a bad man meeting the fate he has ordained himself."

"It is *disgustang*, that's what that is!"

"Yes, m'lady."

Immerwahr came back inside and threw the head in with the others.

Richter nodded. "Apologies for the delay on bringing the bounties."

"Yes, and for what reason did you have to keep these… eh, kind souls in your keeping?"

"We met the brigands on the opposite side of town along the shoreline. That's as far in as they've ever gone. I kept the heads for a minute because I wanted to see if anyone in town would act differently after news of our action at the shoreline spread around."

"And?"

"They've been acting the same, fortunately and unfortunately."

"Hmm, sorry to hear that. Though by now you are surely aware that mercenaries will rarely be treated to anything kinder than sabled bellicosity."

"Aye."

Immerwahr started collecting the heads and stuffing them back in the knapsack. When he was finished, he stood back up, the soggy sack at his hip. He nodded at Richter. "You got something there on your cheek."

A red mark did indeed streak across Richter's cheek, an element of Dahlgren's training, and a whipping from a wooden toy sword of all things. Richter said, "I was training with one of my men." He quickly changed the subject: "We lost our new recruits in the fight."

"All of them?"

"Aye."

"Goodness."

"They did their job, in the end."

"And what job would that be? Absorbing arrows? Swallowing swords?"

Richter shrugged. "The rest of us made it out in part because they didn't."

Immerwahr clicked his tongue and shook his head. "Goodness, Richter."

"We've hired a few more," Richter said. "A butcher, a miller I believe, some daytalers…"

"No minstrel, right?"

"I believe there is a jester."

"Hmm, strange looking man with a cap and bells?"

"Aye. Is that a problem?"

"He's an annoyance, I can already tell," the monk said with a dismissive scoff. "He is absolutely all yours. Do you think any of these new hires are of, how do you say... proper talent?"

Richter shrugged. "Impossible to know. For some men, the stars align just right and they find in battle something they didn't even know they were good at. Others are just all show. You think they'll be good for it then you turn around for a moment and they're already dead. If I had more time, I would run tryouts and better training, but time isn't exactly on our side."

The monk smiled. He said, "I can see a lot of things are on your mind and you have my condolences for being burdened by such a task."

"You're paying for it," Richter said. "It's no burden, it's just a job."

Immerwahr tightened the knots of the knapsack and slung it over his shoulder. He then held out his other hand, a purse in the palm. Richter took it and didn't bother opening it to take count of the crowns – the monk had never been short.

"You should count," Immerwahr said anyway.

"You've never cheated me."

"I know, that's why you should count it. You shouldn't take your own faith for granted," the monk said with a wry smile. "That and seeing you count it out makes a slight assumption about the essence of my character. That I am, how would you say, of malicious devices."

"And... you want that?"

"Being thought of in such a manner is a good thing, wouldn't you agree? Despite my name, being known for always telling the truth is not all that it is cracked up to be. It, let's say, invites the errors of others."

Richter couldn't help but agree. In this world, being all "good" would get you killed sooner than anything. A bad streak could take you far, even if it was feigned. The captain nodded and held out his hand.

"What's this for?" Immerwahr said.

"I know where the brigand leader Kantorek is camping. I'm going to go there, and I am going to kill him."

"And this?" Immerwahr said, gesturing to the hand. "A firm 'goodbye handshake' in case you don't come back?"

The captain nodded.

The monk shook only his own head.

"If you won't count my coins, then I won't shake your hand," he said. "I've never shorted you, and you've always come back. That's how it is, and that's how it will be. So out, out with you."

Immerwahr pushed Richter from the shop until they both stood on the porch. There, a few peasants turned to watch, some horrified that the monk was in the face of the mercenary, like watching a child dance on the rim of a blacksmith's pit.

The monk put a finger in Richter's chest. "And next time, don't make such a fuss! You get the money you deserve!"

Richter looked around. One of the peasants clapped. The captain said, "Feigning 'malicious devices,' eh monk?"

Immerwahr smiled. "Technically it is the truth to them, Richter." The monk cleared his throat and then raised his voice: "Now get out of my sight and do the job I paid you for, sellsword!"

Before Richter could respond, Immerwahr quickly swung around, the sack of heads whooshing with weighty authority, and he strode into his shop and shut the door. A moment later the door opened back up and he stealthily hid himself in the crease. He whispered, "Did you need to buy anything?"

"No, I think I'm good—"

The door closed.

Richter turned around. Townsfolks walked by staring at him, and a group of men stood across the street watching and whispering. As they gawked, the captain looked down at the monk's purse of coins – and counted.

~~~

The captain stared at the company's inventory table. He put his hand to the wood and swept a great length of it left to right, unimpeded both ways.

"Yeah," Crockett said. "We don't have much."

Richter nodded. "It'll have to do."

Dahlgren picked up a spear. Even though he moved it slowly, the shaft creaked like a branch in the wind. "I wager this'll break if I so much as pick my teeth with it."

"Not the greatest gear, I agree," Crockett said. "But the new hires needed something and this is what we got."

"What we don't have is tr-training," Dahlgren said, tossing the spear and then picking a splinter out of his hand. "Who was it you hired, again?"

Crockett brought up his ledger. "A miller, a butcher, a jester, couple more daytalers. Just folks that had been lazing around town. Names are Berthold, Gernot, Minnesang—"

"Let them teach me their names," Dahlgren said. "'Til then, they're nothing but dead men walking as far as I'm concerned."

"Don't let them hear you say that," Richter said.

"Sure. We can let them be little lambs."

Crockett looked at the table. He said, "Do you think it's a good idea to go out with gear like this?"

Richter nodded. "Kantorek is very likely east of here right this minute. We just got done killing a large number of his men and he might not even know it yet. We move now, and we move fast. What we lack in equipment we'll more than make up for in tactics."

"Alright," Crockett said. He did a doubletake on Richter and pointed at the captain. "Hey, you got a little mark there on your cheek."

"Oh hey yeah, Richter," Dahlgren said, grinning. "Where'd you get that?"

"Hmm." Richter nodded. "We'll be heading east. Do you know which way that is, Dahlgren?"

The old man blinked one eye at a time then turned around and guessed and guessed wrong.

"Goodness," Crockett said. "He's actually sloshed. He hides it so well."

"Hells with directions!" Dahlgren said, wobbling on his feet. "Just point me toward the bandits and my smart-hand will do the rest."

Crockett glanced at Richter. "Uh, think he'll be alright?"

Belching, Dahlgren said, "Berthold, Ger-uh, the butcher, and, Minnesang. Those were the names you said a minute ago. See? I'm fine."

"Fine." Crockett said with a shrug. "That was impressive enough."

"The old man sobers fast," Richter said, nodding confidently. "Now, let's go east and collect on this Kantorek once and for all."

Chapter 6. Hunting Kantorek.

THE COMPANY marched out of the ferry town and headed east. Dahlgren stayed on the new recruits, testing their resolve with a growling voice for there were worse things to come than an old man's anger. As they marched further on, Dahlgren turned to trying out their martial abilities, testing them on defense and offense, and giving them a sense of purpose and place within the company itself: namely that of warm bodies on the frontline. He taught them how to hold a shield close to the man next to him, and he tested the pairings with strikes of his sword, clanging it against the wood. Although every man weathered Dahlgren's shouting, the nearly lifelike training of sword-against-shield brought a few men to whimpers. Eventually, the old man sheathed his blade and stared at them and said nothing more and in this silence a vast sea of disappointment washed over the men and some floated in it with somber acceptance while others had reason to defeat it, to surprise the old man and show him that he had missed something, that they were worthy of being there, and with nothing but ocean around them they would still yet swim for land.

~~~

Hitting the edge of the Ancient Road, Richter spotted a very expected sight on the other side and quickly crouched. His company lingered behind him, eyes wide, breathing heavy but quietly, attentive yet fidgety, looking like children about to explode with a secret they were told to keep.

The captain looked back at the troop and put a finger to his lips, and then pointed at Dahlgren and pointed at the men and clenched his hand into a fist. Dahlgren turned and went from sellsword to sellsword, whispering to each, and the men nodded earnestly, their hands tightening around their gear. When he was finished, Dahlgren turned back around and nodded.

Richter took off his boots and held them in one hand as he sprinted over the road in a low stoop, his socks quietly pitter pattering, his black shape loping like a rock skipped across a sea of stone. Behind him, some men asked aloud what he was doing, and a wave of shushes followed.

Making it across, the captain quickly sat down and put his boots back on. He gazed around for a few moments, looking into the bushes and the trees and the branches above. Then he looked at the bodies piled beside the road.

The travelers had been slain by sword and arrow, and their corpses stripped bare. Such ignominy was a good hint of their having been merchants, but the missing ring fingers all but guaranteed it. By comparison, the ordinary sack and hempmade garb of peasants ensured they would at least have some dignity after a bandit ran them through with a sword.

Waving flies out of his face, Richter went around the bodies and there spotted footprints that had come in and the footprints that had gone out. He saw blood on the leaves of the bushes. He saw marks in the trees carved by bored men with rusted daggers. He saw fingers.

Richter looked back across the Ancient Road. A few faces were peering at him through the brush. He raised his hand in a fist again, but this time he tapped the top of his own head before pointing left and then right. One of the faces disappeared, and then a moment later the entire company emerged from the brush and clambered over the road, the jangle and chink and clatter of their gear disturbingly loud in the ever-quiet stillness, no doubt capable of drawing eyes like a tumble of silverware spilled across a pauper's alley.

Grimacing, Richter put one finger to his mouth again and shushed them and with his other hand he waved it up and down like a bird, telling the men to stay low. They hugged their own armors to try and quiet down but as they slipped to the other side they crashed into bushes and slipped and fell and some dropped their spears and one of the daytalers dropped it three times over, each drop spurring a hurried attempt to recover it until he finally booted it over and gave chase like a dog pawing his own toy.

"Gods fucking damned," Dahlgren said as the men crashed back into a lousy, shapeless formation. "That was a bit loud."

"You think?" Richter said, shaking his head.

The old man leaned and looked at the bodies. "Merchants?"

"Aye."

"Think it was Kantorek?"

"Very likely," Richter said. The captain looked at his sellswords. Even with a quick jaunt, some were breathing hard and the sweat poured from them with ease. He pursed his lips. "Dahlgren."

"Aye?"

"I'm going on ahead alone."

"Not sure if that's wise, captain."

"I can scout faster alone." Glancing at the arrangement of fresh recruits making a storm of noise, he added: "I think it'll be safer that way, too."

"I can come with ya, black hat," Trash said, leaning forward with his massive crossbow, his stance awkwardly leaning on his hobbled feet.

"Thanks, Trash, but I'll need to be fast," Richter said. "In and out."

"Maybe take one of the recruits, at least?" Dahlgren said.

"Ahh, leave the cap'n be," Quinn said. "Let 'im go in there with a crossbow he can't shoot straight and a sword that he can pretend is the Reproach of the Old Gods."

"Reproach of the what?" Dahlgren said.

"A relic I one day shall steal. Ol' Cricket probably knows about it."

The paymaster looked up. "You can't steal it, thief, because it's a mythical weapon wielded by an equally mythical great hero—"

"We don't have time for this shit," Richter said. He offloaded a purse of coins, a bandolier of his witch hunting vials, and his quiver of bolts. The former items clinked and clanked too loudly, and the latter would likely get caught on a branch or bush. He left himself one bolt in the crossbow itself and as assuredly as it would pass through the air when fired the captain made certain that he could run through the forest with equal speed and quickness.

Dahlgren looked at the dropped gear. "At least tell us the plan, captain."

"The company's too loud to properly sneak in. If the brigands are fewer than us, they'll hear us and run. If they're of greater number, they'll go on the offense and catch us flatfooted. So… I will bring them to us. You wait here and ambush whatever comes back through those trees, understand?"

"What if it's you?" Quinn said.

Richter briefly lifted his hat. "If you see this first, you hold your fire."

"Yeah sure but maybe one of them bandits is wearing it instead. Maybe yer dead as a pigeon and we all pause and go hey is that Richter, but it isn't Richter, it's someone else, and the not you wearing your shit shoots me in the face with your farking crossbow."

"That'd be the day," Crockett said.

"Hey! I'm being serious!"

"Who said I wasn't?"

"Quiet," Richter said. "And *keep* it quiet."

Dahlgren nodded. "I'll hold down the fort, captain."

Nodding back, Richter said, "Remember, we need to make sure we keep one of them alive." He turned into the brush. He paused and turned back around. "Dahlgren."

"Aye, sir?"

"Please make sure nobody fucking shoots me, alright?"

"I'll try my best, sir."

~ ~ ~

Richter swiftly passed into the forest, paralleling a set of footprints. Heavy boots. Slightly off center. No doubt carrying a haul. The captain started maneuvering around the outside of the traces, his eyes darting back and forth between the tracts where the brigands had moved through, and the roots and branches and bushes and rocks before him, making sure at all times that his feet were landing upon the softest spots possible, and that he would always have somewhere to go forward, to maintain speed and momentum, seeing unto the forest floor as a deer would, surrounded by the certainties of a safe escape in every direction.

A tracker must be of two elements: the mental and the physical. He must know where the prey will go before it gets there. Following directly in its footsteps was the error of green trackers who knew not their follies. The physicality of the pathfinder then comes into frame: how fast can you move through rough terrain. Here, too, green trackers made their missteps. A strong, fit man would assume he could brute force the paths. To simply jump and run as fast as he could. But all men tire, and all men make mistakes when they think themselves superior to the nature which surrounds them. The true pathfinder uses his eyes, spotting the mossy stones to step on and the wet roots to quietly traverse. He eyes the brush to crawl under and the brush to go around and the weak brush he can simply run straight through. He must be as a gnat flying through a dozen webs, nary a single white fiber allowed to grace his flickering wings.

In this way, Richter soared through the trees and closed in on the brigands, first by sound and then by sight, their silhouettes appearing as black arrows rising and falling to the shape of the land. So close did he get to them that their voices broke from murmurs into conversations. He slowed his advance and studied their moves intensely, himself prowling between the trees like an old ghost passing by the windows of its enemies.

The brigands chatted about waiting to see who won the siege of Marsburg and what they could do with anyone fleeing the war. They discussed a family they had set upon and murdered, and they discussed the woman of that family in some detail. As they dawdled, Richter slowed to a stop and leaned into a bush and there sat unmoving. He eyed the brigands slip through the trees back and forth and in total the figures were numbered at four and he waited longer yet to see if anyone would rise from a nap and add to the roster but it remained at four and from this moment forward it would only decline in count.

One of the brigands yelled out he was taking a shit and he fanned his arm in Richter's direction. The rest of the brigands jeered him but all the same took to resting against the surrounding trees.

As the brigand approached, the captain sank further into the brush like an assassin behind a nobleman's curtains. The brigand mumbled to himself as he unbuckled his belt. He took out his cock and shook his head at it.

"Why won't ye work? Why you gotta embarrass me like that? Everyday yer like this. That was a good lookin' gal yesterday and ye still don't got no getup, huh?"

The brigand and his member soon neared Richter to the point the brigand's shadow darkened his stalker's eyes. Completely unaware of the danger, the brigand turned around and dropped his drawers.

Like a spider tiptoeing down its web, Richter slowly leaned and pushed his crossbow through the brush. The man whistled and hummed and muttered tunes about wars he never participated in and leaders who would have hanged him dead had they ever known him. He suddenly cocked his head to the side and belched, but there his head froze in place, catching Richter in the peripheral, the white of his eye glistening as it trembled with what sights it had gained.

"No sound, no movement," Richter said.

The brigand breathed a sigh of relief. "Shit, I thought you was a bear."

"Quit talking."

"Ah, sir, we're just hunters all, if this is yer land we'll—"

Richter prodded the man's neck with the crossbow. He sank his head forward before slowly putting his hands up, but such a movement would be easy to see, for all creatures in the forest are attuned to the strange just as they are to the frightened.

"Keep your hands down."

"Y-yeah, sorry. Of course."

As the man lowered his hands, Richter glanced at the rest of the brigands, but they were none the wiser. He said, "How many are with you?"

"Oh I don't know."

"How many?"

The man swallowed. He said, "Ten."

"I only counted four."

The man cleared his throat. "Well, uh… I'm not learned so I'm not sure what numbers actually mean to be honest. If you say four, then it's four." He held up his hand with four fingers, wiggling them. "This is ten, right?"

"You put that hand up again and I will clip your nuts."

"Ah, yessir."

Richter reached through the brush and under the man's arse and held his trousers down, clumping them into a rag with his fist.

"Staying crouched, I want you to walk backwards with me."

"Ah man c'mon, I'm just out here trying to shit, man."

"Walk backwards."

"Hey man I'm shittin'. It ain't right. I'll shit on yer hand down there."

"You so much as do anything but move backwards and I will have you eating your own cock, understand me?"

"Easy, alright, I'll move. Just sayin' if I shit on yer hand it ain't my fault."

"Marcus!" a voice hailed from the brigand camp.

Richter stared over the brigand's shoulder and saw a silhouette stalking between the trees, its head tilted up and staring out with a layman's eyes. A pathfinder's stare surely would have seen Richter and his hostage, but the brigand fanned his sight over and back again without nary a necessary detail.

"Hey Marcus! You there? Are you havin' a wank or are ye *still* shittin'?"

Richter jerked at the pants and said, "Answer him."

Marcus cleared his throat again. He shouted back to the voice, "Yeah?"

The voice responded, "You doin' alright?"

"Yeah I'm doin' alright. Just ate somethin' that's slow comin', that's all."

"Alright. Just makin' sure." A pause. The sound of brush came, then the sound of the same brush again as the voice returned. "You see any berries out that way?"

Sighing, Marcus sagged his head. "No. No I have not seen any berries."

"Mushrooms, maybe?"

"No... no mushrooms neither."

"Gods damned, they're all gone. Been weeks since I'd seen a shroom!"

Marcus sighed again. "Yessir, I miss them, too."

"Well alright, hurry on back now, yeah?"

"Yeah, sure. Of course."

"Alright." The voice paused again. "And this time don't forget to wipe yer arse!"

They listened to the distant scratch of brush as the man finally departed.

Marcus looked over his shoulder. "He's just joking, I always wipe—"

Richter pulled on the trousers. "Back. Now."

"Yeah yeah, alright, I understood you." As the two shuffled, the man said, "Can I pull up my drawers?"

Richter stared where the three brigands were, now distanced enough to be but black blurs behind green ones. He stood up and tapped the man's shoulder. "Aye, get up."

Marcus stood, his pants around his legs, his arse to Richter, his eyes to his friends. Ever so slowly, he crouched down and pulled his pants up. As he tightened them, he said, "So, are you with the merchants?"

"Sure."

"Ah, sorry about all that." Marcus put his hands down to cinch his belt. "We were just walking on the road when *heyah motherfarker!*"

The brigand spun around and his fist rode between the wood of the crossbow and its strings, corkscrewing the weapon in Richter's grip and the captain blinked and fired but half the cord snagged the brigand's knuckles while the other half ripped the fletching and sent feathers into the air and the bolt shot out in a spinning tumble. Marcus screamed and turned to run, but his hands were ensnared in the bowstrings and Richter yanked him back like a jailor fighting a half-shackled prisoner.

"Help! Help!" the brigand screamed. He turned back around. "My friends are gon' kill you, you motherfark!"

Richter didn't know when or at what speed or even in what order things happened but he let go of the crossbow and unsheathed Adelbrecht's sword and as the man came punching at him, he pierced through the man's gut and out his backside. The captain held one hand on the handle, and his other held the crossguard, his knuckles white, his face wrenched. Blood streamed down the steel and warmed his fingers and pitter-pattered below.

"Faugh…" Marcus grimaced as blood filled the gaps of his teeth.

The brush shook and trembled in the distance, and then again ever closer. Silhouettes crossed behind the leaves and between trees, the shapes carrying concerned chatter as they called out Marcus's name, and the warbling scratch of unsheathed weapons and the clinky-clank of armor jangling soon followed, and a moment later a brigand appeared between trees. His heels skidded as he snapped his head toward Richter and he raised an accusing hand as though he discovered a murder in an alley.

"He's killin' Marcus!"

The scream broke through the trees like a wild animal finding its newborns under attack. Gritting his teeth, Richter put a boot to Marcus and kicked him off the blade. The man fell without a noise, his wormy fingers clutching the earth in clumps as he fell over and silently curled into a ball.

"Get him! Get that motherfarker!"

Taking a few steps back, Richter kept his eyes on the brigands and his feet light on the earth. And he waited. When the first brigand finally got through the bush and planted his feet, Richter took another step back. As the second brigand joined the first, he took another. And by the time all three were sprinting toward him, weapons raised, voices throwing threats, the captain finally turned around and soared back through the trees. Now the pathfinder was gone. Now it was time to be something else: prey.

~~~

"Watch," Quinn said. A few of the new recruits looked over. He held out his hand. "Are you watching?"

"Uh, sure," one said.

"Great. Now don't shit yerself when you see this."

The thief took a dagger and flipped it into the air and then turned out his hip and let it land back into its sheath. He grinned. "Pretty farking nice, right?"

One man nodded. "Nice."

"I can do better," Minnesang said.

Quinn's smile disappeared in an instant. "Shut yer farking whore mouth."

"I'm a trained jester," Minnesang said. "It's not a matter of competition, but of experience."

"Trained jester he says... I'mma train my foot up yer farking arse."

"Hey!" Dahlgren said, hissing a whisper. "Both of you shut yer mouths."

The thief pointed at the jester like a sibling wronged, but the old man's eyes widened and his brow flared. Quinn sat back on his haunches. He quietly seethed toward Minnesang. "'Do better.' Blue hatted queer looking motherfarker. I will *end* you."

Looking up at his cap, Minnesang said, "Respectfully, my good sir, I believe this fine company has room for two jesters."

"Hey, do I look like a jester to you, you mother—"

Dahlgren's handless arm suddenly knocked the thief to the ground. He rolled on top of Quinn with the nub on his throat and his other hand palming the thief's face. As two of the company's more experienced men quarreled, the rest of the recruits stood up and backed away, glancing at each other like children watching a fight between two drunk uncles.

"I said... shut... yer fucking... *mouth!*"

"Get off me!"

"Shut it!"

"Stop touching me with that arm! Seriously Dollgrin it's disgusting!"

Dahlgren pressed his nub into Quinn, driving it toward his mouth, briefly wrenching it between his teeth. The thief turned his head and spat.

"I'mma farking vomit!"

Quinn's hand went for his hip and tried for his dagger.

"Oh ye piece of shit," Dahlgren growled as he pinned the thief's swordhand with his knee.

Minnesang said, "Fellas," airing the word like he was trying it out, and then laughed as he backed away, his jester cap jingling with each step. The fire had been set, no need to blow on it anymore.

Dahlgren reared up with a fist cocked back. He said, "You know it's 'bout time we got to this!"

"H-hey I wasn't going to kill you!" Quinn said. "I was defendin' myself!"

"Hey, yeah," Thomas said, but he had nothing else to contribute as his hands nervously reached out and returned back to himself like the claws of a hawk bounding precariously after a deadly snake.

"Oh thanks!" Quinn said. "Lot of help you are!"

Crockett barreled in and threw his arms around Dahlgren. "Stop! Stop it, already! By the old gods, Dahlgren, didn't Quinn save you from that sellsword? Didn't he save you from Hans?"

Quinn wiggled backwards. "Cricket's right! I saved yer life!"

Growling, Dahlgren threw the paymaster's arms off, then slouched as calmness returned. He put up his hand, waving away further attention.

"Alright," he said. "I'm alright. Just got a little fired up and—"

In an instant, the old man sprawled onto the road, half the company jumping out of their boots as Richter went sliding across the road face first, grit and gravel crunching underneath his chest as he skidded to a stop.

"Richter," Dahlgren said, groaning as he rolled over. "What in the fuck?"

Three men emerged from the brush screaming and with weapons raised and all three promptly set their feet out on stiff legs and had their boots tilted to the heels, skidding to a stop as all the sellswords drew eyes upon them.

"O-oh shit!" one brigand said.

Dahlgren leaned up from his fall and looked at the brigands, then waved his handless arm at the company's newest recruits. "There's your pay!" he yelled. "There's your pay! Earn it! Earn it, men!"

With every one of Richter's trained fighters preoccupied, the company's new hires set upon the bandits like wild animals. Spears awkwardly plunged in and out and someone used theirs upside down like a maid trying to broom out a rat while another man threw his shield like he was throwing a chair in a barfight and at some juncture a blue and white cap went soaring in and bounced and jingled away.

In a matter of seconds, three dead men were crumpled on the ground, surrounded by men getting their first kills, hands rising and falling, beating and stabbing and cutting the corpses into mulch and for a second time the jester's cap went flying in from another direction, bounding back like a chandelier swinging over a brawl.

A quiet settled in, filled by the occasional clatter of weapons, the huff of breaths, the quick planting of feet and stabbing the bodies again at the slightest hint of movement like a cat striking at the death throes of a rat that had put up more of a fight than expected. The men then all turned to the captain and the others.

"They're dead," one said.

"Uh, yeah," Quinn said. "You fellas smoked the shit out of 'em."

Richter nodded. "You did good, men."

Getting to his feet, the captain glared at Dahlgren and Quinn.

"We had an issue," Crockett said, sliding between the men. "But it's taken care of. Right fellas?"

Dahlgren turned to Quinn. "Aye, it's taken care of," he said, nodding.

The thief touched a bruised lip and then nodded. "Uh, yeah. What's done is done, or whatever philosophical shit you peacelovers say."

Little bells jingled and all the men looked over to see Minnesang the jester righting his hat, his eyes studiously glaring upward as he ever so carefully made the wool helm sit prettily on his head. Then he looked down and thumbed over his shoulder. "I know you said you wanted one of them alive, but all of our attackers are in various dispositions very incompatible with life."

"That's alright." Richter adjusted his own hat and nodded to the woods. "We've one left."

~~~

"Marcus."

"Errghhh…" the gutted brigand slowly rolled over. He stared up at Richter. "Ahh man…"

"I know you're in pain," Richter said. He held out his bandolier of vials. "You should know that I'm a healer and I can help you."

The sellswords glanced at each other.

The captain kneeled. "Marcus, I need information. I know Kantorek camps in two different spots in this area. One is a decoy with a runner in place. The other is where he is right now."

"Mmhmm." Marcus swallowed and lifted a finger, weakly pointing it at the bandolier. "And what… what do you have for me, so-called healer who farking stabbed me?"

"Wormwood and balm, mixed with mint for scenting. I've also bandages, of course, and I can stitch you up. That'll hurt, but it will be necessary."

"Hmm…"

Richter continued. "I'll give you a few days of life with which you can take your odds crossing the river or even go to Marsburg, I don't care which, but any chance is better than none."

The brigand's smirk faded. He said, "And if… if I don't… help?"

The captain twisted his bandolier around. Not a one of them had anything useful, but he kept them filled and looking the 'part' as it were. He pointed at one and lied: "In this one is something else entirely. Monkshood. You probably know it as Wolfsbane. If you set me off on the wrong path, I will come find you and feed you this." Richter stared at the man's open wounds. He said, "Actually, I'll just shove it right in."

Marcus swallowed again. He slowly leaned up and pointed. "Down that way is the decoy. It's just one man who stays there. Kantorek usually chooses the fastest of us for that role. If you trip his alarms he will rabbit to the real camp, just… just as you said." The hand moved rightward. "Further that way, you'll pass by some tall trees, probably the tallest in the woods, Kantorek… erggh… Kantorek is that way. There are lots of footpaths that will make it obvious. That's where we were heading when you jumped me and—"

Richter leaned over, Adelbrecht's sword in hand, its steel piercing Marcus's neck. The brigand's eyes went wide and his hands pawed at the air like a kitten chasing moths. Richter withdrew the blade and blood spewed out in two ropes, each gushing pulse lower than the last until it simply frothed from the hole and the brigand's eyes rolled back and he collapsed.

"Goodness, Richter," Crockett said.

As the captain cleaned the blade, he said, "There's stomach bile on the ground over there and I can smell his liver. He had an hour left at most. A very, very painful hour. I did more for him than he deserved." Richter sheathed the sword and turned to his men. "Now let's go kill Kantorek."

Chapter 7. Killing a King.

THE KING OF DRAGONS stood up and wiped a cloth over his cock and then cinched his belt around his pants. He picked his teeth with a fingernail and then swept back his hair, his face garnished with a satisfied grin.

"Not so loud now, are ya?" he said, looking down.

The tent's flap opened and voice came in: "My turn with yer doxy?"

Kantorek looked over his shoulder. "What?"

A bandit stood in the tent's opening, one leg bouncing eagerly while the other wobbled on the stick of a pegleg.

"I-I-I was gonna get it in while I-I-I still can," the one-legged man said.

Kantorek looked back down. Sprawled at his feet was a pale woman with half-lidded eyes and a mouth frozen in the gasps he choked her out in. One of the dead merchant's wives, presumably, though he never bothered to inquire. Nor did he listen much to her protestations about honor, family, legacy, or any of that. Mentions of her husband was probably somewhere in all that blabbering, but the more they talked, the less he could enjoy it, and this one talked a lot. So he shut her up.

"She's no doxy," Kantorek said. "Quite a shame, really."

The one-legged man cleared his throat. "Is she…"

"She's dead."

"Oh…" the bandit augured a finger into his ear. He wiped the wax on his sleeve and said, "I-I-I mean, is she still a little warm?"

"Where are we at on those fortifications?" Kantorek said, still staring down at the corpse, eying the red rings he had imprinted around her neck.

Somehow the wounds still held color, as if pain itself was the last thing to leave this world.

"The fort… oh, right. We're still working on those, Kan—"

"*Name!*" Kantorek shouted.

The one-legged man cleared his throat. "I-I-I mean, we're still working on the fortifications, sir King of Dragons…"

Kantorek dabbed his brow with one of the merchant's cloths. He stared down at the corpse. Her limbs had settled in such strange positions, arms in fight, legs in flight, absent of all else one could presume her fate just by the staggered posture with which she slumped into the next life, eyes still flared toward the one who sent her there. Kantorek threw the cloth over her face.

"Sir?" the one-legged bandit said. "You alright? Want meh-meh-me to get ya some water?"

"I am not thirsty, you fool. I am concerned about our defenses… I thought I made it clear that our positions are compromised. We are missing men, and whoever is on our scent could very well be closing in now. Either we make firm our place in this part of the forest, or we leave entirely. And I plan not to do the latter on account of some upstart monk and his shitarse sellswords." Kantorek stepped toward the one-legged man. "So let me ask you again, and I would like you to be as precise as that twig of a leg you somehow stand on: where are we at with those fortifications?"

Nearly falling, the one-legged man clutched the tent's flap like a sailor going down with the ship, the last man clinging to a doomed mast.

"Any day now," Kantorek said. He mimicked the man's hops with a stutter: "W-w-well?"

Swallowing, the one-legged man cleared his throat and said, "S-so, uh, well… y'know, we got started on them fortifications, but then we was figuring to wait until the hunting party got back. Y'know, make sure we do it right the first time. Cause… cause Rambert was with them, and, y'know Rambert, ol' clever Ram, he'd make sure it was done proper. The fortifications, that is, we'd do them proper with Ram. So we was waiting for him, sir. Waiting for Rambert we was… sir… sir King… King of Dragons."

Kantorek clenched his fist. "I thought I told you that…" he paused. Somewhere in the back of his head, his mind still parsed the sputtered report. He cocked his head. "Did you say the hunting party hasn't returned?"

"Uhh, no, th-they're still gone."

"First our shore party goes missing down the Trading Swords river, that was *ten men*, mind… and now it is midday and I am hearing that you are still waiting on the hunting party to return?"

"Yeh-yeh-yessir."

"Do you not see the problem?"

"Sorry sir, my mind ain't the sharpest," the man said, and then he lifted his wooden leg and tapped the peg as though to say some part of his thinking had gone off with his missing limb. He then fanned his arms out with conciliatory aplomb and smiled halfheartedly. "This is why yer in charge! Yer the big man here! As far as we're concerned, we-we-we think you a man of might and brain, a real thinker, like Rambert but somethin' more."

"More," Kantorek said. "Like what more, exactly? Illuminate me."

The peglegged bandit smiled and then his body shunted forward and he slammed into the tentpole and his arms fenced around it and his pegleg drummed across the ground. Kantorek fell, his arms crossed up shielding his face from a spray of splinters and blood. He looked up to see his man had been impaled by a harpoon of steel, pinning his chest against the tentpole.

"Sir," the one-legged man said. "Can… can you fetch m'leg…"

The bandit pointed at his wooden peg, and then his arm fell aside and his head dropped. Screams erupted outside the tent. Kantorek grabbed his sword and took one step forward.

"Mercenaries!" a passing brigand screamed. "The mercenaries are here!"

Kantorek gritted his teeth and stormed toward the front of his tent, but the word 'there's too many!' broke upon his ears and he came to an abrupt halt. More brigands ran by the tent and into the camp's center. Distant, blurry shapes ebbed and flowed in a fight, the clash of swords and the grunts and howls of men rising. As Kantorek took another step forward, a brigand ran from left-to-right and then fell with an arrow in his back. 'We're surrounded!' one of his men shouted, and seemingly confirming this, another bandit fell right-to-left with an arrow in his knee and a follow-up through his throat.

A brigand skirted to the front of the tent, ducking as a series of arrows zipped overhead. He pointed in all directions. "Sir King of Dragons, we're under attack!"

"I know!" Kantorek said, taking a breath and broadening his shoulders. He waved a hand as though he were a nobleman sending a dish back to its chef. "Form a battleline! I'll be out soon to cleave these sellswords in half!"

The brigand stared uncertainly.

"I'm getting my weapons!" Kantorek said. "Go on then, together we will kill every last one of these sonsabitches or I am not the King of Dragons!"

Gifted with courage, the brigand's face lit up with a wide and knowing grin. He raised his sword and ran into the fray with newfound bravery.

Kantorek, however, turned around and ran to the back of his tent. He lifted the bottom of the tarp and stared out. Nobody stood outside waiting in ambush. Behind him, he could hear the screams and roars of battle and of his men dying. With no further hesitation, he dove under the tarp like a dog with a stolen scrap and he retreated into the forest while his men stood their ground, for surely the King of Dragons would be with them, his name alone sowing fear unto all, and thusly those misguided men met the nameless company of Richter von Dagentear, and the sellswords slew them down, and the brigands died cursing the name of Kantorek the cowardly brigand, and so even absent of blood and body, there died the King of Dragons.

~~~

Dahlgren cocked his sword into the nook of his elbow and squeezed the blood off it. Glancing around, he said, "You know, I think they outnumbered us two to one. Hells, maybe even three to one." The old man sheathed his sword and looked at his captain. "Richter, did you hear me?"

"Aye."

"I'm offering a compliment."

"Aye, thank you."

Richter looked around the camp. Bodies everywhere, limbs contorted in shapes most unfamiliar. One corpse lay face first in a campfire's ashes, the melted hands grafted onto the skull as if offering it as a grey contribution. Most died staring at the sky. Frozen eyes. Gaping mouths. Flesh mottled with flies blackly dancing in their frenzied eating. Between bodies, a litter of shattered shields and spears and staked arrows standing whose fletching rustled like flowers. As the sun broke through the clouds, all the armor glinted, bright and white and blinding, and the grass glistened nothing but red.

"You know," Dahlgren said. "I used to think I'd get used to the smell. But it's always fresh. Always like it's something new even when it isn't."

"Aye"

"You would have done well as a lieutenant in the army, captain."

"Maybe."

"Maybe? This was as fine a tactical battle as I've ever seen. You had them thinking we were twice our number. One even shouted out that we were the Battle Brothers! I'm pretty sure that's a compliment. Crockett! Is that a compliment?"

"Uhh…" the paymaster looked up from a pile of inventory that they were slowly stacking with booty and salvaged weapons and armor. He shrugged. "Only record I have of that company is they killed a criminal named Hoggart. Maybe they've done more since."

"See?" Dahlgren said. "Hoggart and maybe more! We're in league with a premium troop, Richter! Don't be so humble. It is unbecoming for one to feign shyness when their talents are being so lauded."

"Alright, Dahlgren," Richter said, glancing at the old man and giving a nod. "I appreciate your words."

"Good." The old man grinned wryly. "You're welcome."

Crockett said, "Speaking of sellsword companies and their histories, or lack thereof, I did take the liberty of writing down our accomplishment here today." He tipped his quill feather over the edge of his book. "In case anyone was interested."

"Gotta build that renown somehow," Dahlgren said. The old man looked about the battlefield with keen satisfaction as if it was a front yard fence with a fresh coat of paint. "Aye, this one'll certainly be a fine read."

During the battle, Richter led a handful of the new recruits on a whooping and hollering mission, the group sprinting around the edges of the bandits' encampment in pairs, coming to and fro while launching arrows. Meanwhile, Dahlgren led the bulk of the forces down the centerline. Despite the smallness of his band, Richter knew that his enemy would assume their lot to be sane. He knew exactly what they would think: that the only reason there's so few there, is because the rest of them will soon be coming from the trees. And just like that, the bandits were taken by fear. The scant few sellswords running around the perimeter soon took the image of a much larger force and Dahlgren's charge wedged into that fear and broke the brigands. Half were cut down before they could even figure out which direction to turn. Richter and the flanks followed in next and that was that.

But it wasn't a perfect fight by any means.

The captain looked at a nearby corpse. One of his. A new recruit. Mouth agape and a hand frozen to the wound which felled him. His glazed eyes locked upon the man who hired him. A bird sat perched on his shoulder picking appetizers out of his ears. The captain kicked it away. "How many of our own did we lose?"

Dahlgren spat. "Eh, nobody important."

Richter looked back.

Dahlgren cleared his throat. "Ahh, we lost five or six, I believe."

"Any of the new hires survive?"

"Well." Dahlgren paused to break an arrow stuck in his buckler. He used his pinky to bore the shaft out and a tired eye peered through the hole for a moment. He lowered the shield and said, "I think the miller made it. And a butcher. And that other fella, the one with the hat."

"The jester," Crockett said. "Minnesang."

"Aye, Minnuh... uh, the juggling fella. He's over yonder somewhere. Hard to miss," Dahlgren said. The old man crossed his arms, his bloodied chainmail jangling and glinting. "Unfortunately, most of 'em just didn't know what they were doing. That fella going cold at your feet? I saw him jump into a spear. I mean he jumped right into it, Richter, like a fish into a bear's mouth. Another charged a crossbowman without even bothering to raise his shield. Honestly, at the rate they were 'proving' themselves it wouldn't surprise me if one of them just upped and fell on his own blade."

Richter looked at the dead. He said, "Well, they weren't proper fighters."

"No, that they were not," Dahlgren said. "But there is but one way to find out if a man is a 'proper' fighter and yer looking at it."

"Hey!" Quinn hailed from a far corner of the camp. He pointed into a large, grey tent with its front torn astray. "There's a one-legged man in here."

Richter shrugged. "Alive?"

"Dead!"

"That's not very helpful now is it!" Dahlgren yelled.

"I just thought it was funny!" Quinn yelled back, wiggling a pegleg around in his hand. He pointed into the tent with it. "But I think this was the 'King of Dragons' tent!"

"What else is in there?" Richter asked. "Maps? Weapons?"

"Yeah, hold on." The thief looked in. He said, "There's a lady."

"Alive?"

Quinn held open the tarp. He crouched down and leaned forward before finally walking in. The tent flailed and flapped closed behind him. A moment later, he walked out. He looked at the ground. He kicked the ground. He looked at the sky. He would've kicked it if he could. Finally, he looked back at his captain and shook his head.

"Alright," Richter said. He turned to Dahlgren. "Do we have prisoners?"

"That we do. You wanna ask them a few questions?"

"Aye, something like that."

~ ~ ~

The three prisoners kneeled in a row with their arms tied behind their backs. Richter's company hovered around them like birds of prey having already taken the courtesy of a meal or two, splattered in blood and skinflaps and chunks of gore of indiscernible sources, and unfortunately the sellswords stood fewer in number now than when the day had begun which was as awful a portend for a prisoner as any. The belly always had room for a serving of vengeance, after all.

"P-please, we 'aven't done nothing wrong!" one brigand begged.

Dahlgren unsheathed his sword. He said, "I've always been a bit fascinated by what a dead man says to you in the end. A king claims his loyalists will come for you. A holy man swears that the old gods shall damn you on his behalf. The criminal? The bandit? That no-good, road hounding, lady raping brigand? Well, he believes that he has done nothing wrong at all."

"B-but it's true! Kantorek j-just hired me the other day! It was either join him or risk the roads alone! I was just surviving! I'm innocent to all this!"

"Innocence ain't some that returns, little brigand, it is something you leave behind. Forever."

"By the old gods, no! Let us redeem ourselves!"

"Can't. It'd get in the way of redeeming myself," Dahlgren said and he raised his sword-hand. The brigand squealed and ducked his head.

"Hold!" Richter shouted.

Dahlgren's sword froze in the air. The brigand peered up at it, and at the old man furiously staring down at them.

"You've yourself a brief reprieve," the old man said. "*Brief.*"

Richter snapped his fingers. "Trash, would you please show them."

As Dahlgren lowered his weapon, Elletrache the beast slayer walked up. His burly shape and hissing armor of lindwurm scales drew horror from the prisoners. If there were ever a man who knew pain, it was this hobbling, one-eyed cretin who looked like he carried pain around in a wheelbarrow. The brigands cried out as he neared.

"Oh quit yer squirming," Elletrache said. He swung up a large sack and dumped a pile of heads before the prisoners. He crouched down, palming each and turning it face up. "Here, say hello to yer friends."

The prisoners glanced at the heads and then turned away.

"Best take a better look than that," Dahlgren said. "Or I'll have you joining them."

"Aye," Richter said. "Take a good, long look."

The prisoners slowly turned back around and stared. Their eyes widened at the sight. Sometimes they recognized someone they had grown fond of and this drew whimpers and tears. One of the heads was that of a younger lad and the sight of him drew the most sorrow. But none of their stares captured the essence of looking at the ruination of someone they respected, though. At least, insofar as Richter wondered how his own company might land their eyes upon his suddenly bodiless demise.

Richter said, "Which one is Kantorek?"

"N-none," one stammered, drawing glares from the others.

"Yer asking about Kantorek?" Another prisoner immediately got to his feet and jerked his head down at the one who had first spoke: "*He's* Kantorek! That's him! Right there!"

The honest prisoner leaned away. "Wh-what? No! My name's Hugo!"

The prisoners split apart, kicking one another and spitting accusations. In all the chaos, one man even claimed himself Kantorek, a confused admission that saw him instantly fall to his knees and squeal that he had only been frightened in the madness and his name was in fact Packard. Certainly, he was not Kantorek, and the sellswords watched as he soiled himself and they even pitied him a little when he announced what he had done and sobbed that the real Kantorek would never do such a humiliating thing.

Richter sighed. He looked to the tree line. He knew the 'King of Dragons' had made it out. Of course he did: these men were incompetent and easily manipulated, and in their being manipulated they were no doubt strangely loyal to Kantorek himself. Such were the influential ways of a successful brigand that, for a moment, the underlings might obey their leader as though he were indeed king and actual dragons were at his back. The 'King of Dragons' carried no import other than the title providing its wearer with a veritable horse, a few moments with which his believers would throw their lives away while he escaped to live another day.

King of Dragons. What a fanciful title. What a trick.

"Ar-are you the one they call the Wight?" one of the prisoners suddenly said, breaking their arguments and inviting contemplative silence.

Richter turned around. He looked at the prisoners, and then at Dahlgren.

"Kantorek ain't here," Dahlgren said. "These fellas don't know shit."

"Aye." The captain nodded. "Kill them all."

~ ~ ~

As the company stripped the dead of their gear, Richter scoured the tree line. He paused beside an enormous trunk, crouching himself between two massive roots cording through the soil. Beside them, a set of boot tracks that had kicked up chunks of mud and slid awkwardly along a carpet of moss. Its runner had fallen there and planted an image of himself in the earth – hands sprawled, belly down, a little divot where his nose puttied the mud. Then the runner had hurried to his feet and sprinted away.

The runner, of course, being Kantorek.

Richter sighed and wheeled his legs over the roots and followed the tracks further out, taking two steps just to cover the elongated traces of Kantorek's hysterical speed. But as he tracked the signage, his eyes fell upon another sight entirely, something which deeply trenched the forest floor. Something that, unlike Kantorek, strode the earth with calm determination.

"We're about ready, captain," a voice said.

He turned around to find Dahlgren standing there.

The old man thumbed over his shoulder. "Tell you what, captain, we got ourselves quite the haul! New gambesons for chest and head, nice leathers abound, too. What's too cutup we can just slap around the necks and arms, better doing that than paying some smithy or tailor to piece it all back together, oh and of course the big old gods' primary favor: the 'King of Dragon's' war chest! A thousand crowns of spendin' money, to the company, of course. The brigands had been busy around these parts, to say the least."

"Dahlgren," Richter said, his tone an obvious inquiry into matters beyond the material.

"Sir?" Dahlgren's excitement faded. He gripped his sword out of instinct. "Everything alright?"

"Aye, it is, but I do have a question though."

"Sure."

"If you were on a battlefield and needed to run an enemy down, how would you do it?"

"Hmm. Well if I can't shoot them dead then I suppose I'd use cavalry."

Richter looked back to the forest, the imposing foliage proving to be an impressive impasse to his vision, much less to a rider on a horse.

Dahlgren nodded. "Ah, here, horses wouldn't do… no horses do—"

"How about a dog?"

The old man nodded again. "Sure, a wardog could do it. They can be trained to fetch more than birds and balls and no man can outrun a dog. But they're hard to come by. Like men, every dog can fight, but just like men not every dog can fight well. Not to mention dogs are of a friendly disposition. You need a trainer to put that purpose in them."

"The purpose of fighting?"

"Aye, though some dogs enjoy the fight just as men do. You see that with horses on occasion, too. Natural inclination and all that. Sometimes you come across an animal and you can't help but be thankful it ain't human."

Richter nodded.

"But I'm no houndmaster so I'm partly speaking out of school here."

"I've another question," Richter said, waving his arm. "Come here."

The old man nodded and slowly worked his way around the tree trunk and its roots, actions which took considerably more labor than when the captain had done them.

Catching his breath, he stood beside Richter. "Captain?"

Richter pointed at the ground. "Look at this."

Dahlgren looked down. He stared for a moment, then leaned for a closer look. His back popped as he quickly straightened. "Oh shite."

"Aye."

"Hope you weren't thinking a dog could chase that down."

"No, I was not."

Dahlgren stuck a foot into the direwolf's print, his boot small in its middle. The moment his boot touched mud he quickly retreated as though the trace might snap like a trap. He said, "Can't say I've actually seen one of these, but I know men who have and direwolves are awful dangerous monsters by all accounts. I'll let Elletrache know and put the men on alert."

The captain nodded. He said, "Don't try and scare them. Make it sound normal enough."

"Hard to do."

"Just don't quiver when you say 'direwolf' and you'll be alright."

"Did I quiver there?"

Richter smiled. "A little, aye."

"Shite." Dahlgren nodded. "Don't tell no one."

The captain nodded back. "I'll be back to camp in a moment."

"In a moment? You stand out here peckin' flowers and get nabbed by a direwolf and that'll be yer fucking problem, respectfully captain."

"Aye, Dahlgren, as always I appreciate you looking out for me."

The old man stared at the captain a moment longer, then nodded and walked away.

Richter watched him go, and then he returned his gaze to the direwolf's print. Slowly, his eyes went beside it. There he saw a mushroom's stem. Yellow with the cap of it gone. Richter stared at it for a long while. He stood up and took a step further into the woods.

"Captain."

He paused.

He turned around to see Dahlgren standing there.

"I talked to Trash about the direwolf. He says you best get your arse with the rest of us. He had some other choice words but I'll leave 'em out."

Richter turned and glanced at the beheaded mushroom again. Soft, tilting, at the edge of the direwolf's print, and all the same seemingly more dangerous. He nodded. "Alright Dahlgren," he said. "Let's head back to Immerwahr and get our pay."

~ ~ ~

"But... why the whole head?" Berthold asked, the miller struggling to shoulder the knapsack of brigand heads. Its bottom had been soiled red, and the sides of it gruesomely articulated the collective faces pressing against the burlap. He looked about the marching company of sellswords and cleared his throat and said a little louder: "Why do we take the whole head?"

"What's that?" Dahlgren said, snorting as he drank from a goatskin canteen. "You say something?"

"Oh, I'm just wondering... why do we need to take the whole head?"

Quinn grinned. "Well—"

"For the value," Minnesang said, interrupting. "When you provide the whole head, it shows just who it came from. Important men are also noted by their appearance. My head, for example, would be worth quite a lot."

The thief stared at the man with fury in his eyes. "Hey jester, why don't you fetch a few heads outta there and juggle them for us, eh?"

"I'd rather not."

"Oh, that wasn't a suggestion, it was an order."

Richter raised his voice: "The only one making orders here is me. Keep the heads in the bag."

The jester, though not responding, did take a turn in jostling his head side-to-side, bringing his jester hat to a jingle-jangle as he smirked at the thief.

Quinn scoffed. "You've got sound hearing for a one-eared man, cap'n."

"Captain's ear still has the hole you arse," Dahlgren said, smirking between sips on the canteen. "He's just missin' the fold."

"Well then listen up because I got a good farking question!" Quinn pointed a finger at the jester. "Why's this man talking so artic… accurate…"

"Articulately," Crockett said.

"Right, accuraticately about sellsword work, huh? Nobody else think that's strange this fella has just slid right into the job?"

"My talents have taken me far and wide in this life," Minnesang said. "When you sit beside the thrones of noblemen, you gaze upon their work now and again, and upon where their money goes." The jester grabbed at the arms of his cap'n'bell hat and drew them down like winter flaps over his ears. He stared at Quinn and said, "I've seen the heads of many a thief, in fact, and I can say they always look the most surprised in those final moments."

Quinn pursed his lips. He straightened up. "One of these days, I'm gonna take that head of yours and juggle it on a farkin' spit."

"Hey yeah, that's bad luck, threatening a jester," Thomas said. "They say even kings know not to do that."

"This is a kingless land," Quinn said. "And by the way, shut the fark up, Thomas. Nobody asked."

"Quinn, Minnesang," Richter said. "Mind yourselves."

"Yessir," Minnesang said. He looked at Quinn as he let go of the arms of the cap'n'bells, the bells jangling upright and flailing in the thief's direction. The thief stared back. He made little noise aside from the sound of his hands tightly gripping around his daggers.

"Quinn," Richter said.

The thief's hands relaxed off his daggers. "Yes, cap'n, I got my ears."

"Very good, Quinn."

The company walked for a time. The forest seemed to take a liking to them, for the silence which men cast into the woods gently faded, birds chirping overhead and scrounging through the branches in frenzies of building or protecting. Now and again deer could be heard, and on more rare occasions seen, though meeting their eyes sent them away in panicked flurries. Squirrels chewed on nuts and at times threw the husks down at the sellswords.

Dwelling on what he had seen earlier, Richter stopped for a moment and turned around. He waved his arms forward and told his men to keep moving, and that they did. He stared back to their rear, waiting for Elletrache. The beast slayer glanced at the captain and smirked and stepped out of line.

"Ol' Elletrache knows what yer thinking."

"Aye," Richter said. "Is it out there?"

"No." Trash gestured up and around. "Woods're too loud. When things get quiet and peaceful? That is the time to worry."

"If we were to be attacked by such a creature," Richter said. "How do you think we'd do?"

The beast slayer laughed. He laughed again. And again, as if each laugh only precipitated his rediscovering of the original 'joke'. He patted the captain on the shoulder. "Do not worry about these things. You're the one they call the Wight," Trash said, chuckling. "A supposed dead man shouldn't concern himself with life or death nor by what claw or tooth decides such fates."

"I'm concerned for the company, Trash."

"Alright. Yes, this creature may come. If it does, ol' Elletrache shall kill it," the beast slayer said. He lifted a grimy, hairy hand missing the tips of a few fingers. "Or the beast may already be dead. Who knows. The tracking tells us nothing, other than it knew the brigands were there and them it did not attack. Or, maybe the brigands made the track themselves. Wouldn't be an unusual way to set wards around a camp, and I've heard a tavern rumor or two about brigands who dressed themselves like direwolves. Well, dressed themselves with wolves, but stood and stalked like the dires."

Richter thought about it, still uncertain for his company's safety.

"Either way," the beast slayer said. "If yer truly in this sellswordin' business, then maybe it won't be such a bad idea to run this sighting by the holy fella and get ourselves another contract."

The captain shook his head. "I think it best if we have confirmation first. The townsfolk do not like us being there as is, so the last thing we need is to scare them with tales of monsters in the woods and then for it to turn up that there are none."

Spitting a huge gob of gunk, Trash said, "Who cares what they think."

"They outnumber us," Richter said. He smirked. "I know you beast slayers don't fear the peasantry nor their mobs, but us witch hunters do."

"Except yer not a witch hunter no more," Elletrache said. "Yer a mercenary captain. As far as I'm concerned, you tell the holy fella there were *two* direwolves and ask for an advance, hah-hah!" The beast slayer slugged the captain on the shoulder as he walked by to join the company. "But it ain't my business. Sometimes a bit of lying and threatening is the way to get things done, other times maybe yer way of doin' things is the best. You just tell 'em whatever, yer the bloody leader, captain Richter von Dagentear, the guiding light of us mercenaries and the Wight of these here woods, hah-hah-hah!"

Chapter 8. Bad People.

IMMERWAHR HAD ORDERED the building of bunkhouses to help shelter the town's growing population. They were simple structures: long chutes of flatwood and curtained windows, each holding cots or haybeds for sleeping. Further furnishings seemed to take on the personalities of the occupants: cutesy dressers, fashionable adornments to the eaves and soffits, porch steps that jangled with bells to announce arrivals. Of all these buildings, the mercenaries had taken the ones closest to the tree line. Richter had chosen them just in case a mob were to form as it would give the sellswords an out into the woods. But he also chose the corner spot in an act of good faith, to stand vigilant against the dangers of the forest itself.

Sometimes when you share a blanket someone's toes gotta brave the cold and dark.

At least, that is what Richter thought would happen.

"Welcome back," a neighbor said as he tilted on a rocking chair. "You sellsword farks slaughter some more travelers?"

A haggardly woman beside him laughed like a horse choking on its spit. She stood up and went to the railing of their porch and leaned against it. "Sellswords get the rope! They get the river! They get the caaaage!"

Richter tipped his hat to them in a friendly manner all the same and opened the company's bunkhouse door. He stood there, the world's light behind him, his shadow stabbing into the room.

"Hobbs," he said.

The boy was idly half-playing on the floor. His hands moved toys around with the energy of it being more work than fun.

"Alright," Richter said. He entered, the door clattering behind him. A few billowing leaves snuck inside and scratched along the floorboards, skittering quietly as if they knew they weren't supposed to be in there. Richter's boots clopped heavily as he strode across the room.

"You're alive," the boy finally said.

"Aye, I think so."

Richter crossed a window and the scant light illuminated his work: blood caked his hands, blood was upon his jacket, blood was upon his face. And if one stared at him long enough, they'd know it was on his mind just as well.

The boy's eyes lit up as he stared at these glimmers of red.

Richter left the light, his crimson sheen darkening as he went to the washbowl in the room's corner. He dipped his face in, scrubbing the day away, back curled, elbows cocked, moving stiffly like some granitic creature husking his earthen shell. He picked strips of blood away like he was unlatching leeches. He glanced over his shoulder and said, "Don't get too excited."

"Are you hurt?" Hobbs said.

"No."

"Then there's nothing to be excited about."

Richter glanced over his shoulder again but said nothing.

By now, the washbin was filled with red flakes. With his hands in the water, he could feel the flakes prickling as they floated about, and he felt the odd coolness as they glommed onto his wrists like islanded clots. And that's what a man could become: a cold inconvenience the size of a dimple. He turned away from the bloody chunk. "Did you bathe like I ask?"

"I did."

"Did you now?"

"Mmhm. Did you kill the King of Dragons?"

"No."

"Did you kill a lot of brigands, at least?"

"That doesn't concern you, boy, and I still don't think you bathed."

Richter flailed his hands over the water. Bloody droplets spilled undercurrent and curled into the bowl like shadows without magistrate, voidmade wisps borne of distant doings, unshackled from the firmament of the men they once dwelled in. Not a single drop of Richter's own blood in the mixture. Not a single hint of tainting, if it could be called that. Only the purity of killing others, the purity of a task which could be merited by honor or glory or coin. He stared at the blood as it colored the surface red, and soon a crimson reflection murkily stared back.

He dried his hands on his pants and turned and looked at the boy.

"I bathed," Hobbs quickly said, as though accused by stare alone.

Richter crossed the room. He grabbed the boy's hair and turned his head.

"Hey!" Hobbs yelled.

"Let me see your ears," Richter said, turning the boy left to right.

"Leggo!"

Richter let the boy go.

Hobbs swatted at the hand and said, "I wasn't lying!"

"Didn't say you were." Richter stared at the boy. "How're your wounds?"

"Fine."

Richter now grabbed the boy's shoulder and lifted his shirt. This did not gain similar protest from Hobbs, for the matter was of a serious sort.

"I said it's fine," he assured.

What was once a brutish dark purple wound had healed to a bright red. The place where Richter had shot the boy with a crossbow. A permanent reminder that he missed. A permanent reminder that he let a witch go. And on what account? Or on whose?

He cleared his throat. He said, "Sophia's still cleaning these bandages?"

Pulling his shirt down, Hobbs said, "I do it now. She taught me how."

"That's good. It doesn't smell?"

"No. It hurts a little if I bend into it, but other than that I am... peh... uh, peaky."

"Peachy?"

"That's the word. Quinn taught it to me. It means everything is..." Hobbs paused and held his hand up and splayed his fingers apart and wiggled his tongue between them. Richter immediately put a stop to it.

"You don't take nothing else from Quinn," Richter said.

"What? What did I do? Is it bad?" Hobbs said.

"Bad enough," Richter said. "From now on you stick with Thomas like we agreed."

"Thomas is boring, though."

"He is. Boring is good. Boring is safe. Do you hear me?"

"I hear you." Hobbs' eyes went a little slim. He pointed. "You've a cut on your cheek."

"I know," Richter said.

"Brigands?"

"No, it was from this morning. I had been training."

"With Dahlgren?"

"Aye." Richter pointed across the room at a cot where Hobbs' wooden sword lay. "He clipped me with that toy of yours."

"Whoa," Hobbs said, looking at the sword. "It did that much damage?"

"Even the smallest of weapons can do a lot if placed just right," Richter said. He sat down on a cot and took his boots off. He lay on his back, staring at the ceiling as his eyes slowly closed.

"Taking a nap?" Hobbs said.

"Mmhm."

Richter took his hat and slid it over his eyes. Outside, he could hear the townspeople coming and going. The idle greetings which were indistinguishable from the bleating birds, and the long running conversations which carried on in drowned out murmurs, occasionally brought to liveliness with barks of laughter or shouts of disagreement. And there were dogs here and there howling and barking and the occasional hissing wildness of a cat found out when it had thought itself secluded.

The boy suddenly said: "How have your dreams been?"

Richter moved his hat and opened his eyes. Hobbs stood at the foot of the bed staring at him.

"They're nightmares," Richter said and closed his eyes again.

"Mine too."

"It's the forest causing it," Richter said. "Don't dwell on them."

"What are your dreams about?"

Richter sighed. "Darkness. When I was your age, I had a terrible fear of the dark and I guess that has never gone away."

"But is there something in the dark?"

Richter grunted. He didn't like talking about his own weaknesses in this way, but he let the boy in. "Aye," he said. "Usually there are shadows coming after me. These shadows are often in the shape of people."

"Do they ever get you?"

"No." He cleared his throat. "I ignore them and they simply go away."

"Always?"

"Every day the sun rises," Richter said. "A part of me knows of this infinite light is waiting for me and so in my dreams I simply seek it out."

"But what if you can't?

"Not sure," Richter said. "I always wake up. I think it helps that my day to day life has become so rotten that even my nightmares can't compare." Smirking, he said, "I've surrounded my nightmares with worse yet horrors."

"Ah... I see."

Richter waited to hear the boy move away. But he didn't. He didn't so much as move anywhere.

"Alright, Hobbs," Richter said, opening his eyes. "What is it you want to talk about? I know it's not dreams. We've talked enough about those."

"Sorry, I know you need rest. I'll keep to myself."

"No," Richter said. "You've got something on your mind. Out with it."

Hobbs pursed his lips. He said, "The people here hate us."

"Aye," Richter said. "Surely you have the scryer's eye."

"I'm serious!"

"I know."

"They say the meanest things about us."

"We've earned a fair share of it, I'm sure."

"My friends… former friends… they say we're murderers. That we trade blood for coin."

"We do."

"Oh."

"Sellswords will never be trusted," Richter said. "Why would we be? Most mercenaries are a step away from being common criminals, and most *are* common criminals. Put yourself in these peoples' shoes. They don't *really* know who we are. If you aren't being suspicious then you aren't being smart."

Hobbs looked out the window. Two silhouettes quietly moved away.

"Is there anything we can do to prove to them we're good?" the boy said. "Maybe get rid of Quinn or something."

Richter laughed. "As much as I'd like to do that, I think it best you do not worry about these things, Hobbs. It isn't your place."

"Fine," he said. "I won't."

"Good."

A moment of silence filled the room. Richter relaxed into it.

"Richter, am I a bad person?"

Lifting the lid of his hat, Richter said, "Not yet, but you're getting there."

"Har-har."

"I need to rest, Hobbs."

"Alright." The boy pinched his lips closed before squeezing two more words out: "Nothing more."

Richter nodded and closed his eyes. He folded his hands over his chest and slowly his breathing steadied. Though the dark of his hat closed over him, a faint glint of light snuck in, glimmering through some patchwork, the spot where he had long ago shot the hat – Carsten's hat – with a crossbow. Back in the days when an old witch hunter took him from the world he knew and threw him into one he was made for. One little light in all that dark.

"Richter… are *you* a bad person?"

"I don't know."

"But you *do* know. *You're a leader of killers!*"

"Don't say that, Hobbs!"

"What?"

Richter jerked awake. He took the hat away and leaned up.

Hobbs was beside his toys on the floor. "I didn't say anything," he said.

Slowly, Richter took the hat and set it on a dresser beside the bed. He looked at the boy, a strobe of light coming through the window and illuminating his toys, the boy ushering the little soldiers to feigned glory.

"Richter?" Hobbs said. "Are you alright?"

"Aye, just a little tired, that's all."

"I'll stand watch for ya," Hobbs said. He got up and retrieved his wooden sword and waved it forth. "Any evil comes in here and I'll slay it down!"

"Aye," Richter said. "I'll surely sleep well under your vigilance, Hobbs."

The boy brought the sword to his chest like a king's guard of old. He stood by the windows, eying potential threats with a stern gaze.

Richter put his head back to the cot. Above, shadows of the townspeople arced across the ceiling, each of them pausing to point in at the bunkhouse and remark about the man inside, and the man inside fell asleep in their shade.

Chapter 9. Paying Dues.

RICHTER WOKE FROM HIS NAP to find the day's light fading and that Hobbs was snoozing with his sword fallen to the ground beside him and a slip of drool coming out of his mouth. Chuckling, Richter slowly got out of the cot. He snuck by Hobbs. The boy stirred and mumbled something about justice and then Richter opened the door and quietly left the bunkhouse.

A neighbor greeted him with a wave before turning his hand down and cutting his thumb across his own throat. Richter waved at the man in return.

"Kill them with kindness," the captain said through gritting teeth.

He walked to Immerwahr's store, suffering additional peasantry pleasantries all along the way. When he arrived at the shop, he opened the door to find silence inside, and for a moment he stood in the doorway like a man before an empty priory he had expected to be full. The wind whirled behind him, hissing that he was alone in his tribulations, whatever they were.

A dim light glowed in the store's rear, a shadow occasioning itself now and again up a far wall. Richter closed the door and walked toward the back. He heard a steady slurping noise until finally he found the monk sitting beside a few lit candles, his head leaning over a bowl of steamy soup.

"My, this dish is so hot I'd almost think a blacksmith forged it."

"You get the delivery of heads?" Richter said. "A man of mine named Berthold was to deliver them. Quaint fella, used to be a miller, though I suppose that has no relevance on delivering a pile of bloody heads."

The monk's spoon hung in the air. He said, "I'm eating, Richter."

The captain nodded respectfully. "Apologies."

"But yes, I received them," Immerwahr said, taking another sip. His face grimaced at the heat.

"Take it slow," Richter said. "I can just about see embers in that soup."

"Such tasty victuals need not be wasted on the grounds of a constitutionally frail tongue!" The monk proclaimed and Richter could do nothing but roll his eyes at such a misplaced sermonic response. Immerwahr slurped again and just as soon tilted back, his hand fanning an opened mouth. With a grin he tapped the side of the soup bowl. "I just cannot help myself."

"I can see that." The captain grabbed a stool standing in one of the aisles and dragged it over toward the counter. He tilted it. "Mind?"

"Of course not."

Richter took a seat. "You're in a surprisingly good mood considering Kantorek is still out there."

"Mmhmm," the monk said, taking another bite. He then set the bowl down and pointed at it. "You might be thinking that these delicious delicatessens are making me woolyminded."

"I'd never be crossed with such a thought."

"Surely not," Immerwahr said, a soft grin appearing before he snapped his fingers and pointed at Richter's jacket. "Give me the bounty."

Richter retrieved the papered bounty for the 'King of Dragons.' The monk snatched it, folded it, and tore it to strips. He threw the paper aside like a cloud of confetti.

The captain stared at the mess. "You're fine with the result, then?"

"I'm not being dramatic for no reason," Immerwahr said. He leaned back and waved his hand, the candles flickering gently. "Without strength in numbers, Kantorek is finished. He'll either run south to Marsburg, maybe join the lowlanders and their siege, or he'll cross the Trading Swords and head west. Maybe he'll even head north to Sommerwein. If you notice, none of these places involve him staying here. Of this result I am most pleased."

"Maybe he'll go east," Richter said. "Rebuild and return."

"In these woods? I doubt it. Ultimately, to me, that problem is solved whether his bloodied stump of a head is on a pike or being chopped off in some other place. Now, speaking of *delivered* heads…" The monk leaned to a side and then returned upward with a wooden chest in hand. It landed heavily on the desk and its trunk groaned as he opened it. "Let me see…"

He stacked and then slid over two towers of wobbling coin.

Wiping a bit of soup off a coin, Richter said, "Despite Kantorek being alive, you're giving the full reward?"

"Richter, you shouldn't dwell on a man's generosity. Just say something like 'oh, I can't take this' so I can say something like, 'it is my treat,' and then we part ways with profound amicability."

The captain stared over the coin. He said, "I can't take this."

The monk threw out his hand again and said, "Oh please, it's my treat." He grinned as he took another slurp of the soup and, chewing, he raised an eyebrow and nodded toward the rest of the stacks of crowns. "Don't leave them cold. Some stranger might feel bad and try to warm them up."

Richter sighed and took the coins into his purse.

"See? Not so hard." Immerwahr closed the treasury and swung it back under his desk with the brief sound of a drawer opening and being locked shut. He returned to his soup. "I think what I need to do now is figure out what other tasks I can put you to."

Richter remembered the direwolf track he had seen. He also thought about how it might be a faked print, something used to ward people away from the bandits' encampment. He thought about what Elletrache said, and moreso the way he said it – that Richter was a *mercenary* now. No matter what the direwolf track was, he should sell it as an immediate threat to garner more money. That was the mercenary way and—

"Captain?" Immerwahr said.

Richter looked up.

The monk splayed his hands. "Did *you* have anything in mind?"

Richter thought of what captain Adelbrecht would have done.

"Well?" Immerwahr said.

Richter shook his head. "No, nothing certain yet."

"Great! It might actually be good that your activities quiet down for a time. All your moving about stirs the nerves of the laity," Immerwahr said. "You should go join your men, Richter. Show yourself as their captain and all that. Wouldn't hurt to show these townspeople the real you, either."

~ ~ ~

Beneath the night's stars, the pub bristled with song and drink, its candlelit windows passing silhouettes of mercurial black, cutting across the casements like glass ensconced creatures of rock broken and reconstructed along each edge, and out of these figures came the din of guttural laughter strangely earthen behind these watery surfaces, and when the front door opened all festivities belched unto the road and from this sudden belligerence dogs slinked away and the eyes of cats would glimmer, feline glaring full of visceral hate, the same hate with which they had met humans ages ago and with which they would almost certainly see humans off in eons to come, and as the drunken babble emptied unto the street the children there would scram in shrill, crying packs, and they would run into the darkness giggling only to be reeled back, one by one, returning to spy through the tavern windows, whispering amongst each other what they saw, and conspiring ways to sneak in. Such was the manner of the tavern, its banner set to flag the night itself: raucous fun, and delights of merry, and amidst that aplomb, chaos aplenty.

Richter stood at the pub's porch. A passed-out man hanged off its end, a bent woman beside him pulling him up and down by his shirt, the drunkard's head reeling and lolling. She looked over her shoulder.

"It is a bit rude to stare," she said, drool on her lips, eyes crooked.

The captain removed his hat and opened the pub door. A crash of senseless noise hit him, a veritable hammer of cheering and laughter and shouting and music and dance all followed by a strong stench of ale and vomit. Richter glanced back at the woman and she was now slumped over the man, both snoring. He put his hat back on and went inside.

Patrons spilled over the benches in waves of yelling and singing, all the while ale sloshed in the air and frothed beards and spilled across the tables and pooled on the floor. Richter shuffled forward while putting up his hands like a man wading through a swamp with the sun in his face. A bluster of music tailed in from the far wall where a man and woman were in musical combat with lutes, each taking a turn to play out their whimsical jousts, the crowd cheering each coda as though it were a blow of a lance before the opposing musician cracked back with a song more potent than the last.

As Richter waded into the crowd, a coin suddenly plopped into the groove of his hat. He retrieved it and looked up to see a throng of giggling boys. The kids pointed to Richter's right and when he looked there was a well-endowed barmaid leaning over and as she did so another coin fell right into her bosom and she hopped back with a yelp. Richter looked back up and the boys were in hysterics. Smirking, the captain balanced the coin on his thumb and popped it back up and one boy snatched it out of the air like a lizard tonguing down a fly.

In a far corner, two figures waved at Richter. He leaned to see Thomas sitting with Hobbs. He motioned that he was on his way.

But as Richter moved across the room, a bubble of silence followed, those nearest to him hushing all chatter and turning to stare at him until he had passed, then they resumed in hissing whispers and the next closest would take their turn and so Richter passed through the room as though a lanterned figure through a field of crickets, a scythe of silence over the chirping crowds. Even as he passed by the minstrels their songs seemed to dampen, as if Richter dragged a wet cloth over their instruments, their eyes shifting from wild gregariousness to stern stares, until he finally made it through, and as he shuffled into the corner the music grew loudly behind him and the minstrels even got to their feet as if to chase him away with their songs.

Thomas leaned back and offered a place to sit. He shouted over the din of noise, "Don't let 'em bother you, Richter!"

Pursing his lips, Richer threw a dismissive hand and took a seat. Thomas offered a mug of ale. He declined. Thomas offered it to Hobbs, but the captain put his hand out, intercepting it and setting it at the end of the table.

"I'm sure the boy can drink," Thomas said.

"I can," Hobbs said. He reached over the table. "And I will."

Richter pushed the drink further away from the boy. "You shouldn't even be in here."

Hobbs' face soured. "The other kids are."

"If the other kids jumped…" Richter grimaced for a moment, but pushed through: "If the other kids jumped off a bridge, would you do it, too?"

Hobbs nodded. "Probably."

Thomas nodded as well. "I mean there's got to be something down there worth jumping after, right?"

"Right! And it's not every day you even see a bridge! What's the point of a bridge if you don't jump off it?"

"Hey yeah, Richter, what's the point? And you could always stand on the ledge and yell something down," Thomas said, and he leaned up and mimed staring down, "Something like, 'hey yeah, how're y'all doing down there!' And if you don't get no response then you don't jump."

"Because if there's no response that means the others are dead!"

Thomas snapped his fingers. "Exactly what I was getting at!"

Sighing, Richter said, "You're teaching the boy some bad habits."

"Everything out here is a bad habit," Hobbs said.

Both men looked over at the kid.

Hobbs shrank in his seat. "What?"

Richter scooted the mug back over to the boy. Hobbs stared at it as if some joke was being had on him, the punchline hiding in the ale. Richter gestured to the drink, and when the boy's reluctance persisted the captain took a drink for himself then set it back down and gestured again.

"Feel like I'm being had," Hobbs said.

Thomas reached for the mug. "If you aren't gonna drink it I will."

Hobbs hurriedly snatched the mug for himself and stole a sip. Foam on his lips, he set it down.

"Thoughts?" Richter said.

"It's awful." The boy wiped his mouth. "I regret my haste."

"Don't we all," Richter said. He stood. "Thomas, keep watch on him."

"Always," Thomas said. "You saved my life multiple times, I think it is the least I could do to keep the kid safe."

Hobbs stood up, aggressively and almost drunkenly planting his hands on the table. He said, "Hey wait a minute! If you owe Richter for saving your life, then so do I! I demand to repay you, Richter! I just, uh, don't know how."

The captain nodded. "Someday, Hobbs. For now, you be a good lad and stay with Thomas."

"But there's no glory in that!"

"You want glory?" Thomas said. He reached over and slammed the mug down. "Finish that!"

"I will!"

"Then go on ahead!"

"I'm going to!"

"Then what are you waiting for!"

"I have to stretch!"

The captain quietly left the table and crossed the room, the bulb of odd quiet still disturbing its way through the pub's patrons until he found Crockett in a corner playing cards. He looked at Crockett, then glanced at a quaint stack of crowns that would be painfully easy to count for the paymaster. The group of men opposite him peeled back as Richter neared and sensing their upward stares Crockett leaned forward and looked at the captain then at his own stack of crowns then back at the captain again.

"It's my money being lost here," he explained. "Not the company's."

Richter smiled. "I would never have suggested otherwise." He nodded toward the paymaster's shortstack. "I thought you were good with coin."

"Oh he is," one of the cardplayers said, staring up over a rather prodigious stack of crowns that was almost certainly built upon Crockett being the table's fish. The cardplayer tapped the side of his glass mug before taking a drink.

The paymaster shrugged. "I'm learning. Usually, you have to pay to learn something, and the same is true here. It's just more... obviously true."

"Understood," Richter said.

"Hey," one of the gamblers said. "Are you the captain?"

Richter nodded. "Aye."

"I heard you was killing them robbers and rapists."

"Aye."

"Nice. Very nice. Your fat friend here says you don't have a name for your outfit, that true?"

"I haven't given it one, aye."

"So you're a nameless mercenary company?"

"That's right."

Half the table groaned in disappointment while the other half cackled. A moment later, money began crossing back and forth across the table.

"They had bets going," Crockett said. "About whether we were really a nameless sellsword company."

"Of course they did," Richter said. He patted the paymaster on the shoulder. "Don't get too lost here, Crockett. Come morning we'll need to hire some more men and you need to be there for the task."

"Same time and place?"

"Aye."

"You got it, captain."

"'You got it, cap'n,'" one of the gamblers said, snorting.

Richter glanced at the gambler, then down at the man's feet. There was a dagger stashed in his boot, and indeed in the boots of the others. One of the gamblers' hands was nervously tapping on his knee. Richter looked again at their boots and saw one man lightly kick another. When the captain looked up, he saw these two men whispering to each other.

One gambler leaned back. He said, "There a problem?"

The captain leaned over the table.

"You all may rob my paymaster through a game of cards," he said, his stare crossing over each man. "Just know, I got your faces down. If he loses anything besides what he's got in front of him here and you will all have more than just gambling debts to pay, do you understand me?"

"Whoa, Richter," Crockett said. "It's alright, everyone here is great!"

The man with the knee-tapping tic flattened his palm and then put it on the table. Others crossed their feet, stuffing the knives out of view.

"Y-yeah," one gambler said. "It's only a game, right fellas?"

"Aye," another said, nodding. "*Only* a game, fellas."

The paymaster scoffed, oblivious to the fact he had been 'marked' in more ways than one.

"C'mon Richter, take it easy." Crockett looked at the gamblers like a boy desperate to make friends. "He didn't mean nothing by it."

"Oh… I'm sure he didn't," one responded.

"Crockett," Richter said.

"Sir?"

"Don't drink anything tonight."

"I wasn't planning on it," Crockett said. He nodded. "I'll be there with you tomorrow morning, as you asked."

Richter stared at the gamblers. "Aye, you will indeed be there."

The captain walked away and crossed the room again. He found Dahlgren in a corner of the pub, there circled by men of all ages. His good hand and bald nub both gesticulated in the air, helping tell the tale of how he fought Hans the hedge knight, the terror of the once thriving Free Company, slaughterer of squires, and murderer of maidens. A few of the patrons recognized the name and were wowed while others, lest they reveal themselves wet behind the ears, merely pretended to know and mimicked the reactions of those around them. Dahlgren's descriptions of Hans made it so everyone could follow along: the sellsword was an oversized bastard and just about everyone knew at least once big bastard they disliked in their own life.

"So," one of the men said, "You didn't *kill* Hans?"

Dahlgren shook his head. "He bested me, taking this as payment," the old man lifted his nub of a wrist. "But one day I hope to see him again."

"You really think you can take him?" another man asked, a much older fellow whose words scratched through a heavy beard. "Think ye learned somethin' from that first go 'round?"

Confident, Dahlgren took a mug's handle and placed it on his nub and gave it a good spin, the handle rattling around his puckered wrist. He said, "I've learned my own tricks since then. For starters, next time I fight that bastard, I'll make sure I'm twice as drunk!"

The men laughed riotously and some bellyached over it as though it were the first joke ever told.

"Well," one of the drinkers said. "Either I'm three sails to the wind, or yer one of the better sellswords here!"

Dahlgren nodded. "I'll drink to that."

"But, you know, we still want you out of our farkin' town," the man said, staring over the lid of his mug.

The other drinkers glanced at one another. Dahlgren slowly lowered his mug only to reveal a wily grin. He said, "Aye, I'll drink to that as well!"

"Hear hear!" the drinker said, himself now grinning. "But also, fark you!"

"And to the hells with you!" Dahlgren said and threw his head back. "I'll run my sword through your gut if you chance it!"

"Oh, I've got a pitchfork with yer name on it!"

Richter raised an eyebrow. He was rarely one to imbibe, but it seemed the general tenor of the pub had overcome some of the more prevalent differences of the parties involved. He caught Dahlgren's eye and mouthed an inquiry as to where Quinn was. The old man jerked his head back, gesturing toward the second floor where the ladies of the night lined the railing, some empty spaces between them. If Quinn was doing what Immerwahr suggested, which is keeping his hounding away from married women, then it was well enough that the thief had found a proper place to spend his coin.

Satisfied with the state of his men, the captain left the pub. Outside, a few more drunks had passed out, their warm bodies but nests for pawing cats and snuzzling dogs to sleep against. Richter stepped around them and leaned against a porch post and stayed there awhile, thinking, listening, staring, occupying himself with a whole lot of nothing which, for a man such as he, had become something of a luxury in and of itself. As he mulled thoughtlessly, a younger couple went up the porch and stood at the opposite end of it. They whispered, and they glanced, and they whispered some more.

It's rude to stare, Richter thought.

"Sir," the boy spoke up. He looked at his lady friend who nodded. He turned back and said again, "Sir."

Richter turned to him. "Aye?"

"Are you Richter von Dagentear?"

The girl piped in: "The one they call the Wight? My mother said you—"

"No," Richter said. "You have me confused for someone else."

He touched the brim of Carsten's witch hunting hat and stepped off the porch and into the road. He passed between dogs who raised their eyes to him and only when he had gone by did they pick up their heads and put their nose to the air, as if smelling out some secret better followed than truly found. The cats departed the rooftops in silent black leaps, their eyes tracking him in bodiless and hovering yellows. He stepped over a drunkard in the road and the man shouted out a woman's name and he walked past an upside-down wheelbarrow with a pair of whispering kids hiding under it. He scratched the wound where his ear used to be and he continued on and went out into the bunkhouse. He went to the bed and took his hat off and set it on his chest and a moment later he took the hat and threw it across the room.

Chapter 10. Survivors.

KANTOREK LEAPT over tree trunks and barreled through bushes, hands raking away leaves and branches, an awkward and ambling swim through the forest like a starved man ready to forage anything and everything. Thusly he poured into the clearing, still waving his arms out into nothing and the lack of resistance sent him hurtling to the ground and he slid in a wheezing grunt. Both bruised and startled, he clapped a hand over his mouth and lay as still as possible. Here, the black of night was not so strong. Here, the moon had some governance, casting light down like a candle from a hanging bowl, and Kantorek thought himself prime pickings in even this scantest of pale light.

"Hey!" a voice called out.

The King of Dragons ducked his head, his hands in a shiver.

"Hey Kantorek!" the voice hailed again. "Over here!"

The brigand leader looked toward the sound. An obliterated priory sat right in the middle of the clearing, its front half ripped open. Standing in the maw of rubble and hanging stonework, a silhouette waved.

"Here, Kantorek!"

Kantorek nodded and shuffled his way over, running low across the field as though he were approaching a castle while under the fire of its defenders. As he drew closer to the voice and the man who cast it, Kantorek realized it was one of his own.

"Erik?" Kantorek said. "Erik is that you?"

"Yeah, it's me! Gods damned is it good to see you!" Erik said. He turned and went back inside the priory. "Come on in!"

Kantorek climbed the rubble, legs bowing awkwardly as the stones slid out beneath him. An enormous priory bell sat in the midst of the ruins and he rested himself against it. Looking down, he saw giant bones snaking out from beneath the bell and further into the priory. A long spine and thick ribs.

"I think that's a lindwurm's skeleton," Erik said, throwing a hand toward the massive remains like a king all-too-tired of his once awe-inspiring profligacy. "Think the bell fell on it or somethin' I dunno."

Kantorek stared down at the bones. He said, "Any scales left?"

"Naw."

"Damn."

"Yeah."

Erik shuffled further into the priory and threw himself onto a pew. Dust and ash plumed into the air around him, thick enough to be heard scratching and hissing as it settled back down. He pawed his arms out to each side.

"Long farkin' day, no?"

"Yeah," Kantorek said.

"Didn't expect to see me alive, did ya?"

Erik was a man Kantorek had stationed at one of the bandits' faux camps. His job was to interfere with huntsmen, mercenaries, bounty hunters and the like. His position was predicated on speed, his role to lead the assailers aside and eventually loop back around to the main camp. The system of fake and real camps being used in rotation had been working quite well – until it didn't.

"No," Kantorek said. "At its worst, your job was to be dead and us alive."

"Whoops."

"Indeed."

Erik sat staring at him, his arms crowed out to each side, one leg crossed over the other, the foot bouncing gingerly. He looked as if he owned the place. The rest of the priory, from what could be divested of the scant night light, seemed a mixture of tragedies new and old, a carnage of blood and wood and stones and through it all a pungent smell hung in the air, though Kantorek could not tell from which pocket of the disasters it resonated.

"Come on in already," Erik said, patting the pew. "Have a seat." He leaned forward, grinning. "They're all free!"

Kantorek nodded and staggered down the pile of rubble. He took a seat next to Erik and sighed.

"So," Erik said. "Was it the Battle Brothers that farked us?"

"You say it like you hope it was."

Erik threw a dismissive hand. "Ahh, it's not like that. I just think if it were the Battle Brothers it'd almost be a sign of respect. Some unpaid executioner kills ya with rope and twine, eh, that's one thing. But if the king 'imself comes down and lops yer head with some old heirloom passed down generation to generation? That's fine business. The crowd'll remember yer face. You know? Know what I mean, Kantorek?"

"There's been no king in this land since I've walked it."

"Well," Erik said. "I guess they'd *really* remember you then if a king did catch yer neck."

"Yeah, sure," Kantorek said. But he knew the truth: there was no way the ferry town or its runagate monk could ever afford a company like the Battle Brothers. No, the brigand leader knew he'd been bested by some scapegraces looking to scratch a few coins together. But there was another truth there, one which Erik scratched at. That it would be a sort of intrigue to have someone sic the Battle Brothers on you. He spat and said, "Maybe it was the Battle Brothers. They sure as shit fought well enough."

"Ahh, that must've been a sight then," Erik said. "Hells, they went after the main encampment like a hunter after the heart so... maybe it was them. Certainly someone of talent, that's for damn sure."

"You never saw anyone?" Kantorek said.

Shaking his head, Erik said, "Naw, I saw nothing." The brigand kicked up his boots and balanced them on a tilted stone, the grey slab rocking back and forth. "Heard a lot goin' on from yer side of all these trees. Heard a whole heapin' of screamin' and hollerin'. That's when I knew things had gone sour."

Kantorek nodded. "How'd you come out this way anyhow?"

"Ah hells… that's an embarrassin' story, sir. I considered rabbiting back to the ancient road, but I was never one for directions and old gods be damned if these woods ain't confusing as fark and I ain't gone the wrong way." The brigand clasped his hands and looked up at the hole in the priory's ceiling. "But I shant damn them sky farks too much for I found this here priory. With night coming I decided that's as good a time as any to set down pretty and wait til morn. Then I heard your hooves crashing through the trees and I knew it had to be the King of Dragons. Just knew it. And there you was. You came out of them trees swinging and thrashing and took quite the spill into the mud there, but even the royals get a bit o' brown now and again."

"Quite the tale," Kantorek said.

Erik's boots tilted a tad too far and his heels lost claim of the stone and it fell with a clatter. "Hells," he said, and clapped his boots on the ground. He said, "So, how'd you fare?"

"I slew a few," Kantorek said, nodding to his lies. "Two, maybe three. The third I stabbed through, but he still had life in him when Stark grabbed me and said we were surrounded."

"Oh no. But I didn't see Stark with ya."

"He didn't make it. We, uh, fought out of an encirclement," Kantorek said. "Myself and… Stark. But he took an arrow. I tried to defend him but he said no… no! He shouted. He said for me to go on, to avenge the men." The brigand leader looked out into the dark. "So now here I am."

"Incredible," Erik said. "Well, rest in peace to ol' Stark, then."

Kantorek nodded. "Yeah." He looked at the priory bell and the bones beneath it. "You sure this place is safe?"

"Safe enough," Erik said. "You can't see it in the dark, but all around the priory are these totems with lindwurm skulls hangin' off their tops."

"What?"

"Yeah. I think the skulls're scaring away most anything. I'd say it was a kinda queer sight of sorts, but then I remembered we ran into that crazy beast slayer who said there was big ol' lizards running amok in these woods. I think that maybe we're dwelling in his domicile. You remember him, right? That bearded fark with the one eye."

Kantorek nodded. "Of course I remember him."

"Trish was his name?"

"No, it was something like Ellemash or some desert shite like that."

"You tried to hire him, right?"

"I did," Kantorek said. "But he said he had better things to do."

"Like what?"

"I don't know, he just said he had better things to do and then he just sat there."

Erik threw a dismissive hand again. He said, "Ah them kooks, can't take them serious. Beast slayers will tell you a dragon lives in your cupboard just to make a crown or two off the mouse they find instead."

But Kantorek sat thinking about the beast slayer. He remembered the man carried an enormous crossbow with him. And he remembered the peglegged man getting shot clean through with what looked like a harpoon. Kantorek raised an eyebrow as these memories flew by until arriving at an indisputable truth: the beast slayer was working for the sellswords, which meant they might be heading toward the priory.

"Actually…" Kantorek said, bolting upright.

"What is it?" Erik said.

"We can't stay here. Now that I think of it, I think our attackers may have that same beast slayer in their employ."

"Oh?" Erik said, and his face slowly drew wide in realization: "Oh shit. If he's with them, then they'll know about this spot, and then they'll come here! And then they'll do what they did before, but I'll be there this time!"

"Yes, Erik, you have it," Kantorek said. "Now let's get out of here."

"But can we really leave now? It's the dead of night…"

"We leave now and we do it quietly," Kantorek said. He stood and went to the front of the priory, climbing over its rubble and staring into the black forest and up at the moon, one hand resting on the priory bell as if its holy purpose might help divine direction from all the darkness. He turned around. "There's a group of men north of here we can link up with. An old friend of mine runs their outfit. Used to be a sea raider, now he's river running."

"Sea raider," Erik said. "You sure he won't just up and kill us?"

"He's a peculiar fella," Kantorek said. "I mean, he'll burn a town as proper as any raider, but he's a talk first, swing axes later type of thinker. He had a few northern villages setup as tributaries until the barbarians started running wild."

"Well, if he's not a murderous raider than I suppose I'd be game for heading that way, but speaking of seas, you won't be running the ship anymore," Erik said, and when Kantorek glared over his shoulder Erik simply shrugged. "I'm just saying what things are. If you haven't noticed, our group's gon' fucked and farked and fucked again. Unless you think my swingin' dick is enough to account for a whole bad company, you're gonnn have to put hand to plow once more."

"Well you don't gotta be so upfront about it," Kantorek said. The destruction of his band of misfits didn't require much reflection. He nodded. "I know how things are."

"Alright. Just wanted to make sure you'd not gone loopy in the head and had visions of grandeur or anything." Erik got up and joined his brigand leader. They stepped out of the priory together and headed toward the forest.

"You know, this isn't my first setback," Kantorek said. "Couple years ago, I had a bigger band than I did yesterday. Bloody sellswords ruined it, too. I thought maybe if I paced myself this time around, we could really get things going, what with Marsburg and Sommerwein being tied up and all, and these roads still needing that mercantile gold. But it'll be good again. Trust me."

Kantorek spat and cleared his throat.

"And one other thing. We're going to get revenge," he said. "We are going to find that ferry runnin' monk and draw and quarter that sonuvabitch. We just have to get our feet under us, and of course find the mercenaries who did this and kill them to the last man. You got that, Erik? We *are* going to find these shitbird sellswords and make them wish they never crossed us."

Kantorek stopped and looked back.

A huge silhouette towered over Erik, the dark of night obscuring the entirety of it save for the glimmer of scales which reflected the moon like the glint of a million hungry spiders, a series of ferocious eyes which blinkered down two massive forearms in a vortex of twisting white, lighting upon musculature bulbous and powerful, ending at the tensed might of two massive claws. Far above, golden eyes flared wildly and its body heaved upward, muscles and sinews stretching out like the groans of a ship taking an ocean's worst waves, and into the night air the creature rose and rose, its scales hissing against one another like a windblown field of autumn leaves, and drool dripped beneath its gaze and spooled upon Erik's head, the brigand blankly looking up as if it were a string upon a newborn's awestruck face, and the monster growled and its maw opened and even in the dark one could hear the uncinching of its lips pulling away from wetted teeth, and there shimmering in that scant nightlight could one see the slickness of its gums frothing with delight, and the crimson sheen of its most recent mauling.

Erik slowly stared back toward his leader.

"Sir, King of Dragons, I think—"

A rush of wind blew over Kantorek so hard his clothes snapped against his skin. Erik went screaming up into the night sky like a rabbit taken by a hawk and a moment later a massive, scaled forearm slammed the man into the earth. He piggishly squealed between a set of claws like a man a crying out from some ivory cage and he reached through the bars with an utterly mangled arm, his scalped head glistening beneath the moonlight, his eyes fattening out of their sockets as the massive weight crushed him into the earth and his eyes out of their sockets, and in this state the man bloodgargled Kantorek's name just as the lindwurm's maw came down and crushed the brigand, popping his insides across the grass in a squirting splatter.

Screaming and vomiting all the same, Kantorek jumped backward, feet slipping on the grass, arse sliding, hands clenching, feeling chunks of Erik pressing through his fingers. He turned over and clambered across the clearing and made for the tree line. Behind him, teeth crushed a skull and snapped bones. Kantorek covered his ears as he ran as if he were being bullied across a schoolyard.

As he hit the first tree, he threw one arm out and ringed it around the trunk like a maypole and swung himself to the other side, there carefully looking back around the corner. A vague serpent shape violently twisted its body back and forth, and above Kantorek the leaves rustled as if rain were falling and he blinked as flecks of blood speckled down and pieces of Erik crashed through the branches. The brigand slowly stepped back from the tree.

"Oh, oh," he said. "Oh, it's alright. Everything will be fine."

He turned around and stared into a pair of red eyes towering over him, a black matted and furry monstrosity on two legs, one arm clinging to a branch above as though it had just climbed down from the treetops. The arm slowly raked its claws off the branch, falling limply at its side, a sort of unamused musculature in its stance, its massive, silhouetted shape sizing and unsizing in the dark, tips of its moonlit hackles bristling like knives in the night.

"Ah," Kantorek said. "Ah, I see... uh..."

Kantorek slowly turned around. He stopped again.

The lindwurm stood before him, its massive arms postured up, its shoulders touching the branches above. And something else stood beside the creature. Something much smaller. The King of Dragons slimmed his eyes, and as he discerned just what that little being was, he laughed and his mind departed, swirling away in sublime incoherence. A lindwurm. A direwolf. And *that*. What was *that* doing here?

Few men could suffer such sights.

Few could acknowledge such an alliance.

"I can't believe it," he said, his hands climbing upward, his fingers dragging the flesh of his jowls. "Get me out of this nightmare! Get me out!"

Chapter 11. Trouble.

"Richter." A man's voice.

"We have a problem." A woman's.

The captain opened his eyes. Morning light glimmered through the curtains, a cursory red penumbra bubbling across the foot of his bed, and there in its rubricated sublimity the man who first beckoned him: Dahlgren. Beside the old man stood Sophia, and when the captain's eyes fell on her she held out Carsten's hat as though it were a sensitive condolence for rousing him from his sleep. He took the hat and swung his legs out from under the covers and put the ground under his feet. He stared at the bowl of the hat, and the little patchwork on its side. He looked up.

"It's Quinn," Sophia said.

Dahlgren nodded. "He's in trouble."

Richter's thumb picked at his hat's patchwork, and as he did so he noticed he had a cut on his hand he didn't remember getting, and it had half-healed in the time it had gone unnoticed. He turned the hand, staring at the wound and wondering how pain could hide on its own bearer, as if pain itself feared the land upon which it had been given.

The captain sighed and put the hat on. He said, "How bad is it?"

~~~

Richter stood at the end of the bed.

He said, "Who found him?"

"I did," Dahlgren said. "He was out in the mud not far from the pub."

"We know what happened?"

"He slept with a local man's wife and the husband found out."

"For sure, or that's just what they're saying?"

"I have the husband being held on the second floor of the tavern," Dahlgren said. He snorted. "The fucker's proud of what he did, too."

"Did Quinn know she was married?"

"Of course he did," Sophia said as she took a seat and prodded Quinn with a wet cloth. "He was beat to an inch of his life. Ordinary fools don't receive this kind of attention." She paused, collecting herself with a long breath, and Quinn seemed to mirror her with a snarling wheeze. She said, "I don't know if he'll make it. I'm no healer so maybe I'm just in my sorrows, but I've seen plenty of dead men and our thief here just about looks the part."

The thief was wrapped in bloodsoaked linens, giving his body the coloration of a redly mottled cow. His eyes sealed behind welted lids, the flesh puckered tightly in puffed and purpled slabs. His nose snarled as he breathed and his lungs grasped at each breath and let them go with bloodied gargling. Richter thought of the time he found Hobbs in the witch's hut. Except this were not the proclivities of a hexe, but the doings of another man, and just as the witch hunter claimed righteousness in his hunt of the former, the mercenary would find retribution in the blood of the latter.

All the same, he had to ask: "Are we sure he's hurt that bad?"

Sophia scoffed. "I know you dislike the thief, Richter, but please, have a bit of heart here."

"Alright. I apologize," Richter said. "Is there anything we have that could help? Maybe something from one of the stores."

"I asked Immerwahr but he said he had nothing," Dahlgren said.

Richter said, "Did he know about this situation when you asked him?"

"Aye, he was actually helping arraign the fella who attacked Quinn."

Richter sighed.

"What?" Dahlgren said.

"Have you not been paying attention, Dahlgren? This town wants us out of here and the monk is trying to play peacemaker. He can't be seen just giving us what we need. Eventually we *will* leave here and they'll remember everything he did when we're gone. He needs to be in a good position with these people when that day comes or else he might as well be better off leaving with us, understand?"

"Ah, I see," Dahlgren said. "Shit. What should we do, then? Do we just leave town now?"

"Quinn would not survive on the road like this," Sophia said. "At the very least, you have to get those herbs, Richter."

Richter nodded. "Dahlgren, you said you have the man who did this?"

"Aye. He's in the tavern, second floor. I say the sooner we go see him the better."

The captain sighed long and hard. He looked back at Quinn, and then he turned away and affixed Carsten's hat on his head, his fingers still on its lid as it slowly slid over his missing ear.

I can't believe I found ye digging wells, Carsten's voice came to him for the first time in some while. *There you were, a glorified ditch digger, and look what I've made you into: a reasonably talented hexenjäger. Who knows what else you could've been, ha!*

Sophia said, "What are you planning?"

Richter's hand fell from his hat and landed upon the pommel of Adelbrecht's sword. Thoughts and ideas coursed through his mind, and finally he arrived at one, and the voice of Carsten faded out of his mind altogether.

The captain girded the sword tighter to his hip and said, "I am going to be the sort of mercenary captain these damn people already think I am."

~ ~ ~

Richter traversed town with Dahlgren at his side. The townsfolk were already out on the road as though expectants of a holy happening, and in the light of morning they were stewards of their own homes and shops, sentried in stern poses, arms crossed, gazes set, shadows fenced across the mud.

"He had it coming!" someone shouted, but when Richter looked toward the speaker, he could only see their backs hurrying down an alley.

They passed by Immerwahr's store and the monk was already out on the porch with his arms crossed. He saw the sellswords coming and he let his arms down at his side and came out onto the road.

"Captain, I got the man staying put in the first place because he knows that punitive measures here will be done by myself. That's how this town works. Did you hear me? I will dole the punishment here and it will be seen by all the people. This must be a place of law, understand?"

"Dole your law with what lawmen, exactly?" Richter asked.

The sellswords passed by Immerwahr, and the monk gave chase. He caught up and flanked Richter's other side.

"You can't just do this out on your own."

"Watch me."

"The *townspeople* are watching," Immerwahr said. He glanced toward the buildings out of which more peoples were coming to stand and stare. He said, "You're risking far too much, and it's not a risk I can bear to share with you."

"I didn't ask you to share it," Richter said.

The three men arrived just outside the two-story tavern.

"He's up on the whorefloor," Dahlgren said. "Middle door."

Richter stepped up the porch and a hand pinched against his elbow. He turned and looked down at Immerwahr.

"I'm coming up," the monk said.

"If that's what you want to do," Richter said, and drew his arm back and went up the porch. He entered the pub and kicked a chair out of his way, caroming it against a stack of stools which fell off one another and laddered their legs into a pile. The barman looked up from the counter with his fist halfway down a mug. Immerwahr glanced over and shook his head and the barman nodded and looked the other way.

The three men went up the stairs, boots heavy in the quiet din of the pub. A few whores stood outside their doors staring at the men but as they reached the landing the women reared up and leaned out of the way, the cloth of their fineries scratching over the railings. Richter went to the middle door and opened it. A man sat on the bed with his bloodied hands limp between his legs. Crockett and Berthold the miller stood before him with spears pointed. They both looked back.

"Captain," they said together.

Richter nodded. "You two get on back to the bunkhouses."

"Yessir," Berthold said, swinging his spear upright and hitting the ceiling with it. He grimaced and more carefully made his exit.

Crockett was a step slower. He stopped outside the door and looked as though he had something to say, but Richter shook his head.

"This one's not for you," Richter said. "Nor your book."

Crockett nodded and departed.

Richter stepped inside the room, Dahlgren and Immerwahr right behind him, joining him at each flank.

The man on the bed looked up under the dark lids of his brow. "I ain't 'ere on account of fearin' two sellswords with toothpicks for spears," he said. He nodded at Immerwahr. "I'm only 'ere on account of the holy fella."

"You're here on account of me not running you through with a sword," Dahlgren said.

The man grinned. He said, "Then it sounds like yer 'ere on account of the holy fella, too."

As the women stared in, Dahlgren turned and closed the door halfway. He exchanged a look with Immerwahr that suggested he leave.

"I'm not going anywhere," Immerwahr said.

Dahlgren gestured with his lone hand. "I think it is best that you do, monk. This room will soon be profaned and I don't think it wise if the old gods find you in it."

"Even I know that you are not fond of this thief," Immerwahr said.

"I'm not."

"Then why are you here on his behalf?"

"I'm here on the company's behalf." Dahlgren spat on the floor. "There's a difference."

Richter looked back at the monk. "I believe you should take Dahlgren up on his suggestion and leave. This isn't for you."

The monk planted a foot. His clothes wisped around his thin and shaking frame, as though a trembling feather filled their wooly confines. Still yet, he proved indomitable: "This man is a daytaler, Richter! Here he is well respected. He has a family... a wife and a son. They all do good work. This needn't be settled in any gruesome manner!"

"He put his hands on one of my men," Richter said. He looked at the daytaler. "And he did that knowing who we are. He does not fear what he should fear. This makes him dangerous, understand? It makes him dangerous even to you, monk."

"It was a domestic affair, Richter! Men do not think straight in such circumstances!"

The captain spun around, and the monk took a step back.

Dahlgren finally shut the door to the room as Richter poked the monk with a finger. "*You* told me that such issues will transpire through you, and yet this man has circumvented you and your rules and your supposed laws, and now I will also do the same."

The captain unsheathed Adelbrecht's sword. Dahlgren stepped to the corner of the room, pulling Immerwahr with him.

"If yer not leaving," the old man said, "then at least get out of the way."

Looking up, the daytaler gave a bloody smile and said, "Any man who has that done to his wife and stands idly by deserves his portion of steel anyway. I knew he was yer fella, and I seen to 'im anyway and I'd do it again without hesitation."

"You should see to your wife," Dahlgren said. "And what she gets up to come sundown."

"Oh she's been handled, too. She got it worse than yer feller did, but she's got the hide of a mule and the heart of a bastard. She can take it, unlike yer fella," the man said with a sneer. He looked at Richter. "Yer goin' to kill me over somethin' that has so little to do with ya?"

"No," Richter said, shaking his head. "I want you to pick a part you won't mind missing."

"You mean like a leg?"

"I mean anything."

Immerwahr scoffed. "This is obscene."

The man thought. He said, "This'un," and held out his pinky.

"So I'll take that whole hand, then," Richter said.

"D-do what now?"

Holding up his stump, Dahlgren said, "Ye'll get used to it being gone."

Richter turned the sword. He said, "You got three seconds to hold out your hand or I will put this blade through your neck."

"H-hey," the daytaler said. "This is a bit…"

"Three."

"I offer higher pay!" Immerwahr screamed as he jumped between the men. "This is over! Richter! I will give you higher pay for your work here!"

Richter stared down the length of his sword. He said, "I want herbs."

The monk nodded. "I don't think… I can just give those away…"

The captain looked at the monk, and then cleared his throat and said: "If you don't give them to me, I'll take yer hand just as well, and then I'll walk into your store and rob you of them anyway."

Immerwahr's eyes went wide, and he met Richter's eyes in a long, long gaze, the captain communicating a softer intention hidden behind the stern and ferocious stare, nevermind the spoken threat. Richter knew only men of the holy man's resolve could see what he actually meant.

"F-fine," Immerwahr said. "It will be done, just let me—"

"I want it done immediately."

"Apologies, I am nervous, I did not intend to hesitate." Immerwahr nodded again. "I will personally walk you back to the store and get you the goods you need, alright?"

"What about this fella?" Dahlgren said, gesturing to the daytaler.

Richter looked at the man. He said, "What is your name?"

The man leaned between his knees and spat a gob of blood onto the floorboards. He looked back up and said, "My name is Fritz."

"Fritz, I want eighty crowns compensation."

"Sonuvabitch, does it look like I got eighty crowns?"

"That is a lot of money, Richter," Immerwahr said.

Richter nodded. "Consider it compensation for lost services."

"Eighty crowns," Immerwahr repeated. He looked to the man.

Fritz shook his head. He said, "I don't have half that."

"Best find it," Richter said. "Or you'll find out how much that hand of yours is worth."

"Well," the man said. He sat back and glanced at the sword. "Yeah. I'll find yer money."

"If my man dies, you understand what will happen?"

The man nodded. "You gon' set fire to the whole town, eh?"

"Sure," Richter said. "And I'll have you burning at the center of it, understand?"

"Yeah I understand." Fritz turned his head and spat. He said, "Shite. There'd been rumors of ya being a witch hunter, but not just any ol' killer, nah not with a hat like that, rumors are you're the one they call the Wight. That really true then? Are you the lady slayin' *preck* who daggers old hags?"

Richter looked at his sword. Adelbrecht's sword, as it were only Richter's hands upon it, and Richter's visage streaming down the length of its reflective steel, and Richter's actions with which it found new blood. He looked at Fritz.

"Oh, I see it now…" Fritz grinned. "Ye ain't got a clue what you got yourself into."

"We won't be getting those eighty crowns," Dahlgren said. "I say we just end this no good fuck here and now."

The captain slowly turned the sword so the daytaler could see himself in its steel. "Aye, his station is one deserving of the worms."

"Let honor and nobility sing!" Immerwahr said, streaming forward and putting a touch upon Richter's swordhand. He stared at the captain again as he continued: "Let us not dwell on what provoked this conversation lest the fire rush to our heads and have it all unraveled, yes? Th-the agreements were… I'll get you everything you need to heal your man, and Fritz here will pay the eighty-crowns as compensation for lost labor. Until actions prove ourselves to be moving outside the bounds of this spoken contract, we should conduct ourselves as though we intend to fulfill those obligations. Yes? Yes? Are we all in agreement?"

Fritz gritted his teeth.

Dahlgren shrugged. "He deserves worse than a gentleman's agreement."

"Please, Richter," Immerwahr said. "Listen to higher orders."

Sheathing his sword, Richter nodded. "We'll do it your way, holy man."

~~~

The captain entered the monk's shop and the door clattered only once behind him before it immediately swung back open, the monk storming in. Richter leaned against one of the shelves. It didn't take but a second for Immerwahr to scurry around to face him and nearly put a finger up his nose.

"Did I not tell you!" the monk said, shaking the finger in Richter's face. "I absolutely told you, didn't I? I said your men were causing problems, I even said the specific ones to look out for! What were you doing, huh?"

"Killing brigands," Richter said.

"Well, I," Immerwahr stammered. He shook his head. "No! That's not enough! Y-you don't just weasel out of this on account of bandits! You need to mind your men! This whole situation is an absurdity!"

Smirking, Richter said, "You understand I don't actually intend to menace you or this town, right?"

With surprising strength and anger the monk stomped his foot so hard that a few toys toppled over on their shelves. He threw his hands up and said, "Yes, I am quite aware, Richter! I know you're not some barbarian! By the old gods, who do you take me for?"

Richter reached out to a shelf and righted one of the fallen toys. It was the 'camel' he had seen earlier, and just as his first meeting with it he found his hand staying a moment upon its wooden make. He turned and said, "All theatrics aside, Immerwahr, my company's days here are over."

Immerwahr sighed. "I'm aware of that, too, yes."

"My *intention* was to stay as long as possible," Richter said. "Find good men, train them, maybe actually get these townsfolk on my side…"

"These people would never 'be on your side.'"

"Was worth the effort regardless."

The monk pursed his lips. He said, "When do you think you'll leave?"

"Preferably tonight. Tomorrow at the latest. It is only a matter of time until this town turns on us. This Fritz is just one man, but I wasn't making empty statements back there. He knew we were sellswords and he went and did what he did anyway. Put a few more likeminded men together and that is a major problem. The mood is changing here and we have to go." Richter glanced over at the camel, then said, "Of course, I wanted to be sure that when we did leave, you would remain in the best standing possible. I understand full well that you can't be seen affording aid to sellswords hand over fist. Not if you want to keep running this ferry after we're gone."

"Well, Fritz is very likely telling everyone that you're bullying me right this minute."

"Good. If you are seen standing in opposition to me, then the town will see you as being on their side."

"Such a horror, this business," Immerwahr said. Shaking his head, he started walking away. "Alright, let me get you your vulneraries, then."

The monk returned with a sack of herbs.

Richter opened it. He poked around. "Sallowthorn, yellow dock, the base elements, too."

"I began picking those early. I was worried good grass might be hard to find with all the bloodletting as of late," Immerwahr said with a soft smile.

An image of the direwolf's footprint reared into Richter's mind. He quickly said, "Immerwahr, there might be something lurking in the woods."

"Oh?"

The captain closed the sack of herbs. He said, "I found a direwolf track near Kantorek's camp."

"Is that so? And I suppose you're saying this just now in an effort to goad me into hiring you for one last job?"

"No, I think that time has clearly passed." Richter held up the herbs. "But you don't go into the woods anymore, understand?"

"Richter, I don't mean to insult you, but we are in the woods. Woods are all we can go into!"

"Then arm the people. Form a militia."

"After you leave, yes?"

Richter laughed, extinguishing a bit of his tension. He said, "Aye, preferably after."

"I think I can arrange that. Perhaps I could even give the militia captain role to Fritz, as he has proven himself to be a formidable fighter," Immerwahr said. He looked at Richter. "Ah, I'm sorry, I probably shouldn't…"

"No, he'd be a good choice," Richter said, nodding. "A good fighter, and also the flashpoint of this here conflict between 'us.' Giving him that power would truly show the people whose side you stand on. It would set in stone your position here."

The door to the store burst open, two men standing there with pitchforks. Richter instinctively held his hand to his sword.

"I am alright!" Immerwahr said.

Staring in, the two men slowly relaxed, swinging their pitchforks upright. One shouted outside that the holy man was in good health.

Richter sheathed his blade. He dangled the herbs. "I think it is time I get these to the thief."

"Captain," Immerwahr said, catching Richter on the turn. "I'll have you know that a few years back I ran across an instance where direwolves were hunting these woods, stalking them and killing travelers and the like. But there was one small issue: they weren't direwolves. They were merely brigands, using the beasts as cover, wearing furs and wolven heads to play the part. It may insult you as well as ease you to know that those tracks you saw were probably placed there by the brigands themselves with the intention to scare."

"My beast slayer said the same," Richter said, nodding. "So if you can do me a favor then, monk, please pray that I merely fell for some foolery."

Smiling, Immerwahr said, "I would be honored to, sellsword."

~~~

Richter entered the bunkhouse with the sack of herbs. Sophia looked up from the side of Quinn's bed and then in one motion jumped up and took the sack and sat right back down. As she went to work, the captain held out his bandolier of glass phylacteries and vials like a man inquiring his robber if there was more required of his person.

Sophia declined more items and began laying the herbs out on a table, using her nails and thumb to cut the stems and chop them up according to the needed quantity, and as the plants fell into an assortment that looked more rubbish than medicinal, she placed a bowl upon the table and spat into it and spitlaced her thumb and began grinding it all together.

"I'm sure you know some of this," she said between breaths.

"Aye."

"Actually, I'm sure you know all of it."

"Aye, but your hands are better for the task."

"Those witches you used to hunt, they learn this sort of thing as well?"

"Aye, the dangerous ones. They know how to navigate the lines between medicinal and manipulative, elements which are often altered from one path to the other via a single ingredient. For example, if you take that stem in your left hand and add…" The captain paused. He smiled apologetically and said, "Sorry, I did not mean to sour your inquiry in this manner."

"It's quite alright. It was your life, after all, you've a right to reminisce. You were reminiscing, right?"

"I don't know. Probably."

Taking a breath, the homesteader looked up and turned the bowl to Richter, its contents thoroughly pasted. She said, "Anything I'm missing?"

"Color looks good," he said. He leaned in. "Smell is right, too."

"Glad I could be of help then," she said. "Hope such talents don't have you confusing me for something else."

"Only thing I'd confuse you for is a mother or a wife."

Sophia briefly paused, and she stared at her work, her hands hovering above it. The captain had forgotten the fate of her family, a bit of history the homesteader rarely discussed, and its rarity meant his bringing it up cast it into a fiery light with himself stoking the fire. He cleared his throat.

"My apologies," Richter said. "I should not have said that."

"It's quite alright," Sophia said, getting back to the grind, and almost as if to assure herself she added: "It's fine."

Richter hemmed and hawed at the end of Quinn's bed, his fingers playing against the endboard. The thief could barely muster a moan and he frequently settled his head in different positions, looking for angles that might relieve him of his suffering.

The captain said, "Will he be able to get on the road tonight?"

"Tonight…" Sophia said, and the way in which she said it Richter already knew what was coming next: "It'd be too much. We'll have to see if he's still breathing come morning. If he is, I think we'll be in the clear. Health has a way of rapidly improving once you get over the worst of it, but if you rush your way back to good health, you will only worsen. And in Quinn's case…"

"Alright." The captain nodded. "I understand."

Working her thumbs into the bowls again, Sophia glanced back at the captain. She cocked her head. "Something the matter?"

"Something is always the matter," Richter said. His fingers drummed the endboard again. He glanced at the woman and said, "Mind if I say something strictly just between us?"

"Sure. Well, wait, hold on a moment." She leaned forward and cupped Quinn's ears like a mother vanguarding against the vulgar. The thief moaned briefly. Sophia stared back and said, "Go on."

"It is very likely that there is only a short matter of time until the townspeople form a mob and come for us."

"You're certain?"

"A mob is as dangerous to a witch hunter as the witches themselves," Richter said. "I know a mob. I know the way it smells, the way it tenses, the way its blood roils. If we are lucky, we will have the night."

"You don't strike me as a man who levers himself on luck," Sophia said.

"No, I try not to," Richter said. "I considered breaking the ale barrels near the tavern but found them too well guarded. It appears the townspeople will be drinking very well tonight. Our luck will be drained in their mugs."

Sophia's eyes widened in fright.

Richter continued: "There is a certain energy in the air here, and mobs have a tendency to form all at once. I asked you if he'd be ready tonight because it is obvious to me that we should leave immediately."

She gripped her hands tighter over the thief's ears. She said, "Are you planning to abandon him?"

"It would preserve the company," Richter said.

The homesteader's mouth fell open. She stood up. Richter looked at her and her palm was out at her side and he looked her in the eyes and as he did so she slapped him across the face. She sat back down. He fixed his hat.

"Just so you know," she said. "I wouldn't do that to a bad man."

"I know," the captain said. He rapped the endboard. "I speak only to the health of the others." He nodded. "And it is to the others this will go."

~~~

Before nightfall, Richter had the company gathered inside his bunkhouse. Hobbs and Thomas sat in the corner, Elletrache leaned beside the door with his foot jacked against the wall and his arms crossed, Dahlgren sat on a chair with his handless arm slung over the back, his eyes affixed to the missing element, and Crockett sat at a table with a ledger, brushing a quill pen's feather against his nose.

The odd ones out were the miller, jester, and the butcher whom Richter did not trust enough to take part in the discussion, not necessarily because he thought they might sell them out literally, but because they might fall to fear and sell them out by their actions thereafter. Indeed, by Richter's own thinking, the new recruits would be stupid if they were not frightened by the prospect of their newfound employment leading to a bloody lynching, but mobs prey especially quick on the meat and bones of weakness. Succumbing to that fear would only embolden the mob to have those fears fully realized in the worst ways possible.

As for those in the meeting, the captain explained the tenseness of the situation, that the ferry town's inhabitants were growing tired of the company's presence, and that the sooner the sellswords left town the better. He explained the possibly precarious state of Quinn's health and then gave the floor to the company, waving his arm across the room, telling them to freely speak their mind on the matter.

"Ya know, we could handle this a whole 'nother way," Trash said. He grinned. "The ol' Elletrache way."

"Excuse our ignorance, Trash," Crockett said, "and please explain in full what that might entail."

The beast slayer cocked his fingers, pretending to pull triggers. He said, "You just plug a few of 'em dead and you'll rid the rest of their courage."

Crockett shook his head. "I doubt that will endear them to our presence. How on earth could we stick around here with that mood in the air?"

Dahlgren nodded. "Agreed. They would take their umbrage underground and eventually have us in our sleep."

"Hey, yeah, they might do that already," Thomas said. "If what the monk speaks of is true, they might even do that tonight? I say we just leave!"

Dahlgren said, "We can't get on the road with Quinn the way he is."

"But are we willing to wait a day on his behalf?" Crockett said.

Richter nodded. "That is why we are having this conversation. We can stay the night and risk a mob, or just leave now, and..." Richter paused, turning to Sophia. He said, "And I don't think there'd be much point in taking him with us, would there?"

"He'd slow us down," Sophia said somberly. "There might come a moment between transporting him from his bunkhouse to the wagon where we might get attacked. Then we'll... have to make a decision, then and there."

Everyone shifted slightly. If it were a game of cards, it was all show and tell as far as Richter was concerned.

Dahlgren said, "What are your thoughts, captain?"

Richter stared at his hands for a time and everyone seemed to stare at them as well. He then took his hat off and held it in his fingers and began to turn it like a wheel. He sighed and spoke: "If it were me and me alone, I would stay. I know you're all on the payroll and I'm paying you to do a job, but I have to take responsibility for your lot, and staying is what it is. It's dangerous.

It simply is. Now, I also have to think long term."

He continued: "Some of you knew me before you ever met me, you knew me as the Wight, the last man of a doomed village, Richter von Dagentear. Word travels fast in this world, and bad news travels the fastest. This is a ferry town, people come and go and leave in every damn direction. What we do here will have an effect on our place in this world, on our renown, and how capable we are in finding men to fight for us, and it will absolutely have an impact on the work we get." The captain looked up. "I know what I would do, but I wish to hear your words on it. That is why I brought us here."

Again, everyone shifted uneasily.

"Quinn's abandoned us before," Crockett said. "Not saying it would be right to return the favor, but there would be something, uh, poetic about it."

"He came back," Dahlgren said, staring at the floor. "In his way."

"So? The point is he might just leave again, having already practiced it."

"I just want to say that Quinn is a changing man," Sophia said. "Slowly, sure, but he's changing. I can see it in him."

"Only thing he's changing is out of his pants to bed married women!" Crockett said, his voice rising with each word. "And look where the fool has gotten us, woman!"

Dahlgren fell out of his relaxed posture and raised a finger to the paymaster.

"Best ease your tone to the lady, scribe."

Crockett opened his mouth, but before he could say anything Elletrache stepped off the wall and pointed his own finger at Dahlgren.

"Ol' Elletrache knows the fat man is wise in his ways. He'll shrink from you, but that don't mean it is right of you to make threats like that, old man. Not to someone who won't ever fight back in the way he really wants to."

"I've never had an issue with you, Trash," Dahlgren said, looking somewhat surprised.

The beast slayer took another step forward, the scales of his lindwurm armor chittering as they scraped against one another, sounding like dozens of daggers being sheathed and unsheathed all at once. He picked at his eyepatch as he leaned down.

"My eye rarely deceives." He gestured to Crockett. "Very rarely."

Dahlgren looked over. "Wait, do you have an issue with me, Crockett?"

"No, not... an issue, precisely..." the scribe scratched the back of his head. "Well, sorta. Sometimes. I mean, it feels like you don't take me seriously as a fighter. I'm never included in any training and whenever you see me alive after a battle it's like some joke or some accident that I'm still standing."

"But you're not a fighter," Dahlgren said. "You're a historian."

"Paymaster," Richter said. He nodded. "And he's thrown his weight around well enough."

There was a pause in the talking, almost as if everyone was expecting Quinn to jump in with a quip about Crockett's weight.

Dahlgren cleared his throat. He said, "Alright, Crockett. I'll treat you as an equal, if that's what you want."

Nodding, Crockett said, "It is, and I'm glad to hear it."

"Hey, yeah," Thomas said. "Glad all that soft-hearted talk is out of the way but... what about the issue right in front of us? Richter says there's a mob coming and, hey, yeah, that's not great, but how do we know that the monk isn't going to lead the mob himself? If he's so scared about his future here, wouldn't it make sense he'd do just that? How do you know this monk is telling the full truth and isn't just biding his time to stab us in the back?"

"You think I can't tell when someone is lying to me?" Richter said, turning to Thomas.

The servant pursed his lips and cleared his throat. He said, "I just meant, like, hey, you know, to be careful about just trusting someone like that upfront. Y-you never know who they really are."

"At no time in my dealings with Immerwahr have I gotten the notion he was even capable of doing that, much less thinking it."

"He does seem an honest sort," Dahlgren said, nodding. "I imagine this situation has put him under as much duress as it has us."

"It has," Richter said. "He's concerned that the mob will find leadership in another, and that person will then remove him, perhaps permanently."

"Could've offered him a seat with us," Dahlgren said.

"A monk has no position in a company of sellswords," Richter said.

"But millers, butchers, daytalers…" Crockett said.

The captain pursed his lips and adjusted his hat. "We're here to talk about Quinn, and we're here to talk about the mob. I know some of you don't understand what is coming, but I do and I'd like you to trust me on that. So our options are quite simple: we leave tonight, ensuring our own hides while risking Quinn's, or we stay and just see what happens."

"Sophia," Thomas said. "Quinn strikes me as a hardy fella. Are you sure he's too hurt to move? I mean, you're not a healer, no offense… so…"

"I'm no healer, this is true," Sophia said. "But the man is wheezing like his lungs are in his throat and his heartbeat is very slow and uneven."

"Hey, yeah, I don't wanna sound like a coward or anything," Thomas said. "But are we sure that Quinn is… *really* that hurt?"

"Don't wanna sound like a coward he says," Elletrache said. "Then he goes on and talks like a coward."

Richter nodded at the servant. "Thomas, I'll take it as your 'vote' that you'd rather leave tonight."

"I-It's not that I want to abandon the thief or nothing," Thomas said. "I'm just saying maybe if we do leave, he'll be perfectly fine on the road, cause he's not in such a bad sort, you know? But, I don't wanna sound a coward…"

Elletrache whistled. He said, "That's the sound of you falling into the hole yer digging."

Thomas pursed his lips. He looked around. He said, "I mean, does no one else feel the same way? What about you, Crockett? The thief has given you nothing but trouble."

"He has," Crockett said, nodding. "He's also a very talented fighter. Up there with Dahlgren and Elletrache."

"He ain't on my level," Dahlgren said. "Don't even suggest it."

Elletrache spat. "I wasn't even aware we were measurin' each other. How about you and I, old man, you think us equals?"

"Dunno, never seen how you'd do in a proper melee."

The beast slayer held out his hands, the fingers as fat as they were scarred and mangled. He grinned. "You wanna take a guess?"

Sighing, Crockett continued: "*My point being*, I don't let my personal thoughts about the thief get in the way of business. And in the sellsword business… Quinn is good for it. He's good for the job. He's good for us."

Thomas threw a hand toward the window. He said, "If half a town is about to fall on our heads cause we got him stowed up, is that really good for business? I mean, Richter, you're a rational man, you like thinking things out, right? So how many people do you think will get killed on this thief's behalf, huh? If what you say is true, we might end up in an all-out brawl with an entire mob and it'll be nothing but piles of bodies and corpses just like it was at the beach and just like it was in those woods!"

The servant's outburst was met by silence. He found himself at the end of his shouting in a posture of arms astray, legs spread, sweat on his forehead. He took a breath and straightened up and fixed his hair and leaned back against the wall. He awkwardly cleared his throat and folded his arms.

"I don't think you're a coward," Hobbs said, his voice mousing out quietly and slowly. "But I also don't think it's right to leave the thief behind."

Smiling, Thomas said, "Thank you, Hobbs."

"Ha," Dahlgren said. "Like the boy has that much sense!"

"Well you're just an old dog!" Hobbs said. "You can't learn new tricks or nothing! You just bark orders at others!"

"What? What did you just say? And what in the hells are you doing in here anyway? This discussion don't concern you, boy! How about—"

"That's enough," Richter said. The captain walked across the room and stared out the window. He said, "I must apologize for what I have done here."

"Sir?" Dahlgren said.

The captain turned around to face his men. He said, "I am the captain of this company. To put this to a vote was unfair to you all." He looked at the servant and nodded. "What Thomas has said is what has been on my mind since the start. He should not be seen as a coward for stating things as they are." He looked around at the others. "At the same time, Quinn is a valuable member of the company and we must also weigh what his loss would mean. However, I also know that choices such as these must be made with great consideration for our future selves, for what we do here will possibly lay the groundwork of malicious regrets and uncertainties, and these seeds of doubt can plague a man to his deathbed, if not put him there directly."

Sophia stepped forward. "So what is your decision?"

Hobbs grinned. He said, "We're staying!"

"Aye," Richter said, putting on his hat. "We will stay on behalf of the thief, and on behalf of the reputation of the company, and on behalf of ourselves so that we may rest easy in the nights to come."

Chapter 12. What Mothers Whisper Of.

RICHTER SAT on a cot all alone in the bunkhouse. Knuckles to his knees, he had his hands supinated before him. In the fading light, the scarred ridges cut shadows across the skin, wimpling it in dots of black as though markers of an irreversible illness. With every rise and fall of flesh, he remembered. There, a witch hunt. There, a barfight. There, an alley ambush. All in the palms alone. All in the very core with which a man used to grasp the world. He grabbed the world far too often, he surmised, and the world in turn had bitten back its fair share. He turned the hands over and looked at the knuckles, implements which had a far more incisive design, and within a second he looked away and dropped those scarred horrors into his lap.

The bunkhouse's door creaked open. Berthold the miller slowly walked in. He peeked around.

"C-captain, are you there?"

Richter stood up, rising out of the shadows.

The miller jolted. "Oh! Oh, sorry. Didn't see you."

"What is it?"

"I did as you asked. Scouted around, all that."

"And?"

"The townspeople are indeed at the pub."

Richter held his hand up to the light, and turned it palm down. He said, "How many?"

"What looks like all of them."

"Ah."

"Yeah. They're getting drunker than hells and they've pitchforks and torches and the like. They even got this bonfire out front with what looked like a scarecrow burning in the middle of it. And, like I said, they're getting the ale in 'em. They're even singing songs about justice. What kind of drunkards sing songs about justice? It's unnerving."

"Aye."

"Well, uh, the company was mentioned. A lot. I got nervous after a minute and worried some might remember I'm with you guys. I mean— working with you guys. So I left. But what I said is what I aw and heard."

"Alright," Richter said. "Thank you, Berthold."

The miller stood there, wavering in the doorway. He said, "Are we, uh, about to die? You can tell me. I'm the sort that would like to know."

The captain took Carsten's hat off the cot's endboard and put it on his head. He picked up Adelbrecht's sword and cinched it to his hip, then picked up a crossbow and yoked its strap over a shoulder. He walked by Berthold and patted him on the shoulder.

"I'll give you one favor," Richter said, turning to the miller. "You can look at me right now and decide what you wish to do. If you run, I won't blame you, but I just want you to look at me first."

"Uhh…" the miller stammered. He glanced at Richter, then looked away, then slowly brought his eyes back to him. He stared into them. He looked at his captain and nodded. "I'll be here."

Richter nodded back. "Good. Stay inside for a moment, take a breath, collect yourself. Don't let the others see you shaking like this."

Berthold took a seat on the cot. He nodded. "Thank you, captain. You're nothing like the rumors say."

The captain said nothing to the comment as he left the bunkhouse.

Dahlgren stood on the porch, leaning against a post.

"Whole lotta coming and going," he said, gesturing toward the pub.

Richter pointed around the way. "Dahlgren, bring the wagon near to the bunkhouse and make sure everyone is here, armed and looking dangerous."

The old man raised an eyebrow as he looked Richter up and down. "Well if you ain't gussied up. You heading out?"

"Aye."

"To the pub?"

"Aye."

"What for?"

"To do something stupid."

Dahlgren spat. He said, "Hells, that's somethin' I can help with."

Richter shook his head. "No, I think it best I do this alone."

"So be it. What're you planning, exactly?"

"If I told you, you'd stop me."

"Must be mighty fucking stupid, then."

"Aye. You got a dagger?"

"I got a lil' knife," Dahlgren said, taking out a blade that would struggle to cut a vegetable. He offered it. "Want it?"

"Aye." Richter took it, the blade and handle together not enough to even cross his entire palm. He threw back his jacket and sheathed it behind his belt, then kept his hand pressed there to make sure the weapon could always be seen. He nodded. "I'll be right back."

"You know, captain," Dahlgren said. "Just because the town wants our nuts don't mean you *have* to put them on the table."

Richter paused, turning with his armaments clinking and clattering and his jacket swaying briefly open to show the bandolier of vials, and his black hat creasing over one-ear and sloping awkwardly over the absence of the other, and his scarred lips and nose leering in the shadows and his one hand resting on his sword's pommel while the other held the strap of a crossbow.

He said, "Dahlgren, what do I look like to you?"

"Respectfully, captain," Dahlgren said. "You look like a witch hunter."

"Good." Richter stepped off the porch. He turned back and said, "Bring the wagon around to the front of the bunkhouse. Make sure everyone is wearing armor and flashing steel."

The old man straightened up. "You plan on coming back, right?"

"I think the world's been asking me that since I got here," Richter said. He pointed at the bunkhouse's front. "The company, Dahlgren! Get to it!"

"Yessir!"

The captain nodded and headed into the road. Belted at his side swung Adelbrecht's sword and slung over his shoulder bobbled a crossbow with a loaded bolt. Under his coat jangled his bandolier of vials which he had filled with water, spit, blood, remnants of herbs, and anything else he could find that provided color. He stalked across the path with his head down but his eyes up, staring out from beneath the rim of Carsten's hat, the world a scratching black above, and a muddied brown below, and all in between the sublimity of a day's dying sun and the silhouettes of townspeople who paused and turned and stared like sentries waiting for the coming night's first crime.

A massive bonfire crackled outside the pub. Some dark shape sloped into its flames, falling free of the pole it had been tethered to. Women stoked the flames and with every gush bits of burning straw kicked out, spiraling into the air and smarting it with a pungent odor.

Spotting Richter, some of the women retreated to the nearest porch, while others saw fit to stand their ground and hiss and spit at the captain. An elderly man leered out from one of these porches and he menaced a pitchfork at the captain. Richter simply ignored it and walked onward to the tavern.

Berthold's report of the pub itself was almost understated: the building shook with the energy of those inside, chutes of dust ricketing down its outside walls as its burgeoning wooden foundation groaned against the surging capacity.

Balancing on their tippytoes, a few young children gawked through the windows. When Richter took the first step on the porch, the children turned around and screamed and ran off shrieking like birds spooked by the sudden movements of a once familiar scarecrow. As their shrill cries emptied into the night, he steadily went up the porch steps, the weight of his boots wringing groans from the floorboards, and ahead of him the pub seemed to grow louder and louder, as if he were approaching the entrance of a dragon's cave with the quiet certitude of a holy man on a quest. He looked to his side and a pair of men were staring, their mouths open with sticks hanging out of them.

"You *are* him," one man said. "You are the—"

Richter nodded. "Aye."

The front door opened and a drunken woman stood there with her hand to the handle. She looked Richter up and down and then slowly stepped back inside. Richter followed her in as though an invited guest. His ears crackled as the assembly's cacophony washed over him. Table after table of miscreants screaming and belching and singing, telling jokes and laughing and getting into fights that ended as soon as they started, and the barkeep barking orders to the barmaids as they tried to keep pace with demand, for bloodthirstiness required hurriedness to quench. Through it all a minstrel stood at the far end of the floor, there perched atop a tottering stool, his posture wobbling like a gargoyle on a pin as he sang into the crowd a song about the Cattlefold Kid, a rustic ruffian that slayed men with a buzzard's stare, and when you could get him to take a step – *the Cattlefold-foldin'* – you knew you'd won the jackpot.

The cattlefold kid, got nothin' but the deadeater's stare,
Feel his gaze and relinquish your courage, man.
Cattlefold kid will slay you down, man.
Cattlefold kid ain't no crow, man.

Richter walked further in.

Playing cards against the cattlefold kid?
Don't think he has it, do you think he has it?
Over his cards he be gazin' and smartin',
Don't think he'll be a cattlefold-foldin'.

He was a veritable censer, the patrons quieting in the haze of his passing.

You done it and we done it,
We all in the jackpot now!
Cattlefold kid been beat.
Now we play his game.
Now the deadeater's stare we meeeeeeeet—

The minstrel's voice wailed and as the air left his lungs he burrowed low into his pitch and bowed out his coda with a growling final word, the syllable emptying into an unexpected silence. He looked up to find not a soul was looking at him. Shushes and whispers were now his applause and, somewhere, a fork was dropped and its plinking filled the place whole.

Richter stared at them all.

A bumbling drunkard with an ale-stained beard stood up from a pew and towered over the captain. He stunk of many days spent in the pub and not a single moment in the bath in between.

Froth came down with his words: "What you doing in here, scapegrace? You wake up this morning thinkin' it was your day?"

"Is that him?" another said. "Is that the sellsword?"

"Aye, he's their captain."

"The ferryman died by that bastard's hand."

Richter's peripheral grew hostile: silhouettes unsheathed blades and grew large as they approached. In front of him, people spat and menaced him with knives in one hand and mugs of ale in the other.

"We should kill him now!" someone screamed.

"Throw him into the bonfire!"

"Kill the black hat!"

"Stab the sellsword!"

"Burn the witch hunter!"

As the crowd drew in, Richter stomped his foot and slung his crossbow off his shoulder and into one hand, its butt couched against his elbow. His other arm threw back his jacket and uncinched his bandoliers and ripped them off his chest and held them into the air, the glasses clinking together, their contents catching light and scattering it back out in a multitude of colors, speckling the walls in vaguely threatening hues. The demonstration brought gasps and people pressed against one another as they retreated.

"I am Richter von Dagentear," Richter said. "Hexenjäger. Sellsword. Captain. I have been to the Higgarian mountains. I have seen the destruction of Dagentear and I am its last survivor." He turned, menacing the crowd with the bandoliers and their unnatural colors. "I am the one you call the Wight."

The crowd murmured:

"Is that really him?"

"I knew it!"

"He looks just like my mother said he would."

"That's not him, it can't be."

"Am I drunk, or did that black hatted fark just say he was the Wight?"

Richter slowly lowered the bandoliers. He said, "As captain Richter von Dagentear, I am here to fulfill an agreement of eighty crowns, a deal brokered between myself, the town master Immerwahr, and…" He spun and found Fritz sitting halfway up the staircase. He pointed. "And you, Fritz."

The crowd followed Richter's point and arrived at the man.

Fritz stood up, one bruised hand to the handrail, the other poled against the wall. His eyes were sloped, his stare drunken, his legs wobbly.

"Well Ricky Dick, my name is Fritz von Gofarkyourself, and ye ain't gettin' no eighty crowns! Your parlor tricks might work on these fools, but they won't work on me."

Smirking, Fritz took a step, missed the staircase, and thumped down the stairs. He hit the floorboards and on davered legs he bounced up and strode forth, twisting and turning as he used the pubgoer's shoulders for support.

"We had an agreement," Richter said. "Time to pay up."

"H-hey Fritz," one man said. "If you had an agreement, maybe you—"

Fritz shoved the man aside. "Shut it! He's just trying to get at you all! He's only tryin' put on a scare!"

"Eighty crowns, Fritz," Richter said. He shook the bandoliers. "Or I punish you, and everyone else in this room."

Another patron stared at the baubles. "Wh-what's in them things?"

"Death," Richter said. "The slow kind."

The crowd oohed and took more steps back, pressing against each other, some going up on the minstrel's stage where his lute plinked and plunked as it squashed against his chest.

Fritz spat. He cracked his knuckles, the bones sickeningly dense as if he were breaking barrels. "Ain't nothing in those vials but water and piss."

"Just pay the man, Fritz!" someone yelled.

"Shut yer hole!" another yelled back. "You always was a yellowed fella!"

"Fark you!"

A rift started between the drunks. Pushing and shoving and that almost instantly escalated into a single punch. The crowed ooh'd. Sniffling, a man swore an oath to the old gods as he screamed and attacked back. A piece of glass shattered in the back, an expensive error that spurred anger from the barkeep who told everyone he'd be cutting off their ale if they didn't quit it. This threat, unsurprisingly, only spurred further umbrage. Fritz looked at the faltering crowd, and then back at Richter.

In truth, Richter's vials were filled with nothing but discolorations and water. In truth, he may as well have walked into a wolf's den with little more than a stick and a stone.

Gritting his teeth, Fritz strode forward, marching between a crowd that had started to ebb and flow with pushing and shouting matches. Little knots of anger that sparked here and there, scuffles arising naturally as the mob's drunkenness lured it into disarray and self-destruction. Punches went flying. Kicks, too. A chair. A mug. Through it all, Fritz came forth.

Richter took a step back, but his eyes never left the man.

"You gon' shoot me with that crossbow?" Fritz said, his words cutting through the rising din of a bar brawl. "Gon' kill me in cold blood in front of all these people? Is that what you plan on doing?"

Killing Fritz would be easy. A simple shot through the face and the bolt would be clean through the man's head before anyone could register what happened. But in the moment that would come after, it would prove to be such a murderous and malicious act that it would almost assuredly overwhelm the mob's senses, it would throw the cloak off Richter's intended misdirection and trickery, and in the clarity found thereafter they would lynch him as if they were lynching a mangy dog that had dared to suddenly put a bite after its bark. And Fritz knew that, too: despite Richter's weapons, the brawler came forward with a grin on his face and violence on his mind.

Fritz raised his bloodied fists, planted his foot, and cocked his arm back. But Fritz didn't know he was never the true target. The entire bar of drunks was tinder, and Fritz was merely the required flint to be struck.

"I'll beat you like I beat yer thief!" Fritz growled as he charged forward. "I'll cut yer head off and hang it over my door, you sellsword bastard!"

Richter lowered the crossbow and fired. The bolt struck Fritz in the foot, his boot puckering as the bolt pierced through the leather and his step suddenly locked right onto the floorboards. With one foot pinned, Fritz found himself spinning in a bloody pirouette and he launched himself sideways onto a gambling table, breaking it in half and catapulting coin every which way and decks of cards went flying into the air and a gambler fell back against the wall and a second deck of cards streamed out of his sleeve. In the resulting chaos of spilled coin and revealed cheats, the pub's spits of scuffles erupted into all-out war over money and cheating and perceived slights and a whole heap of umbrages which Richter had never even heard of.

The ember had found its tinder.

Fists sailed in and over and around. Men went faceplanting to the floor while others kicked each other in the nuts and more yet took mugs of ale and slammed them into the nearest heads. A chair went flying. Richter crouched out of the way, cinching his bandoliers and holding onto his hat. He watched a man crouch down with him, his fists pumping as he chanted: "hemmenyah hemmenyah hemmenyah!" The captain had no idea what that meant, nor would he ever find out as a pile of men suddenly folded over the chanter.

Richter quickly stood up and dodged around the clump of brawlers. He watched a long table flip upward on its end, its new stature bringing cheers like a holy totem to a throng of terribles, and then it fell back down, clapping a row of men on the heads and flooring them in a heap. For whatever reason a band of drunkards picked the table right back up and started marching it around like sea raiders lofting their ship overland, their shadowed faces cackling as they terrorized the mob with every swing and turn of their craft.

Looking at the front door, Richter saw his exit clogged with angry wives trying to fetch their husbands. Through a window, he could see two old women on the porch pulling each other's hair while children stood by pointing and laughing.

With that route closed, the captain retreated toward the stairs. Mugs soared and ale spiraled across the room in amber roostertails. A dagger zipped past his head and he thought if he still had the ear on that side of his skull it surely would have been shorn. He briefly glanced at the stage to see the minstrel hugging a hanging façade of bedsheets for a stage curtain, his eyes wide as he clambered out of danger. Someone snatched the man's lute and held it up as if he had stolen a golden goose. Someone else snatched it from that man and promptly smashed it over his head, the whole room awarded with a shrill twang of the instrument's sudden death.

Shaking his head, Richter continued for the stairs. He ducked and passed his way through a storm of drunks that ebbed and flowed all over, himself caroming about the crowd like a raft down a stonefilled white rapid. Through the carnage he happened upon four women embracing one another in a slobbering and communal kiss, and they'd part only to shout at the crowd to keep it going, and past them a man with a sword kept getting sheath-locked, unable to draw his jammed weapon until another man picked him up and drove him through the crowd like a battering ram and both men smashed through a window and flew outside. As the kissing women cackled, a boy fell from the rafters, flattening the tribades and giving Richter a clear shot to the staircase. He took it, stepping on the boy and women alike, and jumping for the first stair and hustling up the rest.

At the top of the landing, he bumbled into a group of prostitutes who shrieked and ran back inside their rooms and slammed their doors. Richter tried the first door. Locked. He tried again and the jostle of the attempt spurred screaming from inside. Taking a breath, he stepped back and then kicked the door in, shattering its knob and sending it sputtering and spinning across the floor. A whore jumped over her bed and just as soon spun around and held a dagger over its sheets, menacing him with it.

"I'll do it!" she said.

Three other prostitutes huddled at her back, and she had a certain fire behind her eyes equal to a bear before her cubs.

She jutted the dagger. "Any closer and I'll cut yer farkin' throat!"

"I know you will," Richter said. He looked back down at the pub and couldn't help but be astonished by the level of mayhem. There was no way he was going back down. He stepped into the room.

"I'll cut yer pecker right off!" the whore said, backing away, one hand prodding with the knife, the other hand wheeling the rest of the women away from Richter. "You get anywhere near us and I'll…"

"Easy," Richter said, holding his palms forward. "No one in here is going to get hurt."

Down in the main room, the brawl was slowly quieting down. He could hear a shouting man trying to quell the violence. It was a familiar voice, both in tone and intention.

A leaf of peace in a firestorm: Immerwahr had arrived.

Richter went to a window, his every step mirrored by the women scrunching back against the bed and eventually the wall near to it. Seemingly with every step another one of the troop grabbed something, either a comb, or a pair of scissors, or a tin of makeup, anything to defend themselves with. But Richter kept his distance, choosing the furthest window to look out of. He stared down and saw nothing, no persons nor bonfires. He tore the curtains off the window and threw them toward the women.

"The mob is out of control. It's not safe to go downstairs. Once I'm gone, you all should start looking to make your leave out a window." He pointed at the clump of curtains and said, "It's an ugly fall so I suggest you make a good rope out of those and climb down."

One woman lowered her scissors. She said, "Are you really the Wight?"

"When I need to be," Richter said, and he jumped out the window.

~~~

"Respectfully captain," Dahlgren said, shaking his head. "I think you and I might not have the same definition of stupid."

The captain hobbled to the bunkhouse's porch, took one great breath, and nodded. "Aye," he said, planting himself on the porch's first step.

He swept his hat off his head and ran it over his sweaty brow and then hung the hat on his boot. He gathered another, much longer breath, and then dropped his head between his knees, staring at the earth as if it might be hiding air from him.

"You look whipped," Elletrache said, chewing on a cut of deer leg. He held it out. "Want something to eat?"

"Thanks, Trash, but I'm fine."

Still chewing, the beast slayer shrugged. "More for me then."

Dahlgren walked to the edge of the porch. He looked toward the tavern and the chaos surrounding it.

"Are them fellas going to come here and kill us?"

"Not anymore," Richter said. "They're busy with other matters now."

"You're certain?"

"Dahlgren, you remember Fritz, right?"

"Of course."

Richter brought his head up. He said, "Men like him don't fear much. Men like him can be a problem during times of strain. The safest option for us would have been to hire him. He probably would have made a fine sellsword if he was wanting of that path. But with that out the window, the next safest option would be for us to kill him."

"You killed him?"

[173]

"No. Unfortunately, I don't think Immerwahr would have allowed that, and I have no intention of muddying things for the monk in such a manner. With Fritz, I simply... made a bit of a mess."

Still chewing, Elletrache prodded the leg of deer toward the pub. He said, "Remember, ol' black hat here got that witch huntin' blood. He has plenty of experience with mobs. The pitchfork brandishers, well, they take offense to killing the womenfolk, even if they did think them witches."

Richter nodded. He said, "Much of our training as hexenjäger comes with great concern for the people who employ us. There is a dubious nature to hunting a witch, such as her powers may be that she can inflict innumerable crimes yet leave her victims uncertain from which direction came their calamities. Even when they know it is her fault, there is something that rattles a people's spirit when they see a woman's head in a bag, bleeding and human, empty of her tricks and criminality. It sobers them. And it makes them very angry, and they start to question why they hired you in the first place."

The tavern roared. Its bonfire gushed. Glass clinked as windows broke.

Elletrache spat a chunk of fat out. He said, "I'd seen a mob come after a fella for drawing cocks on walls. I mean, he was drawin' 'em every which way on damn near every building there was. Honestly, now that I think about it, he was a bit of a menace. But his illustrations didn't warrant a lynching, but they saw to him anyway." The beast slayer took another bite and gestured the leg at the captain. "I trust black hat's methods here."

'Fire!' rang out, followed by the only word which ever came after, if only said louder: '*Fire!*'

The three men watched as flames started licking up the sides of the pub. Smoke quickly curled into the sky in belches and long sheets alike. People came crashing out of windows and clambering through the front door and around the back. A woman sidesaddled a second story window and yelled out to the crowd below and then jumped into their arms.

Despite the intensity of the flames, drunken men still carried kegs out of the inferno, holding them like pirates stealing treasure from a sinking ship. A litter of ashy and blackened men lay in the mud before the pub, sharing drinks and mugs of ale, while all around them davered drunks came running with water buckets only to spill them in their stupors, and the dropped buckets only added to the mud and muck and soon everyone was slipping and sliding and yelling at one another about how best to fight a fire they were too drunk to properly assess in the first place, and there before the blossoming inferno did the heat go to the people's heads and they resumed fighting.

Taking a swig from a canteen, Dahlgren belched and said, "You know you fellas get onto to me for being a drunk, but I ain't ever been *that* drunk."

One man was dumped into a wheelbarrow and a throng of children rolled him away with his legs cantilevered over its sides. They threw him into a pile of manure and celebrated their conniving by kicking his unconscious body. Other men clapped buckets over their heads and ran at each other with broomsticks, crashing jousts which aroused much laugher amidst the pugilism and vomiting and halfhearted firefighting. Dogs ran back and forth yipping at the flames, and yellow eyes blinked from the rooftops as cats looked down with almost clerical haughtiness. Most importantly, not a single person was advancing on or so much as even talking about the sellswords.

"See?" Elletrache said. "That there is proper mob dispersal."

Richter stood up. "Aye, I think that should buy us a night."

"Well shit," Dahlgren said. "Now what?"

"Keep low and quiet. Get the company ready to start an hourly watch at this bunkhouse," Richter said. The captain clapped the old man on the shoulder. "Safe to say that this will be our final night here."

~~~

The company spent the evening on rotation with the captain himself occupying most of the watches. He was a light sleeper to begin with, and the town was alight with activity as fights and drunken brawls lurched, ended, and restarted in an unending cycle. Unnerved by the chaos, dogs kept howling. The cats, seemingly borrowing the energies of the evening, took it upon themselves to mate and fight along the rooftops and into the alleys and sometimes run themselves into the dogs who would then, breaking their somber dirges, set upon the cats in scuffles that seemed devilish in the dark, and rank and ruinous in the light. As the evening passed, all these sights and sounds could no longer be differentiated, and the night took on a shrill tone, the tavern's inferno backlighting everything and everyone in a hellish haze.

~~~

Come morning, the peasants were laid out in the mud and scattered across porches and limply folded over railings like clothes out to dry. A throng of children tiptoed about, using sticks to poke and prod vulnerable butts everywhere. Getting their noses picked by these devious souls, a man and woman on a rocking chair snorted awake, glanced at each other, and rapidly departed in opposite directions. Up above, a man slept on a rooftop, snoring as he clutched a rooster at his side, the animal looking curiously comfortable. Once the sun met its feathers, the rooster crowed and the man jolted and threw the bird off the roof. The moment it landed it found itself in a brawl with dogs and cats and there came snarling and hissing and crowing that, despite its viciousness, gently evaporated down one of the alleys.

Dahlgren, sleeping in a wheelbarrow in front of the bunkhouse, roused awake and stretched his arms and efforted out of the barrow like an old horse flopping off the ground and back to its feet. With a slight lean, his spine popped from top to bottom. He then looked at the town and sighed.

"Ah hells," he said. "The pub burned down in full."

Already well awake, Richter stood on the porch cleaning his fingernails. He said, "You expected them to save it, Dahlgren?"

"Expecting? No. Hoping? A little."

"Don't get too down," Richter said, flicking some grime off a finger. "We still have some ale in the wagon."

"But there ain't song and dance in the wagon, nor festivities, nor fun."

"There'll be fun ol' Quinn, though."

"Ahh, fuck off," Dahlgren said. "Respectfully, captain."

"Aye."

"But also respectfully, you burned down the town's pub."

"Aye, I can see that."

"But, just so we're clear, what you really did was burn down their dancing, their festivities, their fun. You've left them only us."

Richter held his hand out before himself, seeing the fingernails all clean. He said, "I suppose that's a shame."

"Captain, they're going to be very, very pissed off. I think we should take this moment to get the hells out of here. They're sobering already and at least one of them will recollect the bastard who made a mess of their pots and pans. Your... uh, face, and hat, and general appearance won't make that a difficult task to accomplish. If we stay here, we might be dead men."

"We stayed for Quinn," Richter said. "Now we'll stay to settle the matter, or did you really think our wagon could outrun an angry mob?"

"Ah sonuvabitch," Dahlgren said, shaking his head. He put his hand and nub on his hips and said, "I truly hope you know what you're doing, captain."

"Have some faith, Dahlgren."

Already, the townspeople were indolent, staggering about the mud, piecing together the figuratives and literals of the previous night, of which the charred remains of the pub proved most spectacularly transfixing. But this laziness would change, and Dahlgren was right about the rage that would come. The captain turned and said, "It's probably best to wake the rest of the company. I want them standing behind me looking as menacing as possible."

The old man looked at the charred tavern, and at the listing, grumbling, mumbling peasants whose voices were steadily growing louder and angrier.

Dahlgren nodded. "Alright. I hope you know what you're doing."

As the company mustered before the bunkhouse, the townspeople were marshaling their own forces just down the road. Richter saw the first few come carrying pitchforks and torches, and this ragged vanguard pointed at the captain and called back to the rest of the slumbering ferry folk, and in the span of seconds a great mob of possibly forty or fifty strong had formed. They had armed themselves with the tools of their trades in lumberjack axes and sheep shears and shepherd poles and hammers and tongs and two men carried fighting roosters which they petted and whispered to.

One man carved a stick in a shabby spear, his eyes glaring at Richter as though he meant for his target to see the very fashioning of his demise. But Richter stood resolute, Adelbrecht's sword sheathed at his side, Carsten's hat on his head, its lid slightly tilted over a missing ear.

"Captain?" Berthold said, coming to the bunkhouse. "What's going on?"

"Hey, yeah," Thomas said. "W-we're not going to fall all of that, are we?"

Richter turned to his company as they met on the bunkhouse's porch. He pointed at each of them and said, "Don't do anything stupid. Don't move quickly, don't breathe strangely, don't sneeze or cough or stare anyone in the eyes too long. Imagine the mob is a wild animal because it is. They're scared of us, but if we provoke or show weakness, they *will* attack, understand?"

"If it's a wild beast," Elletrache said. "How do you plan to kill it?"

"I don't," Richter said, turning around to the throng of furious faces. "Lucky for us, this wild beast has an animal tamer in its midst."

As expected, Immerwahr strode to the front of the mob, himself seemingly dressed for an entirely different occasion: his finest white and grey robe which wispily trailed in the wind. Gold epaulets glinted on his shoulders, perhaps some fineries from his days when he could call his fellow monks his friends. If the monk had ideas of statesmanship and knightlihood, his mimicry was on point, and if there were nothing but hot air filling his attire it would still yet command the crowd which it rapidly marched ahead of.

"Richter von Dagentear!" the monk shouted, his voice cracking with unpracticed fury. "*Merrrr*-cenaries!"

A rock struck the bunkhouse and another sailed up and over, skittering off its roof. Elletrache strode across the porch and balanced his mini-ballista over the railing and just like the crowd murmured quietly in a stammering retreat, like some ferocious storm leaking its way back out to sea.

Immerwahr raised his hands and spoke to the mob to ease their minds, though the appearance of the beast slayer's enormous crossbow had as equal an effect as any monk's words, religious or otherwise. Finished with momentarily soothing the mob, Immerwahr lowered his arms and strode toward the bunkhouse.

"The monk arrives with his pitiful godliness," Richter said loudly with facetious disgust.

"Indeed, 'tis I, a mere man of the old gods!" Immerwahr replied, spinning back to the mob with his arms wide. "Watch, my peoples, as I see to this evil alone, clothed in the protection of the almighties. Let not one of you cast another stone, for the old gods do not reward those whose natures are of their own ill design! And surely enough they reward naked bravery just as they will punish untoward cowardice! Behold my faith!"

Immerwahr turned back to face Richter and slowly stepped up the porch, each footfall heavier than the last, until finally he stood at the captain's level and there the monk's lip quivered before he nodded with a wide smile.

"How you doing, Richter?" he said, their voices just between themselves.

"Could be better. I see you've the friar faithful in good order. Did you give them those rocks or did they find those on their righteous path?"

"Very funny. You should know that I worked well into the night keeping this town from lynching you."

"I knew you would."

"And if I didn't?"

"We'd all be dead, but most of your town would be dead just as well. So, like I said, I knew you'd intervene."

"Hmm. And you're doing all this on account of one common thief?"

"I'm doing it for Quinn," Richter said. He nodded. "And for you."

The monk tilted his head. "For me?"

"Aye." Richter nodded at the mob. "You've been getting too friendly with us sellswords, Immerwahr. Always looking out for us, never truly punishing any of my men, giving me gold, failing to quell concerns about the ferryman's death, shooing away peasants so you could have talks with me. You don't realize it, but your days here were becoming rapidly numbered."

"And of this you are certain?"

"Aye. I thought to take you with us, but that wouldn't be fair. You're a holy man. You can do a lot of good for these people, if only they can get their minds right – which is what we're about to help them do here and now."

Richter looked over the monk's shoulder. The mob stared back, beating their weapons into their palms or the animal handlers petting their roosters' heads. The roosters themselves seemed only focused on each other, as though they'd a history and if their shrewd minds could remember one thing it was wholly devoted to their equally feathered nemesis. Their legs twitched unwittingly in the nooks of their masters' arms, a fight against air, but still yet between each other's air no doubt.

Immerwahr said, "The proclivities of the townspeople aside, you should know that I took actions of my own which you may not have so easily scried."

"Oh?"

"Yes indeed. North of town awaits a wagon with two extra wheels in the bed and a host of tools to go with it. I have also procured more medicine and a few bowls to assist your wounded thief. The wagon itself comes with a donkey incapable of a farmer's encumbrance, but he should suit your needs fine, so long as a few of you are alright walking."

"That is alright and much appreciated. Whose wagon is it?"

"Mine. The one I used to come to this very place after my fellow monks had run me out. You've earned it: I've been shorting you on pay all this time."

"You have?"

Immerwahr pursed his lips. "No."

"As always, you're a terrible liar, Immerwahr."

"Hey!" A voice hailed from the mob. "What's the hold up!"

The man was shushed by his peers. "Let Immerwahr handle this!" someone shouted, and other agreed with an almost hissing tone. "The monk has the old gods on his side! Let him face the wrath of the sellswords!"

Immerwahr glanced back at the mob, their fists clenched, teeth gritted. When he returned to looking at Richter, he took a finger and prodded it into the captain's chest, a move that brought a few gasps from the people.

"So anyway," the monk said plainly, yet still poking with faux outrage. "How do you want to do this?"

Richter looked at the finger poking him. He glanced over the monk's shoulder at the anxiously whispering mob. He said, "You have the right idea, monk, but maybe ante up a bit on the theatrics?"

"Oh, is this not enough? What else should I do?"

"Put some volume on it—"

"I will put the fear of the old gods in you!" Immerwahr suddenly shouted and he threw his arms open as though to illustrate a point of much greater import than their conversation truly carried. Richter, on a whim, took a dramatic step back, as though caught off guard. The crowd ooh'd and ahh'd at the spectacle. The monk lowered his voice, returning the conversation to be between just the two: "I doubt the mob will wander far from the orders of, well, a man of my station."

"Aye, but…" Richter stared at the crowd. "I think I need to get a word in here before your flock thinks me muted and tamed."

"Steel sharpens steel." The monk nodded and gestured with his eyes. "The floor is yours."

The captain cleared his throat. He put a finger in the monk's face and yelled back, "Your peoples should kiss your feet, monk! For if you were not here I myself would kill ten of yours, and my sellswords would lay waste to this shitpile you call a town!"

Wiping spit off his cheek, Immerwahr said, "Pretty good, but did you have to call it a shitpile?"

"Aye."

"Hmm. I suppose it does add some flavor to it. How are they looking?"

Richter stared over the monk's shoulder. "They look concerned."

"Excellent."

"Hey, uh, what's going on?" Thomas said from the door.

"You there!" the monk yelled and wickedly pointed at Thomas. "You will not even dare to threaten my people! You won't even so much as dream of it, you… you little scapegrace scamp!"

Thomas opened his arms as if to say 'what did I do?'

"Alright," Richter said. "Let's not get carried away."

Immerwahr straightened out his garb and nodded. "Apologies."

Richter glanced at the mob. It was unusual for a mob to stand idle for so long. If not properly ushered, they would go find something to light aflame or beat to death, senseless violence being the usual favorite task of a throng of likeminded strangers. The captain thought to bring the falsities and theater to an end lest last night's anger find its old host.

He looked back to Immerwahr and said, "I think we should settle this."

"Indeed. Our bravado is no doubt contagious, even I felt a little hop in my step there."

"Let us settle it like this this, then. We will leave, and you now have the floor to capture these people's hearts and minds anyway you want. Good?"

Immerwahr nodded. "Yes."

Richter stuck his hand out as though to offer it for a shake.

As if that was his cue, Immerwahr jumped back and left the porch entirely. "Our business is settled, sellsword, but I will not sully my hand with yours, given the blood it has spilled and, worse, the blood it desires to spill! You will depart our town and leave my peoples be! In return, we will not interfere with your leaving!"

"Swear it to the old gods!" Richter barked back. "Swear it over the heads of your people!"

"I swear it!"

"Swear it to their dead brothers and sisters!"

Immerwahr stammered a second, looking as if Richter may be pushing the matter a bit too far, as though to say this theater might indeed draw the ire of the old gods themselves and the play would find itself mired in genuine and divine punishment.

Widening his eyes, Richter whispered, "Say a response before they answer for you."

"Ahem, I, uh, I swear it upon our dead, and even those who have not yet been born!"

The people gasped as the monk continued with rising energy: "And you, sellsword! You will not talk to my people, nor they to you! And you will not glance upon them, nor they to you! And by nightfall you will not be dwelling here, nor shall you ever return, for the stars shall find our glorious town ridden of your kind as the old gods rid the world of its disgusting filth!"

Richter spat and nodded. "Aye. Then I shall respect Immerwahr and this so-called militia he wishes to form!"

The monk mouthed: 'militia'?

The captain nodded dutifully. He put his hat back on and yelled out: "This business is settled!"

A man of the mob stepped forward, as though magnetized by the captain and monk. He shouted: "May the old gods bless us as they have blessed Immerwahr! Three cheers for Immerwahr!"

The monk returned to the roaring mob like a conqueror carrying war booty back to his tribe.

Richter turned around as they cheered.

"Quite the spectacle, captain," Dahlgren said. "Could've gotten us all killed, but I suppose if it works it works."

The captain nodded. "Immerwahr can do a lot of good here. We get to keep our thief, and the town gets to keep itself on the right path. Dahlgren, there's a wagon north of town we'll be leaving on. Get it ready now."

"Excuse me," Minnesang said, the jester slightly holding a finger up like a mouse pipping an inquiry into a nest of hawks. "Is this series of events fairly usual for you fellas or is this more like a new thing and not something I can expect to see every—"

"Pack your shit!" Dahlgren said, waving the company back inside. "Did you not hear? We got ourselves a new wagon! C'mon! Quit yer lollygagging!"

Minnesang closed his mouth, then lowered his hand. He shrugged and turned around and went back into the bunkhouse.

"Hey, yeah, that's great and all," Thomas said. "But ain't it just luck that we aren't being lynched right here and now?"

"I think the old gods look out for Richter," Hobbs said.

The servant opened his mouth, then sighed. He kicked the doorframe and muttered, "I'm doing all this on account of some foolish Louis—err, loser... some foolish loser has me doing all this, uh, foolish shite." Thomas looked around a moment and when he saw no one had heard his slip of the tongue he hurried back inside.

Crockett came out of the bunkhouse soon after, one hand carrying a book and the other furiously scribbling notes. Beaming ear to ear, he said, "I got so many adjectives, so many things to say! That... that was incredible!"

"Crockett," Richter said.

"Yes, captain?"

"Please run inventory."

"Oh." Crockett closed his book. He nodded. "Of course. Duty first!"

"All this for some thief," Sophia said, standing in the doorway and smiling. "Thank you, Richter."

"Quinn can thank me."

"Oh, I doubt he'll do that."

"I know."

Sophia laughed. "Yet here you are, doing all this anyway."

The captain glanced at the sellswords scurrying around him, each giving him a dutiful and respectful nod.

"Aye," he said, nodding back. "Here I am."

Chapter 13. A Miracle.

THE WAGON was just as Immerwahr stated: a decrepit piece of wood vaguely in the shape of working transportation. As if that wasn't enough, it was pulled by a donkey with a patchy grey ass and permanently pinned ears.

"It's something," Dahlgren said.

Richter nodded. "That it is."

The captain opened the tailgate and a box fell over. He picked it up, feeling some weight and hearing the jingle of coins, as sure an invite to opening a mysterious container as there'd ever be. And – just as he turned it another way – a little piece of paper fell astray. Richter snatched it midair.

With fresh ink, it said, 'To Richter: a new job. May you sellswords take to this task and never return. – Immerwahr.'

"What's in the box?" Thomas said as he loaded food into the wagon.

"It's another contract," Richter said. He lowered the paper and popped the box's latch and threw it open. Three purses were squashed together in a corner. He tossed them to Crockett and told him to take count. In addition to the purses, there was one letter and a…

Richter smiled.

"What in the hells is that?" Dahlgren said.

Pulling the wooding carving out, Richter said, "It's a camel."

"A what?"

Richter turned. "Hobbs!"

The boy hurried around the wagon with a half-eaten carrot. "This donkey's a real ass! Damn near bit my finger off and—whoa, what is that?"

"It's a camel."

"What's a camel?"

"Somethin' out of the southern deserts," Elletrache said, heaving a pile of shields into the wagon. "Kinda like a horse, but also not at all."

"There you go, something from a desert," Richter said with a shrug. He held it out to the boy. "But it's yours if you want it."

Hobbs pocketed the carrot and took the camel into both hands, eyes wide as though it were an ancient treasure. Rolling his hand along the animal's valleyed humps, he almost seemed wowed by the very passage of his own fingers, the sort of wonderment only a child can have when petting something never seen before. He looked up. "What a strange creature... is it real?"

"Trash says it is, so I suppose it is."

"Whoa."

"Aye."

Dahlgren nodded. "What's that second letter say?"

The captain turned back to the box. He picked up the letter.

"Ooh, the captain can read?" Minnesang said. "I heard that Richter von Dagentear was a man of some education, but it is something else to see it in person!"

Richter glanced over the letter at the jester but didn't bother responding to that. He read Immerwahr's message: 'To my dear friend Richter, I wish you well on the roads. Here is what I need you to do...'

"There's three hundred crowns in these," Crockett said, holding up the purses in one hand and a few coins in the other. "Quite the advance."

Finishing the letter, Richter said, "The camel is meant for a delivery."

Hobbs looked up. "Ah, so I can't keep it then."

"No. Well," Richter thought. "You can hold onto it for now, but *do not* lose it."

"I'd never."

Richter stared at the boy.

Hobbs defended his honor: "I'd never!"

"Who the hell wants the camel?" Dahlgren said.

"That is partly another job for Crockett," Richter said. He held the letter out to the paymaster. "There's a crude map drawn on there that shows a number of roads leading north."

"A number of roads?" the paymaster said, taking the letter. "I thought the Ancient Road itself would be the main causeway."

Richter shrugged. "It seems the work of the ancients has degraded, and there are plenty of paths we could take, some more dangerous than others. Immerwahr warns we need to be wise to it."

Looking the paper over, Crockett nodded. "I'm no cartographer, of course, but I can try and match the monk's map to the company's."

"Good. As for the recipient of the camel…" Richter said. "It's not a person, but a place. Immerwahr only says we should present it to a caravanserai to the north." The captain gave an annoyed sigh, partially outmaneuvered by the monk's deep vocabulary. "Though I can take a guess, I'm not certain what exactly a caravanserai is."

"I was born in one," Elletrache said, coming by and heaving a collection of kitchenware into the wagon. "A caravanserai is a spot where merchants decide t'huddle on the roads. Like a stop for the caravans to rest and recuperate. A rest stop, if you will." The beast slayer leaned on the tailgate with a look of odd nostalgia. "My father loved those places, at least that's what I've been told. I get the feelin' my mother was born in one, too, whoever in the hells she is. I figure she'd be the whorin' sort, on account of my father being a whorin' sort and caravanserais being a place for whorin' of all sorts."

Everyone stared at the beast slayer.

Richter cleared his throat. "Alright, thank you, Trash."

The beast slayer augured a knuckle into his eyepatch. "No problem."

"So that is where we're going," Richter said, nodding toward Crockett. "We follow that map, find the merchants, and present the camel to whoever looks like they'd know what it is."

"Hey, yeah," Thomas said. "Sounds like a plan, then."

"New men," Richter said, turning. The company's three newest hires lined up. He pointed at each, from jester, to miller, to butcher: "Minnesang, Berthold and…"

The butcher looked up as if the world had just seen him for the first time. He said, "My name's Gernot, captain. I killed a few fellas with my cleaver at the brigand encampment."

In truth, Richter only cared that he was still alive, a quality fiercely missing from most new recruits. He smiled and nodded. "You three will—"

Adelbrecht's tactic of putting greenhorns on point returned to mind. He remembered the Free Company deploying new hires to the vanguard and eventual slaughter. Carsten's voice hurried to mind next, as though to shrewdly chastise him: *A mercenary company hires cheap labor for the dangerous work just as any mason or architect would. Why send a seasoned hand to the scaffolding on a windy day when a bumbling idiot will suffice?*

But the truth was obvious, regardless of how unsettling: some men were simply worth more than others.

Richter swallowed and tightened his grip on Adelbrecht's sword. He said, "You three will be on vanguard."

"Vanguard?" Berthold said.

"That means on point," Dahlgren said, throwing his nub toward the donkey. "Front and center."

"Aye," Richter said. "You'll march a stone's throw ahead of the wagon, but never lose sight of it."

"Sure you don't want us closer to the wagon?" Minnesang said.

Dahlgren grabbed the jester, jangling his hat of bells. "Best start listening to orders instead of questioning them."

"Watch the hat, watch the hat!" Minnesang said, righting it on his head like a bird hurriedly keeping a nest from falling from its branch. "My inquiry was simply that: an inquiry. Naturally, I will do as Lord Richter requires." The jester bowed. "I am honored to serve the great Richter von Dagentear!"

"Alright," Richer said. He turned to the others: "You three take the gambesons. We got some strips of leather for use as well. I suggest protecting your shoulders, but it's up to you. Aketon caps should also fit the lot of you. Except you, jester, you can keep your hat if you want."

"I will."

"What weapons can we take?" Gernot said. The butcher cleared his throat. "Ah sorry, my name is—"

"Shields and spears," Richter said. "Those will be your primaries."

The fresh recruits nodded, then stared at the captain as if he might have something more to say.

Dahlgren clapped his hands. "What is this, a dancing ball? Get to it!"

The three new hires hopped to action, scurrying like rats before a scullery maid's broom, though in this case it was Dahlgren's handless arm and menacing stare.

Sophia walked up, face flush and hair sweaty. She had a knapsack of herbs thrown over her shoulder and her hands were covered in green flakes.

"Homesteader," Richter said with a nod. "How is the thief?"

"I've rewrapped Quinn's bandages and his wounds actually don't look half-bad. Honestly, compared to last night, he might be healthier than we think, but he still isn't fully responding to pokes and prods." The homesteader shrugged. "He might recover soon so... last chance to leave him behind, eh?"

"The notion still crosses my mind," Richter said. "But I think we've gone too far on this path to ditch him now. Sophia, make space for him in the wagon. Trash, Thomas, Dahlgren, let's go get our thief."

~~~

Rickety and clackety enough to announce itself a good arrowshot before it could be seen, the company's wagon noisily made its way up the Ancient Road. Tumbling. Tottering. Clapping and clodding. Weapons and pots and pans all alike clinking and clanking. The donkey hawed in protest, but it never stopped moving as Hobbs wooed it forward with a half-eaten carrot, now and again cheating the poor creature from even a nibble.

"You have to earn it!" the boy yelled at the donkey. "C'mon now!"

As they had spent the previous night in rolling watchmen shifts, the company took turns of day spells in the wagon, sleeping beside Quinn who had been wrapped and sequestered near the foodstuffs. Beside him was a bag of freshly baked goods that Immerwahr had slipped into the wagon. Sophia believed that perhaps a bit of wafting smell from them would stir the thief.

"Richter," Hobbs said, coming to the side of the wagon. "The donkey stole the rest of the carrot."

Lowering the wagon's reins, Richter aid, "The donkey *stole* the carrot?"

Hobbs toyed with his empty hands. "It was quicker than I thought."

"Truly he's made an ass of you," Richter said.

"Ha-ha-ha."

Quick as a cat, Hobbs nimbly climbed onto the moving wagon's jockey seat and peeked into its bed. He said, "Quinn doesn't look so bad, you know."

"None of us are trained healers so we don't know how he is, or if he has damage on the inside we can't see," Richter said. "But Sophia thinks he'll pull through, and I trust her on that."

"I hope he makes it," Hobbs said, and then the boy suddenly reached further in, his upper body disappearing, his legs kicking in the air. Finally, he came back out with a fresh roll in hand. As he nibbled, the donkey turned its head and pinned its ears.

"Best keep the good stuff downwind of the donkey," Richter said.

"I am," Hobbs said, and he spoke between bites: "If it was me in the wagon, would you trust I'd bounce back? I mean, I was kidnapped by a witch and poisoned and beaten and you even shot me with a crossbow. Look how I turned out. You'd vouch for my toughness, wouldn't you?"

"A lot has happened to you in so little time," Richter said, "but you're just a boy, Hobbs. Don't get too far ahead of yourself."

The boy pursed his lips and looked down.

Richter tussled his hair. "Aye, you're a tough lad. As tough as they come."

"Only learned it from the best," the boy said, smiling.

Be careful who you make good memories with, the Carsten's voice suddenly returned to mind. *Good memories, light and fleeting in their creation, only get heavier and heavier as time goes on. That's why you're good at what you do, Richter. You know how to work alone.*

The captain stared at the boy, and the boy at him. A lot of hope and investment was in that stare. A lot of trust, too. But Hobbs knew not the real Richter von Dagentear, the reason they called him the Wight. Nor would he ever know, so long as Dagentear's last survivor could help it. Because a boy deserved to be a boy, so long as the world would permit it, and no man should ever trespass on the brief curiosities of youth without good reason.

"Immerwahr told me in confidence that you are a spectacularly strange man," Hobbs said, grinning to himself as he loudly pronounced a new word: "He called you an *indelible force*."

Richter smiled, but Carsten's warning would not quit his mind.

"That's good to hear. Hobbs, I think I'm going to take a rest now" Richter turned, holding the reins held up. "You alright handling the donkey?"

"Done it before, haven't I?"

"Hm." Richter stared at the boy. "Just don't go catching bugs this time."

"Uh huh," Hobbs said, taking the reins. "Lotta jest from a man 'taking a rest.' I know you're just going back there to steal a sweet roll or two."

"Hmm. Let me know if there's trouble, alright? Berthold, Minnesang, and that other fella are on vanguard, but keep your own wits, too."

"Admit it," Hobbs said, staring with a wild grin. Richter remained stone faced. Hobbs pointed. "Admit it... admit it, Richter!"

The captain said, "I'm just going to rest." He let out a small sigh. "And I will be sneaking a roll or two, aye."

~~~

Richter jerked awake. The tarp of the wagon snapped and billowed above, and the wagon tilted and jolted as its wheels made discomfited traversals over the crumbling Ancient Road. As he stared up, the captain heard a crunch to his right, and then another and another. His mind raced over all the creatures he knew of the forest, and quickly concluded at least a few such monstrosities could have snuck inside the wagon. Another crunch came, and then another and another. Quick, chamfering, gargling between bites, a sort of bloodlust slaked between satisfied snarls and snorts.

The captain sprung upright and turned over, his hand to his sword.

Beside him, the creature jolted. Found out. Put there nakedly before eyes it did not expect. About its belly, crumbs. On its maw, berry stains. The food sacks around it chewed through, its carnage caught midstride.

"You," Richter said. "You motherfucker."

Looking over his shoulder, Quinn slowly lowered a butterknife in one hand and a crunchy roll in the other.

"Uh, you're dreaming," the thief said, sweeping crumbs away. "Go back to sleep, captain, go back to sleep… shhh, everything is fine, go back to—"

"You piece of shit!" Richter yelled and he slugged the thief.

A bread roll went flying, crumbs aplenty.

Quinn reeled. "Hey! Shit, man! My bruises! I'm bruised there!"

"Get out of the wagon, *now!*"

"Alright! I'm going! By the old gods, you got fire in that right hand, Richter, anyone ever told you that? You almost hit as hard as that brawler."

"Out!"

As the thief scrambled for the tailgate, Richter booted him in the arse and Quinn barreled out of the wagon, limbs spinning, legs flying, crumbs spraying, and his body crumpled to the road outside.

"Hey!" Sophia screamed as she hurried over. "What's going on? Richter, what are you doing? Hobbs, stop the wagon! Stop the wagon, dammit!"

"Alright alright!" the boy yelled back.

The wagon lurched, the wheels skidding askew.

Richter jumped out. The thief started to stand, but Richter kicked him right back to the ground.

"Augh, shit! Fark!" Quinn said. "Let me explain!"

Sophia jumped between them.

"What are you doing?" she asked. "Stop that!"

"He's a fraud!" Richter said, pointing around her. "He was faking it the whole time!"

The company started to collect around the scene, murmuring in confusion though, absent of information, some still relished in seeing the thief get a sound asswhooping.

Free of the captain's boot and shielded by the homesteader's body, Quinn slowly got to his feet. His linen wraps were in a mess, hanging off his arms in tatters, though the mottling of blood was now rife with a litter of crumbs and smudges of butter and berry jam. He swept his hair back and said, "Now hold on a minute, I can explain. I can explain a lot! You know me, I'm a great talker! Lemme talk!"

Sophia slowly lowered her guard. She turned. "Wait… you're fine?"

"Of course I'm fine!" Quinn said. He grinned as if nothing was out of the ordinary. "Why wouldn't I be fine?"

"I don't… I don't understand. We… we risked our lives for you… we almost got lynched by a mob," Sophia said, her words stumbling as her mind still grappled with the thief's ploy. "We all thought you were dying…"

"Well now hold onto that thought, cause I thought I was dying, too," Quinn said. "But then I got better, and by the time I was back to a sound spirit, you had me all wrapped up and were doting on me and everyone was saying all this sweet talk about me, like how much they liked me, and how much they cared. It really warmed my heart."

Sophia's fist clenched. She shouted so ferociously as she went after the thief: "I will kick your teeth down your fucking throat!"

Dahlgren rushed forth, confused and with his sword halfway unsheathed.

Quinn jumped back, limber as a cat and all smiles. "Dahlgren! Good to see you! This is quite a moment we're having."

"Sophia," Dahlgren said, but his eyes shifted fast. "Quinn? You're up? Walking? What in the hells is going on here?"

"The thief lied to us," Sophia said. She took a huff of a breath and spoke as though she were balancing her words on a knife's edge: "Quinn, you better have a proper explanation as to why you didn't just tell us."

"I was going to say something, I swear, but every moment it seemed the opportunity would pass or you guys kept coming and going. You were all being such sweethearts that I didn't want to make things awkward."

"Awkward!" Sophia shouted. "Make things *awkward!*"

"Yeah? It was nice that you were nice to me. Not every day that—"

The slap cracked over the forest. Birds lifted from the trees and departed as though to chase its echo. Quinn was almost on his knees, holding his cheek, and Sophia waved her hand up and down, screaming in pain and anger. She had never struck one of her children, but the thought had come and gone many a time and all the energy of it never happening seemed to explode then and there. It happened as quick as she could envision it, and a lot of pent-up frustration welted a purple rise on the thief's cheek.

"Holy shit you can hit hard," Quinn said, rubbing his cheek. "You and Richter might want to look into starting a brawling band or something."

Dahlgren shook his head. "Should've left his arse behind. Should have left his dumb, farking, stupid arse in that town and let them have him!"

"Everything turned out fine!" Quinn said. "I'm here, you're all here, everything is fine! What's the big deal!"

"Big deal?" Sophia said, rubbing her reddened hand on her clothes. "The big deal is that we almost got lynched! We almost all *died* Quinn, what part of that don't you understand?"

"He doesn't understand because he was sleeping."

Everyone looked over at the voice like it were a dove flying through the torrents of a black storm.

Crockett stood there with his arms crossed, his face wrenched in the horror of having to defend the thief. He pointed at him and said, "Quinn has no idea what you guys are talking about because he was sleeping. We never discussed the state of the situation with him in the room, remember? For all he knew, we were just being nice and taking care of him. As far as he's concerned, the issue with the town began and ended when that brawler beat him into a pulp. He has no idea what happened after."

The thief looked around. He said, "Wait, what did I miss?"

"Heh." Elletrache smirked and shook his head. "Heh, heh, har har, by the old gods, if this ain't the most ridiculous shit I've ever seen."

Richter stepped forward. He explained: "The townspeople turned against us, Quinn. It had been brewing for some time, but your brawl set it aflame. We didn't think you could survive on the roads, so we stayed the night and fended off the entire town come morning. You don't recall any of this?"

"Uh, no. I slept like a baby last night. Sophia fed me some of that herbal thickness and it knocked me right the fark out," Quinn said. "Hells, I didn't even wake up until just now in the damn wagon. You're telling me that the town came after you... and you stayed, for me...?"

Elletrache snorted and bowled over, hands to his knees, his whole body lurching and laughing, the scales of his lindwurm arm hissing animalistically with every huff. "Most g-g-godsdamned ridiculous shit I've ever seen. M-m-most godsdamned..."

"Fucking hells," Dahlgren said, shaking his head. "I think it best if I just run him through. I'm saying that honestly, captain. Let me do it."

"Quinn!"

Everyone turned.

Hobbs rushed through the throng of sellswords and hugged the thief. "You're alive!"

"Oh, h-hey there," Quinn said, smiling nervously. He said under his breath: "Good timing..."

"Move out of the way, boy," Dahlgren said, unsheathing his sword. He pointed its steel at the thief. "You've a minute to explain yourself."

Hobbs retreated a step. "What's going on?"

"Ah, it's nothing," Quinn said. "Just, uh, us adults having a talk."

"Were you ever truly hurt?" Richter said.

"Hurt?" Hobbs said. "Quinn's eyes are black and blue."

"Th-that they are, boy!" Quinn said, but as he gathered the stares of the rest of the company, he knew it wasn't sufficient. "Look, I honestly, truly, don't remember anything after running into that brawler. I woke up to Sophia and Doll—Dahlgren looking over me. At the time, I could hardly breathe, and I was seeing triple of everything. Within the day, though?" The thief tossed out a hand. "I was swell. A little swollen but swell."

"Sophia was tending to you by the hour," Richter said.

"Well it's not my fault she isn't a proper healer!"

"I've never seen someone so bloodied and bruised," the homesteader said. "I honestly thought he was dying!"

"My insides were," Quinn said. "But, woman, I am a proper fella. Getting bloodied and bruised is a part of my daily diet."

"Is eating your own teeth part of that diet, too?" Dahlgren said.

"No," Quinn said, and he held up a finger. "And I think it's important that I say I don't think it should be, either."

"Excuse me," Minnesang said. "Are you saying the fella at the heart of all that ruckus wasn't really dying? That's something else—"

"*Shut it, jester!*" Dahlgren yelled. "This does not concern you!"

The jester recoiled and shuffled away, his bells jingling with each tiptoe.

"You tell him, Dahlgren," Quinn said.

As the old man huffed, Richter walked in front of him. He put his hand to his steel and lowered it. He slowly walked toward the thief.

"Uh oh," Quinn said.

Richter pointed at the wagon. "I caught you eating our food."

"Oh, that, yeah…" Quinn rubbed the back of his head. "I had to eat something. No offense, Sophia, but your soup would pucker the gods."

"I am offended," Sophia said. "I am offended and I want this man dead."

Dahlgren stepped forward again. "That can be arranged."

"H-hey!" Quinn said, his hands instinctively going for his daggers, only to find none on his person. They quickly went back up, palms out, the thief smiling tenderly behind their naked guard. "Let's talk this out!"

"Your tongue can explain after I cut it from your stinking mouth!"

Richter put a hand to the old man, stopping him a second time. He said, "What Quinn did was wrong, but not worth killing him over. Especially not after everything we did just to get him here.

"I say we should still whip him for it," Dahlgren said. "I can do it. I'll use the donkey whip and thrash him like one."

Quinn straightened up, his linen wraps fluttering in the wind, revealing pale legs and shoulders, and cutting just a bit too far up the groin and wrapping not all that they could. "I'll run. Serious, I'll be gone before I ever let you do that, old man."

"Nobody's whipping anybody," Richter said. He closed the tailgate of the wagon. "Quinn, I'm docking your pay four days."

"Four days!"

"Aye, for the days in which you falsely stepped out from your duties, and additional time as punishment." Richter looked at Dahlgren. He saw in the old man's face that the punishment was not enough. The captain nodded. "You know what? One additional day docked for stealing food."

Quinn's mouth fell open. "Wait that's, four... and..." The thief held his fingers out, three, then four, and he slowly moved his other hand into view with one finger extended. He added a thumb to the mix. He looked up. "Five days of pay? You're taking five days of pay?"

"I'll subtract days," Richter said, nodding at Dahlgren. "If you take the old man's whipping. Ten lashings per day, how's that sound?"

"Five days is fair!" Quinn said. "Very fair, truly."

Dahlgren's grip tightened on his sword. He said, "I'll cut you a deal for five lashings, Quinn."

Quinn shook his head. "Declined."

"Three lashings…"

"We're not making deals here," Richter said. "This matter is settled."

The thief looked around at the company, smiling once again. He clapped his hands together. "Well then! Now that the dust is cleared, I must step aside for a moment for I really, really have to take a shit."

They watched the thief slowly back into the woods.

"You run, I'll follow," Dahlgren said.

"Only taking a shit!" Quinn shouted back as his voice and footsteps faded into the bushes. "Only a shit, promise!"

Dahlgren turned to Richter. "Another chance to leave him, captain."

"No," Richter said. "It's another chance for him to prove himself."

After much howling and groaning at a distance that wasn't all that it could be, the thief did indeed return and did so missing a few strips of his linen wraps. He clapped his hands together again. "Sorry about the delay there. Shall we hit the road, my most kind and gentle sellswords?"

"Quit the falsities and just be yourself," Sophia said. "I think you won't trick the hair off so much as a mole rat anymore."

"Alright then," Quinn said and he tore his linen wraps off, revealing himself in the altogether, standing with legs astride and his hands to his hips. "Fetch me my clothes, woman!"

Chapter 14. Findings.

AS THE COMPANY progressed north, the Ancient Road eroded beneath their feet. The company believed that they would eventually come upon its nadir, a point where the road and its white stones should simply disappear into a plain dirt path, the true center between Marsburg and Sommerwein, and no doubt the most lawless lands between the two cities at that.

The captain and the paymaster talked it out.

"All the maps go dark in these parts," Crockett said. "The trees creep closer to the road, too, making them prime hunting ground for bandits."

Richter stared down the path. Shadows from the trees crept across it and he knew at certain times of the day they may as well be marching through a tunnel of foliage. "Alright. Show me the map."

"Sure." Crockett took a map out of a cannister tied to his hip.

"This one is yours?" Richter said.

Crockett cleared his throat. "Ah, no, that's Immerwahr's. I'm still working on my own map."

"Alright," Richter said, though he eyed the paymaster a moment more. He unfurled the map. It was just as Crockett said: a number of roads weaved vaguely around a firm grey one – the Ancient Road – before both groups pinched off into nothingness, and this long blank space eventually renewed the Ancient Road northward once more.

"That's where we are," Crockett said.

"Where we are is lost then," Richter said.

"Not quite. I've other maps to work off of. Anytime we pass by something of interest, I check the maps to see what all matches up."

"And are any of them accurate?"

"It's a mixed bag."

"Alright," Richter said, handing the map back. "Good work, then. I look forward to seeing your final map, this company sure could use a good one."

~ ~ ~

Before sundown, Richter had the wagon pause for a cook. They ate salted deer meat and fish from the river. As dark washed over them, they lit lanterns and got back on the road. One hour. One hour into the dark of night, the fire of their march shimmering into the tree line, the trees starkly brown and green, then faded grey, then further out but silhouettes, and as the fight of the firelight slackened at those distances the trees submerged into an eternal black, and it was in that penumbra that a man could stare and see anything he wanted to see, and in that deep reservoir of imagination what a man dared himself to see was rarely in his favor, and he frequently looked back over his shoulders, fearfully curious that his imaginations might come true, for in such darkness man's own imaginations had him in their sights.

"Getting a little hard to see out here," Dahlgren said, marching alongside the wagon. "The lanterns are just barely spitting into this darkness."

"Aye," Richter said. "Call in the vanguard. We'll camp here."

He had the wagon turned afront two trees and the company camped in the burrow of their fat roots. Here the earth rolled in uneven berms, and it was against that soft soil that they lit one last lantern, its flame twisting in a strangely sultry fashion as the company sat around it in quiet talks, the dark around them wimpled by the soft gestures of the lantern, the shadows furrowed as they ringed about the trees and about further trees yet. When it seemed that the company's were the only sounds in the forest, Richter killed the lantern and the company turned in to sleep with a rotation of watchmen.

By morning Richter was last on guard and he set about pacing the road and tracking through the surrounding forest, a glowing horizon flaring orange pearls across mildewed bushes and branches and the wet grass below. A pair of deer had passed in the night unheard which bothered him greatly, but no human traces or signs were found. He returned to find Elletrache awake and putting his lindwurm armor back on. Dahlgren woke next and the weight of him moving woke Sophia just as well and she sorted her hair before rising. They two circled around Quinn and kicked him awake.

"Hey, hey! I'm up!"

Dahlgren dug into the thief. "Alright, just making sure."

"My eyes are open, you old man! You blind?"

The old man kicked him again. "I guess I am." And another kick followed. "Ears are also a bit deaf. What'd you say, Quinn?"

"You already answered the first question you sonuvabitch!"

"Alright, alright," Richter said, walking between the parties. He announced to the company as a whole: "I want everyone armed and ready. This is unkept lands we're venturing into. Vigilance is not optional."

The rest of the company geared themselves with an assortment of vaguely usable swords, axes, spears, and armor that consisted of hacked leather and chewed up gambeson. Hobbs and Thomas fed and watered the donkey and within thirty minutes the whole company was back on the road, Minnesang, Berthold, and Gernot on vanguard duty.

By mid-morning they came across an upturned wagon hidden behind a stand of trees. Ransacked, the bed of it wiped clean of goods. Its shredded tarp flailed in the branches above like white kudzu. Nearby, the slain owners. Face down. Here and there apart from one another, the furthest out with broken arrow shafts in his back. The soil beside him held grooves where the killers had kneeled and finished the job. Footprints continued from the body into the forest, undoubtedly heading to the shoreline. Richter assumed the brigands hit the water and then trailed up or down it from there and, in this manner, disappeared.

"Should we be concerned?" Dahlgren said, waving off a few flies.

"Bodies have been here awhile," Richter said.

"Killers still out there, you reckon?"

Richter touched one of the broken arrows in the dead man's back. The feathers were of poor make, and the wood their equal in this regard. He said, "Seems the handiwork of some desperate, poor men."

The captain had the company pull off the road and hide in some bushes for a time with the wagon concealed in the brush. He told Dahlgren to watch the wagon while Elletrache scouted the riverside and Richter himself took to the right flank of the Ancient Road and scouted a few lengths of road and forest there. He found a handful of traces, but the traces – bootprints, kneeling divots, sitting spots, shitting sites – were all too old, and the rest of the signage spoke of little more than the passing of ordinary forest critters. The most interesting find was a rusted knife on the ground, and in the nearest tree a carved heart and a pair of letters.

When he returned to the company, Elletrache was just coming back in at the same time and they convened, Richter giving his report first. The beast slayer then began his, and it was terse and to the point:

"Found some spiders," he said.

"Spiders?" Quinn said. "What do you mean spiders?"

"What do you mean what do I mean? There's spiders and I found them."

"Big ones?" Sophia said. "I mean the only reason a man like yourself would bring them up…"

Elletrache put out his hands in measurement and then widened both arms. "About ye big."

The company gasped.

"Nothin' to worry about," Elletrache said. "They won't bother us none."

"Won't bother us because you killed them?" Dahlgren said.

"Uhh, no. Ol' Elletrache is going nowhere near those suckers. I saw them. I saw they were minding their own business. And then I walked away. No need to complicate matters between man and spider."

"You're talking about webknechts," Richter said. "Is that right?"

"That's the fancy word for 'em, yeah." Elletrache snorted and spat. He could see the horror on the company's faces and he nodded with as much reassurance as his grimly bearded face would allow. "Look, the spiders ain't gon' bother us, alright? These woods're full of animals for them to nibble on. As bowlegged as we might appear, they don't hunt humans much unless they absolutely need to. Now, if yer walkin' in a darkwood and there ain't leaves on the trees then that means there ain't any leaf eatin' animals around. The only warmblood walking is likely you. If yer in a place like that and you see a big ol' spider, then you best run cause yer dinnertime on legs."

"None of this is really helping me ease my thoughts," Sophia said.

"I trust you, Trash," Richter said. "If you say a webknecht won't bother us, then I trust your assessment."

"Appreciate it."

"Question," Minnesang said, his jester hat jingling as he raised a finger. "Supposing a spider does attack us, what should we do?"

"What do you ordinarily do when a spider gets on you?" Elletrache said.

"I usually scream a bit, and then I smack it."

"Alright. Same thing. Just smack it harder."

~~~

The company made their way along the Ancient Road until it could hardly be called that anymore. Gaps in the stonework pitched the wagon into divots and the wheels popped and clacked. Hauling through such terrain, the donkey huffed and puffed as its halter seesawed against one shoulder and then the other. Eventually, the company took to clearing the Ancient Road themselves for its partial displacement was far worse than if it didn't exist at all. They moved ahead of the wagon pitching away the old stones and rocks, making a path of smooth dirt where careful ancient architecture used to be.

"Hey," Quinn said, hurling a cleancut stone of pure white. "You think the ones who made this road would be mad at us if they saw us doing this?"

Sophia tossed a rock herself and swept her brow. She said, "I don't know, but imagining how nice their roads used to be, what do you think their castles and cities looked like?"

"A thief's dream on every corner," Quinn said.

"Not exactly," Crockett said. "We believe that, so austere and amazing were the ancients, thieves didn't even exist at all. The profligacy was total and all encompassing. In those times, a thief simply need not exist for everyone's pockets were full."

"Thieves need not be? But being a thief is in my blood!"

Dahlgren spat. "Most men don't outright admit themselves to be mongrels."

"I'm proud of who I am," the thief said. "It got me this far, didn't it?"

"No bitch mutt knows its place amongst its nearest kin much less its ancient ancestors," Sophia said, hurling another stone. "All it knows is that it's just a dog. Or just a thief, in this case. I wager Quinn here would've been a thief in those days, even if everyone's pockets were full."

Quinn nodded. "Thank ye, fair maiden. Except the bitch part. Only bitch here is Crockett."

The paymaster threw his arms out. "I can't believe you still persist in these manners when I've spent the past days defending you, Quinn."

"So, what, does that make us friends now or something?"

"I don't know, maybe? Maybe if you were right in the head."

A sharp whistle let out. The roadcrew paused in their work. A branch snapped to their right, and the company clattered as they moved together and leveled their weapons and a second later Elletrache suddenly stepped out of the brush with camouflage wrapped over his already green lindwurm scales.

Quinn let out a sigh of relief "Dammit, Trash! Scared the shite out of me. You looked like a farkin' bush giving birth to another bush!"

"Ah, sorry 'bout that, Quinn." The beast slayer picked leaves out of his lindwurm armor. He looked up again. "Where's the captain?"

"Sitting on the wagon," Quinn said. "Not throwing stones, clearly. Or helping out. Or giving a hand. Or doing any sort of job. Or any sort of work for that matter. Or—"

Dahlgren slapped the thief upside the head. "Quit it." The old man nodded to the beast slayer. "You find something?"

"Oh yeah," Trash said. "You all can take a break. I need to show the captain something."

"Find yourself more spiders?" Minnesang said.

"Naw." The beast slayer snorted and spat. "You wish I'd found spiders."

~~~

The half-eaten horse had been found a stone's throw from the main path, its body consumed to the jowls and the eyes plucked. Holding his nose,

Richter crouched for a closer look. The chest and head were all that remained, a smooth, cleanly picked ribcage extending out into the grass. Clouds of flies hurried all over and the captain drew his hand up now and again to prompt them to keep to the meat and not the men staring at it.

Richter stood and looked at the footprints around the carnage. A small set of traces came in, and then a much larger set marched right back out. The captain shook his head. "I'll admit, I don't know what's going on here."

"Yer right to be confused," Elletrache said with a nod. "This here is the work of a nachzehrer."

"I've read of them."

"Read, oh? Come, let me show you what they do."

The beast slayer took up his great crossbow and marched further into the woods. Richter followed until they rounded a tree to find multiple piles of black shite, each a few feet apart, its squatter moving now and again in dribbling displace. Bleached bones stuck out of every mire: human legs, arms, and in one pile the top of a skull, and in another pile was a person's jawbone. Teeth peppered the piles in little nuggets of white and a fat fly sat lazily on a molar like it were an ivory throne.

Elletrache pointed with his crossbow. "I'm gonna go ahead and surmise that them bones are the horse's rider. Supposing them book you read were any good, yer familiar with what a nachzehrer does, yeah?"

"Aye," Richter said, nodding. "They scavenge and grow larger with each meal. A text I read said that smaller ones can double their size in a day."

"Hours, they shed skin and grow muscle about as fast as they can scarf down dinner," Elletrache said. "I've hunted them plenty, but mostly just the little'uns. This one here seems to be gobbling its way to a whole 'nother manner of danger. Those footprints are larger than the span of my hands. It keeps eating at this rate and it'll be king size in no time."

"Is it a danger to us or is it another distant fear like those spiders?"

"Depends. Little'uns scavenge. Bigguns go from scavenging to hunting, and that's when you got a problem." The beast slayer started kicking dirt over the shite piles. "Worst of it is that when nachzehrers get to this size, they'll just eat men whole. You'd hope to suffocate, but ya won't. They eat and chew so fast that air fills their gut. So its bile and acid in its belly that will take ya, and it can take a long, long while. The more it eats, the more you breathe, and the more you breathe the more you get to enjoy being melted alive."

Richter stared at a set of very small footprints that hurried away from the spot, each bit of trace more separated apart from the previous. Trailing these footsteps was a grooved trench where the beast's distended belly had dragged. A chase, or perhaps a lead. Richter flicked a hand toward both prints. "Someone survived and fled out. Looks like they got ahead of it, too."

Elletrache spat. "Sure, and?"

"I think we should see if they're still out there."

"Black hat, there's no cause in seeking trouble someone else ran from."

"Actually, there is," Richter said. "The road's busted and Crockett's trying to figure out if we've passed up any sideroads. Maybe whoever went that way knows something about the lay of the land. Maybe they knew where to go to get away from this thing."

The beast slayer ran a hand under his nose. He said, "If I can speak to it, I'll speak to this: those are footprints, and the fella making them is either dead or gone, and as far as we're concerned them two things are likely the same."

"Aye."

"Hey, it's something worth pondering for more than a simple 'aye', yeah? Ol' Elletrache seen this tale before. I just told you the dangers. These creatures are not to be trifled with, captain. Remember when I told you I saw them spiders? I lied. They weren't just hanging around. They had bodies in their webs. Brigand bodies. They ate those sonsabitches that ambushed that wagon. These are wilds, captain. We need to respect that."

"And your advice is appreciated, Trash."

Elletrache grumbled. He shifted uneasily and snorted and spat. He rubbed his eyepatch and leaned against a tree. "Alright, yer a decent fella and deserve some sincere honesty from ol' Elletrache," the beast slayer said. "So I'll just put it this way: if you send someone out there to go poking around and they disappear, I'll be hard pressed to keep my lips tight that I told you specifically not to do that."

"I won't send anyone," Richter said, "where I won't go myself."

~ ~ ~

Richter and Elletrache returned to the wagon.

"What's out there?" Thomas said. "Is it bad?"

"We got ourselves a nachzehrer," Elletrache said.

"Oh, alright, so… yeah, is that bad? I have no idea what that is."

"A nachzehrer is a scavenging monster. Grey, usually pale eyes, kinda shaped like a naked and fatter Crockett, except with claws and gnarled teeth for eating. Despite all that," Trash paused, hocking and clearing his throat. "Them suckers are easy to kill." He finally spat and then glanced at Richter. "Unless, of course, it's a biggun, in which case you should steer clear."

Thomas looked concerned. He said, "What do you mean, a big one?"

"It means it could be little wee thing, or it could be a big scary thing." Trash scratched his eyepatch. "I'll let ye figger which of the two is 'bad.'"

"I'm going to scout ahead myself," Richter said, looking around the company from man to man. Elletrache met his eyes and shook his head.

"Need someone to come with?" Dahlgren said. "By the sound of things, wouldn't be too wise venturing alone."

"Agreed," Richter said. The captain nodded at the miller. "Berthold, you a quick runner?"

The miller looked around, then pointed at himself. "Me?"

"Aye, you. You push a mill around in circles with your legs, right?"

"Sometimes. Most times, actually."

"Alright, and how fast can you run?"

"I dunno. Pretty quick, I suppose. Just not something I do much of. If you're asking if I got strong legs then yeah, I do."

"Grab a spear, shield, and a leather chestguard. You're coming with me."

"Shouldn't Trash go?" Thomas said. "He seems to know a lot about it."

"Between the two of us we're the only ones here with remotely relevant experience on the matter. I think it best if one of us goes with each group," Richter said, though his knowledge was more of the book reading sort. The real issue was that Elletrache was not a young buck anymore. If they ran into the creature, their best option would be to flee and running was just not in the works for the beast slayer. Richter nodded. "So, Trash will stay with the wagon to help protect it and scout around a little for any hidden paths or roads. If me and Berthold hit trouble, we'll rabbit back and then we can deal with the threat as a company."

"Right." Elletrache looked at Berthold and clapped a hand on the man's shoulder. "Best of luck out there, strong-legs."

The miller smiled nervously. "Uhh, yeah. Thanks."

Richter turned to his paymaster. "Crockett, I want you doublechecking those maps to see if we went up some wrong route somewhere, maybe missed a path in the overgrowth. The Ancient Road may have fallen apart, but trade still came through here so there's certainly a known sideroad we missed."

"A forest can hide open roads easier than people realize," Crockett said, nodding. "I'll see what I can do."

Richter turned back to Elletrache.

"Something on yer mind, captain?" the beast slayer said. "Perhaps rethinking it? Perhaps getting wise to the danger?"

"No," Richter said. "I'm just curious, just how big can a nachzehrer get?"

"Ohhh, I'd say they usually top out at about the size they can kill and eat a direwolf. It'll eat a man alive, but it won't chomp a direwolf unless it wants its guts ripped apart from the inside out. In the grand scheme of things, I think a lindwurm and an unhold giant would still smash a fully grown nachzehrer right and proper, but who knows. At the slayer guilds we like to ponder which of the monsters are most dangerous and a fat nach' ranks high."

Richter stared out into the forest. "You say a big one can kill a direwolf?"

"Oh black hat," Elletrache said, snorting with bearded and throat wrangling laughter. "A big nach' would make a direwolf its bitch."

Chapter 15. Stalker.

SINCE RICHTER'S LEAVING, the town had rallied around Immerwahr, taking to the monk as a sort of savior. He both relished and resented the attention and the faith that came with. On one hand, the sellsword had helped ensure that the monk could continue guiding the town and its people the right way. On the other hand, he had to lose a significant fighting force to do it, nevermind a person with whom he felt a certain, rarely found friendship.

The monk stared out his store window and sighed.

While Richter's misfits and miscreants were no elite band of mercenaries, the captain was clearly wily and clever enough to wield it to victory time and time again. Now, of all people, it was Fritz the monk leaned upon: he had chosen the brawler to head the town's militia. It was a political choice for, like Immerwahr and his theatrics, Fritz was seen as a man who had also stood up to the sellswords.

Immerwahr watched him from his shop windows, the brawler carrying a spear with his boot on it – the one Richter had shot clean through with a crossbow – and he used that spear-and-boot to bully the rest of the men into shape, kicking and poking them like a drill instructor with three feet. Despite these beatings, Fritz was a local hero now, a man who had nearly beat to death one of the sellswords. He was the first to take matters into his own hands, quite literally, and he bore the hobbles and scars of that courage.

A firm and rhythmic *hiyah!* rang out as the men trained. Altogether, there were a solid twenty men in the militia with ten more sidestaring it with muted interest. Unarmored, poorly armed, but full of desire and pride.

"Easy there!" Fritz called out, gathering the attention of a limp-wristed participant. "Keep that weapon up when you thrust! You can't thrust with a noodled cock, and you can't thrust with a noodled arm!"

The men laughed and resumed training. A certain camaraderie was quickly forming between them. Even when they were admonished or humiliated, it only served to harden their resolve, and their commitment to the greater good at that. Immerwahr always knew that desperation and poverty typically drove men into such violent vocations, but it was the intangible threads that helped keep them there. The allure and intoxication of brotherhood, the bonding that could not find purchase in the firmaments of parchment or in the studies of scribes.

"It is coming together, I must say," the monk said, briefly glancing upward at the ceiling and whatever providence stretched beyond. "Old gods, if you all are looking down on me, be sure to also look upon these souls just as well and ensure that if their hands must get dirty least give that dirt some proper meaning, and the acquiring of it be a task of honorable duty, and may their actions instill in them a certain pride to do ever better in this world." Immerwahr knelt his head and added: "And may Richter von Dagentear and those under him find equal ground under your protection, for I do not see in him a man worthy of abandonment, not even in this world. So be it said."

"A lovely prayer," a soft voice said from the front of the store. "And for such a lovely man."

The store's front door fell shut. Immerwahr stared out the window a moment longer, watching the militia try to thrust their weapons in unison, resulting in a haphazard series of stuttersteps and shunted spears that went every which way. Fritz was on the slackers in a second. Chuckling, Immerwahr stepped away from the window.

"Is that a little girl's voice I hear?" he said, coming around his counter. "I've a new set of toys for a lady such as—"

A young girl walked between the rows of shelves, her hands clasped over her chest, her stare swinging from one shelf to the next – and she was covered in blood, little red footprints trailing behind her, unsticking from her soles with each step.

Immerwahr yelped: "Oh my goodness!"

He hurried to the girl's side. He placed his hands upon her shoulders and looked her up and down. "Are you alright? Where are you hurt?"

She smiled. "Would you happen to have something to drink?"

"What happened?"

"A drink, please," the girl said.

Immerwahr held her a moment, then nodded. "Of course. Wait right here. Don't move, alright?"

He darted away, trotting between his shelves so fast and hard that the goods upon them rattled and jangled as he passed. Outside, the '*hiyah!*' of the militia belted over and over in practiced repetition. He grabbed a goatskin canteen and hustled back with shrewd and ungainly form, the sort of staggered flailing one finds in a feeble person spurred by emergency. The girl simply watched him with a reserved stare.

As the monk returned, he lowered himself to her and her eyes beamed alight, flicking upward at him and catching the light of day like two roses swirling through a wintered landscape, reinvigorated and bright and mysterious, and the monk paused and fell into what he was seeing as if through her eyes and her eyes alone the world were true, and all other worlds falsities where he realized he had been lying to himself every single day, that he lived and worked in a falseworld, and the real truth rested behind her eyes, and so the motions of the militia faded, blurred in shape, bulbous in action, and their sounds drew to a quiet din and—

"Thank you," she said softly.

Immerwahr blinked. He let go of the canteen, but his hand held to its lost shape, fingers curled, still hostage to a feeling. He stared at her eyes, her eyes staring back over the frayed goatskin fur as she drank, those eyes but bright whites with squares of his world still yet dwelling in them, the whole world there, the real world that he never knew existed, she was all that could be, wherever she was, she was all that could be, the door to reality, the way to truth and power and—

"You're staring," she said between gulps.

The monk blinked again. "Oh, uh, apologies." His hand closed into a fist at his side, the nails digging into his palm, reminding him that he was still there. "The, uh, declension of the youngsters has gotten to me, it seems."

"So you find me pretty?"

Immerwahr glanced at her, into her eyes, into himself reflected there. He spoke with a dry throat: "Th-that is not what…" He broke his gaze and looked again upon the bloodied tatters which constituted her clothes. He said, "What happened to you?"

The girl lowered the canteen. "I have been busy."

"Busy? Busy doing what?"

"Picking shrooms," she said with a smile. "And making friends."

"Well, these must be terrible friends for you to look like this!"

The girl strode past the monk and went to a window. She pointed toward the militia and said, "What are those men doing?"

Immerwahr straightened up. He did not wish to stare at her but did take a glance at her back: the windowpane shone a blinding light, the sun brighter than he recalled it ever being, and the girl a stark black in that sublimity, silhouetted against a firmament of glowing sunlight as though her entire shape were encased in beat gold. She turned round and her face stole out of the darkness, her eyes flashing through and the monk hurriedly looked away.

"Th-that's our militia," Immerwahr stammered. Keeping his eyes to the window and looking above her, he approached. He knocked a stool over but did not stop to right it. He slowly stepped before the window, wiping sweat from his pate and palms. "We have decided that the best way to defend the town is through a militia."

"Not by hiring sellswords?"

"No... not by hiring sellswords..."

"How about a witch hunter, then?"

"A witch hunter," Immerwahr said with a soft laugh. "A witch hunter is no sellsword. Such a man is occupied by other curiosities." The monk swallowed, his throat dry and crackling. "J-just as his vocation's title implies."

"I see," the girl said. "And are these men of yours any good at fighting?"

The monk mistakenly met her eyes again. Even from the side, even from just a rim of her colors, he was enraptured, and in the slight curve of a pupil he could see himself staring, catching himself in the reflection like a wayward Immerwahr, animalistic in his curiosities.

"Monk," she said.

"Ah, apologies," Immerwahr said, looking away. "Y-yes, the militia is new, but it's getting better with each and every day. What they currently lack in armor and weapons they make up for in confidence and courage."

The girl stared out the window. "Interesting."

The monk cleared his throat. "Are you not from around here?"

"I am not."

"Oh, did you escape Marsburg?"

"I come from Sommerwein. My name is Claire."

"A beautiful name, that one."

"Thank you."

"Now, you wouldn't be the princess of Sommerwein, would you?" Immerwahr said with a soft smile.

"I am."

"You are—" Immerwahr paused and laughed again. "Wait, you are? Oh, you're just fooling, I see. A 'jake' as the laity would say."

"Ah, finally," Claire said, raising up on her tiptoes as her eyes narrowed to some sight beyond the windowpane. "My friend has finally arrived."

The monk followed her stare. He said, "Someone has come with you?"

"Yes. You must understand, I wasn't sure if my orders could be followed this far out. I am quite excited at this development."

"What? What are you talking about? Orders? Where is this friend of yours? I should talk with them."

"He's right there," Claire said, her fingertip against the windowpane.

The monk could not see the girl's friend. He said, "Is he in the woods?"

"Yes. There. Beyond those bunkhouses. Standing in the bushes."

"I don't..."

The monk leaned in, pressing his nose against the glass.

'Hiyah!' the militia cheered. 'Hiyah!'

"I still don't see anyone..."

'Hiyah! Hiyah!'

Claire smiled. "Don't worry. He's coming. I told him to."

'Hiyah! Hiyah! Hiyah! Hiyah! Hiyah!'

"I'm not seeing—oh," Immerwahr paused. "Oh, by the old gods."

Past the militia training, past the peasants walking the paths, down the alley between bunkhouses, and into the trees, he saw it. The creature stood at the treeline, black fur, grey claws, white canines, its doglegs bending its posture into a hulking curl, muscled arms sawing back and forth just above the ground, the palms large enough for a child to sit in for a swing. Its nostrils puckered as it snorted the air and whatever it smelled gave cause for its maw to slide back, quivering and frothing and dripping.

"There he is!" Claire said, smiling and clapping. "There he is!"

"By the old gods," Immerwahr said. The monk pushed against the windowpane. "Fritz! Look out!"

The direwolf cleared the buildings with such speed that a swirl of leaves and dust spiraled behind it and hanging laundry whipped off their lines as though caught in a sudden storm. Hackles bristling, the creature made a mighty leap and sailed into the town center, legs stretched behind it, mighty claws forward, their crescents as sharp and long as any pickaxe.

Fritz turned to face the monk's shop. "Immerwahr?" he said. The militia captain drew his eyes to the store, gazing upon the monk in the windowpane as one would gaze upon the godliness to which the monk gave report, framed by the tint of sunlight struggling through the trees, and there in the sprites of faded light stood a shrunken silhouette of a girl smiling, her skin was of brilliant white with a set of eyes gleaming above like pearled diviners set in some scryer's ivory bowl, and Fritz thought her peculiar, and then the direwolf's claw punched through his skull and emptied out his eyes and brains unto its talons like a spiraling abortion of all that a man truly is, and the man's gullet and lungs were ripped out of his chest wheezing and sputtering, and the rest of the militiamen flinched as blood and teeth splashed across their faces, and they gazed in shocked stares at Fritz who had ceased to be even so much as recognizable within the blink of an eye.

"My newest friend," Claire said, her eyes agleam. "Watch him play."

The militia raised their weapons like drunken sailors would raise oars to fight a hurricane, and the direwolf's hackles bristled and it straightened up like a dark cloud swollen with blood, growls for thunder, claws and teeth for lightning, and there it set itself a storm upon the men: claws carving with waves of red trailing in their wake, the beast swimming through men, drowning them in its own frenzy. Immerwahr watched in horror as the direwolf slashed and sliced and mauled, every span of its movement cutting through the men like a scythe through grass. All the same, the militia tried to attack it like bees to a bear eating their hive, and in return they spun away armless, faceless, headless.

"Run!" Immerwahr screamed. "Run, you fools! Run! *Ruuun!*"

One man speared the direwolf in the back. The monster bolted upright in snarling pain, then wheeled around, ripping the spear out of the man's hands. Yelping, the man fell to the ground, covering himself, and the direwolf promptly stomped downward and skull shards exploded into the air. Growling, the direwolf turned and took the spear from its back and threw it into the sky. The wound, about as brief and painful as a jester's insult to a king, still yet spurred a majestic rage of response: the direwolf accelerated its assault, rapidly drawing down on men in pounces, one to the next, using maw and claw to leave each man in a state of instant ruin.

The monk's forehead rested against the windowpane. "Run... please..."

Finally, there were but two men shoulder to shoulder, and they nodded at one another and charged forth. The direwolf drove its claws through one man's face and ripped his skull in half, so speedy a death that his legs carried on a few steps without him, and the second man screamed and drove forward with his spear only for this assault to be parried like nothing more than a child's curiosity, and the man was snatched up by the beast's claws, hefted overhead, and promptly torn in half, legs going one way, the torso another, and the direwolf in between roared beneath the crimson shower.

All that remained now were the rest of the townspeople.

Immerwahr stepped away from the window as their screams erupted. Blood splattered across the window and clumpier elements clattered against the walls. In the rear of the store, a window shattered and an old man desperately clambered in and emerged between the shelves, slinking out of the shadows with his arms supinated at his sides, the flesh there shorn and glistening with burrowed glass. More people poured into the storeroom and they emerged from it as a mindless mass, spilling onto the floor, latching onto one another, arms and legs entwined, clambering like a horde of rats from a farmer's pitchfork.

"Monk!" someone screamed. "Help us!"

"Pray to the old gods!"

"Pray to them!"

Immerwahr looked at the throng of townspeople, and as he did their eyes turned forward and widened and they shrieked in horror.

The monk turned back to the front of the store.

Claire stood between the shelves, and behind her the direwolf ducked under the door and squeezed itself into the room. It snorted great draws of breath and it shook itself like a dog and blood fanned out, spraying against the ceilings and shelves and floor. Suddenly, the crowd beside Immerwahr shrieked again and in their clumped shape they rolled away from the nearest window. He glanced out to see a giant, snakelike face staring through the pane, and then it passed, a long, scaled tail hissing as it slipped out of view.

"Please excuse my intrusion," Claire said.

Immerwahr jumped backward, knocking himself into his countertop. The girl approached, walking gently out of the massive shadow of the direwolf which stood in firm, hulking obedience.

Claire arrived at the monk's hip and stared up at him, and he down at her, himself once again locked into that world jailed behind her eyes, except now a shape of himself was trapped there, banging its fists against the invisible enclosure, screaming for him to turn away.

"I wish to ask of you a favor, holy man," the girl said. She had a vial in hand and slowly held it up, its yellowed contents fuming in gentle wisps. "Can you do me a favor?"

A sting pried into the monk's nose, the yellow wisps rising from the vial coursing into his lung and warming them. Suddenly, he felt a profound sense of pride and charity. He thought the warmth in his chest must be what it felt like for a knight to kneel to their lord, the day's duty properly fulfilled.

Immerwahr smiled. "You ask of me a favor?"

"Yes, a favor," Claire said. "Tell me: where is the witch hunter?"

"Richter is no longer here…"

"No, don't call him that. Right, now, I want you to call him by his proper name," Claire said, and she raised up on her tiptoes and placed her small hand upon the monk. "You do know his proper name, don't you?"

Though it was but the girl's arm, the monk thought he felt a sword balance against his shoulder, the infinite lordship which weighted it there washing over him. As the crowd of peasants gasped again, the monk kneeled before the girl. He said, "I know his name, yes." He looked up, his whole body shaking. He dared not look in her eyes. He tried to fight the feelings off, he tried to use his resolve in the old gods to maintain some semblance of self. But then the girl's fingers graced his chin, and with the strength of a butterfly's wings they lifted his head until he could do nothing but stare into her eyes again. Weeping, the monk said: "I know where the Wight is going."

"Oh, do not cry," Claire said, wiping away a tear with one hand, and with the other striking a yellow dash of powder on the man's pate. "Be proud." She looked up at the terrified crowd of bloodied peasants. She threw her arms wide, casting a spray of more powder which landed upon their clumped number. "You should all be very proud!"

Immerwahr shrank to the floor. His vision blurred. Behind him, he heard the voices of the laity, their words falling upon him like flowers, rinsing away the pungency of blood, the rot of insides, the mud, the air, the beast. He saw his shelves fall away, tilting like pews being laid to rest, and the girl stood between them, arms wide, receptive to the peoples.

And they met her:

"Oh, are we proud!"

"Tell us what to do!"

"All the world is blessed!"

"We will do as you command!"

Claire put her hands to Immerwahr's cheeks. She smiled at him.

The monk closed his eyes. He felt his heart rise in his chest. If she were a newborn, she was his. His to protect. His to nurture. As an extension of him as his own hands and feet, as an extension of his life as his own breath, his own heartbeat. He bent his head low.

"For what just cause," he said, "shall we be proud?"

"Because I am going to kill the one they call the Wight," she said. "And you are *all* going to help."

Chapter 16. The Hovel.

"Why me?"

Richter stopped. The forest fanned out before him. Endless, ready to be explored. Under better times, enjoyed even. He turned. "You say something?"

Berthold the miller cleared his throat. "I just mean, why did you pick me? I'm new. You barely know me."

"Just watch your corners," Richter said.

"Right," Berthold said, clenching his spear tightly. "Of course."

The captain slid past a thin rail of a tree, pausing briefly to look left and right. Here the forest's trees had started to become lean, pillared amongst the thicker variants, and no doubt the further north they got the slimmer the trees would all become. Between those two types of trees, thick and thin, bushy and railed, it was no doubt the sweet spot for any brigand. He thought if he were a runagate bandit looking for vengeance, this would be just the place to do it. Of course, he also knew that Immerwahr was right, that Kantorek likely fled out of the area entirely and went looking for work elsewhere. But...

Never let idiocy surprise you, Carsten's voice came to mind. *A fool's determination is a quality to be in awe of.*

"If you're wondering why I chose you," Richter said as he started carving a circle into a tree trunk. He stepped back and nodded. "It's because you said you're fast. That's all there is to it."

"Alright then." Berthold nodded back.

"And you *are* fast, right?"

"Fairly spry, aye." The miller kicked out one leg and then sported the

[224]

other, giving his thigh a sound clap. "And spryer yet when I need to be."

"Good."

The miller adjusted his spear and shield, clacking them together as he fumbled them about. He cleared his throat again. "So… I've heard some things about, uh, you."

"I'm sure you have."

"Mostly just idle chatter from the fella that got his face smashed in."

"His name is Quinn."

"Yeah, Quinn. The tonguewagger. He doesn't seem to like you much."

"We don't get along, that is true."

"Yet you saved him anyway?"

Richter stopped at another tree and marked it. He said, "Aye," and continued on.

"Mind if I ask why?"

"He's probably the best fighter we have," Richter said. He turned. "But you don't dare ever tell him I said, that or tell Dahlgren, for that matter."

"Alright," Berthold said and he walked a few more steps and, seeming to end some internal conversation, said it again: "Alright."

In a spell of quiet they traversed the woods, keeping an eye to a little path of dust where the Ancient Road used to be. Only the occasional quarry stone gave any evidence of its existence. Trees now sprouted right through its original path, wooden pillars for ivory majesty. But beneath Richter's feet is what occupied his attention. There, traces of a rotund element had passed through, hints of what the beast slayer believed to be a nachzehrer.

"So…" Berthold said. "Is it true you used to be a witch hunter?"

Richter stopped again and looked back.

The miller held his hands up. "Sorry, I should be spry, not pry! Heh, ahh… apologies, sincerely."

Richter leaned forward and Berthold took a step back. The captain drove a knife into another tree and started marking it. As he carved, he looked at the miller and nodded. "Aye. I was a witch hunter. I hunted for a guild in Marsburg before the siege."

"Mind me asking how you ended up running a sellsword company?"

"Same way I ended up a witch hunter," Richter said. He nodded with a brief smile. "And probably the same way you ended up a sellsword."

"Just sorta fell into it, huh."

"Aye." Richter sheathed the knife and nodded toward the rest of the forest, bushes aplenty obscuring close and far. "You keep stopping to chat like this and a brigand is gonna walk up and pick your nose with a dagger."

"Right," Berthold said and again he brought his armaments close to his chest. "No more talking."

The two walked for a time, the crunch of leaves underfoot, the groan of tree trunks at their ears, birds occasionally fluttering overhead. Richter paused every so often to mark another tree, the placement between the marks themselves just long enough that he could see from one to the other as guidance on the way out.

A forest's constant stream of trees of identical size and shape makes fertile ground for even the most outlandish of constructions to seemingly appear out of nowhere, and indeed Richter came to a sudden stop as the forest gave way to a clearing and an entire two-story building dwelling right in its middle. Berthold bumped into the back of him, clattering his gear again.

"Whoa," Berthold said as he gazed at the building.

Richter grabbed the man and yanked him down, both men crouching behind brush. "Quiet," he said.

The structure sat just off to the side of where the Ancient Road used to run. Its foundation was made of large stone slabs that would be horrid to drag through the woods, suggesting of course that it had been built there long ago when perhaps there wasn't even a forest there to begin with. But however old the foundation was, the rest of it was new: wooden walls, cleancut soffits, a wooden porch with wooden handrails. Despite all the renovations, the front door swung askew on one good hinge, the metal squalling as the wind tilted the frame back and forth.

Berthold said, "What is it?"

"Not sure," Richter said. "Immerwahr's maps mentioned places like this existed along the road. Maybe an abandoned tavern."

"Is it safe?"

Richter raised an eyebrow. "What do you think?"

"I don't know."

"Out here, 'I don't know' is just a *no*, understand?"

"Yeah, alright. Sorry again."

Richter moved around the brush. He immediately found what he suspected and pointed east of the structure. "Look at the tree line over there. See the shapes lumped near the trees? Those are wagon parts. Chopped up and destroyed. And there? Dead deer. Blood in the grass from there to there. Someone's been hunting in these parts and they've been doing it recently."

"But this place looks abandoned," Berthold said. "I mean look at that front door. Who in their right mind would sleep with that thing singing all through the night?"

The door squalled, swung wider than ever before, and smashed down with a wooden calp. It was indeed an annoyance, but the captain wasn't taking chances. He slowly ambled down the tree line and got a closer look at the Ancient Road. He found a signpost sitting crookedly near the path. It had been vandalized with crude stick figures fornicating all over the place. He looked past the signpost and traced the passage of the road itself, seeing it weave around the pub and bend its way back into the forest. One way toward Sommerwein, the other back toward where they had left the wagon.

"What're you seeing?" Berthold said.

Richter nodded. "I think this is a dead end from the northern way."

"You think those wagons bumbled down here and got ambushed?"

"Or they got lost like we are. Look, the river's shoreline is that way, which means the right side-paths through the forest are likely just east of here."

Berthold nodded, though his mind was not of a cartographer's. He scratched the back of his head and said, "But don't you think we should take a look?"

Richter raised an eyebrow. "Take a look at what?"

"I mean, take a look in the building there."

"What?"

"It's there so I thought…"

"What are you even talking about?" Richter said. "You want to just walk in there and look around?"

"Well—"

"Just us two?"

"Well… I thought…"

"I don't want to be heard or seen at all. We're going back to the wagon."

"Alright so it was just a thought I didn't mean to—"

"Do you have any idea how dangerous this place could be? For all we know there are brigands in there, or something worse. And if it were something worse, we'd likely be killed, that is if we're lucky. There are probably creatures nesting in the cellar and—"

Berthold pointed. "There's a kid."

"And maybe even wolves and—" Richter turned his head. "What?"

The miller pointed. "A boy. Standing right there."

Richter followed Berthold's pointing finger just in time to see a little boy running across the faded ancient road from the adjacent tree line. He made it to the pub and jaunted up the porch's steps and stopped there, looking inward, watching the broken door swing back and forth. The boy's clothes were in tatters, long strands whirling from his body. He held what appeared to be a small sword as he stared into the pub with stony determination.

"He looks hurt," Berthold said. "I think I saw a wound on his face and his clothes are slashed."

Richter kept watching. He had to be sure it wasn't Hobbs. Make sure that something hadn't happened at the wagon and here the boy was running for his life, confused, terrified, alone. But as he moved for a closer look, the boy bounded over the busted door and promptly disappeared into the building.

"Should we uh…" Berthold ran a hand against the back of his neck.

Richter swung his crossbow off his shoulder and began to load it.

The miller said, "Hey, now that I think about it, you're right. This is far too dangerous."

Richter jerked back the draw of the weapon and set its pin.

"I just," the miller continued. "I think it be best if we go snooping with the help of others. You know, do it in numbers. Do it in force, as they say. Ha-ha, you know what I mean?"

"Easy now, Berthold," Richter said, bringing the crossbow to bear. "Just like you wanted to, we're now going in."

~~~

The captain stood on the porch as the pub's broken door slipped further off its hinge and now slammed again and again, whistles of wind squeaking away from its clobbering like mice from a hound's bark. He stared into what lay beyond the door – the ungainly shapes of an abandoned pub, upturned stools, disjointed tables, a countertop with mugs, buckets and pitchers, strewn shelves, and from all of these elements cobwebs drifted, floating whisps which

[229]

strobed and glistened like lightning at the faintest hint of light.

"Webknechts," Berthold said under his breath. "Just like the beast slayer spoke of. I'd really rather not run into webknechts, captain…"

"Quit it," Richter said, shaking his head. "You just learned that word and now you see it everywhere. Look. These are just small cobwebs."

The miller shook his head right back. He said, "You're not a beast slayer, you don't know what you're talking about."

"I suppose that's true. But these look like old webs to me."

"Old webs, small webs. Captain, think! A spider is young and small when it starts. But then it grows! And grows! The big chonker is probably stamping around in the cellar or maybe it's up in the rafters ready to lunge!"

Richter looked at the miller. "Chonker?"

"Ehh, yeah, my father used to call big stalks of wheat 'chonkers', just some old thing. Look, let's go get the rest of the company, yeah? I know you're the captain and all, but I'm just being honest that I don't feel good about this place."

"A child just ran in there and you yourself said he was hurt," Richter said. "You want to leave him?"

"I said he *maybe* had wounds on his face…" Berthold licked his lips and then sighed. "Alright. Fark. You are paying me well enough to die in some wretched pub, I suppose risking life and limb is a part of the agreement."

"You're not going to die here," Richter said. "Just fetch me a torch from your bag."

The miller nodded. He turned, setting his spear and shield on the porch, and started picking through his satchel. He took out a torch wrapped in twine and cloth and grass made for rushlights, thick and bristly. Richter nodded again, gesturing that the miller's work was not finished and the man apologized as he returned to the satchel and drew out some flint and metal and he started sending embers onto the torch's bulb until finally one spark caught. A small fire grew and Berthold held the torch up and blew on it, his face carrying a hint of orange. He held the torch out, his eyes in as much awe of it as no doubt the first men were.

"First time lighting a torch?" Richter said.

"Yeah."

"Well, one's sufficient." Richter took it and nodded. "You stay out here."

"Oh, thank the old gods. What should I do?"

"If you see anything, scream, and scream loud. I need to hear it, understand?"

"What should I scream?"

"Just a scream should suffice, but if you find a moment to scream out a bit of detail so that I know what the issue is that might help me just as well."

"And if it's coming after me?"

"Scream while running."

"Alright. Which way should I run?"

"Preferably the opposite direction of that which is chasing you."

"Ah, right. Of course." Berthold nodded. "And same for you, right? You'll scream if you run into something in there?"

"Oh, I'll yell, and I would very much prefer it if you came and helped, but I won't hold it against you if you don't," Richter said. He smiled. "Because I'll likely be dead."

"By the old gods don't say shit like that," Berthold said. He nodded confidently. "You run into trouble and I will be there, I promise."

"Alright, but if that's the case…" Richter pointed at the ground. "You might want to pick those up."

Berthold looked down and laughed as he bent over and picked up his spear and shield, holding them slackly against his chest like a statue of a guard masoned by one who'd never seen a guard to begin with. "Right." He said, smiling nervously. "Can't forget these."

"Keep that shield tight and your eyes open," Richter said. "Don't want you out here getting caught by some brigand with a bow."

The miller held the shield to his chest. "Yessir."

"I don't plan on being in there long," Richter said. He looked at Berthold again, the miller standing awkwardly, tilting his spear to and fro. "Berthold."

"Yessir?"

The captain clapped the man on the shoulder. "I'll be right back."

"Yessir, and I'll be right here, sir."

~ ~ ~

Torch in one hand, sword in the other, Richter stepped into the pub. The floorboards creaked underfoot and as the sound emptied into the dark, he swung the torch, chasing sounds with light for places formerly dark could be newly dangerous. But nothing drew upon him, nothing lunged, nothing fired.

A stark rigidity shaped the pub's emptiness, the torch's light needling through a fallen chandelier and laddering through stacks of chairs. When he looked to the bar, the torch's orange hue cascaded against the metal bands of dusty kegs, casting off their metal rings fiery circlets as though he had set eclipses about the room. He lifted the torch to get a look at the ceiling, half-expecting Berthold's feared spiders to be caught halfway down in their descent, spindly legs sprawled, fat abdomens glistening and silky, fangs dripping poisons. Instead, he merely spied empty rafters and a mottled ceiling.

He swung the torch down, the firelight lurching and reeling as though timid to what it itself might reveal. Even only being there but a few moments, the captain already knew that the building was no place of men, for men corrupted all things and the dark was no different. With every move the shadows receded and regained their dominion in soft penumbras that erred to and fro as though the dark itself treated Richter with prickling caution.

As he walked further in, he took his eyes to the floor and its dust. There he found little footprints. Bootless. Toes and soles cratering and volleying the dust. Distance between each print suggested some hurry.

"Find anything?" Berthold said.

Richter swung his sword as if the words were a lunging animal.

The miller, though he stood distantly in the doorway, leaned back. "Whoa, captain."

"Stay outside," Richter said. "And watch the damn yard."

"Yessir." He paused and turned. "Sorry sir."

"The yard, Berthold."

"Yessir."

Catching his breath, Richter sheathed his sword and hoisted his crossbow. He returned his gaze to the prints in the dust. He followed the traces into a kitchen, his firelight peeling across pantries and glassing reflective fires across hanging pots and pans, his silhouette blinkered and warped in the curved metals. But the boy was nowhere to be seen. He thought perhaps he had hidden in a cabinet or pantry, but the footprints did not go there. Instead, they went into the middle of the floor and disappeared.

"Now that's interesting," Richter said.

He crouched beside the last print and looked down at a slit in the wood that ran a full body's length. A black latch sat in the middle. He set back on his haunches and pulled the latch and swung the giant door up and away, himself rising to handle its size like some old rector before his secreted vault. He gently lowered the door against the kitchen countertops and then stared at a dripping, moss-strewn chute with rounded stone stairs descending like some grey tongue into the throat of the earth.

"Sonuvabitch," Richter said. "If that boy can go down there, so can you."

A soft drip plinked from deep in the dark, and that was all. He crouched and eased himself down the steps like a blind man in a stranger's home, stopping and listening at each landing before gingerly moving on to the next. A sconce emerged from the dark, its gated maw broken and jagged. Beside it, scratch marks ran through the earthen rock, each one deep enough to set his fingers in them. Looking down, he saw similar cuts and divots in the stone stairs. He told himself they were old tumbril marks. But he knew better.

Richter turned. "Berthold?" he said, but the miller wasn't there.

He stared at the cellar's door, thinking and listening, fighting some inner battle about what he should do – and if the marks in the stones were just old daytaler etchings. He thought of what else could make such marks. He remembered the direwolf's trace near Kantorek' camp. If it was down here, surely it would have heard him by now and he would already be dead.

The captain held himself to those stairs and took a breath.

And then he continued, sliding further and further down, the light of the cellar's opening fading behind him, and the darkness swallowing him up from below, his torch not even strong enough to flare his own feet. But he finally found a dirt floor, his boots crunching a cold soil. Despite the chill, a lingering sogginess hung in the air, and hanging moss dabbed his face and neck.

Pushing through the moss, Richter said, "Boy. *Boy.*"

His torch flickered and he air prickled his outstretched arm and a sleek blackness slipped from one shadow into the next. Feet pitter-pattering and slapping soil. Richter instinctively threw his arm out to catch the boy, but the child dodged away, being absorbed into the darkness like two orbs of water colliding, instant collusion, instant alliance.

"Boy!" he shouted.

The captain swung the torch, for if he could not give chase certainly the light could, and there he found the boy standing not far off, his back to the captain, his eyes staring into the darkness as if in communication with it, his little fingers clenching a sword not at all the wooden toy that Hobbs wielded, but one of old iron and older designs, with a rounded pommel and ornamentations that spiraled about the handle. As the captain got closer, he could see the boy's body shaking and trembling.

"Easy," Richter said. He raised the torch and confirmed the boy was not Hobbs and a pang of relief fell over him and he cringed that he had such a selfish thought. He cleared his throat and said, "Easy there. Are you hurt? Can you hear me?"

The boy turned around. Blue tattoos arced over his forehead and red ones crescented in the narrows of his cheeks, his hollow and gaunt skull starkly caged in colors. He stared at Richter like a fish out of water, eyes wide, mouth open and chewing on air.

"It's fine, it's alright," Richter said, setting his crossbow down and waving the boy forward. "It's safe. I won't hurt you."

The boy took a step back. He pointed into the darkness and grunted.

"I can help you," Richter said. "Have you been hiding down here all by yourself? Is this your home?"

The boy glanced at Richter, and then back at the darkness. He pointed his sword toward the darkness and grunted again.

"*Hargravard*," the boy said. He tapped his little chest. "Hargravard."

"What?"

Staring back at Richter, the boy took up his hands and hooked fingers into his cheeks, stretching the skin back until he bared the full horseshoes of his teeth. He stuck out his tongue and said, "*Ehm Hargravard.*" His fingers snapped out of his cheeks, slapping his lips together. His thumb slowly sliced across his own throat. "I slay it now," he said with growling emphasis as if he were saying the words for the first time ever. "I slay it now, *ehm Hargravard.*"

Richter stared at the darkness of the cellar stretching ahead of him.

"Boy," he said. "We need to go."

He stared at the darkness because something was in it. He didn't know what it was, but something was clearly standing in the well of black and he knew it was there as well as he knew anything else in the world entire, just as he knew that the darkness of men carried a sense of familiar disturbance, so too did the darkness of creatures, and when men and monsters occupied that same blackness, a mere torch rarely granted the former any fortune. He knew something was there just as a child knows something sets behind a locked door. And whatever was in the dark was staring back.

"We need to go," Richter said, holding his hand out. "We need to go right now."

The boy shook his head and turned around. He put his hands to his ancient sword and shouted into the darkness: "*Hargravard!*"

"No," Richter said. He snapped his fingers. "Now, boy! We need to go! There is something there! I can see it standing right there!"

A rise in temperature suddenly furled over Richter. Dust pillared down the cellar walls and the moss twisted and prickled his face again. He looked back up the stairs, finding a dim light winking back at him.

"Captain?" Berthold hailed from the entrance. "I know you said to stay outside but—"

"Berthold do not come down here!" Richter yelled back. "Stay up there!"

"Something wrong, captain?"

The boy screamed.

The captain wheeled back around and fell against the wall, his torch shimmering crude, spindly shadows as a giant grey hand spawned out of the black. Richter grabbed the boy and pulled him over just as the nachzehrer's claws snapped closed, its nails clacking like old bones. As the boy fell against him, Richter's torch wobbled and out of the dark it splashed a strobe of grey, glistening flesh, the discolored skin stretching away, some vague shape of the creature itself turning in the dark, groaning as it lurched after fresh meat.

Scraping along the ground, the nachzehrer's arm slowly rolled over and swung back in another try. Richter pressed against the wall as he pointed the crossbow down and fired, nailing the monster's palm to the ground. A terrible growl let out and the hanging moss fluttered to the ceilings and a blast of heat washed past the captain. Deep, guttural chortling belched through the cellar and dust piled down from above.

Richter turned and pushed the boy up the stairs and the boy went scuttling on all fours like a dog. Upstairs, Berthold yelped at the surprise springing from the cellar and there was more yelling and the sound of pots and pans falling and rattling.

The captain turned around to see the claws scraping left to right like a hand aimlessly searching under the bed. Its fingers swung toward Richter and he coiled himself before jumping over its wrist. When he landed, he fell back against the steps. Turning over, he watched as the hand unfurled its fingers as though to take Richter to a dance. Screaming, the captain unsheathed Adelbrecht's sword and drove it forth, the torchlight mirrored in the blade, orange and orange, flickering and flickering before that gleaming steel sank into the nachzehrer's knuckles. The beast screamed and the hand snapped backward in retreat and Richter let go of his torch to keep hold of his sword, the blade unsheathing from the knuckle in a sickening squelch.

"Captain!" Berthold's voice was closer, his footsteps awkwardly shuffling down the stairs. "Captain I'm coming!"

As he sank against the stairs, Richter watched as his torch sparked and hissed into the cellar's depths. Slowly, the orange glow bobbed and rolled and Richter watched as its little light crept over something that could not be.

"Captain!"

Berthold was right over the top of him. Richter turned just in time to see the miller sliding down the steps, dust and rock crackling past him as his booted heels found no purchase.

"I told you to stay upstairs!" Richter yelled. "Is the boy up there? Did you get him?"

As the miller slapped through hanging moss, he landed on Richter's back, his head perched on his shoulder like a bird, his legs strewn out to either end, both men sledding down together in brief and awkward momentum.

Berthold's eyes went wide. He pointed. "Ohhh what in the hells is that! What *is* that!"

Richter turned.

Finally rolling to a stop, the torch washed its light over a horse's head on the ground. Its eyes slowly blinked and looked at Richter. Seeing the captain, the horse whinnied and a mangled leg slapped forth, a crude fetlock scratching against the cellar floor. Above the horse lurched a fat and bulbous belly, greased and rotted with pustules and stretched whitely thin, and the torch's light disastrously went further up, revealing the horse's body limp against the pallid gut, and further up a mouth began, a maw split into four long sleeves of tentacled lips lapping over the horse's bottom half, the slick tendrils licking and lathering the haul, wriggling undulations that sucked the meal into the outstretched mouth, bringing the horse's head up off the ground where it whinnied one final time as the nachzehrer's sinewy lips sealed its meal for engorgement, its beastly jaw unhinging like a snake, its teeth cracking as they jutted aside, and as the beast gargled, the torch slowly lifted to the nachzehrer's skull, its bone akin to a blacksmith's anvil wreathed in flesh, four goatlike horns curling away from where ears should be, and two grey eyes sloshing as they looked at Richter, the pupils murkily afloat in sagging eyeballs.

"Captain!" Berthold screamed. "Oh by the old gods!"

Richter turned around. "Berthold, go—"

The miller was already halfway up the stairs screaming as he went. The captain himself made some noise never to be replicated in the company of others and then he, too, stole up the cellar stairs.

But halfway up, his boots started to slip on the wet stairs and he found himself sliding back down in spurts and jaunts. He threw his hand to the wall, his fingernails scratching along the earthen rock, scratching along those claw marks, his fingertips finding just enough purchase in the groove to keep him from falling all the way down.

"H-hey!" Richter yelled. "Berthold, help!"

A faint light from the cellar's entrance glimmered above, the moss blackly limp in the scantness of his illuminated escape, and then it was gone. As he gritted his teeth in anger, he felt the earthen rock tremble and vibrate against his clenched, lifesaving grip.

On instinct, the captain looked down. He found the nachzehrer wriggling up the first step, its belly slapping upon the slab, the horse lolling from the maw like a brown tongue, sliding in and out on a froth of saliva and guts and blood, a jutting bulb of melted muscle and bone, half-digested and decayed with the organs a sludge, and then the beast vomited it out entirely, the horse mashing into the ground like spilt stew and breaking apart in chunks totally mysterious from the whole, and the nachzehrer's shape sank inward like a nobleman might suck in his gut to fit through a door. Its actual tongue unfurled, oaring side to side as it slapped up the steps.

"I got you!"

Suddenly, Berthold's hands swept under Richter's arms. The captain found himself being dragged upwards, his boots scratching the steps, raining dust. His hands instinctively went outward, one hand still dragging along the claw marks along the walls. Through the moss, through the damp air, down below he watched his torch's light slowly fade and with it the creature itself faded back into its darkness, the last of it a dire pupil jostling in sagging murk like a bowl carrying a dead fish. And then the two men turned in unspoken unison and barreled up the final cellar steps and bailed into the kitchen like two rats scramming from a scullery maid.

"Ahh shit!" Berthold screamed, slamming against the far wall's countertops. "What the fuck was that? What the fuck! What—"

The floorboards bulged, cracking in their centers and spraying splinters into the walls. Both men looked at each other. They then slung their arms out for balance as the ground bowled out beneath their feet and the entire room expanded from its center. Pots and pans twisted off their hooks and clanged to the floor and cupboards bellied outward with their doors swinging and clapping. As the clattering filled the air, a claw burst through the floorboards and sliced forward, four ragged nails squalling as they peeled through the woodwork. Berthold covered his eyes in horror. Richter grabbed the miller and threw him out of the kitchen. Behind them, the room collapsed into the cellar, the kitchenware crashing and sliding into the pit, wood snapping, the ceiling breaking apart and streaming furniture down from the floor above.

"Go!" Richter said, pushing Berthold away. "Go go go!"

Together, the two men hastily sped back outside as noises garbled and snarled in the collapsing kitchen behind them. Back on the porch, Richter spotted the miller's gear: his rucksack, as well as his spear and shield.

"Ah shit, man, I forgot those!" Berthold said, clutching his own head.

Richter dug through the rucksack and retrieved another torch. He lit it in a near instant and swung its flames to the doorframe, brushing the fire over the wood like a hurried painter. As the flames started to spread, he stepped back and heaved the torch into the building. He saw a glimmer of a hulking, black shape shouldering out of falling debris. Glowing yellow in the light, a pallid eye turned its sight toward him. Richter briefly met its gaze, and then he grabbed the miller and fled back from whence they came.

~ ~ ~

"So what is this?" Quinn said, sitting on the wagon's tailgate.

Hobbs sat beside him and held up the wooden camel. "It's a camel."

The thief took it out of the boy's hands. "Is it now?"

"Hey!" Hobbs yelled, giving chase.

"I'll give it back," Quinn said, then he turned and pretended to throw it into the trees.

Hobbs nearly jumped across the thief's lap as he screamed: "No don't!"

The thief returned the hand, camel still in tow. "I'm only fooling, boy." He gave the toy back. "A camel, huh?"

"Aye," Hobbs said, almost nursemaiding the toy. "That's what Immerwahr said, anyway."

"Damn thing's shaped like my sack—uh, I mean, what's it do?"

The boy tilted it. "I don't know. Maybe it slays dragons."

"Why or even how in the hells would that thing slay dragons?"

Hobbs shrugged. "Dunno. You asked. That's my answer."

"Worst answer. Ain't even an answer it's a guess. And a terrible one."

"If you say so."

"It ain't slaying no farking dragons," Quinn said. "It's gotta be doing something else."

"I'm sure it does something. Strange things usually have unusual purpose." The boy held it out in both hands. He nodded. "And I've never seen anything that looks quite so strange."

Quinn thought for a moment. "I suppose in some parts looking strange is doing something."

"If so, you must be doing a lot!" Hobbs said.

Leaning back, the thief said, "Best watch that smart mouth of yers, boy, or I'll widen it ear to ear."

"S-sorry."

The thief shook his head with disappointment. He said, "Dammit, kid, I'm only jaking, you little farker. This is why I don't like talkin' to kids, you lil' shitters take things so seriously."

Quinn hopped off the tailgate.

"Where you going?" Hobbs said.

"To take a shit."

"Again?"

"What do you mean 'again'? Are you counting my squats?"

"No, I just—"

"What are you, the lawman of shitting? Do I need papers to go?"

"No…"

Quinn stuck his hand into the backside of his pants, and then drew it back out. He sniffed it and said, "Ah yeah, I got the paperwork right here. C'mere boy. Right of passage, right of passage!"

Hobbs squealed and retreated into the wagon.

At the company's front, Thomas, Gernot, Minnesang, and the donkey stood watching the road.

"You alright in there?" Thomas said, looking over his shoulder.

"I'm fine," Hobbs said, but his voice quickly went elsewhere: "Go away, Quinn! Go do your business!"

Thomas leaned. He saw the boy at the front of the wagon, one leg out, one leg in. Beyond him, Quinn was walking into the trees, strutting for the gods knew what reason.

Minnesang leaned over and said, "Hey there, you've known the Wight long, right?"

"Long?" Thomas said. He knew Richter longer than anyone save for Hobbs, having known the witch hunter since he stepped foot into Louis von Walddorf's council room. Of course, in that same moment Thomas betrayed Richter from the start, spying on him for the burgomeister, aiding his enemies in the Free Company, and aiding that strange pale man and his scribal counterpart, the two who seemed to desire the whole world as their nemesis. Thomas nodded. "I've known him for a bit, sure. But you should know he prefers to just be called Richter."

"Not the Wight, and not the man from Dagentear?"

"It bothers him, so I try and avoid it."

"But he is the Wight, and he is Richter von Dagentear?"

"You keep asking that," Thomas said. "Were you dropped on your head as a child?"

"A time or two," Minnesang said. The jester jerked back, bringing his cap'n'bells to a soft jingle. "And you're Thomas, right?"

"Yeah."

"Always?"

"Uh, what?"

"I mean, did you ever go by another name?"

Thomas looked around. He said, "Uh, no. Of course not."

"Well that is interesting. And you've known the Wight a long while, too. Sorry, I mean Richter." Minnesang leaned back, his eyes staring keenly at Thomas, his face rounded by his large jester cap, the looping bells seemed to ensconce him in the grip of a blue claw. Finally, he broke a smile and pointed up at the hat. "Do you like my cap'n'bells?"

"Uh, it is annoying. And loud."

"That it is!"

"I'm Gernot, by the way," the butcher suddenly said, leaning into the conversation. "In case you were wondering."

The jester's smile faded. He said, "I was not. And you've a boring complexion, butcher."

"I don't know what complexion means, but I know what boring is."

"And?"

Gernot shrugged. "Ye ain't wrong, but you should know, I killed five brigands that last battle." He proudly held up his hand and mouthed: *five*.

Thomas nodded. "Congratulations."

"Aye, thank ye, thank ye," Gernot said. "I'd never killed a man before. They were my first, second, third, fourth... it all just got easier and easier. It's like when you first start killing chickens, the moment before you chop their heads off you think, what is this? No truly, what is this? I'm seeing something in this here animal I ain't ever seen before, but then you just do it and once that head is gone and the blood is going and the creature's just dead there, well, it's just a chicken again. What questions you had are gone. You know?"

"Hey yeah, sure," Thomas said, though he looked elsewhere, hoping his eyes would glom onto some far structure that would rope him over. As he gazed about, his eyes upon the old man and the homesteader talking.

"I've made something for you," Sophia said.

Dahlgren raised an eyebrow, but tempered his excitement: "Aye?"

"Mhmm..."

Sophia turned and brought forth the black heater shield with the white sword she painted upon it. The old man took it into his one hand and burrowed its point into his leg as he balanced it upright, gathering a good look at its front like some antique collector taking measure of an old copper plate that carried his face in some kind of new unseen reflection.

"That is some fine paintwork," he said. "Menacing colors, too."

"Turn it around."

The old man spun it.

She pointed at the shield's grip, a series of three leather loops with a triangular draw that collected all three into the center. "You can put your arm in there and cinch it tight with a single pull. If you want to loosen it, you just throw off those buckles at the flanks there and the straps will pop."

"I'll be," Dahlgren said. He slotted the shield around his nub of an arm and did as she instructed. The shield tightened to his arm like a snake around its prey. He stood up and moved it, testing where his feet were in comparison to the length and mobility of the shield-arm, and then he joined the practice with his sword-hand, wielding the weapon around the shield, opening the shield to swing his sword in side slashes and overhead chops and thrusting stabs. He drew the shield back to his chest and leveled the sword atop it, his eyes peeled over its lip like two moons over a dark horizon.

"How is it?" she said.

"Proper," the old man said, stepping into a feigned shield-bash, the air whooshing with authority, Sophia's hair lifting gently all the same. He nodded and sheathed his sword and sat back down. "Did you make this?"

"Mmm… bought a shield and painted it. The straps I did myself. Way back when, one of my sons damn near broke his leg in twain. I fashioned something for him so he could manage the daily work while it healed. Just took that same idea and, well, there you go."

"I very much appreciate it, Sophia."

The homesteader stared at the shield's straps. She nodded. "I attached it with the help of one of the ferry town's woodworkers. He did the hard part."

"It's damn near a masterwork, all told," Dahlgren said. He leaned in. "You know I'm going to kill people with this, right?"

The homesteader nodded. "In my aging wisdom, I'm starting to find new ways to romance."

"Is Quinn looking?" Dahlgren said.

"No."

"Well alright then."

The two moved close. Closer. Shadowing each other. Shadowing each other's smirking.

Suddenly, Elletrache burst from the bushes, stomping on a hobbled foot, leaves and sticks scattering about him. He belched. "Is the captain back?"

Dahlgren lowered his head with a sigh. "No. Where were you?"

"Crockett wanted to take a shit," the beast slayer said, and a moment later the paymaster came ducking out of the brush.

"Didn't think it was safe to go alone," Crockett said, his face red from either current embarrassment or very recent stress. He swept some sweat from his brow. "So, uh, thank you Trash."

"Mmm. Only reason I joined ya was cause I was about this close to ruinin' my breeks m'self." The beast slayer nodded at Dahlgren. "Yer lady's cookin' needs some attention. Damn near poison it is."

"His lady?" Crockett said.

Elletrache spat. "How is it that my one-eye sees more than your two?"

Crockett glanced at Dahlgren and Sophia. He said, "Well, I…"

The beast slayer spat again. "Ye've shit on your shoes, paymaster."

"What? Shit on my—ahh, hells. Hells!"

"Also, there yonder burns a fire."

"What?"

Elletrache tightened up his belt and threw a hand toward the skyline.

"Fire yonder," he said. "Burning."

Gobs of black smoke distantly lifted over the forest canopy. Thick, pluming, not the churning of any ordinary campfire. Thomas, Minnesang, and Gernot retreated backwards with their shields readied and their spears timidly balanced in nervous hands. Elletrache picked up his massive crossbow and Dahlgren brought his new shield to his chest and told Sophia to stay down. The company tightened its formation together.

"Something's coming!" Gernot said. "I can hear it!"

Coming from the direction of the smoke, the forest crackled, branches snapping, bushes rustling. Everyone tensed as the sounds drew close.

"If it has more than two legs, shoot it," Dahlgren said.

"Sure," Elletrache said. "But if it walks on arms and looks like a big ol' lizard, best just run."

Their weapons and shields faltered as the sellswords looked over their shoulders at the beast slayer's morale destructive comment.

Shrugging, Trash said, "I'm in debt to the old gods for one lindwurm already, I doubt they'll afford me another. Yer all free to join me in the jackpot, though."

"There it is!" Gernot suddenly shouted.

The company raised its weapons, a creak and clatter of wood and the tension of strings and the clanging of steel.

"By the old gods!" Thomas said. "I see it!"

"Hey did you guys see the—" Quinn walked out of the woods and jumped halfway out of his boots and shouted and covered his head and froze on one leg like a heron. He peeked through his fingers as the sellswords stared at him, their weapons oddly not lowering despite seeing they had been under a misapprehension. The thief shouted like an ambassador might yell up a castle's walls: "Surely you farks did not go through all that trouble of saving me just to kill me, right? This seems dramatic! I can just go, you know?"

The sellswords finally sighed and lowered their weapons.

"Sonuvabitch," Dahlgren said. "We're not going to kill you, Quinn."

"You'd better not," Richter said, suddenly coming through a bush behind the thief.

Quinn screamed again and fell on his arse.

Berthold arrived next, his face ashy and his hands empty of weapons.

"Richter!" Hobbs shouted from the wagon. "You're back!"

"Aye, Hobbs. Please stay in the wagon for a moment, alright?"

Elletrache hobbled forward. "You see somethin' out there?"

Richter nodded. "We saw the nachzehrer. It's dangerous, like you said."

"I warned you, black hat," the beast slayer said, auguring his eyepatch with a knuckle. "Well at least yer alive. How big was it?"

Berthold shouted, "It tried to eat us!"

"Oooh, a big one?"

Richter nodded again. "Aye, you could say that."

The captain leaned against the wagon and caught his breath. He told the boy to fetch him a goatskin flask of water and then drank half of it and gave the rest to Berthold.

Elletrache said, "You two kill it or naw?"

"Found it in a building's cellar," Richter said. He straightened up and looked at the clouds of smoke. "I burned the building."

"Damn," Elletrache said, shaking his head. "A big nach' like that can have a lot of parts worth a pretty crown or two. Shame for it to go to ash."

"We were a little more interested in just surviving," Berthold said.

The beast slayer threw his hands up as if to say 'wasn't there, but the point still stands.'

Dahlgren said, "Did you find any roads out of here?"

"I got a better idea," Richter said, pointing at his paymaster. "Crockett."

"Sir?"

"We got a good look at the roads over there."

"And?"

"Things aren't at all where they're supposed to be. Even if it isn't ready, I'll be needing to see that map of yours."

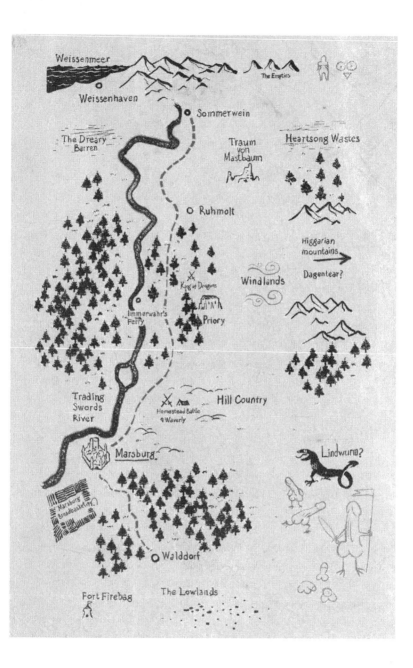

Chapter 17. Mapping.

Richter crossed his arms and lowered his head.

"Cricket!" Quinn howled, nearly doubling over with laughter. "What in the hells is this?"

"No ill will Crockett," Dahlgren said, "but that is one godawful map. I mean, you're missing so many villages. And why did you draw all those trees? How long did that even take? Just draw a circle and say it's a forest!"

Crockett stammered, "Well I—"

"And what's with the cocks?" Quinn said.

"Maybe he fancies himself to be an artist," Sophia said, though her words leaked through smirking lips.

"Yeah. Fancies himself to be a fancy artist if you know what I'm saying."

"The male member is a very difficult item to draw," Crockett said, almost pleading as if he were on trial. "I was just trying something new! We are what we are, there is nothing wrong in renumerating on stenciled replications!"

Quinn raised an eyebrow. "I don't know what half those words mean, but all I see is that you were focused entirely on the cock! On a map! What are they even doing there? Are the tips pointing the way for us? You got signage on them shafts? And why the fark is that one carrying a sword?"

"B-back in the libraries they had these scrolls filled with statuesque drawings, and we were meant to study the human body, which I did, and sometimes in my free time—"

"Draw tits!" Quinn shouted. "Draw some big fat swinging knockers like a normal man!"

"I did! Right there!"

"Where?" Quinn leaned down, staring in the upper right corner. "Those're tits?"

"Yes! And I have the, uh, rest, too."

"Oh is that a cooch?"

The thief put his nose to the page, getting a good look at the extracurricular sketches and a whiff of their implied scents.

Sophia pursed her lips. She said, "That's just a triangle and some circles."

"Actually, I can kinda see it," Quinn said, cocking his head with artistic praise. "Hm. Nice."

"Crockett," Richter said, lowering his arms and raising his head. "If you were having issues mapping the area, you should have told me."

"I thought I could handle it... eventually. The maps I have, they're from all over the place, exchanged by many hands, hard to coordinate into one, uniform and usable picture... cartography is a greater task than I realized."

Elletrache spat. "Lotta words to say we're lost."

"N-no," Crockett said. "Well... well alright, a little lost but I can fix this."

"We're neck deep in the woods and we don't know where we are," Richter said. "This is a serious problem, understand? We can't return to Immerwahr's town for help. If we stay out here too long something will find and kill us. If we wander aimlessly, either something will find and kill us, or we'll end up killing each other."

"Aye," Elletrache said. "This is a sore spot we're in here."

"Cocks are cocks, and tits are tits," Quinn said, as axiomatically as he did emphatically. "But now I'm curious, if he can't draw for shit can he count for shit? How do we know we're getting the right pay?"

"His accounting is fine," Richter said.

"Is it?"

"It is," Sophia said, suddenly drawing the eyes of every man. She nodded.

"I checked."

Quinn laughed. "What? Like you know how to count."

"She's been helping me doublecheck my work," Crockett said. "She knows her numbers."

"Does she now?" Quinn said, raising an eyebrow. "Alright woman, what is five… with… five more, uh, put onto the other five…"

"Added?" Sophia said.

"No, it's got another name. Like it's five and five more but all complicated."

"Multiplying."

"That's it! Alright, what is five… multiplicity… by five."

Sophia said, "Twenty-five."

"Mmhm, alright woman. What's twenty-five but you take away five, but! You take it away all complicated like."

Sophia sighed. "Dividing?"

"Aye! Twenty-five, divi-vi-viding by… uh… five."

"That's back to five."

"Now hold on a minute," Quinn said, holding up a finger. "Numbers go forwards and backwards? Them farkers *move*?"

Richter stepped forward. "Alright, that's enough."

"Hey, no," Quinn said, nodding to himself. "I say this is a good thing! If Cricket over here is training his replacement, pretty soon we won't need to feed his fatass. I think this is great! Cricket, you fool, you never train your replacement!"

"Is that why yer so afraid of the jester?" Elletrache said, picking behind his eyepatch. "Think he's going to replace yer joking arse?"

"Afraid? Naw. Fark Minnesang! That's right I said fark you, Minnesang. I know that ain't your real name. This fark was probably playing ditties for alley rats," Quinn said. "I simply know a fraudster when I see one."

"Excuse me," Minnesang said. Despite his childish and clinking cap, the jester gave a confident nod. "The only fraud here is an upstart thief who thinks himself daisy enough to dance with a devil. I could outjuggle and outduel you any day of the week."

Grinning, Dahlgren said, "Gonna let that slide, Quinn?"

The thief spat and nodded to the jester. "All I see is a dead man jawing."

"Much bark," Minnesang said, bowing slightly. "But so little bite."

Quinn went for his daggers. "Woof, motherfarker."

A quiet voice broke in: "Can I see the maps?"

The thief froze, his dagger halfway out of its sheath, and the jester similarly stood in place, one hand holding his cap while his freehand tilted his spear. Richter already stood between the two of them, his arms out and his mouth open to yell a halt to the matter. Now quiet furled over the lot of them, beholden to a whisper of an inquest.

Hobbs cleared his throat. "The maps... can I see them?"

"Ah, boy," Sophia said. "They have drawings you shouldn't see."

"They're naughty," Quinn said. "They're not for your virgin eyes. Although I suppose the cap'n's seen 'em so..."

Hobbs clucked his tongue and stepped up and took Crockett's map himself. He set down and spread the parchment out in both hands.

Though the map was seemingly useless, Richter found himself blurting: "Don't tear it."

"I'm not." The boy studied the map, his mouth smirking as he found the drawings. With a nod, he looked up. "Alright. Give me the other maps."

Crockett glanced at Richter, and the captain glanced back and shrugged. The paymaster nodded and handed all the maps he had to the boy. Hobbs went to his knees, taking the collection of poor recollections and fuzzy sketches, and he set there puzzling the maps together side-to-side, top-to-bottom. As an image was cobbled together, he stood up and assessed it with his hands on his hips, licking his lips in deep thought, nodding here and there.

Finally, the boy said, "I think I know where we are."

"And how'n the hells do you know that?" Elletrache said. "I'd been hunting these forests for years and even I'm a little turned around."

"The maps at the witch hunting guild," Hobbs said, looking at Richter. "Remember, you left me in the map room?"

"Aye," Richter said. "I remember. I didn't want you touching the tomes."

"Right! And when you were in the dungeons, I still obeyed what you said. 'Don't touch the books, and don't burn the place down with the candles!' But you never said stop looking at the maps. So… I spent a lot of time looking at the maps, just as you told me to. Maybe a little too much time, really. It was either the maps or spend more time cleaning Carsten's chamber pots and—"

Richter held his hand up. "Let's just keep it to the maps, alright Hobbs?"

"Alright." The boy looked back down. He pointed at the paymaster's map and said, "We can't blame Crockett because even Immerwahr's map is too tied to the happenings around his town and has so little information about the Ancient Road. It's just no helpful for traveling the long haul, you know?"

"Don't ask us questions," Richter said. "Just explain what you see."

"Alright," Hobbs said, nodding dutifully. "These other maps lean heavily on unique markers. That's only good if you're going on a hunt in a specific area and want to know how to get back to town, such as you do Trash."

The beast slayer grunted. "I suppose I don't get lost in a pocket."

Hobbs continued: "But knowing smaller areas won't get you from one town to an entirely new one, and definitely won't help you get from one region to another. At least, each map by itself can't do that, but if we put them together… and if you know enough about the details missing in between you can actually see where these side roads truly are. It's almost like a game. You just have to connect the dots! So…" Hobbs crossed his arms and looked at Crockett. "Get me some ink and a quill pen, and I'll fix this."

The sellswords stared at the boy, mouths agape.

"Is he being serious?" Sophia said.

"He's a sorcerer," Quinn said. "The weird wooden toy, his unkept hair, his knowledge. His knowledge! These are all signs. He's painting us a map to all the hells and he aims to take us there!"

"Uh, yeah, maybe Hobbs just pays attention," Thomas said. "And you know something? The boy's got a sharper wit than any lowlander I ever met."

Hobbs looked at Richter.

"Aye." Richter nodded. "Crockett, give the boy your inkwell and let's see what he can do."

~~~

The campfire crackled and the bulb of light shimmered around the sellswords, piping long shadows into the darkness beyond the camp like stakes of a black fence skewered there to protect the flame itself. Despite the gloomy dark, a certain sort of joviality had settled in. There was a spring of humor and jesting oozing from Crockett's drawings which, like a great pot of stew, the company made supple returns to for cracking jokes.

"Alright," Sophia said, hanging an actual pot of stew over the fire. "I think Crockett's suffered enough."

Each man took a scoop of Sophia's soup into a bowl. They grimaced between bites, and the homesteader frowned in disappointment, but she said nothing lest the evening's dagger-like jocosity come for her, too.

"So," Crockett said, taking a seat beside Richter. "Think we're safe here?"

Richter took a scoop of the soup into his mouth. He held it a moment, suffering, then swallowed and nodded. "Aye. While the fire Berthold and I set is likely going to attract a lot of attention, Trash believes us to be safe. He said that when the whole forest is on alert, it's best to stand pat and wait it out. The worst of the woods will ignore us and go investigate, and lesser creatures will remain where they are out of fear of the former group."

"Should I suppose we are one of those lesser creatures?"

"Probably the least of them."

Crockett stared into the fire. "And myself, the least of the least."

Richter set his spoon into the bowl. He looked at the paymaster.

"I failed," Crockett said. "Failed in front of everyone, too."

"You should be embarrassed," Richter said, laughing. "I mean, those drawings, what were you thinking?"

"For a while I was running out of parchment so I just started using the edges and…" Crockett paused, realizing the captain was staring at him. He threw a hand. "Ahh, none of that matters. It's just that ever since the fight at the homestead my head's been spinning, and I guess that was how I was dealing with it. I did not grow up around violence, Richter. The only violence I knew as a child were snowball fights and hitting each other over the head with icicles."

"That's pretty violent," Richter said. He took up the bowl of soup and took another bite. He spoke between bites: "If you're feeling down… I do have something to ask you that might cheer you up. Unless you don't know the answer, in which case I might be doing more harm than good."

Crockett straightened himself up. He nodded. "Try it."

"Do you know barbarian tongue?"

"Uh… a little."

Richter raised an eyebrow. "A little in the way you knew maps or…"

"No, I do know a little," Crockett said. The paymaster snorted and then produced a few gruff grunts with a fist to his chest followed by a long groan.

"Pox on it!" Sophia said, jumping to her feet. "My cooking is not that bad! You are all exaggerating!"

Richter held his hand up. He said, "It's alright, Sophia, the paymaster was only trying out his barbarian tongue."

Quiet fell over the camp. Even the campfire's flames seemed to huddle down, shoring themselves in the ashes.

"Barbarian?" Dahlgren said.

Elletrache put a hand to his massive crossbow. "There be savages?"

"Oh," Berthold said at the edge of the campfire. "I damn near forgot about that kid!"

"Kid?" Hobbs said.

Richter nodded at Hobbs. "Aye, we saw a kid in the woods." He then nodded at Dahlgren and Elletrache. "He had tattoos on his face and carried an ancient looking sword."

"The kid was alone?" Thomas said.

"I don't know."

"I think he was," Berthold said. "I think he was trying to kill that nach... nachzeh..."

"Nachzehrer," Elletrache said. He looked at the captain. "Why would some savage runt go off doing something stupid like that?"

"*Hargravard.*"

The word hung in the air like an unwanted guest, its enunciation and production only possible by the sole tongue present which could manifest it: everyone slowly stared at the paymaster.

"It means kingship," Crockett said, though he quickly waved that off, "but that is a gross simplification. The barbarian tongue is tricky. It can hardly even be called a 'tongue' at all, considering much of it is grunting and other noises I can hardly replicate, nevermind that the meaning of their words are hard to grasp." He nodded. "But Hargravard means kingship, more or less."

Quinn leaned forward. "You tellin' me a little savage king is out here?"

Hobbs leaned even further forward. "Yeah is that what you're saying?"

Sighing, Crockett said, "No, I'm vastly simplifying it. There is no royal concept to the savages. Unlike our nobles, the barbarians cannot be born beneath the weight of a crown. Instead, Hargravard is *proving* oneself to *be* a king. It is central to what spurs barbarians to venture to strange lands and to slay mighty beasts and menace the civilized, for them civilization is a beast unto itself... and all of it is to prove themselves worthy not only to their own people, but to all the barbarians, thus becoming the king. That is why a barbarian king is truly rare, for great accomplishments need first be found, and then triumphed over."

The paymaster stared into the lowered campfire. He shook his head. "I must say, Richter, there is a terrifying complication involved if what you say is true. And I'm sure you know precisely to what terror I'm referring to."

"Barbarians this far south is already terrifying enough," Dahlgren said.

Crockett looked at Richter. He spoke slowly as though he were writing down his own thoughts beside a dim light. "Claire von Sommerwein was supposed to be married off to one of the tribes already, right? That was the original deal between the northern nobles and the savages. Obviously, that agreement is in ashes after the girl fled..." His voice quickened. "But that absence carries meaning! Honor is what governs the savages, shows of strength are laws to them. For something guaranteed to not come to fruition would be a blow to the credibility of a barbarian leader, and such a blow that his own people may have turned against him. For all we know, the tribes have fractured again and are quarreling amongst each other... maybe the kid came down here to prove himself worthy."

"Maybe he came down here to find Claire," Hobbs said.

"Who gives a fark," Quinn said. "I'm with Dollgrin on this one, barbarians this far south is not something anyone wants to hear."

"Yes," Crockett said. "It is disconcerting to say the least. Even if the kid was seen alone, I doubt he got here that way. And barbarians are savages but they're not completely reckless. If I had to guess, the boy very well may have run off, which means other barbarians would be looking for him."

"Hey Cricket, that sort of talk ain't farkin' helping, man."

Richter cleared his throat. He said, "We should—"

A silhouette stood at the edge of the encampment.

"What is it?" Crockett said.

The captain got to his feet. Seeing this, the other sellswords followed suit, a raucous series of unsheathing blades and clattering shields and wobbling spears, and the hurried steps of boots and the men in them falling into formation, something they were becoming increasingly acquainted with doing on the fly and at great speed.

"Who goes there!" Richter said, staring over the shieldwall.

The silhouette approached, and the light disrobed it of darkness and there appeared a man and a small mule. He held up his hand. "Ho!"

Richter held up his own hand. "Announce yourself!"

"I'm a traveler!" the man said. "Mind if I stay the night with you kind folks for a spell?"

The captain slimmed his eyes, spying for any glint on the traveler's person, or perhaps another one entirely somewhere in the trees.

"You can come search me if it'll ease your hearts and hands," the traveler said, lifting both arms. "I don't blame your fears. The old gods know these roads ain't safe for a whisper much less my old arse and mule."

"Alright," Richter said. "Check him, Dahlgren."

"You stay right there," Dahlgren said. He slowly walked over and the man stretched his arms further up. Carefully, Dahlgren patted him down. He then checked the mule, the draught animal carrying pots, pans, panniers, and long spools of rope.

"Find your search to be fruitful?" the traveler said with a friendly smirk.

Dahlgren looked back at Richter. The old man nodded. "He's not only clean, he's a fool. There's not a weapon on him."

The traveler smiled. "What would I do with a weapon, hm? Trick myself into taking risks where I otherwise would not? I wish to only stay for the night, as I said, and I mean absolutely no harm."

Quinn pointed a finger at him. "Have you seen any barbarians?"

"Uh, what?"

"Savages."

"Of northern stock?" The traveler shook his head. "Naw. Don't think I've ever heard of them bastards coming this far south, matter of fact."

Richter said, "You travel these roads often?"

"Used to."

"So you'd say you know them well enough?"

"Aye. See, I'm a bit of a merchant down on his trade and desperate enough to haul arse to Marsburg in the dead of night. I wouldn't be here if I didn't trust my sense of the roads, nor would I have approached yer lot if I thought ye'd strike me dead. Though the way things are going maybe I'm just being wrong all slow like and one of you is about to stick me."

The captain sheathed his sword. "No one is going to do that."

"You gonna let this stranger in?" Quinn said.

"If he's a merchant that knows these roads, then he can help check the maps. Besides, we might learn a thing or two from him otherwise." Richter waved the traveler forward. "Come, stranger, you can stay for the night."

Chapter 18. The Traveler.

AS THE TRAVELER got situated and Sophia prepared another meal, Richter sought out Hobbs. He found the boy sitting on the wagon's tailgate, his legs scissoring back and forth, his eyes to the stars above.

"The traveler checked your maps," Richter said.

Hobbs nodded. "And?"

"Seems you did well. He could at least confirm a few of the roads, and Trash and I ran some inquiries by him to make sure he wasn't bullshitting us."

"Alright," Hobbs said, though a smirk skewered his modest response.

"Alright." Richter leaned against the wagon. He said, "Good work."

"You're welcome." The boy's smirk widened.

"Don't go sniffing your own farts quite yet."

"I'm just sitting here."

"Mhmm." Richter ushered the boy out of the wagon. "Come sit by the fire. The traveler has a lot to say and you've still plenty yet to learn."

~ ~ ~

The traveler set his bowl of soup down. He wiped his mouth and thanked Sophia for her cooking. Unlike the rest of the company, he seemed rather certain it was one of the finest meals he had ever had. He held up two coins to the beaming homesteader.

Richter declined payment. "The meal is on us."

The traveler nodded. He and the sellswords talked for a time, discussing matters beyond their knowing, and beyond their control, such as it is that men recognize themselves to be mere curiosities underneath much greater powers, privileged to only hope that they don't become some pawn in these entities' interests, some unknown sacrifice for a known gain they'd no vantage of in this life or the next. They discussed the siege of Marsburg, and the growing number of creatures in the forest, and that the Sommerwein nobility were hesitant to act with their princess having gone missing, and that northern savages were still quarreling with their civilized counterparts on the matter.

Finally, the traveler looked to Richter and said, "You've a familiar face."

"He's the Wight," Quinn blurted.

"The Wight, sure," the traveler said. He turned his head and his eyes slimmed, his mind carving out the final touches of a once forgotten memory. "No, I know you from somewhere specifically."

Richter said, "Where would that be?"

"In the Lowland Reach," the traveler said. He nodded, seemingly to himself as the memories took shape. "Many years ago, in fact. You were more a boy then, but you've still the same, terrible face."

"Terrible face!" Quinn said with a laugh.

But the traveler merely continued: "Aye, aye... you were with the pathfinders. You and them other fleetfooted lads."

Richter nodded. "You have your facts right, but I must apologize for I do not remember your presence there."

"You wouldn't have because by that time I was half-dead," the traveler said. He leaned back and started rolling up his sleeve, talking as the cloth bulged and furled: "See, most everyone knows the Battle of Many Names, or some part of it, being as it was everywhere and all, nevermind that it collapsed the House of Kaltenborn, shattered us into a kingless future and so on and so forth, but few remember what came in the days before. Few remember that, for a time, we had no notion of all the hells those greenskins would bring down upon us. *Someone* had to find out. I suppose that's just how life is in general, o'course. You get up and move around and do what you need to and it's like any other day… until it isn't."

The traveler rolled his sleeve to the shoulder and turned his arm. A garish, corkscrew of a scar worked its way from elbow to armpit. "I can hardly lift this one," he said, "and those bubbling parts here, and here? That's goblin poison." He let his arm go and then cocked a knee and started rolling up the pantleg. He pointed at his shin where a finger-deep groove ran alongside the bone in a long notch. "Some orc business there. Incomplete transaction, as my father would say. I figure anything more than a glancing blow and my leg would've been on a greenskin's spit for dinner."

"I understand now." Richter nodded. "You were part of the group that ran into trouble ahead of Fort Firebag. I remember the wounded passing through camp."

"Yessir. Yours truly was on a sled pulled by a mule and damn if I didn't feel every bump from Firebag to Walddorf."

"The stories of Fort Firebag are legendary," Crockett said.

Nodding, the traveler said, "That they are. And the keep's resilience overshadowed our own contributions."

The paymaster took out his ledger and his quill pen. He nodded. "Maybe I can help change that. Why don't you tell us your story?"

"Yeah!" Hobbs said. "I'd love to hear it."

Dahlgren looked uneased. He said, "I'm not sure if we should be trading war stories, maybe we talk about something else?"

"I was baking bread for the armies," Berthold said. "I missed all the action and would love to hear about what happened."

Richter nodded. "Only if you'd like to share, traveler."

"Hmm. Alright," the traveler said. "Where do I begin… ahh, well, there'd been talk of greenskins moving in the area west of Firebag, and then some patrols confirmed it, and then other patrols went missing which I suppose confirmed it in another way. So far, none of this was out of the ordinary. Greenskins come, greenskins go. Sometimes they get one over on us, sometimes we get one over on them. This was the way of things. When we set out, we figured it'd be a two or three day hunt. Find 'em, kill 'em, go home. Hells, it'd been done a dozen times before, ain't nothing to it. But you know how men get when they smell the slightest hint of glory, yeah? Yeah. See, we were a day's hike from Firebag staying at a roadside tavern when some rumor got to spreading about an encampment of greenskins being out there ripe for the picking so… we set out after it. To hells with scalps and a pittance of coin, we wanted something to drink to years later! You know, the kind of hokey nonsense you think up when yer already drunk. Well, we figured killing an encampment of those greenskin farks was our imprimatur to glory. Am I using that right, imprimatur?"

Crockett nodded as his pen scratched in a hurried measure.

The traveler stared into the fire. Dahlgren held out a goatskin flask and the traveler took it and drank and did not return it.

He looked up. "That morning went well, too. We found a couple goblins sleeping in a bush of poison berries." He shrugged. "We stove their heads in. Our bannermen though it funny to nail the little legs and arms to a tree so we had ourselves a little fun doing that. Yeah. We had our laughs. An hour later we happened upon a pair of young orcs. Despite our number, they growled and charged us. Two against dozens. We should've taken that as a warning. Orcs are dumb, but they ain't that dumb. But we killed them and we moved on without second thought. We knew by the smell in the air that their camp was real close. And then the first tent came into view, settin' there right dead center on the godsdamned road. That should've been perhaps the biggest of the warnings, yeah? That these dumbshit greenskins would be so grand as to squat right there, central to the comings and goings of all travelers. But we were like stunty dumbarses kicking up a fight with the biggest bear in the bar. We just weren't thinking straight. We got giddy about the glory, sped through a quick prayer, mostly just said we hoped the old gods were watching – *which they weren't* – and then like that we stood shoulder to shoulder, spearmen upfront, a couple talented swordhands among them, bardiches and pikes in the next line, and archers behind them. I tell you what, we were a fine troop. Fine fine fine, yeah. Glinting armor. A couple bannermen with newly stitched flags. Those colors? Sublime. Really caught the sun, they did. And we had a fella with a horn. He'd blow on it a certain way to let us know how things were going. Truthfully, we looked the part. And we were the part, yeah?"

The traveler leaned forward. He poured the ale into his palm and slapped some of it behind his neck.

"Godsdammit," he said.

Quinn leaned forward. "So what happ—"

"'Five seconds!'," the traveler yelled, nodding again and again. "'Five seconds!', that's what my commander barked. That was the countdown to a charge. Ain't but a moment after the words passed his lips that we realized maybe he should've started at three cause we didn't have no farkin' five seconds: the greenskins already arrived on this outcropping above us and they arrived in some godsdamned number. A long, long line of silhouettes as far as you could see. They knew we was coming the whole time and gods did they look furious that we had the balls even be there in the first place."

Dahlgren looked at Richter, his eyes pleading for him to stop the story.

"Sir," Richter said, leaning forward. "I think—"

"Ah! Like I said, we ain't have the five seconds. I should know, I was counting those seconds like they were lifetimes. From the jump, arrows started coming in, their tips coated in poison so if they so much as touched ya, well, yer day was farked. At two seconds these orcs roared down the hill and others yet wheeled around the trees before them which frightened the lot of us. I don't even remember that last second. I think the man next to me said something absolutely strange, absolutely bizarre, like he said he just remembered his old dog's name or something. Fetched a moment from his childhood like his mind desperately wanted to be somewhere else. I dunno, everything seemed to focus in that one second. And I do mean damn near everything, you about see your whole life before you when you see a horde of orcs screaming for your head. It's like their ferocity is a mirror to show you who you really are. It's like their gift to see things in reverse, to walk back the steps that arrived you at your demise, you know? Yeah. And then they descended upon us like locusts: the crash of green bodies upon our shields was like a storm cracking a galley, them big orcs swinging mad huge cleavers, men flying apart, legs and arms soaring, the howling of the wounded and the clatter of pikes tryin' to purchase some blood, some dumbfark poleman wobbling his weapon over my godsdamn shoulder, and all the while them farkin' goblins riding down on them heeled wolves, circling around and nipping at our flanks. I'd never seen a farkin' goblin standing allied with an orc, but there they was, two peas in a very green pod, them motherfarkers."

The traveler took another drink. He continued.

"My shield looked like a farkin' rosebush it was so covered in arrows, but I'd say the shieldwall held strong. Despite all that ferocity and chaos, we were holding. All the weak men were already dead by that point. It was just us stubborn farks left. When your resolve gets tested, the unit tightens up. Shoulder to shoulder, muscles knotted, sweat and mud and blood everything, and you clench your teeth and yell back, you yell shit like 'is that all you got?', and you let them farks know they've a ways to break you yet. This big greenskin with a chain showed up thereabouts and he somehow got around us into the archers and, boy, did he make a mess of those men. But we still held ourselves together, men and shields. So ferocious was the fight that I don't think we had the time to break morale. You could hardly even tell that we were being wiped out. And me and another fella went and killed that chain-swinging orc sumbitch and seeing that monstrosity go down really put a boot up our arses. The men started cheering, roaring, coming to life, the man with the horn started bleating, bannermen were waving the flags with pride. The chaos is what we went out there for, yeah? Despite that initial contact we felt good. Felt like we had it together. Until the warlord showed up."

The campfire crackled. The traveler finished off the goatskin flask and threw it aside and when he did so the throwing arm stayed wide, and his other arm broadened out to mirror it.

"He was a big… *big* orc. And meaner than anything you'd ever seen, and you'd know him mean just by sight alone. He had these crumpled up dead knights stacked on his shoulders for armor, layered there like they was pelts. Horrifying. And he wore a nobleman's chest plate for a helmet, and I think that nobleman's skull was perched above, impaled there on an iron pike. And his weaponry… by the old gods, that weaponry. He had a slab of steel for a shield. I think it may have been the top of a blacksmith's anvil, yeah? Yeah. And in the other hand he swung a massive machete with a blade as thick as my arm. Fellas. Let me say this. Them orcs ain't like us. They don't play games, they don't fool each other, they don't have prancing nobility arbitratin' rules, they don't pay others to do what they won't do themselves, they're not crafty in the slightest, there's not a piece of them that hides from their true selves, understand? They operate on violence and violence alone, and so when you see an orc like that on the battlefield, you know one thing to a certainty: that ain't no battleground yer standin' on. It's his *home*." The traveler turned his head to the listeners, his eyes glistening with fiery tears. "And, fellas, by the old gods, did we ever break into the wrong house that day."

Everyone remained silent, the campfire crackling quietly.

"How'd you get out?" Quinn blurted, and Sophia slapped him on the chest and hushed him.

The traveler smiled, though his lips quivered at the edges. He said, "Good sir, I got out by being a coward."

"You're no coward," Dahlgren said.

"Aye," Richter said. "The deaths of those men alerted Fort Firebag to the greenskin invasion. Had you all been killed, the invaders would have poured through, taken the fort in an instant, and flowed into the lowlands. Your being alive benefited us all, possibly to an extent we cannot imagine."

"Eh, we're all just cowardly refuse, my friend," the traveler said, smiling with a sort of learned and impressed cruelty. "All the good men died that day, and the yellowed bellies went on living, just the sort of coldhearted bastards criminal enough to keep living in this godsforsaken, broken world."

The fire crackled in the silence that followed the man's words. Not even Quinn seemed ready to proffer a joke or anything to puncture the air of tension. All the while the traveler stared into the fire, his upper body tilting back and forth, seeming as though at any moment, at any time when the wrong thought crossed his mind and took hold that he would simply pitch himself into the flames. It would rid him of his life, but more gracefully, at least, rid him of his memories first, replaced by pain he thought he deserved.

Richter hurried to his feet. "Thank you, traveler," he said. "I think it is time we call it a night here and get ourselves some rest."

Looking around at the others, a pang of embarrassment came over the traveler. He nodded repeatedly. He said, "Yeah, yeah, I agree." He looked at the goatskin flask and looked at Dahlgren and bowed. "I'm sorry, friend, I didn't mean to finish it all and toss it away like that."

"No," Dahlgren said. "I think you earned that one."

As the company slept, Richter stood by the wagon. He stared at the embers of the campfire, and at the sluglike shapes of all the bodies surrounding it. He turned his attention to the treetops and stared further into the gloomy night. A faint orange glowed and bristled through the leaves, the building he set aflame still smoldering. The memory of the nachzehrer staring at him with those blank, fat eyes took hold of his mind. Fighting it off, he took a long breath and let it out. Like a child fighting off a nightmare, he took yet another. On the third breath, he heard a branch snap and he paused and instinctively unsheathed his blade and stood silent and unbreathing. Another branch snapped and before the sound could even die he himself snatched a breath and hurried toward the noise. He slipped past tree after tree, traveling further into the midnight wood. Quietly clearing a rise of corded roots, he spied on the other side a very tall, black shape wobbling back and forth.

Richter held his blade close to his leg to prevent any glinting moonlight to catch its steel, and in the same manner he prowled forward like a cat, sleuthing right up onto the stranger until he was within striking range.

"Announce yourself," the captain said, raising his sword.

The shape turned around. It was the traveler. Not even the dark could hide his sorrowful eyes.

Richter stared down and realized the man was standing on a stool. As he looked further up, he saw the traveler had a rope around his neck with the end of it wrapped around a branch.

"You mind kicking this out for me?" the traveler said, pointing at the stool. "I don't think I can bring myself to do it. I've been trying and, well, no dice."

Somewhere far above, a cloud shifted and the moon cleaved in and a good spit of light befell both men.

The traveler looked up as though he meant to wash himself in the light. He smiled. "You think some higher powers have taken some keen interest here? I think it's tryin' to illuminate where you need to kick, so go on and kick it out."

Richter advanced cautiously as though it were himself wobbling on the precipice.

"You want me to kill you?" he said.

"I need ya to kick this here stool out. The rope and fall will kill me."

The traveler had the look of an old dog standing out in the rain just waiting to be let inside. For Richter, the man's eyes were unfortunately familiar. A shared look. One man to others, ages and regions apart. Richter had witnessed a number of witch hunters kill themselves, and most had that look: resignation. Almost the same look they had when the deed was done. Almost as if it were practice. Almost as if to tell others, this is nothing, this is nothing at all. 'Sorry for the mess', that's what he remembered one note saying. It took him and Carsten ten minutes to cut the hexenjäger's body down, wrap it, and set it out for the gravediggers. Hardly a mess at all in some sense, but they knew the man was speaking to something else entirely. Some length of comings and goings and doings. 'Sorry for the mess.' Mess. Four letters for an infinite much.

"I'm not doing it," Richter said.

The traveler clucked his tongue and spat. "Ah, c'mon. I dragged this chair all the way out, too, and this ain't even my first time up here. I just need some help. I can't ever seem to do it alone. Not afraid of heights or nothing. I just get concerned about what I'm doing."

"Right," Richter said. He thumbed over his shoulder. "Had we not met on the road, would you still be there?"

"I suppose the tree and branch would be different." He stared at Richter and then sighed and spat. He said, "Ah c'mon now. You were also there at the Battle of Many Names. You and I know how bad things get. You and I know that surviving ain't always for the best. Now just give it a kick, mercenary. You're not killing nobody if I ask you to do it."

"I'm killing you all the same," Richter said. "Just cause you ask doesn't wash my hands of it."

"Do it, mercenary." The traveler's feet wobbled. His eyes lost the solemnity and pinched with anger now. "Do it, or-or-or I'll... I'll go back to camp and start... uh, I'll start stabbing."

"You don't have a blade."

"I'll find one. Hells, I'll take yours. You'll have to stop me once I start. You'll have to stop me the only way you can. You'll—"

Richter took a step forward and kicked the chair out. The man's legs swung away with the last of the platform until they were left to the air and his neck shunted into the tightness of the rope and he choked on it. His hands balled into fists at his side, the veins rising from knuckles to shoulders, and his neck purpled with the blood rushing into his skull. The captain met the man's eyes, and then he turned around, showing the traveler his back. He only faced away a moment, then spun with Adelbrecht's blade and swung it overhead and cut the rope. The man fell to the ground and the second the rope slackened he went to hacking and coughing.

"Get your fill?" Richter said.

"Ahh fark you, mercenary. Farkin' preck. What kinda killer can't even kill, eh? Fark! Farkin' hells!"

Richter leaned against a tree. He said, "You look as though you've found your truth."

"The hells that supposed to mean?"

"Earlier, you had an uncertain look on your face. Now it's far more certain."

The traveler threw his arm out. "I'm certainly mad as hells!" He felt the rope on his neck and hurriedly heaved it away as though it were a poisonous snake. "Farking sonuvafarking bitch… can't believe I'm still here, and on account of what? On account of what? Huh? You coulda picked through my pockets! I've gold you coulda had! You coulda had my cart, my mule, what goods I got. But no, you leave me settin' here breathing and, and, and – godsdammit – *breathing*!"

Richter let him get it all out.

The traveler went and picked up his chair. He set it upright and sat it in. He threw his hands between his knees. He shook his head. He lowered his voice and said, "Mind if we just set here a minute?"

"Aye, take your time."

The two men dwelled in the dark of night, each faint in the moonlight. The traveler spent some time looking as far away from Richter as he could. A few sniffles and coughs and throat clearings. Despite the silence, these were in fact dialogues going on, crafted both by their terseness and also by what went unsaid. Two veterans of a war, and of the world that produced it.

Finally, the traveler looked up. "How'd you know I'd want down?"

Richter said, "An old friend of mine taught me a trick about things such as this. If you can't decide on something, then you take a coin and flip it. Once it's in the air, you'll know where you want it to land. You'll know where your heart truly is."

The traveler stared at the captain a moment. He said, "So you couldn't flip a damned coin?"

Laughing, Richter shook his head. "Didn't bring my pocket money out here with me, I'm afraid." He nodded. "But it's true. I knew that once you got a taste of that rope you'd be right situated. And I mean that in either way. So if you're really diced up about what I did, you've still rope yet to get on with it, and if you get on with it a second time then I won't stop you."

"I won't be getting on with it," the traveler said.

"Aye. I suspected you wouldn't."

The traveler spat. He said, "Don't get too full of yourself."

Richter nodded.

"You were there," the traveler said. "At the Battle of Many Names. You saw what happened."

"Aye," Richter said. He thought to add that he'd been to many places, and of the litany and lists available to his memories, the Battle of Many Names ranked low in its comparative horrors. Given the traveler's state of mind, he thought it best to keep that dark reality to himself.

"Well," the traveler said. "You ever thought about it, then? You know, stepping out. Permanently, I mean."

Richter nodded. "Sure. There's been a time or two where it seemed the right move. I just didn't because I'm stubborn."

"Stubborn," the traveler repeated. "You mean scared?"

"No, I mean stubborn. A part of me just wants to see how it ends on its own accord. If I do it myself, well, I don't know. It almost seems like I'm robbing the story of its conclusion. That is just me, though. I've no philosophy to tell you on it, no knowledge or insight that may relieve that which ails you because I am not you or any sense of you, not the you standing on a chair with a rope around his neck nor the you who got up this morning or the morning prior. You are you. Any justification for my living is right here standing before you and you've days now to make your own justifications. But they will be yours and only yours."

The traveler shook his head. "Hells," he said again. "Hells."

"I think the hells can wait," Richter said. "Even if we deserve them."

Grumbling, the traveler said, "You know, I think a part of me has earned this. I know everyone's got a favorite old god and you know what mine is?"

Richter shook his head.

"Alder Effour," the traveler said. "Do you know him?"

"The god of renewal," Richter said. "Rebirth. Some monks even argue that he has the power to alter time itself."

"Second chances," the traveler said. He smirked and shook his head. "Perhaps the least proven god there is."

"Careful with that talk," Richter said.

The traveler nodded. "Aye, I probably should be." He stared out into the woods. He turned and said, "So what about you?"

"What about me?"

"Yeah. What's your favorite god? Or are you one of them unholy types."

"No, I have faith in the old gods. Not always, but I do," Richter said. "If that makes sense."

"It does."

The captain thought for a time. Most often, people did not speak to the individuality of the old gods. Their purposes and existences, when combined together, served the entirety of the human experience. Aided, abetted, assisted, however one wished to know that something was on their side. But not every old god had a chosen side.

Richter said, "I suppose the god of chance."

"Arren Gee," the traveler said. "Some call him the god of chaos."

"Chance and chaos do tend to be one in the same, just depends on which side of the circumstance you end up on." Richter nodded, mostly to himself. "But aye, Arren Gee. The god of chance. Aside from that it begins and that it ends, the unpredictability of life seems the surest of its elements. One small decision made in one small moment can have effects on numerous moments unknown. You paint and unpaint entire futures with every choice you make. And cascading around you are those doing the same. Everyone all at once. Constant, unimaginable chaos. Constant, unimaginable uncertainties."

"Surely a busy god, if nothing else," the traveler said.

Richter laughed. "Aye."

"We should probably hush on it, though. Neither of us are in the proper here. We should leave this to the monks. I'm sorry I even brought it up."

"It's alright. The gods put us here, I think they'll allow us some considerations and regards."

"Maybe, but I might spill out something I don't intend. Our makers might not give me a moment's chance to explain. I know my mother sure didn't and she's about as maker as a maker gets. How about your mother?"

In truth, Richter never met his mother. But if there was ever a time to lie about it, now, with the traveler's eyes full of fond memories and his mind flittering with the old gods, and all the creation that dwells between, now was that time. So he simply said: "Aye. She was a wonderful woman, all the same."

"They usually is," the traveler said, nodding and smirking. He looked over his shoulder and laughed. "Shit, you know what's funny?"

"What?"

"I sell rope for a living." The traveler lurched as he chuckled. "You cut my damn product in half, sellsword."

"Just tie two ends together, can't be too hard."

"Very funny sellsword."

Richter rapped a tree. "We should probably head back to camp."

"I don't want to sleep back there. I think I want to take the night out here. Just let myself live as my ancestors did. Just let it in for a spell, you know?" The traveler looked around the dark trees which circled and extended forever. He said, "What's it cost to sleep out here, you think?"

"Sometimes nothing," Richter said. "Sometimes everything."

"Mind staying out here with me to see which one we get?"

The captain nodded. "Aye. I don't mind doing that at all."

"Like flipping a coin, right?"

"Aye. I suppose that's all it ever is."

Chapter 19. The Dragonslaying Bell.

IMMERWAHR'S FEET MOVED BENEATH HIM, but he did not feel the earth, and he knew the wind was blowing but its touch was absent, and there were murmurs abounding from the marching peasants, once profligate with their fears but now assured in their certainties, but he did not lend an ear, and soon their common tongue fell away, as though he had fashioned himself foreign to the homelands, and feeling as though he were losing himself he turned his head and stared back from whence he came, for in sight all things could surely only be what they were, and he stared at the charred teeth of the ferry town's pub, burnt and broken, the slats and foundations crisscrossing into the air with blackened teeth, and by the old gods was the ruin real, and he stared at the bunkhouses laddered across the grounds one after the other, and by the old gods was the abandonment real, and he stared at the muddied road which cut the town in twain, and he stared at the mottled wagons that looked like pillbugs in the fading light, and finally he stared at the store. His store. And by the old gods, his dream had been real, and it were this element that proved to be the last to fade, the building dimpling the darkness before submersing into it, and soon all that could be seen were the yellowed eyes of cats and dogs, glimmers in the black, watching their caretakers go and staring at the runagate monk who once again found his feet efforting at an ill-fitted behest. He felt the wind against him now, and the mumblings of the peasants jumbled into hurried words as they rearticulated her commands, and they bayed much like the cattle they had become, and the monk at last took a long breath and sighed and he followed them as much as they followed her.

~ ~ ~

The monk sat on a pew, legs bouncing, hands fumbling between them. His finger searched for a prayer, his lips muttering ones incompletely. He looked at the front of the priory. The building's front had collapsed, leaving a pile of rubble and the priory's black bell, and under its iron weight the faint white of a giant lindwurm's bones. How these things came to pass was beyond his knowing. With a sigh, the monk turned toward the back of the priory. There, an engraved stone relief held the image of the old gods in a primordial state, anguish and anger and chaos, but in the sum these elements they were in a state of creation, the fount of all life, the frenzy of forming. And in the concaves of the stonework there was dried blood, and three claw marks tracked across its entirety, and this was surely the work of some bestial reality, some issuance that sprang from all inception itself, for as man had come forth he did not come alone, nor could he ever have for then he would not be man.

"You are more resilient than you look."

A voice, spoken aloud, yet delicate as a whisper.

Claire skipped into the priory, her hands out at her sides, her white dress wispily scratching over the edges of the pews. Her bare feet tapped the stone steps like murmuring raindrops. She swept her hand over the defaced relief before spinning to stand behind a lectern at the head of the altar.

"I don't know if it should surprise me, but out of all the people, you were the only one to resist," she said, smiling at the monk with almost motherly pride. "You faltered here and there, but you didn't succumb. I am impressed."

Outside, a felled tree groaned loudly before snapping at the trunk and crashing down, rustling and thrashing as it broke into the branches of other trees. The monk looked out a window, but in the dark he could see only silhouettes of bent backs hurrying to and fro like ants on a moonlit windowsill. Mere shapes hard at work.

Immerwahr said, "What are my people doing out there?"

"Obeying."

"Are you going to kill them?"

"I'm not strong enough to do that," Claire said, tottering on the lectern.

The monk huffed and rolled his fists into his eyes. He groaned at the sheer horror bedighting his body and mind. He threw his hands down and said, "Can you do it again?"

"Do what again?"

"Fool me."

"You wish to join those who are ensorcelled?"

"I would like that, yes. It would be preferable to... this..."

"Hmm. No. I like you the way you are, holy man. You should be happy to have your mind right. Others don't. And others yet *really* don't."

Immerwahr looked to the corner of the room. A naked man stood there with his head facing the stone walls. One hand rested upon a sword's pommel while the other repeatedly clapped its palm upon the top of his head. The monk assumed the man had been doing this for some time as the crown of his hair had all fallen out and the juncture of his flopping wrist had turned purple and black. He also had urine and shit stains down both legs.

"Oh," Claire said, spotting the monk's stare. "That is my bodyguard."

The monk cleared his throat. He said, "Why is he naked?"

"Because I wanted him to be." She stared at the man with the amusement of an owner watching their dog perform a new trick. "It amuses me."

"Who is he?"

"Kantorek I believe was his name," Claire said, her finger tapping the lectern as she thought. "I don't rightly remember, though. It's not important."

"Kantorek is a brigand," Immerwahr said. "And a dangerous one."

Claire smiled. "Not anymore he isn't."

Outside, crashing and cracking and clattering. Another tree felled. Immerwahr looked to the window, but this time the view was completely blocked by a blob of bristling black as the direwolf slowly stomped into frame. Its claws scratched against the wall's stones, producing a clumpy, heavy hiss that raised the hair on the monk's neck.

Claire pointed to Kantorek. "Our naked friend here said that a band of mercenaries were hired to kill him. I know that Marsburg is currently under siege and that so much money is available on both sides that the mercenaries are flocking to it. Which makes me wonder, just what manner of foolish sellswords are footing around out here? Here, a land of almost no value?"

The monk shrugged.

The girl pursed her lips. "Disappointing. That was a rhetorical question, holy man. You should perhaps deploy a bit of theater and esteem me."

"Well," Immerwahr said. "What do you want me to say? What do you want to know?"

Claire held up a slip of paper. "I found this at your store. The handwriting is immaculate, and what it has to say almost equally so. Have you read it?"

"Of course I've read it."

"Has Richter read it?"

"No."

"Why? His name is on it."

"He refused to read it. He seemed to already know what it would say."

"Ah." Claire stared at the letter as though it were a gift that had failed to impress in the manner she had assumed it would. She turned the letter to face him and tapped its signature. She said, "Who is Fuchs?"

"I don't know. I only met him briefly."

"Is it safe to presume he is also a witch hunter?"

"He had the black hat," Immerwahr said. "And a large number of weapons on his person."

"The hexenjäger do not carry heavy weaponry."

"This one did."

Claire pursed her lips. She said, "Where is he?"

"He went across the river."

"That's the last you've seen of him?"

Immerwahr nodded.

"And the girl was with him when left?"

"She was."

"In distress?"

"No. She seemed content. Like they were happy together."

"He was bedding her?"

Immerwahr shook his head. "I don't think it was like that, no."

Claire looked at the paper. She looked at the naked Kantorek still slapping the top of his head. She looked at Immerwahr.

"I suppose it makes sense that you did not recognize me as the princess of Sommerwein, just as you failed to notice that the Lowland Reach's own princess merrily went under your nose as ward to a vagabond witch hunter. Such a dichotomy of persons would raise the suspicions of even the most antlike of intellects, but here you are, mumbling in recollections."

"I'm just a monk... these matters are..."

"Are beyond you, yes yes, I understand. Earthly matters are beyond you, but grandiose holy ones are not, right? It's so very hard to keep pace with what mere mortals are doing when you have to tell us what the old gods are thinking and saying. I understand." Claire smirked. "If this Fuchs and his princess are gone, so be it. I care about one man right now and you know exactly who I speak of. Where is he, holy man?"

"I sent Richter north."

"To do what?"

"Deliver a message."

"A delivery quest!" Claire laughed briefly. Sternness soon reappeared on her face, scowling and determined. "How many men does he have with him?"

"The size was in flux. It is a dangerous business, as you know."

"You don't give me a number and I'll start dropping bodies at your feet, then we'll see who can count and what really is dangerous business."

"Maybe ten," Immerwahr said quickly.

"Are they good fighters?"

Immerwahr threw a hand toward Kantorek. "Ask him."

"Hmm." The girl stared at the naked man. She mused aloud: "Why is the hexenjäger forming a company? Since when do they do such a thing?"

"Richter never spoke of his vocation," Immerwahr said. "Maybe he's simply moved on."

"Hush," Claire said. She continued musing: "Why would he behave in such a manner... if he thought me ordinary, he'd take of me himself... unless he saw me and the lindwurm and... does the Wight consider me a Grimalkin?" The girl smirked at the thought. "If he does..."

Immerwahr stared at the girl as she mused to herself. From where he sat, he could stand, jump forward, and already be in arms reach. When she turned her head, talking to herself, thinking to herself, that would be the time to do it. And then he'd – well, he didn't know. He'd do something without thinking. He'd have to. Thinking about it, especially in the moment, would rob him of the necessary instinct to... to kill. Either way, he believed that once she was gone, his people may yet be free of her invisible leash, and her beasts and Kantorek, too, and she was looking away now, she was thinking and muttering, but most importantly she was looking away, looking so far away, her head turned and the back of her head was so vulnerable and soft and—

The monk sprang to his feet and the pew squalled behind him.

Kantorek stopped patting his head and spun around, the scrape of his sword filling the room with a terse scratch, and its steel was held at full length, unerring as a statue, its tip upon the monk's nose. Immerwahr held his hands up. He looked at Kantorek to see the man's eyes were completely open, the rims a bright red. A line of yellow dust down caked his head, starting at his hair and ending where his nose began.

"You said yourself he was dangerous," Claire said, turning around. "Perhaps he still is, hmm?"

Slowly, Immerwahr sat back down. Mirroring the monk, Kantorek's sword also lowered. He stared for a moment longer, then turned to again face the corner. With a shaking, trembling arm, he slowly started patting the top of his head again.

"Richter is taking me rather seriously," Claire said. "So it must be that I take him seriously. And in this manner, we will marshal our forces and meet when the time is right. And then I will kill him."

"What do you plan to do with my people?" Immerwahr said.

Claire chuckled. She went around the lectern and descended the steps so lightly it looked as though her clothes had simply been thrown without her in them. Gliding between the pews, her hands delicately danced and pranced from one to the next.

"Naughty boy," she said, passing Immerwahr with a stern stare.

She walked to the front of the priory and climbed the pile of rubble that once constituted its entrance. Like a sailor in the topmast, she shouted excitedly to the darkness as though it were land at last. All sounds of work ceased. Tools fell, plopping into the grass here and there, murmurs in the dark. Then, the steady crunch of grass. More and more, converging unto the priory, at first as silhouettes in the dark, then as a throng of faces Immerwahr knew and wished he didn't, all of them now marching without thought.

"The needful," Claire said, pointing at the fallen priory bell.

A group of men shuffled in. Like Kantorek, Immerwahr saw that they each had yellow lines crusted on their foreheads. Without a single word, they walked right to the bell, circled it, bent their knees, and started to lift. Their muscles instantly tensed, bulging and jutting, and the men started growling, some with their backs blowing out, others snapping elbows, but these injuries did not seem to inflict pain for they continued with their task, rigid spines and disfigured arms and all.

"Pleasantly, please," Claire said. "Pleasantly."

Dust and stone hissed and clattered as the bell rose from the ruins. Silently, the men moved it toward the entrance. Outside, another group pushed forward a widely built wagon, the rear of the cart rolling toward the rubble like a ship about to run aground. Just as it arrived, the bell was dumped into its bed with a cacophonous clap of holy and unholy constructs.

"You may feel now," Claire said to the men. "Let it flow."

Granted reality, the men collapsed in howling heaps. Their minds conceived then and there the broken bones and burst muscles. Screaming, they crawled about the ruins clutching spines shaped like snakes while others yet spun in circles, their dislocated arms flailing like maypole ribbons and as each contorted their bodies to subdue one pain it only seemed to commission a new one, and so the men rolled and writhed, filling the air with their moans.

"Look," Claire said, staring at Immerwahr with a white grin.

A throng of women suddenly came forth and began filling the bell with shrooms and herbs, a smoky and discolored haze gently drifting from the bell's center. When they finished, the women turned to the children and helped them climb over the bell's rim, its belly so large that, briefly, each child disappeared entirely before springing back up onto their feet, their heads barely visible above the lip of the bell's rim.

"Look," Claire said. A tender glisten dotted her eyes. She took pleaded to Immerwahr with her hands. "Look."

Immerwahr looked, and he watched.

Every person shared the yellow crust upon their foreheads, and each beamed with happiness, the happiness that seemed to be governed by Claire herself, their cheeks puffed a merry red, their eyes wide with genuine excitement, and even the broken men in terrible pain hissed their feelings through gritted teeth, their shattered arms reaching toward the bell like desert stranded men grasping for the long-awaited oasis.

"Look."

The children started dancing in the bell, their little feet crushing up the herbs and shrooms, and the women backed away clapping their hands with tears in their eyes. A decrepit minstrel with a lute came forward, naked head to toe, his legs bowed as he leaped around like a frog. Landing before the bell, he drew the lute to his shoulder. He readied his other hand, the fingers pinched, but he held no bow. The flesh of the arm itself had been shucked, leaving behind two spindly, white bones, and it was with these glistening cords that he did strike across the lute's strings and played a squalling, horror of a sound, and he danced and spun around the bell, the song twirling chaotically with him, his mouth moaning some simulacrum of the lute itself, and as the swirling noise filled the air the men who had helped lift the bell came to it, shuffling and shambling, and they each gripped their own necks and clenched their nails deep and ripped out their own throats, and as the blood gushed the men climbed upon the rim of the bell and held hands in a circle, their heads to the sky, their spewing necks giving unto the bell a bountiful offering, and beneath this shower the children danced and danced and danced.

"Look, holy man!" Claire wept. "Look and behold my cauldron!"

Chapter 20. The Laager.

RICHTER JOLTED AWAKE, a congress of body parts painfully conspiring against him in an ambush of a morning. Grimacing, he stood up, knees cracking, elbows popping. The tiredness of yesterday had left his muscles, but the weight of his entire life never left his bones. As he caught his breath, he eyed the traveler asleep against a tree, the man's rope in his lap, the noose now unfurled. And there to his side a blue and white image shifted behind a bush. The captain turned to it with his blade halfway out of its sheath.

Minnesang stopped, jester hat in hand, fists clenched over the bells.

"Richter," he said.

The traveler startled awake, snorting and coughing.

"Ah," Minnesang said. "You're with the stranger. We were worried."

Richter let go of his sword. "All is well, Minnesang. The traveler and I had some talking to do."

"Somethin' like that," the traveler said, lumbering to his feet. He turned around and leaned against the tree and drew his pants down and started pissing. Belching rather brutally, he looked over his shoulder midstream and said, "I'll probably be venturing out now. Don't wanna be a bother."

"Your company was appreciated," Richter said. "Come back with us to the camp and I'll set you off with a grubstake. My gift."

The traveler drew up his pants. "I'd much appreciate that."

Richter nodded.

The jester put his hat back on his head. He said, "Well then. It is good to see Richter von Dagentear has made a new friend and is alive and well."

"I don't often make requests like this," Richter said. "But I'm about to start ordering you to call me 'captain.'"

"But Richter is your name, is it not?"

"It is, but you say it like you know me," Richter said. "Except you don't know anything about me."

Bowing, the jester said, "Apologies then, captain."

The traveler walked up with his pants belted by his rope. He smiled. "Ahh, ye've a jester in your party? Fascinatin' addition for sellswords. Say, that's quite a queer hat you got there, fella."

"Thank you," Minnesang said, flicking one of its bells. "It is quite precious to me."

"Should, uh, probably wear somethin' different, though. Y'know? Dunno what good that hat's gon' do ya if someone wants to come and take yer head off."

Richter nodded. "Aye, the aim of the company is to acquire some better gear, including a good helm for you, Minnesang."

"So long as I get to keep the cap'n'bells," the jester said.

"Of course." Richter clapped the traveler on the shoulder. "Now let's get your grubstake and set you back on the road."

~~~

With the traveler's leaving, the company returned to heading north, following tucks and turns based upon Hobbs' mapwork. Unlike the Ancient Road, these paths proved to be dark and dreary, hemmed in on the sides by trees and thick brush, and the ground rough with forest litter from seasons upon seasons. Halfway into the day, some pondered aloud if the boy was wrong. Those who knew not how the sun operated above began to question if they were going in circles. When Richter told them to drop these suggestions, the men changed discussion and soon after a fight broke out about who had spent the most time at sea, where tracking the sun and the stars about it proved most vital. The argument extended on thirty minutes until all parties admitted they were lying and had never once been out to sea, and half of them went so far as to admit they'd never even been on a boat. The deterioration of experiences went further on yet, as some lamented they'd never so much as been on a horse. Another thirty-minute discussion went on about which animals they had been on, but it promptly ended in a flurry of threats after Quinn exclaimed that he had been on all their mothers. At noon, they stopped and ate from the homesteader's cooking and over her roughage they found camaraderie in suffering her talents and by collectively insulting her cooking they got over the day's spats.

As they broke lunch, the company met a sudden and haphazard assault: ten thieves carrying clubs and daggers and hungered bellies streamed out of the bushes screaming for food and money or the heads of anyone who refused to give up either. Caught unhooking the firepot from the spit, Sophia screamed and heaved the hot water, scalding the ambushers and delaying them just long enough for Richter to shout the company into proper formation. As the sellswords formed a line with instinctive hurry, the thieves skidded and broke ground with their heels, coming to an immediate stop like sheep to a cliff. No longer sure of their advantages, they took to dialogue, requesting a more peaceful exchange of food and money. Richter answered by shooting one in the face with a crossbow. Screaming, the thieves charged in. They bashed into the shield wall, but the sellswords did not yield an inch. A beat passed. Breaths held. Then: the shields opened and Dahlgren and the rest fanned forward with their blades and the attackers fell in clumps. Terrified, the surviving thieves fled into the woods from whence they came.

"Sonuvabitch," Dahlgren said. "Sophia, you alright?"

"I'm fine, I'm fine. Just a little surprised."

"They came outta nowhere," Quinn said. "What the fark."

"Hobbs, you alright?" Richter said.

The boy popped out the back of the wagon. He gave a thumbs up.

"Alright." The captain turned to the dead. "They have anything?"

"Nothing," Crockett said, pulling his hand out of a brigand's bloodied pocket. He wiped his hand on the grass. "Not even a crown on them."

"Hey, this guy's got bread," Quinn said, holding up a roll. "There's blood on it, but I think you can eat around it. Anyone want it? Anyone? No? Alright, more for me."

Richter slapped the roll out of Quinn's hand. He turned to the company. "These brigands were so aggressive I Imagine someone in these parts already knows of them quite well. Cut their heads off and stow them. I have a suspicion someone might be glad to see them again."

The thief crouched down and picked up the bread roll again. He clicked his tongue. "Ah man, now it's got dirt on it. Thanks a lot, captain!"

~~~

Just as the day's light began to wane, the company stumbled back unto the Ancient Road. It was as true a sight to the sellswords as land would be to a shipwrecked sailor. The company circled around Hobbs and threw him into the air with three cheers, his little body rising and falling with their whoops and hollers. Richter then cut the celebration short, lest someone hear them and converge. They moved on, though occasionally slugging the boy in the shoulder and giving him wet willies and tussling his hair.

Beneath their feet, the Ancient Road regained its prominence, patching together grandiose stones and fine artistry step by step, as though the travel of the company made some civilized correction upon the wilderness, their very travel mending history. And with civilization came the civilized: the caravanserai drew into view, wimpled wagon tops clearing the horizon, and then their buglike formation lining the sides of the road itself. Even closer, they could see the occupants of merchants and families and across both the protection of caravan guards.

"This ain't no caravanserai," Elletrache said. "This is just a laager."

"What's the difference?" Quinn said.

"I was born in a caravanserai."

The thief scratched his head. "I don't think that really explains it."

"Ho! Ho there!" A merchant wearing golden garb approached. He held his hand up. "Ho there, travelers! Armed travelers, I see…"

Richter held his in return.

The merchant said, "Are you coming from Marsburg or Immerwahr's?"

The captain shrugged. "From one to the other to here."

"Hmm. And is Marsburg still under siege?"

"Unless that has changed in the past weeks, aye."

"I suspect it can hold for quite some time," the merchant said, nodding to himself. "And what of brigands on the road? Did you see any?"

"Immerwahr had us on contracts concerning a—"

The merchant held out his hand. "Just the matter of the road, please."

"We ran into bandits, if that's what you're asking."

"And have you proof?"

Richter retrieved the bag of heads and spilled them out. A few of the watching merchants and families stood up and shooed themselves away.

The merchant stared at the heads as though he were appraising pottery for cracks. "Hmm, they are rather fresh."

"Cooked this afternoon!" Quinn shouted.

Richter looked back. Dahlgren slugged the thief in the chest and pushed him out of sight.

The merchant drew his eyes upon a few of the heads and seemed to glean from their grisly visages some familiarity.

"Hmm, I must admit," the merchant said, pausing to turn one of the head's aside with his foot and then pressing its cleaved face together. "These do look like thieves we ran off two days ago." The merchant clicked his tongue and smiled again. "Well! Your travels here are actually something of a serious matter so I hope you are not offended by my serious inquiries. While this is decent enough proof of your intentions and character, do you happen to have an item for us? I won't say what, I don't wish to give away the code, after all. If you have it, you know you have it."

"I think I do," Richter said. He shouted: "Hobbs! The camel!"

Quick as a hiccup, the boy hurried forth with the carved camel held aloft in both hands.

"Here you go!" Hobbs said. "Just as you left it in my safety!"

Richter took it and held it out to the merchant. He said, "Immerwahr told me a man here would be expecting this and that is all I know."

The merchant strode forward, his silky clothes rustling and scratching with every step. He took the camel and turned it one way and another. Even though he seemed to have been expecting it, the camel's designs still captured his attention like a meaningful surprise. Wherever the camel went, immense curiosity could not help but follow.

"I've never seen one either," Richter said.

The merchant looked up as though the captain had intruded on his thoughts. He said, "Then I believe we both have failed to travel to further out reaches." The merchant turned and held up his arm, the sleeve rolling down to reveal a pale and skinny wrist. He snapped his bony fingers like two reeds clapping together. "Waldo, the package!"

A boy popped out of the merchant's wagon like a prairie dog from its hole. He carried with him a small, but heavy chest. Richter watched as his little feet crabwalked under its weight, his arms stretched to their limits, his fingertips barely holding on, his cheeks ballooned with effort.

"Hobbs," Richter said, looking back. "Are you just going to stand there?"

"Oh, sorry!" Hobbs ran forward, pitching a hand beneath the chest. "Here, let me help!"

As the boys struggled, the merchant handed the camel back to Richter.

"You don't want it?" Richter said.

"The toy? No. Of course not. It's a message that Immerwahr has cleared the way for more travelers and that he is expecting further business. Any brigand could simply tell us the roads are clear just to lead us into ambushes. The camel's purpose is to guarantee the message is true, for who else would have such a thing or, having stolen it, understand its import?"

"And if I'm lying?" Richter said. "Perhaps Immerwahr has entrusted the wrong man?"

"You can lie to Immerwahr all you want," the merchant said. "But there is enough money in this laager that I guarantee you will only lie to us once and whatever profits you have gained between the lie and the truth will soon be lost on you."

Taken aback by the threat, Richter said, "It was only a question."

"A question prospects for future endeavors. A question can hold more truth than the answer it seeks. This is why the wise and powerful listen, yes? What you have asked, I would not ask around men of coin, sellsword. Need I explain that you are not the only one of your sort in these parts?"

"No. Everything is understood."

Grunting and anguishing, the boys put the chest on the tailgate of the company wagon. They straightened up, exhaling huge breaths they had been holding the whole time. Hobbs awkwardly thanked the kid, and the kid awkwardly thanked him back, and then they awkwardly separated. Whatever learned discussion held between the adults was amusingly absent between the children as they diligently tried to avoid so much as eye contact.

"Here." Richter held the camel out to Hobbs. "You can have it."

"Oh, are you done with it already?"

"It appears it has served its purpose."

The boy took the camel with him and, having something of interest, immediately brought it to the other boy, both children cooing and oohing at the strangeness of that which the carving simulated.

Sighing tiredly, the merchant took out a sack of coins and tossed it to Richter. "A hundred crowns for the dead brigands." He took a key from his pocket and unlocked the chest, throwing its lid back with opulent dismissiveness. "And a mere five hundred crowns for patrolling the road, as Immerwahr and myself agreed upon."

The captain stared down at the glinting gold. Immerwahr had said nothing about payment on delivery, much less such a considerable sum of moneys. Briefly, Hobbs' obsession with the camel faded, and his eyes gleamed with the gold in view. Crockett came forward with his ledger in hand and pushed the boy out of the way.

"I'll have it counted, sir," he said.

"I-I can help with that," Quinn said, coming forward with his eyes glowing more than the sun. "Sophia's been teaching me numbers."

"No I haven't," Sophia said plainly.

"What? No, of course you have, and I should practice… my numbers…"

"Yeah I don't think so," Crockett said, pushing the thief back.

The merchant raised an eyebrow to the mercenaries, and then he looked to Richter. He said, "Your company's quite… quaint. Particular, even. Though I suppose the less particular companies are all circling around

Marsburg like buzzards. I won't pretend to know why a mercenary is so far away from where the money is. Your location is a peculiarity, and your peculiarity is in our favor. My curiosity ends there."

"Suppose that's one way to look at us," Richter said.

"I'm a merchant, sellsword. I can't help but judge those on what is in their pockets, and what they think could have been or, worse, what should have been. Do you understand these things as well?"

"Aye." Richter nodded. "Is there anyone in this laager that might be in need of mercenaries?"

The merchant laughed. He said, "Do you believe merchants arrived her absent of such aid already? Of course not. Nevermind that every swordhand you see is getting paid a premium and I do not believe they endeavor to see competition which lowers these prices. There is always an unspoken agreement between a merchant and his guard. A certain pretense of consistency is required for one man to raise his sword in defense of another. That pretense hardens like a stone when on the road. Despite the differences in appearances, the firm and the frail, the guards and those they guard share a bond. A crude one, but a bond, nonetheless. If you want work, you'll have to wait for the next group of merchants to arrive, should they do so without guard themselves which I very much doubt they will."

Richter nodded. He said, "Are there any swordhands in my predicament then? I myself could hire a few."

Again, the merchant laughed. "Did you not hear me? I said the prices are at a premium. No offense, sellsword, but judging by the way you looked at that five hundred crowns I seriously doubt you have the coin to afford them. If I may offer you a glimpse of where you stand financially, one of the merchants here has a man he paid two thousand crowns for."

Berthold leaned forward. "Did he say five hundred crowns?"

"Sophia," Quinn said. "How much is that?"

"It's five hundred crowns, Quinn."

"Wow. Holy shit."

"Yes," the merchant said. "It is an awe-inspiring amount indeed."

"Is this man worth it?" Richter asked.

"Yes, very much so," the merchant said. He bowed briefly. "I believe our business is concluded, sellsword. If you wish to stay at the laager, then you need only ask. The only 'payment' you make is that your wagon becomes a part of the encirclement, that is all. If there be altruism in the hearts of men, it is surely reciprocated here. If you elect to stay, I suggest you do not behave as, how do the youth say... hmm, do not behave as arseholes, yes? But I think you already understand doing that would be unwise."

"Aye, we understand."

The merchant nodded. "People will likely be glad to have you anyway. With notice that the roads have been recently patrolled, I suspect half of the wagons will depart today and start heading south. The rest will conduct some affairs here and wait another week or two to see how things unfold. Some men have investments tied to the conclusion of Marsburg's siege, naturally they're not chomping at the bit to make the wrong move and go get themselves killed on the roads. Your added number, albeit lacking proper employment, will still yet prove to be a useful front to any wayward trouble. And do you know how long you'll wish to stay?"

"A day, maybe a few."

"You do not know. That is a mistake for you, but I think quite alright for us. Well. Any other questions?" the merchant said, his light and gleaming clothes rustling and hissing as a breeze whipped through.

Richter nodded. "Seen anything strange in the woods?"

"Of course," the merchant said, laughing. "Strange sounds, sights, shadows. If you can imagine it, it's out there. Now is it *out there-out there*? That I don't know. Every so often someone goes into the woods and they don't come back. What became of them is anyone's guess. Brigands can be an issue. Internal thievery now and again amongst the guards. A man died on account of a card game so there is still some brutishness amongst us yet. These things happen, I'm sure you understand. We did have some kids find webknecht eggs last week. Caravan guard took care of the critters. No harm no foul in the end, just a lifelong fear of spiders burned into the youth. Waldo."

The merchant's little boy broke free of the camel. "Yessir?"

"Waldo, what did you think of the spiders you saw the other day?"

The boy started to tremble.

Laughing, the merchant said, "See? He is alive, the spiders are dead, yet his fear persists. That is how dangerous these woods are. They are but woods and winds, and yet they can imprint and tattoo us all. Now if you'll excuse me, I must alert the caravan that Immerwahr is ready to receive our business. And good luck with your ventures. I'll be sure to put in a good word to the monk for you. Even a sellsword deserves his renown."

Stepping aside, the merchant slightly bowed and threw his arm wide, as though it had been a gate strewn across the ancient road all along.

"Alright," Richter said. He touched his hat. "Thank you."

"I am not some usher, sellsword," the merchant said. He pointed more sternly. "Take your wagon off the side of the road, please. We will need the room for our departure."

~~~

With news of Immerwahr wanting more business and the roads being clear, the laager momentarily came undone: the circle of carts opened, with half the troop sliding onto the side of the ancient road, while the rest emptied out onto the road itself and rolled south. As the traffic ebbed and flowed, tempers flared and merchants jangled bells at each other and one took up a horn and blew into it which brought brief unity amongst all parties in telling everyone to shut the fuck up. Wheels squalling, one of the wagons edged off the side of the road and half-tottered into the air. A woman screamed and a man yelled at his donkey but the animal persisted despite the calamity behind it and so the cart flipped over in a thunderous crash that saw all manner of yarn and knitting material flitter into the grass. The donkey stood indefatigably on its four feet until the strain of the halter swept its legs and it landed nearly upside down. Even with four hooves to the sky, it still held as belluine and stubborn a stance as ever. A few passing merchants hollered at the wagon driver to do his job right, which prodded the selfsame man into picking up a crocheting needle and menace it toward his critics. This drew out the swords of caravan guards and rather mindlessly the man dared them with his little needle until his wife collected him and spun him away.

"Maybe shoulda kept that camel to ourselves," Quinn said. "It's like we broke the farking place."

"For once, I think you might be right," Richter said. He turned and shouted, "Company! Form... uh, form here."

With claps and whistles, the captain got his sellswords together. He held a brief talk, letting them know that they could wander the laager to their heart's desire. "Conduct yourself as though you represent one another because you do. So you do not steal. You do not fight. You do not squabble. If you converse with someone, learn something. You do not give away anything about the state of our company, though. And most importantly, nobody is to go into the woods. Other than that, enjoy yourselves and be back at the wagon by nightfall. Understood?"

He stared at the sellswords who stared back.

"Aye, captain."

"Yes captain."

"Yessir, Richter."

"You got it, cap'n."

Richter stared at the company. "Alright then, go on about your business."

"Whoohoo!"

"Quietly, Quinn."

"*Whoo.*"

As the day went along, and though Richter had allowed the sellswords to – within reason – act as they pleased, he did spend some time around a number of them, using their talents to help complete some tasks. With Elletrache, he traded for food and supplies, the beast slayer at times recognized and greeted with either fear or distanced respect, and many a time he was asked if his lindwurm armor was for sale. Later, with Crockett, Richter invested some crowns in acquiring historical scrolls and books, much of it just for the paymaster's personal reading. With Sophia, he procured bolts of cloth and a text on healing superficial wounds, the tome coming with extensive drawings to go along with its instructions. "I'll sooner harelip an old god than let Quinn get one over on me again," she had said, holding the book as though it were a heirloom weapon and she was about to start on a quest of vengeance. Richter wished her luck in her learnings and then spent a moment with Dahlgren, refilling the company's stock of ale.

"Ahh, thank you captain," the old man said, testing out a swig. He arced his hand across the merchant's wares. "We'll buy all of it."

The captain stared at the old man.

Dahlgren belched and hurriedly redacted the hand's path. "I mean we'll buy half."

~~~

As the sun drew down, the wagons came together in a great buglike arrangement, their rippled canopies bellied and bony and ribbed, sitting front to back, circling around in collective defense. Campfires shone numerous and bright, inviting warmth to those who would seek it, and a sense of daring confrontation for those who came with ill-designs in mind. As the night settled, conversations abound and a sort of cheeriness held sway over the caravan. After eating another batch of Sophia's stew, which proved as burdensome as ever, Richter returned to the company's wagon and Hobbs joined him to feed the donkey.

"Careful," Richter said. He nodded toward the trees to which the wagon had been positioned. "Notice they have us on the eastern side of the laager?"

Hobbs looked at the trees. "You mean, this is probably the worst spot?"

"Roadside is presumably the safest. There's a bit of clearing on the north and south. East? It's just woods. You could come and go out of there like a killer in an alleyway. They put us in the worst sport, absolutely."

"These are nice folk," the boy said. "I doubt they mean anything by it."

Richter did not rebuff the boy. He knew well enough that the merchants could not just trust a new passerby, and also that by being new to such a place you would, almost by default, be placed at the lowest rung of the ladder. But he also knew well enough that there wasn't much to gain in sullying the boy's trust in others and Richter regretted voicing his observations in the first place.

Hobbs said, "Just why are they so kind to one another anyway?"

"Well, most don't know each other at all. Not by name, anyway. It's the wagons and the wares that give away who they are, and in doing so they know the tasks of one another, and if you simply know the intentions of a man you know him better than you might even know yourself."

"And that's enough?"

"On the roads, aye. Travel is already a dangerous endeavor without inviting the troubles of your peers."

"And knowing the road is rough makes them friends?"

"Business partners, more like it, with the agreed pay that everyone is more likely to keep their heads on their shoulders if they follow the unspoken rules. It is by this momentary brotherhood that they survive." Richter pointed around the laager, a simple sweep of his hand that went over a litany of caravan guards, merchants, families, campfires, and the sturdy wagons themselves. "If someone were to wander into this sort of environment and still seek to make enemies, then he is truly someone of a different nature."

"What sort of nature?"

"Cruel or dumb."

"Or deadly," Hobbs said.

Richter scoffed. He said, "You'd need a small army to break into here."

"Or just be a really big monster."

The two sat in silence. A campfire gushed and people danced around it, their shadows arcing into the treeline like the spokes of a turning wheel.

Richter said, "How was your day with Thomas?"

"Good."

"Good."

The two sat in silence again, the merriment of the laager bursting onward with laughs and giggles and drunken singing.

Hobbs said, "How was your—"

"Productive," Richter said. "I think I had a productive day."

"That's good."

"Aye."

Not wanting to face another silence, Hobbs put some feed in his hand and held it out to the donkey. The animal engorged on the offering, its yellowed teeth chomping with alarming speed, but the boy remained brave, his palm unwavering as crumbs of grains flew off every which way.

Hobbs said, "When these people get where they're going, you think they won't be so kind to one another?"

"A road ends eventually, as does the camaraderie built traveling upon it. After that, who knows. They'll likely end up competitors and, frankly, enough time can make strangers of us all."

"What about our road?"

"Ours?"

"Yours and mine. Ours."

Richter smiled. "We don't share a road, Hobbs, we just share a direction."

The statement seemed to shoot through the boy, his face flinching to the last syllable.

"Ah, I didn't mean it like that," Richter said. "It was more of an indictment of my own self... just, uh, an indictment."

"I don't know what that word means," Hobbs said, but before Richter could respond, the boy nodded. "But now I think I do."

Richter pursed his lips. He said, "My intention is to keep you safe, Hobbs. I intended to leave you at Walddorf and then Marsburg, but things didn't work out like that. But you must understand, being out here with a company of sellswords, much less being around me, it isn't safe and it never will be."

"But I helped you," Hobbs said. "I figured out the maps! I could still go on helping you." If there were any number of words which could drive a dagger into Richter's chest, Hobbs found it and said them plainly: "I could help you kill her."

Sighing, Richter looked at the ground.

"You know she's still out there!" Hobbs said.

"Keep your voice down."

"She's still out there... and she's dangerous. You know she is."

"Hobbs..."

"And if she's out there, then I can help you kill her. I can help with a lot of things! But let's start with that! Let's start with her!"

Richter grabbed the boy by the side of his head, his scarred hand terrifyingly rough in its grip alone. He pulled the boy forward and said, "What do you want me to do, Hobbs? Do you want me to raise you and train you as a hexenjäger and then stand by until you get your first kill? Do you want me to clap my hands the first time you take a blade and put it through a heart? How about when you take your first head? You have to chop it, Hobbs, you want me to teach you how? You have to aim for the neck where the spine ends and the skull begins. It'll cut clean through. Make sure you step back because the blood will spray. If they're alive and you miss, they'll let you know. They'll let you know!"

The boy pushed back. "Get off me!"

Richter let him go.

The boy retreated a step.

The man did the same.

They stared at each other.

"You know she's out there," Hobbs said, tears in his eyes.

"She is."

"So why aren't you doing something about it?"

Richter turned his hands over. They carried so many scars that the stories they told talked over each other. He said, "I'm doing the best I can, Hobbs, but I am not the man I used to be. I am beaten down. I cannot see straight, I cannot shoot straight. I have nearly a dozen people under my care, and nearly as many dead because I lacked it. I've killed brigands I don't care about to make just enough money to realize I don't have enough. I have tortured men in horrible ways to get answers to questions that only I was asking. People hate me before they even know me and then I always give them justification anyway. I am missing teeth. I am missing an ear. I can hardly close either hand.

My knees crack if I stand too fast. My head spins if I move too swiftly. When I wake up in the morning, my back is so stiff I worry I'll never be able to move again. And each night I fall asleep thinking I won't ever wake, and the thought gives me relaxation, it gives me relief, and then morning comes and I'm disappointed, and I have to spend the rest of the day pretending I'm not."

"And yet you haven't shed a single tear or complained once," Hobbs said. He stared at Richter for a long while. He said: "So are you going to do it or not?"

"Hobbs."

"Richter, I'm asking you! I'm asking the *real* you!"

"I know you are and I'm answering," Richter said. He put a finger to the boy's chest. "The witch must die and I will kill her. Me, understand? This is not at all your fight."

"So, what, you just want me to stand here and feed the donkey?"

"Aye."

The donkey turned its head as though to imply it agreed to the notion. Hobbs glanced at it before he suddenly threw all the feed to the ground and stormed off. Richter opened his mouth and thought to chastise the boy but knew it might only worsen things. He sighed and turned to the donkey. Pinning its ears, the animal stared at Richter like a starved man who just had a plate of fresh food slapped out of his hands.

"Don't give me that shit," the captain said. He stared into the laager with his hands to his hips, awaiting the munching of the beast. He turned and found it still staring at him. With a sigh, Richter let his hands drop. "Alright fine. You want a carrot? I'll go get your ass a carrot."

Chapter 21. Incessant Inquiries.

"How do you do it?"

The campfire crackled before Immerwahr. Around him, dozens of faces hovered, pale visages wimpled in the darkness. She had arranged them in rows, and they stared blankly like a shelf of dinner plates. Emotionless. Moveless. Silent. All except for the one she had left the utility of a mind: the monk who sat across from the witch like a councilman from his liege.

"You ask too many questions," Claire said, poking the fire.

In the forest behind them, the lindwurm slept. Immerwahr cautioned a look over his shoulder like a noble with too many enemies. He spied the beast's shape, durable and long, the scales scratching and hissing as its lungs drew and emptied. So long was the lindwurm that it appeared in sections interrupted by standing trees. There its nose and maw. There its claws. There its shoulders. The body. More body. The tail. The tail's wicked end, settled there like a bundle of maces. Each portion of the lindwurm was a monstrosity in its own right. To contend with any aspect of it was to necessarily put your back to its fiercer assets. Fight the tail, and the mouth eats you, fight the mouth and its claws rip you apart, fight the claws and its tail might smash you in the spine. The creature existed as a weapon of annihilating destruction.

However, Immerwahr had taken note that the girl had beset his town with the direwolf. A much smaller, more incisive tool in her repertoire. It, too, stood in the darkness, skulking in and out of it, huffing and growling, no doubt as confused to its purpose and station as a wasp trapped under the glass. But even that wasp still stings.

"Do try to not stare," Claire said. "I can only control them so much."

These were not mere beasts to her but implements of her army. And yet another arrow in her quiver carried certain, albeit poisoned prominence: Kantorek. The once menacing brigand sat across the campfire, legs crossed, body still naked save for a sword laid across his knees. He sat upright and unmoving and with his palms set against his eyes, his splayed fingers shimmering shadows against his own pate as the fire crackled and popped, and in both pallidity and darkness his head looked that of a moth, a natural element hanging somewhere between lure and ward. His mouth sipped breaths, his chest rising and falling in stutters like a fish out of water, now with nothing more than a dribble of the river still on its lips.

"Him you can stare at," Claire said. She ran her hand along the man's shoulder. "He doesn't see much and he only minds what I mind."

Immerwahr stared at the brigand with a sense of pity. As terrible a man as Kantorek was, did he deserve such a demise? Certainly, this was his demise. Certainly, there was no coming back from this. Certainly, there would never be a desire to come back. The moment his mind could be freed, it would necessitate an ending.

"Why do you do it?" the monk asked.

Claire drew up her knees, hugging them. She said, "Did you know that I understand how things are from more than one perspective? That is to say, I understand the ulterior presage hiding in your inquiry."

"I…" the monk swallowed. "Is this a conversation?"

"Did you want one? You seem to want to understand my perspective."

The monk looked around again. The faces of the ensorcelled stared back. He said, "Alright. If you would oblige me…"

Claire swept a hand across her surroundings. The ensorcelled mob. The beasts. The brigand. She said, "I'm aware of the cruelty and evilness which must no doubt be apparent in how I am behaving. I'm also aware that most hexen, that is witches, are terrible cretins who deserve the blade just as much as they beg for it with their actions. To give you a good example, the coven that took me in and taught me the ways of hexen. I would consider them lifelong influences, but they themselves proved shortsighted. Myopically, they did indeed mangle a man of some import for no other reason than it seemed to humor them. He was a very well-known man by the name of Uther, a face of some infamy in Sommerwein and the surrounding areas."

"Uther the swordmaster," Immerwahr said. "I've heard tales of him slaughtering assassins in a bathhouse."

"Yes. A swordmaster that I personally knew. And all the same a man I did once personally wish to die. Wherever he went, children suffered. I saw through his celebrated, public status and the gleam he had in his eyes, I saw the wake of his trespass as surely as a cold wind skirts the curtains. Yet when he was captured on the road, I knew that my wishes were not in the right, nor were they prudent in the moment. What I wish for and what should happen are two different things. They do not exist or justify one another by principle alone. There is also a matter of time and place. Take the assassin's blade, for example. He does not merely kill, he sends a message on behalf of another. The distance between death and circumstantial benefit is the true calculation, for the benefactor can reveal his hand in the matter all too easily with his greed and ambition, and he frequently does. After all, it is typically greed and ambition which brought the benefactor and assassin into league to begin with. These are courtly matters, do you understand?"

"What you speak of is history," Immerwahr said. "The turning of the pages, so to speak."

"Do you understand?"

"Yes."

Claire nodded. She said, "Uther's mutilation by the coven warranted attention. People knew Uther, they knew where he had gone with witnesses abound, because wherever he went, memories were made just by seeing his face, just by seeing his famous hand. With his mutilation, the coven was tracked down with ease, and tracked down by nothing more than common soldiers. You must understand my rage, holy man. I had ensured that Sommerwein's guild of witch hunters would bother us none, and yet the coven took actions so egregious that ordinary men were our undoing. When I had devised an escape, the coven could not come. They were too weak. Not in body, of course, but of mind. They did not perceive things as I do. Experience itself had fooled them, for they thought their powers would save them far better than picked locks and jaunts into the woods."

The girl nestled her chin between the pinch of her knees. Her dress lifted gently to a passing wind, and her eyes danced with the swirling flames of the campfire. She said, "I do not see myself as distanced from the horrors of hexen. Quite clearly, I am becoming well acquainted with their methodologies. But do not confuse my actions as though they are tethered to the moments in which they are manifested. There are thieves of opportunity just as there are those of great conniving and design. Holy man," she said. "What becomes of the man who steals?"

"If he is caught? He is punished."

"And the man who murders his fellow man?"

"The same, although the magnitude of the crime is unquestionably worse."

"And what of the man who kills thousands?"

Immerwahr scoffed. He said, "There is no such man."

"Oh, but there is. There are many of them."

"Not even Uther could do that," the monk said. "It is an impossibility. There is no such man."

"My own father is one of them," Claire said. "I speak of the nobility. I speak of the lords of the land. Those who squabble amongst each other, fighting over the scraps left behind since the age of kings died, since the House of Kaltenborn fell so that humanity may survive the greenskins who once terrorized our borders. And I of course speak of innumerable dead men from eons past, mirrors and echoes of the men of today, shaped in the present as a weaker form yet of undeniable similarity all the same. These ungainly nobles who send hundreds and thousands to their deaths so that they may gain a sliver of land, a purse of gold, a, dare I say, whisper of prestige. The carnage of the coven who met me amounted to the death of one swordmaster. The carnage of men like my father has amounted to the deaths of untold number, and crueler yet, an untold number who are not once remembered, not once celebrated. When I saw the crops which sprung after the bloody summers of campaigning, I sometimes wondered if fertilizer was the utility of those forgettable campaigns and their forgettable dead, and in the evenings my father would be served mounds of bread and he would chew and chew and chew, and though it were a meatless dish I still yet saw the cannibalism within, and I watched him with a certain level of disgust that I do not have the words to convey."

Claire stared at the holy man. She continued:

"When I left the shadow of men like my father, all that has followed me is an air of conspiracy and the boots of hunters. The former simply want their prestige returned. I am of flesh, but a lost princess is ultimately a material matter, understand? And the latter, these witch hunters, they see to me as they would a rat in a grain silo. But I have to ask, holy man, where are the witch hunters for the lords? Who are their correctors? Who can even do it, besides one of their own? So ensconced in power nobles are, they fear little besides those like themselves. And do not fall for the misapprehensions provided by house banners and badges and crests. These divide the peoples, yes, but they do not divide the lords. All lords are cut from the same cloth, a cloth wrapped firmly around the throat of the world."

Immerwahr leaned back. He said, "You wish to change all of this?"

"You do not operate in terms of wishing and dreaming with your gods, and nor do I with my desires. I do not wish to change all of this, I *will* change all of this."

The holy man nodded toward the ensorcelled mob. He said, "And you'll do so by bringing further horror upon the world?"

"I cannot approach this world in peace," Claire said, and her voice did indeed seem drawn out by the weight of the task. "The matter of peace is currently one of pause. As I said, I have read the tomes, I have read the histories. Peace is not a natural word in the tongue of man. It requires translation and, more precarious an element, time to understand. But a snarl, a growl, a shout? These convey with purpose man's instincts and man's intentions, and every man has this tragic vocabulary committed to memory as surely as the hawk knows it must hunt without a single articulation as to why or when or where. But I have seen hawks pacified and controlled." She gestured toward the woods where the beasts lay. "And I have myself taken the greatest of creatures and stilled their hearts. I will have people following me without the need for these cruel behaviors. I am a beloved princess, am I not? In due time, the violent tendencies of man will be quelled, and the people shall flock to me and my cause and nature shall find them all remade."

"But not now."

"No, not now."

"Because of him."

"Yes, because of him. For all this to move forward, he must die."

"What if I were to talk to him?" Immerwahr said. "I could broker a deal."

"You wish to stand on my side then, holy man?"

"No… of course not. I stand against everything you are." Immerwahr nodded to the mob. He said, "I stand for them. I do not want harm to come to them. They are all innocent in this, even if you are 'understanding.'"

"You have desirable traits in you, holy man," Claire said. "But you are as myopic as the coven. Do not allow the witch hunter's somber visage or unremarkable skills to fool you. Richter cannot be trifled with on this matter. I am a witch, and he is the ultimate witch hunter. His resolve is unyielding. He is of one mind and dedication and at the end of his resolution lies my corpse. So he must die, and anyone who stands with him must die. Once he is gone, I shall be free to make full use of this advantageous period. If you truly wish for less bloodshed, holy man, then you should help me kill Richter."

"I will not."

"Why?"

Immerwahr swallowed. "Because I consider him a friend."

"Witch hunters do not have such things," Claire said, snickering like a mother having heard yet another of her child's inane worldly interpretations. "He is a killer with a killer's heart."

"You're wrong. I don't know what man you know as Richter von Dagentear, but the one I have dealt with is nothing as you describe."

"We needn't dawdle on the nature of a witch hunter," Claire said, smiling. "Ultimately, you do not understand the peace I seek because you cannot conceive of something which has heretofore never existed."

"All I see before me is what I've seen before," Immerwahr said. "Another venture of the nobility. Cruel and lost in magicks, I suppose, yet a noble venture nonetheless."

"I agree," Claire said. "That is, for now, precisely what it is. What I shall do will require immense bloodshed, but then it will be done."

"It's never done," Immerwahr said.

"Now I disagree," Claire said. Her eyes bore over the burning fire as though they had set the flames themselves. She said, "Understand this, holy man: the buzzards will have their fill, and then they shall starve."

The fire crackled between them.

Immerwahr sighed and closed his eyes.

The pop of a wheel hitting stone snapped through the air. Both parties looked up and back toward the dark. There, a man stood with a mule and a small cart filled with cords of rope. He looked at everyone, shifting his stare from girl to monk to mob to beasts. He rubbed his eyes.

"We are all what we are," Claire said to the man. "You dream not."

"If I ain't dreamin'," the traveler said, "then this is real new to me."

The girl scooted over and patted the ground. "Come and sit with us," she said. "The fire's warm."

She turned to the monk and nodded.

"Wouldn't you agree?"

Chapter 22. Old Men, New Tricks.

DARKNESS FELL UPON THE LAAGER. A merchant stood on a barrel and blew a bullhorn, a deep, sputtering sound. When he'd the attention of all, he announced that the woods were now to be considered unsafe and that everyone remain vigilant against the stark black that now surrounded them all. A man raised a hand. The merchant shouted "no questions!", and then tried to step off the barrel and promptly slipped out and cracked his back on the tottering barrel and this earned him raucous applause and, despite the dangers which had been pronounced, the peoples returned to their civilities.

Campfires blossomed in pits and here and there silhouettes of men passed betwixt their flames, all laughing and drinking and fighting and never in any sensible order. A certain coziness settled in, the women and children wrapped in blankets and sleepily staring into the crackling flames. Stories were told. Families remembered. Heirlooms promised.

Richter took a stroll through it. His shadow grew and shrank as he passed between the fires, into and out of the orbs of orange like some wayward specter whose provenance swam from one fiery island to the next, and in this illusory form many eyes met his, but not a single word was given.

The captain walked in this silence until he stumbled upon an old man sitting all alone beside a pile of embers and ash. Grunting and groaning, the elder's quivering hand lifted a firepoke and stirred the flames. As sparks crackled and popped, the light reached Richter's boots and the man paused before slowly sitting back. He looked up, his face familiar, his weathered and gimlet eyes peering from under the lid of a black hat.

"Aye," Richter said. "This figures."

Nodding, the old man said, "You look a reaper."

"As do you."

The old man patted the ground. "Come on down here and take a seat."

Richter walked to the campfire which offered as little heat as it did light. Again, the old man patted the ground next to him.

"Don't be a stranger, hexenjäger."

The captain took a seat. He took off his hat and hung it on a boot. The old man did the same with his. They looked at each other.

"You know," the old man said. "Ugliness ages exceptionally well. It changes little, and what does change goes unseen in the whole. You can smash a grape, but there's fark all you can do to a raisin. For the beautiful, age is a terror. It blemishes their perfections. A mirror can only esteem those which it later poisons. But I don't think a mirror does a single thing to you. For you, there is no value in looking at yourself, Richter von Dagentear."

Richter turned his head and spat. He nodded. "Guildmaster Imnachar."

"You were just a little lad when I last visited Marsburg." The old man smiled. "I had heard Carsten's finest was sent to the Lowland Reach to deal with the covens there and that particularly nasty Walddorf wench."

"Aye."

"So what brings you so far north in these interesting times?"

"I should ask what brings Sommerwein's guildmaster so far south."

"Bit of backtalk, eh boy? Though no doubt these questions are destined to share the same answer."

Richter nodded.

Imnachar said, "Is she in these woods?"

"Aye." Richter looked around. "Where are your men?"

The guildmaster leaned back, picking at a drooping eye with a wrinkled finger. He said, "Dead."

"All of them?"

"All of them."

"Her doing?"

"Of course."

"How?"

Imnachar laughed. "The noble family had discovered animal bones and cultish texts in her room. Very concerning elements when a girl that age should be surrounded by dolls and fancying boys. They requested our skills in reviewing her so I sent my best hexenjäger to sit with her. She hexed him. Almost instantly, too. Forspoken, the hexenjäger announced he intended to kill her and that I had given the order. He, of course, was merely a puppet at that point and made little more than theatrical moves to do harm. He was captured and then placed upon one of Sommerwein's torture towers where he screamed to the public what she taught him to scream."

Imnachar stared into the fire. He sighed. "I told the nobles that this so-called plot was the work of one rogue hunter. I threw that hexenjäger under the bridge to ensure the protection of the rest of the guild. It was not easy to do that. He was my best, as I said, but by this point he was gone and I had other considerations to be mindful of. Unfortunately, the Sommerwein nobility had suffered an injury to their majesty, that us witch hunters were operating above and beyond their laws. Claire disappeared soon after and that only confirmed their fears for they assumed we had taken her. They broke down the guild's doors and all of us were put to the question."

"Lord Landon of Marsburg told me that she was captured soon after."

"Her coven mutilated this doddering twat of a nobleman named Uther."

"The swordmaster," Richter said.

"Sure. Swordmaster. Tournament-menace. Kid-diddler. There's a lot of things to call Uther. Most in the public know him as the man who slaughtered a host of assassins in a bathhouse. Ultimately, it doesn't matter who he is.

Mutilating him was a crime that proved impossible to hide. Claire was recaptured almost immediately. Unfortunately, by this point, there wasn't a single hexenjäger to handle her as we were all enjoying the sights and sounds of those lovely Sommerwein torture towers. When those freezing winds are turning your fingers and toes black, you sorta forget your vocation. You forget a lot of things. You forget warmth, even. Last thing I ended up hearing was that she was being transported by some common bounty hunters and soldiers, and that she then, rather promptly and unsurprisingly, escaped."

"None of your hunters got away?"

"A few did, for a time. Two were out in the field when everything went to shit, but they got caught eventually. One they locked in a room with rats and the other got caught by some villagers and, you know, angry villagers can get creative. For the rest of us, dungeons and torture towers. Eventually, they hired a headlopper. I'd almost say that's when our luck improved." The guildmaster laughed. He said, "You know, you get to working with a people long enough, you tend to forget that the line between them trusting you fully and them cutting your head off with an axe is about as thin as the blade itself."

"But you made it out," Richter said. "How?"

"The beast slaying guild is the one who helped me," Imnachar said. He laughed. "Same beast slaying bastards that came after you, in fact. Remember those days when they really thought you were some wiederganger?"

"Aye," Richter said. "Interesting times."

"Well, they wanted to make amends. Not for free, of course, but amends, nonetheless. Together, we made a keymaster rich and myself a pauper. Sommerwein's noblemen wanted to execute me last and make a big show of it, too. Tear my guts out, burn them in front of me, so on and so on. I did take a bit of pleasure interrupting those scheduled affairs. Pissing off the nobles and shitting on the laity all at once? That ain't nothin' if not a proper hexenjäger day. Only thing missing is a wench, a stake, and a lick of flame."

Richter sighed. He stared into the dying fire. He got up onto his knees and grabbed a stick and started shunting the ashes around, getting the embers going, returning the flame to prominence. As it glowed, he saw his scars etch stark shadows across the hand. He realized he was prodding the fire harder and harder, his anger emptying out of his arm while he maintained the resolve to keep it from shouting out of his mouth.

Imnachar's hand fell upon his wrist. "Easy," the guildmaster said. "Easy."

"I need help," Richter said. "Anything. Anything you have at all."

The guildmaster sighed. He sank back as old men do, where even the hardest ground can have the appearance of the softest bed. Each day was just taking too much out of him.

"She essentially killed my finest hexenjäger in a matter of hours," Imnachar said. "How strong is she now? And don't honey it. Just tell me."

"I saw her mount a lindwurm like a knight would his steed."

Imnachar's eyes went wide. He licked his lips. He swallowed. A certain airiness took to his throat as though his tongue was wrestling with the words and nothing could be allowed out.

"Aye," Richter simply said. "We are in serious trouble."

The guildmaster grunted. "If you saw her do this, were you not within range to kill her? Carsten said you were the finest marksman he's ever seen."

Richter stared into the fire. "My... accuracy... I don't know. It's something with my hands or maybe my sight. I was alone when I saw her, so... in the moment, I decided that it would be better to face her when I could find a superior position than to risk missing the shot. Missing the shot implied so much more than just my death." The captain stared into the fire. He decided to omit the fact that he could very easily have shot her when the choice was between Claire and Hobbs. He didn't dare let the guildmaster know which he chose of those two, or that he did it on behalf of a small boy whose life almost certainly had no bearing on anything.

The guildmaster stared at him. He said, "It's a tiring war, is it not?"

"It is, but I can kill her," Richter said. "I just need help."

"You know, Carsten always thought they could be redeemed," Imnachar said, his crooked gimlet eyes staring into the renewed fire. "He believed that us hexenjägers and the hexes were in a dance. An infinite, unending dance that required us to always be with one another, feet over feet, shoulders over shoulders, ebb and flow. And every good dance has a pattern, so Carsten went looking for it. He believed that having witch hunters who went insane, who killed themselves, who quit, all that, he thought that was a good sign. That it meant the same failings could land upon the witches. We are not like men against beasts, after all. We are not, hands lifted from the dirt, backs upright, newly shaped creatures breaking upon the unsuspecting fields and forests. There are elements of civility between ourselves and our foes. Certainly, there's some unique beauty in this relationship. Men and women, purposed for one another in a manner absent of lust, for we are isolated and apart, without touch, without warmth, without sharing, and in these absences we may as well be of different forms entirely, and it is terrifying and it is beautiful all the same. And at some point in the pattern of this hiccupping, bizarre, and unnatural dance, it may come to pass that a hexenjäger and a hexe might hold hands, and lock eyes, and therein finally understand one another as they were always meant to do. That's what Carsten would tell me."

Imnachar cocked his head. "And what does Carsten's finest think?"

Richter said, "I look past the person and seek the power. Faces change, but the power is always the same and always corrupting. With the hexen, I've long accepted that I am no longer dealing with a person, I am dealing with corruption. That corruption cannot be redeemed, but you can stop the vessel which it is using. I think once the hexe understands the power they wield, it cannot be taken from them. No different than any lord or monk or burgomeister or banker. They all cling to it. Always have, always will."

"You were steadfast in that response, boy, and I do admire your certainty. I needed to see it, even. You asked if I have anything to help and that I do. But it is not something for a feebleminded fool to handle and absolutely not for a hexenjäger who poisons himself with doubts."

The guildmaster turned away a moment, the firelight making shadowed webbing of his ribs through his thin shirt, his old body contorting like a broken bug curling up one final time. But, grunting, he unfurled himself and swung back around and threw a bag to Richter. The captain opened it up, stared in, and then snapped it closed.

"Aye, I'd be careful with that," the guildmaster said with a laugh.

Richter peeked into the bag again. "Where did you get these?"

"The yellows and purples? Oh, they be out and about and I, naturally, picked them. Not sure what sort of guildmaster you take me for, but no pureblooded bitch is gonna get one over on me and not have me scrounging like a rat to put a few droppings in her soup." Imnachar levied a heavy finger toward the bag. He said, "You do know what those are for, right?

"Aye."

"You know how to make the concoction, right?"

"Aye."

"You must be taken by the process, you understand?"

"Carsten made a batch with me," Richter said.

The guildmaster smiled, or frowned, it wobbled in either direction and the flames and shadows helped none. He said, "You really must be his favorite. Do you have someone you trust enough to help you?"

"Aye."

"Good. If you manage to do it, I figure there's enough there for you and any friends you got, though I suspect it be best you do not inform them on how the sausage is made, understand?"

"Aye."

"You'll likely lose your mind attempting to make the concoction," Imnachar said, laughing. "But I suppose to stop a Neu Grimalkin anything is worth a try. Certainly, ordinary fancies of the forest will not resist whatever brew she is cooking up."

Richter nodded. He then stared at the guildmaster's arms for a moment. He said, "Do you have a wristed crossbow?"

Imnachar leaned toward the fire, stabbing at it with the firepoke again. "What's that you say?"

"Do you have a wristed crossbow?"

"Come again?"

"Do you—"

"Huh?"

Richter sighed. "Alright."

Smirking, Imnachar said, "You should know better than to ask a guildmaster that."

"Alright," Richter said, nodding. "And what is it you plan to do?"

"Ohh, I think I'll just set here and see if them Sommerwein headloppers ever show."

"There's a ferry town south of here," Richter said. "You should go to it and seek out a man named Immerwahr. Tell him I sent you and he will help."

Imnachar laughed. Or the fire's embers had wheezed, Richter couldn't tell the difference. The guildmaster said, "Carsten is dead, isn't he?"

Richter had tried to avoid the subject. He sighed. "Aye. I believe he is."

"Ah," Imnachar said. "I suppose I won that bet, then."

The guildmaster retrieved his hat from his boot and put it on his chest and he laid down with his eyes to the stars and dim fire to his feet.

Imnachar turned, smiling with cracked lips and drooping eyes. The old man said, "Just one other thing…"

~~~

As Richter returned to the company wagon, Dahlgren met him with a wave of his nub of an arm and a second later his good hand threw something into the air. The captain sidestepped and watched as a wooden sword landed softly in the grass, a soft tuft of noise a humiliating coda to the nearly frightful jerk reaction to having first seen it lofted.

"Yer vision's good," Dahlgren said. "Instincts, not so much. You should have caught that."

Looking around, Richter said, "A bit dark to be practicing, no?"

"That's why I'm giving you the wooden one," Dahlgren said. "Now pick it up already. I'm having myself a moment of clarity." He nodded. "Respectfully, captain."

Richter picked up the sword. He looked up, trying to divest Dahlgren's silhouette from the laager's spotty campfires. Just as his eyes began to pull Dahlgren's shape from the darkness, the old man's steel blade scratched out of its sheath. A lick of firelight strobed its length and as he twirled it around the reflection flickered here and there and back again as though he sparked the air with his speed.

"I get this," Richter said, holding up the wooden sword which reflected nothing at all. He nodded toward the shimmering blade. "And you get that?"

"I know what I'm swinging at. You don't. It's safer this way."

The blade whirled out of the firelight and Richter couldn't see it, but he could hear the old man's worn hand suddenly grip its handle, and he knew somewhere above those knuckles was deadly steel.

Richter took a step forward. He said, "Have you been drinking?"

A whoosh of air answered the question, and Richter sidestepped and slashed out his wooden sword and the weight of it clipped a hard edge in the darkness then rode upward and away. The silhouette of Dahlgren swam by like a fish just under the water's surface, then reappeared on the flank as he swung around, his face faint and flickering, firelight in his eyes.

"Were this a battle, I would've killed you then and there," he said.

"I can't even see," Richter said. "We should wait 'til morning."

"A man swings his sword at you, what do you do?"

"Fight him."

"Ahh, c'mon captain! Let's go over it again: if you got plate or a shield, you can just stand there and block it. If you don't got the armor, then you need to dodge or parry. Most men parry. Very few dodge because dodging requires big fucking balls or an addled pate. Whatever you choose, you always look to hit back no matter what. You always keep your eyes forward. You start blinking and closing your eyes or gods forbid turning your back and yer fucking dead. Nimble fighters, battleforged fighters, hells, even swordmasters all play by these same fundamental rules."

Richter sighed. He said, "Dahlgren, I'm none of those men—"

Yelling, Dahlgren sailed forward, his firelit eyes wide and streaming through the darkness, and somewhere upon the ground was the scratch of his boots across grass, and out to the side a streak of firelight winked off the tip of his sword like a firebug. Richter's eyes took to it like an owl to a mouse and he stepped opposite the shape and he straightened and supinated his swordhand and felt the wood hit the blade and a moment later he planted his foot and leapt backwards – and where he once stood the woosh of Dahlgren's blade passed and the air whispered against the captain's face.

"What are you doing!" Richter said. "That could have killed me!"

"What a parry! And a slick backstep, too!" Dahlgren said. "Yer learning!"

Richter checked for damage, running his fingers over his scars and what little untouched flesh he still had. No fresh wounds. No new blood. The only wound he had was Dahlgren's chuckling laughter barbing his ears.

"Yer alright," the old man said. His blade hissed as it reentered its sheath, the flickering reflection of the campfires dousing into leather. He walked over until he was close enough for his silhouette and Richter's to meet, like two shadows absent of their makers.

"I can smell the ale on you," Richter said, shaking his head. "Bought a few kegs and I wager you've already blown through most of it."

"Aye, I've had a little. Look, I only threw that at half my speed. Any faster and I would've been peckin' yer nose," Dahlgren said. He clapped his nub on the captain's back. "But you are learning to trust your instincts, captain. If this were in the daytime, you would see everything. And you would overthink it. Here, in this faint dark, you behaved as an animal would, by trusting what's inside, and you survived. If you can do that at night, you can do it during the day. Well. Hopefully."

"Ah, thanks," Richter said. He handed the wooden training sword back. "You should take the night off, Dahlgren. The laager's safe enough with its caravan guards. Only a fool would hazard an attack."

"I think I will," the old man said. He balanced himself. Whatever drink he had been imbibing seemed to have suddenly caught up. "Wh-what are you going to do?"

Just one other thing, Imnachar had said. *We're here, then we're gone. At the ends of these worlds of no better and no worse, there is only nothing. I look forward to returning to it. May you have the resolve to brew that concoction well, Richter von Dagentear, and I pray to the old gods that you've the right man in place to help you do it.*

Richter smiled. He said, "I've someone very important I need to talk to."

Chapter 23. The Concoction.

IN THE LIGHT of the laager's campfires, parties carried into the night. With so many merchants around, the evening had ale and mead aplenty, and as the stars rose so too did the drunken rambunctiousness. There, hooting and hollering, the laager's increasingly belligerent and slurring troop gave a rowdy show of force through volume alone, like a hunter screaming at the mouth of a bear den, so unnatural was his courage that the beast knew it best to stay inside. For the forest's beasts, they would not dare go near that which met the darkness of night with sloshing horseplay. And there at the distant rim of the wagons, far from the festivities, Richter and Hobbs sat in the dark.

"Just look at them," Hobbs said. "We're missing so much fun."

"Aye."

The captain watched the boisterous shadows and silhouettes, the flightiness of their imbibed movements. He knew that he and the boy could not venture too far into the woods and stay safe, but at the same time he had to be sure that no one would come and bother them. There in the outer dark between laager and forest, the two sat in what he hoped to be safe isolation. Nothing could be interrupted. Not for what he had planned.

"So what are we doing?" Hobbs said. "Better be worthwhile."

"I hope it is," Richter said, and he unfurled a leather tool roll, revealing a trio of mortars and pestles, the items married to each other in design and purpose. He set them each apart in quiet determination while Hobbs simply observed. Finished, Richter took the bag Imnachar had given him and set it in his lap and then supinated his hands, knuckles upon his knees.

"Alright," Hobbs said, staring at the goods. "What is all this?"

"I am going to trust you with something," Richter said. "And you have to promise me that no matter what happens you will stay right here."

"What are you planning to do?" Hobbs said, his face already wrenched with worry.

Richter took a breath. He said, "I'm going to poison myself."

Hobbs stared at the man for a moment, awaiting the next sentence which would indicate this were some sort of jest. When it did not come, the boy grimaced and then blurted, "Wh-what! No!"

"Quiet," Richter said, holding a finger to his own lips. He put both hands into the guildmaster's bag, descending slowly as though there were sleeping vipers inside and his fingers were to dance upon their heads. He looked at Hobbs. "You know that I am not a mercenary captain, right? That I am, through and through, a witch hunter?"

"I… I think you can be both…" Hobbs said. "And even just… a normal person… like me…"

Richter took a breath. He nodded toward the laager's campfires, and the festivities circling around them, their song and dance trickling through the woods in jovial murmurs. He said, "Everything I do with these people, every job I sign onto, every fighter I hire, ultimately has one purpose: to help me find and kill Claire von Sommerwein. You already knew this but the others cannot. At least not yet. The situation is too unbelievable, and the costs of publicly hunting a princess are too severe. Even the mere rumor that we are hunting royal blood is beyond dangerous. Claire is clothed in the immensity of majesty itself, and she need not bedevil or ensorcell or bewitch to have multitudes following her. It is well enough that she is who she is. But she is, of course, so much more."

The laager erupted in laughter, but now the boy did not look to it.

"I don't like this," Hobbs said. "I think this should stop."

Sighing, Richter said, "Unfortunately, I have seen a great extent of Claire's learning already. I have no doubt at all that her powers might soon be unstoppable. She is likely capable of potent mixtures that can harm even the most fortified of minds and warp the instincts of the oldest of beasts. For that reason, I am trusting you to help me with this, and it must be you alone."

His hands came out of the guildmaster's bag. In one hand, he held a thick-stemmed, brightly yellow mushroom freckled with white dots, its spiny gills as thick as sea corral, bristly and crunchy. In the other, he held a soft shroom of purple make, its cap shaped like an arrowhead, its layers bulbous with pustules that glistened in perpetual dripping. Both were abominable by appearance alone, things so ghastly that no ordinary creature of the forest would ever so much as think to try a bite.

Richter tilted the yellow. "This is a Yeshkun mushroom." And then the purple. "Basaldi."

"No…"

"Both are consumed by the greenskins for their enraging properties. We called their eaters berserkers at the Battle of Many Names. To orcs, the hallucinations only incite the characteristics which were already present. Rage. Fury. Violence. For a human, consuming either one of these could result in a serious illness that scars the body from the inside out, crippling it for a lifetime. Such sufferers do not permit themselves to live long in this world. The pain is too great, understand? But even then, those are the lucky ones, for if it does not attack the body, it instead attacks the mind and dissolves it. A total annihilation of one's senses, of one's ability to grasp reality, pitching the sufferer into an eternal nightmare."

Hobbs grimaced. "No… I… you don't…"

"You need to help me, Hobbs. I need you to do this. No one else will understand. You said it yourself at the ferry town: Claire has to die. Now we go through with it, understand?"

"No, I mean… you care more than that," Hobbs said. He pointed at the laager. "You don't treat these people as if they're just tools. You care more than that. I know you do. You lie to them to keep them safe, sure, but they're still people… they're still worth protecting for their own right… and I know you do protect them, too, no matter what you say. It isn't just about her anymore, it's about them, too."

Richter stared at the boy, and the boy at him. He thought of a hexe and how she might fool a man into being someone else entirely, into being a pawn for her, and though Richter had come to kill many a witch and suffer many a trick in doing so, the boy's simple stare tore right through him as fierce as any potion, trap, or bewitching he had ever faced.

"Right?" Hobbs said, tears forming in his eyes. "They're more to you than just tools… *I'm* more than just some tool, right?"

The captain stared at the boy. He opened his mouth, and then paused. Anything he said here could cause the boy to run off and alert the company. Anything he said might even cause the boy to simply run into the woods. Anything he said could reflect on his own self, revealing something he did not wish to face. Anything he said could lead to uncertainty. Something that weakened him against *her*. Uncertainty. The elixir of existence. With every second that passed, realities were born and others torn asunder…

"Say something!" Hobbs said with pleading desperation.

Instead of saying anything, Richter stuffed the mushrooms into his mouth. The Yeshkun tasted like bitter poison and he retched, and the Basaldi's pustules popped across his tongue and filled his cheeks. He gagged as he chewed. Hobbs threw himself upon Richter, but he pushed the boy back and grabbed another pair and ate them quickly, and another and another. The boy came after him on the fifth and last pair of shrooms, his little hands pulling at the captain's arm with the caps still being held, and Richter ate them in a crazed chomp and then shoved the boy again.

"Back!" he yelled, and in a moment realized he may have been too loud. He looked toward the campfires to see if anyone was coming. The laager tilted, its oval of orange fires wobbling like a plate rattling around on the floor, and reflections of flames shot out in every direction, into the sky, into the woods, and the wagons began to lift upward and turn, one big circumferential roll, wagon after wagon, a belt of carts, a sash of wains, there rolling together like a bug, a great wooden shell creaking loudly as it closed the loop, and through the gap of its hole a crimson moon swirled.

Richter took a breath.

Already it was settling in. Already it was at work. And this isn't at all what he planned. This was nothing more than panic. Absolute stupidity and panic... and he hadn't even properly ground up the other mushrooms yet, the concoction half complete while his mind was almost fully gone. He held his eyes shut and took a long breath.

"You..." Richter said. "Have to be quiet..."

"Oh by the old gods," Hobbs said. The words sounded so far away that the boy may as well have spoken them from the inside of his boots. "Richter! Richer! Ohhh, alright, I'll be quiet. See? I'm quiet. Just tell me what to do! Tell me what to do so you're better!"

Richter reached out, and as he did so he realized his hands were clenched into fists. Blood surged through his arms, the veins undulating like hungered snakes in a sack. He could feel the heat of rage flowing like venom.

"I'm here!" Hobbs said, his little fingers upon Richter's shoulders.

Just with that touch, Richter felt the urge to grab those little fingers and snap them off. He felt that urge in his chest. If his hands wouldn't do it, his teeth would, and if not his teeth, then his very ribcage would spring out and do it, for it had to be done! By any means it had to—

Richter slapped himself.

Hobbs fell back. "Oh by the old gods, Richter..."

Without opening his eyes, Richter held the bag out. "Are there any yellows or purples still in there?"

A moment passed. Hobbs said, "No... but there are other mushrooms."

"Spill those out in killer... in equal parts... into the mortars in equal parts... and start *k-k-k-kill...* grinding them."

"Do the colors matter?"

Richter's teeth clenched.

"Do the colors matter?" Hobbs said again.

Bite his head off.

"No, the colors don't m-m-matter."

"Do—"

"Just put the them in the mortars and grind them," Richter said tersely.

Kill him.

"Alright, I'm doing it, I'm doing it!"

Kill the boy.

He's a threat.

"See? I'm doing it!"

Yes. See. See now!

Your eyes are closed!

Your eyes are closed and he could slit your throat!

What are you doing? Stop him!

Stop him!

Richter bit the inside of his cheek. Blood ran free. Hot. Metallic.

A taste, yes.

An appetizer.

"Hurry, Hobbs..."

He could hear the boy turning the bag up and pouring the shrooms. He could hear the hollow scratch of the pestles at work, grinding again and again, an odd rhythm to mirror the boy's work, as enjoyable as the light scraping of a painter's brush could be as pleasant as the art itself. Ensconced in the noise, the captain leaned backwards, finding a moment of peace as though he were in a torrential river which had emptied into a pond and found there a gentle rest. As he leaned, a cascade of colors burst through the darkness, rainbowing his sanity in a wreath of wonders. And then the colors snapped away, leaving him staring into darkness. Leaving him to his own self and his own thoughts, and with every heartbeat he saw red tendrils spiraling out, little arms reaching, wanting, desiring to grab and rend. Taking a long breath, he fell back even further before planting his arms to keep himself upright.

The grinding of the pestles stopped. Hobbs said, "Are you alright?"

He's asking that to trick you.

Kill him!

Open your eyes!

See the boy!

Watch his hands!

"Richter?"

The captain realized he was grinding his teeth. When he loosened his jaw, blood pooled out of the gums where teeth used to be and he turned his head and spewed it from his mouth.

"Richter!"

"I'm fine!"

"By the old gods…"

"Keep working," Richter said, and the words jettisoned into the darkness behind his eyelids, one after the other: *Keep. Working.* Each word manifested itself into existence by a plethora of colors that danced and bloomed between the letters. In the moment, Richter regretted ever learning how to read and write. He wondered how these words would look if he had no education at all. He imagined—

"I'm done," Hobbs said. "What should I do now?"

Die.

Richter raised his fist. He knew it was shaking, because the whole world of black wobbled and vibrated around him, inducing him to put that fist to use. To export his rage unto the nearest target. His thumping heart demanded it. Slowly, he unfurled a finger and put it to his own lips.

Yes, bite him!

Use your teeth!

Rip him to shreds!

Taking a great breath, the captain tuned his ears to the laager and there found drunken festivities and the sounds of children playing knight and beast and somewhere the sound of a wife barking up a storm about her cheating husband and he heard Dahlgren belch behind all that flurry of noise and he heard Quinn crack a joke at Richter's expense and the whole company laughed heartily to it though soon after he heard Berthold defend his honor and Sophia chastise the thief and in hearing all these things Richter knew he should have heard none, for they all sat so far away yet the sounds were as though he were right next to them, and in this realization of the impossible all the noise cut away in an instant, like a rat spotted in the moonlight, dashing back into the dark with its nibbling crime left behind. Richter opened his eyes.

A pitch-black, granitic golem sat across from him, its shape molten-cooled and ill-formed, the sort of magmatic manifestation the earth made when none were around to look, and even now when none dared to.

"Richter?" the golem said.

Richter.

The word floated from the golem's maw like a fiery belch from a volcano, red and hazy. As Richter leaned away from his own name and its letters, the word swirled and took shape. Legs. Arms. The pairs joining and bleeding onto one another to form a torso. A head appeared. It was as Richter saw himself. A red Richter, slowly coming to stand in the air between golem and man.

The captain closed his eyes.

"Richter?"

Richter...

The red Richter met him in the dark behind his eyes.

Kill him! He's grabbing a branch, you fool! He's going to stove your head in! Kill him!

Brimming with tendrils of rage, the red Richter approached as though there were another set of eyes looking out from behind those closed eyes, the apparition assailing some inner self Richter never knew existed. And Richter ran from it, his mind ringing, his vision spinning, he held onto some nook or cranny within himself, a memory of Dagentear, a memory of a forest, a memory of a branch he had carved his name into. He clung to it like flotsam and the memory took him further down, further down into the realm where the dark wasn't dark at all, where he shouted words – shouted *help*, shouted *no*, shouted *please* – and yet nothing took foot, nothing vocalized, nothing escaped. And from Dagentear nothing did escape and the branch he held onto snapped and he saw his carved name depart the wood and turn red and as the rage brimmed at his back, Richter turned and fell out into nothing.

"Richter?"

...richter...

...is this where you hide what happened at Dagentear, boy?

A white apparition gathered in the dark, the length of its sentence manifesting it, each syllable accomplishing it a leg or arm or hand, and the white words took shape: legs, arms, torso, head, but this shape slumped over, bending at the hip and holding a hand to its back.

"Carsten," Richter said, recognizing the white being. "Please."

You see, boy, the white Carsten said, taking a seat on an invisible chair, speaking out to some distant past, some distant Richter, some boy before the man, some beginner before the expert. *For the shrooms to be properly cultivated, one must be at once thoroughly convinced that they have lost their mind, while at the same time still be of sound enough constitution to realize they* have *lost their mind — and therefore retrieve it in an instant. As you can imagine, producing this concoction is not to be taken lightly. Most who try do not return. It is difficult to explain what I mean… that… and…*

The white Carsten began to fade, and the volume of his words with him.

"No, Carsten…"

"Richter?"

…richter…

A strobe of white lightninged down, revivifying the white Carsten, his dullness suddenly brimming back to life.

…but it can be done… and I'll show you how it's done, Carsten's voice continued. *But you are to never do it yourself. You're too brave, understand? Wipe that smile off your face, boy! It is* not *a compliment! When faced with madness you will be too courageous. You will try and fight it. But true madness cannot be fought. It will grab you, and it will drag you down to its level, and you won't ever come back. Not by yourself.*

"Richter!"

You have to let it in.

You have to let it all in.

Richter opened his eyes and the black golem stared back at him.

"Richter!"

…richter.

A bubbling red Richter foamed from the golem's mouth. It took shape, but as it did the other red Richter drew it into a fist fight, the two crimson images battling in wild and monochromatic chaos, each blow spraying chunks of themselves, their bloodformed bodies disintegrating in bruising pugilism. Rent redness streaked through the air, and in the crimson gloom which brimmed upon every strike, Richter could see a trove of witches giggling and laughing from between trees, most of them holding their decapitated heads at their bosoms, and with every heave of their chests more red Richters emerged, joining together in a giant pool of splattering battle.

"Richter, Richter, Richter…"

…*richter*…

The boy from Dagentear.

The one they call the Wight.

"Richter, it's Hobbs!"

A great crack of white lightning broke across the witches, and as the color faded they were gone. Richter stared forward just in time to see the golem spring forth, its granitic mouth yawning wide like a chasm of the earth, cavernous and dripping with stones so ancient surely it were the truth that the earth had teeth, that the earth had its hungers, and the golem screamed out his name and in a mere instance it formed a massive white apparition as if fashioned by in size by the sheer volume which once contained it and this image ran forth, beaming in the sublimity of its own creation, and it descended upon the red Richters and annihilated them in single blows, and with every strike their crimson shapes unraveled and tailed away into the winds and into the forests and into the night.

"Richter! What do I do?"

"S-stop," Richter said, fanning his hand out. "I… you…"

"Richter! Please, what do I do?"

What do I do?

Three words of immense uncertainty, each letter tumbling down in streams of grey, and the dying red Richters took to the letters like soldiers pilfering an armory, and they armed themselves with this gross uncertainty and fought back against the white Richter annihilating them, and a terrific war unfolded in which Richter could see and hear himself dying over and over, screams of himself as a child and boy and man, and as the battle went on the corpses piled ever higher, some little some long, their little red war climbing through the ages of his own existence, reddening the sky, the great granitic golem towering over it all like some god confused over his own creations.

"Richter! You have to help me! What do I do?"

"N-no… d-don't…" Richter said, his hand trying to wave the creatures away. "You… have to trust… have certainty…"

"That's it, I'm going to get help," the golem said.

All the red Richters froze and screamed and hissed. Richter reached for the creature, but as his arm stretched out, the golem simply rose away, towering overhead, its height soaring above the treetops and into the sky above and through the clouds and into the stars, a swirling white moon brimming on its forehead, itself staring down with two white eyes. The captain trembled at the sight of it and he fell backward and closed his eyes.

A fading Carsten met him in the dark. Shapeless and formless as he was becoming, Richter knew the old man was smiling. He said: *It will grab you, and it will drag you down to its level, and you won't ever come back. Not by yourself.*

The darkness of his own mind flashed as a red arm punched through the blackness, the fist carving it open and then a red Richter pressed inside. Another followed, and another. Just as soon as they filled the space, they joined together and pointed inward. Pointed at the one who watched. Pointed at their maker. Pointed at the one who could undo them.

"Richter!"

The grey Carsten stood up.

You have to let it in, Richter. Let it all in…

He opened his eyes.

"To hells with this," the golem said, the words crackling across the entire night like lightning. Its massive hands reached down, descending like a giant statue falling from its plinth, and one single finger extended downward like a holy totem from the heavens. "Hold still," it said. "Hold still!"

Richter fell backwards. The finger followed. He tried to wriggle away but found himself unable to move. All the red Richters had turned against him: they knew he was there, and each was glomming onto his limbs. Missing teeth and fingers and arms and legs, the red Richters still banded together to stop him. Stop the *real* Richter.

A pressure seized upon his throat. Not his throat, but the inside of it, his tongue receding, his breath gagging. He lurched upward and then fell on his side. The golem's fulminating words arced across the night sky and the swirling white moon cut in half and went its separate ways. Richter's eyes widened as the golem's fingers again drew upon him like the claws of a hawk toward a rabbit, and he shrank backward until they swooped into his mouth and he looked down to see the red Richters fleeing all at once, themselves seemingly slipping from existence as they routed, perhaps stealing into another darkness altogether, one that men were not meant to see. As the golem intruded again, Richter gagged and turned over and his throat was set afire by all the anger welled inside of him, and the terrible golem stood over him stoking these flames until the pain won out, until the pain blackened everything, until the pain gave him the bliss of nothing at all. A nothing in this world, a nothing in all worlds.

~~~

Understand the real horror of trying to harvest this, Carsten's voice said. *You cannot create it with the knowledge that you'll be saved, understand? You must truly lose your mind. Believing that there is a rescue awaiting you prevents proper dilution. You must take it when no one is looking, or when someone does not understand what it is you are doing. You must submit yourself to the chaos of the unknown. You must, in a sense, be taken by the fear – the fear that you will never return. So, you have to create this concoction only with the help of someone you trust. Someone you know who knows you well enough to know that the you, this you inside your head, the* real *you, is being lost. And yes, boy, I trusted you, and you may take that as a compliment. For once, you may do that, and may you one day find someone to return the favor.*

~~~

"I didn't tell anyone. I stayed right here, just like you told me to."

Richter opened his eyes and it seemed as though reality itself were a bucket of cold water. The night air iced over him in an instant, coating the corrugations of confusion and revealing the errors of overthinking, leaving him with a state of mind that was crisp, ready, present. He lurched upward, his hand upon his chest, his lungs filling. He looked over.

Hobbs stood there with a goatskin flask. He held it out. "Water."

The captain took the flask and drank it dry. His arm fell to his side. He looked at the boy.

"I'm sorry," Hobbs said. "I just did the only thing I could think of."

"Did I vomit?"

"Aye."

Looking around, Richter said, "Where is it?"

Hobbs turned and retrieved the bowls. He said, "You were mumbling about the mortars and pestles and the other mushrooms so… well, I made sure you vomited into these. I figured whatever you were trying to do with the shrooms that, uhmm, maybe… you could try again? I mean the parts are still kinda in there…"

"Actually," Richter said, staring at the bowls, his yellow and purple spew swirling with the crushed remains of the more ordinary mushrooms. "That is precisely where it's supposed to be."

"Really?"

"Aye."

Richter retrieved his bandolier of vials and unfurled it across the ground. He took as many vials out as one hand could hold, and with the other hand he gave just as many to the boy.

"We are going to take these vials and start—"

"Are you alright?" Hobbs said.

"What?"

The boy shrugged. "One moment you're writhing on the ground, your eyes closed, your eyes wide, you tried to hit me, it sounded like you wanted to kill me, and you said Carsten's name, and you cackled like an old witch and tore at yourself. Next moment, you're here, already commanding, already looking toward the next step."

Richter stared at the boy. He slowly held up a vial. "We are going to mix the contents into the vials, understand?"

"I understand you don't want to talk about it."

"The vials, Hobbs. We're going to mix, alright?"

"For... later?" Hobbs said.

"Aye."

"You mean... to *drink* later?"

Richter grabbed one of the vials himself and started filling it. As the boy stared at him, he looked over and nodded. "Aye, to imbibe later."

"Th-that's disgusting! Why would you ever do that!"

"Many years ago, a guildmaster and a young hexenjäger figured out that if you consume these shrooms and then regurgitate them, you can defang their properties, leaving behind a mixture that does the opposite: it clears the mind. If given to others, it can be act as an antidote. Unfortunately, we have not figured out how to build a stock of the material. The life of the antidote is about a month after which time it merely turns into a rancid slush." Richter filled a vial. He looked at Hobbs. "The hexenjägers figured this out in an era when a terrible Grimalkin broke upon the world. The desperation of the process speaks for the desperation of those times."

"If they only last a month…" Hobbs said. "Then that means you intend to face Claire soon?"

"Aye," Richter said. "I am building my forces, she is building hers. The forest is our equal here, the seclusion it offers, the transient nature of the peoples who come through." He corked another vial and stared at it. "You know, when I was your age, the woods were my favorite place to be. Now all I see are hiding spots, ambushes behind trees, beasts behind bushes, and hexes in huts."

"Well, once we kill her, maybe these woods will return to how they should be."

"Once *I* kill her, Hobbs. You're not a part of this."

"Except this part here, of course," the boy said, holding out his hands with a litany of vials, his fingers smudged and caked in questionable looking crusts. "You needed me for this."

"Aye, of course. Just not the killing part, understand?"

"Aye, I understand." Hobbs filled another vial, cringing as more of Richter's vomit touched his fingers. He said, "Do witches know about these mushrooms?"

"Not only do they know, they got to them first." Richter filled another vial. He said, "Luckily, the material is so dangerous that most hexen stay far away. Every so often we will get wind of a hexe that has simply disappeared. If she's younger, we assume wildlife got her. If she's older, we think it's because she failed in her exploitation of these very shrooms. Whereas men act foolishly in their youth, age gives the witch the notions that they can do more than they can truly take on. Unfortunately, I believe that Claire already knows how to make her own concoctions of these materials."

"How does it work, though?"

"A guildmaster learned that if you take the Yeshkun and Basaldi mushrooms and eat them simultaneously and raw, have their contents sit in your stomach for a time, and then regurgitate, the stomach will have evened out the potencies while leaving behind a resistance to its original malice. But there is a very peculiar catch that we don't quite understand: this inoculating effect can only occur if the one who eats it is totally uncertain about what is about to happen. If you eat the mushrooms with what we call a 'knowing sitter', the counter-acting potencies are never regurgitated. The elements come out flat and useless. So you do it either alone or with someone who is unaware of what is happening, leaving you completely uncertain that you will come back. I suppose it is ironic that uncertainty is what a hexe preys upon, and it is uncertainty itself that provides the key ingredient in harnessing the mushrooms' powers."

"Exactly how often is this done?"

"Often enough to maintain a continuing understanding of the process, typically at least once in a guildmaster's lifespan with a hexenjäger whose instincts he trusts more than any other."

"What happens if you trust the wrong person?"

"Hopefully you just die," Richter said, corking another vial. "There are tales of hunters screaming endlessly, clawing out their own eyes, jumping until their legs break, pitching their heads into fireplaces, you get the idea. The imbiber's visions become of threats and horrors beyond comprehension. Naturally, they become a threat to those around them. It's not unusual for the imbiber to be murdered by those he was hoping would save him. When this result befalls a guildmaster, he might leave behind a broken guild with terrified hexenjägers almost none of whom will wish to stick around. Many times, hunters realize that an attempt at the concoction was being made only after its attempter has passed. Fortunately, if the eater died in a sea of uncertainty, well, you can still cut open the eater's belly and recover the goods that way."

"Fortunately?" Hobbs said, disgusted as ever.

"Aye, fortunately. It would be a sorry state of affairs to leave this world in such a manner and leave nothing of value behind, aye?"

"I… suppose…"

"As for the Grimalkins, there was a long while where we knew not how to combat such a powerful being other than to simply kill her in the same manner we kill anyone. We operated like suicidal assassins, and that is putting it in as good a light as I can. It took immense courage for the hexenjägers to go after Grimalkins as failure was met with a fate worse than death. Of course, the hexe that has the expertise to utilize such materials is always paired with the talent to ensure you never find her so vulnerable that a simple crossbow or dagger would be her undoing." Richter corked another vial. He picked up another. By now, flecks of mixtures were mottled about his scars, his hands shaking as his handiwork began to strain. "A great many hexenjägers died in those days, and each death was a lesson for someone else to pick up from. There's a reason why the guilds have immense libraries: they double as our graveyards. Every lesson, every learning moment, every advantageous element is someone else's obituary. But, you know, luckily—"

"Richter."

"—Carsten always pulled in the tomes when another guild collapsed and I read every single—"

"Richter."

"—one." The captain looked up. "Aye?"

Hobbs stared at him. "How many witches have you killed?"

Richter shook his head. "You asked that already. You asked it in a priory of all places, and you should know that a conversation which profanes speaker and listener alike is surely an offense to the old gods yet you asked it anyway. Besides, I told you already: I don't know."

"No, I asked you how many people. You didn't know the number, but now I'm asking you how many *witches*. Don't tell me you don't know. Don't tell me you remember all these details and don't know, or that your guilds track everything from day to day and death to death, and you don't know, don't tell me—"

"Fifty-one."

Hobbs fell silent.

Richter held his thumb over the last vial. He said, "I got out of the forties killing a coven around Walddorf. The first of the grouping was a hexe not far east of town. She lived in an old hut. I burned it. She ran out. I shot her. Little while later, I ran into a pairing. I think they were twins. By family, that is. That was rough. After them, a younger one living out in a cabin. I sat with her. I tried my hand at what Carsten believes, this notion of redemption. I said she couldn't stay in Walddorf, but she could head south or north and I'd give her food and coin to do it, too. She agreed. When I stood up and turned around, I saw a hexed man crammed into the ceiling corner, his arms and legs splayed out like a spider ready to pounce. He lunged. She lunged. I killed them both. But the hexe was number fifty. The man I don't know. I don't care. I'm certain almost all of them were recruited by the witch of Walddorf herself."

"The one who almost killed me," Hobbs said.

"Aye. Her."

"Fifty-one."

"She was fifty-one, aye."

"And Claire will be fifty-two."

Richter corked the last vial. He collected the glasses and started piping them back into the bandolier. He said, "The matter of Claire von Sommerwein does not concern you, Hobbs. She's a witch. I am a hexenjäger. Leave it to me. You, you be a kid. I'd very much prefer you just be a kid, do you understand?"

"Fine." Hobbs looked down. He said, "Since I'm being sidelined, what menial task shall I get to? Do you want me to clean the mortars and pestles?"

"We'll bury those."

"Oh."

Richter got to his feet. He tightened the bandolier and then held it in both hands like the lost sash of an emperor. He said, "I feel as though this is obvious but I should state it anyway: the method with which these concoctions were made is strictly between us."

"Well, of course," Hobbs said. He laughed. "If I said a word about it the company would run for the hills."

"However, I do have a serious task for you."

"Uh oh."

"Indeed." Richter took out one of the vials. "Every evening that we camp and eat, I need you to slip this into Sophia's cooking. One vial for each stew will help harden the company against any potential hexing attempts by Claire, if she is to attack us, that is."

"Will they know? I mean these smell awful, so…"

"Sophia's cooking is already a fair bit suspect," Richter said. "I doubt they'll notice an extra bit of… questionable flavoring."

"Alright," Hobbs said. He pursed his lips. "Do I have to eat it, too?"

"Aye."

"Ugh. Alright. I'm not particularly happy to do it, but I'll do it."

"Good," Richter said. "I trusted you for a good reason, then."

"Keeping the secret, sure," Hobbs said. "And also keeping you alive. Nothing too big. Any ol' night, you know? Just another evening of watching you go insane and me shoving half my hand down your mouth."

"What?"

"Oh, did you think you just had a good spewing for no reason?" Hobbs said. He held up his hand and waved it around like it were a magic wand. "Fella in Walddorf had his dog eat up some dishrags. I watched the man shove

[342]

his hand halfway down its throat to get it heaving and vomit those rags back up. So... I just did that to you. It wasn't great. It wasn't great at all."

"I don't imagine it was."

"You just stared up at me, mouth open like a fish, looking like you were screaming but nothing was coming out and then in I went and—"

"You can spare me the details," Richter said. "Let's bury the bowls and then get back to camp. I need some rest."

"Can I ask you one last thing?" Hobbs said, the humorous tinge gone.

The captain turned back around. He nodded. "Sure."

"Did Carsten ever attempt to make the concoction?"

"He did."

"With who?"

"Me."

"You mean... he trusted you fully?"

"Surprisingly, aye."

Hobbs looked down at his own hands, the fingers fumbling and he pursed his lips for a moment. Then he looked up and said, "So you trusted me as he trusted you?"

Richter nodded. "Aye."

The boy's hands started to shake. He said, "Is it alright if I cry?"

The captain nodded again. "Aye."

"It'll just be a little bit."

"It's alright, Hobbs," Richter said, suddenly finding the boy in his arms. "A little bit can do a lot."

Chapter 24. The Steel that Watches.

RICHTER OPENED HIS EYES. As he looked upon the morning sky, a flock of black birds sprang from the nearby trees and crossed overhead. They were lanky with wings so disheveled they seemed to scratch the air instead of effortlessly course through it, and indeed their bodies crookedly swung as though this were either their first flight or certainly their last. In their wake, a single feather fell. Twirling. Swirling. Black with a grey tip. Swishing left to right and knifing down with airy velocity before catching itself and turning back up as though frightened by the fall, too tepid to touch ground, again and again it swam, rocking back and forth, until at last it gently landed upon Richter's chest.

The captain blinked. He got to his elbows and the feather danced away.

"Richter," Dahlgren's voice came in.

"Dahlgren," Richter said sighing. "I know this tone."

"We have a problem."

Richter turned over and got to his feet. The old man awaited him with Sophia by his side.

"It's Quinn," Sophia said. She sighed. "Again."

Dahlgren spat. "I don't know how he goes finding trouble like he does."

"Some men just can't get away from what they are," Richter said. He nodded at the two. "Show me to the thief."

~~~

Richter walked down the line of wagons. Merchants murmured and whispered as he passed. News of an incident, drama in the air, and a hint of excitement. Despite the tension, a cadre of children swirled by in cheery staccato. Mothers hurried to collect the little ones for it was indeed always best for a mother to break the fun. A known face could weather the storm of a child's disappointment. If the children had their fun destroyed by the cruel world around them, then they would learn far too much too quick, and would soon behave in dire ways that did not require their mothers at all.

"This pompous merchant fuck has him," Dahlgren said, catching up to Richter, the old man's weapons and armor clattering with every hurried step. "I thought to just handle the situation myself, but I got wind that he's the man who hired the fella worth two-thousand crowns."

"Is that a bit of fear I sense, Dahlgren?"

"Caution, captain. A man worth two-thousand crowns is either a charlatan or he's plain worth them two-thousand crowns. There lies little wiggle room between, and if he's the latter, well, I've a bit of fear, sure. Money's tight in these territories, two thousand crowns here may as well be ten somewhere else. I'm right interested to meet the fella, but not face first."

"I appreciate your honesty as always, Dahlgren."

"Aye, but all that said, we may wanna slash up a few who get in our way."

Richter raised an eyebrow. "Come again?"

"It's not so much about spilling blood as it is proving that we are not ones to fuck with. I'm sure a few of these chatty caravan guards would oblige my blade with a little rabblerousing."

"Dahlgren." Richter turned. "Ease up, alright? It's morning."

"Apologies, captain. I'm a little riled. Not sure if I'm more pissed at Quinn or the merchants. Just like at the ferry, Quinn's still one of ours. It's a sour look to have someone of our company taken like this."

"If this merchant is as pompous as you say, then surely words are how he navigates through life. I think we can come to an understanding that does not require swords leaving sheaths, aye?"

Dahlgren grunted, but also nodded. "Aye, captain."

A happening between thief and merchant aside, the morning was still yet lively with normal ongoings: merchants cooked breakfast with pots and pans set over fires, meat sizzling and eggs cracked and chunks of vegetables being chopped with mighty thwacks of knives on carveboards, and the odd quiet of a few dogs, staring with submissive eyes at the meal preparations, yet their unending drool gave away the nature of their newfound obedience. But all human eyes now and again stole glances and spoke in hushed tones. From moments like these, Richter had come to learn that the word 'sellsword' is not so easy to whisper and the word 'mercenary' was about as subtle as a whistle. The presence and passing of the captain himself only intensified these whispers, *sellsword, mercenary,* the words tailing after him as though the captain strolled past beds of vipers who sought to hiss him away.

Further up the road a crowd had gathered, their heads turned inward at some other sight. Hands went into the air, some pointing, others carrying sticks and stones, and there was much shouting at their target which, surely, not all of them were crossed by, but there was rarely a bad time to join a mob if one's interests were so suited.

As Richter neared the crowd, one of the heads looked back and his eyes went wide and he started tapping the shoulders of those around him. Soon, all eyes were on the captain and their voices quieted down in turn.

Richter said, "Where is my sellsword?"

The onlookers glanced inward once more and then the crowd parted and an opulent, almost feathery bird of a man stormed out, silk linens flowing, his hair slickly laid back as though permanently wetted, and his fingers glinted with rings and his wrists with bracelets. His legs ruffled and scratched with every step, and even the swing of his arms against his fat belly produced an odd rustling. The only thing which moved more than these displays of spending were his jowls. He reminded Richter of Louis von Walddorf, and on that account, and through no fault of his own, the captain saw this merchant in poor light. But the merchant quickly dispensed any possibility that he and Louis were dissimilar creatures:

"You there, you mercenary cretin!" he shouted, his throat jumping a few shiny necklaces upward. "You! You who has failed to keep your men in line!"

Richter nodded. "Aye, me. Where is my sellsword?"

"You are captain to a man named Quinn?"

"Aye."

"Well, then you shall know that he stole from my wagon!"

The shouting echoed through the woods. Richter raised an eyebrow and glanced at Dahlgren.

"On your order," the old man said, hand to his sword.

Richter shook his head.

Dahlgren lifted his fingers, though the hand still hovered the blade.

Shuffling forth, the merchant's long dress scratched over the ground and rustled between his legs. He stopped before Richter and pointed a finger and huffed, then lowered his hand and screamed: "Son of a farkin' bitch!"

Richter wiped spit off his cheek. He looked down to see his own hand had, almost by instinct, fallen onto the pommel of Adelbrecht's sword. He lifted the hand, slowly, as one might back away from a wild animal which very much wanted a reason to bite.

The captain said, "I'm only interested in knowing where my man is—"

"I scoff at you, sellsword, for your 'wares' are of dubious quality, as is yourself!" The merchant threw a hand up: "Bring the pitiful creature forward! Let us see this waste which has made some ruination of my morning."

The group parted to reveal Quinn on his knees with his hands shackled behind his back. He turned his torso to wave with a wiggle of his fingers. "Hey there, captain. If I could just have one minute, I could explain that this feathery fella here is under a, uh, how do you say… misapprehension? Wow I think I said it right. Sir, you are under a mis—"

"Shut yer farking mouth!" The merchant screamed. He grabbed Quinn and dragged the thief across the Ancient Road, its stones not nearly as kind to the thief's knees as they would be to a wagon's wheels, but both brutally sounded the same as the man's bones clicked and clacked. The merchant threw the thief to the ground and put his boot on his back.

"What the fark!" Quinn howled. "Do you have anvils in those shoes?"

The merchant leaned down and shouted: "Where did you put them? Where are my wares, you stinking thief?"

"Merchant," Richter said. "I believe you are under a misapprehension, as my thief articulated."

"So I did say it right," Quinn said, his face beaming with pride despite his eyes bulging just a little beneath the merchant's weight.

"Misapprehension? No misapprehension!" The merchant pointed a firm finger. "You don't tell me what I know and don't know, sellsword!"

"Well, let us talk ourselves into an understanding then," Richter said. He pointed at Quinn. "But in the meantime, I would very much appreciate it if you take those shackles off my man, and your boot off his back."

"No! No freedom for him! None!" The merchant looked at Richter and Dahlgren before his face wrenched with disgust. "This is it? This is all you bring? One sellsword?"

"Would you prefer I bring my entire company here?"

"Even in full number it would be no good!" the merchant said, grinning. He slowly brought his fingers to his lips. "I'll show you real talent!"

The merchant let out a sharp whistle.

Suddenly, a huge man stood up from the crowd, instantly towering over them and a wash of glinting whites and yellows cascaded as the morning sun struck across his plated heavy armor by which even his face was masked. He slowly walked forward, each step lumbering and heavy, each footfall clinking and clanking armor so heavy that surely in whole this being were the work of a mad engineer's machinations and there could not be a man that dwelled inside. He had a two-hand sword girded to his hip, one massive paw resting on its pommel.

The words 'two-thousand crowns' whispered through the crowd.

Dahlgren planted a foot and placed a hand upon his sword. Despite not wanting violence, Richter found himself doing the same.

As the man came forth, a limp in his step became noticeable, though he still yet carried the armor with effortless motion, the metal shunting and jangling with every step, the gear a thunderclap, the man inside its lightning.

"Lot of armor," Dahlgren said. "I doubt you can move fast in that."

"You'd be surprised," the man in armor said.

Dahlgren cocked his head.

The huge man unsheathed his sword and yoked it over a shoulder and with his other hand he drew up the faceguard of his helmet.

"Sonuvabitch," Dahlgren said. "Sonuvabitch!"

"Hello, old man," Hans said. He nodded at Richter. "Witch hunter."

The last survivor of Adelbrecht's company: the indomitable Hans.

Quinn looked over his shoulder from the road. "Oh fark my life!"

Seething, Dahlgren took a step forward. Richter stopped him. He looked at the old man and shook his head.

"Be easy, drunkard. You should know I have no quarrel with you, just as I said when we last parted ways. Bossman here," Hans said, pointing at his rather loud and angry employer. "He has umbrage with Quinn," the giant sellsword paused to look down. He growled: "The thief."

"How's your limp?" Quinn said, without making eye contact. "Hope yer leg is doing betauggh!"

The weight of Hans' foot suddenly purchased a few audible cracks in the thief's back.

"Shush, thief," Hans said. "Matters of justice need not hear from you."

"Matters of justice? What does that even meauggh!"

"Alright, that's enough," Richter said, raising a hand. "What wares is my man accused of stealing?"

The merchant pointed his finger. "Armor! Leather and chain! And crowns! All gone!"

"Seems awful heavy work," Richter said. "Look at my man. Was he not bruised already? Was he not slowed? How could he have accomplished anything like you suggest?"

"He went back and forth, to your wagon, then to mine, to yours, then mine. A thief with gold in his eyes is like a three-legged dog seeing a bitch in heat. He'll still get it done!" The merchant lowered his head to Quinn. "Did you like what you saw, hm? You just couldn't help yourself, could you?"

"I'm not at liberty to say either way," Quinn said. "Because I don't know what in the hells you're talking about. You speak to an innocent man!"

The merchant bent down, his shiny linens flowering around him as though he had nested himself in a silken rainbow, but despite all these intricacies he hocked up his nose and then spat on the thief.

Quinn recoiled. "Ayy hey! That's too far! Way too far!"

"Is it? Know this, thief: I come from the north where every year raiders arrive by sea. They plunder my goods and kill my friends. They're dangerous, these 'sailors', but every so often I catch one. And I've learned many ways to repay them in kind for their crimes. Many, many wonderful ways."

The thief looked up. "I would like a trial, is that so much to ask? How about a bit of law, yeah?"

"Law? You want law? Ha! I'll show you law!"

"Sir!" Richter said. "There is no reason to get violent."

A mercenary saying the word 'violent' was cause enough for many of the onlookers to take a few steps back.

The merchant, however, stood defiantly in the shadow of his hired swordhand. He said, "The one-eared captain and his one-handed sellsword wish to profane the Ancient Road with a bit of violence, do they?"

"No, not at all," Richter said. He stood up straight as he had seen diplomats and ambassadors do. "I resent this accusation with considerable malice, but if it will help avail you of your anger, you are free to come and search our wagon and campground."

"Oh, that I was already planning on," the merchant said. He waved his arms to the forests. "And I already have my tracker dogs sniffing the woods, because I know this fool stowed my wares somewhere!"

"Then you are being smart," Richter said. "And I applaud your wits in trying to recoup your goods but let us maintain this sentiment of peaceful resolution, aye? You may come and search our wagon."

"That I'll do! You!" the merchant pointed at Hans, then at Quinn. "Watch the thief!"

"Now wait a second," Quinn said, struggling to turn his head up from the ground. "Me and this fella got bad blood. You can't leave me with him!"

"He's right," Hans said. "We do have bad blood. But if yer 'captain' Richter there entertains my bossman with the wagon search, I see no reason to grind you into bonemeal, thief."

Looking at the merchant, Richter said, "Order your guard to not harm my man."

The merchant pursed his lips.

Richter leaned forward. "Peaceful sentiments, merchant, peaceful sentiments. There is no reason to 'profane' anything with blood, aye?"

The merchant blew raspberries with his lips then nodded. "You've a clever tongue hidden in that horrendous, one-eared head, sellsword. Alright. Hans! Do not bring harm to this rat unless I say so. As for you, 'captain', I will see to your wagon now and recover what I know has been taken."

~~~

Richter stood back, leaning against a tree with a boot jacked to its trunk, his thumbs tacked under his beltline, seeming all the picture of a farmer at the end of a day's work. He watched the angry merchant turn his wagon's inventory upside down, the fat peddler's flowery garb slowly falling apart as he dug and tossed and clambered. A crowd of observers stood off to the side, chuckling and humoring themselves by mimicking the merchant's exaggerated rummaging. Hans had dragged Quinn to the scene, presumably to execute him were the missing wares found. He stood with a boot planted squarely in the thief's back. Quinn, however, proved mouthy as always.

"You really got paid two-thousand crowns to work with this madman?"

Hans didn't answer.

"Two-thousand crowns," the thief repeated, whistling sharply. "A lot of coin there, Hans. Do you happen to keep it on your person or in a purse somewherrrghh!"

"Quiet," Hans said, the toe of his boot crunching Quinn's spine.

"Alright alright, I'm quiet, see? I'm quiet." The thief stared at the dirt, watching a worm inch its way across, and in a flash a bird's shadow sailed over them both. He lifted his head. "No hard feelings about the leg, Hans. I saw you still limping so, you know, my apologies about all that. I'm much better with the dagger throws now so if you wanna see sometime…"

"One more word and I will stomp your brains out of your nose, thief."

"Mhmm, mmhmm, mmhm."

In the end, the merchant found nothing.

"Sonuvabitch," he said, throwing a bolt of cloth back into Richter's wagon. "Sonuvabitch, where are my wares!"

"I'm quite sorry for your situation," Richter said. "But in the time you spent upon this witch hunt I imagine that the real culprit has slipped away."

"Hey, hey!" The angered merchant pointed a finger, its tip to Richter's nose, a ring glinting on the knuckle behind it. "Go fark yourself! I know your man is responsible! I know it!"

"Provide proof," Richter said. "Or tell your walking two-thousand crowns to let my man go."

The merchant sniveled. Caravan guards and merchants alike were mightily amused by the situation, and the gaudy merchant turned red in the face from their barely stifled giggling and chuckling.

"No!" the merchant said, gathering his pride and dignity. "I don't think I will let the thief go! He is a thief! I will find the truth in his blood!"

Quinn looked up. He said, "Hey, that wasn't the deal! You found nothing! Your accusations are bullshit!"

"Kill him!" the merchant screamed at Hans. "Kill the thief!"

"Now hold on a minute!" Quinn said. "Richter, help!"

The captain drew out his sword. The rest of the company grabbed every weapon they had and hurried them to the ready. Merchants who had come for the spectacle quickly retreated while their caravan guards jawed at each other, joking that it was high time they got a real show.

One man standing before many, Hans stared at the sellswords with unfaltering poise. His sword scraped off his shoulder as he slowly brought it to the fore. Though it was fitted to be wielded by two hands, the giant sellsword effortlessly waved it in one.

"You kill him," Richter said, "and you die here."

"Is that what you think?" Hans said.

Richter's sellswords moved on uneasy feet. Even though they outnumbered Hans, there was an unfortunate reality: he was not a man who would leave this life without dragging a good number of others with him.

"Kill him!" the merchant shouted. "Do it already!"

"Hans!" Richter screamed. "Hans! We *will* kill you!"

The sellsword grinned.

"Holy fark," a caravan guard said, taking a step back. "The farker ain't even retreating..."

"Richter, get him off me!" Quinn shouted. "Richter!"

Just when it seemed death and mayhem was about to erupt, Hans' foot lifted from the thief's back. Quinn stared forward, his hands trembling, his chest shaking, and he then grimaced and shut his eyes and awaited what was to come. But it did not come.

The merchant stared at Richter with a grin, and then slowly turned his head. He looked Hans up and down. He said, "What are you doing? Hey! I said what are you doing!"

Quinn opened his eyes halfway, half-expecting his neck to feel the sudden, cool pierce of steel. But nothing came at all.

Sheathing his massive blade, Hans turned to his employer. "You thought he had stolen something of yours. We have not found the missing items. Either by man's law or underneath the old gods' eyes, I do not see with what right we could kill this man for a crime you cannot prove he committed."

"Man's got a point," Quinn said.

Hans nodded. "Give me your wrists and I will unshackle you."

The sellsword went to unshackle the thief, only to see Quinn had done it himself already, sliding the chains off and dashing away with a cackle which was mirrored by the laughter and cheering of the onlooking crowd.

"Slippery cunt," Hans said.

"Yeah that's how I prefer 'em," Quinn said, looping a shackle around his finger like a dancer's tassel. He cocked his head to a side. "What? Am I not at least a little impressive? Hey, where's Minnesang? He should see what real talent looks like!"

"Look!" the merchant said, almost howling. "Look at how he behaves! Does he not have the heart and soul of a thief? And you let him go!"

Hans stepped toward his employer, his boots clanking heavier than ever. He said, "Just how much longer would you like to discuss this?"

The merchant dabbed the sweat upon his brow and stammered some response about how much he was paying Hans, and the sellsword nodded and said that was another topic entirely, one which he was quite happy to return to. Hans slowly turned and walked away. The gaudy merchant opened his mouth, and his jowls efforted some words, but everything he wanted to say was garbled by his own disbelief. And so he followed Hans, not once looking back lest he face the mockery of Quinn and his accompanying troop.

With the festivities over, the rest of the crowd melted back to their duties. A few of the caravan guards exchanged monies over what were presumably bets about what would happen. Richter sheathed his blade and the rest of the company slowly lowered their weapons in turn – except Dahlgren, who held onto his sword, his eyes still watching Hans go. The captain put a hand to the man's shoulder. Dahlgren broke his stare, glancing at Richter.

"Let it go," Richter said. "Can you do that?"

"He's a kid killer, captain," Dahlgren said. "We may not see him again, I say we take him while we still can and—"

Richter simply stared at the old man.

"Alright," Dahlgren said. He sheathed his sword. "Alright, captain."

The old man turned and walked away, rallying the company to help clean up the goods the merchant had tossed over in his search.

"Well then," Quinn said, clapping the dirt off his pants and shirt. He held up his chains. "Hey look, free shackles."

"Quinn," Richter said. "Did—"

"Of course I did it. Who do you take me for? I stole *all* that shit."

The captain raised an eyebrow. He was expecting the thief to be more quarrelsome with the nature of his nighttime adventures.

"You cut my pay," the thief said, holding out his hands like a child explaining himself. "What else was I to do, *not* earn money? Besides, I got a little something for the company, too."

Richter shook his head. "By the old gods, Quinn."

The thief nodded with unironic agreement. "They were surely looking out for me, weren't they? Now, had I known Hans was this two-thousand crown monstrosity everyone's been talking about, I probably wouldn't have thrown caution to the wind, but hey, we got out unscathed, didn't we?"

"Where'd you hide it?" Richter said. "That merchant turned over our wagon, but he mentioned earlier that he was running tracker dogs through the woods."

"Oh I planned for those dogs," Quinn said with a grin.

"You didn't poison them, did you?"

"What? No. I'd never do that." The thief's grin widened. "I simply went ahead and put the goods where no dumb pack of bitches would ever look."

Looking at Richter, Dahlgren said, "We can't stay here any longer, right?"

The captain nodded. "Aye, our time here is at an end."

"Good."

Richter stared at the old man. He said, "Dahlgren?"

"Aye?"

"Forget Hans. If he wants to fight for some merchant, let him. We can trust in the old gods that he will have his day."

The old man snorted and spat, but ultimately nodded: "Aye, captain."

~~~

Guildmaster Imnachar awaited Richter at the side of the road. Old and bent, the elder's black garb still drew attention, his dour frame stark against the laager's colorful profligacies. There he stood not just as a man, but as a fount of knowledge and untold secrets, of experiences that would die with him and be washed away with his bones as though they never happened at all. Passersby regarded him as though they walked before an abandoned priory, understanding that this decrepit figure held intangible intrigues far above the corporeal, and that its ruin only belonged to this world and nowhere else.

"Boy," Imnachar said, nodding to Richter. His gimlet eye lifted briefly, staring at and through the rest of the company. "Sellswords."

Richter told his company to go on ahead and he'd catch up.

"Do you know him?" Dahlgren said. "Is he friendly?"

"No, he is not friendly." Richter smiled. "But I'll be fine, Dahlgren."

Imnachar and Richter watched the company trundle onward, the sellswords glancing over their shoulders. Hobbs simply sat on the rear of the wagon, his legs scissoring off the tailgate, his eyes affixed to the duo.

"I see you've the concoction," Imnachar said. "And your mind seems to be in one piece. Congratulations."

"Thank you," Richter said. "I will never make another."

"Not a single soul has made two batches," the guildmaster said. He watched the tail end of the company slowly slip away. "Don't go straight to Sommerwein. If there are headloppers about, they will find you and kill you."

"I figured as much," Richter said, nodding. "One of my paymaster's new maps showed a supposed ferry not far from here. We'll cut our way to it."

"If the boat's out, do you have the supplies to fix it?"

"We're stocked on goods," Richter said. "If the ferry's dead we'll manage. Besides, marching the coastline may be the safest option anyway."

"That right?" Imnachar laughed. "You plan to drown the hexe when you find her? Give her that ancient dunking method?"

"Well, it's funny you say it, because Carsten once fooled us into thinking that water could melt witches. I believed him, too."

"That was my joke," Imnachar said. "That bastard stole it."

Shrugging, Richter said, "I hated that he ever suggested it, because now when it rains, I get this feeling that maybe, just maybe, this time it'll wash them all away."

"Mhmm. Unfortunately, all the rain does is bring the shrooms up outta the ground and give the hexen more playthings to fark us with."

Richer stared at the guildmaster. He held his left hand out.

Imnachar stepped back. "I'm not shaking that."

"Why not?"

"Because the question of whether or not I have a wristed crossbow is still bothering you, and you aim to find out through courteous means."

Richter lowered his hand. "Clever."

"Wasn't born yesterday, boy."

Nodding, Richter said, "I know you got it on you, anyway."

"I don't. Honest."

"That word means nothing from an old fart like you, Imnachar."

"Mhmm. I shan't be seeing you again, boy," the guildmaster said. "So I'll just say it: if you come to the life beyond this one hands empty of a Neu Grimalkin's scalp, then me, Carsten, and the rest of us ornery farks are going to cane the everloving shite out of you. Now get going… and good luck."

Chapter 25. The Scent of Beasts.

EMBERS. ASH. SMOKE. The building had burned down long before Claire got there. She stared at the charred remains, wooden rods, black as can be, still yet implying some purpose as a pub or parlor. But most curious of all was in the rear of the building, where cellar doors had been blown off their hinges and whatever entity exited in this manner moved with ferocious speed and incredible weight: all along the traces of the wreckage tread giant footsteps and deep trenches where the being had gouged the mud in retreat.

With hissing scales, the lindwurm coursed forth and angled itself beside the smoky ruins. It poled one arm into the ground, tilted itself aside, and gently reached a hand forth, something infantile in its curiosity. The moment it touched a chunk of wood, a portion of the building collapsed, spewing clouds of black and causing a clatter of material, and the lindwurm roared and the swirling ash blew backward and flames seared in the ruins as though it were a dragon of yore learning the elements which the earth had gifted it.

Claire looked into the forest. Her direwolf whimpered behind a tree.

A stench filled the air. Thick. Balmy. It reminded her of the torture towers in Sommerwein, how looking up from the crowd you could but see colors: red trickling through the floorboards, sparkling if the sun were out, and the black silhouettes that moved as though shadows in revolt of the light, shadow against shadow until the red came. But if you walked up those steps, if you got to where the torturers stood, and you looked at their handiwork as they did, then you smelled what they smelled. The blood, and the bowels.

But the direwolf's nose did not smell blood nor bowels. The direwolf had picked up a scent of something else entirely. Something it feared by instinct, its apprehensions breaking through the spell she had put upon it.

"What was here?" Immerwahr said, walking with his hand over his nose.

Claire pursed her lips. "Some sort of monster, it appears."

She walked to the road and looked for human traces. Two pairs of footprints crossed and darted into the trees, cutting east. Her eyes looked at the footprints a long while. Sighing, she returned to the mudded trenches of that which had fled the cellar, the monster having left a rounded groove in the mud as though it, too, dragged a cauldron with it.

"Two or three men came here," Claire said. "They met the monster inside. It fled out, heading that way," Claire said, nodding west into the trees. She turned around, pointing east. "And at least two men fled that way."

"We should keep going," Immerwahr said. When Claire met him with a curious gaze, the monk swallowed and said: "I do not mean to offer advice, my nerves got the best of me. I only fear the return of this supposed monster."

Claire smiled. She said, "Yes, I can see you are not a man of action. That is quite alright. But your fear has destroyed your knowledge of these roads. We are not on the right path. We've strayed." She pointed east. "If we follow their tracks, then surely we will come to the right road once again."

Immerwahr bowed his head. Not out of respect or a sense of humility to royal blood, but because he feared the look on his face might give him away. He knew these roads very well, and knew the road they were on was an abandoned one, and if she kept walking up it they would be led astray. He knew it was Richter who had been here. He knew it in his soul, as though the old gods whispered to him these things.

"My intuition is rarely wrong," Claire said, suddenly at the monk's hip, looking up into his eyes. She took his hand. "Come now, holy man. Let us make amends of our travels."

The hexe turned to her cauldron. Standing before it, the ensorcelled mob listed in two columns, long ropes across their shoulders, slackly limp between each body. She raised her fingers and made a motion, then cupped her hands and whispered. Despite being right beside her, Immerwahr could not hear the words, and yet the mob perked its heads up in a collective shunt of bodies and motion, and they slowly started pulling the wagoned cauldron east into the woods. As the cauldron rolled by, the monk turned away, not wishing to gaze upon those who danced inside it.

"Have no fear, holy man," Claire said. "There is nothing to fear when you are with me."

Immerwahr's eyes lifted. He couldn't help but for one moment see her cauldron and those within it. The little ones, laughing, giggling, dancing, and all the while the motions of their bodies churning the materials of a witch's brew. He pinched his eyes and looked down. He said, "Please, let them stop."

"You think them insane because they dance to a song you cannot hear," Claire said, staring up at the monk. "But who gave them the song? Who is it that sings to them? I do. And do I look insane to you, holy man?" Her eyes furrowed, her stare long, her dress treated gently by the wind, her hair but a wisp of movement. "Do I look insane to you?"

Chapter 26. Breaking Webs.

THE COMPANY traveled north, grousing and grumbling about having been prematurely kicked from another public's good graces. As the tempers rose, the thief suddenly whistled and cocked his head and pointed off into the trees.

"Here," he said, barreling into the forest. A moment later, he screamed.

Chasing after him, the company found Quinn standing before a pile of webknecht eggs, and in entwined in one of the webbed and dripping sacs was a dog, its tongue panting, its puppy-dog eyes wide and sullen, an ironically defanging stare given that its mouth was wrenched in a growling snarl.

"Sonuvabitch," Quinn said. "Damn dog scared the shite out of me!"

Beside the mutt was a pile of armor, armor attachments, chainmail coifs, and a purse of coins, the items sitting in the broken shell of a huge, green egg. Richter noted little footprints all around, showing the thief had indeed made numerous trips. He couldn't help but respect the effort.

"Hey, yeah," Thomas said. "What in the hell are those?"

"Eggs," Elletrache said. He looked over, grinning. "Webknecht eggs."

"Oh by the old gods, not the spiders!"

"They ain't 'ere, quit yer howling, tenderfoot."

"Quinn," Richter said, looking at the webbed goods. Why did you hide the stolen goods here of all places?"

"Ah, captain, remember that green-silked merchant who talked to us at the head of the laager? Well, at least I was listening, dunno about you farks, but I heard what he said about the spiders causing a spook. I asked the kids where they got frightened and they pointed me the way. Of course, I asked them if the spiders themselves were gone, which they said they were. Now, I noticed some of them merchants had dogs, so I knew I couldn't just execute my plans without keeping them in mind. Dogs and us thieves, we have history… anyway, the eggs were the perfect spot. Everybody was scared of the area already, all I had to do was goop up the goods in some spider slough so no hound would catch the scent."

"Except this one," Elletrache said, nodding at the mutt.

"Well of course there's always one determined bitch in the pack," Quinn said. "Sometimes that's just how it goes. But look at 'er, she's stuck. She ain't snitching on nobody."

"Just how many trips did you take?" Richter said. By the traces, he knew it was three in and three out, but he was curious if the thief would lie, maybe if he sought to hide something for himself.

"Ahh, three total," Quinn said. "Busted my ass getting it all here, too. Was gonna make a fourth but I was ragged and the morning light was coming and, well, there was no fourth trip on account of being 'caught' and all, which I wasn't! I wasn't caught! I had nothing in hand when they snooped me out, I was merely, at the time, looking with keen interest into their wagon, understand? I was never actually caught, I want to make that clear."

"We got it," Richter said.

"No, I mean put that in your book," Quinn said, pointing at Crockett. He nodded. "Never caught. Write it. Write it!"

"Never caught… alright," Crockett said, shrugging and writing a note.

Minnesang leaned over Crockett's shoulder. He said, "You shouldn't use so many capital letters."

The paymaster jerked his ledger away. "Stop spying on my work!"

"Minnesang," Richter said. "Go watch the wagon, please."

"Aye aye, Richter von Dagentear."

The captain sighed.

"You know," Hobbs said. "We should take the dog."

"Eh, take care now," Elletrache said. "Dags have a natural fear of webknechts, but this one didn't seem to give no shites and came snoopin' anyway. That means that there dag is of fightin' stock."

"Or maybe it's just dumber'n'hells," Dahlgren said. "Even a big bear would know not to get into that muck."

The dog reared up, trying to free its hindlegs from a crackling spindle of webbing and goo. Its paws stretched far but the tension snapped it back into the spider egg. Energy sapped, she whined tersely and sat back down.

"Whatever it is," Richter said, "It is in our way."

He drew his crossbow and aimed it at the dog.

"What're you doing!" Hobbs said.

Richter lowered the weapon. He nodded toward the animal. "The dog is in the way of the goods. Last thing we need is one of us losing a finger to some mutt and we're not leaving without the thief's goods."

"But you can't just kill it!"

"It's not our friend, Hobbs. It belongs to the merchant and was sent here as a tracker. If we cut it loose, it'll just go fetch its owner."

"Wh-what if we got some sticks… and twine… and just fished the gear out of the eggs?"

"That'll take all day," Quinn said.

"Aye," Richter said. "And we will still be leaving the dog to die a terrible, slow death."

"But if we take the goods, the people won't know!" Hobbs said. "The proof will be gone!"

"Aside from all our footprints and clear evidence that, for some strange reason, we all collectively stepped off the road to the very spot the dog had sniffed out." Richter shook his head. "They'll know."

"But…"

"I'm doing it a favor, Hobbs. You can go on back to the wagon if you don't wish to see or hear it. I'll give you a minute to clear out."

The boy pursed his lips and turned away, escaping into the arms of Sophia who rubbed the boy's back and told him it'd be alright. But the boy did not leave the scene entirely, he simply stared over the nook of the homesteader's arm, his eyes glancing at the animal and the man who sought to exterminate it.

Richter aimed the crossbow again. The dog stared back, the barbs of Richter's bolt betwixt its eyes. Its ears flicked forward and the nose snorted, for if it were to be sent on a track of its own death surely it had picked up the scent then and there. Taking a breath, Richter nestled the butt of the crossbow tighter against his shoulder. The sellswords stared at him, their eyes glancing between man and beast. Richter put his hand to the weapon's trigger.

"Can't miss from this distance," Quinn said, nodding. "Even with your shaky-arsed hands. I mean, you still could. Would be embarrassing as fark."

"Shut yer mouth, Quinn," Dahlgren said.

The dog tilted its head, ears flopping.

Richter kept staring at it, and the dog at him.

"Ah hells," Quinn said, throwing up his hands. "The captain don't have the heart for it."

"I can do it," Gernot said. The rest of the company looked at him as if they totally forgot he was within their ranks. He swallowed and nodded. "I'm a butcher. I've butchered many a dog."

"Butchered dogs?" Dahlgren said. "For what?"

"Meat and fur and neighborly squabbles." Gernot nodded and then quickly continued before anyone could dally on the last of his points: "It ain't easy killing such a creature, but I can do it."

"Wait," Quinn said. "Who are you again?"

"Gernot," the butcher said. "I killed five some-odd men at that big brigand's encampment. Two more after we broke lunch the other day."

"What, really?"

"Yeah, I—"

"Enough of this," Richter said. He reset the crossbow's firing pin and then set it down.

"Ah for farkssake," Quinn said. "Cap'n's gon' sentimental."

"That ain't wise," Elletrache said. "That ain't wise at all, Richter."

"We'll just see," Richter said. He approached the dog, hands out, palms to the mutt, his feet as light as feathers. "Easy now," he said, caution in his breath, calm in his words. "Easy now. Easy…"

The dog growled. Richter slowly put his hand within reach of the dog's bite and the huff of the animal met his fingertips like the heat of a fire. The dog's nose wiggled. It sniffed. A moment later, the lips drew back, baring its teeth. Richter did not falter. It was merely a show. It was merely bestial fear. And a human's steady hand alone could conquer that. And indeed, the dog suddenly turned away and threw its head back and forth as it tried to escape, its legs kicking and jumping, the webbing and goo only sinking further and further into its fur. Richter grabbed a chunk of the white webbing and the dog howled as if the man were the spider itself come to make use of its sticky remains and the dog responded with a quick snap of its jaws.

"Whoa, captain," Dahlgren said. "Maybe you should…"

"It's fine."

Each peeling back of webbing was thanked with a snap of the dog's jaws. Richter worked for the animal's freedom, nonetheless. Thick spit and foam mottled his scarred, yet steady hand. Suddenly, the dog's maw pressed into Richter's knuckles, and he felt the beast's teeth chamfering against his flesh, some bizarre crossing of aggression and civility, something a dog might do in trying to appeal to the strongest of its pack. When one leg broke free, it flopped back and forth as though it had been tossed down a stairwell, and then the other leg got free and it planted itself all paws to the earth and barreled away in a heartbeat. It made it a few trees distance before it spun around and stuck its head low and arse in the air, tail pointed upward, its teeth bared, lips quivering and frothing as it growled, and then the dog barked at its liberator and spun again and took off, heading south through the forest and presumably back to the laager.

"Aye, you're welcome, too," Richter said.

"Hey yeah," Thomas said. "That mutt looks like it's going back home."

"It sure does," Dahlgren said, shaking his head.

"We should go kill it!" Quinn said, pointing a finger at the quickly diminishing blur of a dog. "He's gonna fetch that fat farkin' merchant and march back here with Hans! He'll bring Hans! Did you forget about Hans! He has a Hans!"

Richter nodded. "No point fretting in it now. We'll just be sure to watch our rear and make do with what we have. Besides, if they do come, we'll be better prepared, right Quinn?"

The thief sighed. "I regret helping."

"And we regret a lot of things about you, too," Dahlgren said.

"Everyone, start picking up the gear. Clean it if you can, too." Richter started walking back toward the wagon. "Crockett, inventory this gear."

"Yessir."

As the captain passed Hobbs, he nudged the boy in the shoulder. He said, "Happy?"

"The dog won't come back," Hobbs said. "It won't say a word."

"I know," Richter said with a nod. "I trust you on this."

~~~

As the wagon trundled north up the Ancient Road, Richter took a moment to glance back. The road ran straight down the columns of trees and unto the horizon and somewhere beyond there it ran past the laager which could no longer be seen. But Richter could see it going on ever further – he could still yet see the forest crowding around it, still yet envision the seesawing of the road's quality, the ebb and flow of it through time and the recklessness of the men who stewarded it, and he could see the road making it back unto the ranchlands north of Marsburg, passing Sophia's homestead, passing the corpses of Meinrad and his men, somewhere in the grass there Waverly the tailor still coffin-sat as Crockett had propped him, and he could see the road all the way to Marsburg itself, unfurling under its gates. And there he could see siege engines and their soldiers hard at work. Lowlanders and sellswords alike, before them the city of Marsburg, nearly bottomless in its wealth yet nearly all aflame above. And in those flames he saw Carsten the guildmaster.

Richter glanced back down the road, imagining the laager itself manifesting there at the horizon as though it were a worm hellbent on breaking the world, barreling after the company like some serpentine cretin made of wagons, clacketing machinations for a body, frothing gold out of its mouth, a mad knight of a merchant riding its head while screaming matters of accounts and debts, declaring vengeance into the sky, scrambling the scriptoriums, stripping time of its vigor, and with this annihilating force the merchant-knight would drive the monster upon the company and it was this idea, horrible and maniacal all the same, that pleased the captain. Because at least it would be over, and absurdly so.

The one they call the Wight should have a death which deserves the name, the guildmaster's voice returned to him. *Don't you think so, boy?*

~~~

Hobbs stood playing with his own fingers, the way in which a child might knit together his thoughts before letting them be known.

"What is it?" Richter said.

The boy sighed. "Why'd you let the dog go?"

"I don't know," Richter said. "Truthfully, Hobbs, I do not know."

"Well. I'm glad you did."

The two walked for a time, the wagon trundling beside them, the donkey at its head slapping its hooves down

Hobbs suddenly said, "Maybe you did it because I didn't want you to kill it. Remember, like the kidnapper in the wheelhouse?"

Thedrick, or Theo for short. Richter was surprised the boy even remembered him at all – the captain surely had let the memory fade.

"I didn't kill that man because he had boobytrapped the entire building."

"That's what you told me, and that's what you told yourself. But you were lying. I knew you were. You were lying to make me feel better."

"Maybe."

"You don't have to do that," Hobbs said. "You can tell me the truth anytime."

"Well," Richter said, thinking. He said, "Action is truth, is it not?"

"Sure, I suppose."

"I let the dog go, so regardless of what words I speak to you, what does that action mean?"

The boy walked for a time, thinking on it, and Richter glanced at the boy. He couldn't help but realize he himself was still seeking the answer, and he winced at the thought that the kid would arrive at the answer before him and—

"I think it means you care," Hobbs said. "What for, to what end, I don't know. But the care is there, you know? Somewhere and meaning something. But I think it's well enough that you do care. Well enough, indeed."

Richter had thought of his own answer, but it melted then and there, lost from his mind like a good dream to an even better morning.

He nodded. "Aye, maybe you are right."

"No, not maybe," Hobbs said. "I'm certain I'm right."

~~~

Despite its flagrant invitations of trouble, Quinn's impromptu thievery did solve an issue for the company: every sellsword was now well armored. It wasn't the best of gear, but leather chest plates with pauldrons across the shoulders was vastly better than rat-chewed gambesons. Even Sophia wore a leather set, clumsily donning it like a child wearing her dad's clothes. Beside her, Hobbs tried on a leather cap that slouched its lids clear down to his nose.

"We're looking a little more proper," Dahlgren said, watching the company strap up. "Like we can take on some real fighters now."

Richter nodded. "Aye. Thanks to a criminal, no less, and his crime which we now partake in."

"A crime," Dahlgren said. "But a worthwhile one."

"They weren't going to sell it to Marsburg anytime soon anyway," Quinn said, pridefully jacking his thumbs into his belt, his fingers tapping his sides where two daggers were sheathed. "Half the laager set out, but that other half were just settin' around wanting to see who won the war so they could sell their goods to the highest bidder. They're the fence sitters of the group, and as far as I'm concerned, fark those fence sitting farkers."

"Very poetic as always, Quinn," Sophia said, tightening her straps.

The thief ran a finger down his nose and winked.

"We don't need to justify this in any sort of way," Richter said. "Dahlgren is right. It is what it is. We have gained from someone else's loss. Even if we wanted to make amends, it is doubtful that the merchant would hear us out. And even if he did, he'd still yet determine himself to punish us. We've damaged his prestige and for that there's little repayment."

Quinn held his finger up. He said, "And most importantly, Hans would just kill us all anyway. I mean, we're all pretty sure about that, right? You saw his armor. Dollgrin, back me up here."

"He has a new set," Dahlgren said begrudgingly. "He looked... considerably more dangerous than the last time I saw him."

"So, hey, yeah," Thomas said. "I think I missed this knight..."

"You were hiding," Dahlgren said. "Best not see you doing that again."

"Never again," Thomas said. "But, hey yeah, so do, uh... any of you know him? Or did you... talk to him?"

"He ain't exactly easy to talk to."

All fitted up, Sophia leaned against the wagon. She said, "Thomas, this Hans is a hedge knight and even I know him well enough. He used to come to Marsburg for the jousting tournaments, usually representing a Sommerwein nobleman. My husband, rest his soul, did meet him once. Sold a pig to him and his troop. I think he had a few young squires with him. None of them gave us problems. From what I have heard he was quite good in those tourneys, too. They said he only lost to Uther von Ruhmolt, and after that loss he disappeared from the circuits."

"The Uther match was rigged," Berthold said. The miller joined the conversation as though they were all hunters trading stories of a great and foul beast they had seen in the woods. "I have heard it many times over that whenever Uther faced a man on horseback who could beat him, he simply paid the man off to take a fall. It makes sense to me, anyway. Uther's old and Hans is in his prime."

Dahlgren spat. "Hans is a murderer, that's what he is. Killed two children at a tournament and fled out. Bounty hunters don't want to confront him, and the lawmen don't want to bother on account of his connections with some of the lords. Now, his morality is dictated by coin and coin alone."

Jingling his jester bells, Minnesang said, "You guys seems rather hung up on this fella."

"*Minnesang*," Quinn said, seething that the jester dared to even talk.

"I'm actually curious as well," Berthold said. "Hans knew you two."

Quinn shook his head. "Me and Dollgrin got into it with Hans a few weeks back. I left Hans a dagger in the thigh. The old man lost his hand. Real good work there, Dollgrin, really helped out. Hans ended up having us dead to rights, but let us go. We're alive, but that was pretty embarrassing."

"Hans will get what's coming," Dahlgren said.

Quinn rolled his eyes, but in a rare show of constraint did not continue the conversation.

"I saw Hans eyeing you," Hobbs said, looking at Thomas.

The servant raised an eyebrow. "Me? He was eyeing me?"

"More like just a glance, but it almost seemed as if he recognized you," Hobbs said. "I think he smelled you out when you were ducking away."

"Why, uh, why was he doing that? I don't even know him!"

"Probably wanted you for lunch," Quinn said, laughing.

"Hah-hah, hey yeah, that's probably it."

"Dunno why yer laughing," Quinn said. "You weakest link motherfarker."

Richter had his fill of the sellswords squabbling amongst each other and hurriedly put his hand up and gave his voice an equal measure of raise: "That's enough! We have better things to do than reminisce about some sellsword."

"Question," Quinn said, holding up a finger. "Real quick one."

Sighing, Richter nodded. "Go ahead."

The thief cleared his throat and straightened out his clothes. "Ehem, so... you know, in addition to all these fine pieces of leather armor which, you know, are protecting your hearts and bodies and all that, you know, very, uh, very important stuff..."

"Stop trying to butter us up," Dahlgren said. "Just get out with it."

Quinn scoffed. "I wasn't buttering, I was... setting the mood..."

"You were buttering," Richter said. "Just be yourself."

The thief looked at the company. Nobody was having his facetious modesty. He laughed and then shrugged and leaned against the nearest tree. He said, "Fine. Along with all the fine gear you're now using, I also stole some crowns from the merchant. I was curious if I'd be seeing a larger cut of that money on account of my, how do you say, 'contributions.'"

"You want payment for your crime?" Richter said.

"A hundred crowns sounds fair, no?"

Richter remembered that the thief had been honest with how many times trips he had made in his stealing. He decided to offer a deal: "Fifty."

"Seventy-five?"

"Fifty."

"Alright."

"The rest goes into the treasury," Richter said. He snapped his fingers. "Crockett."

The historian straightened up, his leather chest plate looking more like a beige bib than proper armor. He nodded. "I'll deduct it from the treasury."

"Alright," Quinn said, grinning. "You cut my pay, I work to get it back, I see how this relationship is. Carrot and stick approach."

"No," Richter said. "I'll also have Crockett reinstitute your normal daily wages, but you pull anything like this again and I'll hang you."

"Now that's a good deal," Quinn said, unironically.

Dahlgren spat and said, "If you need me to put him in line, captain, I'm more than ready."

"Aye," Richter said. He turned around. "Hobbs."

The boy was standing small in a leather chest piece, looking like a man wearing a barrel for armor, his arms out, legs stilted. He stiffly waved his limbs around and said, "This isn't really fitting me."

Richter snapped his fingers. He said, "Put that back in the wagon. You protect yourself by hiding, understand?"

Sighing, Hobbs took off the armor and heaved it into the wagon.

"And feed the donkey," Richter said.

"Yes, pa," the boy said, and in a moment, he toe-tapped and stood on the edge of his feet as though caught stealing from a king.

All eyes looked over.

Hobbs' mouth dropped open. He said, "Uhh, yessir," and hurried his way to the front of the wagon.

"Pa?" Quinn said. "*Pa?*"

Richter waved his hand. "Hobbs only meant—"

"Hahahahaha!" The thief bowled over and back with laughter. The rest of the company snickered.

Sophia smirked. "Every boy does need a father…"

"Quit it," Richter said. "Let's just get back on the road. We don't know what dangers these forests still hold for us yet."

Chapter 27. Changing Directions.

A SERIES OF THOUGHTS ran through Richter's head again and again: gather men. Gather supplies. Gather money. Keep building the company. Keep making it stronger. And then – face her and kill her.

"So we're leaving the Ancient Road," Quinn said. "And the plan is…?"

Find her. Kill her.

Richter spat. He said, "There's a ferry out a ways. We're going to see if it's in service. If it is, we cross and hit up the towns west of here. More money and talent can be found there than in these woods. If the ferry's busted, we'll see if we can rebuild it. If not, we'll continue on along the shoreline. Ground's firming up and the wagon will tread just fine if we need it to."

A few bells jingled. Everyone looked at Minnesang, the jester raising a finger. He said, "Perhaps we should head south to Marsburg. Plenty of work to find there for mercenaries, yeah?"

"Can't do that," Dahlgren said.

"And why not?"

"It's complicated."

"Explain."

"Cap'n," Quinn said, throwing a hand to the jester. "Mind tellin' me why we still have this fark here? Cut his ass loose. He asks too many questions, and he ain't smart about it like Berthold is, or that other fella."

"Gernot," the butcher said.

"Yeah, whatever."

"We need all the men we can afford," Richter said, nodding to the jester.

"Even the peculiar ones who keep thinking outloud when they shouldn't."

Minnesang bowed. He said, "It was only a suggestion. If I get paid, I go where you tell me to."

"Aye," Richter said. "So why are you talking, then?"

The jester bowed again, but this time he retreated a few steps before straightening up, and when he did there was no grin on his face, nor any look at all, as if he were a staggering chess piece that had been solved of a briefly animated life.

Dahlgren said, "Think we should run scouts? Maybe a picket?"

Richter shook his head. He said, "We don't have the manpower for it." The captain turned and touched the wagon. "We stick to the wagon. This is our castle, understand? Anyone attacks, we retreat to the castle. If we are ambushed we retreat to the opposing side." He turned to point himself down the road, then swung out an arm. "Left flank, right flank, understand? I want to make sure everyone knows their right from left."

"I can count now," Quinn said, scoffing and brushing his chest with pride. "You don't have to worry about me gettin' that all mixed up."

The company stared at him. A few sighs were had, and others simply shook their heads.

"Are you expecting us to get attacked, Richter?" Sophia said.

"Aye. When we were at the laager, a merchant mentioned that brigands had attacked and probed their defenses. If you noticed, we spent our night on the eastern flank of their setup. Despite being new arrivals, nobody attacked again. Further out east is just more forest, as far as your eyes can see. Nobody's living out that way. But here," he paused, thumbing over his shoulder, "Is likely where bandits would actually go. Off the main roads and near fresh water. If they're anywhere, they're here."

"Captain," Berthold said. "Can I ask you something?"

Richter nodded. "Sure."

The miller opened his mouth, and then screamed and fell out of formation, dropping his spear and clutching his shoulder – an arrow hanging out of it. Another arrow flew in, whistling until it *tokked* against the wagon.

"Ambush, ambush!" Richter yelled. "Move to left, move to left!"

The company sprawled in every direction, some wheeling around the wagon, others falling to the ground and rolling under its bed. Crouching, the captain stared into the forest and caught a trio of silhouettes moving between trees. He took out his crossbow and fired it at one and the bolt caromed off a tree trunk and spiraled up into the branches. A distant bowman leaned around a tree and returned fire. The shot whistled overhead. Another arrow zipped in and shattered against Elletrache's lindwurm armor, spraying the beast slayer with shrapnel.

"Sumbitch," Elletrache said, leaning away from the wagon's corner and picking splinters out of his beard. "That almost got me."

"What do you see, Trash?" Richter said.

The beast slayer spat. "Brigands, of course. Just a handful."

Hobbs leaned out the side of the wagon and threw down a crossbow. "It's loaded!" he said, and a second later the tarp tufted over his head as an arrow shot through, the boy flinching with his shoulders up to his ears.

Richter stood and pushed the boy back into the bed. "Stay down!" he yelled as pair of arrows burst through and sailed right by him, the tarp snapping outward in pinched folds and the trees beyond him *tok-tok'ing* as the arrows slammed into their trunks.

The donkey honked as an arrow pierced its hindquarters and it jerked on its halter and jaunted ahead, jostling the wagon forward, suddenly leaving half the company sitting in the open. Dahlgren threw up his shield and it collected a few shots while Elletrache turned and raised a shoulder, the lindwurm armor turning the shots into shrapnel.

Richter waved. "Go, go! Keep up with the wagon!"

Tok-tok-tok, arrows belted the wagon and the trees. Another one sailed through the donkey's ear and it jerked forward again and twisted its head around nipping at air as though an eatable bee had done the damage.

Screaming and hollering, the brigands in the trees started drawing closer. Richter could see that they wore cloth and shredded gambesons and some aketon caps. They almost looked like the company did just the day prior.

"Charge!" a brigand growled out. "Kill them all!"

The voice was hoarse and hungry all the same.

Shapes poured out of the woods. Richter questioned what Elletrache considered to be a 'handful.'

"Hey, yeah," Thomas said, "Th-th-they're coming!"

"Let them come!" Dahlgren said, clapping his shield with his sword

Richter drew an invisible line from left to right. "Shieldwall, shieldwall!"

The company gathered together, with shields of all shapes and sizes, their colors disparate, and the height of the sellswords themselves gave the wall of wood a bubbling, incoherent appearance. And yet it held firm. Shields held tight, spears leveraged in the nooks where the mobile bastion had closed together, and like that they met the bandits in open battle.

~~~

Collision. Two brigands dead upon the spears. The sellswords lowered the weapons, shucking the corpses free. More brigands poured in. They sidled between the spears and landed blows upon the shields. More yet poured in behind them, causing a collision and the company bent its knees and slid back in the mud. More brigands tried to go around only to meet Elletrache and Quinn on the flanks, both men game for one-on-one combat. Within a single minute, every bandit had been stabbed, slashed, and ultimately slain.

Richter stood, bloodied sword in hand, catching his breath. A breeze passed through, lifting the branches and bushes and he spun his steel toward the movements, mistaking the blurs for more brigands.

"It's alright," Dahlgren said, wiping blood from his face. "We're clear."

The captain sheathed his blade. He started a search of the dead bodies. Inspecting the corpses, the company realized the battle itself may have been an act of mercy for the brigands. When each bandit's clothes were ripped away, little more than bone and pale skin could be found beneath. No crowns. No food. The weapons at their sides not even worth taking, their bows looking like they had been crafted the very day of their use.

"Everyone on our side is accounted for," Crockett said, coming around the wagon. "Cuts and bruises here and there but beating hearts all. Berthold took an arrow to the shoulder, but the armor made it only a flesh wound. Looks like Quinn's recent, uh, acquisitions, helped quite a bit here."

Richter looked at the pile of corpses. He said, "Roll the bodies into the road. Let them know what happens if they cross us. And if anyone does happen to be following us, they can find it just as well."

~~~

Within hours, the company was beset by another ambush. Five men in total, the attackers totally outnumbered, but what they lacked in quantity they made up for in desperation. They were slaughtered. While the company picked through the remains, ten more men attacked using slings and thrown rocks and branches for clubs. One of the bandits managed to break through the shieldwall and smash Dahlgren atop his helmet, but his steeled brow deflected the blow with ease, and the assailant lost his nose in the ensuing slash of a counter, and then his life in the follow up thrust. The rest of the bandits were quickly slain, the last of them pinned to a tree by the shaft of a shot from Elletrache's mini ballista.

After this ambush, the donkey stood on three legs, one lifted into the air. Hobbs stood beside the animal trying his best to console it. The boy had tears in his eyes as he ran his hand over the matted, bloodfilled fur. He whispered into the donkey's ear and the donkey perked up and seemed to hear him and it stamped all four feet to the ground, ready to carry on. But Richter knew another attack like this might hobble the beast for good.

"Well," Dahlgren said, walking up and cleaning his blade. "This batch had naught all on 'em, too."

Richter looked at his company. The sellswords' armor was holding, but in just a few fights the leather garb had taken slashes and dents. After one brigand nearly stove Dahlgren's head in, the captain knew it was only a matter of time until one of the reckless attackers got lucky.

"I'm quite enjoying this," Quinn said, grinning. "I say let them come!"

"No," Richter said. He pointed at the bodies. "Cut their heads off."

Dahlgren cleared his throat. "Eh, respectfully captain, I don't think anybody around is going to be paying us money for some random heads."

"I know. Put the heads on spears and hoist them off the sides of the wagon. Let these bastards see what we can do."

"Uh, captain…"

Richter looked at Hobbs consoling the wounded donkey. He sighed and walked to one of the brigand's, put his boot to its back, and sawed his sword into the nape of its neck. He drew the head up and threw it aside.

"This is not a conversation, Dahlgren," Richter said. "Cut their heads off and put them on the spears."

Chapter 28. One Step at a Time.

Immerwahr stared at the road. He said, "Changing the world, huh."

"You should be proud of your people," Claire said. "They fight well."

"They're dying…"

"And you are free to not watch."

Before the monk and girl, the ensorcelled mob descended upon a caravan. The guards protecting it shouted out and unsheathed their weapons and dove into the melee or shot bows from the wagons. Like chickens in a coup invaded by a fox, the merchants themselves went every which way, some opting to fight, others running for their lives. Weapons slashed and smashed, wagons were thrown over, and people were grabbed and pulled into the mob where they disappeared. The mob itself sounded unnatural. It moved as one, and instead of the shouting and screaming that followed any such grouping, they merely oooh'd, mouths agape and cooing, battling as though they were a wind escaping a hollow, fleshen geists looking for bodies to inhabit.

"Why not send your beasts?" the monk said.

"Oh," Claire said. "My beasts are here, too."

In the trees to the left of the road, anyone who got too far from the wagon was pounced upon by the direwolf and shredded in an instant. To the right of the road, the lindwurm picked off the runaways, clawing them in half or battering them with its tail, shattering their bones and sending entire bodies soaring through the trees. As the merchants continued to run for their lives, the beasts both hurried to the prey, pouncing from one to the other in growling frenzies.

"Must you treat those who are fleeing in this manner," the monk said, turning away. "Just let them leave. They are not your enemies."

The girl smiled. "My military acumen is not so sharp, but I do believe I shouldn't let anyone escape. Or do you suggest I let them run so that they may return from whence they came and alert them there to the nature of that which approaches?"

Immerwahr glanced at the girl and then avoided her eyes. He said, "My understanding of military matters is also dull, I must admit…"

Claire took the monk's hand like a child's first handshake. She stared at him warmly. "Then let us learn together, holy man."

As the ensorcelled mob pressed down on the guards, they were readily cut down, easily dispatched by blade and bow. But as they dwindled in number, they still yet went on grabbing the guards one by one, pulling them into the fleshy, naked mass where the mob bodied them like clustered bees.

"As for the melee, consider this a harvest," Claire said, nodding toward the action. "Some of these men are fighters and I would prefer them alive instead of treated with the, how do you say, niceties of claws and canines."

"They're killing your…" the monk paused. "They're killing my townspeople."

"I know."

"You're losing your fighters! You should… you should protect them!"

"And you only say that because you want me to keep them alive, for to you they matter. But to me, I need a different resolution. I cannot feed every mouth here. It is preferable that the mouths I do feed understand how to swing a sword. These guards will be useful. An upgrade, if you will."

Immerwahr grimaced as he looked back at the battle. Many of the mob had fallen aside, mortally wounded by cuts and slashes, some even missing limbs. One man crawled back up to his feet, picked up an arm which had been chopped free of his shoulder, and went back swinging it like a club.

"This will take a few more minutes," Claire said, nodding like a general watching his cavalry finish off a routed enemy. "I shall be by the cauldron."

~~~

Bubbling, frothing, splashing. The little ones frolicked in the mire of the cauldron, stirring it around and around, caking its corners with paste that sizzled as it dried against the metal. Claire watched them with motherly warmth, then her face soured as she turned to her newest prisoners: the caravan guards. Speckled in blood, smattered in sweat, heavy breathing, heads down, hands slung between the knees. Some sitting with their eyes closed, stealing sleep or practicing for another kind of sleep altogether. Defeated. Claire had seen such men return from battlefields. These were nothing new, these men or the images they presented. It was instead a boy that captured the girl's interest, and she slowly stepped away from her cauldron and pointed at the child.

"You look familiar," Claire said.

The boy looked up, his eyes wide.

"What is your name?" she said. "It isn't Hobbs, is it?"

The boy shook his head. "It is Waldo."

"Now *that* is a curious name. Waldo, do you happen to know a Hobbs?"

"My master," Waldo said, his chest huffing. "Where is he?"

"Your master is right here," Claire said, fanning her fingers against her chest. "And you should always answer the questions of your master."

Swallowing nervously, Waldo nodded. He said, "There was a boy north of here… I think his name was Hobbs. I didn't talk to him much, though."

"And was he with anyone?"

"Some men. And a woman, I think."

"What kind of men?"

"Fighters."

"Sellswords?"

Waldo thought for a moment. The caravan guards kneeling around him exchanged glances. The boy said, "Yes. I believe so."

"Was there a man with this group that wore a black hat?"

"Yes. He had a black hat and a strange face."

"Was his name Richter?"

"I don't know. He reminded me of a story my mother used to tell."

"About the one they call the Wight?"

"Y-yes. I didn't ask him if it was him, but he looked like him."

"Quite ugly, yes?" Claire said, smirking.

"He was scary-lookin' if that's what you mean."

"Mhmm. And do I scare you?"

Again, the caravan guards exchanged glances. One raised his hand. Claire turned her head to him like an owl spotting the long-awaited mouse.

"Ma'am," he said. "There's no reason to bring us any harm."

In the woods, a briefly lived scream shrilled out followed by the chomping and crunching of the lindwurm having a meal. Claire cocked her head. She said, "If I wanted to bring you harm, would you and I be having this conversation? Your lot... you... hmm, ten? I was hoping for more. You ten will not be suffering harm. On the contrary: you will be joining me."

Claire stepped aside. She fanned her arm to the cauldron, and to the contents splashing about within its belly. She said, "Any man who resists goes in the pot."

Kantorek sidled up to Claire with a jug in hand, his other hand limply laid atop his head. Its wrist had been seesawed black just by the mere endless motions she had demanded of him. The hand itself now sat atop his head like a hat, the tips of his fingers now tapping like spider legs in final pulses of submission to her will. His appearance stunned the guards as though Claire had dashed a slaver's whip across the lot of them. They watched as Kantorek held the jug out with blind and unfeeling orderliness.

Claire put her little hands into the jug, caking them in yellow. Fingers dripping, she turned to her prisoners.

"Only question now is, do you prefer the cauldron, or do you prefer me," she said, slowly approaching the guards. "Tilt your heads up if you prefer me. There you go. That's good. I'm glad we are all in agreement. Some of you are crying. That is quite alright. Let it all out while you can. I'll not allow you the tears later. We simply have too much to do."

~ ~ ~

"Ten caravan guards with leather armor and an assortment of swords and spears," Claire said. "I'm supposing that is a good military addition."

"For some things," Immerwahr said.

"And do you consider yourself a man of war?"

"N-no… but…"

"Then why are you talking?"

Swallowing nervously, the monk nodded and took a step back. He watched the girl from behind. She stood in the middle of the road, staring down it with the poise of a conqueror choosing their next target.

"Leather armor," she continued. "Probably good enough to handle whatever Richter has on his end. Though if there's a laager further up, I don't want to risk losing these men against it. That would certainly be a waste. And he's probably with them, too. If he is… do I send everybody all at once?"

"You should establish a picket and send scouts."

Claire whipped her head around.

Immerwahr bowed his own head and took another step back.

"What did you say?"

"I..." the monk cleared his throat. "I said you should set a picket and send scouts."

"What is a picket?"

"Forward posts," Immerwahr said. "They run ahead of the main party. If there lies danger ahead, they can help warn you of it."

"A vanguard."

"Not... exactly. More like..."

"A dinner bell."

"Well..."

"I'd rather not split my forces," Claire said. "I'm sure you read of these pickets in a book somewhere. So have I. But we are not a full army. It may be the case that Richter would be plotting a trap for us and would more than gladly whittle my numbers portion by portion. I would be daft to hand him such victories."

"Yes, yes of course..."

"But a scout... hmm. I don't need a scout either. I know where the laager is. I know half if not most of its forces are now my forces. I know that Richter is up there somewhere. I don't need a scout. No no no... you're trying to fool me with your blabbering."

A bead of sweat formed on the monk's cheek. He said nothing because she was right. He was trying to prod her into making terrible tactical decisions, hoping that, on his end, Richter would make the most of these mistakes. In reality, every retort she had was the truth. But a part of Immerwahr's ploy did get through – the girl thought on his suggested element a beat longer than she should have, and instead of leaving it behind, she mused on it.

"No, a scout is pointless, but something else… maybe a bit of a shock force would suffice. When my father would battle the barbarians, the savages would send madmen and reavers to try and shatter the resolve of the more civilized before the main forces could arrive for the pitched battle. I don't have such ferocious fighters on hand, but I quite like the idea nonetheless…"

Claire turned around. She stared at her contingent of an ensorcelled mob half-naked and exhausted, the ten caravan guard who stood in rigid formation like statues, their foreheads now caked in yellow crust, and beyond them was the cauldron in the wagon, now pulled with great speed by lengths of corded rope, and sitting atop the wagon was the limp-wristed Kantorek with the dead stare, and beyond him the beasts.

"Shock and awe," Claire said, her eyes going over her retinue. "Shock and awe. Who do I send to do this? Or… *what* do I send?" She looked to the monk. "Any thoughts, holy man?"

"N-no… well, actually…"

"Shut it. I already know the answer." A grin stretched across her face. "Oh yes, I know the perfect answer. Something to knock on Richter's door and, perhaps, blow it right in."

Chapter 29. The Man in Black.

RICHTER'S COMPANY moved beneath the tottering of spear shafts poled at the wagon's four corners. At the length of the weapons themselves were bandit heads, planted there with mouths agape and eyes wide. In moments of pause, the buzzing of flies filled the air.

"It's a bit grim," Sophia said, glancing at the heads.

"Aye." Richter nodded at his handiwork. "But these men are dead and there is no coming back from that. Now they help spare others what they have suffered."

"I'd say it's working something proper," Dahlgren said, waving a fly from his face. "I see shadows in the woods, but never the men with them."

Four times the company spotted silhouettes moving in the surrounding forest, and four times those silhouettes retreated. Although spearing heads for presentation was a barbarous act befitting a cruel king, it had undoubtedly saved numerous lives in the process, particularly the lives of those they were scaring. Most importantly, though, the donkey was left alive. Even if Richter's company slaughtered another attack, the animal itself would likely die in the process. The captain simply could not afford that. Not with all the arms and armor and tools and foodstuffs they needed to transport.

"Ah, there's another one!" Quinn said, pointing into the forest.

A group of bandits stood in the trees. Hesitating. Whispering.

"You don't want this?" Quinn barked at them. "You don't want this?"

One brigand picked up a bow and half-lifted it in a partial draw, the arrow's aim somewhere between the trees and the wagon.

"Ah boy, don't do that!" Quinn yelled. "Oh, that would be a *big* mistake!" The brigand wavered. He lowered the bow.

"Good job!" Quinn put his boot to the neck of their proverbial courage: "Best to walk away thinking you'd been beaten, then to come down here and remove any doubt, and also get yer farkin' heads removed just as well!"

Dahlgren spat. "Alright Quinn, that's enough. Let them run. You keep badgerin' them and you'll put a fire in their arses to attack just outta spite."

"Let them come, we can take them."

"Well I'm tired of fighting," Dahlgren said. "So stove it."

"You're getting older yet," the thief said. He grinned and smugly crossed his arms. "Personally, I don't think I've ever turned away a fight."

"Yeah," Sophia said. "We've noticed."

~~~

The company moved, now and again accompanied by the appearance and subsequent scurrying of bandits. It reminded Richter of his youth, traversing the forests of Dagentear, his very presence spooking the birds and squirrels from their hollows, and his ears would hear their escape and his eyes would dart only to catch the fading shapes of them, the shiver of a branch departed, a tumble of leaves fluttering down. It was now as it was then: they turned and left, and Richter gave them no harm aside from a curious gaze.

Richter eventually ordered the company to stop and they ate a meal with one eye to the food and the other to the trees. As instructed, Hobbs slipped a vial of Richter's concoction into the meal. The sellswords moaned about Sophia's cooking, and Richter found himself cringing as the homesteader cried out that she had just purchased new spices and it should be better. The captain consoled her by saying her medical acumen was a very worthy and needed addition to the company. Indeed, Sophia tended to the sellswords one by one, mending little cuts and scratches. Dahlgren looked half-white in reams of sloping and crisscrossing cloth, the old man having acquired more wounds in a span of the past week than he had his entire soldiering career.

"This one will close on its own," the homesteader said, her finger pinching a wink of a gash on the old man's forehead. "Is the pain alright?"

"It smarts," Dahlgren said. Ever the pragmatist, he added: "But a head can't limp, so I'd rather take ten more of these than even one cut to a knee."

Crockett lowered the wagon's tailgate and spread a map across it. "Per the merchants' maps, the ferry shouldn't be far. Straight shot down the road."

"No side roads to get lost down?" Richter said.

The paymaster pursed his lips.

"I'm fooling with you," Richter said. He clapped the man on the shoulder. "You got us on the right track, and that is well enough."

"Thanks," Crockett said. "But... I do think we should be concerned about all these bandits. If they're out here, there's certain to be some at the ferry itself, no?"

"Aye," Richter said. "And I imagine if there are brigands there, then they likely booted out these ones we've been seeing in the woods. Which means that—"

"Hey!"

Everyone paused. Heads turned. Quinn was walking ahead of the wagon, pointing and yelling down the road like a man trying to scare off a dog.

"Hey!" he threw his arms wide in bravado. "You want some too?"

But a man wearing a black cloak and hood stood unmoving on the path. He had his hands jammed into his beltline and his legs spread in a fearless posture. Weighted heavily across his back was a very sharp, sun-winking bardiche to go along with a sword on his hip. Suddenly, more men slipped out of the treeline around him, all similarly black. Steel weapons glinted with perfected sheens, bringing sharpness to axes and swords and polearms, and they wore metal nasal helms and kettle hats and squared flattops, their chests covered in chain mail and furs and heavy lamellar layering beneath, the chinking and clanking of their approach filling the air with ominous intent.

"Hey…" Quinn's voice died as he slowly lowered his hands. "Oh shit. Oh shit, Richter! Cap'n! Captain!"

The thief turned and ran face-first into Richter.

"H-hey, these aren't ordinary bandits," Quinn said.

Nodding, the captain said, "I know."

Behind Richter, his company bustled forward and formed a motley line, altogether armed with spears and shields, bows and arrows, some crossbows, and hurriedly adorned leather armor.

"Orders, captain?" the old man said.

"We can't fight them," Richter said. "They'll kill us all."

Dahlgren grimaced. He said, "Captain?" again as though he had misheard. "Should we run?"

"I suspect they have a plan for that if we do," Richter said. He looked at his company. "Just stay quiet and don't do anything stupid, understand?"

The man in black stepped forward, leaving a good dozen of his fighters behind. As he strode ahead, his face became clearer. Richter could see a tattoo of a spindly fishhook starting from one ear and skewering across his skull before looping around the other. Metal piercings dotted eyebrows and ears and lips, adornments of valuable silver and gold, not the sort of treasures a man attaches to his own flesh lest he were utterly confident that no thief would have at them in the only way they could be taken.

Richter took a step forward. He raised his hand.

"Ahohoy!" the man in black said with a grin. He spoke with a sailor's slick and salty accent: "By the seas, you all should be dead!" He leaned forward, taking in the sight of the bandits' decapitated heads still yet towering above Richter's wagon on speartips. He gave a thumbs up. "Very spooky. I mean, it don't scare me none, but little does anyway."

"We're trying to get to the ferry west of here," Richter said. "If you operate it, we'll pay for passage."

"You'll pay for passage," the man said. He laughed. "Good stranger, a little of what you got don't beat everything of what you got."

"Captain," Dahlgren said again. "We should take the initiative. Let Trash shoot that man dead from here, and then maybe they'll fall into chaos."

Richter sighed. "Dahlgren. We cannot win this fight."

The old man sank back. The rest of the company exchanged glances.

"My name is Eppo!" the man in black announced. He threw a thumb over his shoulder. "As you suspected, I run the ferry just up the road and, much like yourself, I deal with a lot of ballyhooed bandits up in this area. You wouldn't happen to be a ballyhooed bandit yourself, would ya?"

"We're sellswords," Richter said.

Eppo smirked. "Sellswords." He leaned left and right, staring deep into the company, his eyes dancing along their mended wounds and their shot-up wagon and the maimed donkey. He nodded. "Interesting. On these roads, fellas always be coming and going and screaming and dying. So much of that screaming, too. That's just the worst of it. The screaming. On the ocean, you don't get much of that sorta thing. A man goes overboard and the ocean screams for him, cause the ocean was always screaming for him."

"They're sea raiders," Dahlgren said. "Eppo's a northern name and his accent is straight out of Weissenhaven."

"Weissenhaven?" Berthold said.

"It's a port town west of Sommerwein," Crockett said. "Some say all the hells on earth can be found in its alleys and that—"

"Psshpsshpsshpssh," Eppo said, mimicking their whispering. "You all should be more respectful. Either raise your voice or don't say nothing at all. You really don't want me getting any wrong ideas, you know?"

"You haven't attacked us yet," Richter said. "Why?"

"Goodness, you sound like a man staring into a grave wondering why he ain't in it yet!" Eppo laughed. He turned back to his men. They laughed. Their armor clinked and clanked. Their weapons winked. Eppo pointed at Richter. "I like you." He put both hands low and bobbled them like weighted scales. "You got big balls, friend. You're also smart."

The raider took a few more steps forward, his eyes firmly on Richter.

"I'd my men watching you," Eppo said. He looked at Quinn. "The ones you think you were scaring away. The ones dancing in the shadows yonder. And these men told me that someone of great use might be in your company." Eppo took more steps forward. "They told me you might be the Wight."

"My name is Richter."

"The Wight," Eppo said as if to correct Richter of his own name. "I know of you from me mum. You were said to be a pale, ugly fark, all skin and bone, like a revenant coming out of that wayward town, whatsitsname."

"Dagentear."

"Richter von Dagentear," Eppo said. "The boy tattooed by chaos and carnage, the ash of his own village upon his flesh, comin' out of there looking like a skeleton steppin' and fetchin'. And here you are, all these years later, all the same look to you. I'll be damned, ahohoy, I'll be damned."

Eppo smiled.

"Alright," he said, thumbing over his shoulder. "Come along then."

The company stared at the raider, not one man taking a step forward.

Eppo frowned, his jewelry jangling. "Oh, sorry, we're not in negotiations here. You pause one more farking second and I'll gut every single one of you like a fish and use your guts for chum. I think comin' to the ferry is a fair deal, yeah? Sound good or no? I said, does it sound good?"

Richter nodded. "Aye. We'll come with you."

"No, I asked if it sounds good."

The captain sighed. "Aye, it sounds good."

"Alright!" Eppo clapped excitedly as though his 'dog' finally learned a new trick. "It's a little bit of a walk, but not too far. Oh, and take them heads down off them spears. I got a man who likes noses and ears."

"Of course he does," Quinn said.

"What was that?" Eppo said. "Did you say something?"

Richter turned. "Keep it in line, Quinn. If you want to prove yourself worthwhile to the company, now's the time to do it, and you do it by not being yourself for a bit, alright?"

"Sure, cap'n."

"Everything in order, Richter?"

The captain turned around. "Aye. Let's see to your ferry."

"It's a good view," Eppo said, grinning. "You'll just love what's sitting across the waters."

Chapter 30. The Steel that Wars.

"Hans!"

The sellsword opened his eyes. His employer stood over him.

"Sleeping on the job are you?"

"I was."

"Well get up."

Hans sat up, a simple movement that came with a lot of moving parts.

"I don't know how you sleep in all that armor," the merchant said.

"You get used to it."

"Is that how you sleep when yer alone? Just lying on the ground ready to be robbed?"

"Nobody's robbing me," Hans said, and the growl with which the words came out served as proper security as any on the matter. He got to his feet, his height towering over his fat and silk-laden employer and, despite the rotundness of the merchant, Hans still proved the larger man by muscle alone.

The merchant looked him up and down like a mother would a daughter late to her own wedding. "Well," he said. "We're leaving."

Hans nodded. "As always, your monies, your choices."

"Not just leaving, mind. We're heading south to the ferry run by the Immerwahr. Apparently, that Richter's wily, *and thieving*, sellswords did confirm in part that the roads are safe enough to travel. I would have liked to have left with a group, but I think it's well enough we can go alone." The merchant grinned as he stared at his enormous mercenary. "Are you up for this? I don't pay thousands just so you can sit around menacing peasants."

"If we run into problems," Hans said. "I can handle it."

"Good." The merchant smiled and his nostrils pinched as he sucked in the morning air. Letting out a satisfied sigh, he said, "I can't help but feel it in my bones that Marsburg will soon be open again. Open and thriving! And I want to be there for it, supplying all those poor, starving peasants with the goods they want. The goods they need. The goods they *deserve*."

"Sure," Hans said. He leaned over and picked up his massive two-hand sword and yoked its strap over his shoulder. In a similar motion he picked up his metal helm and cupped it in a hand. He stared at his employer, briefly imagining himself spiking his helmet into the man's fat head, and in this imaginative strike he saw gold spilling out where brains should be. It was a scenario he had seen himself doing many a time, yet not once in any of his long, long stares did the merchant pick up on the fact that his imaginary self was victim to numerous and grisly murders at the hands of an imaginary Hans. An imaginary Hans not too far distanced from the very real Hans.

"You know, my father had this feeling sometimes," the merchant said, proudly beaming. "Like you could taste the good fortune in the air."

Hans pictured himself gouging the man's eyes with his thumbs, his nails plumbing the depths, mushing into something wet and soft, and his fingers would then grip around the skull and crack it open like a seashell.

"Right?" the merchant said, turning to him, head whole, eyes gawking.

"Right." Hans snorted and blew the snot out of his nostrils. Finished, he threw a thumb over his shoulder. "I'm gonna go take a shit."

"Be quick about it," the merchant said, staring up at the sky with a grin. "Money awaits us, sellsword! And through my sound and profound business mind, you too shall realize yourself to be quite the beneficiary!"

Hans grumbled again as he stepped away. As always, the sellsword marched through the encampment of wagons like a leper, the women and children fleeing from his sight and men only glancing at his back. It was in these mostly silent observations that Hans came to fully accept when and where he was: a long time away from the roar of the tournaments, from the fights that the minstrels would write poems of, from the victories that warranted him any woman he wanted. A long, long time away from all of that, and there was no going back.

The laager's shitting hole was a giant pit in the ground with a series of horizontal sitting poles circling it. Just stumpy enough to sit on and hold yourself up, and the pit itself was home to a slippery ladder in case one was ever so poorly fated as to fall in.

A trio of merchants were already squatting over the pit, their pants at their ankles, their asses in the air, and their mouths busy with chatter. They briefly quieted down to look at the coming sellsword wearing plates of steel rounded out with spaulders and cowters and at the edges of his armor they could see the tightened lamellar leather layered beneath, an assortment which few men could afford, and even fewer had the stamina to wear all day. They watched as this equally regal and lethal man lifted his metal plates and drew down his pants and took a squat.

The merchants looked at him as if they had just watched a tortoise leave its shell, and then they returned to their talks.

"I got word that if you offer nine crowns a pop for your goods then people will snap them up faster'n if you'd had it at a flat tenner."

"Well why not just round it to ten and get yourself an extra coin'a'sale?"

"Cause then they won't make the buy. See, the nine looks cheaper."

"Well it is cheaper."

"Right, but cheap enough to get them to buy, right? And that's the point! They do buy! Is it not better to 'ave a sale of nine'ah'coin, than no sale with a ten marker out front?"

"But I just sell 'em at ten cause that's their worth."

"Look. Yer just not understandin' my point."

"Shitfarkin'fire!" another merchant piped in. "I just want Marsburg to be open already!"

The shitters leaned forward. One said, "You just want to handle them womens they got!"

Another nodded. "They've some fine whorehouses, I'll admit."

"Well, I dunno about now. Don't imagine there's much to eat behind them walls. Be like dicking down a dried salmon or somethin'."

"I'm still game for it. Farkin' fish scales be finer than southern silk when you're on the road this godsdamned long, and I won't apologize for being a man of flesh and blood, cause I'm just that, I'm a man of flesh and blood."

"Don't gotta say it twice."

"Said it twice cause that's just how true it is."

"Well alright, seeing as how yer horned up, why don't you get one of them road lasses if ye got that itch."

"I don't need none of that sickness with the squishness."

"Oh dear, we got ourselves a medically mo-ral fella here."

"No, it ain't that, it's just that if I lower myself to dicking down road squatch I think I might just go on and rope m'self."

"Yer just scared some mouthy bird will speak of yer manhood in ill light."

"I don't give a rat's arse what some damn jangleress mouths off about."

"Now if you had a biggun I suspect you'd have responded different..."

"You shit talkin' m'stinger?"

"Good sir, I can *see* yer stinger, it shit talks itself."

"Now hey, fellas, either of you ever visit that redhead in Marsburg?"

Hans cleared his throat. The men hushed.

The sellsword said, "Can I ask you men something?"

The merchants looked at one another. One said, "Y-yeah, sure."

"Why do you act like I got nothing to say?"

"Wh-what?"

"I walk over here and nobody says nothing. Like I'm some ghost."

The men looked at each other again. "W-well, how're you doing?"

"I shouldn't have to ask for common decency," Hans said.

"L-look," one man said. "It's just a matter of many here knowing who you are. Knowing wh-what you did… to them kids."

"Oh, they wasn't kids," another man said, defensive in tone. "I-I think they were older. Al-almost men, even."

"They weren't," Hans said. "They were kids. I killed their father in a tournament. Smashed his head in so hard that the only thing they could get out of his helmet were his teeth. Afterward, I was sitting on some priory steps when the man's kids came up and stabbed me in the back. I unsheathed my blade and turned all at once." The sellsword looked at the men. He said, "Is there something wrong with me defending myself?"

A long quiet filled the air. One of the merchants leaned forward. He said, "B-but did you have to cut them in half like that?"

The merchants gasped. "Hush, you! He didn't mean that!"

Hans sighed. He drew up his drawers and picked up his steel helm.

"We don't mean nothing ill by this fool's chirpin'," one man said.

Hans walked away. At his back, he could hear the men chastising one another and worrying that the sellsword would remember all their faces.

But Hans simply departed the laager and went into the forest, his armor clinking and clanking with every step, and it seemed as if the noise of his own progress only grew louder as the din of the merchants faded behind him. In walking, he thought about having crossed paths with Richter again. What were the odds that would even happen? And what were the odds he'd not find it within himself to kill the man then and there? He knew the bastard was responsible for the death of Captain Adelbrecht and with him the demise of the Free Company. He also heard rumors that Sommerwein and the surrounding villages had gone onto purging the witch hunters from their lands, and goodness if there wasn't a right black hatted little shit in Richter von Dagentear that might pay out a shiny crown or two.

He looked back toward the laager, barely visible through all the trees. He pondered leaving north to go and see if he could join some bounty hunters and help them catch Richter. It would certainly be worth a lot of coin. But then again, it was only potential coin, when currently he had an actual couple thousand crowns deep in his pockets and with more to come, too. The fat, smelly, greasy merchant employing him nearly drove him mad, but the pay was what it was. There were certainly cheaper ways to lose one's mind.

"To hells with the witch hunter," Hans said. "Let him find his own demise."

Hans set his sword against a tree and dropped his helmet beside it and lowered his drawers and took another squat. A grunt. Another. Then he wiped his arse and drew up his drawers and started refitting his armor. He tightened the leather vambraces over the cowters and repeated it with his spaulders, throwing one hand out behind his back and yanking each strap down with strained, teethgritting crookedness. With the elbows and shoulders snug, he jacked his thumbs into the gaps of chest armor and ran them north to south and then back up again, feeling his armor firm against the chest. Just perfect. Content with its fitting, he knuckled the armor's exterior and listened to the sound: dense, shortlived, a sense that the only thing that could break through was a spear shunted at full force and even that would likely be sent astray.

With the torso taken care of, he threw a leg up and planted a boot on a tree. He tightened the leathers there and made sure the metal braces were fitted right and that they didn't past his gambeson and start cutting into his leg. He hated when they did that. Gingerly and slowly, he pulled his other leg up and set it against the tree. This leg's thigh carried the wounds of Quinn's throwing dagger. It provided a constant throbbing, but once pain like that is constant then it becomes a way of life, and the pain goes away. You live near the rush of a waterfall long enough and it's nothing more than just another noise, no matter how loud it might be.

Peace with pain or not, Hans pictured the thief in his mind and gritted his teeth and said, "I shoulda killed that motherfucker."

He stomped his boot down and felt something crumple beneath it. He took a step back. A clay shard stuck out of the ground. Using the toe of his boot, he shoveled around and eventually nudged out a mortar and then the pestle with it. He stared at the two. He drew up his eyes and noticed bootprints. A pair of little ones, and a pair of a man's.

"Richter," Hans said. "What in the hells were you doing out here?"

As Hans leaned down, a scream rang out. He bolted upright and looked toward the laager. Another scream. Another. And another. Screams building atop one another until they were nothing but mindless, hair-raising shrieks.

"Now that's something," he said, staring toward the chaos.

Hans carefully weighed out his options: that which could and would attack a laager in broad daylight only did so in force, and by the time he got back to the wagons the assailers would no doubt have the momentum of a successful ambush and then some. On the other hand, he had no food or water on his person so fleeing into the woods was a perilous prospect at best. But mostly… it was the merchant's money that tilted the scales. His employer had a lot of it. And Hans wanted all of it.

More screams snapped through the forest. It seemed as though the throat of suffering was being throttled in all its woes.

"Yeah," Hans said, sliding his helmet on. "Time to get paid."

The sellsword picked up his sword. A foolish hero would run in, but Hans knew better. He knew to pace himself, to not deplete his energy before he even got there. The sellsword, armored head to toe, simply jogged back toward the merchants, not letting all the shrieking and screaming fool him into an exhausting sprint. They never wrote it in the martial books, nor in the scribes' war stories, but it was fatigue that killed most men. All the skills in the world meant nothing if the muscles that manifested them from mind to reality could not lift the needful. It was so that Hans had struck down numerous men. Standing over them in the end, themselves staring up like tired rabbits, hearts all a'pounding, sucking up the last of the energy, sucking up the last spurt of life so their eyes could widen just that little bit more, almost as if the body was insulting them, telling them look: look at your own demise, hold still and look! And Hans obliged them the sum of their mistakes.

As he curved around the bushes and up and over the tree trunks, the laager grew in between the slits of his helm, and the slits of the trees passed in shimmering vertical imagery, here and there natural panes which gave glimpse of wagons and peoples and debris and corpses, and now just debris and corpses, and only debris and corpses, and there a fire, and there smoke. There a dog limping away. There a headless chicken spinning in circles.

Breaking into the laager's center, the sellsword met a sudden, eerie silence. Wagon tarps billowed and snapped. Barrels creaked as they rolled back and forth. Campfires crackled with their firepots pitched into the embers, the soups bubbling and frothing wildly. A sight drew his eye and the point of his sword with it: an overturned wheelbarrow scuttled across the grass like a bug. Someone murmured inside like a whimpering mutt.

Hans lifted the wheelbarrow. A merchant screamed and fell on his back, arms out, hands shaking back and forth. "Ahh! Aaahh!"

"Hey." Hans pointed away. "Where are the attackers?"

"G-go away!" the merchant said. "Th-this is my spot!"

"Where is everyone?"

"I don't know! Not my problem!"

The merchant unfurled like a trapdoor spider and snatched the wheelbarrow and slammed it back down. He scooted away and, knowing the man's mind broken, Hans knew there was little purpose in chasing him down.

"Pssst! Hans… hey!"

Hans looked over to see his employer hiding under a wagon like a dog under its owner's table. The merchant waved his hand.

"Get over here!" his employer hissed. "The hells am I paying you for!"

Hans jogged over and leaned down.

"Thank the gods," the merchant said. "You have to get me out of here."

"Where are the brigands?" Hans said.

"Brigands? What? There's a beast. A terrible, fast one."

"I'll kill it," Hans said. "Whatever it is."

"Are you daft, sellsword? Don't even think of it. We're leaving before it comes back, that's what we're going to do. Now help me out of here!"

The sellsword pursed his lips. He crouched and held out his arm. "C'mon then. Just know you'll be paying me extra for this."

"Wh-whatever you want," the merchant said.

As the merchant clasped on, the sellsword bent back. For a moment, the employer's weight was all that it could be: a godawful anchor of uselessness forged by decades of decadence, and then the weight snapped away and Hans yelled as his feet slipped out from under him. Landing on his back, he quickly leaned up to see that he had his employer's arm in hand, muscles and tendons wiggling in the air, the bracelets and rings oddly hollow in their suddenly cold clanging. He looked past his own feet to see the fat merchant being effortlessly dragged back under the wagon, and suddenly a silhouette clambered atop him, and the merchant screamed and the wagon rocked back and forth and then the frenzy stopped almost as soon as it started.

"Hey," Hans said. He grabbed his sword. "Hey!"

A black shape with bristling fur planted itself on all fours and stared under the cart, red eyes penetrating through the shadows.

Hans flinched. "Oh shit."

He threw the merchant's arm away and kicked backward before hurrying to his feet. The beast barreled under the wagon snarling and roaring, its arms thrusting with the speed of snakes, snapping out of the shadows and wrenching great clumps of earth as it crawled with lashing, slashing haste. Clattering, the wagon shunted back and forth until the direwolf cleared the weight of it and before the wheels could so much as crash back down the direwolf had already made it halfway to the sellsword, its massive arms fanned out at its sides, claws hungry, mists of blood spraying off its mane as it soared forward, maw opened, bloodlust in its eyes.

The sellsword took a breath. He evened out his feet. Planted his weight.

"Come on then," he said. "Come on then!"

The direwolf supinated its arms and the claws unfurled. Hans balanced his sword in both hands and in the blink of an eye the beast bounded forward, soaring left to right in strides so lengthy the sellsword had to turn his whole head to keep up. Hans dug his right foot into the earth. He lifted his blade and the edge followed the beast's approach like a hunter tracking a bird. Roaring, the direwolf leapt through the air and swung. Hans clapped his forearm against the center of his blade's steel and caught the attack in a crossing parry, slicing down the direwolf's arm like he was shearing a sheep. It howled as it skidded across the mud, one arm bracing itself upon the earth and the other curling against its chest. As it came to a stop, the beast held up its arm where a chunk of flesh had been flayed and then it looked up at the one who had done it. The direwolf's mouth drew back, its lips shivering in fury, blood and foam spewing between its razor-sharp teeth.

Hans let a breath out. Pacing. One. Two. He breathed again.

The direwolf took a step forward, and then another, and another.

"Come on then," Hans said again, replanting his feet. "Come on then!"

Growling, the direwolf went to all fours and burst forth. Hans couched his sword's pommel against his shoulder and half of the blade rested in the nook of his other arm. He lifted the blade like a pike, keeping the tip aimed at the creature's chest. The middle slit of his helm shimmered with the dark monstrosity. He breathed. And then the two slits beside it. And then all the slits were blinkering as the beast rushed in. Hans turned his feet, digging down for now the very earth was a needed ally.

"Come on then!"

The direwolf leapt through the air. Hans pointed the sword upward, its tip aimed directly at the beast's heart. He grinned at the animal's folly for this was the natural state of things. Man against beast, the latter could only unwit itself, for the former knew all. But suddenly, the airborne creature's arm shot down to the earth and clawed into the mud, dragging its flight back to the ground in an instant, and before Hans could lower his aim the creature drove itself under the sword and slammed the sellsword backward and his arms flopped over the direwolf's shoulders like a child being carried away. His sword slipped from his hand before his finger and thumb pinched hold of the handle, great strength indebted to so little, and he managed to bring the blade back into his grip and then he slammed into a wagon, cratering its side as planks cracked and wood and dust blew out and a keg punched open and ale spewed in fizzing geysers and his armor clenched tight to his chest and squeezed and Hans blew out his lungs in a gasping wheeze.

A massive mitt of a hand turned its claws against his armor and pushed him against the wreckage of the wagon. The creature towered, and for the first time in a long while the sellsword had to look up. The beast's chest heaved, its mouth open, its tongue flailing as it breathed, sheer, raw power emanating.

Hans slowly brought his sword to his side.

"Come on then," he said. "Come on—"

The direwolf broke upon him in a frenzy of claws and through the jumbling of his helmet Hans could see blurs of black as the direwolf's nails hissed against his steel, but not breaking through the armor the assault hurried with bestial frustration until the direwolf planted both claws against the sellsword's chest and ran them down the steel in an ear-piercing squall.

Hans screamed and pressed his back against the wagon and used all the counterforce to kick the beast right between the legs. With a muted grunt, the direwolf took one step in retreat, stared at the man in a moment of disbelief, and then reared back and delivered a mighty bestial kick, blasting the sellsword through the wagon entirely, breaking the cart in half and tumbling him onto the other side on a litter of wooden slats and broken barrels and gushing wash of spilled ale.

Rolling over, Hans let out a long groan. He lifted his helmet for another breath, but as he drew it in, his chest swelled and rejected it and he choked and spewed blood instead. He stared at his crimson coated gauntlets and blinked the sweat out of his eyes. He brought both hands up and realized neither of them had his sword. His eyes widened. More sweat poured into them. Eyes stinging, sight blurred, he sent his hands through the grass, horror in his slapping palms, desperation in his prodding fingertips.

A glimmer of his steel flickered as he knocked into the sword by happenstance. He blinked his eyes clear and shouted in glory and reached for the sword, but as he grabbed its handle a shadow crossed over him and a massive pair of hands drove down onto his forearm, crushing it into the earth, and the beast's head cocked down sideways, drool and blood frothily dripping out the side of its maw as its eyes stared into Hans' helm, knowing the man inside had much to pay for.

"Just don't let go," Hans muttered, his eyes affixed to his blade.

The direwolf twisted its grip.

The armor crunched and leather straps snapped apart and the bones within fared no better.

Hans screamed and planted his left hand and hurried to his knees. The direwolf let go and grabbed him by the neck of his armor, drew him onto his feet, rolled its claws into a fist, and threw a punch. By sheer instinct, the sellsword rolled his shoulder and thick, bricklike knuckles glanced off a pauldron and rode up and blasted the top of his head. He spun away, and his helmet spun with him, rattling and clattering, and he caught it and held it down because if he lost that he was certainly doomed, and though his right arm was broken, the hand wasn't, and he told that hand with every ounce of courage that it was not to let go of his sword, and as he made this instruction the direwolf snarled and closed in on him and the sellsword suddenly found himself being lofted into the air, carried effortlessly, and as the weight shifted down a moment, he could hear the clinks of pieces of metal falling through his suit of armor and the sloshing of blood as though he wore chalices for protection and was at a feast of his own making, and then he was gone.

Airborne. Weightless. For a small moment, Hans remembered his childhood fascination with catapults. He once sat in one and was a hair's breadth away from loosing himself into the sky like a ball of soon to be dead fun. A whole lot of trouble could have been saved there if his father hadn't leapt across the spoon of the weapon and cleared the boy of it. And then a glimmer of light caught Hans' eye, and he saw his sword spinning above him, straight and long, swimming there in the blue sky, glinting like a salmon in an infinite river, and like a bear Hans went after it, pawing for it, pawing through all that crystal blue, pawing after a memory, pawing after the present, pawing for his future, and he got his fingers on the blade and pulled it to his chest and then his back slammed into the earth and rolled up on his shoulders and he flipped over and his feet stiffly poled into the ground and then he was in the air again and chunks of armor went spiraling away as buckles broke and straps flailed and a boot came off and then his back crashed once more and this time he simply slid across the grass, and for all his memories in life, for all that he had done and not done, when he looked down he had his godsforsaken sword in his godsforsaken broken and bloodied arms.

"Just need a chance," he said.

The sellsword got to his feet. Half his helmet had been cratered, the molds of metal pinching against his cheeks. When he tried to plant his feet again, he slipped on the sock of a bootless foot. When he lifted his sword, he did so with his left-hand. Not his primary. Better than most men, but he wasn't facing a man. The heat of his own breath soggily mildewed in the helm's slits. He blinked the sweat out of his eyes, but a blink was all it took for more to fall in. When he righted himself, he felt blood seep through his gambeson and break warmly across his chest and lines of it ran down his arms and his back and his arse and his legs. He looked down to see his half-naked legs standing without protection, and his chest piece smashed to ruin with a concave reflection of himself in the rent metal where the beast's kick had landed.

"You're doing great," he said to his reflection. "This is fair enough."

The direwolf roared through the broken wagon and charged after him.

"Fair enough," he said, awkwardly heaving the sword up. "It's fair."

He stared the beast down. It narrows in his already narrowed vision.

"Life is fair," he said. "Always been. This is just the way it is."

Black fur. Red maw. Snarling. Growling. Roaring. Feet pounding across the mud. Every step filling the air of the emptied laager. Just man and beast.

"Of all the ways," Hans said, his sword wobbling unevenly. "This is the fairest."

The direwolf planted its feet and launched. Black fur. Red maw. Barking. Brown fur. Small maw. Snapping. Blurring. Blur against blur. The direwolf tilted. Its arms swung sideways. Its legs turned, its body tilted. The sellsword blinked. Too much sweat. He threw off his helmet. The direwolf appeared in full, enormous and murderous and distracted, a hunting dog clasped onto the nape of its neck, its hindlegs whipping side to side as the black beast shunted and rolled. Hans' eyes went wide. He limped forward, sword dragging behind him. The direwolf planted itself on all fours before reaching back for the dog. Howling in pain, the dog let go and tumbled down the side of the direwolf. When the beast cocked its head to find and finish the hound, a shadow passed over them both, and the sword swung down and the direwolf's arms tensed, and then it fell to the earth, body stiff, its head rolling in the grass.

Hans dropped his sword and collapsed to the ground. He pitched his head between his legs and spewed. Blood and breakfast. Shaking his head, he started pulling off all his armor, piece by broken piece, the entirety of it now worth as much as a dinner plate in divorce. Half-naked, he got back to his feet and limped across the laager. Campfires still burning. Broths still churning. Tarps flailed and snapped as he passed, their frayed edges hissing.

"Yeah," he said.

Grunting and limping, Hans made his way to his employer's wagon. He tore its tarp, ripped it into finer strands, and made himself a sling. Seething, he lowered his broken arm into it. Now that the fighting was done, the injury was making itself known, throbbing and pulsing with pain. He wondered if it would heal. If not, he'd get better with his left. He knew he would. Looking back into the wagon, he retrieved a belt and threw it around his waist. Then he grabbed a hatchet and used its flathead wrench off the last of his armor. As it fell away, he took a breath. His lungs filled. Nothing hurt on the inside, and that mattered most. Content, he looked for a chest. Found it. Broke its lock. Didn't bother counting the crowns, just took it all. Now a few thousand coins richer, he hobbled back across the laager.

The dog sat waiting for him. Panting. Tail swishing.

"What're you so happy about?" Hans said. "I ain't taking care of you."

The dog corked its head aside, ears perked.

"Oh yeah, you think you deserve something? Go on, get."

The dog barked and started humping the direwolf's corpse.

"Quit that," Hans said, booting it away. "Dumb bitch, you don't even have the tools for it."

Hans collected some bounties from the direwolf: he chopped its hands off and flayed the fur about the shoulders and chest. Finished, he grabbed the beast's decapitated head and held it up. The dead eyes were befogged in spools of swirling grey, the gums caked in drying froth, the canines mottled red. And then Hans raised an eyebrow, noticing a streak of crusty yellow painted down the front of the beast's head. He put his finger toward the material.

"Best not touch that," a voice said. "It's been hexed."

The sellsword spun around. The dog growled.

An elderly man in all black staggered through the laager's campsite, a black hat at his side. He pointed. "That, there, the yellow... it is her work. Richter was right. Claire von Sommerwein is a Neu Grimalkin."

"And where were you? Hiding, hm?"

"What, are you Richter's pap?"

"No."

"Then stow it. Go back to hiding."

"You should listen to me," the elder said. "That beast was a guardian. A soldier. One of many hexed elements which protects the hexe herself." The old man pointed further up the road. "Richter von Dagentear went north. I believe he cut in at the first break in the road. He's heading to a ferry. You need to go and tell him she's coming. Help him fight her if it comes to that."

Hans limped across the laager and picked up a knapsack. He stowed the direwolf's head in it and cinched it shut and threw it over his shoulder. Walking back, he kicked the headless direwolf across the grass until it fell into the campsite's shitpit where it landed with a splash but did not sink.

The old man opened his hands. "You must tell Richter, sellsword."

"I don't have to do shit, old man," Hans said. "Best steer clear of me."

And like that the sellsword limped down the road with his money and his trophy and a dog that wasn't his but followed all the same.

Chapter 31. From the Seas.

THE RAIDERS AWAITED the return of their leader and his 'catch.' Each man bore tattoos, the art of some variety: fish. Fishhooks. Blades. Kills. Lost family. Lost loves. Lost bets, if one cock tattoo was anything to go by. Many had stacks of black teardrops. Richter presumed these to be an accounting of either raided villages or something worse. Something not easy to take from this world, but they'd still yet taken a good deal of it. Altogether, the group stood beside a pair of wagons which they were using to 'gate' the road, and Richter presumed these carts had been stolen and that not a single one of their previous owners was still around.

Grunting to himself, a bald raider strode forward wearing a necklace of human ears while a string of human noses spun around a finger. As if these weren't menacing enough, the man wore thick leather armor with iron studs. When he grinned, his teeth were all silver and in them stood Richter's company, cavities in reflection.

"Ear-Manny," Eppo said, raising his hand to the terrible raider.

"Welcome back, sir," Ear-Manny said. The string of noses jiggled as he rubbed his hands together. "What ye fish?"

"Sellswords."

"Mmm... they look soft."

Eppo threw a thumb over his shoulder. "Don't touch 'em, Ear-Manny."

"Aww..."

"I said don't touch 'em, Ear-Manny!"

"I heard ya, I heard ya."

"Now, Ear-Manny…"

"Sir…"

"They got some heads you can have. Bandit heads. Fresh."

The bald raider's face lit up. "Are they in one piece?"

Eppo nodded. "They are, Ear-Manny, they are."

"This makes Ear-Manny happy," the raider said, raising his necklace of noses and nibbling on a bit of dried flesh. "Very happy, this makes me!"

Quinn sighed loudly. "We are farking dead. Absolutely wrecked."

"Keep calm," Richter said. "Like I said, we are alive for a reason."

"Yeah, the reason being that we're about to be these maniacs playthings."

"There you go whispering again," Eppo said without even turning around. He held a hand up and wagged his finger. "Best quit that chit chat, sellswords, you get me?"

Silence lingered. A pause. Eppo put his hand down.

"Yeah, you get me. Alright, come on then. In we go."

The company walked between the wagons. As expected, Ear-Manny took the brigand heads from the company's spears, his hands delicately caressing them, fixing their hair, and dabbling on their noses and ears.

On the other side of the wagons, Eppo's band of raiders threw themselves down onto boxes and crates and barrels, others rolling up what looked like fancy dresses and using them for pillows. Some played cards while others tossed dice. In total, Richter counted a dozen men.

As the company went further in, Richter spotted a line of rope had been staked into the edge of the Trading Swords' shoreline, and beside it floated a ferry raft, its edges crashing and grinding against the rocks.

"Richter!" Eppo suddenly shouted as he turned around. "Let us properly meet! I believe that our first greetings were of minorly ill tempers. It doesn't set anyone at ease to go on with that behind us, so I want to try again."

Eppo held his hand out. A black glove with iron studs on the knuckles, and the leather creased in old, bloodcrusted grooves. The raider turned it gently. "Richter, please don't make me ask twice for a bit of civility."

The captain shook the hand.

"Now that is a grip! Now that is some firm, firm pleasantries! Alright, alright. Now, introduce yourself."

Richter looked down. The raider's grip tightened.

"Go on," Eppo said, smiling tensely. "Introduce yourself."

"I'm Richter von Dagentear."

"Ah, Richter von Dagentear! Richter von Dagentear, everyone!" Eppo said, turning left to right, using his free hand to point at the captain. "Look at you, Richter, just look at you! Scarred hands. Big black hat. Glass vials. And, of course, yer uglier than a cobbler's foot. Ahohoy, you truly look like the cretin my mother spoke of. The Wight, the *Wiiight*, she used to say, as though you were there in the dark awaiting her. But you're not in the dark lurking like some creature. You're just a man."

Eppo would not let go of the handshake. He turned, swinging Richter with him, his hand over the captain's shoulder like two drinking buddies.

"Walk with me, Richter! Walk with me!" Eppo threw his head back in bizarre laughter. The underside of his chin was mottled with scars as if he himself had been brought out of the sea by a fisherman's hook, and as his mouth fell open in hoots and hollers, Richter could see the rind of a lemon resting against wooden molars. The captain looked over his shoulder and made a motion for his company to not panic. They listed near a wagon, the sellswords all looking tense with their hands not far from their weapons. The raiders, by comparison, lazed about, having seen this show before.

Eppo spoke businesslike: "See, I am but a simple sailing man though, as you can see, I must now take the pity of the river and not the embrace of the ocean! You and I are at the ends of two very different predicaments, Richter von Dagentear. As I said, ordinarily we'd already be turning you into chum, but you ain't chum, you still got all yer toes and fingers, right? And ordinarily, I would *like* to be running this ferry, because hells if this ferry ain't but the easiest money we'd ever made! But there is one small problem for me and my boys and that wee problem is one you're going to help us with." He straightened up and clapped his hands. "Hugo!"

A raider stood up.

Eppo waved him down. "No, not you, the other Hugo."

Another man stood up. "Aye, sir?"

"That's the peckerwood Hugo I'm looking for. Hugo, bring us a head."

"Aye aye, sir."

"You'll like this," Eppo said to Richter. "This is up your alley, as we'd say in Weissenhaven."

A pair of spears suddenly rose into the air, each tipped with a decapitated head. Hugo brought them forth, the heads swinging into each other and apart like some strange matrimonial ceremony seen to with macabre puppets. Hugo twisted one of the heads such that its sunken eyes faced him.

"Hugo, what the fuck?" Eppo said. "I said only bring one!"

"Ah, sorry, sir." The raider threw one of the spears away, the head clunking into a crate with a sickening clap. He held out the other spear, his eyes filled with pride. "I like this one," he said. "It's my favorite so far."

"We know you like that one," Eppo said. He waved his hand forward. "C'mon now. Bring 'im here."

Hugo staked the spear into the ground and slowly backed off like a man timidly loaning his neighbor a tool he knew he was never seeing again.

"We'll take good care of it Hugo," Eppo said, shooing the man. "Now go on. Go sit down."

"Aye aye."

Eppo stared up at the head like a man would stare at pieces of art: lips pursed and a tinge of confidence that said he could do that. He then slowly brought it down to eye level, a bulb of flies ensphering it, their buzzing fierce against the change in scenery. The raider stared at Richter through the swarm.

"You notice anything about this head?" Eppo said.

Richter looked at it. Long blond hair braided with chicken bones. Thick neck. Firm jowls. Big ears. And a blue tattoo arcing over the forehead, almost like a wave, the wrinkles of the pate the rocks of a fleshen shore – and almost the exact shape of the tattoo he had seen on the boy in the nachzehrer's den.

The captain looked up. "Are there barbarians across the river?"

"Wow!" Eppo said, genuinely astonished. "You are one quick fuck! Here I was trying to do a little theater and *schlick*," the raider clicked his tongue. "You go right through! Ahohoy, you really are the Wight, the face of a tumor and the humor of one, too! Yes, this here head belongs to a little barbarian bastard. Well, the rest of him was not so little, really."

"He had a huge cock!" Hugo shouted from his seat.

"Yes, thank you, Hugo!" Eppo said. He looked at Richter and nodded slightly. "It was formidable."

Richter said, "How many savages are there?"

"It's not the number that concerns us," Eppo said, "but their ferocity."

The raider's faux joviality faded as he pulled Richter toward the shoreline. There, the raiders' ferry raft scratched and crunched into the rocks. It was large enough to fit a whole wagon and then some. Despite the roughness of the raiders, the craft was far superior to the one Immerwahr's town had been using. Richter figured that it was either built by the raiders themselves or perhaps even the ship they had come in on repurposed for the task.

Eppo pointed across the river. "There."

On the opposite shore stood an encampment of very large and half-naked men. A stand of spears fenced their shoreline and, much like Eppo's, these were adorned with the heads of their victims.

"Those heads you see belonged to my men. Gerold, Torkel, and Hugo,"

Eppo said. He nodded. "Yes, we had a third Hugo."

Richter slimmed his eyes and counted the savages. Eight in total, and then nine as one emerged from the waters, a fat fish clenched in his mouth, his arms pumping in the air, a glistening blond mop of hair swishing as he met a roaring and grunting hero's welcome from his camp.

"You, Richter, are going to go talk to them," Eppo said. "I imagine the dumb brutes are a superstitious sort, the second they lay eyes upon the Wight himself they will surely run for the hills and—"

"That's a foolish plan," Richter said. "And an unnecessary one."

"Foolish? Sure? Longshot? Sure. But it'd really toot my fuckin' boots if I could clear them barbarians off my damned ferry and you, Richter, are in no position to negotiate."

"I know why they're here," Richter said. "I know what they want."

"Oh, oh ahohoy… this better be good. Alright, Richter, tell me then."

"I saw a boy in the woods a few days ago. Blue tattoo, just like on the head back there. He was carrying an ancient sword and hunting a nachzehrer."

"One boy hunting a beast?"

"The boy spoke of *Hargravard*, a kinging notion in the savage tongue. We believe he was hunting a beast to prove himself worthy."

"You speak their tongue?"

"I've a scribe in my company who has some knowledge of it."

"Shit… I knew I should've kidnapped a few of those instead of always taking their ink bottles and their fat heads…"

Richter cleared his throat. "If these barbarians are not leaving, it means they're waiting for someone or something. It likely means they're waiting for that boy to return. If I go across that river, I die. If you go across that river, you die. If we all go, we all die. The only way out of this is to find that boy."

An eyebrow lifted, Eppo said, "You're pulling my strings."

"I swear by the old gods I am not."

[416]

Eppo glanced across the river. He said, "I really, really, *really* like the idea of watching you float on over to their shore. The thought of seeing someone like you maybe taking an axe through the head just gets me going. I mean, it would be funny, right?" The raider shook his head somberly. "Alright. Let's say we look for the lad. How would we ever find him in these woods?"

"I'll go fetch him easily," Richter said. "I'm a pathfinder. Cutting through the woods and finding things in them is precisely what I do."

"Ahh, what now? Who is in charge here? Just because I'm keen to your idea here doesn't mean mine is dead in the dirt and it sure as shite doesn't mean you're running this ship!" Eppo said. "Your ass is staying right here. *I'll* choose who goes and… and you know what?" The raider's piercings and jewelry jangled with frustration. He pointed a finger. "If the men I choose don't get back within one day, I'm shuttling your pale arse over to them barbarians in a fucking gift basket, how does that sound?"

Richter looked at his company. Of their number, a few would do well if chosen. And a few would be his doom. He thought of Arren Gee, the god of chance, the god behind every roll of the dice. He looked back at the raider and nodded. "Sounds like a good deal."

Chapter 32. Searchers.

RICHTER EXPLAINED the happenings and finished with Eppo's selection of men: "Trash, Thomas, and Minnesang."

"Me?" the juggler said. "Why me?"

"Because the raiders think you're a daisy puller and your hat is annoying."

"Ha!" Quinn howled. "Hahahaha!"

"I can take the hat off," Minnesang said, his voice incredulous as to how no one else thought of that simple solution first. "Richter von... captain... I respectfully wish to stay by your side in this instance. I am, clearly, a man of some martial talents, I can balance a dagger and throw it just as well."

"I can do that too," Quinn said and he slapped the jester upside the head.

The jester's cap'n'bells flew off, but Minnesang snatched it midair like a cat catching a bird. He stared at the thief. "Do not touch my cap again."

"Or what? You'll juggle my farkin' balls?"

Richter stepped between the two men. "We don't have time for this. Minnesang, it wasn't my decision, it was the raider's."

"Captain, sir..."

"What part of 'wasn't my decision' don't you understand?" Richter said. He nodded and clapped the man on the shoulder. "Look at it as a good time to prove yourself, jester."

"Aye," Dahlgren said. "You should be honored to join the ranks of the other up and coming greens like, uh, well I guess just Berthold there."

Berthold nodded for the given respect, the miller's eyes glistening a little as he looked away, sniffling but proud.

"And me," another man said.

Dahlgren looked over. "And… uh, I suppose that fellow."

"Gernot," the man said. "I'm the butcher. Why doesn't anyone—"

"Ol' Elletrache ain't got any problems with being chosen," the beast slayer said. "I'll lead this here expedition and fetch the lad."

"Thank you, Trash," Richter said. He turned and snapped his fingers. "Crockett! Map please. The one that Hobbs did, of course."

The captain and the selected men stood at the back of the wagon with the hatch down. A map was unfurled across it, some scribbled markings of where they were and the extent to which the forest stretched onward around them. With the help of Hobbs, Crocket had filled out the rest of the map.

"We're here," Richter said, putting his finger down a piece of shore just north of Immerwahr's ferry. He dragged his finger across a line which broke east. "This here is the road we just came down. Here, here, and here are where the bandits attacked us. This right here is the merchants' caravanserai."

"Laager," Elletrache said. "It wasn't no caravanserai."

"Right. The laager is here. The Ancient Road cuts through it. South is where the roads bled out into multiple paths."

"Yar, where we got lost."

Crockett leaned forward. "Again, sorry about that."

"Oh no worries, Cricket," Quinn said. "See, initially wolves and birds and shit would've eaten our corpses, but now our eyes and ears get to join some bald maniac's toy collection. We've definitely improved from being lost, ain't that right captain?"

"Shut your fucking mouth, Quinn," Dahlgren said. "Ye ain't even going on this trip so what are you complaining about?"

"Hey I get paid to kill and I kill very, very well. Between the lot of us, I'm probably the best fighter this company's got and it's damn time someone farking said that out loud!"

Dahlgren turned to face the thief, his hand to his sword. He stood there a moment, then made eye contact with the captain. The old man nodded and stepped back. "Alright, Quinn. You say what you want."

"Damn right I'll say what I want."

"Burning daylight with your chirping, thief. Go and sit down," Trash said and pushed the thief away. The beast slayer put his fat finger on the map. "This'n the place where you saw the nach', right?"

Richter nodded. "It was from there where we last saw the boy fleeing west. If he's still glory hounding, I suspect he'd still be hanging around there."

"Don't think he'd venture south?" Elletrache said. "Followin' the waters'n'all."

"It doesn't matter, because we don't have the time to look that far."

"Ah so we're truly huntin' on a prayer," the beast slayer said and grunted out a laugh and turned to Minnesang and Thomas. "Remind me to fetch some pots and pans for this here snipe hunt, fellas."

The captain's finger stopped on a spot west of the nachzehrer's den. He said, "You look here." He hit the spot again. "Here, understand?"

"What has you figurin' he's there? Instinct?"

"Aye, something like that. If the boy's got his wits, that's where he should be. Somewhere between proving himself and leaving entirely, but close enough to the river to get the food and water he needs."

"And it's not too far from the nach' he be huntin'," Trash said. He scratched under his eyepatch. "How much time you say we got to look?"

Richter sighed. "A day."

"Oh hells."

The captain looked at his men. He spoke quietly, "Come tomorrow morning, they're ferrying me to go meet with the savages."

"Tomorrow morning's considerably less than a day, captain."

"Aye."

"Hey yeah, does the boy have to be alive?" Thomas said. When the others stared at him, he quickly added: "I'm just wanting to clarify, that's all. I mean if we find him dead should we still spend the effort hauling his body out or what? Is it worse if the barbarians see him like that?"

"I think it's a good question," Minnesang said, defending the servant.

"Crockett?" Richter said. "What do you think?"

"I'm not sure. A body alone could be worthwhile, or it might make the savages think we killed the lad. I'd hate to think what the they would do then."

"Barbarians coming over here is better than them not," Richter said. "We might have a fighting chance in all that chaos." He looked at the three chosen and nodded. "Bring him back, no matter how you find him."

"Can do," Elletrache said. "Does this boy look any different than I suspect he does? Bit o' wild'n in him, bit o' tattooing and the like?"

"Aye, you can't miss him: he's about the height of Hobbs, but bigger in body and with a large tattoo going across his forehead."

"Is he armed?" Thomas said.

"He might have a rusted sword on him," Richter said. "He didn't attack me with it, but then again I wasn't trying to steal him away from his quest."

"Look, captain, this is easy enough," Elletrache said. "If he's out there, we'll find him. I don't know about these two other jokers, but Eppo got the best man for it in me."

"Thanks, Trash."

"Mmhmm."

"Just to clarify, I'm a jester," Minnesang said. "Not a joker."

The beast slayer grunted. "Right. Eh, look captain, I can leave these two twiddling their dicks and hoof it alone. It'd be faster that way."

"I know," Richter said. "Unfortunately, Eppo's decided to send two men as well so I'd rather you three stick together in case something happens."

Crockett said, "You think they'd cause problems?"

"Hey, yeah," Thomas said. "Doesn't he want this all to work out?"

"I think Eppo is earnest," Richter said. "But I don't think he has as much control over his men as he thinks he does. Stay alert, alright?"

"Stay alert because…" Thomas said, "…they might attack us?"

Richter nodded. "Something like that, aye." He leaned in. "If you get a whiff of them about to stab you in the back, you go ahead and do it first. You have that on my command, understand?"

The three nodded and Thomas said, "I'd hate to stab a man in the back, but I'll do it if I need to, captain. I'll do it for the company."

"For the company," Minnesang said, nodding.

Elletrache spat. "Shit I'll do it just to survive."

"Good," Richter said. "Have everything you need, then?"

Elletrache took the map. "Can I have this, Crockett?"

The paymaster lofted a hand. "I've made backups so that's all yours."

"Good." Elletrache stowed it in his pocket with the care of crumpling a dishrag. He looked at Thomas and Minnesang who, by comparison to the beast slayer, looked like two paperdolls endangered by a stiff wind. "Hells. Don't you two piss yerself. Ol' Elletrache was made for this'n wood hunt and – hey! Hey you two! You farks put that down!"

The sellswords turned. A few raiders stood in the distance holding the beast slayer's giant crossbow. They flinched at the man's growling words, and then grinned and set it down and backed away like they meant no harm.

"Shit," Trash said. "Sooner I'm away from these jokers the better."

Chapter 33. The Ancient Hexenjäger.

THE COMPANY SAT AROUND THE CAMPFIRE, its flames dimpling the pockmarked sands of the shoreline, and wimpling the rises in the river, occasionally catching a fish in a strobing glimmer, a wink from the depths. Beyond them the sun lowered unto the horizon, its rays starting to catch the mountains and hills there.

Warming his hands, Quinn said, "I can't believe they left us our gear."

Dahlgren spat. "They got the upperhand, thief. Any one of us so much as scratches a blade from a sheath and they can butcher us in under a minute. I reckon with some good certainty they left us armed to give them any good reason to jump to it. Some raiders are right savages and like to have their 'fun' in their own way."

"You think that's right, cap'n?" Quinn said.

Richter nodded. "Eppo knows these are dangerous lands and would want as many bodies as possible available in case something bigger and nastier comes along. He knows we aren't a threat to him, but unlike some, he's smart enough to understand that isn't a good enough reason to just lay waste."

"Aye," Dahlgren said. He threw his hand toward the river's waters and across them. "The raider wants us around in case those fellas come over."

The company turned to look across the river. At the opposite shore, the barbarians' silhouettes still proved robust and rowdy despite the fading light. They tackled, they fought, they wrestled. Sometimes they threw one another, grown men spinning through the air as if some giant entity meant to skip them like rocks across the river. The chaos of these festivities took as clear an existence as the scalding swords which might hiss and glow in a blacksmith's shop, for surely in a sense the might and main though fleshen as it were still yet came of familiar make as the metals which came from the mountains, and of this there was something to behold in these barbarians, as though the earth itself were a craftsman and these men its finest products.

"You don't think the savages would be scared of you, Richter?" Sophia said, coming to stand beside the captain.

Laughing, Richter shook his head. "My understanding of them is that they do not carry fear because they are not allowed. I believe, if anything, they'd only see me as a trophy to claim and boast about."

"Oh, I'm sure they've got women back home that'll smack a bit of fear into 'em and oop – what are they doing now?"

The barbarians started hooting and hollering, little beads of noise that barely crossed the river but still yet animalistic even in their minuteness. One of the barbarians held congress with the others, and he took his hands and shaped them as though he were holding bowls of disparate weight. After this gesticulation, the savages whipped off their furs and leathers and thrust their members back and forth, another item which the distance did little to conceal.

"I think they saw you," Richter said.

"Yeah that's about usual," Sophia said, watching cocks flopping every which way. The homesteader turned. "Can I ask you something?"

"If it isn't about savages, sure."

"I wanted to ask about the… other you. The hunting you…"

"Alright."

"I mean the witch hunter you."

"I know," Richter said, smirking. "I'm not going to dagger you like a hexe for asking the wrong question, Sophia. Go on and ask what you want."

"Yeah stop hemming and hawing," Quinn said, poking the fire literally and figuratively.

The homesteader said, "I'm just wondering why there are no women witch hunters. After all, don't the witches prey upon men specifically? A woman could get around that easily, could she not? Seems so obvious."

Richter nodded. "The obviousness of the question is only matched by how rarely I hear it."

"Maybe you're just around too many men. You know, us ladies can be observant, too."

"Hmm. My guildmaster used to say that women master the movements of society as shadows master the movements of their makers. Back in the age of kings he said that when a woman came to power there was a great unsettling amongst womankind as a whole, for such prominence could draw a lantern upon them and reveal that they've been far more involved than they ever wanted to let on. You can accomplish quite a lot in the vastness of another's misplaced assumptions."

"And what do you think?"

"I don't know. I'm not a woman and I don't live in the time of kings."

"Attaboy cap," Quinn said. "Just pretend to not know."

Richter smiled. He went to the campfire and sat down. He gestured for Sophia to sit beside him and she did.

He said, "I would say that women tend to be quietly observant which is something of a shame. You came to me carrying qualifiers and a distanced sense of concern as though your question would spur something out of me. It's an unfortunate reality, this state of things between you and I, whether we are strangers or familiars it has no doubt remained the same."

"Sorry, Richter," Sophia said. "I didn't mean to couch the question in such a cautious way. But… I'm still curious."

"You've a right to be. To understand why there are no women witch hunters, you have to understand something not only about the history of the hexen and hexenjäger, but you need to understand something about history itself and its existence as a kind of perpetual poison for certain minds."

Richter paused and stared at the homesteader, gauging her.

"Go on ahead," she said. "I'm interested."

"Hey, wait," Hobbs said, leaning forward with a wooden sword in one hand and the carved camel in the other. "The last time I asked questions like this you butted in and told Carsten to get lost."

"Shush, boy," Dahlgren said. He nodded. "I'm curious as well, captain."

Crockett had his quill pen and ledger out. He said nothing, but out of all the ears perked his were the highest and he almost shivered with anticipation of hearing something he had not found in a book.

"Alright." Richter took a breath. He said, "Nobody has a full account of our history, and by our history I mean all of our history, understand? We only know that there was an Ancient Empire. We see it all around us in buildings of strange designs, the roads, the structures, the place of oracles that even today the holy men squabble over. I've personally seen faceless statues as big as watchtowers, I've seen boats smashed on mountains so far inland it disturbs the curiosity just as well fulfills it. So you have to realize that this Empire is still here, utterly present in its absence, understand? It unsettles most of the scribes that something so massive could disappear, as it does put into place the transience of man. If an entire empire could fade into nothing then surely we are of very little import, aye? Often, a man can only be something for just a moment in his entire life. Perhaps he delivers a message that wins a war, or he makes an offhand suggestion that improves the wagon and makes him rich, but in the eternal before and the eternal after, he is nothing. He doesn't even return to nothing, for in the grand scheme of things he was never *not* nothing. He is faced with this reality the moment he wields foresight or intuition."

Richter stared into the fire, then briefly glanced at Crockett.

He continued: "Scribes, in their lust to write everything down, were in truth seeking to preserve themselves, to fight against this tyrannical nothingness, only to happen upon something infinitely greater than them, something that, like any ant or peasant or king, all the same, fell into dust. They found an Ancient Empire governed by people whose names we will never know and yet whose very skeleton we wander through with a vague sense of acknowledgment that someday it will be us amongst them, bones upon bones upon bones. You must understand how horrifying this realization has been for even the most intelligent among us, driving some so mad that they seek tricks of charlatanry and chicanery, and some have even delved into the perversions of necromancy."

"Necromancy?" Gernot said.

"Shhh," Quinn said. "Shutup, Berthold."

"My name's not—"

Quinn shushed again, as fierce as a schoolmaster on a week's start.

Richter cleared his throat. He continued.

"The hexenjägers know that the hexen prey upon man's insecurities, his fear of the unknown, his abject terror when placed at the feet of uncertainty. We have no reason to disbelieve that this fear, this resource if you will, also existed in the time of the ancients. Many guildmasters believe the hexen and hexenjägers operated on the perimeter of the Ancient Empire, dueling one another in secret wars for true control of the institutions within. But as we do not even know the names of the emperors that presided over this empire, we also do not know the true starters of the hexen and the hexenjäger. But, to answer your question, we do know that they did have men and women fighting together. The guilds in general were different – more soldiering, more knightliness though in those days I do not think knights existed. But there was a pride in hunting evil, and evil in those days was said to be vast, powerful, even magical. Some claim that the evils of that time still live among us now, wandering the land in secret, a sort of malevolent intrigue which menaces man and beast alike, and beside them track the likes of ancient hunters and warrior priests made immortal, entities trying to protect us, and like the ancients, doing so without ever leaving the shadows."

"Like necrosavants," Crockett said.

Richter shrugged. "The nature of those beings is of considerable debate between the witch hunting and beast slaying guilds. I think that—"

"Wait," Sophia said. "Let's keep it on topic: you said women *did* fight witches. So, what happened? Why the change?"

Richter nodded. "To get to the heart of your question, I have to incriminate man and woman together. The reason women are no longer in the witch hunting guilds is because of Grimalkin. She was the grandest of hexen, the one whose existence in those eras required whole armies to defeat."

"Grimalkin," Sophia said. "Even I have heard of this being."

"Aye, she lives on in the tales of laity and nobility alike. But she is no mere tall tale. We have found mentions of a very real her in the dusty tomes, and we also came upon her visage now and again in old, worn-down relics."

"I don't understand what she would have to do with women witch hunters, though. I know she was a powerful creature, but... there are many of those around, are there not?"

Richter sighed. He said, "The reason she was the grandest of hexen is because she, herself, was a hexenjäger."

The campfire crackled. Eyes shifted, looking to see if they heard right.

Hobbs said, "A witch hunter was the greatest witch?"

"Boy," Quinn said. "Why ain't you paying attention? That's just what he said. Get out of here!"

The thief threw the carved camel down the shore, causing a brief moment of shouting fright from Hobbs. He hurriedly rescued the camel and came back to camp with it cradled in both hands while he menaced Quinn with his wooden sword.

"Right," Richter said. "*If* the texts are true, or at least our interpretations of them, Grimalkin was in fact a hexenjäger guildmaster. She knew everything about us. She had both worlds in her palm: those of the hexen and those of the hexenjäger. It would be as though a flame had learned the ways of water, and no matter how often you doused it, it would burn on. You can see how such a being would prove troublesome. As I said, the guilds once operated in the open as soldiers, proud of what they did. Grimalkin put an end to that. The sheer scope of the danger she presented ensured that the guilds purged themselves of their women overnight. Most were killed out of the fear that they, too, would turn into hexen. The guilds became paranoid and closed off. Grimalkin, meanwhile, spread her forces over the lands. Monsters and men alike filled her ranks, all equally ensorcelled. She claimed to be fighting higher powers, but of course she would say something like that – an army of hunters were after her."

Richter sighed. He continued: "The hexenjägers, once proud soldiers of the good and righteous, turned to secrecy. They became experts in matters of subterfuge and espionage and eventually, after what may have been hundreds if not thousands of deaths, Grimalkin was defeated. In her final moments, she donned her hexenjäger garb and proclaimed to the world that she was simply one of us. It was her final spell, a hexing which has not come off the vocation since. The world blamed the guilds for the troubles she wrought and so the remaining hexenjägers were in turn purged by the world they had helped preserve. To this day, the one thing a hexenjäger fears more than a hexe is the very village who hired him to hunt her."

The company sat in silence again. Perhaps looking for help in digesting what they heard, they looked at the savages across the river. But the barbarians were merely sitting about their fires, still and quiet as though they themselves had been listening. Crockett closed his ledger and held it firm in both hands.

"Well," Sophia said, breaking the silence. "Thank you, Richter."

Nodding, Richter said, "For all I know, what I said could be nothing more than falsehoods and myth."

"But you don't think so," Sophia said.

Richter shook his head.

"Why not?"

"Because the hexen don't think it's false, either. The hexen pursue the role of Grimalkin amongst themselves. Evidence very much suggests that many covens are in fact like schools of scribes with the individual members working together toward some hidden knowledge. My specialty as a witch hunter was tracking, hunting, and killing these covens." Richter stared at the fire. He said, "In truth, I don't know if my guild cared much about the damage the covens caused to their surroundings so much as they wanted to either procure said knowledge or have it destroyed."

"And what did you care about?"

The captain stared at his scars. "I think I just simply enjoyed being good at something." He dropped his hands. "Any more questions?"

"Aye..." Hobbs said. "Did you ever hope to become a guildmaster?"

"No," Richter said. "And as I've said, all of that is a past life now."

"Ah, yeah, right right right," Quinn said. "But these guildmasters must be like some of the baddest of motherfarkers, yeah?"

"Aye, only a select few can take on that role."

"The elite of the elite?"

"The best of the best," Dahlgren reiterated.

"Cream of the crop," Berthold said.

"Bell of the ball," Minnesang said.

"Prime cuts," Gernot said.

"Alright, alright, that's enough," Richter said, holding his hand up. "To answer your question, aye, the guildmasters are our best. Very few live long in our vocation so those of age are quite formidable indeed."

Chapter 34. Masters of Domains.

CLAIRE STOOD AT THE EDGE OF THE PIT. Flies welcomed her stare with idle buzzing, their feasting song oddly humming and hymnal. Her white dress gently shifted to the whims of breezes as though it had carried her to the horror, lofting her upon it like a fresh leaf might swirl onto a bloody battlefield. Down in the pit's mire, a man stared back up at her, his white eyes the only element of his cretinous being that could be said to be human at all, and she thought him dead until they blinked. He was trying to gain certainty that what he was seeing was indeed real, and he cocked his head side to side, blinking more and more.

"Are you an old god?" he finally said.

The hexe crouched. Beside the man floated the direwolf's headless body. Flies swarmed the corpse, an orgy of anonymous wings which gave the fur a strange, white glisten.

"H-hey… help me out," the man said. "Can you help me?"

"Help you?" Claire said.

Green scales hissed as the lindwurm slithered up beside her. Snorting starkly the beast's breathing rumbled down its throat like tumbling stones and growling on return. It towered over Claire and stared down, a razored gaze locked upon the direwolf's body. It snorted again and shook its head, its long neck of scales chittering in waves. Grunting in confusion, it stepped back and walked around the edges of the pit and stared down again, perhaps hoping to surmise something of truth which no first glance could ever offer, like some dog unsure if its owner is asleep or something more disastrous has happened.

The lindwurm lowered its head into the pit and put its nose upon the direwolf and the corpse flies reared up in a ferocious buzz and the beast drew its head out and violently shook it in a rattling growl.

"I'm sorry," Claire said, looking at the beast.

The lindwurm's mouth drew back and its teeth, long as a child's forearm, dripped with foam as they unsheathed from shivering gums.

"I'm sorry," Claire said again.

With viperlike speed, the lindwurm struck its head forward and screamed into the pit, its long neck undulating, its claws sundering earth, and its tongue ran out, long and whipping, spit and gore and saliva spewing, and the pit itself welled out beneath the fury, the mire rippling into a depressed alcove, the man down in it finding himself sinking into a sudden bowl of filth, his hair and clothes lapping backward, and he cried out and shot his hands up and screamed for help but not a soul could hear him, and then the lindwurm's mouth snapped shut, a coda which cracked echoes into the trees. Finished, it spun and stormed into the laager. Demolition followed. Wagons pulverized or effortlessly made airborne, and an unending roar followed the lindwurm's snarling rage.

Down in the pit the alcove of feces collapsed back in on itself, swallowing the man whole save for a hand which slapped the surface in search of something to hold onto, and then it sank just as well.

Claire looked up to see the lindwurm cast an entire cart into the sky and in a flowing whip of its body spun its tail through the air and obliterated the cart, disassembling it so thoroughly it looked like straw showering away. The monk ducked as shadows of debris sailed by, the trees rustling as they were sprayed with nails and slats and old merchant goods.

"Th-there is a survivor," the monk said. "He seems... to know you."

Wiping tears away, Claire took a breath and said, "Show me."

~~~

Claire stood behind Kantorek. The brigand's discolored arm had blackened from wrist to elbow to shoulder, but the hexed man's swordhand still remained with strength as he menaced his blade at the prisoner.

"I can hear you, little one," the prisoner said. "No need to hide."

The witch stepped out a moment.

"Ah, there you are." Surrounded by the ensorcelled mob, the old guildmaster sat cross-legged on the ground with his hands on his knees. He smiled at the girl. "There's the witchling I know and love."

The girl nodded. "Guildmaster Imnachar."

"Aye," Imnachar said. "Why don't you come closer?"

"Where is Richter?"

"I can't but hardly hear you. Come closer, girl."

"No."

"Do you often say no to your elders? Why would you do such a thing?

She nodded respectfully. "A hexenjäger always has his tricks."

"Hm…" the guildmaster smiled again. He put up a finger and dragged it under an eye, pulling at the saggy skin. "My eyes fail me worse than my ears, but you do seem a little grown up since I last saw you."

"Did you enjoy watching your hexenjägers die?" Claire said.

Imnachar's smile faded.

The witch continued: "I heard they screamed upon the Sommerwein torture towers. I heard their blood seeped through and they used moss-lipped sea buckets to catch it lest the hexenjägers' blood poison the land. Why the commoners were so fearful of men who screamed so mightily is beyond me. I feel as though such screams should humanize them, don't you agree? Like when the shriek of a gutted pig sounds a little too familiar on the ears."

Imnachar snorted and spat. "You wench."

"Ah," Claire said. "So you can hear me."

The guildmaster looked at the naked ensorcelled mob surrounding him, each of the pink bodies leaning inward like the poles of a fleshy palisade. More absent-eyed caravan guard stood at a distance. Behind the witch herself stood a quaint and nervous monk stepping back and forth on uneven feet. Nearby, another wagon met an explosive demise in the lindwurm's mourning.

"So you do have a lindwurm," Imnachar said, shaking his head. "I always knew you had this in you. I always knew the second them stories came out about you and the coven. I knew I should have poisoned you."

Claire cocked her head. "If you were so certain that you should have, but didn't, then all it tells me is that you are uncertain about death itself. But you fear death, and certainly fear the Sommerwein torture towers where my father would have made death wait for you. I'm sure your witch hunters appreciate your decision to not follow through on your so-called certainties. You lived, they all died. Good job, Imnachar."

The guildmaster looked away, seeking perhaps a familiar face in the crowd, or at least one that could understand his plight. Sometimes even a menacing cat can take pity on the bug whose legs it just removed. But only empty glares met him, most of them sideways or gated behind swaying, sweaty hair, staring as if they could never blink again, the eyes red and veiny.

Claire said, "Who killed the direwolf?"

Imnachar laughed and shook his head. "A sellsword did that."

"One man?"

"As big as two."

Claire smirked. "You lie. One man could not have killed the beast."

Imnachar shrugged. "You should come closer," he said, leaning forward. "I'd much like to see this Neu Grimalkin so proud of herself."

Claire remained where she was. She tilted her head and whispered.

In an instant, the ensorcelled mob closed in on Imnachar, grabbing the old man by his arms and yanking him to his feet. They ran their hands up to his shoulders and then tore away his shirt, revealing his skinny and pale frame mottled with disease. His body flailed against their grip like a staked scarecrow trying to leave with the wind.

Growling, he spat at the mob. "Weakminded fools, the lot of you!"

Claire stared at his arms. No wristed crossbow. No bandolier. Just skinny arms and a ribbed chest. A shrewd, broken man, his belly concave, his hipbones struggling to keep his pants up. But Claire knew an aged guildmaster held great reservoirs of knowledge in places unseen. Little niches of nuance, learned passages aplenty, studied instances, scripted responses, thousands and thousands of years of doings bundled behind a blotched and pallid pate, its wrinkles rolling and moving as though some manmade miasma of what was inside still bore out, such were the ways of the world's elite, aura emanating, and as the guildmaster raised an eyebrow it was akin to a swordmaster smiling as he stirred a bowl with a spoon.

"You need not be afraid of me," Imnachar said.

The witch looked up to the sky and whispered again.

Beyond them, another wagon clattered to the ground and then the lindwurm slowly stomped over. The mob separated out as the beast towered over the procession, its shadow long and angular and potent. It slowly coiled and nuzzled its nose at the side of the girl, careful to keep its scales flat lest they shred her just by touch alone. Claire walked out from behind Kantorek's guard. She ran her hand carefully about the lindwurm, her fingernails scraping along the scales with clicks and clacks.

She looked at Imnachar. "Tell me where Richter is."

"Carsten Corrow's brightest and best," Imnachar said. "If you go looking for him, Richter will kill you, witchling. You can be damn sure of that."

"Tell me where he is and I can make this short," Claire said, stepping forward again, leaving Kantorek and the lindwurm behind. "Tell me where the witch hunter is, and I'll make it quick."

"And if I don't?"

"I'll skin you alive," Claire said. "My cauldron could use a new coat."

The guildmaster looked at the cauldron and in doing so stared at Immerwahr. He shook his head. "The old gods will see your betrayal, monk," the guildmaster said. "They see us all, inside and out."

Immerwahr pursed his lips. He tried to move, but to one side were the caravan guards and to the other the length of the lindwurm's tail which he had no interest in leaping over.

"Aye," Imnachar said. "Yer not hexed at all. Of all the men and beasts here, yours is of proper mind. A broken little lapdog, ain't ya?"

Claire laughed. She turned around. "Holy man, ignore this fool's—"

A grunt and a clatter. By the time Claire turned back around, Imnachar had wrenched his arms free of the mob and fallen to his arse. Both feet swung into the air. With one hand he yanked a pantleg back, and with the other he went to the trigger of a wristed crossbow wrapped about his ankle.

Eyes wide, Claire yelled out for Kantorek. Instantly, the brigand brought his blade to the fore and charged forward. At her other side, the lindwurm's scales chittered like the blades of a thousand kings guard unsheathing to protect their majesty, and just as soon as Kantorek had advanced, he simply disappeared in a sheet of fanning green as the reptilian beast broke forth in instinctive guardianship.

Imnachar gritted his teeth.

The lindwurm coiled haphazardly before the guildmaster, its shapes squirming and tumbling as though it were being boiled in its own rage, energy unending, power overwhelming, animal ferocity at its core.

But man had his ways: a crossbow bolt the mere length of a finger zipped out of the wristed crossbow with the authority of a king signing off on a war. The lindwurm shrieked backwards, coiling like a snake thrown into a wall, scales rippling nose to tail, and it rankled upward and whipped its head side to side, the guildmaster's bolt having found one of the beast's eyes.

The beast whipped its head side to side squalling and screeching before it planted its arms and leapt over the ensorcelled mob and fled out. As its tail snaked by, Kantorek, still following Claire's command, quietly walked into the slithering scales where he violently spun on contact, his flesh unseaming in a dozen slashes, his organs spewing and trailing out and his blackened wrist caught a tip and was ripped off entirely and then a foot shunted off the ankle and his momentum dropped him hard into the scales where his body squelched greasily as it came undone as his torso twisted completely over his hip and in this mangled state he finally corkscrewed and unfurled across the grass in a long stretch of crisscrossing flesh and guts, his sword itself uneventfully falling where he once stood.

Immerwahr, though a monk and not privy to combat, stared at the weapon as though it had been forged for him. Forged there by the flagged forces of men, the resources of earth, and the circumstances of the gods. And it were the gods, he thought, whom must have ordained it be so, wiggling and gesturing such that things fell where they may and only where they may. Swallowing nervously, the monk stepped toward the blade.

"Don't you even dare!" Claire shrieked.

If the gods could ordain the sword, then they could ordain her.

The monk took a step back.

"Richter awaits you, witchling!" the witch hunting guildmaster screamed from his back. "You think you hunt him, but you know not what you face!"

The girl spun to Imnachar, her fists tight and her cheeks red. Yet, despite all that vibrating rage, all that came out of her lips was a quiet whisper: a pair of simple words which quelled the color from her face. The syllables floated forth, minute yet beautiful, delicate and profound, the eyes of all turning to the sounds like they were but stark butterflies skittering a brutal winter's night.

Imnachar's eyes widened. "No!"

Claire smiled. Her ensorcelled mob descended at the speed of a collapsing cave, a fleshen wall swarming in wriggling, grunting mass, and beneath that glistening, sweaty rubble was the old guildmaster screaming for mercy. It were humanity's first feast, the slobbering and drooling and snarling of cretins who knew food but not its flavors, who knew necessities but not the spice of pace, and so they bestially hooked their fingers into the every inch of the old man and his body jerked around as though buzzards were fighting over it, and once the first bone broke the rest followed, a series of hollow cracks, dominos of torture, and the old man growled out as his ribcage was ripped apart and hands puttied into his organs and there began to scoop and shovel and from his mouth they pulled his tongue and from his arse they pulled great lengths of rope and in this manner he was finished.

"By the old gods," Immerwahr said, staring over the curve of his pinched elbow, sheltering his face with it. His eyes looked away, then back again. He shook his head. "By the old gods."

"Yes," Claire said. "Speak to those cretins as much as you want."

The girl whispered again and the ensorcelled mob returned to a standstill as though they had done little more than take one step forward and one step back. Pitter-pattering blood splashed down from their fingertips and mouths.

"Th-that was a guildmaster," Immerwahr said. "A man of… import…"

"Yes, I'm quite aware of what a guildmaster is, holy man."

"But there was no dignity in that…"

Claire said, "He lived a life of false dignities. He dignified his station with corpses of pitiful witches. Bodies upon bodies, many of whom wanted nothing to do with him or his people, but who were just different enough to warrant his gaze and his flames. Witch hunters speak of great terrors, but that is a falsity. They are the terror, and he is merely one head of that terror."

The monk looked at the girl, his eyes wide.

"Ah, yes," Claire said, nodding respectfully. "I'm quite aware I am something of a terror myself. But you should be happy I am here." She pointed at the pile of remains. "I gave him one good moment here. I showed him that he was right all along. I took away the uncertainty of his crimes. I took away the doubt which lingers in men like him when the halls grow cold and the fires dim. He died knowing he was right. That's a gift, holy man."

Immerwahr's hands shook at his sides and he clenched them into fists.

Sighing, Claire turned away. She looked at Kantorek. In its pained escape, the lindwurm's scales had run roughshod over the brigand's body. Only by the blackened hand could Claire even see it was her bodyguard. But then her eyes fell upon the brigand's sword laying in the grass. She picked it up.

"Monk," she said.

"I don't... I don't really wish to talk any further if that is alright."

Claire held out the blade. "Take it. Go on now, take it."

The girl's eyes furrowed and what glimmer ran across their colors spurred the monk and he hurriedly took the blade. He held it by the handle as its steel length limply fell into the grass.

"I-I don't know how to use this," the monk said.

"Yet earlier you were reaching for it."

"N-no, no I wasn't." Immerwahr stared at the girl. When she stared back without blinking, he steadied himself. His hands tightened around the handle. He said, "I will kill you with this."

"Hmm."

"I will. If you leave me this weapon, I'll..." he menaced it, but the sword's weight proved awkward, the steel of it bobbing with much error. But he pressed on: "I'll kill you! I swear by the old gods, I'll kill you!"

"If you want me to hexe you, holy man, you'll certainly have to try harder than that. Besides…" she took his armed hand and turned it and the blade with it, approximating his stance into that of a well-trained guard. "…if Richter has more men like this guildmaster, then I need those who are equally loyal to the cause, no?"

"I… I don't…"

"Just think of duty and pride." Claire raised the sword until its metal chilled against her neck, the edge a cold pinch, and she stared upward at the man holding the blade as though she were being knighted by an executioner.

Immerwahr swallowed. "K-k… I'll kill you… by the old gods I will."

Leaning her neck into the steel, Claire said, "You swear by the old gods that which you will not do. You tarnish enormous brokers of power with pitiful assertions that not even the ants would believe." She smiled. "To do these things at my feet, at my back, at my face, this is loyalty in and of itself. Whether you know it yet or not, your words and your energies have already placed me above your gods and, truly, there is no greater honor, holy man."

She turned and kissed the blade.

And the blade fell aside.

And the monk wept.

Chapter 35. Near Abroad.

"A barbarian kid in all this forested mess?" Minnesang said, holding the lengths of his jester hat in each hand, stretching it like a rabbit he meant to skin. "There's no way we find the lad, but there are so many ways in which we find something else, and something else is never something good. I'm talking bears, wolves, maybe some direwolves, lotta wasps out here, bears…"

"You already said bears," Thomas said.

"Ah that's right. Bears…" the jester held his finger out, wiggling it back and forth as though to shake some truth out of it. "Bears *and* beehives!"

"Bees can't kill men," Thomas said. "The hells you talking about?"

"I've seen one lone bee kill a man. Pecked him right on the cheek. His face turned red and he fell over dead."

"Sure it wasn't one of your jester pals playing a trick?"

"No, because I always work alone," Minnesang said.

"What kind of jester works alone?"

"Hey!" Elletrache faced the two men, his lindwurm armor chittering, his beard full of leaves and twigs. "You two quit yer bitchin'."

"Oh I wasn't bitching," Thomas said. He thumbed over. "Minnesang here was just concerned—"

"Whatever it is, it's sore talk, and I'd just about had it, alright?"

"Ah man," Minnesang said, holding his gut. "I must apologize. My stomach is upside down right now and I suppose it's getting the best of me."

Elletrache looked the jester up and down. He said, "Keep it tight. We've not far to go, which means you all need to be on your toes because ol'

[441]

Elletrache don't have the energy to carry yer water."

"Alright," Thomas said. "We got it, Trash."

"Good."

Looking up through the trees, Thomas angled the way with which the light pierced through. Evening would soon be upon them, and as the light diminished any hope of finding the boy would vanish right along with it. If Eppo the raider was a man of his word, then Richter wouldn't be far behind those evaporating hopes.

Suddenly, a hand hit him upside the head. Two raiders walked by snickering. "I doubt that boy is hidin' up in the branches, you dumb fark."

"Hugo, was it?" Thomas said, rubbing the back of his head.

"Yeah," the raider said, pointing a thumb at his own chest. "I'm Hugo. The *best* Hugo, mind you. That other twat at camp named Hugo is just that, a twat. Useless sack of shit. Oh and," Hugo paused, slapping a hand into the other raider's chest. "This here is Egil. He don't talk much."

"Hey," Egil said.

"See?" Hugo said.

Thomas nodded. "Yeah, sure."

"Yer captain's as good as dead," Egil said.

Hugo slapped the man's chest again. "Gods dammit Egil, keep yer mouth shut! Didn't I just say ya was quiet?" Hugo looked at the three sellswords. "But yeah, yer captain's farked. We ain't findin' no boy out this'a'ways."

"We'll find him," Elletrache said.

"And if'n we don't?" Hugo said.

"We're not going back emptyhanded," the beast slayer said, nodding.

Hugo pointed at the beast slayer. "Seeing as how yer guaranteeing we go back hands' full, I call dibs on that fancy lizard armor yer wearing."

The beast slayer glared. "Announcin' some intentions there, raider?"

"Just barking out a bit of interest, that's all." Hugo leaned forward.

"Look, if it's any interest to ya, we're nothing to Eppo. Look at us. There's us two, and you three! He clearly means to rid himself of us, right? I say fark this place entirely. All five of us should just head south together and knock heads."

"That ain't happenin'."

"But maybe it's best if it did."

Elletrache sized up the raiders, his eye balancing the strength of each. While the beast slayer, Thomas, and Minnesang outnumbered them, the two raiders had all the right scars in all the right places, and their eyes did not waver from Elletrache's stare. All the talk about them being outnumbered meant nothing. If anything, it was meant to slacken the slayer's alertness.

"But we can table this here discussion," the raider said, grinning.

"Yeah," Elletrache said. "Right."

The beast slayer turned around and took a step and then held the foot in the air. He stepped back, looking down, then hurriedly crouched.

"Find ya somethin'?" Hugo said.

Elletrache stretched a hand across the grass, combing the folds and divots. Following the broken blades, he looked up and saw more crookedness jigsawing away from his point. He stood. "Yeah. The boy's close."

Thomas said, "What'd you find, Trash?"

"Footprints," Elletrache said. "Fresh ones."

Hugo looked down. "Well shit, them are some'n lil' footprints!"

"My stomach," Minnesang said, hand to his belly. "Fellas, hey… I gotta… you know… let loose…"

All the men stared at him.

Scrunching his face, the jester looked at Thomas. "Can you come with?"

"Come with?" Thomas said.

Hugo smirked. "You want 'im to hold yer cock too?"

Minnesang shrugged. "These woods are dangerous. I don't think it's good to just wander off alone." He looked around for approval. "Right?"

Elletrache snorted and spat. He said, "We just found a strong trace of the little lad and you wanna peel off to take a shit?"

Despite the barb, the jester's self-concern did not fade. The beast slayer scoffed again.

"Ah farkin' hells. Alright, Thomas, take 'im behind some bushes then. If you run into trouble, call out." Elletrache looked at the two raiders. "We'll be doin' the same."

Hugo cleared his throat. "Eeeh, oooh, aaah, there. You'll hear me right and proper now. I don't scream often, but I'll do it right, heh."

Sighing and looking at the jester, Thomas said, "You really want me to watch you take a shit?"

"Yes! I'll just be a Minnesang minute!" the jester said, smiling as if he'd reached the end of a comedic act.

All he heard in response were groans and the beast slayer and raiders turning around as though to shield themselves from the crushing, almost bruising attempt at humor.

"By the old gods, Minnesang," Thomas said, shaking his head. "Now I know why you work alone."

~~~

Thomas followed Minnesang through a series of bushes which slowly gave privacy in walling away the raiders and beast slayer. Around them, the light leaked down in crisscrossing patterns, as though the sun had shattered against the canopy and spewed its debris, the two men rooting through the splintered and glimmering remains, one man holding his belt tight while the other gazed at the canopy above.

"You really too scared to shit by yourself?" Thomas said. He looked down and realized they had come far. He snapped his fingers. "Hey, this is private enough, man."

Minnesang stopped and turned around. He stood up straighter than ever before, like some child might imitate the orderliness of a passing soldier.

Thomas said, "Yeah? Is your stomach alright now?"

"What are you doing?" Minnesang said, and not a single shred of the sing-songy tone was in the jester's words, and the sudden flatness had Thomas take back a step as though all this time Minnesang had been a puppet with a squeaking gastromancer's mimicry, and now for the first time the growling voice of the unseen puppeteer had come down.

The jester shook his head. He said, "Do you not recognize me? I thought you'd have come to me first, but I suppose I gotta spell it out."

"Hey… wh-what?"

"Louis was right, by the way. Richter does not make himself an easy target. I was gonna get him at that ferry town then he upped and poked the hornets' nest and got them peasants going. Then later I had him in sight only for that damn rope traveler to get in the way. Bloody hells. That man is more weasel than Wight as far as I'm concerned. Richter von Dagentear, blech."

Thomas opened his mouth, croaking for the right words.

"Louis von Walddorf, Thomas," Minnesang said. "He has a bounty on Richter's head."

"Louis…"

"Yes, Louis. The burgomeister, you remember your employer, right? By the old gods, how long have you been out here?"

"Louis wants Richter…?"

"Yes! Louis thinks Richter hired someone to assassinate him. Some albino git, I believe. But the killer half-arsed it and left Louis for dead when the job wasn't done. The burgomeister's properly farked up is how I hear it.

Can't talk well or something. Naturally, he's so sore about the affair that he's offering fifteen thousand crowns for Richter's head. Twenty if you can bring him back alive, but we both know that's not happening."

Words swirled in Thomas's head, his thoughts trying to grapple onto one at a time: Louis. Richter. Assassinate. Louis. Richter. Assassin—

"Hey," Minnesang said, clapping Thomas on the shoulder. "You there?"

Nodding hurriedly, Thomas said, "Y-yeah, I am. I'm just a bit surprised that... uh... the price has gotten so high..."

"Don't be too surprised. Louis is about to be running Marsburg. The man has gold to burn," Minnesang went on, his hands out as he counted: "I mean, there's also fifteen thousand for the head of Claire von Sommerwein. The lowlanders still don't know if Sommerwein will join the war and her being missing is causing the lowlanders to sputter and hesitate at the gates of Marsburg. I doubt the lass is anywhere but in some ditch. Then again, if I find her alive, I'll be taking more than just her head, know what I mean?"

"Fifteen thousand..." Thomas said. The amount clarified things and he drew his eyes upon the jester. "But of the two targets, you're here to kill captain Richter?"

"Preferably get them both, of course, but I knew you were working that witch hunter already and figured if you were having trouble, I could pitch in. Divvying some spoils is better than taking all of none."

"Right... no problem with that at all," Thomas said, nodding.

"So what was your plan?" Minnesang said. Not only had his tone and demeanor and stature changed, but even his smile, a sort of new wickedness formed upon his lips. "Were you going to poison him?"

"No..." Thomas said. "Not poison... Hobbs and Sophia watch those pots real close... and Dahlgren's usually by the homesteader's side."

"Yeah that was trouble for me, too."

"Anyway, I was just going to wait until the next town," Thomas said, swallowing so nervously that he nodded as confidently as he could to mask it. "Y-you know, let him get lost in a crowd and do it there."

"Crowd work, nice, nice. I like the style. Hey, I got a question."

Thomas choked on his spit. He snorted and swallowed. "Y-yeah?"

"Yeah. Is that Quinn fella working for us? I couldn't tell if he was actually giving me shit or just trying to play some part to slip in. I mean he never shuts the fuck up."

"What? Quinn? No. He's just a dipshit," Thomas said, shaking his head with very real confidence now. "Louis would never hire a man like that."

"Oh thank the gods. I tire of working with the wrong fellas."

"Right, right... hey, h-how... I mean, what were your plans? How could you kill Richter and get out without anybody knowing?"

"Same as always: I was going to use this," the jester said, taking off the cap'n'bells. He grabbed two of its arms and pulled them apart and a sharp whine let out and the circle of the cap zipped so tight it would have cut off a finger. Clumps of wool wafted down as the jester slackened the cable. He grinned. "In case you didn't catch that, I got a fine-wire garrote hidden in the cap. The rim is the noose, and if you pull on these two arms it snaps closed. Pretty nifty, huh? I killed a fella up there in Ruhmolt with one of these. Got the burgomeister of Grasmarkt, too. You know, the one who owed Louis money? Now he owes nobody nothin', heh."

Thomas's mind was running. "Hey..." he said. "Hey..."

"Ayo, Thomas," Minnesang said. "So we going to do this or not? I say we cut loose back to camp and then take care of business come nightfall."

Thomas swallowed nervously again. "Ehem, well..."

"Or we can go back there and take those three out. You know they think us dandies, which means they won't suspect anything and we can peace two of them at the drop of a hat, heh, then it's just a question of who we leave last. I suggest that wobbly, grouchy fuck."

"Elletrache."

"Yeah, the beast slayer. It'll be some proper skunkwork taking him out, but I think we could manage. Or we could leave one of the raiders, I suppose, but they both look like hardscrabble fucks itching for a fight."

"Hey yeah… true. Say, how does it work, again?"

"Huh?"

"Your implement there… your hat. How does it work again?"

"Oh, once this is pulled tight over their neck then it's all over," Minnesang said. He put the hat back on his head. "And once the strings are taut, you can start sawing. Just muscle the two points here back and forth, like cording wood. Don't take but a minute for the head to pop right off. It stays in the bag, too, so you can make a quick exit. Genius, no?"

Nodding, Thomas said, "Ha-ha, yeah… very genius… and I suppose later you can pull the head out like a magic trick."

Minnesang laughed, his voice still disturbingly different. "Now you're talking! Shit, I think we've dallied long enough. Let's head back."

"Right."

"The slayer right?"

"What?"

Minnesang thumbed over his shoulder. "We'll peace out the two raiders and leave the slayer for last. Just making sure we're on the same page."

"Oh, right. I'll, uh," Thomas thought. "I'll go on your first act."

"Nice. Louis always did speak highly of you. Said you were like a rat with wings, something of a worldly delicacy, but not afraid to get his hands dirty." The jester turned around and started heading back into the bushes. "By the way, I'm more than willing to split the rewards with you at sixty-forty. Way I see it, you've been buttering Richter up. But I don't think waiting for a town is the go move anymore. That raider is absolutely sending him over the river. At some point, we gotta get him away from the camp and get it done. If they send him over to the barbarians, we'll never get his head back from those savages. After him, I might go ahead and take the head of that Quinn fella, I'm pretty sure he knows I'm up to no goofgh!"

Thomas shunted the cap down over the jester's neck and pulled the strings back. A muffled scream quickly cut out as a fan of blood sputtered out in a sheet of red. Gargling, the jester jumped in desperation and the leap jaunted Thomas forward, his heels skidding until they slipped out from under him and both men hit the ground. Tufts of blue and white wool gently snowed about the men. Gritting his teeth, Thomas hurriedly sawed the wires back and forth. Minnesang went to writhing and kicking, his boots scratching up the leaf litters, and all around in the bushes and trees it sounded as if rain were falling, sprays of blood pittering and pattering amongst the greenery, and Thomas closed his eyes as this warm rain fell upon his face.

~~~

Elletrache crouched. Drawing water north to south, a creek cut a tinkling path through the forest. Alongside its rocks and mud were small footprints that had gone across it multiple times and in all directions. The beast slayer stood up, his hands to his hips, gazing from one trace to the next, and then doing it again as though to make up for the absent labor of his missing eye.

"Kid's been around here," he said, nodding. "Probably still is, too."

The two raiders walked up, one of them crushing the boy's footprints.

Hugo snorted. "Wussat you sayin'?"

Elletrache pointed. "The little lad's been using the creek as a watering hole. Curious bit is, why ain't he just usin' the river instead?"

"Maybe he's dumb?" Egil said.

Hugo nodded. "I wager that he is." The raider mimicked the beast slayer's hand movements. He said, "This a way and that a way and this a way." His hand fell. "We ain't gon' be nothin' but twisted around trying to see which'a'ways the little shitter went."

Elletrache shook his head. "Naw, it's actually a simple matter. We stay here, and we stay quiet, and that boy will return. Patience is all we need."

"Can I ask ya somethin', beast man?" Hugo said.

"Yeah?"

Hugo nodded at Elletrache's shimmering scales. "How'd you get on killin' a lindwurm? You and a team do that? Use a big ol' trap or somethin'?"

"No," Elletrache said. "I killed it myself."

"You," Egil said, smirking. "You killed a lindwurm by yourself?"

"That's right. I had some luck on my side, but yeah."

Chuckling, the raiders looked at each other then over their shoulders at the bushes. As they turned back around, both men drew out handaxes.

"You still think you got that luck on your side?" Hugo said.

"Ah." Elletrache slung his huge crossbow off his shoulder. "This is what we're doing?"

"As far as we're concerned, Eppo can get farked," Hugo said. "Stupid git don't know what he's doing. Me and Egil here, we're better than him, better than the rest. It don't have to end ugly, beast man, but we'll kill you outright. Don't you go thinking otherwise."

Elletrache eyed each man so intently that even his eyepatch wiggled, his absent stare muscling back and forth. He said, "Yer still just talking, though."

"Mmhmm. We've only interest in yer armor." Hugo carved his axe through the air as though he were carving the lindwurm's scales free of their slayer. "Take it off and give it to us and we'll be on our way. You can go tell Eppo and yer shitfark captain we did it. We won't care none at that point."

"These are lindwurm scales," Trash said. "You have any idea how long

I've been tryin' to make a chest piece like this?"

"Real happy for ya meetin' yer dreams," Hugo said. "But go on and take it off and we'll be on our way, promise. Be taking them lindwurm teeth you got around yer neck, too. After that, we'll let you go, and those two rats takin' shits in the bushes? They can live, too. I think that's a fair trade."

"Oh and I'll be wantin' that crossbow yer fingerin'," Egil said, exchanging a wily smirk with Hugo. "I played around with 'er at the camp. Fancy bit o' property, but I thought she could use some work."

"You touched it?" Trash said, his grip tightening around the weapon.

Egil licked his lips. "Oh I put my fingers all over 'er. And I think it best you just go on and hand over that harpooner all friendly like, too. You fire 'er and, well, you'll be making a big mistake. Like Hugo said, we're willing to letcha walk free. Don't do otherwise. Otherwise is the grave, understand?"

"We will kill you," Hugo said. "And them other two, too. Don't waste their lives on account of yer greed, beast man."

"The crossbow," Egil said, clamoring for it. "Hand it over."

As Egil took another step closer, Elletrache drew up his crossbow and pulled its release bar. Instead of ripping off a shot that would have obliterated the raider, the weapon groaned as its machinery failed in a series of staccato snaps and breaks. Trash turned it to see the mechanisms bent and crooked and that the ratchet had been clogged with a web of thin almost invisible twine, and as he stared at the contraption the twine snapped and the withheld tension slammed the metal against the underbelly cratering the wood and cutting straight through his left hand. Shrapnel and metalworks and fingers and a thumb cascaded into the air as the frame of the sabotaged weapon disintegrated and the taut ropework ripped in half and the harpoon harmlessly limped out of its chute. Tearing his mutilated hand out of the shredded wire and woodwork, the beast slayer screamed and fell back against a tree, a flopping mop of an appendage wiggling before his lone eye.

"Ahh," Egil said, shaking his head. "Done told you to just hand it over! Now ye've one hand less to do what we asked!"

Trash looked up just as the two raiders swung their axes down. He turned and Hugo's axe crashed into his armored shoulder, the lindwurm scales crackling as they accepted the challenge. Egil's axe swooshed by and sank into the tree with a clap. Acting fast, Trash smooshed his bloodied limb into Hugo's face, causing the raider to gag and step back. With his other hand, the beast slayer ripped his lindwurm necklace off his neck, grooved a serrated tooth between his knuckles like a claw, and uppercut it right through Egil's wrist, quickly sawing between the forearm's bones. The raider howled out and fell backward as geysers of blood sputtered from the gored arm.

"By the old gods, Hugo!" Egil shouted. "My arm! My arm!"

"Egil!" Hugo turned to Elletrache. "You motherfucker!"

Trash turned the tooth over and swung it in a wide hook. Faster than expected, Hugo swung his axe again and the beast slayer's fist met steel, the axehead splitting the hand in half from knuckle to wrist. Howling, Trash fell back against the tree as the raider drove against him, his metal armor squalling against the razor sharp lindwurm scales.

"Die you fuck!" Hugo growled, bringing the axe down once more.

Roaring, Trash launched forward and headbutted the raider, the slayer's old, worn pate clattering like an old shovel. Stars and white fuzz filled Trash's vision. Old sights for the beast slayer. He blinked them away and saw Hugo stumbling backward and clutching his face. The raider spat out a tooth and gingerly touched a crater where his nose used to be.

"Sonughabetch," Hugo said. "Sonughabetch!"

Trash looked at his own hands. Missing fingers and thumbless on one, and the other looked like a crab's claw, having been nearly cleaved in half by Hugo's axe. Using the claw, he tried to unsheathe his own handaxe out of from behind his belt, but his mangled grip could only prod and pry, the weapon's handle slipping away over and over, the wooden handle splintering and scraping against his wounds like fire. Finally, he pinched his last thumb and a movable ring finger over the handle, shakily drawing it up like a nobleman eating an expensive delicatessen at the end of a lengthy spoon.

"Furgh you!"

Trash looked up. Hugo barreled in. The two men met, one-eye and two eyes and four fists followed, slugging back and forth, knocking teeth out, bloodied knuckles cracking cheekbones and digging into eyesockets and denting foreheads, and with every strike Trash's fingers went limper and limper yet with paling appendages flopping about until it seemed he was swinging red mops around, painting Hugo's face red by one means or another.

"Farghin' hellsh," Hugo said, swaying backward on his feet, eyes blackened, nose sloped, blood pouring from a missing ear. "Hellsh," he sputtered again. "J-jusht gib it up, mahn. Jusht gib awss the ahhrmor."

"Us?" Trash said, wiping his wiggling remains of a hand across his bearded, slathered maw. He spat out an ear he didn't remember biting off. "You all alone now, fella."

Hugo opened his mouth, then he looked toward the creek. Egil lay dead in the water, his gashed arm bubbling so much blood that it overran the natural current, turning it a dark, frothy red as it lapped away. Tiny fish glimmered in their newfound environment. Gritting his teeth, Hugo turned back and pulled a dagger from his boot.

"*Thomas!*" Trash screamed. "Thomas get yer arse here now!"

Roaring, Hugo charged in once more.

Forced to think with his feet, Trash slid his toe under his huge crossbow's fallen harpoon and kicked it up into the air. In the same motion he caught it in the carriage of a bent arm and planted its nock against the tree and couched its length and weight in the nook of his elbow. Hugo had already left his feet by the time the metal rod swayed in his direction, and he could not but widen his eyes as he plunged himself upon it, sliding down the harpoon with a long, angry gargle.

"Motherfargher," Hugo spat, his blood freckling the beast slayer.

Despite the impalement, the raider's dagger hand suddenly went up and over in a graceless swoop, and Trash's eyepatch fell off his head and a sheet of blood ran down from his scalp. Elletrache flinched as though in surprise.

"Motherfargher!" Hugo screamed, his dagger-hand wildly slashing.

Trash let go of the harpoon and wrapped his arm around the back of Hugo's head. Simply opening his arm in this manner left him open to more of the assault, and he felt the heat of his face as the slicing continued unabated. Gritting his teeth, he ducked his chin and took the wounds as he leveraged his arm deep behind the raider's neck. Once the hold was in place, Hugo's attack stopped, and his eyes turned to the beast slayer, and then Trash promptly plunged Hugo into the lindwurm scales like a child into a birthday pie. When he pulled back, Hugo's face never fully left the shoulder for strands of flesh bridged the gap between, and the raider's visage appeared as if it were some confectionary being poured into shape by an unpracticed baker.

"You want my armor, huh?" The beast slayer growled. "Then have it!"

Trash slammed Hugo's face back into the scales and this time when he let go the raider stood in bloodied silence, his eyes lacerated and dripping, his eyebrows uncinched and flopping like dogears. The beast slayer let him go and Hugo promptly fell. His head bounced off the ground and the ruins of his face splashed upward and misshapenly landed like some grisly scaremask knocked askew.

"Yeah," Trash said. He limped forward. He looked toward the bushes as he stumbled and yelled out: "Thomas! Thomaaughh!"

A horrible chill befell his foot and Trash jumped up howling. When he put his foot back down it gave out under him and he buckled. He watched the front of his boot tumble away, his toes wrapped in the tight leather like raisins in a roll of bread. He looked back to see a prone and faceless Hugo lunging off the ground like an old snake, his mangled face fluttering to reveal an opened maw and then he clamped down on Trash's mangled hand, bringing teeth into tendon.

Screaming, Trash kicked the axe away and pulled his hand out of Hugo's mouth, cords of nerve and muscle stretching before they snapped free and bloodily whipped both parties. Using his elbows, he clutched the harpoon in Hugo's belly and wrenched it side to side like some mad sorcerer before his dire makings. The ribcage cracked and Hugo's heart went with it, the raider briefly lifting his hands into the air before collapsing dead and unmoving.

"Thomas…" Trash said, leaning on the harpoon and catching his breath. He lifted his head and yelled: "Thomas! Thomas get yer arse here *now!* Thom*aughFARK!*"

Just taking one step, Elletrache's halved stump of a foot rolled its open wound right into gravel and the beast slayer fell. Through sheer adrenaline, he had completely forgotten the wound itself.

"Sonuvabitch," Elletrache sputtered, staring up at the sky. He rolled over and looked at the bushes, the greenery blurred in orbs of red as blood ran into his eye, the fading light of the sun speckled and fading and bright all the same. He mustered a breath and let it out in a growl: "Thomas!" He paused. "Thomas! Minnesang! Ya farkin' precks!"

No answer.

"Sonuvabitch. Son of a farkin' *bitch.*"

Elletrache shook his head and started crawling toward the creek. With every shunt, the scales of his armor dragged mud to go along with the chunks and flecks of Hugo's flesh. Grunting, the beast slayer finally pulled himself to the creekbed and dropped his face into the cool water. He gingerly set his mangled hands in, strips of red gently stirred in the slow current. He then dropped his halved foot into the creek and worked its water over the stump.

"Thomas!" he yelled out again. The name seemed to empty into an uncaring realm. Elletrache shook his head and slurped up some of the water and spat out the blood in his mouth. Throat clear, he reared back and yelled again with better clarity: "Thomas!"

Suddenly, the creekwater thinned to a dribble, the last of it trickling away like a silk sheet slowly being pulled off the edge of a bed, leaving behind a glistening yet quickly drying forest floor. Elletrache turned around and looked upstream to see a massive nachzehrer squatting atop the creek's fount, the beast's round belly rising and falling in quick gasps, the rest of its flesh smoldering in black and grey streaks, contrails of hazy smoke lifting off it. The beast's arm slowly swung out and grabbed onto a tree. Drapes of flesh flailed from the bone, but its strength proved unerring as it shunted forward, effortlessly puncturing the tree trunk with its claws and showering itself in a cascade of leaves and bird nests as it pulled itself forward.

The beast slayer took another breath. "Well fark."

Elletrache turned over and dragged himself out of the creek and stood up on one leg, hopped twice, and fell back down. He picked up his eyepatch and knotted it back to one piece. Behind him followed the grunting and sloppy issuance of the nachzehrer grinding its belly over gravel. As the beast slayer's mangled hands finished the eyepatch, he slung it back over his head.

The beast's belly grumbled as it neared, its tentacled and unhinged maw undulating and dripping with hunger. So hungered and wanting, its distended belly folded under its own weight and dragged behind its rump like a child stepping over its own blanket.

Pursing his lips, Elletrache dragged himself to his lindwurm teeth and picked them up and he looked toward the bushes again, but Thomas and Minnesang were still nowhere to be seen. He assumed they saw or heard the fight and fled, that or they saw the beast and fled. One and the same. The beast slayer spat and yelled out: "Thomas!"

Spindly shadows slowly enveloped Elletrache, the beast calm in its approach, knowing well the state of its prey, that this was no hunt, but a mere scavenge. Elletrache spat and damned much of the world with a few mutterings and then he clenched his necklace of lindwurm teeth in his crabhand and he shifted his eyepatch over his good eye to blacken out the world. Behind him, he felt the weight of the earth depress, gravel and rock crackling, and drool dripped upon him, and he could hear the gargle of the beast's belly as it excitedly awaited its next meal.

"Thomas!" Elletrache screamed. "Run! Run! *Run*! R—"

~ ~ ~

Quite unfortunately, Minnesang's implement worked exactly as intended: the assassin had no chance of escape once his own garrote tightened around his neck. The wire sliced through skin and muscle and as Thomas sawed it back and forth the string started grinding its way through bones. Feet kicking, arms waving, the jester thrashed and fought, and with each move a sheet of blood fanned out, landing in scattered dribbles like spits of rain. Thomas wrapped his legs around Minnesang and when the jester jerked one way, the servant quickly shunted in the opposite direction. The metal squalled, the wool hissed, and Thomas's arms jerked backward. Rolling over, the jester's neck presented a smooth muscled remnant as clean as any executioner could hope to present. Looking down, Thomas found the would-be assassin's head sitting in the hat like a pumpkin in a satchel. It stared back, quite a grimace having been carved out of its visage. Exasperated, Thomas fell back onto the earth and stared up at the forest canopy. He drew in sips of breath, one after the other, and he felt the man's warm blood already cooling on his face.

"By the old gods," he said. "By the old gods."

"*Thomas!*"

The word broke through the bushes like a flushed bird.

The servant leaned upright, holding himself up on his elbows.

"Elletrache?" he said.

"Thomas get yer arse here *now!*"

"Elletrache, I'm coming—" as he sprang to his feet, the garrote loosened and the sudden new momentum catapulted the jester's head into a bush. As it crashed down the branches, two little hands reached out and caught it. Thomas jumped back with a yelp. Before him, a young boy giggled as he looked at a freshly decapitated head.

"Oh shit," Thomas said, seeing a tattoo on the boy's face. "It's you."

Beyond the bushes, more shouts hailed: "Thomas! Thomaaughh!"

Looking up, the boy stared at Thomas with bemused curiosity.

Thomas pointed at the ground. "Stay right there, alright?"

"You," the boy said, and he nodded. "You, Thomas. He," the next nod went to the jester. "Minn… Minneh…"

"You speak our tongue?" Thomas said.

The boy held the head up as though it were the first fish he ever caught. He growled and grunted, then lowered the head. He nodded. "I… try."

"Thomas!" Elletrache's screams were louder than ever. "Thomas get yer arse here *now!* Thom*aughFARK!*"

"Hey, yeah," Thomas said. He pointed a finger at the boy. "S-stay right there, I have to go help my friend, alright? Do you understand?"

Elletrache kept screaming. And someone else was screaming, too.

Thomas looked toward the direction of the screams, then slowly turned his gaze to the boy. He said, "Are there more like you in the woods?"

The boy shook his head. He pointed all around the woods before landing his finger upon his own chest. He grunted and said, "Hargravard."

"Ah, right, sure," Thomas said. He pointed at the ground. "Stay here, alright? Do you understand 'stay'?"

"Thomas!" Elletrache howled again, and the beast slayer's urgency was mirrored by the echo of his shout.

"You, stay," Thomas said again and he turned around. "Elletrache, I'm coming—"

"Run!"

Thomas stopped.

"Run! *Run*! R—"

Silence.

"Trash?" Thomas said. He stared through the bushes. "Trash?"

Little fingers wrapped around his hand. He looked down.

"Run," the boy said, jerking his head over his shoulder. "Run run ruh!"

Looking toward Elletrache's screams again, Thomas waited to hear another. But nothing came. Nothing came at all. No sounds. And the longer he stared into the woods, the more it seemed the forest floor spun out from under his feet, and the trees bent and turned, like ears to a sudden silence, and out of these looped sights his imagination ran wild with devised horrors.

The boy jumped clapping. "Run run ruh!"

Thomas blinked. The forest floor wobbled flat and the trees righted the way they should be. He shook away the fear and plucked the jester's head out of the boy's hands and threw it into the bushes. He then put his arms down and picked the boy up and slung him behind his back.

"We're going," the servant said. "Understand?"

"Run!" the boy shouted, his voice giddy. "Run run ruh! Run run ruh!"

~~~

"Oh shit," Thomas said. "Oh man."

The boy glommed onto his back, Thomas paused now and again to look and see if Elletrache, or whatever attacked him, was following. Staring back through the trees, it seemed as though the forest stretched itself again, great halls of wooden pillars with carpets of green and brown, the light of the fading sun slanting in as though through windows, the corkscrewed shadows twisting up all sorts of trouble for a fearful mind. He wiped his forehead of sweat and returned to the retreat.

"You," the boy said. "Tired. You, tired."

"Hey, yeah," Thomas said. "You don't need to keep saying that."

"You, tired. You a tired man. Very tired."

"Uh huh."

"You no run run ruh!"

"No, I don't run run ruh."

"Very tired man, you are."

Thomas stopped and leaned against a tree. He felt his heart pounding so hard he thought he heard it knocking on the tree's trunk. Giggling, the boy jumped off his back like a goat off a haybale. The servant turned around and slid down to his arse in an exhausted heap.

"I think something bad has happened," Thomas said, shaking his head. "Oh man, I think something really, really bad has happened."

"You," the boy said, pointing. "You bad."

"No, something bad. I think all those men are dead."

The boy looked back from whence they came. When he turned around, he said, "Hargravard."

"Right, sure," Thomas said. He wiped his brow again. "Hardavahd."

"Hargravard."

Thomas leaned forward onto his knees, took a breath, and got up.

"I don't know if we can make it back before nightfall," he said, grimacing at the day's dying light. He looked at the boy. "Do you understand that we should hide? Do your people even know what hiding is?"

"Hide, wear, armor, yes, Hargravard, yes."

"Right…" Thomas looked away, pursing his lips as he assessed the nearby trees. He spotted an alcove where three trees had sprung out of the soil in a shared cluster, their branchless trunks stalking over the forest floor like a bird's foot. He pointed at the arrangement. "We'll stay there."

"Stay?"

"Yeah, stay. Like, non-Hardavahd, understand?

"Hargravard."

"Hey, yeah, hargra-har-alright, just come on."

~ ~ ~

Thomas held the boy in his arms, the two snug in the nook of the trees. Pale moonlight bled into the woods. Every second, Thomas thought he was spotting a wolf or lindwurm or brigand hunting after them, but a second later it would appear only to be a bush swaying in the wind, or a branch stooping low as a bird landed upon it. And in time, his eyes approximated things as they should be, and the misapprehensions of darkness gave way to known imagery: there the twisted tree, there the trunk blasted by lightning, there the bush with half its leaves gone, part spindly, part edible, and there a bird flitting back and forth as it stealthily assembled its nest. And in the center, his own eyes, and between these places that was all there was.

"I think we're safe here," Thomas said.

"Har—"

"Hargravard," Thomas said. "I know, I know."

The boy leaned out of his arms and turned around. He pointed at the servant. "Hargravard."

"Oh, I'm Hargravard now?" Thomas said with a bemused whisper.

The boy shook his head. He said, "Minnesang."

"No, I'm Thomas."

"Thomas."

"That's right, Thomas."

For a moment, the boy sat, his white eyes hanging in the darkness. He blinked and said, "Assassin."

Thomas shook his head. He put his hands to himself. "I'm Thomas. No assassin. Just Thomas."

"You... kill Minnesang..."

As the words fell over him, Thomas sighed and he found himself moving his limbs around as though the boy's words had disturbed him from a restful sleep. He said, "Hey, yeah, we don't have to talk about that, alright?"

"You... kill... Richter."

"What? No. I killed Minnesang," Thomas said. "Only Minnesang."

"Louis is your captain?"

"Louis? What? Just how much did you hear?"

"Louis. Richter. Assassin. You... kill Richter?" the boy said, and his hands fanned out, carving a large bowl into the air. "Huge reward. You kill Richter and this is... huge reward, hew-yah reward!"

Thomas's eyes widened. "Why are you saying this? Don't say that."

"Huge reward, hew-yah reward!" The boy clapped his hands and pointed at Thomas and then at himself. "You, I, we kill Richter!"

"N-no," Thomas said. "Stop saying that."

The boy smiled. "Yes, kill Richter. We... reward... I Hargravard, you Hargravard. Richter... kill... reward..." the boy paused, his fingers dancing.

"Huge! Hew-yah! Hew-yah reward for you, hew-yah reward for me! We kill Richter for hew-yah reward!"

Slapping his hands over the boy's mouth, Thomas pressed him into the nook of the trees. "Quiet, you have to be quiet! You... you have to stop saying these words, understand? Stay quiet! No more talking! Understand?"

"Kill Richter," the boy said, grinning sheepishly as he practiced out these foreign words as an apprentice might hammer in a piece that he finally figured out how to do. Though the barbarian tongue frequently gave way to grunts and growls, the northern vernacular shared some sounds of the barbarian's, making their repetition all the more joyful: "Kill Richter, huge reward! Kill Richter, huge reward! Kill! Richter! Huge! Rewaaard! Hew-yah reward!"

"Shush, shush! Stop!"

"Huge reward, kill Richter!" the boy's words turned to a sing-songy tune as he jigged his shoulders side to side in an excited dance. "And then I... Hargravard. I... king. Kill Richter, I king." The boy stopped, his shoulders dropping. He looked at Thomas. "Wh-wh-where... is this Richter?"

Thomas stared at the boy. The man's eyes were full of tears. He said, "Can you be silent? Do you know what silence is?"

"Wh-where is... Richter? Lew-ess... Louis... Richter..."

"Please. You can't say these words. You just can't, alright?"

"I. Hargravard." Smiling, the boy pointed at Thomas. "You. Assassin."

Chapter 36. Tracking a Pathfinder.

THE LINDWURM curled itself beside the cauldron's fire. Hours after the wounding, its eye still carried the rod of Imnachar's crossbow. Each time the beast looked around, the shaft swept along with its sight, the wood grinding against the rough, scaled ridges of the socket itself. For the beast, it seemed as though it now and again forgot the wound, falling asleep and then rising from a slumber and snapping its head around, confused about its suddenly half-blackened world. Such was the nature of a mind driven by instinct, forever damned to recollect its wounds in fits between the days. Claire tried to pull the shot out, but the pain inflicted seemed, for a moment, to return the beast to its origins, its teeth bared and its good eye glaring at the girl as prey, and so she let go and whispered to it and she had tears in her eyes and she said she was sorry for losing the direwolf, that she should not have been so stupid, and that she would not lose the lindwurm, no matter what, and then the beast fell asleep, the huff of its snores enflaming the cauldron beside it.

In the middle of the road, Immerwahr stood over a pile of. They were half-naked and hardly armed. All bony ribs and open mouths and hungry tongues. No doubt these maladies had determined them into untimely demises. No doubt it was Richter's company which they thought to attack and failed. When starving, death became but another parcel in all negotiations, and one which could even be seen as a compromise. Killing such men could be a matter of ultimate relief and so the monk whispered blessings upon them.

"Holy man," Claire said, walking across the road. "Talk with me."

The monk looked over to see Claire staring at him. He nodded and picked up Kantorek's sword. He walked by the ensorcelled mob, the naked gang set out in a long line, cross-legged with their backs bent and their shoulders red from rope burns. They lifted their eyes to him, and so quiet was the evening that he could hear their collective eyelashes fluttering, and the dry creaks of what little wetness broke in those shifting stares, and some mouthed whispers, words as soft as a breath across a butterfly's wings yet all the same seeking an anchor in a reality that had been stolen.

"Here," Claire said, pointing at the ground. "Sit down here."

He sat.

She sat.

The darkening forest loomed, and in the distance dozens of eyes stared from the ensorcelled mob and blades shimmered from the similarly postured caravan guard. Naked flesh. Leathered bodies. Steeled weaponry. Glowing across them all the orange hue of the cauldron's flames. As Immerwahr looked at the line of hexed, their eyes blinked in sequence, from front to back, a great fluttering like a fire arrow blinking between past the poles of a fence. But it was a superficial light. No gleam, no life. And staring into those eyes was akin to putting your hands before a fire which provided no warmth. It was an error. Persons made mirages, yet touchable all the same.

Claire said, "It is a shame you knew of them before they knew of me."

Immerwahr looked forward. "What is that supposed to mean?"

"An appropriate question." The girl leaned back, planting her arms onto the dirt, her eyes to the night sky and its infinite glories. "When I was a child, my father showed me these plants which consumed mice. Did you know this, that there are little greeneries which will eat live animals?"

"I did not."

"What do you think of it?"

The monk moved himself around as though the notion of such an idea had sent little bugs crawling up every inch of him.

"Yes, I would be unsettled too," Claire said, nodding. "The plant came from the east. I didn't inquire as to a more precise where, for in some sense when you see the little nightmares of a land you instinctively fear what more oddities might trample overfoot. But by some eastward land it came, and by a scribe's presentation I gazed upon it. Shaped like a cup it was, and strangely smoother than any silk. But we weren't there only to ogle. Thusly, if not in a manner preordained, a little mouse comes along. Maybe it smells something sweet. Maybe the plant knows what the mouse likes. There is no cheese in there, but something else. Something we haven't figured out. The mouse climbs up and falls in. It slides to the bottom. It cannot get out. In time…" Claire flipped her hand once, then back again. "It dissolves. The plant drinks."

"Why are you telling me this?"

"I'm curious, holy man, when such a new novelty comes to the fore, what would you do with it?"

"I don't know."

"Truthfully now, how do you think the mice fell in?"

"Fell into the plant?"

Claire nodded.

Immerwahr cleared his throat. He said, "You put it in there."

"Yes. More than one, even. Novelty must be multiplied and expedited. Surely nothing you wouldn't wish to see twice is particularly unique. That is the charm if not backwardness of all that is wonder. Wonderment, by its nature, finds its own demise. All that is mundane was once amazing. Now we can walk through life seeing so little of a world filled with so much. Our very eyes grind down the glint and glow until all that remains is a husk. Many of our elders have this sense of things. A sense of seeing it all. It's not that the light of their life has gone, but that the novelties have been extinguished."

"Their health flags as it naturally should," Immerwahr said. "Nothing more."

"Perhaps. Perhaps." Claire nodded with each word. Her eyes still stared at the night sky. "However, I read one scribe's work that said we as people live longer or shorter lives depending upon the novelties of our times. That in the eons of the past, people lived for hundreds of years for that is how long it took to consume the novelties which surrounded them. Life was more spectacular, and thus life was longer. But now, today, you pass this road, and you've seen most all roads, you see a castle, and you've seen most all castle, you witness a battle, and you've seen most all battles. For nobles in particular, boredom becomes an antagonist of its own."

"What a privilege."

"Indeed."

"I take it your fancy plant became little more than a used novelty then?"

Claire finally looked down from the stars above. "After a week, the scribe and nobles moved on from the plant, yes. The sheen was gone. A plant which eats flesh became nothing more than another plant. Just like that. Of course, my curiosities were not so easily satiated. A mouse falls in and gets eaten, and that is all there is to it? No, no no no. Of course not. There's something else to be seen in this relationship between flesh and plant, is there not?"

Immerwahr nodded. "Taking the fallen mice out."

"Mmhmm." Claire smiled. "Even as a child I could see that people, whether poor or rich, pursue a vicarious connection with power. Real power, after all, is exceedingly fleeting."

"Thank the old gods."

"Yes." Claire nodded again. "I used to watch from my towered window a vagrant, and this vagrant would spend his idle hours throwing crickets into a spider's web for no other reason than it gave him immense power in the confines of that particular relationship. It seemed pointless if not cruel play to some, but I understood its nature. Being the highborn that I am, I have also seen the way wealth weighs upon the world as though it were magic. With a flash of gold, a man's lips can be loosened, his loyalties melted, his swordhand raised, almost as if that gold were akin to the puppeteer drawing upon its strings. People will one day widely accuse me of ill magics yet ignore this mysterious element which already exists before them, the one that can send whole armies sweeping across the world all thanks to a shiny glint."

"Love also has this power," Immerwahr said. "But you have not experienced it. At this point, you would be lucky to even be in its aura."

Smirking, the girl looked up at the stars once more.

"Funny you say that. Despite resolving to save every mouse that fell into the plant's trap, the mice never did love me, much less thank me," she said, her voice vaguely strained as though reminiscing of a man who never said he loved her. "They simply went on their way. They're mice. They've no sense of such affections. But in time, though, the mice learned to avoid the plant. Stranger yet, the freshly born mice never had to be taught anything. They seemed to inherently understand the realities of this new world I had guided their parents out of. I was astonished, to be honest. As I said, we all pursue power in our own little ways. There's something all the more emboldening about saving that which knows not the slightest hint of your having meddled."

Claire swept a blade of grass from her dress. "In time, the plant died. I had killed it. Not directly, of course, but by my curiosities. I had taught the mice to avoid it, and the mice in turn flourished about the room. Unlike the vagrant with his crickets and spiders, I no longer wished to feed the plant directly and the mice themselves now killed off all the insects. A certain dearth in diet befell this little plant. When it finally curled, I sat beside it, candle in hand. Watching and nothing more. A part of me felt obligated to see it out. I had crafted the world which deprived it of its carnivorous hunger."

Immerwahr nodded to the ensorcelled. "Your handling of a plant and mice has nothing to do with these people. These are actual lives and they deserve a far more dignified life than the one you have fooled them into."

The girl nodded. "Holy man, you do not speak lies. Quite naturally, these people deserve so much more. But we must maintain perspective. When the world is at stake, the suffering of a few is not to be narrowed in on."

"Notions such as these are plainly monstrous."

"Are they now? When the nobles charge their armies forth and dozens die by the second, do you suppose that they pause their ambitions to mourn each and every one of the fallen? And why do they even throw these armies around in the first place? One campaign feeds into another and another. They know not what they do, they simply go and go again until an enemy archer gets lucky or they fall off their horse or they drown in a river, and then the scribes bow their heads and righteously commit to the books that this, this man with a cloak of corpses trailing behind him, was a hero until his directionless road came to a pointless end. And then another nobleman comes along and sees this and says yes, that is my path, and everyone's natural intuition is so scandalized that they cannot see the obvious. And the obvious is that the error is in the man just as much as it is in the world which chooses to ensphere him in myth."

"And what myth what that be?"

"The myth that anything he accomplished mattered in the slightest. His existence is his own, and it is annihilated upon its completion. Nothing else remains. If I open the tomes of history and I see this man, and this one, and this one, and they're all doing the same thing, killing and conquering and dying, and the land renews in their absence so the next one takes his place to repeat the process, harvesting great depths of pain and suffering so that he might enjoy ten or twenty years to himself. Dare I ask what it is that I am reading, holy man? People hear of these stories with a sense of wonder as though nothing is at cost. The people who suffered the fires of conquest did not get to have these moments of wonder. And it is those people I remember. They do not get a page in the books. They rarely get more than a sentence, and rarer yet more than a number. A hundred dead here. A thousand there. Again and again and again. Many, many numbers beside one name. Endless lives turned into ink, little underlines to go beneath the name of the one who brought them carnage in the first place. What a truly, truly horrific end."

"I suppose your doings will not be meaningless, is that right?"

"You're not listening to me well enough, holy man. Please give me some credit here. The answer to such a question is: I don't know." Claire pursed her lips and shrugged. "Maybe I'm wrong. Maybe I'm simply a new menace, this could very well be true."

Claire got to her feet. She walked toward the adhoc wagon which hitched her cauldron. A few children stirred in the pot itself, but she cooed them back to sleep with a few words. Turning, she whispered to the ensorcelled mob and their eyes, once blinkering in straightline patterns, all flashed open simultaneously and in the same motion they got to their feet. Wordlessly, they marched before the cauldron's wagon, took up its ropes, and started pulling. The cauldron jostled, the brew hissing as it shifted and its surface broke upon the little bodies which stirred it into being. Hearing the crack of noise, the lindwurm roused from its sleep and its one-eye spun about, the other clacking the wooden shaft along the rim of scales. Claire whispered to this being just as well, and it settled and slowly followed alongside the wagon, head swinging left to right to gather a faltering perception of things. And then she said a few words to the caravan guards and they turned with precision and fell into formation and marched at the rear of the cauldron.

Passing Immerwahr, Claire said, "Come along now, holy man."

"I thought we were sleeping," the monk said.

"What once was is now gone," Claire said. "I make this decision arbitrarily of right and reason. I make it by instinct. We will push through the night and come morning we will see to this ferry and the ill-shaped, perpetual habit of a man that dwells there."

Though Immerwahr did not wish to loft a question which roused her back into a rightful mind, particularly because he believed her leaving the Ancient Road was incorrect for surely the Ancient Road was where Richter remained, the monk's curiosity did get the best of him. He said, "That guildmaster never told you where Richter went! How do you know that he has gone down this way?"

Claire laughed as the wagon jostled and creaked beneath her. She said, "Imnachar was guildmaster of the Sommerwein witch hunting guild. I destroyed that guild, holy man, and I poisoned its hexenjägers in the eyes of the nobility and laity alike such that they were sought to be executed in total. Imnachar's bones should be bleaching atop a Sommerwein torture tower, but instead he was down here, which means my father's bounty hunters and executioners are probably looking for him. Do you think Richter and this man did not converse? Imnachar would not tell Richter to keep to the Ancient Road because he'd run right into those hunters. No no no, he'd tell him to leave it, and the first path I see has fresh wagon tracks and that's enough for me. Frankly, holy man, that guildmaster needn't tell me anything," she said, cackling. "I only wished to have him betray Richter, to break him and his hexenjäger spirit. Alas, the guildmasters, as much as I despise them, do tend to earn their seats by some virtue of merit."

Immerwahr stammered. He thought she had been going off-track on a longshot chance of catching up to Richter. The monk thought the witch hunter would assuredly stick to the Ancient Road, head north, and collect more men with which to fight. With just a few of her words, he now knew she was completely right. As his eyes watched the departing mob, caravan guards, and lindwurm, he realized Richter and anyone with him was doomed.

"Now pick up that sword, holy man!" Claire yelled. She clapped her hands. "Steady your faith, for a very proper morning awaits us!"

Chapter 37. Lost and Found.

THE TRADING SWORDS river lapped against the shore, gentle in the morning light. Before it, the company of sellswords and a band of raiders stood, and between them kneeled Thomas the servant, his hands supinated, at the length of each the weight of a dead child: the barbarian boy. Richter stared at the corpse with a long sigh. The tattoos which once swept about the child's skin now ran staggered, broken, misshapen, colors washed out in bruises and dried blood. His hair had clumped into dried strands, hanging from his head like branches. It seemed as if every sort of martial defilement had befallen him, from blunt smashes to sharp slashes. Articles of Thomas's shirt wrapped the boy in attempts to mend, but Richter knew that if he were to unwind the wraps a whole lot of the child's insides would plop right out.

"By the old gods," Hobbs said.

Richter put his hands over Hobbs' eyes. "Sophia."

The homesteader gathered the boy. Hobbs protested, but she hushed him in a motherly manner he had not heard in years and he quieted.

Eppo snorted and spat. He dug the toe of his boot into Thomas's chest. "Hey, crybaby, where are my two men? Hugo and Egil, where are they?"

"W-w-we were attacked," Thomas said. He wiped his eyes and then looked down at the barbarian boy. "We found the little lad and we were coming back and then s-s-something attacked us."

Looking at the corpse, Richter said, "Can you describe what it was?"

"It was a…" Thomas looked at the child for a moment. He swallowed. "It was a nachzehrer! A big one! An-an-and some little ones! Elletrache and the raiders fought the big one, and th-they told me to run! So I did."

"Did Minnesang run with you?"

"What? Oh, yeah, Minnesang was with me. He-he-he didn't make it. Something took his head clean off…"

"That's a shame," Quinn said, garnering a few daggering stares.

Eyes full of tears, Thomas continued: "…their… their claws were so sharp! And they snatched the boy out of my hands and they cut him and hit him and stepped on him and it was terrible! I managed to get him back, but by then… it was too late." Thomas looked down again, but this time he turned out his arms, showing little cuts and bruises. "I got hurt, too. See?"

"Elletrache is dead?" Crockett said.

Thomas nodded. "I think the big beast got him."

"Ah," Quinn said. "Fark."

Crockett snorted and pursed his lips and stepped away. He stood at the treeline with his arm against a trunk and his head slackened into it and the company's ledger swung limply at his side, pages unfurled, sweeping back and forth, each one awaiting new entries he did not wish to put in.

"I have to confirm this," Richter said. He looked at Eppo. "And I can confirm if your men are dead, too."

"No, don't!" Thomas yelled. "The woods are not safe!"

Eppo stared at the savage boy's corpse.

One of the raiders behind him spat and shook his head. "Eh yo, Egil and Hugo were our best fighters. They wouldn't go down like that to some scavenging nachzehrers."

Glaring at Richter, Eppo said, "Egil and Hugo wouldn't go down to no two-bit sellswords, either. You, coward, describe what unfolded."

"H-hey, yeah," Thomas said. "I s-saw them fight for a bit, they were vicious, but I th-think that… that… the big nachzehrer… it ate them. Ate them all." He looked at Richter somberly. "I think it ate Trash, too. It ate the beast slayer, captain. I'm very certain that we shouldn't go into the woods."

The captain lowered his head.

"He might still be alive," Crockett said, turning around from the tree. "I mean, if the nachzehrer was a big one… even if Elletrache got eaten, he might still be alive. For another day or two while… while he's digested."

"What?" Sophia said, a hand to her mouth. "Is that true?"

"Could be," Richter said. "Some of the slayer texts have accounts of men being retrieved from the bellies of those beasts."

Gripping his ledger firm, Crockett stood upright and said, "I say we find that nachzehrer and get Elletrache back!"

"N-no," Thomas said. "The woods aren't safe! We should stay here!"

Richter stepped over to Eppo. The raiders around him put their hands to their weapons and their jewelry jangled in threatening tunes.

"Easy men," Eppo said. He nodded. "What you got to say, sellsword?"

"I can go into the woods," Richter said. "I'll see what happened. I can even lead some of your men with me, however you want it."

"There's no reason, Richter," Thomas said. "Why is no one listening to me? It's too dangerous!"

"Be calm, Thomas," Richter said. "Let us talk."

Eppo looked at Thomas, he looked back at his own men, and then he looked at Richter.

"Naw," Eppo said. He jerked his head. "Tie him."

The raiders came forward, chains in hand. Richter took a step back, but Ear-Manny grabbed him with great strength and pulled the captain forward, and into the hands of the rest of the gang he felt weightless as they dragged him away. Behind him, he heard his sellswords prepare themselves for battle.

"Tell your sellswords to stand down," Eppo said. "Tell them or they die!"

"Stand down!" Richter screamed. Water filled his boots. The raiders pulled him into the Trading Swords river and down the shore of it until they got to their ferry raft.

"Richter!" Hobbs called.

"Stand down!" Richter screamed again.

The captain found himself briefly swung upside down as the raiders lofted him onto the raft. Huge, thick chains rankled across the wood of it and they cinched to a bracelet and clasped around his arms, the other end of the tethering going to the raft itself.

"Eppo, listen to me," Richter said. "The savages will kill me."

"Probably, but like I said, we're out of time."

"You have all the time in the world! Just wait!"

"Mmm, no."

"Before he goes," Ear-Manny said, his bald, pale face staring down at Richter. "Can I take his ear and nose?"

"Maybe…" Eppo said, smiling. "But, ah, he's garish enough as is."

"Eppo, listen," Richter said. "You said it yourself, Egil and Hugo were your best fighters. Do you really think a jester, a servant, and a beast slayer could kill two hardnosed raiders?"

"Heh, nose," Ear-Manny said.

"Shush, Richter," Eppo said. "I'm a man of my word. You should take solace in the fact that your company will be allowed to leave. Albeit, without their gear and, of course, without their captain. Of course, you keep wriggling and talkin' to me and, ahohoy, I just might change my mind. So here is what we're going to do. We're going to—"

"Kill Richter."

Eppo paused. The voice came from behind and he snapped upon his raiders. "Who said that? Who farkin' said that?"

The men looked amongst themselves. "Hey, wasn't us, sir."

"Kill Richter."

"Oh really, wasn't one of you? I'm the one in charge here!" Eppo said.

"I'm the one who decides when we cross that line! Remember the last time you didn't listen to me? I collected teeth, don't make me do that again! It was like pulling – ech! The point is, we need this sellsword *alive*, got it?"

The raiders looked amongst themselves. "Genuinely, sir, it wasn't—"

"Kill Richter…"

This time, the voice arrived with company. Everyone turned and looked toward the road. A dozen naked men and women stood on the path, each holding a clay pot to their bellies, their eyes affixed to the fighters. Gaunt figures flared with bony ribs and over their shoulders were what appeared to be rope burns. Despite these maladies, their voices sang a song both melodic and dutiful: "Kill Richter. Killlll Richter. *Kill Richter*. Killllll…"

Eppo cocked his head. "Who the fuck are these people?"

"Look like villagers, sir," a raider said. He smirked. "Naked and out of their godsdamned minds!"

"Killlll… Richter."

The hair on Richter's arms bristled and he felt a chill down his back. Something about those two words was undeniably hollow, like hearing the last of an echo from a mere whisper. As the drained, lowly incantations neared, he looked into the trees.

"Eppo," he said. "We need to—"

Pushing Richer aside, Eppo strode toward the mob like a farmer shooing birds. "Stay back! This is our ferry and nothing's free!"

The mob slowly pushed through the wagons, skirting their wheels and blindly driving them aside with the weight of their bodies and the determination of their souls. Despite the obstacles, their eyes never broke from staring at Richter. In their hands, the clay pots stayed perfectly upright, clasped like holy idols, carried forth with seamless grace while their mouth sputtered desires for death.

"Killlll Richter. *Kill'im.*"

"Sonsabitches won't listen, huh?" Eppo said. He took up a bow, nocked, and aimed at the mob. "We are open for business, but that means we talk! You talk, you live! You take another step and you die!"

Naked and unafraid, the figures trudged forward.

"Maybe they ate some shrooms," one of the raiders said.

Richter gritted his teeth. "Eppo, you need to listen—"

"Shut yer farking trap, Wight," Eppo said. The man's fingers tensed, his lips pursed. He did not seem ready to strike down unarmed peoples and in that Richter found something endearing – something almost appreciably human buried behind all the stolen armor and pierced jewelry and general disguise of an otherwise murderous raider.

But the mob, still trudging forth, took the choice for him.

Eppo squinched his eyes and his shrewd tattoos stretched and his hanging jewelry jingled. "Ah, I say let the old gods sort this out in the next life," he said and loosed.

A sharp whistle, a crack, and a man dropped to his knees, an arrow sticking out of his eye socket. His arms swung out, one of them turning the clay pot over and spilling its contents in a splattering gush. Eppo and the raiders cheered and told the mob to go back from whence they came.

But Richter stood upright, his hand by instinct clutching his black hat as he stared at the pot's spilling liquid: its color a curious orange, glistening over strange chunks of additives. It was as he had suspected: Claire had the knowledge of elements that only elderly witches should. Worse...

"She's found us," the captain said under his breath.

"What's that you say, Wight?" Eppo said. "You don't like my shooting?"

"S-sir!" one of the raiders called out. "L-look!"

Eppo turned. The mob continued to advance, unwavering, and the shot man's mouth opened as he spoke: *"Killllll Richter!"*, each syllable bursting blood upon his chin.

Richter grabbed Eppo. "Don't let them get close!"

"Hey hey!" Eppo shouted back. "Get your hands off me, sellsword!"

"Eppo, they are *hexed!*"

The ensorcelled mob jolted to Richter's voice, their backs crackling as the spines whipped to his sounds, their teeth flared, legs bowed. In their hands, the clay pots rattled in the grip of fervorous fingers, and the orange liquid foamed to their tops and leaked over the edges in soft sizzles.

"Oh no," Richter said, his hands falling from Eppo.

"Kill Richter! *KILL 'IM! Kill'im kill'im kill'im!*"

Her words poured through the ensorcelled mob, her own excitement lively upon their lips. And with her in their ears, they came forth in a sudden sprint, their mouths stretched back in wild moaning, their eyes white and wide. Clambering forth in a naked mass, their legs swung stiffly, knees locked, shins and legs crooked, wheeling through the sand and mud in an inhuman gait, the *tft-tft-tft* of their feet kicking through sand filling the otherwise unnatural silence of their assault.

"What in the old gods," one of the raiders said, taking a step back.

Richter turned and pulled at the chains holding him to the raft. The links ripped across the wood in an ear-ringing zip until they snapped to a stop, almost flipping the captain off his legs. He turned again to Eppo.

"Cut me loose!" he yelled. "Eppo, unchain me!"

"Sir," one of the raiders said. "Sir, the naked folk…"

"Get in formation!" Eppo screamed at them. "Front, center, go, now! If they want a fight, we'll give it to them!"

Richter stared at the mob, their clay pots held firm in their screaming assault. He yelled at the raider's leader. "Eppo! Do not let them get close!"

"Motherfark!" Eppo screamed. He turned around. "If you say one more word, Richter, I'm going to cut you out of those chains by your wrists!"

When the raider turned back around, Richter planted a boot against the raft and pulled. The chain ripped tight against his wrist, and every inch the metal cut down the skin purpled and blood slid free in trickling lines.

"Richter!" Hobbs screamed.

"Captain!" Dahlgren yelled. He took a step forward, unsheathing his sword at the same time.

"Whoa whoa whoa!" Eppo said, pointing at the old man. "No, absolutely not! You all stay right there! You take one step closer and I'll kill—"

"Kill Richter!" the shrill words fell over the shore like cold raindrops: "*Kill'im kill'im kill'im!*"

"You, you, you, and you! And you, too!" Eppo yelled at his own men. He pointed toward Richter's company. "Head them off! The rest of you stay and slaughter these naked farks!"

Eppo's raiders split in half with one group heading off Richter's company and the other maintaining a defensive stance against the ensorcelled mob.

Watching the heavily armed and armored raiders move toward his company, Richter looked again to his sellswords. Dahlgren met his eyes. The old man's hand clenched the handle of his weapon. But the captain slowly shook his head. Dahlgren's grip tensed, then loosened, and he slowly put his sword back into its sheath and he held his hands out to the raiders like some criminal cornered down an alley. The raiders, following Eppo's own orders, lowered their weapons in half-stances, all the while everyone turned and glanced back at the coming mob.

"Eppo, listen to me," Richter said. "Do not let them get close! You cannot let them get close!"

"Your wrists, Richter," Eppo said, menacingly. "Best shut yer trap!"

Richter grimaced. "You don't understand."

The ensorcelled mob shouted again, two words so rhythmic and staccato they seemed as though beaten out of their chests with drums – *kill* – *Richter* – and they came forth in a warring march, the clay pots held over their heads like mothers trying to save their infants from a flood – *kill* – *Richter* – and in this purpose they met Eppo's men, and the raiders obliged their naked bodies with the certainties of steel, swords and spears and axes, and their thundering voices chilled – *killergh* – blades upon flesh, axes upon necks, spears into bellies – *Richterghhh* – but as the raiders slew the mob down, Richter saw the hexed men and women lift those pots of dark materials and smash them upon their killers, and glistening orange liquid coated the unsuspecting and the ensorcelled leaned forth, hanging on with both arms like lovers to departing spouses, and with dying breaths they transmuted their orders, whispering the voice of that which commanded a designed demise, and hearing their words the raiders slowly turned and looked at Richter, their own eyes now as wide as those they had just slain, and their mouths stretching far back, their tongues now levying the words given to them:

KILL.

RICHTER.

Eppo walked forward, pumping his fist. "Good work, men, good work!"

But the sopping, orange-caked raiders pushed their leader aside. He yelled out and demanded the man who did it be grabbed and punished only for another raider to push him to the ground and step over him. Hearing Eppo's yelling, the raiders holding Richter's company at bay turned around. They looked at their old friends and brothers in battle, and then glanced at Eppo. Murmuring confusion followed their discord at the sight.

"Wh-what's going on, Eppo?" one called out.

Eppo got to his feet and chased after his raiders. "What is this, a farkin' mutiny? What're you doing? Get back in line! I said get back in line! Just cause you kill some naked sods doesn't make you farkin' high and mighty!"

As a group, the ensorcelled raiders stomped across the shore and into the shore's waters and around the ferry raft to which Richter was tethered. With one final try, the captain yanked at the chains holding him, gritting his teeth as his arms poled out, the cuffs hooking into his wrists, blood flowing free. He felt the chain briefly jerk back, and when he looked up the bald head of Ear-Manny gleamed the sun's light as he leapt off the raft, soaring through the air, arms wide, ears and nose necklaces jangling, a dead stare in his eyes. They collided and together sank into the Trading Swords river and five more raiders followed like hungered pups upon one teat, and they frenzied themselves in the waters, there in whispered rapture taken by her designs, taken by her intentions, to do one thing and one thing only…

~~~

"Kill. Richter."

The syllables danced off Claire's tongue.

"Kill. Richter. Kill him. Kill him. Kill him."

She cocked her head, turning her ear to the distant reports. The sound of a man being beaten and drowned. The sound of his mouth pursed, grunting and grimacing as he thrashed, fighting to not let the water in. The sound of her own words spoken back by his killers, echoing her command: kill Richter, they said, and kill Richter they would.

"Beautiful," she said, wiping a tear from an eye. "Absolutely beautiful."

Immerwahr watched her. The weight of Kantorek's sword had never been heavier in his hands. There, a brigand's blade. What poor innocents had the blade profaned? Could he redeem it? If he brought it down upon the girl, would that do it? Would it redeem Kantorek himself, for it were his own actions, evil and cruel as they were, which brought his weapon here and now, glinting hopelessly before a far greater evil, a worldly crisis in the form of a little girl with far too much knowledge and far too little experience.

The monk gripped the handle.

Claire turned. "If you seek blood, holy man, then you need only put your head in that cauldron, and you shall indeed find the future you envision."

Immerwahr softened his grip. The sword's point pattered into the ground. He nodded as if his intentions were mundane instead of macabre.

"Do not worry yourself, holy man," Claire said. She nodded toward the caravan guard. "Richter's demise will be, all in all, quite peaceful. You see…" she smiled, and the crusts of yellow upon her own pate crinkled in their dryness. "I can hear it already. I can hear the writhing and gargling of the man. I can hear the choking breath of the one they call the Wight." Tears formed in her eyes and she shook her head with uncorked glee. "Oh, how I wish I could share this sound! Oh, how I wish I could share it with you, holy man, oh how I wish you could hear! Hear the death of Richter von Dagentear!"

~~~

Hobbs screamed, "By the old gods they're going to kill him!"

Just a small jaunt away, the shore of the river splashed and foamed, a half-dozen black clad bodies rising and falling into it, and the captain's boots and hands coming up and disappearing all the same. The chain attached to Richter's ankle rattled and clinked as it ripped back and forth across the raft and the raft itself dipped into the waters as though a fisherman had caught a line on something far bigger than his craft could account for.

Eppo's raiders, those who had not been hexed, stood before the sellswords, both parties with their weapons out, threatening each other as tremendous uncertainty about what was happening gripped them. Richter's sellswords pleaded for them to act, but the raiders seemed sure this was only a ploy, some sort of trick to even the playing field so the sellswords might win a fight they, just a few minutes ago, had no chance in.

As confused as anyone, Eppo stood on the shoreline screaming at his ensorcelled raiders as they plunged Richter under the river. "We need that man alive! What are you doing! Cease, you fools, cease!"

"Oh Dahlgren," Sophia said, her hand to her mouth as she watched Richter's body flail in the waters. "It's horrible!"

Quinn pursed his lips. He looked at the Trading Swords river. The waters lapped limply at its shore, but the currents beyond that streamed with effortless might, a quiet torrent just beneath the surface. Hardening his nerves, the thief stepped wide of the raiders and into the river.

"What are you doing Quinn?" Crockett said.

As the raiders and sellswords alike eyed him, Quinn tore off his gear and stormed into the waters. The raiders stared, not sure what to do as the thief maneuvered around them and started up the shore, his legs stumbling in and out of the depths, each step sinking him further than the last.

"To hells with this shit!" Quinn screamed.

Crockett stumbled after him. "Quinn you can't swim!"

"Gotta be easier than watching this shit!" Quinn screamed back, arriving just outside the raiders drowning Richter. Behind him, the sellswords started threatening the raiders and the raiders the sellswords. The confusion bearing down on all was about to explode.

The thief looked down, the water at his waist, the current lifting his legs now and again, threatening him with elements he knew not how to contend with. He gritted his teeth. "Limpdick motherfarkers, I gotta do everything."

"Quinn!" Crockett shouted. "Don't! You'll drown!"

"Fark off, Cricket," Quinn said, and there the thief took a sip of breath, gritted his teeth, and dove in.

~~~

"You're beet red, my boy. Whatcha doin'?"

"I was holding my breath!"

"Why?"

"So I can feel the fire in my lungs."

Richter's father stared at his boy, and the boy at his father. The man's face washed back and forth, white and grey, dissolved into spirals, full of motion but absent of purpose, drifting like the foam of ale yet to settle, as stirred by its very pouring as the man's face was by the drawing of its weathered memory. It had been many years since Richter had seen his father's face, and by now he was certainly older than his father ever was, and in this way he even allowed his imagination to fall short on purpose. It would be simple to pretend to know what his father looked like, some mirrored visage of his own self, but that couldn't be. A reimagination of his father could only be an imagination of the disappointment therein. Life had become far too real since he had last seen the man and moments of fancy so far and few between he had not the practice to see the man who had brought him into this world, because that man had existed in a time when Richter knew so little and the man was but a totem of all things seen and unseen and to be seen. But the man he spoke to now was his father all the same. And for all the lusterless swirling where a face should be, there came the slight glow of warmth, and the familiarity, and the comfort therein.

"If you want to hold your breath, do it somewhere useful."

Richter looked up. "Somewhere useful?"

"Aye. For example, holding your breath under the water," his father said, gesturing to a river that Richter hadn't even noticed before. The man drew up a trotline wriggling and flailing with trout, their line of bodies glistening, heads crystalline, like they were ornaments of some unseen civilization. Smiling, his father said, "I bet these can hold their breath longer than you."

"Nobody can!" Richter exclaimed, though his voice was not of his own, and nothing of volume came out of him, only that, as in all dreams, things were said and understood simultaneously, sounds absorbed, ideas inherent.

He took a great breath and then plunged his head into a rush of water. Coldness. Brisk and smooth. Glimmers of fish. Not scared of him, just idle and staring. Around them, the grey rocks with green mossy domes which roped downriver like hair in the wind. He could hear the murmurs from the surface above. The shouts of excitement, of support. And then he felt the fire in his chest. It swelled. More pressure than heat, and then heat itself, and then both. He gargled. He took a breath by instinct, gulping it in desperation. Water filled his lungs and it seemed knives unfurled inside of them. He drew out of the river and fell back onto the shore and turned to his side and spat and spewed and gasped for breath in between.

"You're alright," his father said. "You're alright."

"My chest hurts…" Richter said. "It's burning."

"I know. And you have to let it burn." His father's shadow stood over him. "The lungs will demand to be quenched but, when you are surrounded by nothing but water, you can't let it in. You let that fire die, you die. You set that fire to burn as long as you can. You set it to burn even if you have to stick your hands into the ashes and embers to keep it going, do you understand?" His father lowered his hand. "Because if you burn it long enough, well, someone will see the smoke. You just have to trust that someone will see it, understand?"

"I understand," Richter said.

~~~

A dozen hands formed a fleshen anchor upon Richter's chest, their weight the weight of the hexe's authority. The black clad figures looming over him seemed more shimmer than human, the glint of sunlight which strobed across the river's surface eliding the natures of that which was occurring, and he seemed a part of two worlds, the thrashing of his limbs trying to break free, and the unsounded hollow of the river into which he peacefully sank.

By now, the fire had arrived. Iron claws gripped his chest, caging his lungs in a searing pain that crackled and spiderwebbed mercilessly, a hearth overrun with flames desperate to be quenched. His body demanded breath, and his mind bounded between the certainty that if he took it, he would drown, and the uncertainty, the growing delirium, that perhaps he could take a little sip of breath, just a little, and for him the world would break its rules and allow him this respite for all natural order.

Burn as long as you can.

He thought of his father. He thought of a river. He thought of jagged mountains and white snowcaps. He thought of trees as far as one could see. He thought of Dagentear. He tried to make free with the past, to come to it and mold it and turn it into what it should have been, direct it to the majesty it never found, but as the hands knuckled him into the river these thoughts slipped him by. Emptiness replaced them. The past disappeared precisely as the past does and was meant to do. He did not think of his life at all. He began to think of that which would come, the existence of a new world in which he would be absent, and in this necessary exclusion he saw a boy standing alone. He saw Hobbs. Hobbs cast out into a wilderness. A white face in a sea of black. Where would he go? Where would he be? What would Richter miss?

I'm terribly sorry, Hobbs. I'm terribly sorry I won't be there for you.

[486]

The words left him, and the water came in, and the fire died.

~ ~ ~

"Richter!"

The captain opened his eyes.

Shimmers gave way to a frothing white which burst into the light of day and the blue sky above and the grey clouds and the green treetops and the sounds of the river gushing as he left their drowning torrents and the splashing of men fighting one another to put him back under.

Richter blinked and saw the hexed raiders being struck with blades and hacked with hatchets, and he felt the weight of the hands, pound by pound, release from his chest, and he felt the air upon his lips and he drew his mouth open and spewed water from his lungs and he took a great breath which filled him like ice, and the standing raiders tried to shove him down once more, but his back refused to descend. Something earthen and true had slid behind him and refused to budge, keeping his head just above water.

Bleeding all over, Ear-Manny the towering and bald raider blanky stared down, the last of the hexed lot, his massive, yellowed hands plunging into Richter's chest over and over, his bald head glistening with the stew of the hexe's mixtures, his necklace of ears and noses jumbling and dimpling the waters, and Richter watched as an axe sank into the man's shoulder, and a knife stabbed into his side, and finally Dahlgren's sword sliced through the raider's neck and a red sheet fanned over Richter as the raider's eyes rolled back and he stiffly fell into the water like a tree cut from its stump.

Freed of all weight, Richter swung upward. The company met him, Dahlgren, Crockett, Thomas, Sophia, Berthold, the butcher, and Hobbs, their hands collecting their captain, keeping him upright as he haggardly drew breath. Six black clad bodies floated around the group, each corpse gently skirting into the river's mainstream where the current took them away. Richter stared at them until his eyes went wide. He broke free of the company's hands and dashed through the waters and grabbed a drifting body before the river could claim it. He hurriedly turned it over. There, a man, blue in the face, eyes closed, hands fenced out at his sides, water spilling from his nose and mouth. It was he who was the earthen matter, the rock at Richter's back, that which pushed him out of the river and into the air, the one who gave him life when the ensorcelled wished to see it extinguished. The very man which stole from death itself: Quinn, the thief.

~~~

"Kill...Richter... Kill..." Claire's voice died. She cocked her head. "Wait, something is wrong."

Immerwahr glanced at the girl and, seeing her distressed, he looked at those she had hexed. Ten caravan guards stood with their backs upright and unmoving. The witch's sudden loss of confidence did not spread amongst her followers in the way it would have from an ordinary commander. Whatever realm the men had fallen into, they were fully inculcated.

"Something is terribly wrong," the girl said, her hands clenching and unclenching. "I can hear him. Why can I hear him? Why is he full of life? Holy man! Why can I hear the Wight? Holy man!"

"Uhh, I don't... I don't know..."

"Give me an answer!" she screamed, her voice crackling through the woods. "Why can I hear him?"

The caravan guards blinked.

Immerwahr stammered. "B-b-because he's alive?"

"Alive!" she screamed back. "Alive you say!"

Claire huffed. Usually, the sight of a little girl red in the face with her fists clenched earned little more than a roll of the eyes and, if the day was of friendly make, a suggestion that she calm down for there was time yet to be upset over grander and far more important things. But most little girls did not throw tantrums while commanding men absent of their minds, nor keeping an invisible hand to a belluine leash, seeing great beasts bandy back and forth to given tasks like barnyard animals.

As she roiled and shook with rage, Immerwahr again thought to strike her down. He saw himself nodding, agreeing with her that she should be mad, and then in a moment, turning the sword against her, slicing – or was it chopping? – as hard as he could. He'd never seen such damage in the moment. Only see the effects of battle in the aftermath. To see it live, nevermind to wield the hand of wrath itself, would be wildly different. Maybe he would even enjoy it? Steel against a little girl's skull. Split her from pate to teeth. He knew he could do it. Aim right and then just close his eyes. The weight of his body behind the swing would take care of the rest.

"Holy man."

Immerwahr blinked. He looked over.

Claire sat on the makeshift wagon, its crooked wheels still burdened by the priory bell. Waldo sat in its mire, his arms over the lip, his head down as bubbles frothed and burst around him and a terrible steam lifted and wafted.

"Holy man," Claire said again. Beside her nobody remained. The lindwurm beast had gone. The caravan guards were gone. "I tried the peaceful option," she said. "For the second time, I have tried the most peaceful route. For the second time, I have tried a route which you no doubt placed in my mind in a manner of, what is now obviously, subterfuge."

"I-I'd do no such thing," Immerwahr said. "My suggestions are only suggestions."

"You've hexed me with your old gods and your desperations and your sweat and your filth, every word darkened with ulterior motives. Even the sweetest suggestions were intended to undermine me, were they not?"

"N-no, of course not. I only speak from the heart."

"That is the problem then," Claire said, her lip curling. "Your little heart."

The monk looked up the road. He could see the spoors of the scaled beast breaking into the forest, deep trenches of footprints and the scarred bark of trees which it had merely brushed past. On the road itself, he saw the military-esque march of the caravan guard, heading out with certainties and purposes beyond his knowing. It seemed the girl was sending a full assault now. One that would not only kill Richter, but everyone around him.

"Did you really think I would allow you such freedom?" Claire said.

The girl struck the side of the bell. Grounded as it was, it made no noise at all, but Waldo the boy cocked his head back, his mouth to the skies, hollowed and holed, and he muttered: "*Gong.*" And when she hit it again, he repeated: "*Gong. Gong... Gong...*"

"Come now, holy man," Claire said. "Kneel before a proper holy totem."

Immerwahr refused, but in the gleam and gloss of the priory bell, an image of himself did move. He narrowed his eyes at it, and then looked down to see his legs moving on their own. He shouted that he would no longer follow her lead, and he shouted that he would kill her, and he moved his arms to swing the sword and strike her down, but no such action came. And as he walked on legs not of his own drive, not of his own corded muscle, he saw the selfsame shadowy image draw into detail upon the priory bell, and in his reflection he saw himself, sword in hand with a two-hand bidengrip, steel upright with authoritative guardianship, and as he looked at himself in that black mirror, he saw a wash of yellow on his forehead. He screamed. He screamed as hard as he could, and the cauldron bubbled and frothed in gentle response, and the girl chuckled and not a bird lifted from the trees, not an echo came back to tell him he screamed at all, for the selfsame shadow in the priory bell did nothing but stare, and did nothing but exactly what the witch commanded it to do, for Immerwahr the monk was no longer himself, he was but the shadow of his own mind.

Claire tapped the side of the bell.

"*Gong... gong... gong...*"

Immerwahr kneeled.

The girl smiled.

"Beautiful holy man," she said. "Let us pray."

Chapter 38. Kings of the Wilds.

SOPHIA ROLLED Quinn onto his side as he spewed. A film of watery vomit crackled across the shoreline's sands. Emptied, he gave a bubbling wheeze as his body trembled to sudden chills. The homesteader patted him on the back.

"Is he dying?" Richter said.

"I don't know," she said. "He had a lot of water in his lungs but it's out."

Dahlgren spat. "We sure he's really hurt? The last time he was like this…"

Quinn vomited again. A bit of blood swirled in the froth.

"Hey, yeah," Thomas said. "That looks real enough to me."

Richter put a boot to the thief's hip. He jostled the man. "I don't know if you're lying to us again, Quinn, but there's no lying in what you did. For that, you have my thanks."

The thief wheezed again.

"Sumbitch," Dahlgren said, shaking his head. "Those raiders had you completely surrounded, captain, and he went and did that. We couldn't even get through so he just… dove into the waters and snuck between them and went under and next thing I know he's lifting you up. Damn thief didn't even know how to fucking swim and he goes and does that."

"In a sense," Crockett said. "He *did* drown."

The paymaster crouched before the thief with his ledger and an ink-dabbed quill pen. He leaned forward and whispered to the thief and he wrote something down and he showed it to the man, and the thief wheezed again in return. The paymaster smiled and nodded and he whispered again and patted the man on the shoulder.

"Put him in some bushes," Richter said. "Somewhere so he's safe and out of sight."

"You think there's more to come?" Thomas said, his eyes wide.

"Aye." Richter looked at Eppo down the shoreline, the raider's fighters staggering around him. "There's more to come and everyone is going to need to be on the same page if we are to face it."

~~~

"A witch!" Eppo screamed. "You're telling me a witch's uh uh, uh what, forspoken bullshit tricked my men? Some mystical bullshittery, that right?"

Richter nodded. "Something like that, aye."

Eppo's lip curled, his jewelry glinting alongside his incredulity. When his brow furrowed, his hooking tattoos bunched and crunched, his folded skin giving them serrated edges.

"You have to understand," Richter said. "This is—"

"I thought your witch hunting days were behind you, sir Wight!" Eppo said, his furrowed face suddenly stretched as it exploded in outburst. "Gods, why in the hells did I even bother to let you in? The farkin' myths are true! Every single one of them. You're nothing but a portend of terribles!"

Richter raised an eyebrow. Despite Eppo's consternations, the raider wasn't exactly disagreeing with the notions that a witch was about to descend upon them with bestial fury and that whatever had just attacked them was only the start. Compared to a long list of peasants, merchants, burgomeisters, and lords, the raider's rather sudden understanding was almost a shock.

"Bahh, fark it all," Eppo said, his face relaxing. "I know it's true. My men do, too. Something was off about that whole goatfuck right from the jump."

One of his raiders spat. "This ain't our first dogfall wit'a'witch, neither."

Eppo nodded. "Ayyup, ayyup. We ran into one out near Weissenhaven. Took two of my men under her wing. When we tried to get them back, they fought on her behalf. They said she was the most wonderful thing they'd ever seen, but the witch was covered in puss and boils and looked like she was two-hundred years old! She cackled while we killed our own men, and when we were done with it, she was gone. I don't even know what she had to gain from that. She said nothing to us. Just laughed and laughed."

"I am sorry you had to experience such a thing," Richter said. "But we need to focus on the present."

"Alright," Eppo said, looking around. "I've... three men left."

"Four," said Hugo, ostensibly the last of his kind.

"Right, uh, that Hugo, too," Eppo said, though it was clear this particular Hugo was the least valuable and therefore least memorable of the three known Hugos. "So five including Hugo and myself. You got whatever pile of trash you call a mercenary company, not to mention a woman, a kid, and a man retching river water. There are barbarians at our back and a witch to our front. So... I think me and my men are just going to hop on one of those rafts, hightail it out of here, and see what comes of what."

"Yeah fuck this bitch business," one of the raiders said. "Let's sail."

The rest of the raiders nodded in agreement.

"You mean travel downstream," Richter said.

"Yeah, that's right."

"Not sure if you have forgotten, but there is a war downstream," Richter said. "You ever notice Sommerwein's boats aren't coming this way anymore? Lowlanders scout the western shores the nearer you get to Marsburg. They'll think you're smugglers and shoot you dead."

"Oh ho ho ho, Richter, sir Wight," Eppo said, shaking a finger. "Don't think I don't know about the other ferry town south of here! We'll just land there and make free with those peasants."

"We just left there," Dahlgren said. "Last we saw, the township was talking about organizing a militia. They're not exactly proper fighters, but I wager they outnumber you five to one."

Both the sellswords and the raiders had enough men to ruin one another, so the threat from the raiders themselves had dwindled with their dead. To this, Richter was happy. Unfortunately, he still needed the men to help with whatever Claire had in store.

So, Richter piled on some lies: "In fact, the ferry had chainmail and fine steel and wouldn't trade any of it to us. Considering they just had a problem with a local bandit gang, I don't think they'll be very warm to your arrival."

Eppo snorted. He said, "Then we'll just go downriver a bit and hop out in the half-a-ways. Plan something from there. Maybe hit the roads."

"Sir," one of the raiders said. "The laager is just east of here. Even if we cut in, our only options are north and south, the laager or the ferry…"

Eppo slapped the man's hand away. "I got my sense of direction, godsdammit! Don't need you telling me shit!"

But another raider piped in: "Even if we go down the river a half-a-ways won't we run into what all killed Egil and Hugo?"

"I'm alive," Hugo said.

"The other Hugo, dipshit."

"Oh, that Hugo."

Eppo sighed. "Hugo, whenever we talk about an important Hugo, we ain't farking talking about you."

The third Hugo pursed his lips. "Aye, sir."

"I have another plan if you're willing to work with me," Richter said. He looked from raider to raider and then to his own sellswords. "Maybe something that will help everyone."

"Let me guess," Eppo said. "I just need to trust you."

"Aye."

"Ahohoy…" Eppo said, but despite his incredulity he rolled his eyes and threw up his hands. "Alright then, let's hear it."

Richter said, "The plan is simple. Fortify the shoreline and prepare for whatever the witch is throwing at us next. She is not a general. She does not have military experience. Everything she knows comes out of a book or from the spoken word of a lost coven. While she is dangerous, everything she does is still a first for her in some sense. She'll make mistakes." Richter nodded toward the dead bodies around them. "She already has, right? We now know she's coming, so let her forces break themselves on our defenses."

"I'm supposing there's another element to this plan," Eppo said. "One which involves you going else-a-wheres."

Richter nodded.

"Alright, sir Wight, what is it you plan to do?"

Hobbs said, "He'll find the witch and kill her."

"Boy," Richter said, whipping his head around.

Shrinking back, Hobbs clutched his wooden sword and camel. "Sorry."

"So you'll go out alone," Eppo said. "And find her and kill her?"

"Not exactly." The captain looked at Berthold. "I'm going to take my fastest sellsword with me. We'll cut through the trees and flank her." He nodded toward the tree line where Elletrache and the rest had gone in search of the dead savage boy. "Just as well, I may yet still find our lost men. But time is of the essence. Either we start in on this now, or you all depart and go somewhere and die another day while we deal with it alone. Hells, maybe we all just hop on those rafts and we cross the river and *all* go talk to the barbarians. There are no great options here, so choose."

Eppo pursed his lips. "Just give me a moment, alright?"

The raider stared at the ground, and then at the shore. Dancing off their ropes, the ferry's little rafts looked like brown seashells caught in a trotline.

Water lapped up through the wooden slats, washing through the rafts' centers and foaming over their sides. Eppo stared at them like a man who had come to the deserts in search of treasures, and here he had but a dried out oasis, naught all but emptied hands to stare at while he took a consolatory shade.

"It'll work," Richter said. "You just have to trust me, just as I trust you and your men, and just as I trust my company."

"Alright," Eppo said. "We'll take your plan."

Richter turned and hit Berthold in the chest. "Grab your gear, Berthold." As the miller nervously stepped back and picked up his kit, Richter pointed at the makeshift wagons near the front of the ferry. "Pull your fortifications back to the shoreline. You need to shorten the angles necessary to cover. My company's wagon can join to widen it. I suggest tearing the tarps off and layering them between the panels. Use what you have to keep armoring it. Pots, pans, anything, understand? But walling against the shoreline is our best move here. Whatever comes, make them work extra for it."

"And do I get to command your men?" Eppo said.

"You command yours as you wish, but Dahlgren here will command the company in my place."

"Aye," Dahlgren said, strapping his arm into his shield "I'd be most honored, captain."

Eppo said, "What if this witch of yours has an army behind her? If she can forspoke that many peasants, and even get my men on her side with little more than some wash and filth from pots, what else might she have in store?"

Richter looked around. He stepped closer to Eppo and gently pushed him back a few steps.

"Uh oh," the raider said.

Quietly, Richter secreted his belief: "The witch may have a lindwurm."

"Excuse me?"

"Please," Richter said. "Keep your voice down."

"You're telling me a witch has a farking lizard and you want me to keep my voice down?"

"Listen, alright? Your men and mine can kill it, but you have to maintain composure. The beast isn't fully grown. It's a youngling about half the size of its mother."

"Its mother? Where is its mother?"

"Remember that beast slayer you sent out with your men?"

"Yeah."

"He's wearing her."

"Oh shit."

"You understand why I'm telling you all this in quiet, right?"

Eppo turned and spat. He leaned down and picked up a bardiche and nodded. "Yeah I know. Better to face fear on instinct than to let it sit in your belly and strengthen itself over time."

"Good," Richter said, honestly impressed by the raider's quick analysis. "Very good."

Although Richter had never been on the high seas, he knew sailors combating storms might fall within the same purview of soldiers fighting battles on land. If a storm was unavoidable, sometimes it was simply best to let the tempest come and have men face it with their instinctive might and main. The other option – to alert them to what was inevitable – only caused them to dwell on it and, as time drew out longer and longer until that inevitability came, it would unease them until the time of reckoning arrived, and by then they'd be so relieved to have escaped the inexorable weight that they'd be happy just to die if only to have it over with. It was a sort of destructive mentality that leaders needed to safeguard against, a choice wedged somewhere between tactical foreknowledge and total ignorance.

"Well, sir Wight," Eppo said. "Got anything else left to your plans? Cause our backs are still to the wall here."

Richter said, "Do you know about Fort Firebag?"

"Even a far northerner like me has heard of that one," Eppo said.

"Alright." The captain nodded at the floating rafts. "That's your Fort Firebag. If push comes to shove, you hop on those and cut yourself loose and take your chances downstream."

"Your version of Fort Firebag is to tie slabs of wood together and have a bunch of men cling to 'em like rats? Didn't the fort go out with a bang?"

"Aye." Richter smiled sheepishly. "And who says this one won't?"

"Fucking hells." Eppo threw a hand out. "Alright then, get whatever you need, sir Wight, and get your arse going." He let out a sharp whistle and started directing with his hands. "Alright men! We're pulling those wagons back! Hop to it! Line 'em here and line 'em here!"

As the raiders went to work, Eppo looked back at the captain. "Whatcha waitin' for?"

Richter shook his head. "Nothing. Just want you to know that if I come back here and you've betrayed me or done something to my company, I will hunt you down to the ends of this earth. There isn't a dark corner or shadowed land I don't know of. I will find you, understand?"

Eppo reeled back with a wily grin, his jewelry winking and tattoos scrunching. He said, "Ohh, sir Wight, I hear ya there! I hear ya. I also don't doubt the potency of the threat so I'll match yer offer!" He tilted his bardiche toward the rafts. "If push comes to shove and I gotta get on a farking dingy to survive, it's yer head I'mma be having, understand?" His fingers danced in the air like creeping spiders. "I don't know all the scary bits of this world, but I have friends in many places, and I have favors owed, and I have monies hidden. I'll find a way to find ya, do *you* understand?"

"Aye," Richter said with a nod. "Sounds like we have a deal then."

"Wanna shake hands on it?"

"No."

"Good." Eppo turned around. "Ahohoy, hurry it up, men! We need those wagons pulled back here yesterday, chop chop!"

Richter girded Adelbrecht's sword to his hip, tightening the leather straps with a sturdy yank, and then he drew up a crossbow and yoked it over his shoulders. He picked through the raiders' gear and took a pair of forearm gauntlets made of leather and studded iron. Solid armor, but still light enough to not detract from his speed. Geared up, he walked by Crockett who said nothing but nodded and wrote in his ledger. He passed by Dahlgren and gave him some words of encouragement. By the time he met the tree line, Hobbs was standing there, wooden sword in one hand, wooden camel in the other.

"Will I see you again?" Hobbs said.

"Aye."

"But see me again in *this* life, right?"

"Of course, Hobbs." Richter smiled. "I'm not about to cut you loose on this world yet, boy."

~~~

"He had something. He knew. He had something and he knew. Of course he knew. Of course he knew. The Wight. The damned Wight! Even a piddling hexenjäger would know, but him? He'd... ahhh..." Claire paced back and forth.

The surrounding forest scratched and clattered as light winds swept through, breezes that couldn't even hope to mask her mutterings. "But all the knowledge in the world won't save him now. To hells with the holy man's apprehensions! Ahhh, to the hells, to the hells..."

She paused.

She looked into the trees. Trees and trees. As far as the eye could see. Branches tottered and lowered and twisted. Imaginative little things. West and east ran the road. Dirt and mud. Windrows where her wagon had trod. Beside the path, more trees. Shadows cast. Shadows swaying. Leaves now and again sputtering by. Free and wistful. The hexe's eyes widened. The corners crackled. The brow lifted. No hint of obscuration. Nothing that might fade the future she saw for herself.

"By the old gods," Claire said. "He is going to kill me."

The monk rocked back and forth with his sword between his legs, the blade clacking between boots in steady, perfect pendulum. She strode past him and hauled herself up on the wagon. What had once been a steady boil had since quelled into a quiet bubbling. The little merchant boy Waldo sat in the mire, his face slaked in dripping orange, his arms cast out over the lip of the cauldron to hold himself up. He looked at her.

Claire held up a pot and dipped it in and smelled it. She sighed. She stared at the boy, his eyes having never left hers. She put her hand to his shoulders and rubbed them and smiled. He smiled back. Tracks of tears were upon his cheeks, but in the moment nothing more could come. She moved her hand down his arm and unto his hand and slowly pried his fingers off the iron. His arm fell into the mire and half his body went with it, like a man falling off a cliff in a half-swing. He looked at her again, his eyes wider, but in a gentle, curious sense, as though he had just asked a question that could only possibly have the most delightful of answers.

"I have to make more," Claire said. "It has to be better than him."

She rode her hand down his other arm. She stopped her fingers upon his. The boy smiled. She smiled. She lifted his fingers. He sank. He sank so slowly. His eyes never leaving hers. So slowly. She looked away. The boy made a noise. When she looked back it was only the top of his head, an island of hair skirting the surface, and then he was gone.

"Holy man," Claire said.

Immerwahr's sword stilled. He turned around and walked to her. She pointed at the cauldron and whispered. The monk nodded. He stepped up onto the wagon and stood beside the cauldron. He lifted the sword and stabbed it into the mire and started stirring. In moments, the steel of the blade would catch, like a fishing rod upon unseen moss, and the monk would grit his teeth and jerk it free, and then he'd stir again.

"Stir it faster."

The holy man's sword caught on something in the mire again and he raised his weapon and pounded it down like someone mulching grain. He staked and twisted and staked again. A certain darkness came to the mire's color and Claire hurriedly went to her reserve of herbs and threw more in and she screamed at the monk to stir faster.

"Faster! Faster!"

A strong wind blew. The surface of the mire tilted. Shadows enveloped them. All around, the leaves and branches hissed and clattered. Such a place, the forest. Its endless towering trees. Its drooping woods that swayed, drawing figures out of one's head, dancing creatures at the rims of one's sanity. The cooing of its birds. The squelching of mud. The great belching of the ground. The great belching. The great belching. The great...

Claire turned around. She screamed. Pale, pustuled, black and grey and long-clawed, the nachzehrer stood between two tree trunks, its arms poled to each, its belly distended, its lining slashed agape. As it hunkered over like a drunk, its tentacular lips sickly drooped and wiggled. Blood spewed down from its gullet, and one slab of its four-parted mouth lifted as though an eyebrow to a question. When it stepped forth, its claw folded a tree, snapping its trunk in half and casting it down in a great thrash. The beast slowly slid into the mud of the road like a boy upon a winter sled. It skidded sideways before gently knocking into the wagon, the cauldron hissing as it spilled.

Retreating, Claire yelled for Immerwahr to leave the wagon. Still stirring the cauldron, Immerwahr's eyes were at even level with the nachzehrer, two little silhouettes of himself standing there in the reflection of the beast's white orbs. With a single nod, the monk took his stirring sword from the cauldron, turned, and jumped down. He landed and did not move another step, standing like a statue absently staring off while invaders pillaged its maker's village.

The nachzehrer stared at the monk and grunted, disinterested in the free meal. Instead, it moved its massive arms, the flesh flailing from them like drapes, and wrapped its claws around the cauldron and effortlessly lifted it off the wagon. The beast then sank back on its rump, tilted its head back, and drank. Sizzling and sloshing, the mire emptied into the beast's maw. A mangled Waldo slid down and caught onto one of the beast's lips and it simply picked the boy out like spinach from a tooth and threw him over his shoulder, the corpse crashing through distant trees never to be seen again.

"No no no no..." Claire said, stammering as she stepped back.

Blubbering and farting, the nachzehrer chugged and chugged. The cuts upon its chest expanded, the fat audibly expanding like tensed leather. Finished, it dropped the cauldron and the weight of its iron smashed the front of the wagon like a shot from a catapult. The beast groggily stared at the girl and monk, then it belched and turned and it sloshed its way back from whence it came, trees breaking and snapping in its path, all the while with each step it burped and groaned and rubbed its distended stomach.

Claire waited to make sure the beast was gone, then she hurried around the wagon and to the cauldron. As tears fell from her face, she gathered what pots she had and tried scooping what all could be saved of her brew.

"Holy man," she said. "Help me! Help me, holy man!"

Immerwahr turned. He looked at the girl. "Well hello there," he said with a sudden, unwieldly fresh smile. "It appears I have nothing to stir with my sword. How is it you would like me to help now?"

~~~

Three wagons bound together. One donkey standing outside their walls, chewing grass and staring back at the humans who had, seemingly, penned themselves while giving it the freedom. As one group, the raiders and sellswords numbered, at best, ten actual fighters. Eppo and his four remaining raiders, and then Dahlgren, Crockett, Thomas, Sophia, and the butcher. Hobbs sat beside a recovering Quinn. He put the carved camel before the thief and told him he could have it, but the man pawed it away mumbling. The boy cleaned him and told him he'd not hold it against him, that he'd keep the camel for him when he was good and ready to have it.

Dahlgren slung his arms over the top of a wagon, his eyes to the forest. Eppo joined him. They looked at one another.

"Alright I'll ask," Eppo said. "What happened to your hand?"

The old man lifted the nub. "Hedge knight took it."

"In a tournament?"

"No. Open field. I was trying to kill him."

"While he was taking a shit or something?"

"No, he was fully armored and ready to go."

Eppo clicked his tongue and shook his head. "That's an oops."

"Maybe. I was a bit drunk."

"Was, huh," Eppo said. "I saw you sneaking a sips just a minute ago."

"Chugged a carboy or two, actually." Dahlgren nodded. "I drink fast."

"Ahohoy… can you even see straight right now?"

"I can talk straight enough."

"Talking ain't what swings a sword," Eppo said. He shook his head and spat and shook his head again. "Fark me. A drunkard and... what even are these sellswords? Only one of you who looks dangerous is the fat man, and that's cause he might kill you just by falling on you."

Crockett looked up from his ledger, but by now he had weathered many an insult and took this one like a rock receiving a raindrop.

"We make do," Dahlgren said. "How about I ask you something."

"Yeah sure."

"You from Weissenhaven, right?"

Eppo smiled, his hook tattoo stretching. "Yessir, the one and only. Grew up in the alleys beside the port. I take it you're from Ruhmolt."

"Aye, I guarded the lordship there for a time," Dahlgren said. "But I haven't been north in some years. Life just..." he moved his arm, the missing hand still yet approximating great lengths of happenings in its physical curtness. "Well, life just swept me south, I suppose. I fought for the Landons for a while. Good pay. Retired early. Unretired early. Now I'm here."

"Now I'm here," Eppo repeated. "I always find myself saying that. So, old man, have you come to terms with me and my boys? A soldier from Ruhmolt certainly has had his fair share of run ins with raiders."

"Aye," Dahlgren said. "Killed many. Pillagers. Plunderers. Rapists."

"Eh, we're all killers, but we're also all not like that," Eppo said. "Well, Ear-Manny was. And Egil and Hugo, too. Three absolute maniacs at the end of the day, but good fighters are exceedingly rare to find, as I'm sure you're aware. You take what you can get. And men like Ear-Manny, Egil, Hugo... well, I allowed them their obsessions."

Dahlgren looked to the river. "And what about that Hugo?"

Eppo followed his stare. The last of the Hugos was on the rafts, tightening their tethers to the ferry line. "Ahohoy... that Hugo. Yeah. He's something else. Not a good fighter. Not much in the way of bravery. Sorta just follows orders. But he's alright, I suppose. You know. For a Hugo."

Looking up from his work, Hugo said, "You say something, sir?"

"No Hugo, you're doing good!"

"Thank you, sir! Almost finished."

They watched the daft raider bobble and wobble on the rafts, each step lurching them into the Trading Swords river. Noticing that he was being watched, Hugo straightened up and gave a little wave of his hand. Behind him, the water sank in a sudden crescent as though some god were sweeping a scythe through it, the clarity of the river wedging inward so starkly that fish flew between the gaps of open air, a great watery canyon bubbling and frothing as it poured toward a green center, and then Hugo was hurtling skyward and one of the rafts exploded into shrapnel and water gushed upon the shore and the lindwurm burst from the river and snaked onto its shore, head low, body undulating with uncorded strength, its massive arms wheeling and slamming as it crawled out with tremendous speed, and so quick was its appearance that a great tide of the Trading Swords river gushed upon the shore with it, unfurling like the arrival of an ocean's wave.

"Oh," Eppo said. "Aho… ho…"

Beached fish slid up into the grass and to Dahlgren's feet. He drew out his sword. The lindwurm planted both arms into the mudded shore and roared, massive teeth flared, tongue flailing, spit flying from its maw, the raiders and sellswords grimacing and holding onto their hats and helms. When it finished, its jaws snapped shut, clapping loud enough to produce an echo.

"Sophia!" Dahlgren shouted. "Get Quinn out of here!"

The homesteader jumped to her feet. With Hobbs, the two picked up Quinn and started dragging him into the tree line.

As Dahlgren looked back to the beast, a shouting raider sailed past him with a lumberjack's axe raised high. He chunked its blade into the lindwurm's shoulder. Green blood sprayed on the man and he spun away screaming as hissing smoke curled from his eyes. The beast growled and swept around and its tail coiled and then unfurled like the snap of a green whip and the black clad man went skipping across the river like a rock.

The other raiders backed off immediately.

"We don't stand a chance!" one yelled.

Corking its head side to side, the lindwurm's one eye tried to augur its newest wound, the beast growling at the pain as if rage could mend it.

Dahlgren stepped forward, a hand over his eyes. He grinned.

"Look at its eyes!" Dahlgren yelled. "It's half-blinded!"

The lindwurm's scales shimmered in a glistening, green wave. It turned its head toward the raiders and sellswords, the guildmaster's crossbow bolt clacking around its eye socket as it gazed about in half-measure.

Dahlgren unsheathed his sword and tightened his shield. He fanned his arm from side to side. "Go wide! Stay on its flanks!"

"Go men!" Eppo yelled. "Slay the beast!"

"Polearms and spears!" Dahlgren yelled. "Keep your distance! Watch the tail! Don't let its blood get on you!"

"Fuck all that!" Eppo yelled, bardiche readied. "Just kill the bastard!"

Screaming and howling, the sellswords and raiders sailed forth with axes and swords. The lindwurm pawed backward, lifting one arm and then the other like some dog that suddenly found itself in an ant pile. Men ganged up on its flanks, driving their blades underneath the scales, sizzling blood hissing off their steel as they drew the weapons back. The beast reeled and wriggled, its head swinging from side to side, its blackened vision seeing its attackers in silhouettes and blurs, every one of their movements paired with a terrible slash or piercing upon its flesh.

"It doesn't know how to fight!" Eppo said. "We have a chance!"

Almost as if hearing the raider, the lindwurm's throat rattled and shook, and it channeled from the depths of its belly and let out a ferocious roar, its head waving side to side, the breath and heat of it wilting the men, causing them to cover their ears and dive for the dirt. When it finished, the beast vibrated with rage, green blood leaking down its muscled arms, the grooves of its strength tightening as it clenched the earth, claws crushing through the sand and gravel of the shore with bestial fury. It snapped its mouth shut and a plume exhaled from its nostrils.

"Uhh, old man," Eppo said. "What's it doing?"

"Trash," Dahlgren said, turning instinctively to a beast slayer who was no longer there. "Ah."

But a beast slayer wasn't necessary to know what was happening. The first thing an animal learns is its mother's smell, and the next is how to survive without her. And learning how to survive is learning how to fight.

"O-old man!" Eppo yelled. "What is it doing, man?"

They watched as the lindwurm's neck tightened and the scales crackled as they uniformly snapped down like an army of shields closing formation, bringing the beast's coat of scales to look more like one piece of plated armor. Its eye narrowed as it lowered its head to the height of its attackers, seeing them from their level. Now they weren't ants indistinguishable in their numbers. Now they were prey. Cattle. Ready to be slaughtered.

"Fall back!" Dahlgren yelled. "Fall back now!"

A clump of the shore cast into the air as the lindwurm launched. Its growl passed forth like the roar of a storm caught in a lightning strike. Swiftly, effortlessly, and with annihilation in its footsteps. Here, there, bounding, jumping. Poles of muscled green swept left to right, massive trunks of momentum that obliterated the raiders with fist and claw and tooth and tail. Men turned into blurs, standing in one moment and flying away in the next. Natural instinct took over: while the beast's upper half moved on the raiders, its tail worked elsewhere, coiling before lashing whiplike snaps that lifted men off their feet and tossed them into the trees, or taking their legs out from under them and spinning them through the air, weapons and armor flying.

Yet, the raiders still attacked, dumbly walking into danger with bardiches and poleaxes. One jumped on the lindwurm's back to stab it with a dagger. He was grabbed and fed into the lindwurm's maw, its giant teeth tearing out his ribcage and spilling his guts onto the sands below. Another raider met the tail, a quick swish that saw his spine fold in half.

"Tell your men to wait until I've got the beast's attention," Dahlgren said, stepping forward with sword and shield. "Once I do, attack its tail!"

"And what exactly are you going to do, old man?"

"I've still got ligaments," Dahlgren said. "And I'm going to use them."

Banging his shield, the old man marched toward the lindwurm.

Chewing on a raider, the beast slowly turned around, rolling its body like the snake with two arms that it was, unsettlingly fast, yet strangely human in its deliberation. Head cocked, it watched Dahlgren in its half-stare. It dropped the dead man from its maw and its tongue probed toward the old man.

"That's right," Dahlgren said, walking into irreversible lengths of danger like a mouse before the shadow of the hawk. "Look at me. Look at me good."

Steadily, the old man started moving sideways, walking himself into the beast's blind spot. Each step he went, the beast lost sight of him and it brought its neck back in a questioning coil, then its head lurched side to side until it picked him back up again.

"If Trash can kill your mother," Dahlgren said. "Then I think we can kill little ol' you. Now look at me. Keep looking, you stupid sonuvabitch."

The lindwurm huffed and snapped its mouth and the clap of scaled lips echoed into the forest. It leapt forward. Dahlgren lifted his shield. He stole a moment's glance around his shield's side. A green boulder, fist clenched and coming fast. Dahlgren adjusted his shield. It slammed against his shoulder and skidded him backwards as though he were on ice. Before the hand could retreat, Dahlgren lowered his shield and swung, nicking one of the lindwurm's digits. Green blood gushed forth, sizzling against the old man's chainmail.

Dahlgren took a moment. He felt his bones more alive than they had ever been. Fire ran through him, an energy he thought he'd forgotten.

But the lindwurm hadn't forgotten him: it swung in again. This time, it learned and instead of striking the shield, it grabbed it, the beast's massive fingers wrapping around the edges. Dahlgren lifted into the air as it pulled up. Grunting, he slashed the straps Sophia had made and dropped back down. The lindwurm took the shield into its mouth and crushed it, tonguing the wood like a cat having eaten a beetle.

While it chewed, the old man wasted no time: he ran beneath the beast, standing between two poled, muscled arms like a man between trees. He slashed his sword left, right, and as blood sprayed and smoke drifted from his armor, he planted his sword and drove it upward. The lindwurm roared and its head corkscrewed around, the massive skull waving back and forth like a lantern bobbing at the hand of a roadagent divining dangers out of the dark. As its good eye found Dahlgren, the head snapped firmly into place. The old man looked back, seeing himself in the yellowed sheen, black pupil and black man and grey steel, and in his own eye he saw himself blinding the lindwurm once and for all.

"Have it!" Dahlgren screamed and drove forth with the killing blow.

A knee popped, a burst felt leg to hip to neck. Some horrid pang of the nerves turning against him, setting his flesh aflame with sudden pain. His assault decentered. His elbow uncorked awkwardly. The steel sword ran amiss, scratching the side of the lindwurm's eye and caroming away, and the old man's broken, staggered momentum carried him right into the lindwurm's awaiting hand.

Dahlgren gasped for air as the fingers wrapped around his body and he suddenly found himself airborne. His chainmail's grinded. His chest clenched. As the lindwurm turned its squeeze, his breath sputtered from his lips and blood pressed against his skull as his eyes bulged. The lindwurm's eye returned, now gazing at him from the length of its neck. There, Dahlgren saw his reflection again, an old, decrepit man whose best years were behind him, and certainly with no years to come. And then the eye closed and the maw slickly drew open. Teeth. Razored. Endless. A froth of raider blood and the glint of chunks of broken armor stabbing into its gums. Licking back and forth, a long tongue and an issuance of steamy breath behind it.

"Sonuvabitch," Dahlgren said, and closed his eyes.

He felt weightless, that it crushed his throat and heart with its teeth, and sent him on his way to the great beyond. Wind whistling. Nothing beneath, feet finally free of the earth. And then his other knee exploded as he hit the ground and his body crumpled and folded. Jarred awake from what he presumed to be his death, Dahlgren looked up to see the lindwurm roaring, a dagger winking from the side of its gum, a glistening toothpick.

"You don't touch him!" a man screamed hoarsely. "Nor his boots!"

Dahlgren looked down the shore to find a wobbling, angry Quinn. The thief held up another dagger and flipped its blade between his fingers and threw it. The knife clanged off the side of the lindwurm's eyebrow, drawing little more than a incredulous blink.

"Alright Dollgrin!" Quinn yelled. "Get your sword and stab its heart!"

The old man looked in the mud. His blade was lost. Sunken in the chaos.

Quinn threw another dagger. It pinged off the beast's head and flipped harmlessly away. The thief's eyes widened. "I swear to the old farking gods, old man, if you don't slay this farking dragon right the fark now!"

The lindwurm slowly stomped down the shore, one arm wheeling before the other. A litter of dead raiders sank beneath its weight while wounded ones desperately crawled out of the way.

"Hero shit, Dahlgren!" Quinn yelled, stepping back. "Slay it, old man!"

"I don't have it!" Dahlgren yelled back. He tried to stand. His knees gave out. Gritting his teeth, he looked at the thief and screamed: "Quinn, run!"

~~~

"Did you hear something?" Berthold said.

Richter looked back. He looked up. Waited. Shook his head. "What was it?"

Berthold waited a moment. He shook his head. "Not sure."

"Alright," Richter said. "Stay focused, miller. We've work to do."

"Right, captain."

The two men continued into the forest.

~~~

"Dahlgren you motherfarker!"

Sitting in the treeline, Sophia and Hobbs watched Quinn, the thief stumbling backward as he yelled.

"The damned fool," Sophia said. "How did we let him slip?"

In the flurry of the lindwurm coming ashore, the three retreated to the tree line with the boy and homesteader dragging the thief. They hid him in a grooved trunk and themselves poked their heads in and out of it like prairie dogs as the combat unfolded. When Quinn recovered his means to talk, which was in essence a swordmaster recovering his blade, he quickly got to his feet and went out. The two tried to stop him, but he was as intent as he was woozy. Now he stood a good stone's throw from the lindwurm and total annihilation.

"We have to do something," Hobbs said.

"Do something?" Sophia said. "The only one who can do something is him." The homesteader poked her head over the trunk and cupped her hands over her mouth: "Run, Quinn, run!"

Maw dripping in salivation, the lindwurm stomped forward, its one-eye piecing together the size and shape of the thief with sways of its head like an artist's brushstrokes painting its scene. Broken bodies littered the shore in its wake, some moving, many not. Further beyond, Gernot, Thomas, and Crockett took shelter behind one of the wagons, the three men given away by the oblivious donkey eating grass behind them, the animal disinterested in the sheer scope of carnage happening right in front of it.

"Why aren't those three doing something," the boy said.

"Did you not just see what that beast did? Nobody stands a chance," Sophia said. "Let's go, Hobbs. Richter would not want you here. We can still leave and I will keep you safe until we get back to—hey!"

The boy darted out from the treeline. He didn't know why, he didn't know by what force or impulse, only that his feet moved, and in going his hands picked up his wooden sword and the camel carving. He felt the brush of Sophia's fingers chasing after his heels, just missing ensnaring him and dragging him back to safety, and he heard her cry out in frustration and then cry out his name in horror. He wanted to turn and tell her it would be alright, but there wasn't the time, and there likely wouldn't be any truth to it anyway.

"Quinn!" Hobbs shouted.

The thief looked over his shoulder.

"Lil' runt?" Quinn said. "What in the hells are you doing!"

"Richter wouldn't leave you behind!"

The thief turned around, his last dagger in hand. The beast stomped closer, its tongue prodding in and out, its head still swinging left to right.

"One last throw," Quinn said. He coughed, his chest still swollen with the Trading Swords river, his throat all afire from spewing it out. He aimed the lindwurm up, straight down the narrows of his blade, the beast's verdant visage growing fatter and broader and all the scarier by each stomp of its arms and yet... all the easier to hit.

The thief lunged forward. Elbow cocked. Arm ready. Foot planted. Fingers pinched.

"You got this!" Hobbs yelled.

"What!"

Elbow corkscrewed. Arm diagonal. Foot displaced. Fingers scattered.

The dagger sailed through the air – sideways and sidewindering and spinning and it glintingly and harmlessly sailed over the lindwurm and pattered into the mud with the quietest insult to every ear that heard it.

"Sonuva-farking-bee sting!" Quinn turned around. "You distracted me!"

"I-I-I didn't mean to!"

"Ahh shite just go!"

The thief went to push Hobbs away, but the boy dodged him.

He held up his wooden sword. "I still have this!"

"Oh, that! Great! In the meanwhile, let me take this!" Quinn said, snatching the carved camel away. He turned around. "Here you farking go, you disgusting lizard!"

The lindwurm snarled and planted its arm in a quick beat, sliding forward in the mud as its eye drew wide, staring at the camel in total confusion and curiosity. Slowly, its arms encircled the thief and boy, hemming them in like sudden, emerald walls, the scales shining like treasures, the clawed hands threatening instant death.

"Uhh," Quinn said, looking for an escape.

Mewling and hiccupping, the lindwurm keeled its head forward, the steam of its breath sending the man and boy's clothes fluttering

Quinn stepped back. "Uhhhh... Hobbs... Hobbs what's going on?"

"I-I-I don't know!"

Mud squelched beside them, the beast's claws trenching inward. Its tail slithered, the scales hissing as it coiled around the two. Darkness surrounded them and the lindwurm's one-eye stared down from above, like some serpentine totem come alive to prey upon its worshippers. Like a cork into a bottle, the head descended into the coiled arms and tail, its neck throttling side to side as it shook, its sharp scales chittering as its curiosity loosened it from its weaponized, murderous state.

"When it eats me," Quinn said. "You run, alright? I'll put up a fight. I'll make it work for these bones."

"H-how?"

"I dunno. I'll bite its tongue. What the fark does it even matter? You just need to run."

The beast's breast closed in, its breath churning in its lungs, and the pump of its heart, chugging, a rhythmic pace of the innerworkings, the engine behind its power and violence. Thumping. Growling. Foam drooled from its lips, blossoming between teeth, its maw filled with chainmail and iron studs and a few fingers and a chunk of someone's flesh. It slowly turned its head, left, right, each time its one-eye narrowing in on the thief from one angle and then another.

"What's it doing?" Quinn said.

Hobbs watched the beast carefully. His eyes went wide. "The camel!"

Quinn looked down at the carving. It was still clenched in both his hands, upright and presented like some gift to a vizier.

The thief lowered it. "The camel? What about it?"

As the camel lowered, the lindwurm's head shunted with speed to keep it in sight.

Hobbs nearly jumped out of his shoes. "It doesn't know what it is!"

The lindwurm's wheeled again, and each curve and turn found it closer and closer until finally it snaked inward, its eye right to the camel's nose, its sight upon its peculiar humps and foreign make. So close was its gaze that Hobbs and Quinn both appeared as fat, stretching reflections in the curvature of its yellowed eye. Suddenly, Quinn snapped his fingers.

"Hobbs! Your—"

The boy beat him to the punch: screaming as hard as he could, Hobbs stabbed forward with his wooden sword and sank it into the lindwurm's eye and plunged the beast into total darkness. Beset by blindness, the lindwurm roared and reeled back and all its limbs and tail moved in every direction, governed by panic alone. Quinn grabbed the boy and moved to step out, but the dangerous scales sliced by, and the thief gritted his teeth and took Hobbs into both arms and fell into the mud, the boy at the bottom of him and the thief screamed something that had been yelled at him more times than he could count: "Don't move!"

Mud squelched. The earth shook. With every ferocious and frightened breath, the air warmed. And then: water. Splashing. Enveloping. A roar cut in half, garbled by the river and then returning, confused and bubbling.

Quinn sat up and the two looked toward the shore.

The blind lindwurm flailed into the Trading Swords river, churning it into a bubbling foam. It shrieked in terror. It shrieked for its mother it knew to be gone. It shrieked for the one who had hexed it. It shrieked for sight. It shrieked for now it knew nothing, and knew not how to fix what was broken.

And so they watched its shape and limberness tumble and twist and slip away, sinking into the middle of the river until, finally, at last sight of it, they saw its head poke up out of the rushing water, one eye carrying the shaft of the guildmaster's bolt, and there in its other eye stood the skewering wooden blade, a toy hewn from an ordinary tree and there wielded by an ordinary boy to destroy an extraordinary creature.

Chapter 39. Gluttonous Things.

"Wait... did you hear that?" Berthold said again.

In truth, Richter knew some sort of carnage had befallen the shoreline. Whatever was happening, he could only trust that everything was working out as planned. He had built his company for a purpose, built it to withstand what all the hexe could throw out it. Now it needed to do its part while he did his.

Richter nodded. "Let's stay focused, miller."

The two traveled through the forest with speed, Richter's eyes following the tracks of the five men who had marched in, as well as the reversed tracks of Thomas who had returned alone. A sudden flash of blue caught the pathfinder's eye and he skidded on his heels. Berthold stopped and crouched with his spear readied.

"What do you see?" he said.

Richter waved a fly away. He said, "It's the jester's hat."

Walking up, Berthold shouldered his spear and leaned forward. Minnesang's cap stuck out of the verdant surroundings with sparkling aplomb. But it wasn't the pure blue-and-white adornment they remembered. It was covered in blood.

"I suppose that confirms the jester's dead," Berthold said.

"Seems so," Richter said. He looked ahead and, following his instinct, chose a bush and walked through it. Minnesang's body lay on the other side.

Berthold seized up at the sight of it. "Ah hells, something ate his head."

Richter waved more flies away as he crouched. He slowly pushed the jester's body to get a better idea of the damage. Sticky blood crackled as his body turned. The neckhole was like a slab, as clean a cut as one could get, like something one would find in a healer's studies. He slowly let the body back down. When he stood, the flies buzzed mightily as if to see him off.

"This isn't right," Richter said.

"What's not right about it?"

The captain pursed his lips. "I don't know."

"Well, Thomas said a nachzehrer took his head off. Not much else to it."

Richter stared at the corpse.

"Stay focused," Berthold said. "Right, captain?"

Nodding, Richter took a breath and steadied himself. "Right. Let's go."

The captain discarded all hesitation and tore through the bushes knowing full well the miller was right: he needed to focus. It was at this speed that his eyes failed to approximate the wall of grey hiding behind a bush, and as he broke through its branches, he fell out the other side and his hand puttied into the belly of the giant nachzehrer squatting there. As the captain reared back, Berthold blew through the bush and landed against him and together they smooshed their faces into the slick, mildewed distension.

Berthold peeled himself off the flesh like a man unsticking himself from the mud he put a full night's rest into. Grey skin stretched from his cheeks, batlike webbings from the side of his head that snapped back to the belly and set it wobbling. Richter unplugged his face in turn, a grey mesh stretching from his face like the rind of a fish's fin. It snapped free and flailed back into the belly, jostling it as good as any punch. Both men fell back into the bush.

"Oh shit!" the miller screamed.

Richter said nothing, but Adelbrecht's sword sang from its sheath.

The nachzehrer slowly turned its head like a drunkard discovered by his wife at the bar. Eyes slumped from its sockets, the corners full of crust, the cheeks wet with may have been tears. Its massive claws lay supinated at its sides. Gargling, its belly bubbled with each breath. Despite seeing the two men, the nachzehrer simply turned back away.

Screaming, Berthold sank his spear into the beast's belly.

"Hahaha!" the miller yelled. "Take it! Take it you greasy bastard!"

As he rammed his spear in again, the tip broke through the belly. When he jerked at it to return, it wouldn't give, and then a moment later it sucked out of his hands and disappeared.

"Get back, Berthold!" Richter yelled, his sword readied.

But the nachzehrer's arms lay forgivingly at rest, and as the words left the captain's mouth the beast's belly popped: the speartip returned from within and sawed left to right, unfurling the creature's belly until the flesh and fat pushed outward and folded over and a terrible orange gush flooded past the men and a moment later a green and white ball slid out onto the ground. Belching, the nachzehrer's hands rose up in the air, its four-tentacled mouth licked about, and then it fell backward, squashing an entire bush flat and shaking the trees around it, soft leaves twisting downward in a jostling hiss.

"Holy shit," Berthold said. "I killed it. We'll have to tell Crockett!"

Richter ignored the miller's feat, instead crouching down to look at the green and white thing which had slipped out of the beast's stomach.

"Elletrache?" he said. "Trash, is that you?"

The green and white unfurled, a man's arms and legs stretching out, the flesh as pale as bone. From toe to pate, he had not a single hair on him. He was solely clothed in a chestpiece of lindwurm scales and his flesh bore a shining, white hue like some ivory totem rainslick beneath a pale moon. As the man turned, he revealed an eyepatch and he lifted a mangled hand and gently skirted it from one eye to the other and grinned up at Richter.

"Y'know what, captain? Ol' Elletrache has seen better days."

"Holy shit," Berthold said, glancing to the skies, half-expecting to see some great deity peering back down.

Richter said, "Don't move, Trash, let me get a look at you, alright?"

The captain looked at the beast slayer, the man's body stretched at full length in white monochrome, there transpicuous and transparent like some drowned earthworm beside a gutted fish it helped lure. When Richter's fingers touched the slayer, he seethed and recoiled.

"Yeah," Elletrache said. "That smarts, captain."

"Shit," Berthold said. "Holy shit."

The beast slayer groused. "Would you tell the wobbly kneed miller to stop profaning. He's gon' let the old gods know I'm still alive."

"M-maybe they want you alive," Berthold said. "Holy shit."

"Berthold," Richter said. "Let's get him to his feet."

"Yessir."

Richter looked back down. "You can walk, right?"

"I hope so." Elletrache nodded. "Just mind the lindwurm scales."

Pursing his lips, Richter nodded back. The two gently placed their hands under his arms, the flesh wet and slick and warm to the touch. As they lifted him upright, he hissed as though the very air through which he passed did him harm. He gritted his teeth as his soles and toes touched grass. Every inch of his flesh glistened white.

Elletrache turned his hands. Fingers missing. One of his palms split in twain. He looked at them and shook his head. "Sumbitch."

"Where are the raiders?" Richter said.

"Dead on account of quarreling with me," Elletrache said.

"They attacked you?"

Holding up his brutalized hands, the beast slayer nodded.

"Eppo…" Berthold said, gripping his spear.

"Naw," the beast slayer shook his head. "I think they was operatin' on their own accord. Them two shitters still alive, Thomas and that jester fella?"

Richter said, "Minnesang's dead. Thomas found the boy, but he didn't make it. He said other nachzehrers attacked."

"I didn't see no other nachs," Elletrache said. "But the scavengers do usually move in packs. Wouldn't surprise me if there were a few little'uns running around out here. Shame about the lad. Where's the company?"

"On the shore. Are you alright, Trash?"

"Naw. I got ate, captain. I'm far from alright."

Berthold said, "How… how was it?"

"Uh, well, I couldn't tell shit from Sommerwein in the belly of the beast, but if the nach' was going to eat me, he was going to pay for it, that's how I saw it. So I wriggled and wrassled and let my lindwurm scales make free with his innards until he got sick. Then one moment he drank all this farkin' shit."

The men looked down. A wash of orange liquid lacquered all over the nachzehrer's distended belly, brimming along the rinds of its opened and unfurled flesh, and pooling about the forest floor.

"Ever since the nach' dropped that down the hatch, I've been feeling a bit out of touch. Like my head's gone foggy, though not in a bad way. I'd even say it's helped with the pain. I mean, I'm still hurt something awful, but, y'know, in a hazy sort of way."

"I don't think I do know," Berthold said.

Richter crouched and put a finger into the orange mire and smelled it.

Elletrache grinned and gingerly rubbed his belly. "I wager that nach' needed a good ale to go along with this here sausage."

Staring into the forest, Richter's eyes tracked and traced the path of the nachzehrer: claw marks on the trees, orange flakes in the surrounding bark. Weighted footsteps, orange in the toed divots. Troughs of mud where the distended belly slid, orange along the creases. Leaf litters, orange in their veins.

Claire von Sommerwein.

He took his eyes back to the dead nachzehrer and studied the sheer amount of orange liquid pooled out before him.

"She has a cauldron," Richter muttered to himself.

"What was that, captain?" Berthold said.

Richter turned. "Berthold, get Trash back to the shore."

"Yessir." The miller didn't protest, but at the same time he was struck with a look of concern. He said, "But are you going to continue… alone?"

"Aye."

"You're not leaving us for good, are you?"

"Naw, he ain't." Elletrache laughed. "I know that look in the captain's eyes." Arms raised and teeth gritted, the beast slayer staggered forth like some sunburnt man stepping on glass. His pale, bony-white face proved strangely foreign without its beard and unruly hair, but all the same his smile was genuine. He gave a ragged thumbs up. "I'll proffer a prayer to the old gods for ya, captain, if that little runt is who you think she is."

Chapter 40. Red on the Shore.

"Hugo!" Eppo said, staring up a tree trunk. "You're alive!"

The last of Eppo's raiders lay sprawled and suspended in a tree, his arms and legs hooked over the branches, his back against the trunk. He looked down. "Eppo, there're squirrels up here. They're staring at me."

"Well, you're in their home."

"Am I alive?"

"Yes. Come on down, Hugo."

Rather haphazardly, Hugo uncorked his arse from its seat and drew out his limbs for the branches. He slid down the tree in skirts and scoots. When he hit the ground, his knees buckled and he fell back and hissed, though his hands had a hard time finding which of his bodily pains hurt the most.

Eppo raised an eyebrow. "Oh Hugo, you've been hit in the head."

"I have? That part is the only one that don't hurt any."

"Uh, well…" Eppo touched the side of Hugo's head. His hand grooved into a deep, purple dent. He withdrew his hand and pursed his lips.

"How's it look?" Hugo said.

Eppo smiled. "Well, if you can't feel it, I think that's good enough, right?"

"Buttered pies and mountain tops."

"What?"

"What? Are you deaf?" Hugo's eyes blinked one at a time. He said, "I said, 'yeah, I agree.'"

Eppo pursed his lips again. "Alright, Hugo. Let's get you to your feet."

The two walked out of the trees and took to the shore. Every other step had to carry over a corpse, and every single body proved to be another raider.

"Everyone's dead?" Hugo said.

"Yes," Eppo said. "Unfortunately, the sellswords made it out alright."

"I fell up a down staircase."

"Huh?"

Touching his dent, Hugo said, "I asked if the sellswords going to kill us."

"Uhh, maybe, but I think they need us for now," Eppo said. He looked back at the mercenaries. Dahlgren, the old man, moved around reordering the shore with a tactician's eye. Turning back, Eppo said, "I think we could work for them if we play our cards right."

"I dunno," Hugo said. "Maybe Eee… Eee… and other… other me…"

"Egil and Hugo."

"Y-yeah, Eee and Ooo… what I meant was… oh I don't feel good."

Eppo put one hand to the dent in Hugo's skull and then used his other to rub the back of the man's head. "Maybe your words got knocked back here somewhere. Try now."

"Eagle me again."

"Egil and another Hugo," Eppo said, nodding. "You got it."

"You know," Hugo said, looking up with a smile. "I think I can still fight, sir. Honestly, I feel like I can take on the world and all the cats in the bag."

"Right… good to hear, Hugo."

"Hey!" Dahlgren shouted. He tapped the top of his helmet and then pointed up the road. "I'm seeing men on the way!"

"Friendlies?" Eppo said, and grimaced at how stupid of a question it was.

"Why in the hells would you ask that?"

"I know, I know, I got it. We're on our way."

Eppo grabbed Hugo and started dragging him toward the sellswords.

A group of ten men were marching down the road. Unlike the naked mob, they came armored: leather with iron studs, and the appropriate arms to match in an assortment of spears and swords and shields. They moved as one, five behind five. Eyes forward. Boots clodding in unison, their march seemed routine, a strange sort of automation in its nature, so unfaltering they looked like wooden soldiers scooting across a general's war map.

The sellswords and raiders gathered behind their 'fortress' of wagons.

"I want clemency," Eppo said. "Otherwise, we're gone."

Dahlgren looked over. "Shrewd, raider, very shrewd. That's up to captain Richter to decide, but you help us fight these bastards and I'll put in a good word, how does that sound?"

Eppo looked at Hugo.

Hugo looked at Dahlgren. "So, you like kissing old women, eh?"

"What?" Dahlgren said.

Sophia leaned forward. "What did he just say?"

"Hey!" Eppo said, nodding hurriedly and waving away Hugo's words. "You have a deal! We'll stay and fight!"

"Right…" Dahlgren pointed at the wagons. "Let's pull these in and wedge them close to the shore!" He looked at the caravan guard which swept down the road steadily as ever. "I don't see a bow on a single one of them so if they aim to kill us, we can at least put 'em in a funnel or have 'em trying to climb over the wagons. Better than nothing, anyway."

The raiders and sellswords got to work, hurriedly dragging the wagons inward, pinching their sides against each other, leaving their closest edges sinking into the shoreline's mud.

All the while, the caravan guard approached, their march steady, unhurried by the defenders' preparations. The uniform clapping of their step finally staggered as the group broke free of the tree line and their formation unfurled. They lined up in a wide breadth, each man an arm's length away from the next, altogether stretched along the riverbank such that the wagons and their defenders were effectively surrounded.

"Whatcha want?" Dahlgren yelled.

Starting from left to right, the ten caravan guards turned their heads, each man jumping in as though to provide one sentence of a singular speaker:

"The Wight, Richter von Dagentear."

"We know how he looks."

"She said to kill him."

"I do not see him."

"She told us."

"Yes."

"He is hiding."

"Kill those hiding him."

"Yes, we must rid him of his helpers."

"Then it is decided, to kill Richter they must all die."

In unison, the caravan guards brought their weapons to the fore, a sudden crash of noise as if a storm's rainfall fell all at once. Dahlgren, Quinn, Thomas, Crockett, Gernot, Eppo and his last raider, Hugo, uneasily braced themselves against the strange horde. Sophia and Hobbs clutched one another at the edge of the adhoc fortification, the homesteader's eyes on the rafts, her mind ready to escape downriver at a moment's notice.

The caravan guard took a few steps forward. A guard bumped into the donkey which chewed absentmindedly before the army. He stepped back.

"No, this is not Richter," he said.

Quinn laughed. "They're dumber than hells this should be easy—"

In an instant, the caravan guard's sword ran upward, cleaving into the donkey's throat, causing it to spit out its food. A second later, another guard drove his sword down from above. The blades met and the beast's head fell away with a thud and its four legs jerked pointedly before tottering over.

Another guard crouched and peered into the gaping neck wound. He looked up at the others. "Richter is not hiding in here."

Eppo's eyes went wide. He turned to Dahlgren. "Uh, just what sorta enemies have you guys been making out here?"

The guards returned to their steady, inward march, the circle of their formation ever so slowly closing in on the defenders.

"Rid them of his helpers," they said. "And eviscerate the Wight."

Dahlgren spat. He said, "Alright men. Remember, they have to come to us. You take from them anything they want to put on the table, understand? Don't just go for heart or head! If they put fingers down, I want you taking them. If they give you a nose, slice it off, if you see a boot in the sand, stab the motherfucker. Cripple them right into the damn grave."

Sophia knelt by Hobbs. She tidied up his shirt as if it were a normal morning and as the motherliness passed, she said, "I want you to run, alright?"

"Run? You want me to be a coward?"

"No, I want you to be smart."

Behind them, the men started clapping their weapons on their shields and banging the wagons. They hurled curses and spit at the oncoming caravan guard. Almost like chickens squawking at the fox as it is seen and then again as the beast figures out the coup's latch, the raiders and sellswords raised their voices as the guards neared. Then, a rush of footfalls outside the defenses. A bang. The wagons' edges drove back, skidding into the mud, trenching it. Sophia lurched. She instinctively grabbed Hobbs as the sound of battle erupted all around them, swords clanging, spears clattering, shields deflecting.

Warring shadows danced across Sophia's face, menacing in their speed, terrifying in their frequency. Blood flecked the homesteader as a dismembered hand suddenly landed between her and the boy. She grabbed it like it were a rat fallen into a grain sack and flung it into the river. The second it was gone, a pair of fingers plopped into the sand, and a heap of indiscernible flesh after.

"Alright!" Sophia said, pushing Hobbs. "Get to the raft!"

Resisting her pushes, Hobbs yelled: "I have to get to Richter!"

A leather-armored hand soared down and grabbed the boy, yanking him upward. Sophia screamed and stood up, spinning to the caravan guard who had the boy in his hands. With no weapon on her, she punched the man in the face before desperately plunging her thumbs into his eyes.

Bleeding from the sockets, the guard simply drew the boy up and inquired softly and blindly: "Where is the Wight?"

Hobbs screamed.

A glint of a blade passed.

The man's arms fell, and Hobbs with them.

Dahlgren moved between boy and caravan guard, his shield bashing the suddenly armless man away. Another guard clambered over the top of the wagon and Dahlgren sank his sword into the man's throat, only for the blood to jet out with each sputtered word: *where is the Wight.*

Another guard reached over and grabbed Sophia by the hair. Screaming, Dahlgren swung in after her attacker, but more guards met him. Beyond them, Crockett and Quinn fought off two men, and Thomas was shrieking as he shielded himself against a guard's repeated blows, and Eppo the raider gave a war cry as he sank an axe into a man's head. Hobbs stared at the battle, bodies upon bodies, fists being thrown, blades slicing, crimson running down the sides of the wagons, red on the shore.

"Run, Hobbs!" Sophia screamed as a chunk of hair left her skull.

Downriver was no escape. Now, the only escape was killing Claire. Grimacing, Hobbs got to his feet and sprinted with purpose. A little boy out of a big battle. Legs churning. Breath heavy. And through a gap in the wagons he went, passing under the storm of swords, blood raining from their clouds. And in this manner, he soared up onto the path, and behind him the caravan guards, dying and fighting, all the same shouted: *"Find Richter. Find Richter."*

Find.

Richter.

Chapter 41. Insulting the Majesty.

AS RICHTER FOLLOWED the nachzehrer's path, more and more of a hexe's brew appeared, its unnatural orangeness brimming against the browns and greens of the forest. Even the nachzehrer's stumbling traces appeared equally strange, no doubt that it had confusedly staggered to and fro as the brew took effect on even one of the strongest stomachs in all the land.

But what it all told was a simple fact: she was close.

"Close enough," Richter said.

The captain unsheathed his sword and knelt to the ground. Kicking out his legs, he tucked his pants into his boots, and then his sleeves into his gloves. He took out the vial with the potent hexenjäger concoction and uncorked it. A stinging smell was quick to his nose, a pungency urgent in its pursuit of poisoning breathable air. Slowly, Richter dribbled some on two fingers.

"Close enough," he said again.

He snorted the concoction up one nostril and then the other. Each dab felt like rakes dragging across his brain, a fierce burning that saw his vision momentarily blurred, and a pain that keeled him forward, his lips pursed as he groaned into gritted teeth, his fists clenched, each of them violently shaking as though he were some monk losing faith at the altar itself.

"C-c-close enough," he stammered.

Pain such as this could not pass, but he did not have the time nor energy to dwell on it. As the fire ran to his head, he straightened up, took a breath, and drank the rest of the concoction. Unlike a strong brew that was quick to leave the mug and stir the belly, the concoction proved slow to exit the glass, and the captain steadied himself as he, bit by chunky bit, drank the entirety of it, each swallow bringing what felt like a stone's weight upon his belly, and, soon after, another fire upon his insides.

When he was finished, he threw the vial aside and staggered to his feet.

Before him, the forest shimmered. Trees tripled in fading penumbras, the selfsame shapes ghostly shifting and spinning around one another. He saw little heads pop around the corners of their trunks, blank white eyes staring at him, and great monsters soon after, the nachzehrer, a giant spider, and two infinite lindwurms moving in unison, two rivers of scales slithering along in twisting sequence, unseaming the earth, all of these sights spilling forth.

Richter blinked.

The terrors disappeared and his sight stabilized. Trees stood where they should be. Nothing of the imagination attacked. All that remained was a task.

His father spoke to him: "Don't stray far, boy."

And he lied as he always did: "I'd never."

Richter tore through the forest faster than the wind could course its columns. He spun around the trunks and clambered through the bushes. A sort of nimbleness could nary be matched in all of Dagentear. With glee he couldn't help but smile and feel the breath burning his lungs and the air sweeping his hair and crackling his ears. And for all the physicality, all the might and main of the little one, it were his eyes that took in most glories: there of the brown and green and plain he did augur out the deer and frogs and the strange. Footpaths. Footprints. Many together. Creatures chasing creatures. Traces. Blood. Feces. Stems. Grass. Even the slightest, singular blade caught in its verdant bend. His eyes saw all, and his mind carried the certainties with which to tackle that which he saw. The spoors went on. Leaf litters dashed. Trees denuded. Bear-ravaged bark. Old elk horns. The skeleton of a wolf. By its prints, it had come in alone, there readied to face death. Animalistic, yet something more. There! An old arrowhead. And there! An axe grown over in the trunk of a tree. And there! A halved copper sword. Blade rusted. Hilt obscured. A place of battle, winner unknown. If only time itself could be tracked then the boy would surely have seen all things. Ahh, a cave! Deep, dark, the wind cooing between its earthen teeth. Old campfires outside it. Sticks with dark tips, signs of bat fowling kits. A one-wheeled tumbril tumbled onto its flawed side, the lone wheel creaking in the wind.

And so it went on. Forest. Trees. Copses. Lumberjack brakes. Adze saws abandoned. And… and a terrible hut. The domicile whispering, a murmuring echo of a lost occupant. Beyond that, the great Higgarian ranges. Mountains jagged. Enormities looming. There together the great stippling of firmaments, the old gods gazing through the earthen spines and the stone cogs and the bones of men who dared to assail either, to climb these pillars of existence around which all things moved. Clouds above. Fog below. Only mountains in the middle. A man tells a boy to not stray. The boy strays. Then, a great fire. As the sky was blue, the earth turned red. Flames. Screaming. Ash. Screaming that ended, ash that never did. Caked in it. Survived it. Alone. Moved on. More forests. Every tree its own story. He carved his name. Maybe one day someone would recognize it. One day they do. They see him in impossible isolation. They don't see a boy. They see the Wight.

Have nothing, give nothing. Take what can be took. Steal. Work. One job, then another. Digging wells. Honest living. Sudden duty: find the child. He is found. Tongueless, but alive. A call to action: war. Pathfinding. Scouting. Reporting. There, more forests. Swamps. Drooping trees grown into curves by the evil which lurks. Greenskins. Terror. Survival. Carsten. Training. Trees. Forests. The leaps and bounds slowed. A pop in the knee. Months to feel alright. Can still run, but slower. The air no longer crackles in the ear, it barely even lifts the hair. The hair itself recedes. No wants, no desires. Trees. More of them. One trunk after another, one bird, one deer, one elk, one wolf, one hunt, one witch, one corpse, one war, one boy. Until.

Her.

Richter jumped from the tree line. Slow. Lumbering. Enraged. Claire knelt beside a tipped-over priory bell, her hands scraping orange liquid from its crusted rim and putting it in a jar. She looked like a doe in the road, white-dressed, faint colorings, urgency in all things, frailness inherent. He broke upon her in a hobble, his first step heard as she turned around and his second step seen at such close proximity it was as though he had teleported there. She clenched her own face, the once-held pottery smashing at her feet.

She screamed: "No! No no no no!"

Black hat. Black clothes. The grim visage of infinite trouble. He snatched her with one hand and menaced her with the sword in the other. She kicked and wheeled around and he caught her and pinned her body to his hip and put the sword to her throat.

"Holy man!" she screamed. "Holy man!"

~~~

"Never lie, boy, you hear me?"

"Yes, father."

"Word one of untruth to me and I'll hide your rump."

"Yes, mother."

"Ah, look at him, the boy who refuses to lie."

"Not even a little white one?"

"Not even one to get you laid?"

"What is that, some holy text?"

"He's pretending to read, that's his lie!"

"Did you steal the treasury from the priory?"

"He did! An outright admission to his crime!"

"If yer to be that honest, keep a foot in the stirrup."

"Ah, the man who couldn't tell a lie."

"I'll take one of them wooden swords."

"Goodbye, friend."

"Do not fear, holy man."

"Holy man, why can I hear him?"

"No! No no no no!"

"Holy man!"

"Holy man!"

"Immerwahr."

"Immerwahr?"

The monk opened his eyes. No, not opened. They had been open all along, but only now did he see. Only now did he gather what he could. But reality proved vague. Even as he gazed with a diviner's intent, the world's shapes and sounds drifted, illusive, fading as a dream into a morning routine. He blinked. He blinked and that was all he could do, and all that was before him was the forest, and his outstretched hands holding a sword.

"Immerwahr?"

"Holy man!"

Blinking, Immerwahr turned.

Richter and Claire stood together.

The monk stepped forward. He raised his sword.

Richter! he shouted, mouth unmoving. *My friend! It is so good to see you!*

"Immerwahr!" Richter shouted back. He held Claire to his hip, the girl kicking and screaming, her legs pedaling through the air with every jaunt.

Oh my friend, Richter, what is it you are doing?

Richter aimed his sword at the girl, but Immerwahr swung down with his own blade. The captain instinctively twisted his sword and the metals met with a stiff clang. Unpracticed and unbalanced at each end, both men fell away, carried by their collective inexperience. The girl slipped free, dipping out of Richter's grasp. She started for the trees and he slid a foot out and tripped her. She fell into a pile of pots, shattering them into shards. As she howled, the captain caught a glimmer in his peripheral. He brought his blade to the fore. It met the glint, sparking something brighter, and he fell into the side of the wagon while a parried Immerwahr staggered back across the road.

Why are we fighting?

"Immerwahr!" Richter shouted. "Immerwahr it's me, Richter!"

Laughing, Claire said, "Kill him, holy man! Kill him!"

Richter spun to the girl. He knew not what he looked like in that moment, he only knew that no living soul had reacted in the way she did, sinking, flinching, grimacing, like her soul had been hollowed out and the husk remained, cobbled together by the very fear which had devastated it so.

My friend, that is just a little girl!

As the hexenjäger stood over her, Claire screamed. A terror that tore at her throat, a scream that died at the length of her breath for it surely used all of it. She turned over and tried to get to her feet. She took one step before the captain grabbed her by the nape of her neck. As she spun in his grasp, she met the hexenjäger with a pot of her brew. It shattered across his face and knocked his black hat off his head and caked him in dripping orange.

"Be still," Claire whispered. "Be still, be calm, follow me. Be still, be—"

Richter raised his hand and swept the liquid from his face. As his palm peeled it all away, what remained behind was unaffected and undaunted alike, there, the glare of the Wight.

"F-follow…" Claire's eyes widened as her hexing failed. "H-how?

Richter's grip tightened and he slammed the girl headfirst into the side of the cart. Her skull cracked against the wood and her legs gave out and limply dangled beneath her.

No, Richter!

Immerwahr rushed the captain.

Another glint. First afar, and then close, and this time Richter's parrying blade was not fast enough and Immerwahr's steel went caroming across his chest and he felt his breast catch fire. As the captain stumbled back, his bandolier fell to the ground, its leathers cut clean through. Unpausing, the monk awkwardly swung his sword back in a rushed flurry of an assault, Richter turning his sword up and having it yank and jerk one way and another as it deflected each oncoming strike.

Most men parry, Dahlgren said. *Very few dodge because dodging requires big fucking balls or an addled pate.*

Richter looked down. He listened to Dahlgren's words and leaned back. The monk's blade glinted by and purchased a piece of his chin, and then the captain bent back forward, planted a hobbled knee, and thrust his blade and its steel staggered a moment before freely sailing through.

The monk grunted. He spat blood and more drained from his nose and ears. Adelbrecht's sword – *Richter's blade* – had ran him completely through.

Richter? It's me… Immerwahr… where was I?

"Immerwahr," Richter said, steadying the monk with a hand to his shoulder. "Immerwahr, can you hear me?"

"Oh, he can hear you…" Claire said, woozily getting her feet under her. "Because now you have truly freed the holy man."

Richter looked at the monk. "Immerwahr, are you there?" He pursed his lips as the monk's eyes began to glisten, and his face faded of color. "Immerwahr? I can help you, but you have to tell me it's you. Is it you?"

Immerwahr looked at his friend. "Richter…" he said.

Ah, the captain. The protector of the ferry town. Of all the men who came and went in this world, you in the black hat are surely a rarity of absolute and unexpected kindness. Richter. Looking for a just cause. Richter. Seeking relief. Richter. Killing me.

"Never lie, boy, you hear me?"

"Yes, father."

"Word one of untruth to me and I'll hide your rump."

"Yes, mother."

"Ah, look at him, the boy who refuses to lie."

"Not even a little white one?"

Immerwahr stared from the depths of his own history.

Richter pleaded for any sense of the monk. "Immerwahr… friend…"

The monk smiled. The captain gritted his teeth.

"Frehh…" Immerwahr swallowed. The damage had been done. There was no coming back. He was awake now, he saw where he was, he knew all that had transpired and that an end was soon at hand. One determination existed: he could only ensure that certain wounds were not to be left open.

"For…" He brought up his sword. "For…"

Richter didn't buy it. He waited, his hand trembling upon his own sword.

"Immerwahr, are you in there? I know you're there, I know it!"

Claire laughed. "He is! Show him, holy man! The hexe is gone!"

Just one little lie.

No wounds.

Only healing.

"For…" Immerwahr gritted his teeth. "For Claire von Sommerwein!"

A glint of steel.

The scream of a man.

In sudden silence, the monk fell back. A holy man's blood arced beautifully. Red. Bright. Untethered and free, and at the length of its roping shimmer Immerwahr met his shadow and his shadow met him. He groaned. Eyes to the skies. Back to the earth. Hands playing with the clouds. And then in this manner he eased away. Unmoving, he still seemed to go, his flesh whitening as the life leaked out, as though color itself had weight, and the pallid remainder proved the balance of the darkness to which he went.

Richter clenched his sword. Not Adelbrecht's sword. *His* sword.

"Kill yourself," Claire whispered. "Kill yourself, too."

Taking a breath, Richter wiped his face and the hand drew back with the blood of the monk and the orange mixture which the hexe had smashed upon him. He stared at the combination with roiling hatred.

"Kill yourself," she said again. "Kill yourself, too. Kill yourself."

Though the words were soft and left the hexe's tongue like petals from a flower, the captain heard them as clearly as a battalion's warhorn. But they did not have the commanding effect. He heard them, and they were just words. Only words. He wiped the orange liquid from his face and turned around and stared at the witch.

"My brew and a holy man's blood," Claire said, sinking against the cart. "Nobody could have resisted that."

Richter ignored her. He stared about her wagon, his eyes quick upon the traces and tracks. Footsteps leading in. More than a dozen men, it seemed. And the grooving path of a lindwurm's tail. And the trenched roadwork of the cart which, once weighed mightily with the priory bell, had since been freed of its burden, the holy relic spilled into the road and caked there with the hexe's magicks.

Claire fell to her knees. "I surrender!"

The hexenjäger stood before her. His shadow long. Death its compass.

"N-nobody could have resisted that…" she said again. "Nobody."

Richter lifted the sword, aiming its blade at her neck.

"You can't kill me," Claire said.

Gritting his teeth, Richter steadied the blade.

"You can't kill me," she said again. "I'm too important. Too important to Sommerwein. Too important to Marsburg. I'm too important to you, Richter. You kill me and they'll all know. Everyone in the north will know.

They'll hunt you down and kill you and everyone with you. My father is renowned for the terror he wields. Sommerwein's ferocity is forged by endless years of battling the savage barbarians."

Her eyes lit up at the word.

"Y-yes! You can take me to the barbarians, Richter!" She held out her arms. Her little wrists. Pointed, knobby things. Weak. Brittle. Easily broken. And all the same potent offerings, like lit tinder before a summer's field. "You can take me to them, Richter. You—"

The captain grabbed her with unhinted speed, almost a punch and snatch, at once throttling her backward and again pulling her forward. He threw her to the ground and unyoked his crossbow from his back and shot it. The girl flinched, turning aside as mud scattered and her dress gently skirted. She looked down to see the bolt stuck in the mud. When she looked back up, Richter was upon her, sitting on her chest like a beast to its fallen prey. He yanked the bolt from the ground and grabbed her tiny wrist and pinned it.

"End your hexes," Richter said. He held the bolt's tip against her wrist. "I can see the tracks of your army heading toward the river's shores. End your hexes, now, or I will flay you with nothing more than this little notch!"

"How do you know you're not back in the homestead?" Claire said. "Or maybe you're still in Lord Landon's castle with me? Maybe we're still in that room, just us two talking. Did you ever consider that, Richter von Dagentear?" She said his name like he'd said it long ago. When he first spoke his name to her and immediately regretted it. She said his name like Fuchs writes it, beautified and dripping with allurement: "Richter... von... Dagentear." She smiled again. "Did you ever consider that your mind is lost?"

Richter paused. He nodded. "Aye. I had considered that."

"Good. Because I can hear the hissing of your—"

Claire screamed.

With a bony crunch, Richter took her little finger.

"End your hexes!" Spit and froth fell upon her face, the man's rage following his words as he menaced her with the bolt again. "End them!"

"I'll do it!" she yelled, her feet kicking up and down. "I'll end them!"

"Now!"

She turned aside and spoke toward the road: "Listen to me, my loved ones, listen to me! You are all free! Go free and—"

Claire screamed again.

Richter drove the bolt between the knuckles of her middle and ring fingers. He twisted. Blood bubbled. Her feet kicked up and down again.

"Do it the right way, hexe," he said. "Do it the right way or I will be the hexenjäger your kind speak of when the night is dark."

The girl's eyes went to him.

"We used to think you enjoyed it," she said. "We used to think you relished the hunt. But now I see nothing in you. I see a husk. A pile of bones wreathed in meat and muscle, thrust through this world by the strength of its broken heart and little else. We had you all wrong, Richter von Dagentear. You really *are* the Wight." She smiled again. "At least I can take some solace in knowing that I'll be your last."

Richter raised the crossbow bolt into the air.

Claire turned her head. She whispered down the road.

Soft and simple. Words which one would secret to a baby. Words which you knew were heard no matter where they went. Words which you could look upon the listener and know they had your secret in them. Deep. Very, very deep. A secret told and not lost. A secret told and vaulted. Richter pursed his lips. His heart raced. When she was finished, she turned back.

Richter knew the task was done: a tear ran down the girl's cheek, bleeding its way through tracks of mud, and he knew she had lost her army, lost all that she had worked for, and an entire future with it. But something was off.

"Did they listen?" Richter said. "Did your army stop fighting?"

Claire sighed. "They already have. I cannot hear the voice of my beast. I cannot hear the voices of my soldiers. They were all in a battle, beautiful and loud, and now I only hear silence. Whoever you placed upon the beach has already won, Richter von Dagentear. You've won."

Richter nodded. He saw truth in her eyes. That's about all he could see after her dreams had been shattered. Truth usually was the rock upon which those shards were made.

"I'll go to the barbarians," Claire said. "Marsburg can be saved."

The hexenjäger stared at her.

The hexe stared back.

"Richter?" she said.

He threw the crossbow bolt aside. He crouched past the girl and as he did so he grabbed her and dragged her across the mud. She made a noise, and then she spoke to matters of war and peace and he ignored her entirely. He passed by Immerwahr's corpse. The monk's eyes hadn't shut. He saw all that he could to the very end. Richter looked away. He pulled the girl to the lid of the fallen priory bell and he rolled her to the mound of mud built there in the waves made from its weight and there he put her face into the mud and held it there, its earthen depths squelching above her ears.

Arms punched and legs kicked. To Richter, these may as well have been sticks skirting in the wind. It was the great irony that so much power resided in something so little, as something so little could be felled with such ease. Such was the pernicious reality creeping at the corners of royal life. All the wealth, glory, and power did not stop you from having flesh, a few bones, and a cord of muscle all to protect what made you, you.

The effects of his own concoction were starting to wane. He began to see red again. He saw red Richters spawning from the very arm poled against the back of her head. They roped down like pirates wheeling around their masthead, and they joined his fingers in helping pin her down.

"Yes, kill her!"

"Kill her, Richter!"

"She has to die!"

"Kill her!"

But the words did not come from them nor from himself.

Richter looked up.

Hobbs stood in the middle of the road. White. Pure white. And pointing. His mouth opening and closing in excited shouts.

Kill her! he said. *Kill her!*

The boy's image slowly drew dour. Crimson unfurled from his maw and ran down his chin and washed the white out of him.

Kill her, Richter!

Soon, the boy was all red. Caked in it. Slaked in it. Cursed by it.

"Oh Hobbs," Richter said, shaking his head. He looked down. The red Richters yelled at him to continue, but the captain gritted his teeth and, shivering with violent fever, he pulled his arm up and pulled Claire with it.

The hexe gasped for air as she sloshed the mud from her face.

Richter set her down and he sat himself back on his haunches, collecting himself. Steady breaths. Fingers clenching and unclenching. Toes doing the same. A hexenjäger's training to help clear the mind. The girl kicked backward and rolled into a ball, arms clasped over her knees, her terrified eyes upon the hexenjäger who had suddenly reeled back into being a mercenary captain.

"I hear little feet," she said. "And a loud heartbeat."

"Someone had to stop this," Richter said, staring at her.

Hobbs' footsteps pitter-pattered until his feet skidded on their heels. "Immerwahr!" he shouted. The boy's shadow scurried by. They heard him fall upon the monk. Heard him shaking his body.

"Richter!" Hobbs shouted.

"I'm alright."

"The monk…"

"I know."

The boy sobbed, but the pain was brief as Richter heard the sound of Immerwahr's sword being dragged off the ground.

"Hobbs," Richter said. "Hobbs don't."

"She has to die."

The boy stood with the monk's sword, its weight carrying it into the earth. Crying, Hobbs stared at the girl. His white face. A face cleaned by tears. The selfsame image of his sublimity shimmering down the steel of a heavy blade he could hardly hold in his little hands, but the weight of his task needn't much strength to complete it. Only one little strike upon one little girl.

"Please don't," Claire said. "Please."

Richter stood up. He towered over them both.

"Boy," he said. "Don't."

Hobbs gritted his teeth. The handle slipped from his fingers and the blade fell to the ground.

"I can't do it."

"I know."

"I want to. I want to so, so badly… and yet… I can't…"

"I know," Richter said. The boy fell into his arms. "That's why you are who you are, Hobbs."

"I'm sorry."

"Nothing to be sorry about. You stay right here, alright?"

Hobbs nodded.

The captain walked over to Claire. "Get up," he said.

Shaking, the girl slowly got to her feet. Her face was tracked with mud and her clothes caked in it.

"You deserve death," Richter said. He looked at Immerwahr's corpse. "But this world will bring good out of you yet."

Claire swallowed nervously. "What good can this world bring out of anyone? It hasn't changed for thousands of years. All I wanted to do—"

"I don't care what you want," Richter said. "The time for that is over, do you understand me?"

Chapter 42. Hargravard.

LEAVING THE SHADE of the forest path, Richter instinctively put his hands out and stopped both children.

"What in the world?" Hobbs said.

Claire gasped. "Oh no."

Both children glommed onto Richter's arms.

The barbarian sat on the shoreline and though there were others like him, *he* was the savage of the group. His arms and shoulders sinewed with every breath like the lumbering of some vast warship afloat in a modest harbor. He wore the head of a brown bear, the savage's eyes staring through its teeth like some echo of the beast's slain ferocity. Scars shaped his face as if they were scores on an anvil, jaggedly etching across his forehead and down his cheeks and cutting pale roads into a brown beard, no doubt the clawing remnants of the bear's final mauling, leaving behind a warning that its slayer was not to be trifled with. The savage's great power lay buried under pelts made of unknown tundra animals with pauldrons of thick white manes matted over his shoulders and more yet worn as bracers, and as the wind blew these frosty furs gently skirted like steam. Girded to a hip was a cleaver made of an enormous antler, the points reinforced with metal tips, the bone beam enameled with paints that seemed to mimic spiritual rites either in commemoration of or damning those the weapon and its bearer had killed.

"Don't give me to them," Claire said. "I beg of you."

The captain unsheathed his sword.

"No Richter," Hobbs said. "They'll kill you!"

Richter gripped his sword. "Both of you hush."

Beyond the boulder of a man stood the rest of his warband, most of similar might and main. Richter's company sat on the shore, heads down, too drained to fight on. Picking through the company's goods, the barbarians seemed content with robbing instead of killing, or perhaps preserving the lives of those they defeated was in some form a humiliation in their own culture.

At the shore itself, a barbarian took a torch and set it to a raft. Flames crackled and flickered over a body wreathed in leaves and grass, its little hands grasping an ancient sword. The barbarian bowed and took his boot and kicked the boat and it gently skirted into the Trading Swords' current. Richter knew it was a funeral rite for the savage boy.

The bear helmed savage growled out: "Hargravard!"

Hobbs yelped as the barbarian suddenly jumped to his feet, springing forth like a rock out of a catapult. He marched through the sloshed mud with the ease of a young soldier cracking his boots across a brick street. The earth simply gave way to his trespass.

Richter pushed Hobbs and Claire behind himself.

The savage's shadow fell upon them in a bulbous and barbaric hurry.

"Richter!" Hobbs yelled.

The captain swung his sword. It mutely stopped midair as the barbarian caught the blade itself. Barehanded. Richter looked up. He felt the man's strength vibrating through the steel. Blood slowly trickled from the palm and then in an instant the sword was snatched away, Richter stumbling forward with empty hands. Turning, the savage hurled Adelbrecht's sword through the air and it went flipping and tumbling before splashing into the Trading Swords river where it would sit for eons beyond all present living beings.

"Hargravard," the savage said, almost as though speaking to the river. He turned around. "Hargravard."

"The boy was killed by a nachzehrer," Richter tried to explain.

Slowly, the barbarian lowered his head. The bear's teeth closed in and, monster within monster, the savage's eyes glared from between its canines. Richter held his ground, his own eyes leering from the dark of a witch hunter's hat. The jaw of the bear helm slowly folded Richter's cap, pinching it down until the two stood alone in a cave, the savage's helm the earth, Richter's hat the darkness, and in between were two men and two unseen yet infinite fires.

"You," the barbarian said. "Leader."

"Captain."

"*Leader.*"

"Aye."

"The boy," the barbarian said. "Hargravard."

"A beast killed your boy."

"Not Hargravard." The barbarian smiled. "Not my boy. *Yours.*"

Dark blinked to light as the barbarian suddenly pulled away. He stared down at the captain and looked at the boy and then at the girl. A moment later, he whistled in the tune of a bird from his lands and turned and growled at some of his men. They nodded and growled back and made gestures that would provoke fights in civilized realms, but between them it seemed as though this language allowed for certain masculine obsessions.

Crockett was plucked from the circle of prisoners. He wasn't brought forward so much as pushed and then pointed the rest of the way when his wards tired of guiding him. Slowly, the historian trudged through the muck and mud, stepping over dead raiders, caravan guards, and naked ferry town villagers. He arrived in a fit of sweat and labored breath. The barbarian looked at him and shook his head with disdain.

"Fat man," the savage said. He growled and pointed at Richter.

"Give…" Crockett paused, clearing his throat. "Give him—"

"Who is alive?" Richter interrupted, looking beyond the paymaster. "I need to know."

"C-captain, I think it best if we focus on matters with the sav—"

A tuft of the paymaster's hair went flying from the back of his head as though he'd walked backward into a low-hanging beam. Seething, he crouched and nursed his wound and the barbarian grabbed him and drew him upright, the rather large and rotund Crockett being manhandled with startling ease. The savage growled and pointed again.

"Ah, right," Crockett said. "Uh… give him the girl, Richter."

The captain spat.

The savage turned and spat as well, his the more audible of the bile.

"Don't just hand me over, please," Claire said. "This is what my father always wanted, and nothing my father does is wise…"

Richter pushed the girl back. He said, "The barbarians could easily take her from us, so why is he merely asking?"

"An agreement was made. He wants to see it owned to." Crockett nervously looked at the barbarian. "Taking her isn't the point. He wants it done by our rules and customs."

"Can he understand us?"

"He knows a few words."

"But can he understand us?"

The barbarian growled.

"He understands us as you would animals."

"We're something more."

"Not to him." Crockett lowered his gaze. "Richter, please… the fact they've even allowed us to live…"

Richter looked down. Claire held onto his wrist in the trustful manner a little girl might glom onto her mother and walk whilst her little eyes sailed elsewhere. But Richter stared through it, remembering her for what she was.

"I can get you great wealth," Claire said. "Great power, even. I can set aside the hexencraft. Or I can use it to help you. I'll help you with whatever you want… I'll help you with Marsburg, even… just… don't…"

The captain pushed Claire forward. She went screaming and curled into a ball at the feet of the savage. She yelled that she did not wish to go. She yelled for her mother and cursed that the woman had died and left her alone in this world. She cursed her father who still yet lived and had doomed her to this fate. She cursed an endless trove of ancestors, names and titles flying from her lips in almost holy recital, each being dragged through the proverbial mud as surely as they were spat into it. The barbarian stared at her without emotion. He turned to Crockett and growled again.

The barbarian put his hands forth as though gripping an invisible crown and then placed its implied eminence upon his own head.

"Crockett, tell him he has his princess," Richter said. "Now he can go be a king elsewhere."

"No," Crockett said, tears welling up in the paymaster's eyes. "It's not about that… he wants something else…"

"Crockett?"

The historian nodded to Hobbs. "He wants Hobbs."

"Me? What?" Hobbs said. "I'm nobody."

Richter said, "They want him because of the savage boy's death?"

"No, Richter." Crockett sighed. "They saw Hobbs kill a lindwurm. He *proved* himself worthy, proved himself to be… Hargravard."

Hobbs shook his head and shouted: "I didn't kill it! I blinded it! The river killed it! The beast drowned! I swear! I'm no hero, I'm no king!"

A meaty, hairy hand went for the boy. By instinct, Richter pushed himself against it, both hands to the savage's forearm, gripping it like a thick branch of a tree and pulling with all his might to keep it away from the boy. The barbarian froze in place and his gaze slowly moved upon the captain, his bear helm tilting ever so slightly, his pupils fattening as though he wanted Richter to see himself in them and see the mistake he'd made.

The blow arrived fast. Faster than the savage's size and girth and power would suggest. Richter found himself on the ground, head spinning, nose leaking, his vision spliced as his left eye was swallowed in the puffing of a rapidly purpled lid. Through it all, he still saw the shape of Hobbs. Small. Diminished. Blurry.

"Richter!" the boy called.

Woozily, Richter got to his feet. He swung his fists. The shots landed. The damage, however, accrued as though he were punching a rock. Grumbling, the savage moved again. Swift. Catlike. Richter found himself stumbling backward, hands clutching his chest, his lungs gasping for air.

The savage stood with his arm half-cocked, the rolled fist freezing the momentum which had plunged it into Richter's sternum. He slowly lowered his arm and spat and growled. "Admirable," he said, his accent so thick it was as if a stonecarver were chipping the words off his tongue. "This pride, heavy. But this pride… it stops now. Do you all… understand?"

"I…" Wheezing, Richter looked at Crockett. "I thought you said he only knew a little of our language."

"Well," Crockett said. "He knows the words you'd expect him to."

The savage stared at Richter like a cat having clawed its meal into a mangled yet still breathing ruin. Looking down at his handiwork, a certain sort of pitying appeal gleamed in the savage's eye. This gaze widened as the captain straightened up and put his hands out before him, fists clenched again.

Richter saw four of his own arms, waving back and forth in some squidlike pugilism, half-real, half-image, but full of determination. Unfortunately, his vision also doubled the barbarian, and in turn set the shoreline and river shifting atop each other like a deck of cards being cut and shuffled. Despite these maluses, Richter knew that ordinary diplomacy would not work here. He knew that if he were to win anything, he'd have to do it in the barbarian tongue. He'd have to speak their language.

"Alright," Richter said. "Let's fight."

"Richter," Crockett said. "I don't…"

The barbarian put a hand to the paymaster's mouth, muffling him. He smirked at the captain. A breeze eased through, scooting on like a nervous patron's chair in an all too quiet tavern. The Trading Swords river stilled, its water lapping quietly against the shore, and the men who stood or sat in its mud watched with quiet appreciation or tremendous apprehension.

"Pride," the barbarian said. He turned his hand and blood dripped from the palm. "Bravery. Such things meet… when they shouldn't."

Richter took a step forward. The savage laughed and held his hand out and shook his head. He turned to Crockett and grunted and thumped his chest and he mumbled lowly and then growled loudly, his language seemingly taking every valley and peak it had in its range for surely Richter had earned a manner of the tongue's eloquence. Finally, the barbarian barked out to his clan and then turned and nodded, a final stop in most all languages.

Fists still up, Richter said, "What did he say?"

"Your, uh, diplomacy seems to have earned us a reprieve." Crockett gestured for Richter to put his hands down. "He's making us an offer."

Richter's company was gathered and pushed forth. They came staggered and exhausted. Following closely behind were Eppo and Hugo, the last of the raiders. Grunting along in guttural geniality, the barbarians joined them, each savage armed with weapons hewn from earth and animal alike.

"Captain," Dahlgren said as he stumbled closer. "Good to see you alive."

"Aye," Richter said. "Looks like my trust in you was not misplaced."

"Soldiering is what you hired me for, soldiering is what you get." The old man sighed. "Unfortunately, our luck ran out the second these half-naked mean muggers decided to come over."

"We're still alive," Richter said. "So let's just take this one step at a time."

Fixing his bear helm, the leader of the savages leaned back, making sure that that all were present. Satisfied, he turned to Crockett and nodded.

Crockett said. "Uh, I suppose we can conduct some business now."

"What did he say this time?" Richter said.

"Since you have sought to parlay in his language, the barbarian now wishes to parlay in ours."

"What?"

"He wants to make a deal," Crockett said. "You have two choices, captain. Either we can all fight one another, barbarian against civilized, or you can offer one steward to go with the children. That steward can be you, of course. I don't want to speak out of turn here, but if we all fight them—"

"Hey I know this math," Quinn said, his voice hoarse, but his powerful, innate drive to be heard not the least bit quelled. "We fight them and we die! Sophia, back me up!"

Nervously looking around, Sophia said, "Yeah, that checks out."

"Checks out!" Quinn said, beaming.

"This man…" The barbarian turned to Richter. "Important?"

Richter shook his head.

"Ah cap'," Quinn said. "You don't gotta tell him that. He doesn't even know us. Give me some authority, even if it's just for pretend."

The barbarian leader unsheathed his antlered weapon. "Unimportant man says unimportant things." He growled. "Intruder on our trade."

"Oh, uh," Quinn faltered. "Apologies."

As the barbarian stepped forward, Crockett hurriedly produced a few growls and grunts and waved his hands. The barbarian leader stared at the historian. A smile crept across the savage's face and he began to laugh and he nodded and girded his weapon back to his hip. He growled and nodded again.

"Captain," Crockett said. "The barbarian wishes to know your answer. Either… we can all fight, or one of us can go with the children."

Sighing, Richter said, "The savage knows the civilized ways well, considering he gave us two options, but in truth only one."

"That's fine," Hobbs said, grabbing onto Richter's hand, the boy's light touch weighing heavy upon its many scars. He smiled. "We can find a way out on our own. We always find a way, right, Richter?"

Richter looked at his company. The downtrodden. The old. The hated. The forgotten. A group of veritable castoffs way in over their heads, islanded in the vast ocean of an uncaring world. Altogether, a motley crew, some deserving of everything coming their way, others just along for whatever comes next, but the captain knew he was looking at nothing but dead men if he were to walk away. Dahlgren proved himself an excellent sergeant, but no one was there to truly captain the company were Richter to depart.

"We'll go together, and then we'll escape," Hobbs said quietly. "C'mon."

"Thomas," Richter said. He nodded at the servant. "I want you to go with Hobbs and watch over the boy."

"What?" Hobbs said.

"Sir?" Thomas looked equally confused. "Oh, I mean… I suppose…"

"No!" the boy screamed. "No, Richter! No!"

The barbarian grunted at Crockett. The paymaster grunted back. Slowly, the savage smiled. He pointed at Thomas and thumbed over his shoulder. In a heartbeat, the barbarians took the servant and dragged him from the group and started tethering his wrists together.

"Richter!" Hobbs shouted. "You're going to choose them over me?"

The captain crouched. His knees cracked. His lungs wheezed. He took off his black hat. "You'll do great things, Hobbs. You and…" The captain stared at Claire. She stared back, slumped over a barbarian's shoulder with her protests having died. Richter said, "You and her can do great things. Many people will be saved because of you, Hobbs. The politics are beyond your years, but thousands of lives will be spared, do you understand this?"

"I don't know thousands of people," Hobbs said. "I just know you."

"You have to understand," Richter said. "Please tell me you understand."

"I don't understand! I don't!" Hobbs shouted as he was pulled away. "I don't understand! Richter! Richter! When will I see you again?"

Richter got to his feet, wobbling on a wounded stature. He pursed his lips and cleared his throat. He strode forward. A barbarian pushed him back.

"I just have something to give him," Richter said. "Crockett, tell them!"

The paymaster hurriedly translated again, and the barbarians looked to their own leader for guidance. The savage nodded like a king allowing a messenger past his guards and just like that the barbarians gave way.

As Richter stumbled forward, Hobbs caught him in a hug. Clenching, firm, never wanting to let go. But the captain pushed him back, holding him at arm's length, and with the other hand he offered his black hat.

"Take this," Richter said.

"When will I see you again…" Hobbs said. "Richter… please…"

Richter pursed his lips. He turned the hat and placed it over the boy's head. He lifted the lid and stared at the sullen, wet eyes beneath. He said, "I'll be wanting it back, do you understand?"

Hobbs stared at the ground. He said, "Alright."

The captain hugged the boy. He said, "Alright then."

A sea of hands fell upon them both, separating them. Despite the savages' strength, it seemed more like the two simply drifted apart, Richter left stranded in the mud, Hobbs disappearing in a wash of enormous barbarian muscle and pelts and clattering weaponry.

"I'll watch him closely," Thomas said, standing beside the captain.

"No," Richter said, getting to his feet. "You will protect him, Thomas."

"I will. I'll do everything I can. You can trust me on that!"

The barbarian leader watched his men gather Hobbs, Claire, and Thomas onto the ferry rafts. He looked back at Richter.

"You no follow," the savage said. He raised his antlered weapon and cut it across his own throat. "You... understand?"

"Aye," Richter said, nodding at the barbarian. "I understand."

~~~

RICHTER COULD ONLY WATCH as the boy shrank across the Trading Swords river, his silhouette swallowed by distance, and Richter grimaced for it seemed as though a sword were being pulled out of his chest, his heart hollowed, his blood set to boil against the proverbial blade. And then Richter could see nothing of note, only a little black shape, a moving and living memory, but an inevitable memory, nonetheless, drifting away in the moment of its manifestation, constructed in the lost connection, and like a man whose wound sputtered in the absence of the steel which had created it Richter gasped for air and sank back against the ground, breathing in a world which had longed done him nothing but harm. And there he sat for a time, suffering another of its damages. He simply sat and waited, like any wounded man, for a sense of things, for an accounting of that which the final tally could not be known only experienced. A boy found. A boy lost. A soul revived. A soul darkened. A breath taken. There, the balance of things. There, the man was. Wounded, but was. And he sat on the earth to which he would eventually go and he looked up at the skies to the heavens he hoped to eventually be. And he nodded to neither place in particular. And then he got up.

~~~

Birds dotted the sky. Wheeling overhead, staring down with clerical rumination. Silent announcers of that which has happened and all the same the arbiters of that which will inevitably occur again. Death. Regeneration.

"How's the eye?"

Richter looked down, his purpled lids flaring. The paymaster grimaced as though he just watched a valued tome ripped in half.

"Tell me how you really feel," Richter said.

"Ahh, it's nothing. You'll get over it." Crockett gathered a closer look, his own eyes slimming as he appraised the puckered flesh. "Just, you know, don't touch it."

Richter nodded and looked around. All along the shore and beyond lay bodies in various states of wretched unmaking. Wounds manmade and gruesomely natural all alike, the work of fantastical beasts and fantastical human imagination at their most potent stages.

Crockett had spoken to him of the lindwurm's assault. How it ravaged the raiders who seemed intent on killing it for some future monetary gain. Or, at least, that was Crockett's assumption. He explained that everyone, including himself, was partially woozy from the pots of orange liquid which had splashed about the shore from the day's first assault. He spoke of Dahlgren's daring charge against the lindwurm, buttressing his shield to take it on while the rest attacked the beast. He spoke of how this did not resolve in the old man's favor but that, in the final moment, a certain thief stepped forth and saved the day. Again.

"I thought Hobbs saved the day?" Richter said.

"Whoa," Quinn said, walking by. He stopped, naturally. "Let's get one thing straight here. Hobbs wouldn't have been nowhere near that lindwurm if I hadn't strolled out there and taken it on, man against beast. Put that in your book, Crockett. Say I spearheaded that charge."

"A one-man charge?" Crockett said.

"That's right. And I spearheaded it."

Dahlgren spat. "If you're making that argument, then it's really me that killed the lindwurm."

"He's right," Sophia said. "Dahlgren walked out there first, which then set the stage for all that followed."

"I didn't see no old man out there," Quinn said.

"Oh please, you were yelling his name," Sophia said. She mimed the thief with a haughty feminine veneer: "'Oh Dahlgren, where art thou? I hath wandered foolishly into danger and now I need a strong man to save me!'"

"Pretty spot on," Dahlgren said.

"No it ain't," Quinn said. He pointed at Crockett's ledger. "Put in there that... uh..." The thief realized the captain was staring at him. Quinn relented. "Alright. Hobbs killed the lindwurm. The boy stabbed that sumbitch in the farkin' eye with a wooden sword and then it rolled into yonder waves and drowned. It was the craziest farking thing I've ever seen."

Crockett looked at Richter.

The captain raised his hands. "Don't look at me. I wasn't there. You put it how it happened, paymaster."

"Yessir."

"Gonna miss that little bugger," Quinn said, staring across the river. "I mean, I don't think he added nothing to the company being just a little kid and all, but, still. I feel an absence, you know?"

The company nodded amongst themselves.

Crockett looked at Richter. "We could go after him."

"Let's sit and reorganize for a moment," Richter said. He stared down the shore. Eppo and Hugo sat against a tree like shackled men awaiting their sentence. They surely couldn't run into the woods, and they were not yet certain of the captain's ideas for them. Richter nodded. "Offer the raiders our modest wages to work for us. If they don't accept, let them walk. If they do accept but got any kind of sneering or look about them, let me know."

"Yessir," Crockett said.

Richter took his eyes to all the gear littered about the shoreline, most of it thrashed to bits by the battle with the beast. "Let's pick up whatever's left out here. Scrap it. Junk it. Sell it. We should perhaps head back east and find those merchants again. Get some herbs and cloth for Elletrache."

"Ol' Elletrache is quite alright," Trash said, though the beast slayer's nachzehrer-burnt body had cooled to a wormlike white, his paleness unsettlingly smooth, and his hairless body a strobing horror of glistens for he was an odd-shaped man at every length. "Beside m'hands and m'foot, I ain't ever felt better than I do now. I feel... cleansed."

Lacking his beard, Elletrache looked like another person entirely, and lacking human pigmentation, he appeared of another world entirely. All the same, the beast slayer's attitude remained true.

"Sure, Trash, sure," Richter said, nodding. "But I think it best we get you some care just in case, alright?"

The beast slayer spat. "Hells. If you say so, captain."

"And after all that," Crockett said. "We go after the boy?"

Dahlgren spat. "You'd want us to venture north, into the frozen wastes, to hunt down a child taken by barbarians?"

"Yes," Crockett said.

"No," Richter said. "We won't do that. You all deserve to earn a livable wage. There is no money in chasing down Hobbs. And there is no reason, either. He's a tough lad. He doesn't need me—he doesn't need us helping him out." The captain nodded. "Everybody understand?"

Sophia looked away, as did Quinn. Crockett wrote something in his ledger, his penmanship oddly slower than normal.

"Aye," Dahlgren said. "We understand."

"Hey! Hey captain!"

The group turned to see Berthold dragging a long pole from the shore, the wooden rod scratching across the sands. He paused and wiped his brow. "They… the barbarians… I think they left this behind."

Berthold planted the rod into the ground and tilted it upward. A black cloth limply clumped around the rod itself.

"Looks like a standard," Dahlgren said. "Maybe a treasure of theirs."

With the help of a stiff wind the black cloth unfurled, suddenly snapping at full length, and revealing in its center the stitched emblem of a white bear's head, the maw stitched to be open and snarling.

"Gruesome looking," Sophia said. "Did they leave it as a gift?"

"It's an old bear banner," Dahlgren said. "Knowing barbarians, they wouldn't have forgotten it. The bear is of great importance to them, especially the white ones."

Berthold looked unimpressed. "Should I toss it?"

"No, don't do that!" Crockett said, snapping his head up from his ledger like a mother seeing her child approach a melting pot. "Items like that are worth quite a lot to those obsessed with the savages, particularly those who have never *met* the savages themselves. We can sell it for a large sum!"

"We're not selling it," Richter said. He grabbed the banner from Berthold and walked with it in hand, feeling its weight. Down its shaft a tether of black cloth wispily fluttered in the wind. The captain touched it and smiled.

Running between his fingers was the final scrap of the Bear Merchants banner from so long ago, the one Hobbs had taken from the doomed caravan out of Walddorf. Dahlgren was right: the barbarians didn't forget the banner. Instead, they had been convinced to leave it by Hobbs himself. Somehow, the boy's heart had already demonstrated command of his new surroundings. Blood is blood, courage is courage.

"It was left for us," Richter said. "And we'll take it."

Dahlgren grinned. "Aye, I like it. Every company worth its salt should have a battle standard, and this white bear is certainly one to fear."

"So, we have a banner of, uh, grisly sorts," Crockett said. "And we have loot to sell, food to eat, and coin to spend. Question is, what do we do now?"

"I've an idea," Quinn said. "How about we finally name this company?"

Crockett said, "Well—"

"I'll go first: Battle Brothers!"

"We've discussed this, Quinn. Another company has that name."

"Sorry, I misspoke," the thief said. He grabbed the banner and stretched it out and pointed at the beast in its center. "*Battle Bears*."

Pinching his eyes, Dahlgren said, "By the old gods."

"What? What's wrong with that? You put a bear on the banner, you put a bear in the name. It makes perfect sense!"

As the company argued once more, Richter looked at the standard's white bear, its maw stitched into a fearsome growl. It was hard to believe that such a creature could ever be felled, and harder to believe yet that anyone who succeeded in doing so saw fit to place their trophy upon a simple banner. He wondered what other monstrosities the barbarians faced in their lands.

"Fine!" Quinn said, throwing up his hands as the entire company finished burying his ideas. "We'll just be a nameless company forever!"

Sophia smiled. "All the same, glad to see your back in spirit, Quinn."

"Bullshit aside," Dahlgren said. "Where are we heading, captain?"

Richter thought. Marsburg was still under siege. West and east were either too poor or too dangerous. All that was left was one place, perhaps the most dangerous of them all. Grimacing, he touched his chest where the savage's fist had plunged, knocking him to the ground with complete ease. A dull pain ached there, but it would pass… if only to make room for more.

The captain looked at his company.

"How many of you have ever been to Sommerwein?"

Epilogue. The Last Witch Hunter.

THE PUB WAS ALIGHT with drunks and its barkeep whirled to keep up with their thirst. Ale splashed from mugs and music rang from a minstrel's lute. Wobbling on her tippytoes, a young lady stood on a table and sang:

Did you see the night show
With the moon high and the stars low.
Light and light and light, all lay in sight!
Gather thine eyes, gaze upon yer prize.
Here in mountains conquered,
Sommerwein's got no wine!

The lady kicked a mug across the room and fell back knowingly and trustingly and there a group of men caught her in their arms. Great cheers sprang through the crowd. Ale sloshed and refills were ordered. The barkeep wiped the sweat from his brow and hurried ever faster, grinning and grimacing as he truly earned his commerce.

Nestled in a dark corner, Arvid the scribe sat like a rat in a barn full of cats, shrunken and still, but all the same he still clapped under the table in modest applause. Certain energies simply could not be resisted, and gayful drunkards were a peculiarly convincing sort.

"Sommerwein's got no wine!" the tavern cheered. "Sommerwein's got no wine, hey!"

"Yeah," Arvid said under his breath. "Sommerwein's got—"

Hinges squalling, the tavern door flung open and clattered against the wall. The crack of wood on wood hushed the tavern in frozen flinches, all that could be heard was the drip of spilt ale. As a chilly breeze swept through the room, three men entered, bringing with them an air of authority.

Two of the men wore plates of armor and glinting chainmail layered beneath. Longswords girded to their hips, gauntleted hands firm upon the pommels. A third man was unarmored and far more diminished, but in this comparative manner he seemed all the more important. Naturally, Arvid knew his role by appearance and demeanor alone: he was a levy master, known in the north as a conscriptor. Pale, shrewd, standing crookedly as if his cruel task had bent him over the years. He reminded Arvid of himself.

Strangely, in all the new silence, the dingy odor of the room could now be smelled, as if the stench of piss and ale and other elements were spared the nose by the overwhelming of the ears. Levity gave way to reality.

"Sirs?" the barkeep said. "Can I help ye?"

Clearing his throat, the levy master unfurled a scroll. "By decree of…" He paused. He looked at one of his guards. "Do you smell that?"

"Aye sir."

"What is that?"

"It's a tavern, sir. Could be anything."

The levy master sniffed. "Must be a tavern for dogs."

"Aye sir."

Shaking his head, the levy master continued: "Ehem, by decree of the Sommerwein royalty, all able-bodied men are to be accounted for in service of military duty. Those who are fit for said service will be pressed into it for the duration of one campaign which shall be resolved upon the liberation of Marsburg's farmlands from occupation by lowlander scum. Resisting conscription shall be treated with time on the torture towers…"

As the conscriptor went on, Arvid looked at his hands, pondering if they were dainty enough to avoid the army's call. The scribe couldn't afford to be pressed into anything. Not now, not ever. And if they did, they would surely find who he had left in the bed of the tavern's rented room. And once they found him, what would happen then? What hells would break upon them all?

With a papery scratch, the conscriptor's scroll rolled back up. "Any questions? No? No questions? Alright. Women, you may leave. Men, stay."

He turned and pulled at a table. A few patrons rose from their seats like doves flushed from a stand. As the women departed, one man tried to slip out with them, but the levy master's guards turned him around.

"Go back," the guard said. "Don't make me tell you again, coward."

"You've nowhere else to be right now," the levy master said with an almost motherly tone. He pulled the table to the center of the room and stood before it with bureaucratic pride. Satisfied, he promptly sat down and set out a red inkwell and beside it a black one. He unfurled a second scroll and let its length limply roll over the edge of the table itself. As he flattened the crinkles out of the paper, he looked at one of his guards and nodded.

"I'm ready."

"So it is then!" the guard yelled, his voice booming, remarkably louder than the levy master's. He swung his hand. "Every swinging dick lines up here and here! You, barkeep! You've men yonder somewhere?"

The barkeep shrugged. "You mean like in the rentals?"

"Aye. If they're men and they're breathing, we want them here."

"Well, uh, I suppose just that one there is rented out," the barkeep said, pointing toward a room at the rear of the tavern. Arvid's room.

Overhearing this, Arvid slunk down in his chair. He'd been in the corner hoping to disappear into the shadows there. He very well may have gotten away with it just as well, but he had brought with him a certain individual, one he had hooded and gagged and left 'asleep', infinitely asleep, yet infinitely awake all the same. Near and abroad in all respects. A figure not meant to be seen by anyone for they would not understand what it was they were looking at. There couldn't even possibly be enough time for them to understand.

The guard stomped across the room and knocked heavily upon the door. "Come on out."

A muted groan responded in turn.

"You've five seconds!" the guard shouted. "Or I'm kicking this in!"

Arvid stood up. "Good sirs!"

Both guards half-unsheathed their blades and for a moment Arvid was proud of himself for having the constitution to draw such a response out of hardy, well-martialed men.

"G-good sirs," Arvid continued. "I am but a traveler. I have a very ill partner and I do not think it is wise to stir him as he needs his rest."

"We'll judge his health for ourselves," the guard said, and he turned around and banged on the door again. "Come out!"

As the guard threatened the door's hinges and unveiling all that Arvid wished to keep secret, a noise and sight swept into the tavern, there standing at its front door so prominent an image it may as well have glowed. Ethereal. Unbelievable. Cloaked in grey and gliding in like a moonlit mist on a cold night. Her features drew glints and gleams even from the most dour of firelight, and it were the fact she clearly wished to hide herself that made these flashes of appearance all the more remarkable. She moved with the sort of feigned demureness only the learned royals could maintain, her posture and walk akin to a highborn gracing the stillness of a courtly promenade.

Within just that moment alone, Arvid knew exactly who she was.

"Get out of here, girl," one of the guards said. "Come back tomorrow if you need."

"Prin…" Arvid mouthed. "Prin…"

"Yes yes," the levy master said. "The principalities will have their men, yourself included my dear, hiding friend. Girl, as the guard said, you may go."

"N-no… princess," Arvid said. He raised a finger. "Princess! Her! She's a princess of the lowlanders! She was the one to marry Lord Landon's son!"

Every man in the room stared back over, eyebrows scrunched in scrutiny. The girl stood with a coin purse nervously jangling between hands.

"By the old gods," the levy master said, lowering his pen. "Is it her?"

"I'm… I'm not…" she stammered. "I just wanted to inquire if this establishment sells shrooms. I'm… no I am not a princess, sorry."

The words fell upon the tavern like the whispering plea of a murderer caught with a dripping dagger in hand.

"I'm not—" the girl cut herself off, fleeing with a quick turn and jaunt. The closest guard dove in chase, but she ducked away just in time.

"Seize her!" The levy master shouted: "Those who aid in seizing her will be free of Sommerwein's soldering duties! And… and have one-thousand crowns as a reward!"

Chairs screeched across the floor. Tables were flipped. Mugs went flying, their ale raking against the walls. Shadows blossomed fatly, cruel intents before bright lights, and the creatures which created them now gave chase for the girl and if not her then her clothes, tearing strips away as she efforted an escape from a collapsing pile of desperate souls, and when one drunk fell and grabbed her ankle, she too fell, clapping against the disgusting tavern floor.

"Fuchs!" she screamed, reaching for the door. "Fuchs!"

A stabbing cold bristled over Arvid and he looked to the front of the tavern to see its door flying off the hinges. He could not see what transpired other than a shadow swept in behind one of the levy master's guards and a moment later both his arms were flailed out, fists clenched, teeth gritted, and eyes crossed. He fell forward and as he did so a spear's shaft swung up, there planted in his spine. The second guard unsheathed his longsword and as his legs moved there were two noises in quick succession, leathery and steeled, and a glint of light to follow. Arvid blinked. The guard's body bolted upright with feet fixed to the floor, and in this manner his legs crossed one another and he fell into a stool while his head rolled across the barkeep's countertop.

Arvid's mouth fell open and he pushed himself back into his corner.

"Seize her!" the levy master screamed. "Seize her—"

Another two quick sounds and a glint of light.

The levy master stumbled back a step, pawing at an axehead burrowed in his pate, and then he fell forward, smashing his little table in half and sending red and black ink splattering everywhere. Arvid looked to the front of the room to see a man in black moving swiftly like a shadow free of its maker, pouring into and out of every space and crevice. This shape was attacked on all sides by the tavern's drunks, and the man in black welcomed them. He kicked a chair into the legs of a drunkard and as the assailant folded over the wood, the man in black produced a crossbow and shot a bolt through the back of the man's skull. He threw the emptied crossbow into the face of another attacker and a moment later Arvid could see a black cloak burst open, and what lay beneath shined mightily with what he thought at first was armor, but clearly wasn't armor at all – instead there glinted rows and columns of weapons. Swords. Knives. Axes. Folded crossbows. And belted carefully between them: a bandolier of vials.

"Motherfark—"

Another drunk fell silent, a hair-raising shriek of a sweeping scimitar taking half his head clean off, leaving him his tongue but no thoughts with which to use it. Spinning, the man in black felled another two in one stroke, and spinning again he threw a net which cluttered three drunkards together and they screamed as he set upon them with slashes, his curved blade looking like a stinging whip as it crescented in and out, each pass spraying blood against the walls in smooth, calligraphic lines. When another drunkard moved to help those under attack, he was stopped in an instant. Arvid couldn't even see what killed him, other than some ungodly manifestation of physical force by which the drunkard had idiotically stepped into, like a curious child stolen away by a river's ferocious undertow.

When the man in black was finished, insofar as every threat had been swept aside like dust motes by a broom, he raised a curved blade and pointed it at the rest of the tavern, the steel of it humming as it vibrated, its violence still singing. Every soul which could still breathe huffed on what they thought might be their last breath and the survivors raised their hands as if to say they wanted no part of it. The man in black gestured over his shoulder. Captured in terror, the survivors looked at one another.

"He means you can leave!" the princess yelled. "Go! Now!"

The crowd fluttered like dry leaves, nothing but hissing and scratching as they fretfully carried themselves out of the tavern, their eyes to the man in black and the princess, and strangely they nodded courteously at both, a sort of noble dignity to end the frenzy, as if they were more than happy to depart but didn't want to appear too hurried about it.

In their absence, a terrible quiet filled the room. Blood dripped from every wall and post and table and chair, a pitter-patter that sounded like the morning after a good night's rain. The man in black cleaned his scimitar and sheathed it. He walked across the room and gathered up those terrible blades he had flung and thrown and cleaned those and opened up his coat and added them to his armament like a bricklayer. When he closed his jacket again, his gaze suddenly darted.

Arvid shrank into his seat, curling there like a bug. "Sir sir sir sir!"

But the man simply put his hands out, the fingers constructing shapes.

Looking at them, Arvid shook his head. "You want me to leave?"

The girl came forward. "He's asking why you didn't."

"Oh, uh, I... was scared," Arvid said. "That's all."

The man in black's eyes bore down on the scribe, his pupils narrowing. Black hat. Black clothes. A bandolier. He reminded Arvid of Richter von Dagentear, the man who had resisted the call of Davkul, but this was no ordinary witch hunter. This man was something else. Something far deadlier.

"Fuchs," the girl said. "Let him go. We need to leave anyway before more people come."

Again, the man's hands moved from one shape unto another.

Sighing, the girl said, "I know you can handle them, but that doesn't mean you should. The last thing we need is a bounty on our heads!"

"I'll go," Arvid said, rising slowly, hands up. "I'll go."

Fuchs planted a foot as he put a hand on his scimitar.

"No! He's harmless!" the girl said. "Cease this carnage, please."

Arvid stood as carefully as any man ever could. He held his hands in the air and tiptoed between the blood and body parts on the floor. As he made his way around the two travelers, the man in black glared at him, his head affixed and turning slowly like an owl's. The girl meanwhile stared at the table, hurriedly collecting fallen crowns that had been flung from dead men's pockets. A small amount of coin being swept into hands worth untold thousands... little hands worth more gold than Arvid had ever seen... gold he could use... that could help him... help him spread the word of the one who waits... spread the word of Davkul...

He's harmless, Arvid thought. *I'm harmless. Just look away. Just look away.*

"T-take it easy, Fuchs," Arvid said with a cowardly smirk. "That was your name, right? Fuchs is a good name."

Fuchs grunted and finally looked away.

In an instant, Arvid grabbed the girl. The obsidian blade, the ancient, black dagger forged in a dark age, slipped down the sleeve of his shirt and into his hands and he pressed its edge against her throat. Two quick sounds. A strobe of light. Screaming, Arvid fell to the ground. He clutched his right arm – or a fiery sponge of flesh where it used to be. Shrieking in pain, Arvid took a breath and when he looked up again he saw his reflection curving down the crescent of a curved blade, and at the end of its length two eyes stared ferociously down at him, the man in black ready to strike again.

But the blade wavered for Fuchs' eyes were staring down. They widened and for a brief moment the man in black seemed as if he were any ordinary man. Then he knelt in a hurry and picked up the obsidian blade.

"No!" Arvid screamed, but an invisible chain of pain seized his entire side and he fell to the floor clenching the stump which remained of his arm.

Fuchs stared at the dagger, and then at the girl.

"I'm cut," she said, bringing her palm away from her neck. A single drop of blood ran down. "But it's just a small cut, it's nothing serious."

Fuchs sheathed the black dagger amongst his armament, there a mere black item in a wall of steel. Growling, he turned and swept the girl up in his arms. Whatever words his fingers could communicate, they were doing nothing now but shouting as they gripped her firmly.

"I'm fine!" she screamed. "What are you doing?"

The man in black carried her out of the tavern, leaping out onto the porch, and like a shadow carrying a sheet, they were gone into the night.

"No…" Arvid said. He took his hand off his shoulder. Blood caked his palm. He looked down to see his arm on the floor. Muscles and bone alike flat, the quickest and cleanest of cuts. "I've not yet… served my purpose…"

He slowly got to his feet.

"Helfgh megh…"

Arvid turned as the levy master's arm flopped after him. Half the man's face looked in his direction, and the other half the other. Blood pooled in a canyon of bone and meat where one of Fuchs' blades had trenched itself.

"Help you?" Arvid said. "Help you? Yes. I'll help you. I'll help you, help me. You'll help me. You'll help me!"

The scribe drifted toward the rented room, knocking over a stool and stumbling into another. He slammed against its door as he took the key from his pocket. Its metal greasily slid between his bloodied fingers and with an unpracticed left-hand he fumbled the key into the lock and jerkily turned it.

With a stiff crack, the door popped ajar. Arvid put his bloodied fingers against the wood and gently pushed it inward.

Gargling, the levy master sputtered again. "Helfgh megh… plergh…"

"Help me," Arvid said, staring into the room's darkness. "I'll help you, and you'll help me."

The wiederganger stood in faint moonlight. Hunched. Arms hanging at its sides. White orbs leered from the sockets. Bundles of leeks, celery, and garlic hung off it, items trying to mask its reek. Sensing Arvid, it slowly turned. Hips and knees cracked, guttural pops that emptied out of the decayed body's gaping holes. It groaned as its eyes slowly lifted toward the scribe.

"I know, I know," Arvid said. "You must be very hungry."

Turning around, the scribe looked at the levy master. The man's head turned, left, right, each eye gaining a new perspective on the monstrous creature shambling out of the room.

"Yes," Arvid said. "I will help you, and you will help me."

Blood spewed from the levy master's split face as he gargled on his own scream. He kicked his legs and tried to scoot backward. Knees popping, shoulders clacking, the wiederganger shuffled toward him.

"Wergh!" the levy master gargled. "Wergh! Noergh!"

The wiederganger dropped to the ground and buried its face into the levy master's. Its teeth gripped the muscle and crunched the bone and it tore and ate as it relished in the fundamental task of its former life. Its staggard slowness gave way to frenzy and carnage. The levy master's legs kicked up and down, his arms pounded the floor. Knocked a stool over. A mug. His fingernails grated into the floorboards and hissed as they dragged across the wood. All but little noises between the big, crunching ones.

"Do not fret," Arvid said, watching from above. "Death is not the end for you. Death is a divide, do you understand? Are you listening? Death is a divide, and Davkul awaits in the land which balances between."

Silence answered him.

The wiederganger drew its head up like a pig from a trough. Blood and ligament dripped from its face. It stood. A moment later, the levy master groaned and slowly stood just as well. Half his face had been torn away, one socket shredded and below it rows of crooked teeth seen through a shorn cheek. But its one remaining eye, now a pure white orb, lifelessly yet dutifully stared at the scribe. The levy master groaned.

"Welcome back," Arvid said. He motioned his arm to the rest of the room. "If you don't mind, please spread the word."

Made in the USA
Coppell, TX
11 September 2023

21478862R00340